RELICS & THRONES

RELICS & THRONES

Book Three of Warriors & Mages

V.K. Dixon

XHP
xenia house press

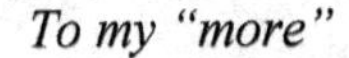

To my "more"

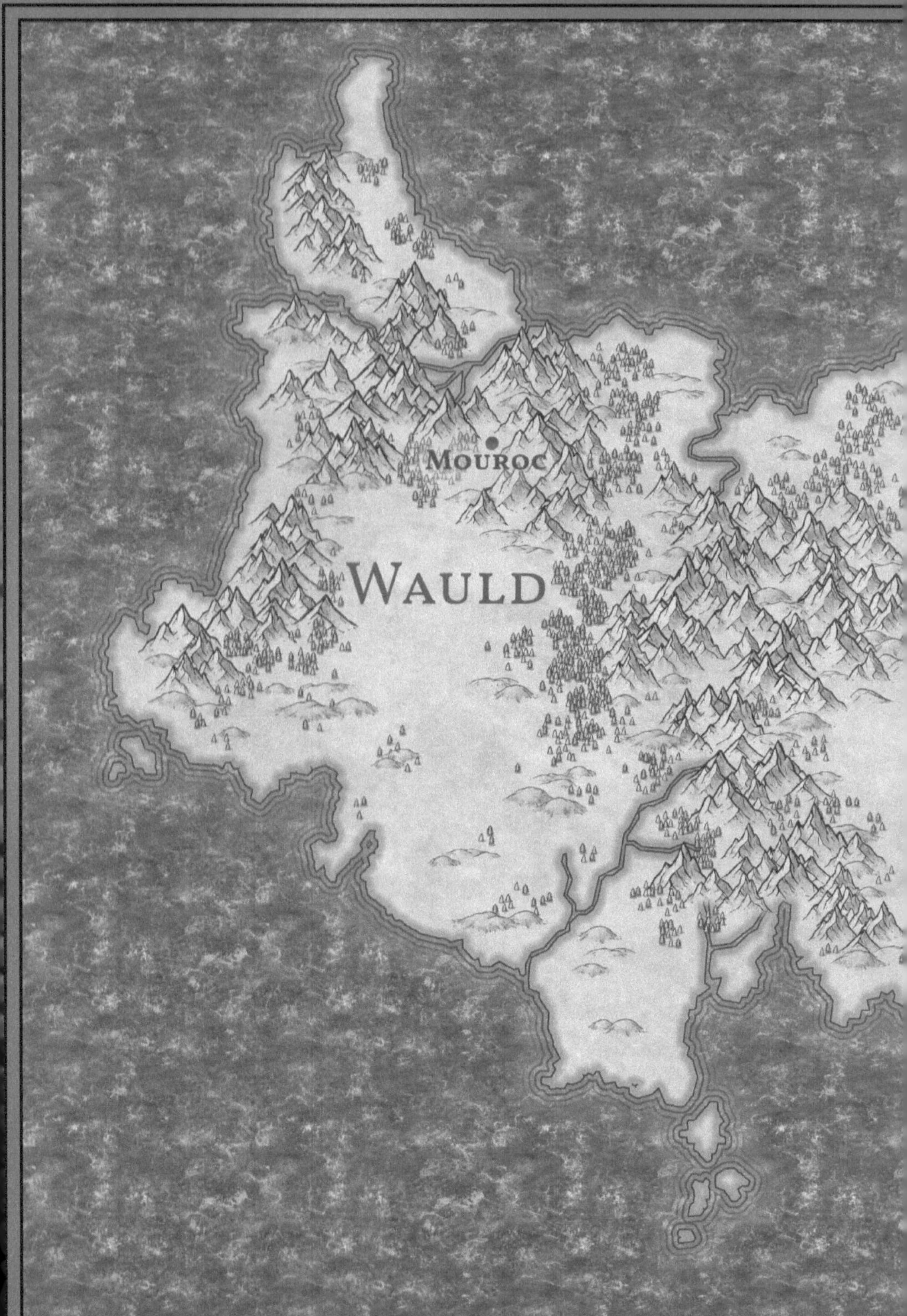

MOUROC
WAULD

RIA
Keves Island
Isle of
Allund

Part I: Warrior & Mage

The Heavenly Allore has taught us of our need for one another. Let us heed and follow his voice. One Mage to one Warrior, we shall create as the Creator created.
Quote attributed to Aanir, Warrior of the Ateris, the first Men of Terraeus

OAUK
KINVAURA
THORPE
BAULTGATE
SCAUTLA
LOTHES
LIVINGSTONE
STRATHY
MOUROC
LOCHEARN
ANAUSAN
BROHAUNE
LOCHALINE
VAURINVER
MITHVEN

CHAPTER ONE

Evylin

37TH OF CHRONOS, 1574

The steady drizzle of Waulden rain pattered on Evylin's hands as she drew back on the reins, the horse's gait slowing in response. Surrounded by mountains, the capital city sat in a valley edged by a wide, rapid river. The soft gray clouds overhead blocked the late morning sun, casting a dreary tint over the scene. Lush trees dotted the plain, growing sparser as they approached the moss-mottled city walls. The sprawling settlement reached out like a hand over the terrae, with farming communities and watchtowers extending its grasp.

"That's it?" Rafferty asked, his horse sidling up alongside Evylin's. "Doesn't look like the home of a maniacal tyrant."

"What did you expect?" said Isla Freye. The Wind Mage's honeyed foreign accent tinged her every word with warmth. "A city made of war machines, slave drivers, and iron bars on every window?"

"Well . . ." Rafferty shrugged. "Something like that."

Evylin grinned at his confusion. She'd rather expected a more desolate and villainous lair herself. However, to her surprise, the palatial city of Mouroc looked much like Ephria's own capital. Granted, it was larger and landlocked. The massive city butted up against a mountain with five interior walls separating its various sectors. At the foot of the mountain, on a hill overlooking the city, the columned palace rose, its deep purple banners snapping in the breeze.

Their large party had come to a stop just shy of two miles away from the gates, ten riders staggered on a tree-covered road, hoods up against the ever-misting rain. As the spring air warmed the atmosphere, they hardly needed their wool cloaks anymore. But the protection from the weather was only an additional benefit to keeping their appearances hidden.

At the head of the group, Isla led the way with her brother-in-law, Auden, at her side. Nearer the back, their sister, Ilain, rode with their Alliance companions, Emmaas the Warrior and Jarrad the Terrae Mage, while the rest of the Ephrians clustered together in the center. Rafferty and Ethenn flanked Evylin while Thom rode at Deckard's side near the front.

Looking over his shoulder, Deckard met Evylin's gaze. The corner of his mouth lifted in a faint smile that she couldn't help returning. The whole morning had been that way. Surrounded by others and pressed by the urgency of reaching safety, they'd been forced to keep their distance from one another, only permitting themselves to exchange short glances and longing looks.

Despite being married for over three months, Evylin finally understood what people meant by "the honeymoon stage." She was desperate to get her husband alone while at the same time feeling more nervous in his presence than ever.

"We'll need your help to get in," Auden said to Deckard, turning slightly in his saddle.

Attention drawn away, Deckard faced the Day Mage. "What can I do?" he asked.

"Mouroc is heavily guarded," Isla explained. "As Auden, Ilain, and Evylin's images are on Blount's Writ of Attachment, they can't just ride in. You'll have to put a shroud over them."

Deckard's jaw tightened for a second, and Evylin wondered if he was fighting his desire to abandon his magic. He ran a hand along his lightly stubbled jaw. "Won't the guards be suspicious of three saddled horses with no riders?" he asked.

"It's perfectly believable that we're traveling with fresh mounts," Jarrad said. "You merely need to shroud three people. And you *do* have the Night Relic. It isn't like you'll run out of power."

Still, Deckard hesitated.

Evylin nudged her horse forward to join him. "What is it?" she whispered.

He turned to her slowly, his green-blue eyes lingering on the towering stone walls rising in the distance. "The city is so large," he said. "It'll be loud. I'm worried I won't be able to keep my focus."

Scanning the landscape before them, Evylin realized that he was right. Even from their distance, it seemed that a hum drifted to them on the wind. And despite their time in the Keeps, Deckard was still new to drawing on his magic.

Once inside those thick walls, they would be directly in the thick of the noise and action. Evylin remembered their arrival in Ephria City two months ago. At every turn, there was something new to see. The architecture, the people, the movement, the sound, the colors, the life: It all pulsated and demanded attention. With the constant opportunities for distraction, it would be a struggle for her to maintain a grip on magic, let alone have to shroud an entire group.

"In that case . . ." Evylin shifted in her saddle. "Hold my reins."

"What?" Deckard's brow pinched even as he followed her instruction.

Without taking the time to explain, Evylin skillfully positioned herself to step from her horse onto the back of Deckard's. She settled in behind him, wrapping her arms around his waist. "There," she said, planting a kiss on his cheek when he tried to look at her. "Now, you can have my focus too."

He gave a soft laugh. "I'm indebted to you."

"I'm sure I'll find some way you can repay me."

"Quit flirting," Thom said, despite flashing an amused grin. She was relieved to see the lightness that had settled into his eyes as he watched them, his former jealousies gone. "We've got a hideout to get to."

Plans settled, Evylin tied her horse to Deckard's while they determined that Auden and Ilain should ride with Emmaas and Ethenn flanking them. The two Warrior men would stagger their positioning at the rear to ensure additional space so the Calders' horses didn't bump into any wandering guards or travelers, potentially alerting them to the riders. A shroud hid objects from view; it didn't block them from any of the other senses. The Calders and Evylin would have to be as silent and contained as a unit as possible.

Evylin felt Deckard's ribs expand as he took a deep breath. A tingle spread through her arms, wrapped tight against his abdomen, the sensation heralding the accessing of his magic. Then she watched as Auden, Ilain, and herself grew hazy, their forms increasingly faint as the shroud covered them.

Isla surveyed the seemingly empty space where they had once been visible. "Impressive," she remarked, then turned to Jarrad. "Lead the way, Hoult."

"With pleasure, Freye."

Jarrad spurred his horse, circumventing the rest of the party to take the front. Isla remained at his side, the rest of them falling in line. They continued down the road to the line of people waiting to enter the dark stone walls of Mouroc. Dozens of carts, wagons, horses, and individuals made slow progress as the city guards thoroughly questioned and searched them. Blount's writ had been effective and widespread, forcing their troop to stay clear of settlements for the last few weeks. They'd only managed to make it through the border crossings due to possession of the Night Relic and Deckard's unexpected magic.

Now, Evylin could feel the faintest thrum of power as they inched closer and closer to the gates. Guards in dark gray uniforms with the deepest amethyst accents milled all around the muddy entry point. Made of wood and metal, the hulking gates were set into a stonework frame.

When their turn came at the gate, Evylin felt Deckard's frame tense. She looked over her shoulder, watching as Ilain and Auden cautiously worked to keep out of the path of the guards. Knowing how hard he was working, Evylin leaned deeper into him, trying to transfer her focus into him by sheer physical contact. He drew in a sharp breath through his nose but otherwise showed no sign of recognizing her attempt to assist.

At the front, Jarrad and Isla came to a stop as the guards approached. "Highlord Hoult," said the lead guard. "Didn't realize you'd left the city."

"Had some business for the lady," Jarrad said casually. Then he withdrew a hand from under his cloak, tossing something to the guard. "Birde sends her regards."

The guard weighed a small pouch in his hand, grinning. "Always a pleasure to do business with the lady." He stepped back and waved them through. "Welcome back, milord."

"It's good to be back, Vauster," Jarrad said, nudging his horse through the gates.

Moving past the guards, Thom leaned nearer Deckard to mutter, "If they were just going to bribe them, why have you go to the trouble of . . . ?" He wiggled his fingers in a mock of magic.

"Because I don't imagine they had one hundred fifty gold pieces to cover the bounty on our collective heads on them," Deckard replied, an edge to his tone. "A bribe can stop a search only so long as the recipient doesn't see a more valuable alternative."

"Right," Thom muttered. "And even the hint of an Ephrian woman or two redheaded siblings would draw attention."

"Exactly." Deckard's jaw tensed as he murmured, "Though I'm not comfortable with their incessant use of bribery and violence."

Thom furrowed his brow. "It isn't as though they have much choice," he whispered. "Would you rather they had left us to Blount?"

"Of course not," Deckard said in a firm tone, annoyance creeping under the surface of his reply.

His irritation was, no doubt, caused by his impeccable scruples. While Evylin didn't necessarily find bribery to be altogether honorable, she did accept it as a useful tool. However, she understood that Deckard wasn't likely taking issue with the bribe and the violence used to facilitate their escape so much as the gray morality shown by the

Alliance in their limited acquaintance. This was the group of individuals they were supporting in the takeover of their government. Deckard was an upstanding Allorian; he would desire to serve an authority beyond reproach. But Evylin had to wonder if an organization with his impeccable moral standards could even exist. Was such a governing body possible in the face of such a ruthless adversary?

Unable to speak for fear of being heard by others, Evylin brushed her thumb against Deckard's stomach, hoping to soothe his concern for the moment.

Immediately, he grabbed her hands and jerked them higher on his torso. "As much as I appreciate such affection," he whispered, the words rumbling against her chest, "that's making it a bit difficult to focus."

Looking over his shoulder, Evylin could only see a slight flex of his jaw beneath the reddish-brown stubble. She only had to wonder at his reaction for a few spare seconds before realizing how low her hands had unintentionally drifted. Her cheeks heated even as she fought to maintain her poise.

"My apologies," she breathed against the hood of his cloak.

The city was a buzzing hive of sound and activity around them. Hundreds of people milled about the dirt-packed streets, running, pulling carts, shouting, laughing, slamming doors, hammering, cheering, arguing, buying, selling, and living their lives. Evylin found the scene jarringly similar to the hustle and bustle of Trollenston on market days, albeit on a far grander scale. Jarrad and Isla led them through the first sector, evidently the poorest one if the ramshackle houses and citizens' dingy clothing were any indication. The narrow streets made it so that Ethenn and Emmaas practically had to herd Auden and Ilain's horses to ensure strangers didn't jostle them.

Shortly, they arrived at a secondary gate. The guards there knew Jarrad too. This time, he didn't bother to toss them coins but exchanged a quick word with the head of the outpost. Evylin wondered if their easy passage was because they were friends or if the man was a member of the Alliance too. She assumed it could be both.

The next sector of Mouroc was nicer, though infinitesimally so. The houses were of a sturdier build, and the streets weren't as narrow, but the residents looked little better off. On they went, through the next gate—Jarrad did toss out another bag of coin there— and into the third sector.

The improvement was immediate. Fewer people crowded the streets, which, though unpaved, were in much better condition. The buzz of noise was deadened to a pleasant hum. The houses gradually rose in size and respectability. All the buildings were arranged in groupings, with small alleyways cutting alongside each one. Business began to cut in amongst the abodes, reminding Evylin again of Trollenston but on a far grander scale.

Then they reached the center of the sector.

The buildings grew tall, rising three and four stories above their heads. Their gray stone and brick façades were designed with a sense of refined architecture, giving the groupings the appearance of a single massive structure rather than individual premises. It looked remarkably like the Loclight District in Ephria City, and Evylin gaped with wistful awe. She thought back to the townhouse she and Deckard left behind, three barren stories that they intended to make a home. She wondered if they'd ever get that chance.

Jarrad led them to their final stop in front of a four-story triangular building that appeared to be a conglomerate of businesses. The light rain still pattered against the iron-cased windows. Trees and vining vegetation climbed portions of the tall walls. People drifted in and out of shops on the far end while a young boy sprang forward from the shadow of the alleyway. "Aye, yeh needin' stablin' fer yer herses?" the lad said in quite a fierce Waulden accent.

"Aye," Jarrad replied good-naturedly.

"Ah, Highlerd Hoult, I's wanderin' when yeh'd get back."

Jarrad flipped the boy a coin and said, "Let's keep my arrival to ourselves, eh, Coalum?"

"Aye, milerd!" Coalum quickly snuck the coin into his pocket while they dismounted.

Emmaas stepped forward, helping the boy gather the horses together with a kind greeting. Auden helped his sister down from her horse, then patted the Warrior on the shoulder to acknowledge that their steeds were clear to be taken away.

Deckard carefully assisted Evylin, their comrades blocking their action from the view of the street. His continued silence was surely due to the extended taxing of his magical reserves. Evylin remained close to him, her hand tucked into the crook of his arm to continue the sharing of her magical strength.

"This way," Jarrad summoned, leading them around the corner to the entry of the establishment. Clay planters sat on either side of the door, bright white and yellow flowers welcoming them. A metal sign hung above them, announcing that they had arrived at the Crimson Clover Hotel.

"What's a *hotel*?" Ethenn whispered to Rafferty, and Evylin leaned closer, curious as well.

"It's a really big inn," Rafferty explained, tone confident. "They've got 'em in Loclight too." Though he'd grown up in a village just as small as Evylin and Ethenn's, his work as an "entrepreneur" (in his case, a smuggler) provided him ample experience with individuals who had explored far more than the small settlements of Estshire.

Holding the door open, Jarrad ushered Isla in first; then, with a murmur of coaching from Deckard, Auden, Ilain, and Evylin entered while the rest of the group followed. The Crimson Clover was good to its name, the walls covered in deep red damask wallpaper and dark wood paneling wrapping around the lower half. In the foyer, a large fireplace crackled, two chairs and a sofa facing its warmth. A lantern-like chandelier dangled above their heads. To the far right of the room, a staircase twisted out of sight. And to the left, a reception counter awaited their arrival.

A man stood behind the tall wooden desk, head dipped over a book. Seeing his customers, he marked the page, shut it, and straightened his posture. His eyes shimmered brightly as he smiled. "Good day, Highlady Freye and Highlord Hoult," he said. "A pleasure to have you in our walls once again. Who are your companions?"

At the front, Isla returned the clerk's smile. "Good day, Maurus. These are our Ephrian friends."

The clerk, Maurus, nodded. He was a pleasant-looking man, somewhere in his early fifties, should his soft wrinkles and silvering temples be any indication. Pale as most Wauldeners were, he bore a smattering of freckles all over his skin. "Wonderful. We've been expecting you," he said cheerily.

Jarrad leaned against the polished high desk with lazy ease, gave his greeting to the man, and turned to Deckard. "You can drop the shroud now."

With a relieved sigh, Deckard's shoulders relaxed. The haze around Evylin and the Calders disappeared, yet the clerk showed no signs of surprise at their sudden appearance.

"Ah!" he exclaimed instead, eyes twinkling. "If it isn't the Calders. Been a long time since I've entertained your family. Now, my rooms are filled with them."

Ilain chortled merrily. "Auden, Isla, and I hardly constitute filling a hotel, Maurus."

The man scratched his graying beard, lips lifted in amusement. "I suppose that's true."

"But then again," a man's voice called from the staircase. Tall and trim, he leaned against the railing with a regal air. Bright, clear blue eyes stared at them underneath golden brows. A well-kept blond beard graced the jaw of his narrow face.

Evylin's heart lurched, and Deckard's hand clamped onto her arm, drawing her behind him as Thom, Ethenn, and Rafferty gaped in shock.

They'd been betrayed.

Blount started down the carpeted stairs, a familiar wry grin on his lips. "You've forgotten to include me," he said, his Waulden accent somehow less posh than Evylin remembered.

Deckard, Thom, and Ethenn went for their weapons, and Auden and Ilain rushed forward—but then Evylin realized it wasn't to attack. No, the pair were laughing. They were excited.

Meeting at the stairs, Ilain crashed into the prince first, their arms going around one another. And that's when Evylin understood.

Grabbing Deckard's wrist, she halted him from drawing his sword. "Wait," she instructed.

Pausing at her word, Deckard glanced from her and back to the Calders and Blount—who was not Blount. His posture remained tense even as he hesitated.

"Oh, firebrand, you smell fearsome," the man was saying, laughing along with the woman. He pulled back and took her face in his hands. "How are you ever going to snag a man looking like a drowned rat?"

Ilain slapped his cheek playfully. "I'm doing just fine, thank you," she retorted. "Believe it or not, I had two men fighting over me recently. Granted, it wasn't as romantic as you might think."

The man looked genuinely impressed. Then he turned and swept Auden into a rough, masculine embrace. "Auds," he said, scanning him. "How many times have I told you? You look horrid with a beard."

"What about you?" Auden said, gesturing to the man's blond scruff. "Since when have you gone wilding?"

"It's just temporary," he defended. "I didn't feel that your arrival warranted a shave. Now, if you'll excuse me—" He pushed Auden and Ilain out of his way, those sharp blue eyes landing solely on Isla. He took a deep breath and stepped forward.

Isla, ever calm and collected, met him halfway. He stood nearly a whole head taller than her, his pale complexion contrasting heavily against her bronzed skin. "o, love," she said. And with that, he took her in his arms, kissing her soundly.

Deckard's brow rose, and Evylin smirked.

When they'd finished their passionate embrace, the man and Isla drew apart, and the Blount look-alike faced the Ephrians. He seemed to grasp immediately that Deckard was the leader, holding his hand out to him. "Vayden Calder," he said, his smile revealing a kindness Evylin doubted Blount could ever possess. "You're the folks traveling with my siblings?"

Shaking the man's hand, a slow smile spread over Deckard's lips. "Yes. I'm Colonel Jonn Deckard," he returned. "It's, uh—well, it's a surprise to meet you."

Vayden's eyes crinkled, giving away his age and distinguishing him from Prince Blount even further. "Same here," he replied. "Welcome to the Alliance."

"Thank you," Deckard said. Reverting to his natural role, he angled to introduce his troop. "This is my wife, Evylin, my brother, Thom, and our friends, Ethenn and Rafferty."

"Nice to meet you all," Vayden said, eyes passing over them each with curiosity.

"You look just like—Ow!" Rafferty cried as Evylin's heel connected with his shin.

Though he didn't know the Calder family's backstory, she didn't want him to offend the man.

"No, it's all right," Vayden said with a laugh. "You're right; I do."

Thom eyed him with interest. "You're their brother?"

"I am."

"Why do you look like Blount then?" Rafferty demanded.

Vayden leveled him with a calm stare. "Because I'm his brother too."

Rafferty's nose scrunched, turning to Auden and Ilain. "Your father is King Blount?" he demanded, and Evylin saw his mistrust growing.

"Biologically," Vayden interjected, drawing the weasel's attention back to him, "he's *my* father. However, my true father is Daultun Calder."

Isla slid her hand around her husband's arm. "Shall we move this conversation somewhere more comfortable?" she asked.

Watching the exchange from the sidelines, Maurus the clerk perked up. "Graicelle is in the kitchen, preparing for noonday," he said. "I'm sure she'd have a little something to restore your energy, should you like."

Vayden surveyed his siblings and the Ephrians. "What do you think? Food first? Or would you like me to show you to your rooms so you can rest?"

"Food," Evylin, Rafferty, Thom, Ethenn, and Ilain all chimed in.

Jarrad stood. "You all have a splendid time," he said. "I'm off to check in with Birde before the evening festivities."

"Did Emmaas head out too?" Vayden asked.

Isla nodded. "He wanted to see his family."

Vayden smiled at his siblings, wrapping an arm around his wife. "I know the feeling."

Then he turned to the Ephrians. "This way."

CHAPTER TWO

Down a hallway on the ground floor, Vayden led the troop to the rear of the hotel. They passed several rooms for rent, the deep brown carpet muffling their tromping footsteps. After months on the road, Evylin's feet were unused to the cushioned flooring. It was odd being in a building, to begin with. Since they'd entered Wauld, they'd slept under the sky, rain, trees, and open air. Now, she couldn't decide whether she felt comforted or smothered by the dark walls and the unnatural glow of the yellow lamplight.

They entered the kitchen, a large, brightly lit space that opened into the dining hall. A row of windows revealed the courtyard behind the hotel, the drizzle of rain tapping on the glass. Tables and chairs filled the hall, enough for two or three dozen patrons to dine. A massive stone hearth filled the opposite wall. A young woman, perhaps a few years younger than Evylin, stood at the tall bench, chopping sausages. Another, older woman loitered at the fire, stirring one pot while surveying a few others.

The Calders were greeted with enthusiasm by the young woman, who was quickly identified as Graicelle, the daughter of Maurus, the manager of the Crimson Clover. It was evident that this hotel was a front for Alliance business. In what capacity, Evylin didn't know, but she assumed it functioned as a safe house or a covert meeting place.

"Please," Vayden said to the Ephrians and his family, "have a seat. We'll bring the food over shortly."

"We don't mind helping," Deckard offered, but Vayden waved him off.

They drew two tables together to suit their large party. In the shuffle to take their seats, Deckard was placed at the head with Evylin on one side and Thom on the other. Ilain readily took the seat next to Evylin, pulling Isla to sit next to her, creating a women's side of the table while Rafferty, Ethenn, and Auden were left to line up next to Thom, leaving the opposite head seat for Vayden, nearest to his wife.

"Do they have ale in this fine establishment?" Rafferty asked.

"They do," Isla said, settling her silver skirts around her. "However, I wouldn't advise that you drink any."

Rafferty lifted his white-blond brows. "Watered down?"

"Not at all," she replied. "You're simply in for a night of imbibing. It'd be best to keep your head on straight for the approaching meeting."

A look of pure excitement drew Rafferty's eyes wide while Thom leaned forward to ask, "The Alliance is keen on raucous parties?"

"The Alliance is keen on community," Ilain corrected, the brilliance of her rings contrasting strangely with her unusual, drab gray outfit. "We believe in living life to the fullest while building lasting connections. Often, that dynamic includes alcohol. It helps loosen the tongue and encourages . . ." Her eyes flashed to Ethenn, then she smirked. "Intimacy, both of the platonic and romantic variety."

Evylin and Deckard exchanged a look.

"Don't make our gatherings sound illicit, Lain," Auden chided, then addressed the rest of them. "They are wholesome events meant to inspire deep conversation and familial attachments. There's nothing raucous about them."

"Tell that to Vayden," Isla murmured.

Ilain snorted, a glimmer in her eye as she cast a look toward her brother, who was gathering refreshments in the kitchen. "Ah, yes. He rather embarrassed himself by professing his undying love for Isla at a celebration a couple of decades back," she explained. "I believe he broke his wrist when he fell off the table."

"It still gives him pangs when the weather's foul," Isla confirmed.

"You mean every day here in Wauld?" Thom returned.

Isla gave him an amused grin.

"So that's what we have to expect this evening?" Deckard asked. "A celebration?"

"Well, first," Vayden said, appearing at the table bearing a platter of meats and cheeses on one arm and a basket of bread on the other, "you're to expect a meeting of the Administration. Darling," he turned to Isla, "would you mind helping? My wrist is killing me today."

Isla took the basket proffered toward her. "It's your other hand, love."

"That it is," Vayden replied with a wink.

Following close behind him, the older woman from the kitchen placed glasses in front of each of them with a deft hand, then plunked a pitcher of water on the table and scurried back to her work at the hearth.

"Thank you, Mrs. Howerth," Vayden called, then took the seat next to Isla. He eyed Rafferty's hand, already in the breadbasket. "Shall we say grace?"

Rafferty's wily fingers stilled, then slowly withdrew a slice of rye. "That's right," he said sourly. "You lot are religious."

"You're not?" Isla asked.

He smirked. "Allore and I have our agreements."

Vayden reached out and took his wife's and brother's hands, grinning at the weasel. "Then you won't object to showing gratitude, will you?"

Evylin sucked in her bottom lip. She wasn't particularly religious herself, and prayers for meals were more of a familial habit than devout practice. She wondered what the Calders—and the Alliance at large—would say if they learned that she didn't fully espouse their views. Then Deckard's fingers slipped around hers, and she wondered what *he* would say about that. One of the first things she'd noticed about the captain who joined her family's dinner was his fervent "by your grace" as her father concluded the prayer. They'd never discussed their respective faiths, but now she worried he'd be disappointed to learn that hers was lacking.

Eyes closed, Evylin struggled to pay attention as Vayden's deep baritone filled the air. There were a great many things she and Deckard had never discussed. Their marriage was so quick, so unexpected, and they hadn't had time to question the efficacy of their union. Were they really a good match? Yes, as unexpected as it was to discover he was a Mage, and she was a Warrior, did that mean they were well-suited to one another? Certainly, the Calders touted the coincidence as Allore's way of marking them as one another's perfect balance. But then, that would make Auden as much her match as Deckard, and she certainly didn't believe that to be true.

The mumbled "by your graces" said around the table brought Evylin out of her disconcerted reverie. Deckard's hand lingered on hers before reaching to fill her glass with water. She watched his movements with growing unease. Should she broach the subject with him? There was so much they didn't know about one another. She hadn't even told him about Ryen. If she loved Deckard, shouldn't she be open with him about every area of her life, even the most broken, devastating parts?

"You mentioned a meeting," Deckard said, setting Evylin's glass in front of her. "Is it one we're required to attend?"

"I wouldn't say you're required." Vayden sat back while the Ephrians and his siblings snatched up the food hungrily. "But I would recommend you join."

"The Administration wants an account?" Ilain asked.

"Can you blame them?" Vayden replied, then glanced at his wife. "You've forced their greatest spy to reveal herself."

Ilain rolled her eyes. But it was Auden who spoke. "We didn't have much choice in the matter."

"No," Vayden allowed. "But they'd like an accounting of your mission anyway. The archminister has called for an impromptu hearing."

"A hearing?" Deckard asked with a startled scan of the table.

Evylin didn't feel any less unsettled, but Vayden held up a hand to forestall their concern. "It's merely a term," he assured them. "None of you is on trial. The Administration simply wants our most influential members to gather so they can understand the situation to its full extent."

That didn't make Evylin feel any better. "And what is the situation?" she asked.

Vayden's bright eyes shone in the light as he gave a dry grin that looked strikingly like Ilain's. "I should think you'd be aware of it," he said. "Seeing as you're in the midst of it yourself."

"You mean," Ethenn interjected, "this meeting is simply to hear what we've been up to these last two months?"

"More or less," Vayden confirmed.

"And," Auden added, "for us to request additional aid."

"What sort of aid?" Evylin asked.

"Finances, supplies . . ." Auden glanced at his brother and sister-in-law. "Members."

Lifting her chin, Evylin looked at Vayden and Isla with renewed interest. "You want to come with us?" she asked.

"If the Alliance will allow," Isla confirmed.

"Regardless of whom they allow," Auden said, "we need help now that we've lost two of the Relics."

Frowning, Evylin met first Deckard's, then Thom's stares. Though she thought Auden was correct, she didn't know how she felt about adding additional members to their party. It had been the seven of them for so long now that she could hardly imagine life any other way.

Eight, Evylin corrected herself. Hewitt was still with them, even if he was a ghost.

Evylin glanced at Deckard, wondering when he could bring her uncle back to her again.

Suddenly, the kitchen door burst open, slamming against the wall. They all whirled just as a youthful peal rent the air. "Mama!"

Isla gasped, leaping out of her seat. "Reya!"

In a frantic collision, Isla embraced a girl who looked to be in her early teens, with dark hair and pale skin. They clutched one another in a mess of tears, kisses, and murmured words. A sudden swell of homesickness clutched Evylin's heart. It'd been so long since she'd been held by her mother, a feeling she hadn't realized she missed so dearly.

Isla was muttering to her daughter in a foreign tongue that Evylin didn't understand while Vayden, Auden, and Ilain rose together. Then the mother spun to slap her husband with a sharp *smack*. "You didn't tell me she was here," she said, clinging fiercely to the teen.

Vayden smiled kindly even as he held a hand to the red mark blossoming on his cheek. "My darling, I wanted it to be a surprise," he said. He turned back to the others with a dry look. "I always forget how temperamental Schonese women can be."

Isla held her daughter closer even as the girl giggled in her embrace. "Papa brought me because he knew you'd be coming soon," she said, the features of her face a blend between the sharpness of Waulden and the fullness of Schonese. "I told him it was a bad idea to hide it from you. Hello, Aunt Lainy, Uncle Audy."

Rafferty sniggered at the nicknames while the family exchanged their greetings. Evylin smiled all the while. She hadn't known that Auden and Ilain had a niece. Granted, she hadn't known they had a sister-in-law either. And once again, she realized she didn't know very much about the people who surrounded her.

Thoughtful as ever, Deckard rose to set another chair at their table for the young Calder girl to join them. She sat between her aunt and mother, chatting blithely . . . until she spotted Ethenn across from her. The young girl blinked, taking in the strapping Warrior, then blushed deeply. She scanned the rest of the table, swallowing visibly. "Hello," she murmured.

"Hello," Evylin said, thinking of her own nieces. She'd never particularly gotten on with children, but this girl was old enough and the Calders were witty enough that she thought she might have some sporting conversation.

Vayden took his seat once more, nodding to the teen. "This is our daughter, Reyana," he said, then introduced her to the Ephrians.

Reyana shrank in her seat as the Ephrian men said their hellos. Her eyes kept darting between Ethenn and Thom, and she pressed closer to her aunt as though to hide, though Ilain wasn't very adequate cover, being trim as a post.

Granting the young girl mercy, Deckard started up the conversation with Vayden again, asking more about the meeting. However, Evylin was more interested in hearing Reyana's whisper to Ilain. "You have very attractive friends," she murmured.

Ilain patted her hand. "Yes, dear," she whispered back.

Reyana's eyes locked on Ethenn, who was failing to keep his eyes on his plate as though he knew he was being observed. "He's quite muscular," she said in a hushed tone.

"That one is mine, darling," Ilain replied. "But you can have the broody one in the corner."

Reyana snorted softly in laughter and put a hand to her mouth, making it so that Evylin couldn't pick up whatever she muttered next.

"And what is it that you do for the Alliance?" Deckard asked, drawing Evylin's attention back to the conversation.

"At present, I'm a bit of a glorified messenger," Vayden said with self-derision. "My age has caught up to me, you see. When I was younger, my likeness to the prince made me an invaluable asset. I often traveled under the guise of Prince Blount, helping to undermine the monarchy's authority in various military outposts or by retrieving sensitive information. I was quite successful in impersonating him until these wrinkles betrayed me."

"They make you look distinguished," Isla said.

"They make me look old," he corrected good-naturedly.

Evylin disagreed. She'd hardly noticed the lines on his face until he'd pointed them out himself. "How does that work?" she found herself asking.

The whole table turned toward her, and Vayden's lips quirked up at the corner. "How does what work?" he asked.

"Blount—Mages and their extended youth," she clarified, then looked at Ilain. "You said you're in your forties?"

"Forty-three to be precise," Ilain confirmed.

"Yet, you look younger than I," Evylin said.

Ilain brushed a hand through the air. "That's purely because you weren't readily using your magic until these last few months. It's why Jonn looks older than Auden despite being fifteen years his junior. The magic of Mages *and* Warriors keeps them young. Now that you're both accessing your magic, you won't age like normal humans. You'll stay looking youthful until . . . Well, likely for another century. Maybe two if you Bond."

"That's not—" Deckard began, but Ilain cut him off.

"Not a topic you'd like to discuss," she said reproachfully. "Well, forgive me if I think living longer and improved lovemaking is beneficial."

Evylin blushed, and Deckard blanched, while Ethenn choked on his food. Immediately, Rafferty began to laugh hysterically, and Thom covered his amused grin with a hand. The Wauldeners regarded them all with bemused expressions.

"I don't understand what—"

Isla took her daughter's hand, silencing her as she explained, "Ephrians are more reserved, Reya. They don't discuss things like marital intimacy in mixed company."

"And especially not in front of children," Thom added.

Reyana's face went red. "I'm thirteen," she said with great offense.

Thom failed to hold back a smirk. "My apologies, ma'am. I only meant to defend your honor."

That caused the girl to deflate as her whole face went bright red.

"As it is," Ilain went on, "most magical individuals appear in their mid-twenties to thirties for the majority of their lives. Look at Isla—" She gestured to the Wind Mage. "She's seventy-two."

"I beg your pardon?" Thom said with incredulous disbelief.

Evylin had to agree. Isla looked no older than her.

The woman in question shrugged. "I'm only half Waulden, so I'll likely die sooner than the average Mage. I was born in Schon and was only brought here when I was Reyana's age, which makes me less powerful as well. It's a wonder I haven't started aging yet."

"It's because you're stronger than you give yourself credit for," Vayden said supportively.

"I'm under no illusions of my abilities, love," she said. "And in fifty years, I will die happily at your side."

Evylin wanted to ask about the disparity in a marriage between magical and non-magical individuals but thought this was neither the time nor did she have the relationship with either Isla or Vayden required to make such an inquisition.

Instead, she returned to the topic of the couple's occupations. "You are both spies, then?" she asked.

"Were," Vayden corrected. "I aged out, and Isla's been compromised."

Evylin turned to Isla. "You said you were with Lady Renaul for three years."

Isla nodded, smiling knowingly as Evylin's eyes darted to Reyana. "That is correct," she said. "I haven't seen my daughter or my husband in three years. Nor was I able to contact them for fear that the duchess would discover me."

The Ephrians stared at the small family in alarm.

"That's asking a lot of a family," Deckard said.

"It's what we do in the Alliance," Isla continued, drawing her daughter closer. "We sacrifice everything for the sake of a better future—for our children."

Evylin met Deckard's stare. The sentiment made her feel unsettled. She didn't think Isla meant to pressure them or to suggest they offer the same sacrifice, but the weight of her words was still there. If they wanted to secure a better future, what were Evylin and Deckard willing to sacrifice?

Rafferty leaned forward, elbows propped on the table, as he gestured to Isla with a slice of cheese. "If this is a recruitment speech," he said, silver eyes glowing, "it's shit."

Vayden chuckled. "I assure you that we aren't bothered with recruiting you."

"Because you already suckered us into that when your siblings duped us before?" Ethenn said brusquely.

Evylin couldn't help her wry grin, feeling a similar cynicism.

"We didn't trick you," Ilain said with terse enunciation.

"You lied," Ethenn returned, not quite looking at her.

"It was our job."

He picked at the bread on his plate. "And duplicity is completely different from trickery."

A beat of silence passed uncomfortably as the table watched the pair. Deckard looked ready to interfere while Vayden narrowed his eyes, a brother watching out for his baby sister. Then Rafferty sniggered.

"He's got you there, firebrand," the weasel said.

Ilain glared at Ethenn even as she spoke to Rafferty. "If you call me that again, I'll burn your stupid mustache off."

Rafferty self-consciously brushed down his white-blond stubble. "It's the only facial hair I can grow," he said defensively.

"I promise you," Vayden interjected, an appeasing tone to his voice. "It was never the Alliance's intention to dupe you into anything. Auden and Ilain have made many sacrifices themselves, doing what they must to ensure the salvation of all our people. You were never intended to join them in the first place."

"We weren't?" Evylin asked.

"We'll get into that at the meeting," Auden said. "But no, you weren't, and no, we didn't bring you into this intending to force you into our services. We asked your forgiveness in Virwoud, and you all agreed to help us despite our lies. Once this mission is over, if you choose to go your separate ways, you may."

Deckard's jaw tightened, reminding Evylin that the claim wasn't wholly true. Auden had used Deckard's desire to make Evylin happy against him, eliciting his promise to join the Alliance at the end of their journey together. As Deckard would never go back on his word, it appeared their future was set.

An air of discontent rested over the table. Despite the Calders' apologies and placating remarks, the Ephrians weren't ready to trust them. Not when every act they'd experienced by the Alliance was riddled with deceit and manipulation.

Clearing his throat, Thom spoke. "I think," he said calmly, "that this is a conversation better discussed when we aren't so tired."

Deckard nodded. "Yes, thank you, Thom, you're right." He looked at Vayden and Isla then. "And you have a family to spend time with. We appreciate your welcome and hospitality, but we don't want to forestall your reunion any longer."

Vayden's chin lifted in gratitude. Whether or not it was genuine, Evylin couldn't tell. "In that case," he said, rising, "allow me to escort you back to Maurus. He'll have your rooms ready, I'm sure."

As one, the Ephrians rose, their chairs scraping against the wooden floor. Ilain remained in her seat a few moments longer, her fingers tapping against the tabletop in agitation. The men began to move away, but Evylin paused and leaned down.

"Don't take it personally," she whispered. "You're still our friend."

Ilain's eyes widened, then she laughed. "Oh, Evie," she said with a sigh. She stood, grinning like her old self. "You are delightfully obtuse sometimes."

"Excuse me?" Evylin said, unsure if she should be offended.

Ilain dipped her head closer. "I'll give you a hint," she said, slipping her arm through Evylin's. "What's five foot, seven inches with shaggy brown hair and a blush to rival Reyana's?"

Evylin smirked. "Ethenn."

"Precisely."

Allowing Ilain to lead her out of the room, Evylin moved behind the group and back into the hotel's lobby. Maurus awaited them at his desk, reading his book. Evylin tried to catch a glimpse of the title but failed as the clerk handed out keys and gave directions to their rooms. He'd given them an entire wing on the third floor, it seemed.

"Best rooms in the place," Maurus said. "You'll find the bathing chambers at the end of the hall, one for the men and one for the ladies. My son, Hendrin, brought in your saddlebags." He gestured to the stack behind the counter, and Thom and Ethenn began to hand them out. "And earlier, he lit the stoves and stocked each room with additional provisions. You'll find some new clothes, soaps, oils, those sorts of things. If you need anything else, don't hesitate to ask."

"Thank you," Deckard said, taking both his and Evylin's saddlebags.

Maurus smiled. "It's our pleasure," he said, eyes darting to the empty foyer. "What with what all you're doing for our people."

Vayden, Isla, and Reyana parted from the troop on the second floor, heading to their previously acquired room. Evylin glanced after them, wondering what they intended to do with their daughter if the Alliance approved their place on the team. They couldn't bring a thirteen-year-old along with them to recover the Relics. Would they send her to live with family? Did the Calders have other family? Ilain had mentioned their parents living in the province of the Highloft Moors, but that was at least a week's journey from Mouroc. Would they send the girl such a distance alone?

Up the next flight of stairs, they found their rooms at the back of the building, nearest to the bathing chambers. Six rooms lined the hall, one each for Thom, Rafferty, Ethenn, Ilain, and Auden. A final room for Evylin and Deckard was at the very end— Maurus had been specific about its location, telling them the other rooms were singles and wouldn't suit a couple. Though Evylin only caught a glimpse of Thom's room across the hall from theirs, the reason was evident in that brief sighting alone. The singles were narrow, small spaces, though well-lit by a tall window and well-dressed with single-person beds.

However, stepping into her room with Deckard, Evylin felt that Maurus had vastly undersold the difference. Their room wasn't just larger—it was a suite. The crimson wallpaper and mahogany paneling continued through the room, little gold flecks in the damask catching in the oil lamps' light. A small stove sat in the corner, heating the room with a two-person table at its side, already dressed for tea, while a kettle awaited warming over the burner. Heavy draperies pulled back on either side, a grand window flooded the room with light. It overlooked the back of the building, giving a glimpse of the triangular courtyard. A golden chandelier, simple but elegant, hung over a settee with brown paper-wrapped packages waiting to be opened. At the back of the room stood a wardrobe and a changing screen.

And in the center, a large, four-poster bed with crimson curtains and matching bedding beckoned her.

Deckard shut the door, and Evylin's shoulders slumped as she stared at the bed. "Do you think we have time for a nap?" she asked.

A soft chuckle escaped him. He moved to set the saddlebags next to the packages on the tea table. "It's," he glanced at the clock on the side table, "a quarter past two, and Vayden said the meeting is set to begin at seven, so I'd say, yes."

Evylin sighed and flopped face-first onto the bed. "Praise Allore," she mumbled into the comforter. Then she lifted her head to look at Deckard, propping herself on her elbows. "When is dinner?"

He took a seat at the foot of the bed. "We just ate, and you're already concerned about dinner?"

"We had a snack," she corrected. "And I haven't eaten properly in months. Now, when Vayden was giving you our schedule, did he happen to mention when we'll be eating?"

Deckard smiled fondly. "He did."

"And?"

"The meeting includes a meal."

Evylin pursed her lips. "Well, at least we'll have nourishment while we listen to people drone on for hours."

"You expect the meeting to be boring?"

"My father is a magistrate," she reminded him. "I grew up going to 'hearings.' All of them were boring. And none of them had food."

"Poor child."

Evylin poked his thigh. "Don't mock me," she said. "I'm testy when I'm hungry and even more so when I'm tired."

Deckard snatched her hand from the bed and kissed her knuckles. "So I've learned. But may I make a suggestion?"

"If you must."

"Perhaps you'd enjoy your nap more should you take a bath first."

Evylin sucked in her bottom lip, enjoying the tender way Deckard was looking at her, yet feeling shy all the same. "Are you suggesting that I smell poorly?" she teased.

He shifted farther onto the bed, moving to sit at her side. She rolled over to look up at him, and he dipped his head lower. "Not at all," he promised. His fingers traced the edge of her braid, which trailed across the comforter. "I'm merely thinking of your comfort."

With Deckard hovering over her like that, Evylin found words rather difficult. She wasn't yet accustomed to the newfound intimacy in their marriage. For all their flirting and time together, for all their kisses and united feelings, her body still faltered when she thought of being *with* him again.

Evylin wondered if he could see her unsteady pulse thrumming through her veins. She didn't know whether she wanted him to kiss her or if she wanted to run from the room and hide. "Then perhaps," she murmured, the words coming out in a breath as she held his green-blue gaze, "you ought to move away so I can get up."

He drew his thumb along her jaw. "Perhaps you're right," he said, then leaned closer.

Evylin's hand shot up, pressing against his chest to keep him back. "Jonn," she warned, "if you kiss me now, I—I'm not sure I'll be able to stop."

His jaw twitched with a faint smile that turned into a grimace. "I'm not sure I would be able to either," he admitted, then pulled away with a heavy sigh. He climbed off the bed, reaching for her hands. "Come on. We ought to get ourselves moving so you can get to your nap."

Evylin let him pull her from the bed, even as she groaned. She wasn't sure whether to be grateful for his practicality or annoyed by it. As he helped her search through the packages and gather supplies for a bath, she found herself wishing she'd let him kiss her, nap be damned. But being the conscientious and solicitous man he was, Deckard sent her off into the hall, arms loaded with a fresh change of clothes, a towel, and soaps, with the promise of a fresh pot of tea on her return.

While lounging in one of the oversized tubs within the women's bathing chamber, Evylin decided she was, in fact, grateful for Deckard's practicality. It'd been far too long since she'd had a good soaking bath, possibly since their time in Loclight two months ago. Even at Renaul's, the servant had scrubbed her skin with a fury, rushing through the process.

Now, Evylin leaned back, luxuriating in the steam and allowing the pads of her fingers to wrinkle.

When she began to doze and the water took on a chill, Evylin finally forced herself out of its embrace. She toweled off and slipped into the new clothing provided for her by the Alliance. Though not a perfect fit, they'd done well enough. She tucked the white blouse into the light brown skirt she'd chosen, the petticoats soft against her legs.

Forgoing stockings, Evylin slipped out of the bathing chamber. The carpet tickled her toes as she darted down the hall to their room. Using the key Deckard had placed in with her supplies, she opened the door. The heady, floral scent of olifera and illus tea wafted to her nose.

"Oh, that smells divine," Evylin remarked, then frowned, realizing Deckard wasn't there. "Jonn?"

"Over here," he called, peeking out from behind the changing screen. "I'm just putting things away."

Evylin crossed the room, setting her belongings on the tea table on her way. She found him tucking folded piles of clothing into the wardrobe. "Jonn," she said again, smiling. "We aren't staying here for . . . Well, surely, not longer than a few days. Why are you wasting time stocking the wardrobe?"

"It's not a waste of time," he said. "No matter how long we're here, having piles of clothing and personal items strewn about the room will be a nuisance."

As a matter of course, Evylin had often left clothing and personal items scattered about her room. But she decided not to inform Deckard of that habit.

Tucking some of her damp, towel-dried hair behind her ear, Evylin scanned him. "And you chose to do this instead of bathe because . . . ?"

He shut the now-stocked wardrobe and smiled at her. "Because I wanted to have the room ready for your return so you could drink your tea and take your nap without worrying about cleaning up."

Though that was the last thing Evylin would have worried about, she found the sentiment charming.

"Now, come," Deckard said, taking her hand. "If I timed it right, the tea should be perfect."

Letting him seat her at the table by the stove, Evylin watched as Deckard went about pouring her tea. "That's usually the woman's job, you know," she teased.

He grinned. "Perhaps I like doing things for you. How do you take it?"

The unwelcome realization that they didn't know one another well enough to possess this basic information came back as Evylin blinked at the teacup in his hand. "Oh, uh—with cream and sugar."

"Really?" Deckard hesitated, then added the accoutrements.

Evylin rolled her eyes at his condescension. "Not all of us are so brave as to drink it black," she said, remembering how he took his tea from his stay with her family in Whickam Village. Perhaps she did know him better than she thought.

Deckard chuckled, setting the cup before her. "Yes, well, we mere mortals have to prove our bravery to you Warriors somehow."

"Says the Mage who single-handedly saved our lives."

He gave her a reproachful look as he went about tidying the bathing supplies she'd left by the settee. "If you're referring to our escape from Renaul, I very clearly couldn't have done that without Isla, Emmaas, and Jarrad's help."

"Agree to disagree. Jonn," she leveled him with a pointed stare, "you don't have to clean up after me."

"I know," he promised. "As I said, I like to take care of you."

"Yes, but—"

"Evie," he raised his brow, grinning, "I don't mind."

Doubtful, Evylin let him carry on, sipping her tea as he draped her towel over the changing screen with precision. Then he tucked her dirty clothing into the basket for the chambermaid to pick up in the morning.

Once he was done, Deckard gathered his own bathing supplies. Evylin realized she was staring but didn't care to stop. He was always so graceful, so controlled in his movements, almost like he was born to be royalty rather than a farmer's son. In the dim afternoon light, his hair looked more brown than usual, highlighting his more Ephrian features. While he could never be considered broad, he still bore a brawn thanks to his hard work as a soldier. She knew just how deceptive that trim figure of his was, hiding his strength.

Tapping her fingers against the porcelain teacup, Evylin considered how she might forestall his bath and convince him to linger for a few minutes. They still had four hours until the meeting. Plenty of time for them to enjoy one another's intimate company, for him to bathe, *and* for her to still get her nap.

A smirk tugged at her lips. She didn't think the convincing would be all that hard to accomplish.

With a fresh towel and a new set of clothes draped over one arm, Deckard met Evylin's stare, but evidently, he didn't notice the lasciviousness within it as he asked, "Have you amused yourself?"

"Pardon?"

He stepped closer, tapping the dimple in her cheek. "You're smiling."

"Mm, yes. I was having some rather entertaining thoughts."

"Oh? Might you share them with me?"

Evylin bit her bottom lip, suddenly embarrassed under his attentive gaze. "I was thinking about you," she said into her teacup.

"And you find me amusing?" he asked, sounding pleased.

Somehow, Evylin found enough courage to look back up at him and whisper, "In the most *diverting* way."

Deckard's brow lifted in surprise, catching her suggestive intonation. "I see," he murmured, his tongue darting out over his bottom lip. "In that case, I feel I must advise you to be careful, Mrs. Deckard. You're liable to give a man inappropriate notions with such a speech."

Evylin tipped her chin up at him. "That's rather the intent. And it's Private Deckard, sir. I'd ask you to address me properly."

"Well, then, Private," he bent forward, hand on the arm of her chair, his face only inches from hers, "I must beg your forgiveness."

His lips touched hers then in a gentle, affectionate kiss. It appeared to be his only intent as he began to pull back, but then it turned into a second, heartier kiss that sent a wave of tingles through Evylin's veins. A spike of magic egged her on, drawing her to reach for him when a small splash of tea spilled over onto her hand.

Evylin jerked back, righting the cup. She intended only to set it on the table behind her, but then Deckard stepped away, a soft chuckle slipping out of him.

"I think," he muttered, "that was good timing."

"I don't," Evylin murmured.

"Mm." Deckard stared at her, lips pressed together as though fighting an internal battle. Then he heaved a labored breath. "I'm going to bathe."

Evylin opened her mouth to suggest he wait, but no words came out.

Deckard must have understood her intention anyway because he smiled tenderly at her. "Finish your tea," he said. "When I come back, we'll continue this . . . conversation, shall we?"

Without hesitation, Evylin nodded vehemently.

"Excellent," Deckard said, turning and walking out of the room.

Evylin propped her elbow on the chair arm and dropped her head into her hand. Why did she feel like such an inept schoolgirl around him now? They were married. They were in love. They'd consummated their union two nights ago, removing all boundaries between them. And yet, the thought of taking him to her bed once more made her tongue thicken and her words flee. Was that normal?

A nervous laugh escaped her. She shook the thoughts off and sipped her tea in the empty room. Her anxieties wouldn't matter, she knew. Once they started, things would take their natural course as they had at Renaul's. She might begin with insecurity, but she'd end up in the blissful comfort of her husband's embrace.

Smiling at the thought, Evylin let her mind wander to other things as she finished her tea. The Alliance meeting would start in four hours. She wondered what the hearing would entail. A recounting of their travel, Auden had said, and a request for additional support and members. Would the Alliance approve that request? If so, would they send Vayden and Isla with them alone, or would other members join their cause?

Still unsure how she felt about more Alliance members joining their band, Evylin set her empty cup on the table. She drifted to the bed, leaning back against the pillows. Though she liked the Calders, she wasn't sure she was ready to have more devout members around, spoiling their fun little band. It seemed that every day brought new reasons to continually disrupt the troop they'd once been, trained by Hewitt as part of the Ephrian Army.

And what if they determined they didn't support the Alliance? They knew so little about the organization. It worried Evylin that they might discover some unsavory monarch at the helm or a cause they were unwilling to champion. The Administration they were meeting with appeared to be part of the governing force, but what did that even mean? Was this the same group of individuals who'd decided to wheedle the Ephrian soldiers into working for them? Their penchant for secrets and manipulation made her all the more uncomfortable. But then, Deckard's promise to serve them bothered her too.

What if they discovered the Alliance wasn't worthy of their help? What if they were cruel and tyrannical like King Blount? Or insipid and selfish like King Ephren? Would Deckard uphold his promise then? Or would he break it, to hell with whatever consequences came?

Evylin took a deep breath, staring out the window as she stretched her legs across the bed. And yet, what if the Alliance was true and noble? What if the Calders were right? What if this plan to return Allund to its original state, to the nation of Allore's calling, was pure and righteous? Deckard would certainly hold up his end of the bargain in that case. But would that include their own Bonding?

Playing with the buttons on her blouse, Evylin considered the idea. Could she be happy with that life? Life as Deckard's Warrior, Bonded to him, body and soul.

A smirk tugged at her lips. Yes, she could be *very* happy with that life. A hundred years with Deckard would never be enough. She'd settle for two centuries quite cheerfully.

Evylin's thoughts devolved over the next several minutes. Deckard would return soon, coming to claim his continued "conversation." She rolled onto her side, imagining him lying beside her, kissing her, touching her . . . and then promptly fell asleep.

CHAPTER THREE

The gentlest touch drew Evylin to open her heavy-lidded eyes. Deckard's deep voice thrummed through her ears, reaching down into her heart as he whispered her name. She rolled into the touch, his palm warm against her cheek. At last, he had returned.

Deckard pressed a kiss to her forehead. "It's time to go," he said softly.

Evylin's eyes flew open. "What?" she gasped.

Smiling down at her, Deckard's form was outlined by the bright amber light of sunset. "Well, we have a few minutes still," he said. "I thought you might need time to prepare."

Evylin stared at him in shock. "How long have you been back?"

He shrugged. "A little over three hours."

"You didn't wake me?"

"You were tired." Deckard's thumb brushed her cheekbone. "I wanted to let you sleep."

Evylin didn't know how to tell him that she'd rather have lost sleep to him and his affections than be well-rested. Women in Ephrian society didn't discuss such brazen topics, not even with their husbands. And while she normally didn't care about being perceived as a decorous lady, this was Colonel Jonn Deckard—he prized propriety more than most things. Perhaps he wouldn't appreciate her wanton thoughts.

Capturing his hand, Evylin held his gaze. "Next time," she said, "I give you permission to wake me."

He smiled, but Evylin wondered if he'd listen. He always was a bit too courteous for his own good.

Rising, Evylin asked about the time. They had fifteen minutes until they were expected in the foyer, where Vayden and Isla would escort them to the meeting. Not long, but just enough time for her to slip behind the changing screen and brush down her sleep-mussed hair in the looking glass.

"What were you doing all this time?" Evylin asked, readjusting her blouse.

Deckard's voice drifted to her from the other side of the screen. "Preparing. Thinking. Reading."

"The Alliance gave us books?"

"I found *your* book in your saddlebag."

"Oh." Evylin grabbed a woven shawl from the wardrobe. She'd forgotten that she'd brought the novel with her, but it was small, and she readily tucked it in with her belongings when they were preparing for their journey into Wauld. "Do you like it?"

Deckard waited patiently on the settee as she turned the corner. He wore a steel-blue coat and tan trousers tucked into his black boots. His eyes practically twinkled in the evening light. "It's no 'King's Knight,'" he said playfully, "but it'll do."

As Evylin approached, he stood, and she brushed his smooth jawline. "You shaved," she lamented.

"Was I not supposed to?"

"I've told you before," she said, angling her face toward his. "I like you with a bit of scruff."

"My sincerest apologies," he replied. "But I *don't*."

Evylin laughed as he took her hand, guiding her to the door. "In all your preparing, thinking, and reading, I take it you didn't consider joining me for a nap," she teased.

"I considered it," he admitted. "I just decided against it."

"Why?"

"I don't nap."

Evylin narrowed her gaze in disbelief.

Deckard shrugged, opening the door. "It doesn't agree with me."

She scoffed. "Napping agrees with everyone."

"I'll take your word for it," he said, turning the key in the lock just as the door across the hall opened.

"Almighty, you two took your time," Thom said, slipping out of his room. "I was waiting by the door for the last twenty minutes."

"Why?" Deckard asked just as the next two doors cracked open, Rafferty and Ethenn spilling over their thresholds.

"Time to go?" Rafferty said.

Deckard surveyed his men with incredulity. "Were you all waiting to go down with us?" he asked.

"Of course," Rafferty replied. "What, you thought we'd like to small talk while the Calders continued their family reunion? No, thanks."

Deckard sighed, and Evylin smiled. All three soldiers were dressed far more casually than their commanding officer, coats hanging open over their tunics, and only Ethenn had bothered to shave. They followed behind Evylin and Deckard like a personal guard.

"How did you three pass your afternoons?" Evylin asked as they descended the stairs, her hand tucked around Deckard's arm.

"Napped," the three men said in unison.

Evylin tossed Deckard a sly grin, to which he shook his head in amusement.

When they entered the foyer, they found only Vayden and Isla waiting. "You were late," Vayden said kindly, "so I sent Auds and Lainy on ahead with Reyana."

"Auds and Lainy," Rafferty quipped. "I do love a good nickname."

"Don't call her that if you want to live," Thom warned.

Vayden gestured for them to follow. "We'll go through the back," he explained. "The Alliance owns this whole set of buildings through various members, so we have ready access and viable excuses for our organization as a whole to visit the business. It makes meeting vastly easier, and it keeps individuals like my siblings and our Madam Warrior safe from prying eyes."

"Then the meeting isn't in the hotel?" Deckard asked.

"Oh, no, there isn't a room large enough," Vayden said. "There's a banquet hall on the far side of the complex. People rent it out for parties or dances. We use it for our meetings."

Going out through the kitchen's back door, they stepped into a triangular courtyard. The stable ran the length of one side, two alleyways splitting off from opposite sides. Lamps lit the space as the spring sun made its final descent, casting it in a dark yellow glow. A patch of grass filled most of the space, wide enough for only a few horses to graze at once.

Vayden and Isla led the way, he in a dark brown coat and she in a deep green dress. The couple stood in great contrast to one another. She was surely a whole foot shorter than her husband, and he was the epitome of a pale Wauldener while her Schonese heritage shone prominently in her black-brown hair and bronzed complexion. Yet, despite their three-year separation, somehow, the pair moved with a sense of comfort and awareness of one another that Evylin could only hope to achieve with Deckard someday.

When they reached the far side of the courtyard, Vayden opened another door. "After you, darling," he said with a sly grin to his wife.

"Thank you, love," Isla said, trailing her fingers along his arm as she stepped through. Then she motioned for the Ephrians to follow her. "This way. Most of those attending should already be here. And I won't have them stopping you to put in their bids for joining our venture."

They moved through a storage room, then a back hall, and finally into an entry space where two double doors hung open, leading into a grand hall. A large fireplace nearly filled an entire wall at the back of the room, heating the space. The vaulted ceilings featured large, yet simple, chandeliers. Black and brown square stones tiled the floor, and the walls were paneled in wood.

A great clamor of voices filled the hall with conversation and laughter. Four tables lined the room, three running parallel down the hall with enough room for twenty people at each, while the fourth stood before the fire, with only eight individuals sitting along its length and facing the others. It was evident that the dozens of attendees were perfectly at ease and in welcome company despite the blatant disparity in their stations. There were men and women dressed in the finery of the wealthy, some even possibly ranking as nobility. Others wore more middling suits and dresses. Even a few were in all but rags—likely the best attire they owned. Yet, the rich spoke with the poor and the poor with the rich as though they were the dearest of friends.

That is, until the Ephrians' presence was noticed.

The room fell into silence for but a moment before the murmurs began. Evylin inched closer to Deckard as Isla led their way to the far-left table. A gentleman dressed in all the trappings of wealth rose as they neared, but Vayden called from the back of the group, "Sit down, Clovis, or I'll make you."

Chagrined, the man dropped back into his seat while the people around him guffawed good-naturedly at his embarrassment.

From the back of the table, Isla gestured toward the center, where five empty seats awaited them. "Those are for you," she instructed as Vayden stepped up to her side. "We'll be across the table."

While the couple split off from them, they walked down the length of the floor, attempting to keep their heads down and ignore the obvious stares of the Alliance members. When they stopped at their seats, Thom tapped Deckard's arm and slipped around him, taking the one at the end while Deckard held the middle chair out of Evylin. Shortly thereafter, they were positioned—Ethenn, Rafferty, Evylin, Deckard, and Thom across from Auden, Ilain, Reyana, Isla, and Vayden.

As it appeared they were the last to arrive, one of the gentlemen at the head table rang a bell, signaling the start of the meeting. Several lines of serving staff funneled into the room, carrying trays of food while the gentleman stood. "Good evening, my friends," he called in a steady Waulden accent. His gray hair and wrinkled face marked his age to be somewhere near seventy, but his sharp gaze betrayed no wizened mind. "It is wonderful to see you all together once again, despite the circumstances."

With discomfort, Deckard adjusted next to Evylin. She felt just as uneasy as he, though she struggled to pay attention as platter after platter of food was set before them. Roasted goose, braised trout, meat pies, boiled potatoes, glazed carrots, fresh figs, glistening cherries, and lemon tarts. Her fingers twitched as another server placed a tiered dish of mini sausage rolls directly in front of her. The man at the head table was still talking, though, and no one had reached for the food except for Rafferty, who got a swift kick from Ilain across the table.

"As always, we will commence with the meal," the gentleman was saying, "before we proceed to the hearing. Today, we are thankful for the return of our treasured members, Highlord and Highlady Calder."

The siblings dipped their heads in gratitude at the recognition, though Ilain's lips also quirked proudly in the corner. They'd both cleaned up as well. Auden's wild beard was gone, and he'd tied back his overgrown hair. Dressed in a rich blue frock coat, he looked far more pulled together than he had since the Annaltide Day celebration in Loclight.

And Ilain—she'd accepted her return to civilized society with open arms. She wore a scarlet gown of luxurious silk, its low-cut bodice embellished with red glass beads that shimmered in the light and brought attention to the sheer organza sleeves that sat off her pale shoulders, the beadwork trailing down to her wrists. If that weren't enough, her copper hair cascaded with renewed curls, and her jade green eyes were lined with the most delicate application of pigment.

Though Evylin was sure Deckard would call Ilain's dress improper or unladylike, she couldn't help finding it immeasurably stunning.

Based on how Ethenn completely avoided looking in Ilain's direction while his neck turned the shade of her dress, he felt the same.

At the head table, the gentleman said a devout prayer over the meal, then bade them all enjoy the feast. It took no time for the Alliance members to take advantage of his permission. The room filled with chatter once again as people tucked into the meal with vigor. The serving staff continued to pass through the hall, offering to fill glasses with fragrant wine.

An older woman stopped next to Evylin and Deckard, pitcher in hand. "Schonese red, sir?" she offered.

"No, thank—" Deckard cut himself off, eyes widening. "Did you say Schonese?"

"Yes, sir."

Without hesitation, Deckard lifted his glass to her. "Keep it coming."

The woman smiled knowingly. "Yes, sir," she said, then offered the same to Evylin.

Once she was gone, Evylin leaned over to him. "Who are you?"

Deckard's brow pinched together as he took a sip. "I don't know what you're talking about."

Evylin smirked. "Try not to get too drunk," she said. "I'd rather not nurse you back to health in the morning."

"It's Schonese wine," he protested, lifting the glass to his lips once more. "And I don't get drunk."

Evylin laughed, turning as she heard Auden say her name. He was talking to a beautiful, dark-skinned woman on his right, gesturing to the Ephrians in turn as he introduced them. The woman's cunning eyes scanned the troop, nodding thoughtfully, though she looked disinterested in Auden's conversation. On her other side sat Emmaas Caarney, the Warrior who'd helped to save them from Renaul.

Scanning the rest of the table, Evylin caught sight of Jarrad Hoult near the front of the room, in deep conversation with those around him. But the rest of the attendees were strangers to her. The great majority of men and women were undoubtedly Waulden, while a smattering—like Emmaas and the young woman at his side—were clearly Ephrian. She wondered how many of her countrymen had defected to join this rebel organization's ranks.

"Who are those trussed-up peacocks up front?" Rafferty asked Ilain, drawing Evylin's attention.

Ilain swallowed a sip of wine. "You mean the ministers?" she replied. "They're our ruling body for the time being. There are eight, four men and four women, to represent balance. Though this is just the Waulden Administration. There are eight others across the border who handle Ephrian affairs."

Evylin leaned forward in interest. "Is Lord Carlile one of them?" she asked, thinking of the white-haired man they'd met in Banbury before saving Prince Ephren's life. The lord worked as King Ephren's most trusted advisor, but as they'd discovered later, he was really a double agent for the Alliance.

"No," Ilain said. "Carlile is simply a member, though an influential one."

"Politics," Rafferty grumbled. "Tell me, Lainy: Where's the drama? Who hates whom? Who's scheming? Who are the rivals?"

Ilain grinned wickedly. "And take the sport out of the discovery? No, no. You'll have to weasel out that information yourself."

Over the next hour, they ate their fill and laughed more heartily than they had in what seemed to be months. After much reflection, Evylin managed to pinpoint the exact moment: their celebration after rescuing Prince Ephren. Her heart pinched, thinking of Hewitt. She wished he were here, seated at her side. He would know what to do and what to say to the Alliance's requests.

Deckard's hand brushed hers on the table. "What is it?" he whispered in her ear.

Magic prickled at her senses as he leaned in, but the feeling floated away. "Nothing," she murmured.

His fingers wrapped around hers, brow rising knowingly.

A sad smile tugged at her lips. How well he knew her moods now. "Just thinking of Hewitt," she explained.

Deckard's chin dipped, his eyes darting across the table before meeting hers again. "I can let you see him again," he said. "So long as I have the Night Relic, I am strong enough now."

Her heart pattered hopefully. "I would like that. Very much."

"Tomorrow," he promised.

Evylin's smile grew, and she opened her mouth to thank him when the bell rang again. The chatter quieted as the attendees shifted in their seats, turning to the front of the hall. A man stood from the far-right table, moving to stand at a small writing desk. His orange hair flashed in the lamplight as he opened a book and rattled off an opening speech.

Once the clerk had finished announcing the start of the meeting, he lifted a pen from the desk. "Now, we shall proceed with the agenda," he said in his nasal Waulden tone. "We are here to receive the account of Highlord and Highlady Calder on their mission to retrieve the Ateri Relics of Allore. With your permission, Archminister Fishere, we will have Highlord Calder bring forth the report now."

The gray-haired gentleman who'd welcomed them before the meal nodded his assent.

The clerk gestured toward Auden. "Highlord Calder, if you please."

Pushing back his chair, Auden stood, clasping his hands before him. "Good evening, all," he said, his accent thicker than usual. "It's a pleasure to be back, enjoying the companionship of like-minded men and women such as yourselves. During our time in Ephria, I was in regular contact with Lord Carlile, but since our return to Wauld, our communication has been impeded. While I assume he forwarded my updates to you, I take it you'd like me to give an account of my sister's and my entire journey."

The archminister lifted his hand in an approving wave.

Auden cleared his throat and began his recounting. "As you know, Ilain and I took the Fire Relic from Doorstunds Reach on the thirty-ninth of Terraen, and we fled to Ephria thereafter. Upon our arrival in Ephria City nearly two weeks later, we stayed hidden on Lord Carlile's estate while he was away with Prince Caspar Ephren, intending to enact his staged kidnapping."

Deckard shifted in his seat. Evylin didn't have to guess at his discomfort. The kidnapping could hardly be considered "staged" when the prince was, in fact, kidnapped, and the lives of several men were lost in the process. However, she also recognized there had been no true danger to the prince's life in the plot, as it was only intended to scare the king into action.

Auden went on to explain the change to the ploy's enactment due to the arrival of the Ephrian Army's Third Volunteer Company at Banbury, led by the then-Captain Deckard. Upon meeting Deckard and Evylin, Lord Carlile knew the kidnapping would not succeed. Not while a dedicated military officer was in the area. But as they couldn't stop the plot, they'd have to shift it.

Beyond that, Carlile had recognized Evylin as a Warrior during their dinner and wanted to confirm his suspicions. While Auden didn't explain how Carlile had known, Blount had also recognized Evylin's magic purely upon looking at her. She made a note to ask Ilain about that in the future.

"Upon Lord Carlile's return to Ephria City," Auden continued, "he informed us of his revised plan, then introduced us to King Ephren. Through careful manipulation of the king's ego, Carlile and our story convinced him of the necessity of retrieving the Relics and stopping the war, lest the Waulden king be successful in killing his heir in the future. At which point, King Ephren formed what he called the Order of the King."

A smattering of derisive laughter passed through the room.

Ilain grinned smugly as Auden continued, "He assigned these fine soldiers," he swept his hand toward the Ephrians, "to act as our personal guards, assisting us in reclaiming the Relics. Shall I introduce them?"

At the archminister's nod, Auden went down the line.

The woman to the archminister's immediate left sat forward to ask, "Didn't Carlile's report list six soldiers?"

Auden's gaze flickered to Evylin. "Yes, Minister Birde," he confirmed. "Unfortunately, we lost him at the hands of Prince Blount's ambush."

A collective rumble passed through the room.

"This was how you discovered the prince's involvement?" another female minister at the far end asked.

"It was."

Archminister Fishere took the lead. "Blount attacked you himself?"

"No, Archminister."

"Then how did you come to this conclusion?"

Auden told them of their experience in the Water Keep, the discovery of Blount's identity, his torture resulting in the divestment of the Relics' locations, and their escape. "When he informed them of how Rafferty stole the Day and Fire Relics from an ignorant Blount, the weasel piped up.

"You're welcome!" he called, tipping his wine glass toward the ministers.

Another smattering of chuckles filled the room before Auden continued. He explained the Ephrians' discovery of the Calders' lies, the subsequent reveal of the Alliance, and the soldiers' agreement to continue assisting the Calders in saving their countries. He covered their long journey through Wauld—leaving out the most dramatic parts and completely ignoring the tumultuous nature of Evylin and Deckard's relationship, to her gratitude. Then he reported Caustin's capture of them and Renaul's plans to give them to Blount.

At that point, the archminister requested that Isla give her account of the events at Renaul's. Her story matched everything Evylin already knew—she'd been working with Renaul for the past three years as her steward and personal guard, she heard of the plot to capture the Calders and Ephrians, and she requested aid from the Alliance to help rescue them from the mad noblewoman's clutches. Emmaas and Jarrad arrived, and the plans were set into place.

Isla also pointed out that though Renaul managed to take three Relics from them— a great loss—she failed to obtain the things Blount wanted most.

"Which are?" the archminister prompted.

"The Night Relic," Isla said, then her eyes darted to their side of the table. "And the opportunity to Bond with Evylin Deckard. The prince is quite fixated on her, as evidenced by his recent letters to Lady Renaul. He wrote, 'Her role is more important than anything—in truth, she is even more important than the Relics.' I believe this supports our theory of his increasing mania, suggesting early signs of the Deep."

While several members murmured in the crowd, the ministers regarded one another cautiously. "I see," the archminister said at last. "We will discuss that in more depth momentarily. First, how was it that you managed to retain the Night Relic?"

"It wasn't just the Night Relic, sir," Auden said, still standing. "Corporals Rafferty and Loxley also managed to hide the Wind Relic."

Archminister Fishere raised his graying brow. "How?"

"During our time in Wauld, we discovered that Corporal Loxley is a Warrior," Auden said.

Several "oohs" passed through the room.

"And Colonel Deckard is a Mage."

Now, a collective hum gathered. Deckard drew a hand along his jaw, and Evylin brushed her knuckles along the side of his leg under the table. He gave her a half-hearted smile of gratitude for her support.

"An Ephrian Mage?" Minister Birde exclaimed.

"It appears," Auden said, "that his grandfather was Waulden."

While the murmuring continued, the archminister indicated that Auden should return to his explanation.

"Corporal Loxley handed Corporal Rafferty the Wind Relic," he said, "and as a smuggler, he managed to hide it away on his person. And evidently, Caustin's men didn't search him *that* thoroughly."

Rafferty sniggered softly.

"As to the Night Relic, Colonel Deckard managed to alter its appearance, so they mistook it for only a common family crest. I believe he must have used some form of shroud."

The archminister's gaze narrowed. "If Carlile noticed Mrs. Deckard's magical abilities—"

"Private," Deckard, Thom, Rafferty, and Ethenn corrected as one.

Evylin pressed her lips together around a smirk as the room fell silent.

The archminister stared at them. "I'm sorry, what?"

The soldiers deferred to Deckard as he replied, "Her correct address is Private Deckard, sir."

A wry grin split the archminister's wrinkled face. "My apologies, Colonel," he said, his genteel tone blithe. Then he turned to Evylin. "And to you, Private Deckard. I hope I didn't offend."

Approving of the gentleman's good humor, Evylin returned his grin. "Not at all," she said.

Archminister Fishere turned back to Auden. "How is it that there were two Warriors and a Mage in one company without Carlile's notice? Without your or your sister's notice?"

"The only explanation I can offer, Archminister," Auden said, "is that none of them knew of their magic and, therefore, were not using it to where we could recognize their power."

Immediately, Ilain's hand shot up, the vibrant gemstones on her rings glittering in the table's candlelight. "I have a theory," she said, then dropped her hand as the room stared at her.

Auden gaped at his sister, but the ministers appeared amused.

"Of course you do," Archminister Fishere said as though a theory from Ilain was expected. "Do share, Highlady Calder."

Ilain rose, the beadwork on her bodice twinkling like starlight. "With pleasure," she said, then threw a wink at Ethenn, who was failing miserably at keeping his eyes off her. Granted, that seemed to be the point of the provocative gown.

"As my brother mentioned," Ilain began, authority evident within her words and drawn-back shoulders, "we lost our sixth Ephrian member at the hands of Blount. What he didn't tell you is that Major General Hewitt Glaas was Private Evylin Deckard's uncle and a Warrior as well.'

The archminister's brow shot up. "Another Warrior? Finding two together is . . . Impossible. You're telling me that you found three?"

"I'm telling you, Edmaund, that I've found the solution to your Warrior problem."

The room was deathly silent.

Ilain didn't falter under the direct stares of dozens of people. She simply held the archminister's gaze as though he were her equal—her peer. And perhaps he was.

"Hewitt chose this team," she went on, her hand sweeping over the five Ephrians. "He trained Evylin from childhood. She's a fully-fledged Warrior thanks to him, and though she could use more training with her magic, I'd defy any of our men to beat her. Then you take Jonn, her husband, whom Hewitt chose for her after only three days of knowing him. He knew they were right for one another. A Warrior and a Mage."

Evylin and Deckard exchanged a look, his thumb pressing against hers beneath the table.

Ilain motioned generally in Ethenn's direction, not deigning to look at him. "Hewitt handpicked Loxley out of hundreds of soldiers. Hundreds who *weren't* Warriors. If you count up the odds of three Warriors among nearly five hundred men, that's less than a single percentage. And while it's greater than the presumed ratio of magical to non-magical individuals, what if our numbers are wrong?"

The ministers all considered her words thoughtfully, even as Ilain continued, "Jonn is a Mage—that's a fluke of his heritage. Evylin and Ethenn? They're two out of one million."

"This is your theory, then?" Archminister Fishere said. "As a Warrior, this Major General Glaas was able to sense the magic in them."

"Exactly."

The ministers began conferring with one another as the crowd resumed its murmuring, heads bent together.

Evylin drew in an unsteady breath. Was it possible? Had Hewitt sensed Deckard's magic from the start? Was that how he'd known they were a good match? Moreover, was it magic that drew Evylin to Deckard in the first place? If Hewitt could sense magic because he was a Warrior, that meant Evylin could, too, didn't it?

Evylin looked up at her husband, finding his green-blue gaze turned to her already. Had she always known, innately? Was her love for him nothing more than a Warrior drawn to a Mage, magic drawing magic?

No. Evylin leaned closer to Deckard, the arms of their chairs getting in her way. Whatever magical pull she felt, it wasn't the cause of her love. She'd chosen Deckard— consciously. Not Thom, Rafferty, Ethenn, Auden, nor any other man she'd come across in twenty-seven years. Only Jonn Deckard had captured her affection and her desire. Not because he was a Mage but because he was the only man her heart could love.

Archminister Fishere held up his hand, signaling for silence. "This is a potentially astounding and impactful discovery, Highlady Calder," he said with weighty intonation. "One that we will need more evidence of before it can be officially accepted."

"Where else would you go for evidence?" Ilain asked. "You've got four Warriors of your own in this room."

Glancing at his fellow ministers, Fishere accepted the idea. "All right, Highlady Calder, we'll put your theory to the test. General Waaver, Sergeant Caarney, Major Olsen, and Lieutenant Lohen, please rise."

Around the room, chairs scraped against the tiles as the four Warriors stood. One man at the farthest table and one in the center, both with rich tans and burly builds like Ethenn. At their table, Emmaas and the woman at his side stood as well.

Remembering that Emmaas's granddaughter was a Warrior, Evylin marked this woman as his relative. Though vastly shorter than her family patriarch and with a complexion more of a tawny brown than umber, they shared the same strong cheekbones and full features.

The archminister greeted the four of them with a grateful nod. "I'd ask that you all consider my question carefully before you reply, as this could be an imperative turning point for our people." He leaned forward to impress the inquiry upon them. "Can you say with any certainty that you have a sense of when a person carries magic within them?"

The Warriors took their time, thinking and hesitating. The room filled with anticipation, waiting for their answers. Evylin scanned the room, trying to puzzle out the concept herself. Could she sense when others were magical? If there were Warriors attending the meeting tonight, surely there would be other Mages beyond those of their acquaintance. Was it possible that she could identify them by intuition alone?

The man at the far side of the hall cleared his throat, calling their attention.

"General Waaver," the archminister recognized.

The general crossed boulder-like arms over his broad chest. "While Commander Loew might have more knowledge of the texts than I," he began, "I don't remember reading anything about this phenomenon. And with the literature destroyed centuries ago, we can't consult them. However, if you're asking for my personal experience alone . . . Then yes. I have discovered a dozen or so magical individuals that others failed to spot. Not regularly, mind you, but often enough that it seems unlikely for it to be a coincidence."

"I concur with General Waaver," Emmaas said. "There's much about the Warriors' way of life that we have yet to rediscover for ourselves. But from my own life, I can say there's a certain air about those with magic."

"A certain air?" the archminister repeated as though asking for clarification.

Emmaas's granddaughter took over for him. "It's a feeling in your gut," she said, her voice tinged with the same sultry accent as Isla's. "You look at someone and know there's something different about them."

"That's a bit too hypothetical for proof, I'm afraid."

"But it *is* provable," she returned. "If you put a Warrior in a room with twenty individuals and they find the one with magic, *that's* proof. You can try that experiment hundreds of times until you're satisfied. It doesn't matter if it's a gut feeling if it works."

The archminister brushed a hand along his silvery beard. "So you've experienced this sensation yourself?"

"Only a few times," she confirmed. "But that's all that matters, isn't it?"

"I agree with Lieutenant Lohen," the third man chimed in from across the room. "This is a matter that should be further investigated."

"Mm." Archminister Fishere nodded. "Thank you for your input, Officers. We will give your recommendation serious consideration." He turned back to Auden and Ilain as the clerk scribbled notes in his ledger. "Your theory appears to be believable, Highlady Calder. But the question remains: Why didn't Lord Carlile notice the other three magical people amongst your team? I'll grant that he's not a Warrior, but he is trained to recognize magic when he sees it. Why did he only notice Private Deckard?"

"I can tell you why," Rafferty muttered to Ethenn under his breath.

Ignorant of his remark, Ilain answered, "Carlile only spent time with Evylin and Jonn. He was barely around Hewitt and Loxley for more than a handful of minutes, and that was at a distance."

"And how did he miss Colonel Deckard's magic?"

"He's a Night Mage," Auden interjected. "Existentials are notorious for hiding their magic, particularly when they are unaware of it themselves."

Bridging his hands in front of him, Archminister Fishere leaned forward in his seat. "Colonel Deckard," he called.

Deckard startled upon being directly addressed. "Yes, sir?" he replied, voice strong and amenable as a good soldier's should be.

"You never had any idea of your power's existence within you?" Fishere asked.

"No, sir."

"Hm. Thank you, Colonel." He turned back to Ilain. "Your theory is looking quite plausible, Highlady Calder. And it seems Lord Carlile's reputation remains intact," he said with a small smile.

"Now, to the matter at hand," the archminister said, leaning back in his seat. "We've had an adequate recounting, and it is the Administration's duty to confer before determining our final course. That said, are there any requests you'd like to put forth to be voted upon between us?"

Ilain resumed her seat as Auden readily gave his reply. "Yes, Archminister. We require additional aid on our journey. With only two Relics and the final, most dangerous Keeps ahead, if we're to complete this journey and secure the future of Allund, we'll need assistance."

"You mean more members added to your party?"

"Yes, sir."

The expressions of several ministers grew discontent as the archminister considered the request. "More members mean slower movement, more chances to draw attention to yourself, and higher financial cost," he said. "We are here to support you, but these concerns greatly affect us all."

"I understand, sir," Auden replied, voice steady. "But I'm not asking for a whole troop or any great purse to finance us. Only three or four more members intended to offset the loss of the Relics and the danger of the Keeps. That small number will not affect our speed or reveal our cause. And the cost is worth the reward."

The ministers turned to the archminister in expectation.

"Before we take this to a vote, I assume you have specific individuals you'd like to accompany you on this journey?" Fishere said.

"We do."

"And they are?"

Auden hesitated only for a second before answering. "We'd like Mr. Vayden Calder, Highlady Isla Freye, Highlord Restin Forsen, and . . ." He paused, and Ilain nudged him pointedly.

He cleared his throat and added, "And Sergeant Emmaas Caarney."

A collective grumble passed through the room. Evylin didn't recognize the name

Restin Forsen, but she assumed by his title that he was a Mage. Several people muttered things like, "Of course," "Should have known," and "Could have seen that coming." The ministers appeared no less surprised.

"You ask a lot, Highlord Calder," Archminister Fishere said, his good humor fading. "I presume you have strong arguments in support of these additions."

"I believe my cases to be quite sound, Archminister."

"Please explain."

Hands still clasped before him, Auden nodded. "Of course, you know, Vayden's work with the Alliance has been compromised for quite some time. He requested to join us, to do something of great impact once more. With his knowledge of Blount, he can be a valuable asset as we work to subvert the prince's plans.

"As for Isla, she can no longer work as a spy. Blount knows she's against him, meaning she can no longer work in Wauld. We are returning to Ephria immediately, giving her a place when you will have none for her here."

Auden shifted, gesturing across the room toward a man Evylin couldn't see. "Restin was my alternate at the start of this mission," he said. "If I couldn't go, he was to take my place. As such, he is uniquely qualified to join us. And we could use a Time Mage to help us prevent the worst from happening."

He returned to face the ministers. "Finally, we have two untrained Warriors. Emmaas has worked with Isla for more than a decade. It makes sense for him to join us and develop the magic of Private Deckard and Corporal Loxley."

Several of the ministers' expressions softened, while others appeared just as irritated.

Fishere nodded. "You present a reasonable case, Highlord Calder. Very well." He began to rise, and the other ministers followed suit. "We will confer."

Together, the Administration stepped nearer the hearth, huddling to speak privately. The hall filled with casual conversation while they waited. Evylin found herself tugging on her rings as she considered the idea of having four more people join them on their journey. Her eyes drifted to Emmaas, unsure how to feel about his training. The only instructor she'd ever had was Hewitt, and she had no interest in replacing him.

Leaning over to Deckard, Evylin whispered, "What do you think of this?"

His head tipped down, their shoulders brushing. "I don't know," he admitted. "Auden is right; we need the help. But I'm not sure . . . I'm still not convinced about all this."

Evylin furrowed her brow. "About all of what?"

She didn't get an answer as the Administration's conference concluded. They returned to their seats, and the audience turned to listen with bated breath.

Archminister Fishere set his hands on the table in front of him. "We have come to a unanimous conclusion," he announced.

Evylin's chest expanded with uncertainty.

"We agree to *some* of your requests," Fishere continued. "We will allow Highlady Freye and Mr. Calder to join your mission. However, Highlord Forsen is needed to keep the Order of the Age in check. We cannot risk his loss. And Sergeant Caarney is required to assist Highlord Hoult here in Wauld. That said," he held up a finger, "we do agree that you require another Warrior for training. Therefore, we'd like Lieutenant Lohen to take the position."

Auden's eyes flashed with something like excitement while Ilain rolled her own.

"As Sergeant Caarney's granddaughter, she has trained under him since childhood and can provide thorough instruction. With her previous experience in the Fire Keep, and as she is yet unassigned to a Mage, we are happy to lend her to your cause."

"Thank you," Auden said with a bright smile.

The archminister's stare grew serious, and Evylin could have sworn it flicked to her just before he added, "One last thing: As Highlady Freye made particular note of Prince Blount's fixation on Private Deckard—"

Evylin and Deckard sat up straighter.

"We are removing her from your team."

"What?" Evylin, Deckard, and Thom said together.

Fishere continued without regarding them. "We require Private Evylin Deckard to remain in protective custody here in Wauld until the threat of Prince Rouland Blount II is removed."

CHAPTER FOUR

Their group's reaction was immediate. Deckard, Thom, Rafferty, and Ethenn jumped to their feet together, irate expressions across their faces as they each protested. Auden blinked, clearly baffled as he stood with his mouth slightly ajar, while Ilain glared at the Administration as though they'd lost their minds.

And Evylin simply sat at the table, staring at her plate.

The pronouncement made sense in a horrible way. She'd already determined at Renaul's that she'd kill herself long before Blount could force her to Bond with him. If he truly was determined to possess *her* as his Warrior, continuing their quest put her in greater danger than ever.

"That's out of the question," Deckard said, his voice steady despite the depth of anger in his tone.

The archminister was unmoved. "We're concerned for your wife's safety, Colonel. Surely, you understand that."

Deckard hesitated for only a moment. "If she stays, so do I."

"So do we all," Thom added with Rafferty and Ethenn's approval.

Archminister Fishere sighed with an air of long-suffering patience. "You do realize that by refusing to continue this mission, you are prolonging the time in which she'll need protective custody, not to mention prolonging a nearly two-century-long war."

"We need her, Edmaund," Ilain said sharply.

Fishere sent her a disapproving glare. "We need her alive and not Bonded, Highlady Calder."

Evylin thought perhaps she should speak up for herself, but what was there to say? She was caught in indecision herself. She could stay with her husband and friends and risk being captured by Blount, or she could remain behind, trust them to save two countries, and know that she'd never have to face a future as Blount's unwilling Warrior.

"Now that Blount has discovered the existence of the Warrior he intends to take," Fishere continued sharply, "do you think he'll stop? More likely, he'll forestall his desire for the Relics if it will help him obtain her."

"He doesn't even have all the pieces for the ceremony," Ilain protested.

"What is that to him? She's a Warrior. He's a Mage. He can wait a hundred years with her as his prisoner, and she'll be just as viable as ever," Fishere said, then his sharp eyes scanned them all. "As you don't seem to understand, allow me to clarify your situation. We received news from one of our spies this evening. Blount arrived at Lady Renaul's estate in Keale the morning after your escape, and in his anger at losing you and two of the Relics, he killed her."

Evylin blinked.

"Blount commandeered Officer Caustin from Lady Renaul's services and had a servant post a letter to the Orders detailing his plans to leave Keale and journey to Carrickbrack, where he will meet with a band of Mages before continuing to Ephria and the Terrae Relic."

Fishere surveyed the troop, only Deckard remaining on his feet. "You have, at most, two days to catch him. Should you pursue a crossing at the border, your path will take you right alongside Blount and his Mages. Should you return to Verlund Reach and attempt to cross through the Night Keep again, your path will take you right into the hands of the Night Mages traveling to join Blount. Am I making your predicament clear? Private Deckard is in imminent danger."

A beat of silence passed through the hall.

"And what about Lieutenant Lohen?" Deckard pressed, searching for any hole in the Alliance's reasoning. "She's not Bonded, is she?"

Fishere didn't appear bothered by this fact. "The prince doesn't have an obsession with the lieutenant. And she is fully trained."

Another fine point, Evylin thought.

"What if I don't want the job?" Lohen asked abruptly, rising from her seat once more.

Auden gaped down at her as though personally affronted.

Fishere's eyes narrowed. "Are you rejecting the assignment, Lieutenant?"

Lohen shrugged. "I haven't decided. Perhaps Isla is correct. Perhaps Blount is so fixated on Private Deckard that he wouldn't give a damn about me, but who's to say he won't simply decide any female Warrior will do? I'm putting myself at great risk based on a narcissist's whims. Beyond that, I'm not entirely certain what my assignment would be. Am I to be a Warrior to the Calders or train the corporal? And potentially the private, should she join us."

"She won't be joining you," Fishere said, then hurried on before Deckard could object further. "I fail to see the exclusive nature of those jobs, Lieutenant."

"They aren't exclusive, sir," the lieutenant agreed. "But it is a necessary distinction. If I'm first and foremost a trainer on this mission, then the private and corporal are my priority. If I'm to be a Warrior to Mages, then the Calders will take precedence. Should life or death be a factor—which sounds likely—I will need to know where to put my focus."

After a deep breath, the archminister turned to each side of his table to hear the thoughts of his fellow ministers. He nodded in approval at their muttered replies before turning back to the lieutenant. "It seems to us that your priority should be training up our Warriors. As highly as we value the Calders, they are both strong enough to rely on their own powers, each other, and the remaining team members for assistance. Corporal Loxley is in far greater need of your services."

Rafferty snickered at the statement, elbowing Ethenn.

Lieutenant Lohen eyed the men for a moment before giving a firm nod. "Then I accept," she said. "But if you'd like my professional opinion as a soldier, you're being ridiculous. Private Deckard is far safer with her husband than she is without him. Keeping her here is asinine. Thank you for your consideration." And with that, the lieutenant resumed her seat.

A ripple of discontentment blended with laughter around the room. From far down the table, Thom snorted in amusement, and Isla smirked.

Evylin took a moment to glance at Lieutenant Lohen, feeling grateful for her honesty while wondering at its validity. If she were safer with Deckard, wouldn't it be best for both of them to stay protected in Wauld?

Archminister Fishere lifted his eyes to the Heavens before calling for silence once more. "With that settled," he said crossly, "might we return to the issue at hand? We value Private Deckard's safety. As such, we do not want to put her in harm's way. Can you not see the reason in that?"

"I see no reason in separating me from my wife," Deckard insisted.

Evylin stared up at him along with the rest of the room, breath caught in her chest. Turned away from her as he was, she couldn't see his expression. But his taut jaw and fists pressed against the table told her all she needed to know of his mood.

"Will you refuse this assignment, then?" Fishere asked, tone blatantly terse.

"Forgive me, sir," Deckard said, sounding anything but repentant. "But we were never offered an assignment. Your agents manipulated us into your service. We are not members of your organization, nor are we your soldiers. Therefore, I do not recognize you as my commanding officer."

A ripple of dissatisfied whispers began to spread through the room. Auden, still standing, stared at Deckard in disappointment while Ilain held her chin high, despite the seething expression on her face.

Archminister Fishere's hands clutched together on the table before him. "You don't believe in our cause?" he asked.

"I don't rightly know what your cause is," Deckard returned. "I know you want to reinstitute Allund. I know you want Mages and Warriors to help rule in some way. I know you claim this is a message from Allore above. That's all. And it isn't enough for me to stake my life or the lives of my wife, brother, and men upon."

"It was enough before," Ilain countered.

Deckard glared at her. "But now, your leaders want to take my wife from me. I'm afraid my good faith has reached its end."

Seeing the rising animosity in the room, Evylin reached up and took Deckard's hand. He glanced down at her. "Carefully," she said softly.

Deckard dipped his chin in understanding. Evylin supported him and his questioning of the Alliance. She no more trusted them than he did. But they were in a room filled with dozens of their members and only five on their side. And she didn't particularly care to go against Ilain and Auden should the conflict escalate.

However, she felt the need for answers herself.

Pushing her seat backward and rising, Evylin finally decided to speak. "Only this afternoon, Highlady Freye told us that the Alliance is built on the sacrifices of its members," she said, almost faltering as the gathering turned to her. She swallowed the lump that immediately came to her throat. Suddenly, she realized that Deckard was the one for great speeches. It was her job to stand by his side, wielding a sword, not speak in front of the masses.

Then Deckard entwined their fingers, and a tingle of warmth spread up her arm, emboldening her.

Evylin stepped farther into the aisle next to him. "Well, we have made sacrifices too," she said. "We defected from the Ephrian Army to the detriment of our futures. We've defended the Calders and secured five Relics at the risk of our lives. I lost my uncle to your cause."

Evylin's voice cracked on those words, and several heads dipped respectfully. "I think you owe us an explanation of what that cause is," she concluded.

Archminister Fishere regarded Evylin and Deckard, standing side by side in the aisle. The corner of his mouth lifted in what bordered on a smile. "You both make excellent points," he replied. "Very well. Allow me to clarify our cause."

The elderly man leaned forward, a solemnity in his gaze that assured them he took their charge seriously. "It is the Alliance's core tenet to restore Allund, as you mentioned, Colonel. Not to the unjust state it was nearly two centuries ago, but to the divine province that Allore ordained more than a millennium past."

Evylin shuffled her feet, uncertain how much of his grand rhetoric she could trust.

"We intend to accomplish this," Fishere continued, "by first reclaiming the Ateri Relics, which are fragments of the Creator Divine's very self. Since they've been locked away, their absence from our realm has set our world into a slow degradation. With their return, we shall restore Terraeus to its true nature by granting each Relic to a Bonded couple of corresponding resource. At which point, we will establish our rule in Allund as an oligarchal democracy. Granted, all of this can only take place once we've overthrown the Waulden and Ephrian monarchies, which we intend to accomplish by means of the power granted to our Bonded couples with those Relics.

"We will give both Ephren and Blount the opportunity to surrender," he explained. "If they refuse, they will either be incarcerated or, if they turn violent, executed. But we'd prefer to avoid that outcome."

Evylin glanced at Deckard, unsure what to think of these plans.

"Now," Fishere said, "if you'd like a full report on our governmental structure, such an endeavor would take several hours, and as I'd rather not bore my members who are already familiar with those details, I'd be happy to meet with you tomorrow should you like to review the specifications of our plans. Does that answer your question?"

Evylin forced herself not to chew on her lip, finding her brain too full of political elocution to come up with words of her own.

"Not entirely," Deckard said slowly. "But well enough. I'd only ask: What if the people of Wauld and Ephria don't want to be part of this new version of Allund? What if they prefer their lives to remain the way they've been?"

A handful of individuals scoffed at the idea, but Archminister Fishere regarded the question with earnestness. "I'm sure many Mages of Wauld do prefer things the way they are at present," he said. "But I can assure you that the people do not. Though some of our members here in the Alliance are nobility, we are not a league of the elite. The majority of our people are normal citizens from settlements throughout the continent. They are the merchants, the farmers, the tailors, the bakers, and the smiths. Their futures are not defined by grand or entertaining tales, but they are the individuals who make our choices. They are the ones who gave us—" He gestured to himself and the rest of the ministers, "our jobs. We have thousands of Wauldeners and Ephrians who have rallied to our cause, only a small number of whom hold any sort of wealth or noble blood. The Alliance has no interest in claiming power for the sake of ego or ambition. We don't care for glory or honor. We only seek to provide a better future for our children and to serve Allore's holy charge from the beginning: to care for Terraeus, to create as he created, and to serve the nature of his divine balance."

A deafening applause and clamor of approval filled the room as the archminister finished his impassioned speech. Fists were raised as men and women whistled and cheered their support. The Calders sat with their heads held high, proud of their leader's proclamation. Even young Reyana let out a whoop of excitement.

The sound surrounded the five Ephrians. Rafferty appeared unimpressed, lounging in his chair. Ethenn stared at his hands, deep in thought. And Thom's eyes were on Evylin and Deckard, as though waiting for their reaction.

Evylin met Deckard's gaze, his expression inscrutable. She couldn't deny the stirring of emotion in her chest. The archminister meant his words. These people—the members of the Alliance—meant them too. This was not a band of selfish anarchists. It was an organization of devout Allorians, determined to uphold the commission of their deity.

But Evylin wasn't religious.

So why did she feel the urge to join them?

As the cheering died down, it was clear the archminister was waiting for their response.

Deckard steadied himself, resetting his grip on Evylin. "Thank you, sir," he said with his usual refinement, "for sharing your convictions. They are both insightful and reassuring."

When it was clear Deckard didn't intend to say anything more, Fishere spoke. "I can appreciate your hesitation, Colonel, and I resent that your introduction to our organization was one fraught with mistrust and coercive action. I assure you that such a practice is not our preferred method of presenting ourselves. But I hope you can forgive the duplicity, knowing that secrecy and underhanded techniques are necessary when you're a rebel faction."

"As a soldier who has betrayed his own country," Deckard said stolidly, "I'm in the unique position of understanding completely."

Fishere gave a single, appreciative nod.

"Regardless," Deckard added, and the archminister's ease disappeared, "that doesn't negate the fact that you'd like to separate me and my wife."

"I wouldn't *like* to," Fishere said. "I feel it's best for her safety and the safety of our people. Do you know what would happen if Prince Blount had the opportunity to Bond?"

"I'm sure I wouldn't like to find out," Deckard replied. "But that doesn't change the fact that I won't be leaving without my wife."

Fishere raised an eyebrow. "Then you won't be leaving."

A handful of men rose to their feet throughout the room, a show of force marking their position with clear intentions. If Evylin tried to leave or if Deckard or any of their friends tried to take her on this mission, they would be stopped.

Ilain muttered a curse and dropped her head into her hand as the three Ephrian soldiers rose too. "You're making matters worse, Edmaund," she warned.

Fishere regarded her. "The entirety of Wauld is looking for Private Deckard. To allow her to leave our protective custody is to hand her over to Blount. Renaul's capture of you is proof that you can't keep her from him forever. There are hundreds of other nobles just waiting to prove themselves to the prince, and the entirety of the Orders of the Night, Wind, and Flame are looking to assist him in his endeavors."

Evylin's heart pattered traitorously. The danger was abundantly clear and frightening. Should she leave the Alliance's custody, she would be putting herself directly upon a path to be forced to Bond with Blount. Even if he didn't capture her on their journey to retrieve the Relics, they would have to face him eventually. And yet, if she stayed in Mouroc, she was as good as taunting Blount to find her, to take her.

Unless . . .

The answer struck Evylin with its obviousness.

Evylin dropped Deckard's hand, stepping forward, her mind made up. "Sir," she said, drawing the archminister's gaze, "I don't believe you've asked my opinion on the matter."

Fishere blinked, then let out a thin chuckle. "By Allore's grace, you're right. My sincerest apologies, Private Deckard. What is your opinion?"

Without letting herself question her decision, Evylin answered honestly. "I agree with you," she said.

She felt Deckard approach from behind her. "Evie—"

She ignored him, continuing, "It is dangerous for me to continue this mission. Blount already has four Relics. Seeing him Bonded would secure our defeat. Though I would like to say I am brave enough to withstand his coercion, I don't know what a century of torture might do to me."

The words tasted bitter on her tongue, and she felt Deckard bristle. "But there is one course we haven't considered," she said.

"And what is that?" Fishere asked.

Evylin turned to Ilain. "Can an individual Bond with more than one person?"

Ilain's nose scrunched instantly. "No," she said as though Evylin had suggested a particularly heinous crime. "Bonding is the picture of balance—one Mage with one Warrior, one of them male, the other female. It is unbreakable and indestructible. Even if a person wanted to, they couldn't Bond a second time. Not so long as their first partner lived."

With a nod, Evylin turned back to Fishere. "Then we have our solution," she concluded. "Jonn and I will Bond."

"Evylin!" Deckard's voice landed like a hammer on an anvil as the rest of the room was filled with murmurs, both of approval and surprise.

Archminister Fishere's eyes narrowed. "You're asking to Bond with your husband?"

Before Evylin could reply, Deckard's hand latched onto her arm. "Give us a moment, would you?" he said, then began tugging her down the aisle.

Evylin knew he'd be surprised. She'd even anticipated his frustration with her for making this decision on her own. But in the end, she knew it was the only course left. If it were between Bonding with Blount or Bonding with Deckard, there wasn't a question in her mind of which she would prefer. She loved Deckard. She intended to spend the rest of her days by his side. And if taking such action ensured that future—if Bonding protected her from Blount and provided them both enough power to guarantee their success, to secure her husband's safety—she would do it in a heartbeat.

But would Deckard?

He pulled her out of the hall and into the foyer, the low-burning lamps casting blue-purple shadows into the corners. The hum of surprised conversation still drifted to them as he released her. Immediately, he began to pace the tiled floor, then he stopped to face her.

"Evylin, you can't be serious," Deckard began, his brow pinched together in concern. "You know that once it's done, there's no going back."

A sliver of worry worked its way into Evylin's gut, but she determined not to let her uncertainty show. "Jonn," she said with a smirk, "if you're looking for a way out of our marriage, I'm afraid it's a bit late."

His lips quirked in the corner, but he fought off a smile. "That's not what I'm referring to," he replied, voice low. "I don't want to be a Mage forever."

Sighing, Evylin stepped closer. She set her hands on his arms comfortingly, holding his gaze. "I don't think you have much choice," she said. "You *are* a Mage just as I am a Warrior. We always have been, even if we didn't know it. And I don't think there's any escaping that truth. Not so long as we're together."

Deckard's chin dipped even as his eyes held hers. "So you want this to be our life? Working for the Alliance? Being part of their regime?"

Though he didn't say it, Evylin could hear his true meaning. He'd promised to give her the life she wanted, to make her happy in whatever way he could. And he wanted to know, was this the way he could fulfill that vow?

"I don't know," Evylin admitted honestly.

The path before them was riddled with danger. They could potentially lose their lives. But it was also filled with hope and the chance to see a truly brighter future for Allund and for the people they knew and loved. She knew what life Deckard wanted. He'd told her early in their marriage that he dreamed of having a family, of a wife and children to love and provide for. While he hadn't revealed much more of that dream to her, she rather thought having Deckard's children would be an exciting adventure of its own.

But what sort of family could they have as a Warrior and a Mage? Would their work with the Alliance take them from their children just as it had taken Isla and Vayden from Reyana? Where would they even live? And would their children inherit magic too? Or would it skip a generation like it had for Emmaas's family? Worse, were they destined to see all their children and grandchildren leave this world before they even drew near the twilight of life?

Evylin could see those questions swirling in Deckard's worried gaze even as they plagued her.

Reaching up, Evylin smoothed her thumb over the crease between his brows. None of those unanswered questions mattered. She only knew one thing.

"I want to live," Evylin whispered, resting her palm on his cheek. "And as long as you're there, I don't really care what that looks like anymore."

Deckard's chest rose and fell with deep, halting breaths as he stared back at her. He looked at war with himself, his jaw tight and his expression perpetually pinched. She couldn't tell if he was disappointed, hurt, or angry. His tongue darted out to wet his bottom lip before he drew his shoulders back, standing to his full height. He didn't speak but gave her a steady nod.

Offering her his hand, Deckard led her back into the room. Evylin ignored the expectant stares of those around them, watching Deckard's tight posture carefully. Was she pushing him into something he didn't want? It was the right choice, wasn't it? Not only would it protect her from Blount's machinations, but it would also deepen their connection and secure their safety. She knew he wanted those things too. But was this cost too high?

Once they reached their previous position by their seats, Deckard met the archminister's gaze. "After discussion, it seems that the best course of action is for

Evylin and me to Bond," he said, his delivery flat. "As Highlady Calder stated, it resolves the issue of Blount's desire to Bond with Evylin himself, and we agree that it would benefit our mission as a whole. Beyond that . . ." he faltered for a moment, then concluded, "it is what we want for our marriage and our future."

There was a beat of silence as the entire room turned to hear the archminister's reply.

Evylin's hand trembled around the tension of Deckard's grasp. Worry pricked her heart like a thorn. Her announcement had been impulsive, fueled by her desperation to protect herself from Blount. She'd been self-centered, only imagining what she wanted for their future. And now, she'd publicly pressured him into a life he'd never wanted.

"Very well," Archminister Fishere said with ready agreement.

Evylin's heart sank.

"The Administration heartily agrees to the benefit of this decision. Mr. Nowen," Fishere turned to the clerk, "make a note of this and prepare the necessary arrangements. We will perform the Bonding ceremony of Colonel and Private Deckard tomorrow night. After which, we will send off the Calders, including Mr. Calder and Highlady Freye, our new Ephrian friends, and Lieutenant Lohen to complete their mission. Now, if there's nothing else . . ."

Fishere paused, surveying their party.

Evylin knew she should speak up. She should tell them that she'd changed her mind; she and Deckard needed more time to discuss this life-altering decision. They didn't even know what Bonding entailed. Evidently, it involved a ceremony, but of what sort? And what would Bonding do to them? Ilain had called it a binding of hearts, a fusing of their souls. What could that possibly look like?

Opening her mouth, the words didn't come in time before Fishere moved on. "Excellent," he said, then regarded the room as a whole. "With that cleared up, we have concluded our business. Highlord Calder, please submit your final requests to Mr. Nowen for processing. Should you need anything, I will return to visit the Crimson Clover in the morning to oversee affairs. In the meantime, you are all dismissed to enjoy the rest of your evening. May Allore's grace be with you."

"Allore's grace," the crowd called back.

Only Evylin and Deckard stood, unmoving, even as the rest of the room rose from their tables. She could feel the tension in his muscles, the firm grip he held on her hand. What had she done to them? Her mind raced, trying to cobble together what she knew about Bonding. It was so very little, and she'd committed them to it.

"Well," Rafferty said, drawing her from her thoughts far too quickly, "that was eventful. What a fun little surprise you had up your sleeve, Eve."

Across the table, Ilain smirked. "Indeed, it was."

Deckard shifted Evylin closer as the other attendees began milling around them. A few Alliance members made as if to approach, but Vayden leaned forward with a furious glare in his eyes, threatening violence if they didn't bugger off.

"We just want to show our gratitude," one woman proclaimed in offense.

Isla raised her brow. "You want to politic, Suette," she returned. "Or, at best, you want to say that you shook hands with the saviors of the nation."

Suette turned away, disgruntled.

"Here," Vayden said, motioning to a couple of the men and women around him. With their help, he shifted the tables out of the way so the Ephrians could join them away from the fray of departing members. "We'll wait here until the storm has passed."

Pressed close in the narrow space, Auden turned to Deckard. "I want to apologize," he said. "I didn't realize you all felt so bullied into our cause. It was never our—"

"Oh, come off it, Audy," Rafferty interrupted, a wily grin on his lips. "We don't care about that. What we don't appreciate is being herded like some unruly flock of sheep."

Thom gave a firm nod. "We believe in your cause—"

"Speak for yourself," Rafferty interrupted.

Thom gave him a dismissive frown before turning back to Auden. "We just didn't fully know what it was until this evening."

Resplendent in her scarlet gown, Ilain elbowed him. "You could have asked."

He smirked at her. "Affairs of state aren't my preferred topic of conversation. Nice dress, by the way. It really sets off your—" His eyes darted to her cleavage for a spare second. "Charming wit."

"Why, thank you, darling," Ilain said, brushing her fingers along the beaded bodice. "It was a gift from an admirer."

Vayden scoffed. "A bribe is more like it," he said.

"It's only a bribe if the inducement in question influences the decision of the individual it's intended to persuade," she returned. "And it will not."

"Bribery, eh?" Rafferty sniggered, hopping up to sit atop the nearby table. "Who's trying to induce your favor, lady flame?"

"Major Olsen," Ilain said.

Ethenn's brow furrowed. "Wasn't he one of the Warriors who stood up earlier?" he asked.

Ilain sent him a suggestive glance. "He was indeed."

"Olsen has been in love with Lainy for the past fifteen years," Vayden said casually. "She just doesn't care to return the feeling."

"Love is a loose term," Ilain said flatly. "He wants to be Bonded, and I'm one of the few remaining candidates not spoken for."

"Speaking of . . ." Vayden murmured, then smiled as Lieutenant Lohen approached. "Welcome to the party, *naladar*."

The lieutenant gave him a flat stare, though her dark eyes twinkled with humor as she slipped in at Isla's side. She said something in Schonese that made Vayden, Isla, and Reyana laugh. Then she gave a quick scan of the Ephrians. "The night's festivities are proceeding at The Rook," she said. "And Imelda, the tavern's owner, requested I inform you all that the drinks of our Ephrian champions are on the house."

"Free drinks?" Rafferty said, then catapulted off the table. "What are we waiting for?"

Though Evylin would usually be excited at the prospect of such an evening of frivolity, she couldn't quite find her smile. All through the exchange, Deckard had grown more and more tense by her side, his grip on her hand ever tightening. Whatever her intentions, she'd made a mistake mentioning the Bonding. She owed him an apology for pushing him into the choice.

While most of the crowd had exited the hall, Vayden, Isla, and Lohen had to stop a few stragglers from approaching them. They left through the back door, the cold night air prickling their exposed skin. Evylin struggled to get a breath in as they walked across the courtyard. She thought to pull Deckard to the side to tell him they should return and find the archminister. They could take it back. They didn't have to Bond.

But as Vayden opened a door to their right and Isla guided their troop inside, Deckard's fingers tightened once more, drawing Evylin ahead toward the Crimson Clover.

While their friends disappeared into the tavern, Evylin let him divert their path. He was right. They needed to talk and figure this out. They passed through the kitchen and the halls to the foyer, proceeding up the stairs. She didn't bother finding excuses along the way. She would apologize, and they would work out how best to explain the situation to Fishere.

They weren't ready to Bond.

Deckard released his grip on Evylin to unlock the door. Then he set a hand to her lower back, ushering her inside.

Feeling the agitation in his sharp movements, Evylin began her apology as he began to shut the door. "Jonn . . ." The words stuck in her throat, and she had to swallow them down.

The door latched, and he turned the lock.

Trying again, Evylin made sure her voice was filled with earnestness as she said, "Jonn, I'm so sorry."

Deckard faced her, his brow drawn low. "You're sorry?"

Evylin nodded, hopeful he'd see her contrition. "I am. I wasn't thinking, and I—I know I should have talked to you before . . . We can talk to the archminister. We'll convince him—"

"Evylin," he cut her off, a slow, baffled smile spreading across his face, "I'm not upset."

She blinked. "You're not?"

He took a step closer, the smile growing amused. "No."

"Oh." Evylin smoothed her hands over the back of her skirt, somewhat embarrassed. "So . . . you didn't bring me up here to reprimand me?"

Deckard approached steadily, the shadows of the room catching on his sharp features. Only the low-burning lamps lit their room in an amber haze. In their flickering light, his hair took on more of a red tint.

"No," he said. "I did not."

"Oh," she said again, the breath slipping out of her lungs as understanding dawned.

Deckard closed the gap between them, reaching out to sweep her hair over her shoulder. "Why would I have any cause to be angry with you," he whispered, "when you asked to be bound to me forever?"

A faint laugh escaped her as he leaned forward, his nose brushing hers. "It does sound rather ridiculous," she managed to say, "when you put it that way."

"Mm," he agreed, his hand settling on her waist to draw her closer.

Evylin's heart skipped nervously for a whole new reason. "You were just so—so serious, and . . ." she stammered. "And tense."

His lips pressed gently to her cheek. "I was serious because I was struggling to keep my emotions in check after you told me that what mattered most to your future was if I were in it."

Evylin closed her eyes as his fingers traced her collar, skimming her neck.

"And I was tense," he whispered against her skin, "because my patience was running thin."

Smirking as his lips brushed hers, Evylin drew back to say, "I have no doubt that your patience would have lasted."

He grunted as his fingers worked free the buttons on her blouse.

"You're the most patient man on Terraeus."

"That," Deckard said, his voice low and husky, "was before."

CHAPTER FIVE

Thom stared at the row of tankards on the wall behind the bar. The small tavern was too loud for his liking. Its long, narrow confines held far too many people for its smattering of tables. Every chair and table was full, the length of the wooden bartop packed with those sitting and standing as they talked and drank. A solitary bard played the mandolin in the corner, adding to the cacophony of sounds.

When they'd arrived in The Rook's tavern room through a hidden door in a storeroom, their band was welcomed with cheers and excitement. Thom recognized many of the people from the meeting, surprised to discover that the tavern was, like the hotel, completely occupied with Alliance members. Though he supposed that would have to be the case with Auden and Ilain's faces plastered on Blount's writ. Vayden readily began to introduce their team—they all ignored the missing presence of Deckard and Evylin—while Auden and Ilain were swept into conversation with old friends and comrades.

Ushered into the space, they found themselves at the front of the tavern, an ample-bodied woman asking what they'd like to drink. Shortly, she returned with tankards of ale and glasses of wine. Everything devolved from there as Rafferty settled into his finest role. He told story after story, regaling the Alliance crowd before tricking them into playing cards.

While Rafferty conned them out of their money, the rest of their party slowly branched off from the large front table. Vayden and Isla wandered away to sit in a half-booth at the far side of the tavern. As they'd sent their daughter away under the supervision of Graicelle from the hotel, the couple preferred to enjoy their time alone. Auden moved to visit with a group of fellow Mages, and Ethenn wound up talking with Lieutenant Lohen and Emmaas in the corner. Ilain entertained a small crowd, sipping her white wine as they asked her questions about her time in Ephria.

And Thom . . . He felt more alone than he had in some time, even though surrounded by a hundred or so patrons. So he drifted off to sit at the bar, thinking that if he was doomed to *feel* alone, he might as well *be* alone.

Setting his ale on the counter, Thom rested his hands around the cold clay tankard. He wished that Deckard and Evylin hadn't left. He didn't blame them. If he had a spouse, he would far prefer to be alone together after the ordeal they'd survived as well.

Thom glanced back at the front table. Rafferty would happily welcome him by his side, but he didn't particularly care to watch him play tricks. Not in the midst of the existential crisis Thom was going through. Of course, that was melodramatic, but that's how it felt. After years of living as the victim, he was finally owning up to his faults and trying to fix them.

The only problem was that Thom didn't know how to do that. How did one stop being a foolish git after nearly twenty-eight years of narcissism? He wasn't exactly sure. But the best path he could determine was to make up for his past behavior to Deckard. Thom had to become a better man. He had to prove himself to his brother, stop worrying so much about what people thought of him, and put others first.

And the problem there was that he didn't know how to do those things either.

Deckard was the one who took care of people. He was the leader. He saw beyond his feelings and desires and got the job done while Thom wallowed and blubbered and failed. And Thom couldn't see a way out of that miserable existence without his brother nearby to lead him by example.

He pressed his lips together and wiped away a droplet of ale. Laughter rang out from the front table. Rafferty doled out some cash as he "lost," obviously lulling his audience into a false sense of security. Thom wondered if the Alliance would kick Rafferty out for swindling so many of their members tonight.

Suddenly, a fire-bright presence appeared at Thom's side. "You're moping," Ilain said, then turned to the barkeep. "Imelda, could I have another, please?"

The woman took her wine glass and began refilling it while Ilain leaned against the bar. Her rich red dress did wonders for her figure, making her appear more voluptuous than she was. Not that Thom knew firsthand. He'd simply seen enough women to know when things were illusory. And by the way Ilain rested against the counter, her torso slanted just right, she was evidently aware of how the dress played to her more provocative assets.

"You are stunning," Thom said dryly, gesturing to her stance. "Are you flirting with me once more?"

Ilain accepted the wine glass from Imelda with a gracious "thank you." Then she gave Thom the most searing glare he'd ever received. "Why would I ever flirt with *you* again," she said with venom, "when you've ruined what might be my one chance at happiness?"

Thom raised his brow, keeping his expression in check despite how his gut twisted. "That's an excellent question," he said. "It begs another, though."

"Does it?"

"Mm. Why are you talking to me in the first place?"

Ilain eyed him. "Perhaps I intend to punish you."

"By gracing me with your sparkling presence?" Thom scoffed and turned back to his ale. "Consider me reprimanded."

She didn't reply, but neither did she leave.

Surrounded as they were, Thom didn't think it was the right place to have the conversation they ought to have but took a long swig of ale and did it anyway. "I'm sorry," he said, meeting her angry glare. "I made a mistake. One in a long line of thousands. I would have said something sooner, but . . ."

Ilain twirled the stem of her glass, waiting.

Thom took a deep breath. "I'm gonna fix it," he promised.

"How?" she demanded.

"I don't know yet."

"Hm." Ilain tapped a finger on the bartop, pursed her lips, and then pushed herself to stand. "Good enough. Come with me."

"Pardon?" Thom said, baffled.

Ilain didn't bother to explain. She grabbed the collar of his coat, and he grappled to get ahold of his tankard before she pulled him from the counter. Across the narrow room, she dragged him to Vayden and Isla's table. The couple sat closely on the L-shaped bench, and Ilain took the seat closest to her sister-in-law.

"Sit," Ilain ordered Thom, pointing to the chair next to her.

Cautiously, Thom glanced at Vayden and Isla—who were both watching him with interest—before doing as told.

"How many have you had tonight, Lainy?" Vayden asked, nodding to his sister's wine glass.

"You know I have a high tolerance," Ilain returned. "And we had a large meal."

Isla smiled knowingly. "Not even we Mages possess that high a tolerance, dear."

Suddenly understanding the reason for Ilain's additionally ostentatious demeanor, Thom chuckled. "You're drunk?" he asked.

"I'm not drunk," Ilain said. "I'm tipsy. Seems you should know the difference."

"Because I drink so much?"

"Because you're friends with Rafferty."

Thom opened his mouth to reply before realizing she was right. The weasel did have a habit of pushing spirits on his friends at an abnormal rate.

Vayden watched their exchange thoughtfully, then leaned toward his sister. "For my sanity, try not to overdo it, Lain."

"It's a bit late for that," Ilain replied with a tip of her glass in his direction. "You don't have to worry. I've got Thom to protect me should any men have nefarious designs on my person."

Feeling the lightheadedness of the ale hitting his own system, Thom frowned at her. "I'm not exactly at my best at the present moment," he said.

"You're never at your best," Ilain retorted, then turned back to her siblings. "You're sending Rey back to Mum and Da?"

Though Vayden looked ready to pursue the previous conversation, Isla spoke first. "We are," she said. "Veris and Lorna Grenwoode are returning to the moors themselves, so they offered to take her with them."

Ilain made a face. "Poor Rey. That'll be a dreadfully boring trip."

Isla grinned. "She is looking forward to being with your parents and the horses again. Though she requested to join our mission as well."

"Of course she did."

Thom felt like an interloper sitting in on the family exchange. After the past month of developing a friendship with Ilain—a true miracle if there ever was one—he found himself interested in learning as much as he could about the enigma of the Fire Mage. She was strange and confusing to him. He'd come to see the similarities they shared between their passionate, strong-willed personalities. But where Thom was prone to cynicism and a sense of inferiority, Ilain was confident and crafty. She wore a façade few had the opportunity to crack, and he was determined to discover what was truly underneath.

As though sensing Thom's thoughts, Ilain turned to him. "You've got yourself an admirer, you know," she said.

"What?" he replied, confused by the sudden diversion.

"Reyana," Isla clarified. "Our daughter has worked up an infatuation for you."

Now, it was Vayden's turn to say, "What?"

Isla patted his hand. "Don't worry, love. Infatuations are merely part of growing into a young woman."

Thom let out a small grunt of disapproval, though he didn't think any of them could hear it over the chaos around them. "I assure you," he said to Vayden, "I won't be returning her interest."

"I should hope not," Vayden said sharply. "She's still a child."

Ilain's gaze, somewhat glassy from drink, drifted to the front of the tavern before returning to her brother. "Thirteen isn't quite a child."

"But neither is it old enough for romance," Isla countered.

"It most certainly is not," Vayden agreed, looking thoroughly uncomfortable with the idea that his daughter might not be quite as childlike as he'd imagined.

Ilain shrugged, then took a deep sip of wine, eyes shifting back to the front of the room.

Vayden muttered something in Schonese, at which his wife chuckled. Then he reached over and set his hand on top of Ilain's wine glass. "Why are you drinking yourself into a stupor?" he demanded.

Though she scowled, his sister crossed her arms and sat back. Her eyes flicked away again.

Thom followed her line of sight and smirked. "If I had to wager a guess, it probably has something to do with that," he said, pointing to the far corner, where Ethenn, Emmaas, and Lieutenant Lohen now sat conversing with another woman who had joined them, her chair drawn very near to the young man's.

The woman was quite beautiful, with tight golden curls and porcelain skin. She had a sharp nose like many Wauldeners, but it only served to give character to her otherwise soft and youthful face. She wore a dress of sky blue, its flowy fabric draped with a demure, romantic flair, while the fit gracefully indicated an ideally feminine figure beneath its delicate folds.

And she was clearly entranced by Ethenn.

"Ah," Vayden said, then frowned. He looked at Ilain. "I don't understand. I thought you liked Ivry."

Ilain took another swig of wine, her bare shoulders growing tense. "I have no personal problems with Ivry. She's a fine Mage even if she is a scheming hag."

"Oh," Thom said, then laughed. "Oh, I see. She's a Mage."

"And Ethenn is a Warrior," Ilain said flatly.

Thom looked over at the pair. The woman, Ivry, was smiling brightly at Ethenn, and, admittedly, she had a lovely smile. As expected, a crimson-red flush was creeping up from under Ethenn's collar at Ivry's attention. What was unexpected was that Ethenn was talking to her and smiling back.

When Ivry's hand came to rest on Ethenn's forearm with evident flirtatious intent, Ilain knocked back the rest of her wine and stood. "Excuse me," she muttered.

Thom, Vayden, and Isla watched with interest as Ilain stormed across the tavern and right up to Ethenn and Ivry. The couple looked up at her approach, Ivry saying something that looked like a greeting, though Thom couldn't hear the words. Ilain didn't bother to reply. She ignored the woman altogether, grabbed a handful of Ethenn's coat, and hauled him to his feet. Ethenn appeared to protest, but Ilain didn't pause as she yanked him along behind her, carting him through the tavern to disappear into the storeroom from which they'd entered.

After Ilain shut the door behind them with enough force to rattle the frame, Vayden turned back to Thom. "As an elder brother," he said, "I feel I should ask: Should I be concerned?"

Thom raised his brow, amused. "About Ilain? No. About what she'll do to the boy? Probably."

Vayden's brows hung low in confusion. "She . . . likes him?"

"You should ask her about that," Thom said. "Look, I'm not exactly privy to how things work here in Wauld, but of all people, you don't need to worry about Ethenn taking advantage of Ilain. If anything, she'll take advantage of him."

Vayden and Isla shared a look, and Thom worried he'd said the wrong thing. "Sorry, no—not like that," he corrected. "What I mean to say is—"

"We understand," Isla said. "Ilain is determined to marry a Warrior. The problem is she hasn't met one she likes enough to pursue."

"Or at least, she hadn't," Vayden added, his eyes on the storeroom's door.

"Right," Thom muttered, then sipped his ale awkwardly. "So . . ." He cleared his throat and looked at Isla. "You go by Highlady Freye. Do Waulden women not take on their husbands' last names? Or is the convention a Schonese thing?"

Isla's dark eyes glimmered slyly. She set her hand on Vayden's, which rested on the table. "It's a precaution," she said. "We aren't legally married due to our work with the Alliance. I needed to remain single in the eyes of the monarchy and the Orders."

"But," Vayden added, "we are married in the eyes of Allore, and that's all that matters."

Thom waved a hand. "I may be Ephrian, and Heavens knows we love our traditions, but the officiality of your union or lack thereof doesn't bother me. If you said you'd done the ceremony yourselves, I'd still consider it binding."

Vayden dipped his chin in appreciation. "And what about you? Are you married?"

"No," Thom said with an immediate, self-derisive chuckle.

"Engaged?"

"No."

"Courting someone?"

Thom raised his tankard and said, "No," then took a sip.

"Interesting," Vayden said.

Thom was about to ask why it was interesting when Lieutenant Lohen dropped into the seat next to him. "Vayd, I'm going to need you to talk to your brother," she said, sipping from a short glass tumbler. An inch of amber liquor swirled at the bottom when she set it on the table.

Thom raised his brow. He'd never met a woman who drank whiskey. Granted, such distilled liquors were quite expensive and often reserved for the nobles or vastly wealthy merchants.

Vayden grinned at the lieutenant. "Auden's driving you to drink already?"

The woman grimaced. "He won't leave me alone."

"Tell him to shut up," Vayden suggested. "It's always worked for me."

"He's not trying to marry you," she argued.

Vayden and Isla laughed while Thom eyed the lieutenant with renewed interest. Ilain had told him that Auden was once in love with a Night Mage named Maura, but that she was lost to the Deep. While he knew the Day Mage was capable of romantic attachment, he struggled to imagine him attempting to woo anyone.

"Huh," Thom said with a smirk. "What sort of lines does he use to win you over?"

"I beg your pardon," Lohen said, her thick black eyebrows dropping low over her almond-shaped eyes.

"Well, I can't imagine he's a good flirt. What does he say? That his dedication to Day magic speaks of his faithfulness?"

That got Vayden to chuckle while the lieutenant continued to study Thom. "Are you having a laugh at my expense?" she asked.

"Not at all," Thom replied, amused. "I simply can't fathom what it looks like for Auden Calder to have caught feelings."

She drew back, her trim figure muscular like any Warrior's would be, but somehow still petite. Her unembellished dress bore almost a military cut with a square neckline that matched her no-nonsense expression. Its deep color reminded Thom of the reddest wine, setting off her light brown skin. She was attractive in a foreboding manner, one that suggested no man should dare to approach her, as they could never hope to match her superiority. Thom had to admit he was impressed that Auden had plucked up the courage to make a move, though he couldn't fault his taste.

As Thom finished his assessment of her, it seemed she also completed her evaluation of him. A slow smile spread across her lips. "I don't think we've officially met," she said, holding out her hand. "I'm Breata Lohen. You can call me Brea."

"Thom Deckard," he said, not surprised by the unusual strength of her handshake.

Drawing back, Brea returned to the previous conversation. "Auden doesn't have feelings for me. He has ambitions for himself."

"Well, he does have *some* feelings for you," Vayden interjected. "He likes you well enough; it's just not in a romantic way."

Brea lifted her glass. "How flattering."

"He desires to save Maura," Isla added. "It's a noble pursuit."

"I don't have any interest in being part of anyone's noble pursuit." Brea turned to Vayden once more. "If I'm going to travel with this group, I need you to tell him that he's picked the wrong Warrior."

Vayden gave her an apologetic shrug. "Alma's already promised to Grey. Unless we find another female Warrior, Auden doesn't have other choices."

"What an honor, being a last resort."

Thom let out an amused huff just as the storeroom's door opened. Ilain strode out of the room, head held high, and Ethenn stood in the doorway, a look of pure confusion on his face. Thom scanned Ilain for any sign of mussing, but every bit of her scarlet dress and fiery hair was in place. Evidently, she'd not shared her true feelings with Ethenn.

When Ilain joined Auden and his friends, Ethenn ambled uncertainly into the tavern. He glanced at Thom's table before bypassing it to sit with Rafferty at the front of the room. It appeared that Thom had more apologies to make.

He glanced down into his empty tankard, then caught Imelda's eye and gestured for her to bring another.

"Isn't that your third?" Brea asked.

Thom turned back to her, surprised. "Are you counting my drinks?"

"I count everyone's drinks," she said.

"Why?"

"Because drinking makes people ridiculous," she said with a pointed look in Ilain's direction. "And I like to be prepared in case I need to intervene."

Thom tipped his chin toward the whiskey tumbler in her hand. "I don't imagine that'll aid your endeavor."

The corner of her mouth twitched. "I can't get drunk."

"Lucky," Vayden muttered.

"It's a side effect of being a Warrior," Brea explained at Thom's baffled expression. "The more I drink, the more my magic rises to counteract the alcohol's effects."

Thom shook his head. "That doesn't make sense," he said. "I guarantee you, I've seen both Evylin and Ethenn get drunk."

"They're both young, rather inexperienced Warriors. The greater your connection with your magic, the less the alcohol affects you."

"Doesn't that take the point out of drinking?" Thom asked.

"Not if you actually enjoy whatever it is you're drinking," Vayden said, lifting the glass of wine in front of him. "Being drunk is a distraction from the drink in your hand."

Thom grinned. "You'd make a poor drinking buddy," he said, then thanked Imelda as she set his new tankard in front of him.

Turning back to Brea, Thom tipped his head toward Auden and Ilain near the front. "I have a potential solution to your problem," he said.

"Do you?" she asked.

"Indeed." He gave her a wry grin. "I've helped with this sort of thing before, and . . . well, that didn't work out as planned, but that has more to do with the fact that they wound up wanting to be together after all."

"I'm very confused," Brea said.

"Aren't we all?" Thom replied. "Here's the deal: You want to get Auden off your back, and I can help with that. You see, I've lost my flirting friend."

She quirked one of her dark brows upward. "Your flirting friend?"

Thom pointed to Ilain.

Brea, Vayden, and Isla turned to follow the direction he indicated. When they turned back, Vayden was frowning. "You were flirting with Ilain?" he asked, a hint of agitation in his tone.

"Purely platonic, I promise," Thom assured him. "But then I was sort of a shit, and even if our plan hadn't backfired, Ethenn got jealous enough to beat the fear of Allore into me."

Their faces scrunched in confusion simultaneously.

"Ethenn beat you up?" Brea asked.

Thom nodded. "Nearly killed me. He *would* have if Deckard and Hewitt hadn't stopped him."

Now, they fully gaped at him.

Thom cleared his throat, ready to move on. "Point is," he turned to Brea, "so long as you're sure you don't want to be with Auden—no matter what—I can flirt with you and get him off your back."

"You're offering to flirt with me?" Brea asked.

Thom nodded. "Yeah."

"And that helps how?" Isla asked.

"It won't," Vayden said. "Auden isn't interested in Brea for himself. He wants to marry and Bond with her so that—as the most powerful Day Mage alive with the Day Relic for support—he can find a way to heal his lost love."

Thom raised his chin in understanding. "Maura," he said.

Vayden frowned. "He told you?"

"Ilain did."

"Hm."

Thom furrowed his brow. "But if he marries someone else . . ."

"Auden loves Maura more than he loves the chance to be with her," Vayden said. "He's willing to sacrifice a future with her in order to save her life."

"And as selfish as it may be," Brea said, "I'm not willing to be the price of someone's sacrifice."

Thom could understand that. As virtuous as Auden's efforts might be, it seemed a terrible thing to ask of someone else. "But," he remembered, "Ilain said that Bonded couples are destined to fall in love with one another. Wouldn't that sort of . . . make up for it? After all, Bonding is the pinnacle for Warriors and Mages, right?"

Brea's stare was cold. "Ilain can't see past her own nose."

Glancing at Vayden, Thom expected him to defend his sister. Instead, he sat patiently as his wife spoke. "Bonding is not everything," Isla explained. "It is good, it is beneficial, but it is not the only way to have a valuable life as a Mage or Warrior. Take it from me." With her final words, she set her hand on Vayden's arm.

"Do you—" Thom paused, then decided to risk crossing a boundary. "Do you mind telling me how that works? Being twenty years older than your husband and knowing that he'll die before you?"

"I don't know that to be an inevitable future," Isla said. "I am half Schonese. That means I will never be as powerful as a purely Allundan Mage. That directly translates to my lifespan as well. I may live to be nearly two centuries, or I may only live shortly past my first."

Thom turned to Vayden. "And having a wife who will look to be in her twenties in perpetuity doesn't bother you?"

Vayden chuckled, lifting his wine in a mock toast. "There are manifold benefits and minimal drawbacks."

Thom scoffed and turned to Brea. With her smooth skin and impeccable figure, she looked no older than Evylin. "And you're what? Eighty?"

With a smile, she said, "I'm fifty-five."

"Ah, a year younger than my mother. Good for you."

Brea hooked her arm around the back of her chair. "Age is a number. Maturity is what matters."

"That's nice," Thom said with a smirk. "Too bad I'm wildly immature."

Her dark eyes sparkled as she swirled her whiskey. "You're good at this flirting thing," she noted.

"Why do you think I offered?"

Brea glanced at Vayden. "You're sure it won't work?"

Thom didn't fail to notice the way Vayden looked between them with curiosity in his eyes. He twirled the stem of his wine glass between his fingers. "You're Auden's last hope of saving Maura," he told her. "He has nothing to lose by pursuing you and everything to gain by convincing you. He won't stop."

Brea let out a sigh, took a sip, then turned back to Thom. "In either case, keep *this*," she gestured to him, lounging in his chair, "up. If I'm going to be pestered, I may as well have some fun in the meantime."

"You just waved your hand at the whole of me," Thom replied. "What sort of instructions are those?"

She placed her elbows on the table, leaning toward him. "You're very amusing."

"Thank you, but I'm going to need more of a directive if you want my assistance."

Brea's smile softened her whole face, making her far less formidable. "This is going to be fun," she said.

"*Nota te cares envela, Breata,*" Isla said in rapid Schonese.

Thom glanced at her, confused, but Brea ignored her. "How's this for a directive?" she said, eyes locked with his. "Be yourself, and I think we'll have a splendid time together, Thom Deckard."

He tapped his thumb against the tabletop. "I'm not sure you want that?"

"Why not?"

"I'm known for being a shit."

"Sounds entertaining."

Thom leaned forward then, grinning. "All right, you're on. Lieutenant Breata Lohen, prepare to be amazed by just how immature I can be."

Her eyes sparkled. "I look forward to it."

CHAPTER SIX

38TH OF CHRONOS, 1574

"Quit that," Rafferty said, kicking at Ethenn's foot.

"Sorry," Ethenn mumbled. But he couldn't stop his knee from bouncing under the breakfast table. They sat in the Crimson Clover's dining hall, the bright morning sun doing the Creator's work, reminding him what an idiot he'd been for drinking so much the previous night.

"Intoxicants are for dullards and heathens," his uncle's voice rang in his head. *"Wise men stay away from the stuff."*

Ethenn wasn't a wise man. He never had been.

Rafferty reached over and slapped Ethenn lightly across the face. "Kid, I don't know what's got you so agitated," he said, silver-gray eyes narrowed. "But if you don't stop shaking my damn porridge, I'll give you something to be agitated about."

Heat flared up Ethenn's collar as he glared at his friend. He tightened his grip on his fork, choosing to take his anger out on the metal. From the second he'd awoken, anxiety set him on edge. It rankled in his gut, unsettling him as he went about his morning. He'd like to blame it on his hangover, but he knew that wasn't the truth.

Ethenn forced his leg to go still, dropping his gaze to the scrambled eggs on his plate. They were the color of that woman's hair—Ivry, the Water Mage. The moment she sat down last night, Ethenn knew why she was there. He was a Warrior, an asset in short supply. She wanted to use him for her personal gain, the same as any female Mage might.

As Ethenn was coming to the conclusion that his life would be desperately wanting without a Mage to stir the magic inside of him, and Ivry was a beautiful woman with a sweet smile and soothing voice, he'd accepted her advances without hesitation.

Then Ilain had shown up.

Ethenn didn't know what he'd expected from the Fire Mage, but anger hadn't been it. Jealousy, perhaps—after all, she'd made no qualms about wanting a Warrior for herself. Maybe she'd even demonstrate possessiveness. But anger? Bright, seething, unquenchable fury? No, he hadn't seen that coming.

Once Ilain had grabbed Ethenn by the coat and begun dragging him through the tavern, he decided it wasn't worth making a scene. He'd follow her, listen to her tirade—whatever its cause—and move on with his evening. It didn't make him any less resentful of her treating him like a child, pulling him into the storeroom to reprimand him, but he would hold his irritation in check.

Ilain had shut the door behind her with a fierce *click* that rattled the walls. "What," she hissed, "do you think you're doing?"

Ethenn stood in the storeroom, uncomfortable but unflinching. "I'm not sure what you mean," he replied dully, working to keep his emotions in check.

"Ivry is a Water Mage," she said.

"I know," he said. "She introduced herself."

Ilain crossed her arms, drawing his attention to her decolletage for a spare second. She noticed his distraction and smirked. "Do you also know she intends to Bond with you?" she asked.

Ethenn lifted a shoulder in a half-assed shrug. "I assumed so."

She glared at him then, incensed. "And you didn't reject her?"

"No."

A sharp huff of disbelief flew out of Ilain. "Do you *want* to Bond with her?"

"Her?" Ethenn scoffed, the hold on his emotions slipping with the alcohol in his system. "I don't know, Ilain. I just met her."

She drew back like he'd slapped her. "But you want to Bond . . . with someone?"

Taking a deep breath in, Ethenn lifted his eyes to the ceiling. He could feel the heat creeping up his back, and he tried to gain control of himself once more. "Maybe," he admitted weakly.

"Maybe?" she demanded.

"Probably," he corrected himself. "I've been thinking about it these last several weeks since you told Evie and Deckard about it, and . . . It seems like my best future is a Bonded one, so yeah, I'd probably like to Bond with a Mage."

Ilain stared at him for several seconds. Even in the dark room with only a single oil lamp lighting the space, she looked like a brilliant flame. It was no secret that Ethenn was attracted to Ilain. She was impossibly gorgeous. Her loose red curls flowed over her shoulders like molten copper brushing her ivory skin. That scarlet dress did things to his pulse, assaulting his imagination. But he held his ground, keeping his head down as he stood under her inspection.

A slow grin lifted Ilain's lips. She took a step forward. "Why didn't you say so?" she said, her raspy voice fraying his resolve. The heat spiraled up along his collar as she came another step closer. "You know my situation, Ethenn. I need a Warrior."

He retreated a step, bumping against a crate.

"If you want someone to Bond with—" Ilain stood before him now, a dare in her gaze. "If you want *me* . . ."

The heat was at his throat now, coiling higher to choke him.

"All you have to do is say it."

His breath caught, her jade green eyes all he could see.

Ilain set a hand on his chest. He pulled back immediately but found himself pressed against the wall. And she was still there, face only inches away now. "Do you want me?" she asked.

The blush crept up Ethenn's jaw and into his cheeks. Everyone assumed his blushing was due to embarrassment or shyness, as if he were only a foolish child. It had nothing to do with innocence. No, Ethenn could perfectly imagine what it'd be like to grab Ilain's wrist, whirling her around, pinning *her* to the wall. His hand twitched as he envisioned the beads of that bloody scarlet dress underneath his touch.

Ethenn blinked, fighting his staggered breath. No, the blush had nothing to do with innocence. It had everything to do with stifled rage and need, fury and desire.

Ilain's eyes flashed between his, waiting. "Ethenn—?"

"Yes," he said through gritted teeth. His voice sounded angry to his ears.

He could hear Ilain's careful intake of breath. Then she stepped back, her hand falling away. "Good," she said imperiously. "We'll Bond, then."

And with that, she strode out of the room, leaving him to stand there, irate and baffled all at once.

Staring at his breakfast plate, Ethenn still wasn't sure how it had happened. Or what precisely *had* happened. It wasn't as though Ilain admitted to feelings. If anything, she'd confirmed what he'd worried about from the moment he discovered she wanted a Warrior—she only wanted someone to Bond with.

Last night, his head had been muddled with drink, desire, and confusion. After nearly two months of pining, he'd felt his control slipping. And he'd finally admitted what he never should have: He wanted Ilain. But surely, she hadn't meant what she said. She couldn't have truly agreed to Bond with him so easily.

Rafferty's hand slammed down on the table before Ethenn even realized he'd begun to bounce his knee again.

"Trouble in paradise?" Thom asked, appearing at their table with a plate in his hand.

Ethenn and Rafferty looked up as Thom took one of the empty seats. "Loxley's got ants in his pants," Rafferty grumbled. "And he's ruining my breakfast."

Thom eyed Ethenn curiously. "Something on your mind, ki—Loxley?"

It didn't escape Ethenn that Thom had narrowly avoided calling him "kid." It was a piss-poor excuse for an apology, but it was a start. They hadn't spoken much since their fight outside of the Time Keep six days ago, but Ethenn could see that Thom was contrite.

Still, he hadn't decided whether to forgive him or hold onto the grievance.

Ethenn stabbed a boiled potato. "Not really," he mumbled.

The kitchen door opened, and Ethenn's head whipped around of its own volition. Two strangers entered. He turned back to his plate.

Rafferty gestured to Ethenn with his spoon. "He's been doing that ever since we got here," he said with a smirk. "So I'd say it isn't so much a *what* on his mind as a *who*."

"Ah," Thom replied.

Ethenn ignored them.

Thom tapped a fork on the edge of his plate. "This wouldn't have anything to do with your chat in the storeroom last night, would it?" he asked.

The heat crawled along Ethenn's spine. "What's it to you?" he muttered.

"Right." Thom shifted, his chair creaking. "Look, I owe you an apology. Things . . . they got out of hand. What was going on with Ilain and me—"

"I don't care," Ethenn interrupted, feeling the immediate flush of anger spread into his neck.

"It wasn't real."

"So you said."

Thom grimaced. "No, you don't understand, Ethenn. I was upset—I was hurt that you outed me like that, and I—"

"You, what?" Ethenn met his gaze then, struggling with his rising fury. "You wanted to hurt me, too, so you lied?"

"Yes," Thom admitted.

Ethenn nodded. "I know."

Thom's lips parted, fumbling for words. "You—you do?"

"Yeah." The heat was nearing his ears now. "Ilain didn't want me, so she asked you to flirt with her to deter me. Then she found out I am a Warrior, and it backfired, seeing as how she needs one. Well, don't worry. I won't hold it against you."

While Thom sat there continuing to gape, Ethenn returned to his meal.

"This is tense," Rafferty said, a cheerful smile on his face. "It's great. You should have another brawl; that'd be entertaining."

"I've had enough near-death experiences, thanks," Thom muttered.

"Hate to break it to you, Thommy, but we're heading out in the morning," Rafferty said. "We're bound to face death a few more times until this Relic situation is sorted."

Ethenn ignored them, working with all his internal might to push down the anger that consumed him. He'd learned not to show it. Clenching his jaw, tightening his fists, furrowing his brow—nothing physical helped ease the anger within. It wasn't until the last few weeks of training with Evylin that he discovered the best way to chase away the rage.

With a slow, determined breath, Ethenn stared at his plate, unseeing. A tingle spread over his skin like small pinpricks of ice. He imagined the heat receding, the coolness of his magic freezing it low in his gut. Magic never got rid of the fire, but it could quench it for a time.

The kitchen door opened, and Ethenn's magic spiked. He took a sharp inhale, the scents of the dining hall becoming far too vibrant. Roasting ham, cooking smoke, peppered sausage, aged cheese, burning wood, boiling oats, and, above it all, the sharpest tinge of heather.

Ethenn turned to see Ilain walk in with Auden, Isla, Vayden, and Reyana. The ember in his stomach caught, the heat rising once more.

"Well, we've lost Loxley," Rafferty said with a dramatic huff. "Say, Thommy-boy, I saw you talking with that stunning Warrior-lieutenant last night. What's she like, eh?"

While Thom mumbled some reluctant reply, Ethenn watched Ilain and her family gather their meal in the kitchen. The Crimson Clover's kitchen provided three meals a day, served as a buffet. The hotel owner's daughter, Graicelle, walked around serving drinks and clearing plates. There weren't more than a dozen other patrons present, and while Ethenn recognized many of them from the meeting the previous night, he couldn't remember their names.

Ilain finished filling her plate first and began to turn, surveying the room. She was dressed far more modestly today in a dark blue dress that reminded him of the wild berries in the forests of Estshire. It made her hair flash even brighter in the morning light.

Her eyes landed on Ethenn and his table, lingering on him, her face inscrutable, before turning to walk to a long table at the far end of the room.

The second her back was to him, Ethenn bolted out of his seat, muttering, "I'll be back," to his friends.

"Where're you going?" Rafferty asked.

Ethenn didn't bother to reply. He hurried across the room, sure the rest of the Calders wouldn't be far behind Ilain, dodging tables and the scattered diners to step in front of her. Ilain came to an abrupt halt, the sausages and potatoes on her plate wobbling as her eyes grew wide. And the heat seared across his back.

Staring at one another, Ethenn found his jaw clamped shut as Ilain waited. Beyond her shoulder, he could see Isla and her daughter beginning toward them. He had to speak up now, or he'd lose his chance.

"Could I speak with you?" he asked just as she said, "Good morning."

"I suppose so," she replied as he awkwardly added his own, "Good morning."

Again, they stared at one another.

The anger scorched his spine.

"Would it be all right if I had my breakfast before we spoke?" Ilain asked.

Isla and Reyana were there then. "Good morning, Ethenn," Isla said. "Would you like to join us?"

The girl stared up at him, her cheeks bright red.

Turning to the mother, Ethenn could feel his jaw flex with agitation. He'd wanted to get Ilain alone without drawing others into it. He already looked like a fool after last night; there was no need to make himself a greater one today.

"No, thank you," Ethenn said just as Ilain began to say, "Go ahead without me, Isla. I need to speak with Ethenn."

"All right," Isla said, taking her daughter's arm and leading her to the far table. Vayden and Auden were close behind, both men eyeing Ethenn and their sister.

The heat rose to burn the edges of his collar.

Reluctantly meeting Ilain's gaze, Ethenn pushed against the feeling. "We can sit over there," he said, pointing to the table at the opposite end of the room. While an older couple sat two rows away, it was the most secluded of their options.

Ilain nodded and let him lead the way. Once they were seated, Ethenn clasped his hands on the table. Ilain ducked her head and muttered a prayer, then took up her fork. She met his eyes with expectation.

Suddenly, Ethenn's throat was tighter than a bowstring. He had to clear it twice to get any words out. "Do you, uh—do you know why I wanted to talk with you?" he asked.

A sly grin lifted the corner of her mouth. "Don't you know?" she teased.

So she wasn't going to make this easy.

Ethenn sighed. "Listen, I—I wanted to apologize. I was not . . . sober last night," he said.

Ilain raised her full fork, her brow quirked in amusement. "Neither was I," she said before taking a bite.

"Good—I mean," Ethenn shook his head, "not good, but good that we both were in a rather compromised position." He paused, then grimaced. "Not that that's good either."

Steadily, she watched him fumble, not bothering to stop him.

"What I mean is," he corrected again, "it's good that we both understand that neither of us meant what we said, and so we can easily forget about the whole thing."

That got Ilain to set her fork down. "What whole thing are you referring to?"

Ethenn blinked. Didn't she know? Had she been so drunk that she'd forgotten their exchange? He rather hoped so.

Cautiously, Ethenn said, "Do you remember—?"

"My intoxication wasn't *that* great," she said, a twinkle in her brilliant green stare. "Of course, I remember our conversation. What I'm asking is what part of that conversation do you want me to forget?"

Ethenn had to think about it for a moment. "The whole conversation."

She frowned. "Are you backing out of our agreement?" she asked with indignation.

That set the heat flaring up his neck and into his cheeks. "We didn't agree to anything," he said tersely. "I said that I . . . When you asked if I . . . And I admitted I did, so you said we should, and then you left. That isn't an agreement. That's a—a . . . I don't know what that is."

Ilain patted the corner of her mouth with a napkin, then carefully spread it back over her lap. She settled her hands demurely on the table, meeting his wary gaze. "Very well, allow me to formally submit my proposal," she said, then continued before he could get a word out. "Corporal Loxley, I am a Fire Mage in need of a Warrior husband. As I find you more pleasant than any other male Warrior I've yet to meet, and you would like a Mage to Bond with yourself, I would request that you marry and Bond with me so I can take up my place as Highlady Chancellor of the Order of the Flame when Allund comes into its power, and so I can satisfy your desire to be a Bonded Warrior and your desire to have—" She paused, smirked, and concluded, "Me."

Ethenn gaped at her, the heat covering his ears.

"Do you agree to my proposal?" Ilain asked.

Quite sure he'd never heard anything more ridiculous in his twenty-one years,

Ethenn struggled to find the answer. Did he want Ilain? Damn right, he did. She was somehow the most alluring, graceful, and powerful woman he'd ever witnessed. She was bloody gorgeous too. But she was nothing like what he'd imagined a wife to be.

Ethenn had grown up happy. He had a small family—just him, his parents, and his baby sister, Terrina. They'd lived on the outskirts of Trollenston, content and peaceful. His father started taking him on hunts when he was only six. As a boy, Ethenn always imagined that that would be his life. He'd grow up, fall in love with a woman as loving and tender as his mother, and raise his own family in the glens of Estshire, hunting with his sons.

Then everything changed, and slowly, through the years, Ethenn's dreams collapsed into rubble.

Now, he was a Warrior, and that life wasn't accessible to him anymore. Sure, he could marry a sweet, gentle, non-magical woman, build a home with her in the quaint countryside, and have a family together. But he now knew that woman would die well before him, and no matter how much he loved her, she'd never be able to give him that rush—the sense of total clarity and perfection—that a Mage could. Their children would have a father who outlived them too. And what sort of life would that be?

Ilain Calder was everything Ethenn hadn't wanted. She was fierce, dangerous, driven, and significant. She was fire embodied. A life with her would look nothing like the dreams of his youth.

And yet, he wanted her. Deep in his soul, he longed for her, to feel her fire fill his veins and bring him to life like nothing else could.

But she didn't want him.

Until now.

Ethenn knew it was foolish. Even if she was right, even if she fell in love with him due to their Bond, he'd always know she didn't love him for him. She hadn't chosen him because of who he was but because of what he could give her. And that would always be between them.

A wise man wouldn't put himself in that position. He'd protect his heart from such devastation. A wise Warrior would choose a Mage who held the same love for him— even if that was none at all. There would be no disparity between them, no chance for resentment. Mutual affection or indifference—that was the wisest course.

Ethenn wasn't a wise man.

Here sat the woman not of his dreams but of his deepest desires, and she was offering herself to him.

He might be a fool, but he'd rather be a fool with her than without her.

"I agree," Ethenn said, "on one condition."

"What's that?" Ilain asked, her words unusually light as though she'd been holding her breath for far too long.

"That you understand how I feel about you," he said, lowering his voice. "I'm not accepting your proposal because I want to Bond with someone. If that was the case, I'd pick Ivry. I don't have any feelings for her, which is the same way that she feels for me. We'd be entering into a partnership as equals, which is what should be done. But I don't want to be your equal, nor do I particularly want to be your Warrior."

Ilain's expression pinched, confused.

Ethenn swallowed down the fire in his throat, sure his face was nearly red with the fury surging through his veins. "I want to be your husband," he said. "I want to protect you and make you stronger. I want to be to you what Deckard is to Evylin and what she is to him. I don't want to be the one you go to for a joke or light conversation. I want to be the one you go to because I belong to you. I want to take care of you and love you, to be by your side for the rest of our bloody, eternal lives. And if you don't want me that way, that's fine. I'm not asking you to reciprocate. But you have to know that's what I want because if we're going to do this, then by Allore's might, I'm going to love you, Ilain, and you'd better be damn sure you're ready for that."

Mouth agape and flaming eyes locked with his, Ilain didn't say a word for a long time. She just stared at him as his blood boiled through his body, keeping him from feeling embarrassed. Then a little wrinkle formed on her nose as she smiled. "Our lives aren't eternal," she said.

"Semantics," he returned.

"You love me?" she asked.

He didn't bother to hesitate. "Yes."

"You don't know me," she whispered.

"No," he agreed.

She pressed her lips together, shifting uncomfortably in her seat. But a small laugh escaped her. "Well," she said, smiling more brightly than ever. "That's good to know. Thank you."

"You're welcome," Ethenn said, then the embarrassment started setting in. Had he just bared his soul to her? What an idiotic thing to do.

"So we're in agreement?" Ilain asked. "We're going to marry and Bond."

The heat nipped at his scalp. "Yes," he concurred slowly, the truth not quite settling in.

Ilain pursed her lips, then let out a small hum. "In that case," she said weakly, "there are a few people we need to talk to."

CHAPTER SEVEN

A thin sliver of morning light peered through the curtains to wake Deckard. The white-yellow beam drew a line across the foot of their bed and up to his face. He squinted, shifting away from its assault, moving deeper into the comfort of the blankets and Evylin's arms.

With a sleepy smile, Deckard angled to look down at her, catching only the smallest glimpse of her in the darkness. Having doused the lamps the night before, the thin beam of sunshine was the only source of light, casting the rest of the room in shadow. He accepted the gloom, settling into the sluggish atmosphere.

Rarely did Deckard allow himself to linger in sleep. In his youth, he'd set a routine of early mornings and devoted improvement. A habit he continued to the present. But after last night. . . .

Warmth radiated into Deckard's arm, side, legs, and chest from Evylin's body, which was tangled with his. Almost from the start of their marriage, they'd begun to sleep close to one another. What had begun as a means to keep Evylin warm in the cold winter months of travel had grown into a strange habit neither of them could break. In all that time, they'd carefully watched just how intimately they allowed themselves to touch. Now, things had changed.

Though it was only the third night together after the consummation of their marriage, they'd already found a new level of comfort with one another. Evylin practically lay atop him while he held her close, not a scrap of clothing between them—

a suggestion of Evylin's to which Deckard had wholeheartedly agreed. His hand now rested on her bare hip, his mind regaling him with visions of the rest of her.

Readily, Deckard found he was tired of not being able to see his wife in the darkness. Carefully, he extricated himself from her. He'd become somewhat of an expert in the task. She was a heavy sleeper, which helped. However, they'd never slept quite as twisted up in one another's embrace, so he found it a greater challenge than usual. Still, she only stirred once as he climbed free of the bed.

The frigid air nipped Deckard's skin as he darted across the room. He only had one mission and wanted to accomplish it quickly. He jerked the curtains back, letting the light flood the space. The slightest rustle of blankets alerted him to Evylin's disturbed sleep, so he hurried back to begin the gratifying process of enfolding her into his arms again.

Evylin roused as he slipped his arm beneath her neck. "You're cold," she mumbled, the words low and slurred.

Deckard kissed the top of her head. "I know, I'm sorry. Go back to sleep," he whispered into her hair.

Without another word, Evylin snuggled into him. Their legs twisted together again as she settled her cheek on his shoulder. He let his hand drop back to her hip while running the other along her arm and back. Her breathing soon returned to its slow, rhythmic pulse. The blankets still covered all but the tips of her shoulders and head.

Propped up by his pillow, Deckard savored the moment. In the serenity of sleep, Evylin took on a more youthful look. Her muscles relaxed fully, her lips parted, and her foot twitched beside him. Her brow, normally so animated with expression, lay unaffected. So often, her hooded eyes lifted with her gregarious and teasing smiles, but now they turned down with a contemplative tilt. Her dark brown lashes grazed the very tops of her cheeks, drawing his eyes down to the solitary freckle that so often got swallowed up by her smile lines.

Deckard drew his fingers up from her shoulder to the rounding of her cheek to sweep away the loose wisps of her hair. *This is it,* he thought, *the culmination of everything I'd hoped for.* He'd imagined one future his whole life: a future in which he'd serve his country and build a family, a future marked with love for and dedication to others. Now, he stood at the precipice, holding his wife in his arms as they worked to change the nations around them.

Though Deckard still had reservations about the Alliance, Archminister Fishere's speech had put him at great ease. He might not be willing to promise his life to their service, but he was happy to assist them in overthrowing their currently corrupted overlords.

However, there was the problem of his promise to Auden. *"I want your word that you'll join the Alliance in whatever capacity they ask of you."* Those were Auden's exact words. Deckard hadn't quite figured out how to handle that expectation. Even then, Deckard had known that the Alliance would request that he and Evylin Bond. Now that they were doing that, what else would that promise require of him? Was it even something he *could* fulfill? He wouldn't go back on his word, but it wasn't solely up to him to uphold it either.

Evylin hadn't made promises to Auden. She was free to do as she pleased. So if the Alliance asked Deckard to do something she didn't want to take part in, how would he handle such a plea?

Brushing his fingers across Evylin's shoulder, Deckard drew a circle over her lightly tanned skin, marveling at its softness. Then he frowned. He'd always been pale compared to her, but the disparity of their different hues had narrowed. She'd lost so much of her color in the overcast skies of Wauld. When he first met Evylin, she'd glowed with warmth, her complexion like rich cider, and her hair a deep walnut. This dreary country had dulled that radiance.

Time in the sun would refresh her outward appearance, but Deckard wondered if a future in the Alliance would dull the woman she was internally. No matter what they asked of him, no matter the promise he'd given Auden, he'd made vows to her long before, and he wouldn't bind her to a life any less than she deserved. That was his priority. He wouldn't let her be stifled. He would give her adventure and wonder, unencumbered by the world around her. Should the Alliance's requests prove to require anything that would conflict with that goal, Deckard would have to accept the mark on his integrity and break his promise to Auden.

Deckard pressed another kiss upon Evylin's forehead. Yes, he would take her wherever she wanted to go, do whatever she wanted to do, and live whatever life would make her happiest because she was all that mattered.

Evylin flinched at his touch and pressed her face into his neck, letting out a soft hum of agitation. She rolled farther on top of him, her shoulder blades emerging from the blanket to catch the sunlight. "It's too bright," she grumbled, voice muffled on his skin.

Enjoying her attempted escape from the morning, Deckard chuckled. "Are you complaining about the one day of sunshine in Wauld?" he asked, and she groaned in response, eliciting more laughter from him. "You're such a grump when you wake."

She lifted her head just enough to glower at him. "And you're too cheerful. We all have our faults."

Catching her face in his hands before she could hide it again, Deckard held her deep amber gaze. He smiled at her sleepy scowl. "Good morning," he said, running his thumbs over her cheekbones.

It took a moment, but her small dimples pierced her cheeks as she pressed her lips together, attempting not to smile.

Considering it a victory, Deckard leaned in to kiss her. "Did you sleep well?" he asked, resting back against the pillows.

Evylin shifted over him, her weight a pleasant pressure against his ribcage. She tucked her wavy hair behind her ears, then propped herself up to meet his gaze again. "I slept very well," she said, then raised her brow. "Though I certainly could have slept longer had someone not opened the curtains."

"I would apologize, but I'm afraid I'm not sorry."

"You're not sorry to wake me?"

"Not at all," he said, pleased by her shiver as he ran his fingers along her back. "I was getting lonely."

Evylin chewed on her bottom lip, her eyes dropping despite the smirk that pulled at the corner of her mouth. Even now, naked and wrapped together, she still blushed at his hint. "Is that so?"

Deckard nodded, content with the slowness of their touches.

Her fingers traced his collarbone. "That's awfully selfish of you," she said.

"It's difficult being selfless all the time," he teased.

"Mm." She failed to hide her grin. "I can't decide whether to punish you or be grateful you're finally showing some sort of failing."

Deckard scoffed. "I have plenty of failings. You know many of them."

"Oh, yes, you're right." She pursed her lips as though in deep thought. "First," she ticked off one finger, "of course, you're unbearably patient. Second, you care far too much about people. Third, you're infuriatingly kind. Fourth—"

He grabbed her hands, laughing with embarrassment. "Stop, I understand."

Evylin gasped in faux shock. "Pardon me, sir, but I'll need you to let go of my hands."

"For what purpose?"

"I'm not done yet," she said, then broke free of his grip. "Now, where was I? Oh, yes. Fourth."

Deckard shook his head, tipping it back to stare at the crimson canopy above them.

"You love me," she continued, "so that proves you're mad. Fifth, you are immeasurably and cruelly handsome. Sixth . . ." She paused, tipping her head to the side in exaggerated ridicule. Her eyes scanned his face as his dropped to hers again, which lingered on his lips. "You're far too good at kissing. I don't believe anyone should be capable of such power."

Deckard screwed up his face, the flattery adorably irritating. "What sort of power is that?" he asked.

Leaning in, Evylin drew the tip of her nose along his and whispered, "The power to dominate my every thought."

The slow, gentle touches were no longer enough. Deckard closed the gap between them, his hands gripping her arms as his lips met hers. She responded with the same desire and enthusiasm, her fingers sliding up his neck and into his hair. Most often, their kisses began softly and cautiously. Now, after the past several minutes of skin-on-skin touches and flirtations, neither wasted time on such gentility.

Eager to get on with the venture that lay before them, Deckard's hands wandered while hers cradled his head, keeping their kisses deep and impassioned. The tingle of magic met him, coiling low in his gut, present but patient as though satiated by her touch.

It didn't take long for their activity to conclude, their embrace fierce as they gasped against one another's skin. Despite their limited experience, Deckard had surmised that it was the most pleasurable, frustrating sensation in the world, so wonderful and consuming that he clung to her, desperate to hold onto the feeling for as long as he could.

Evylin angled her head to kiss his neck, sending a renewed shiver through him. He tightened his grip on her thigh. "I don't know what you're trying to do," he whispered, voice hoarse. "But you're pressing your luck."

Her laughter tickled his ear. "Really?" she whispered back, kissing her way to his mouth once more. Their lips met with a kiss that drew out his groan. "I hadn't thought you'd be done with me yet."

"While I would love to comply, I'm afraid you'll have to be a bit more patient than that."

"Patience is your strong suit, not mine."

He raised his brow. "I'll have to teach you, then."

With some coaxing and explanation, Deckard convinced Evylin to sit up with him. He hurried to grab two of his shirts from the wardrobe to help with the cold, then returned to enfold her in his arms. He leaned against the headboard as she leaned against his chest, their fingers interlocked.

"Do you know how much I love you?" he asked, sure that she did.

"Yes," Evylin said, pressing closer to him. "Because it's how much I love you, an immeasurable amount."

"There would never be a number high enough." He bent forward to kiss her with quick and gentle pressure before resting his head back.

Evylin smiled and began playing with the plain, platinum wedding band on his finger. They sat in contented silence, enjoying each other's company as they so rarely were able to do. Even if they had been this comfortable in their marriage from the outset, moments like these were few and far between, particularly since joining the Calders.

Deckard had always hoped for a romance like theirs—one that felt easy, secure, and passionate. He no longer feared driving Evylin away with his love; he knew she no longer feared giving hers to him. After all this time, they were finally confident in their united affection.

"Jonn," Evylin said, her head propped against his shoulder, "are you worried?"

Deckard couldn't help his bemused smile. "There's a lot to be worried about these days," he said. "Are you referring to any specific issue? Or am I to be generally worried?"

She gave a soft, half-hearted laugh. She'd taken his left hand in both of hers as she continued to twist his ring. Used to her habitual tugging on her own rings, he grinned, knowing she'd turned to him in her concern. "I'm referring to tonight," she said.

"You mean, am I worried about Bonding?" he surmised.

"Yes."

He pressed a kiss to her temple. "No, I'm not worried about that."

She turned her face up to him. "Not at all?"

"What do I have to be worried about?"

"I don't know," she said. "But that's the problem, isn't it? We don't know anything about Bonding. Yet, we've agreed to it without asking for an explanation."

Deckard hadn't considered that particular detail. He knew what the Calders said of Bonding—it was the height of a Warrior and Mage's achievements. It made them stronger, enhancing their powers. A side effect he didn't care for, but a helpful one in their present situation. It was an oath of trust, fusing their souls to become one power, mind, and heart—an acceptable, if strange, outcome. A Bond was an unbreakable vow more venerated than marriage. He couldn't quite comprehend that but was perfectly willing to accept it.

With a flick of his wrist, Deckard caught Evylin's hand and laced their fingers together once more. "It doesn't matter," he promised. "Whatever it requires, whatever it does to us, I don't care because it means I can take care of you and love you for the rest of our lives."

"Which will be centuries, apparently," she said sourly.

"It seems so."

Evylin drew away just enough to look at him. "It will make our magic stronger."

Deckard cocked his head. "Why are you pressing me? Do you want me to be upset, to stop the ceremony from happening?"

"No, I just—" Evylin sighed. "I don't know. I'm just afraid my impulsive decision is going to drive a wedge between us."

"Evie," he cupped her cheek, drawing her close again, "*nothing* will come between me and my love for you. Not even magic."

"And what about the Deep?" she whispered.

Deckard flinched. He'd forgotten about the Deep, the madness that could afflict a Night Mage. Ilain assured him that not all Night Mages succumbed to the Deep's hold, but Auden was certain he would. After unintentionally summoning a ghost, Deckard already seemed stronger than he should have been, given his experience and training. And that didn't bode well for his sanity.

"Well, that's why I need to meet with the highlord that Isla mentioned," Deckard concluded. "If he's truly able to help train me, surely he'll be able to help me avoid that fate too."

Evylin sucked her bottom lip between her teeth, her hesitation clear. "And . . . what about Hewitt?" she asked.

That made Deckard pause. "He asked that I release him," he said gently. "If Highlord Obel can teach me how . . . I feel I must honor his request."

"We leave tomorrow," she said.

Deckard waited, unsure where she was taking the conversation.

"If this highlord teaches you how to release him," the faintest glimmer of sorrow shone in her eyes, "will you do it immediately?"

"As promptly as I can," he confirmed. When her chin dipped, he added, "But not before you've had the chance to say goodbye."

She let out a relieved breath, leaning into him once more. "Thank you."

Deckard held her close, whispering, "Always," against her temple.

They remained there for some time, breathing and existing together. Deckard closed his eyes, relishing the moment that had felt so impossible only days ago. Her soft hair tickled his cheek. She smelled of the faintest, exotic vanilla from the oils after her bath, a departure from the typical scent of loam, grass, and sweat from their travels. Somehow, he couldn't decide which he preferred.

In Deckard's mind, Evylin was vaster than reality. She was grander than anything Terraeus could be worthy of. Luxurious perfumes were a worthy, if meager, means of displaying her magnificence. And yet, Evylin was also wild. She was a Warrior, at one with the terrae and the world around her. To mask her natural scent was to dampen her, diminish her.

Evylin's fingers trailed from Deckard's hand to his wrist. "Jonn?"

"Hm?"

"Do you want to know why I asked to Bond with you?"

"Do you want to tell me?" He felt her nod against his shoulder. "Tell me, then." Deckard loosened his grip to let her turn to face him. The morning light gilded her cool brown hair.

"Well, yesterday," she began, her eyes on his collar, showing her embarrassment, "I was thinking about everything—you know, about the Alliance, your promise to Auden, about Blount, and . . . all those things. And I wondered, what would I say if the Alliance asked us to Bond?"

He wrapped his arm around her waist as she played with a button on his shirt. "In that moment," she continued, "I realized I'd say yes because Bonding with you would be a privilege. What's more, it would make me happy—*very* happy—knowing I'd get to spend nearly two centuries at your side.

"So there we were in the meeting, and they were worried about Blount, and I thought, why are we fighting this? The answer was so obvious. I couldn't stay behind because we have to win this war; we *have* to defeat Blount. Still, they were right. We couldn't risk him taking me. Even if it didn't give him power immediately . . . I would have given in. One day, perhaps after decades of torture, I would have. And I couldn't risk that."

Finally, Evylin met Deckard's gaze. "So it seemed the only answer left was the one I wanted most anyway." She smiled. "Because I want a life with you, Jonn, not just a few months. And it seems to me that Bonding is the best way to ensure that."

Affection spread through Deckard's chest. He opened his mouth to reply but couldn't find words sufficient enough to express how her admission made him feel. Everything inside him desired the same thing. Not months, but years—centuries of life—with her. He'd told her back in the countryside of the Shires that he intended to be a good husband to her, to do everything in his power to make her happy, no matter what that looked like. That was the promise he'd made her. And he intended to spend every moment of his life fulfilling that vow.

Forsaking words, Deckard kissed his wife. Her arms wrapped around his neck as he drew her onto his lap. He trailed his fingers across her thighs to slip under the hem of the shirt she wore. These were the slow, tender kisses they shared most often, testing, exploratory, and gentle. Even as their touches grew more intimate, their lips were unhurried in their caresses.

Evylin sighed as his hands slid up her bare back. He fought a smile, determined not to cause any impediment to the continuation of their kisses. She settled a hand on his jaw, growing more intense in her ardor. He was scarcely less eager.

A sudden, irritating trio of knocks sounded on their door.

They froze, lips still pressed together as their eyes flew open.

Another knock, and Evylin pulled back. They turned to glare in the offending sound's direction.

"Jonn," Thom called from the other side. "It's me. Open up."

Evylin quirked her brow at Deckard, a twinkle coming into her eyes.

Deckard didn't return her amusement.

Thom started knocking again. "Jonn, I have to talk to you."

Evylin slid off Deckard's lap.

"I'm going to kill him," Deckard grumbled, climbing free of the blankets. The cold floor seared his bare feet, and he cursed as Thom started knocking again. "Give me a second!"

Chuckling at his irritation, Evylin leaped from the bed, kissed his cheek as he struggled into his pants, and moved for the changing screen. Flirt that she was, she began to remove the shirt before disappearing from view.

Sure that he was about to have a conniption, Deckard crossed the room and yanked open the door to glare at his brother. "What?" he snarled.

Thom furrowed his brow. "What's wrong with you?" he asked, pushing into the room. "Where's Evie?"

Evylin's hand appeared above the screen. "Here."

"Ah," Thom said, then took in the bed and Deckard's disheveled state, raised his brow, and said, "*Ah.*" He grimaced and murmured, "Sorry."

"Do you have a reason for being here?" Deckard asked.

"I do," Thom said, then gave a dramatically flourished bow. "I'm officially a page. Archminister Fishere is here—Lord Fishere, as his title is, apparently—and he's requested that I usher you down to his office on some pressing Alliance matter."

"His office?" Deckard asked, shutting the door.

Thom took a seat at the corner table. "Your room is fancier than mine," he noted. He shrugged. "The nobleman owns the place. Maurus is just his manager. Fishere comes in every so often to check the books and such. Why is it so cold in here?"

"That's an excellent question," Evylin called.

Deckard didn't bother to divert his attention to lighting the corner stove but moved to finish dressing. "Did the Archminister say why he wants to meet with me?" he asked.

"Not exactly," Thom said. "Only that he requires your presence in a meeting, and he's sending you off to meet with someone else afterward. Granted, I got all this from the clerk's daughter, so I might've missed something."

"Mm." Deckard tucked his shirt into his trousers, then grabbed his boots. "Hopefully, one of these meetings will include Highlord Obel."

"Who?"

"The Night Mage."

Thom nodded. "Right. I assumed one would be about tonight's ceremony, what with you two Bonding and all."

Evylin appeared from behind the screen fully dressed, a light blue skirt swirling around her hips. "Then why ask for only Jonn's attendance?" she asked. "If it's about Bonding, I should be there, too, shouldn't I?"

"I should think so," Deckard agreed. He snagged his coat from the wardrobe and shrugged it on, turning to Evylin. "Are you ready?"

"Just about," she said, sitting on the edge of the bed, tying off her boots. She slipped a small dagger next to her ankle and reached toward the nightstand. "Here."

Deckard caught the Night Relic. "I'll be glad to get rid of this thing," he said, draping it over his head. He tucked it out of sight, then buttoned his coat.

Thom watched the process with an expression of worry. "You could always give it back to Rafferty or me," he offered.

Though the idea was tempting, Deckard shook his head. "We only have two Relics left. Rafferty can keep one safe easily enough, but I'm the only one who can alter the appearance of this one. As it doesn't affect me like it does others, it's best that I keep it for now."

"But why doesn't it affect you?" Evylin said, joining him and Thom at the door. "You should ask Highlord Obel that question."

"I will," Deckard promised.

They headed for the stairs, Thom and Evylin keeping pace on either side of him. Deckard couldn't help but let a faint smile emerge. For once in his life, everything seemed to be going right, at least relationally. He and his wife were in love. He and his brother were friends. So what if they were fighting for their lives? They were soldiers— that was their job.

Now, he just needed to ensure his magic didn't ruin everything they were working toward.

CHAPTER EIGHT

Arriving in the foyer, Deckard split off from Evylin and Thom. He headed for the clerk's desk while they went toward the kitchen in search of breakfast. Maurus was waiting for him, readily pointing him to the door behind the desk, stating that Lord Fishere was inside and expecting him.

Deckard thanked the man, slipped behind the counter, and stepped into a small office. Despite the light brown and cream wallpaper and the singular window that lit the space, a wall of cabinets made the cramped interior feel even darker and more constricted.

Behind the large desk sat Fishere, his gray hair catching the dim light. He wore a rich frock coat of deep blue that contrasted heavily with his ivory cravat. Though he was clearly aged, the man carried an intelligence in his eyes that engendered respect.

Two crimson chairs faced the desk, one occupied by a woman, while three men stood at the back, crowding the small room.

"I apologize," Deckard said before realizing who these additional individuals were. "Have I arrived early?"

"No, no," Archminister Fishere said. "We were waiting for your arrival to begin, Colonel."

Deckard's response was late in coming as he held Ethenn's gaze for a prolonged, confused second before turning to the Calders quizzically. Ilain sat in the chair while her brothers stood behind her.

Drawing in a breath, Deckard worked to clear his confusion. "I hope I didn't keep you waiting long," he said to the archminister. "What is this meeting about?"

"We'll get to that in a moment," Fishere said, then motioned to the chair in front of Ethenn. "There is a seat open if anyone would like to take it."

None of the men moved.

Fishere waved a hand dismissively. "Very well. At the request of Highlady Calder and Corporal Loxley, we have assembled to process their formal appeal for marriage."

Deckard blinked, certain he'd misheard.

"As per protocol in the Alliance, the appeal must be met with a short hearing to ascertain the validity of such a union," Fishere continued before Deckard could ask for clarification. He addressed the Calders with a glance. "For the benefit of the colonel and corporal, I will explain the process of such hearings and subsequent betrothals, shall I?"

All three Calders nodded their agreement.

Fishere turned to the Ephrian men. "In the Alliance, we revere marriage and do what we can to protect the bonds of its holy estate, so they are entered into with the utmost care. We strive to keep personal regulations minimal. However, as magical individuals carry the touch of Allore, we require hearings such as these for any Warrior or Mage who wishes to enter a binding union, whether with another Warrior or Mage or with a non-magical individual."

Deckard furrowed his brow. "You mean you require this exclusively of magical people?" he asked.

"Yes," Fishere confirmed. "Due to their power and extended years, they are held to a higher standard. We believe their gifts grant them an Allore-given responsibility to take care of others. Therefore, we have a process when one of them—or in this case, two—wishes to marry."

Though Deckard wasn't fully comfortable with such proceedings, he kept his thoughts to himself. If Ilain and Ethenn weren't bothered by this, then who was he to stop them? Appealing this method of governing was an issue for another time.

"While our fledgling government does require the notice of all marriages," Fishere went on, "we specifically require Warriors and Mages to present their supplication to the Administration for approval. As the archminister, I am warranted to approve or deny your request myself. While each case varies—such as if a Mage wants to marry another Mage or a Warrior wants to be with a non-magical individual—since Highlady Calder as a Mage and Corporal Loxley as a Warrior wish to marry, creating the possibility of Bonding, we take extra care to ensure the union is good and beneficial to both of you as well as to our nation.

"So," the elderly man clasped his hands on the desk, smiling, "the purpose of our meeting here today is to verify if it is in the best interest of Highlady Ilain Calder and

Corporal Ethenn Loxley to join in holy matrimony for the sake of one another and the people of Allund."

The realization of what was happening finally hit Deckard. Ethenn and Ilain were asking to be married. Why? He'd known the young man had feelings for the woman, but she'd seemed ambivalent toward his affections at best. And suddenly, he felt he was back in Whickam Village, watching himself be duped into marriage with Evylin— which turned out to be the best and most difficult thing that had ever happened to him.

"Now," Fishere said, looking directly at Deckard, "part of our hearing includes the benefit of what we call advocates: people who stand at the side of the Warrior or Mage to give counsel. As Mr. Calder and Highlord Calder are here to advocate for their sister, Highlady Calder, I asked Corporal Loxley who he'd like to stand at his side, and he's chosen you, Colonel Deckard."

Raising his chin, Deckard turned to Ethenn in surprise. The young man met his stare unflinchingly. Perhaps he, too, had considered the similarities between their unions.

"I'm honored," Deckard said to Ethenn. "I hope to provide the best advice I can."

As Ethenn returned his smile, Fishere nodded approvingly. "You'll do just fine, Colonel," he said. "Let's proceed to the hearing, shall we? Corporal Loxley, we'll start with you. Please state why you believe your marriage to Highlady Ilain Calder will be in her best interest as well as the interest of Allund."

Ethenn turned to the Archminister, eyes wide. His hands gripped the back of the chair as the faintest blush crept above his jacket collar. He opened his mouth to speak, but nothing came out.

"Archminister," Ilain said, drawing their attention. "Ethenn isn't known for his eloquence, verboseness, or openness."

Fishere gave her a fatherly grin. "He needs to explain his position, my lady."

"He doesn't have a position on the matter beyond his feelings for me."

"I can speak for myself, Ilain." Ethenn's sharp tone cut through the room, drawing them all to stare at him. His fingers were almost white on the chair's back, but he held Ilain's gaze with resolution.

While Ilain blinked in shock, Deckard, Auden, and Vayden watched carefully. Used to Ethenn's quiet nature, Deckard had to admit his assertiveness at this moment boded well against Ilain's more forceful personality. He'd feared the Mage would cow the young man too much for him to be of any true use to her.

Fishere appeared amused. "Do share, then, Corporal," he said.

Ethenn straightened his shoulders to address the archminister. "I'll speak of the benefits to Allund first," he said. "I'm not wholly certain of all the . . . outcomes, but Ilain and I want to Bond, which means we will be as Allore intended and capable of serving Allund as a nation in whatever way the Administration sees fit. As Ilain is the most powerful Mage in two centuries, I should think our union would be of great use to your government and, thus, a great boon to the people of Allund. You can correct me if I'm wrong on that, sir."

Fishere said nothing, so Ethenn continued, "As to our marriage being in Ilain's best interest . . ." He paused as though to keep himself from faltering as the red flush spread up his neck. "I love her. I would do anything for her. As she wishes to marry a Warrior and Bond with him, I don't believe there is a single other man in this world so uniquely qualified to ensure her happiness."

The room was silent as they let his words sink in.

Deckard shifted awkwardly behind the young man. Had he sounded this impassioned when he asked to marry Evylin? He doubted it. Because, despite the interest he'd held for Evylin at the time, he hadn't loved her. He'd only wanted to.

But Ethenn . . . If his words were true, he already loved Ilain.

Did she love him in return?

"Well," Fishere said and flashed a grin in Ilain's direction. "It appears you misjudged your young suitor, my lady. I'd say that was satisfactorily eloquent."

Ilain returned the dry grin, though her eyes kept darting to Ethenn as though she was surprised by the feelings he'd expressed.

"Thank you, Corporal," Fishere said. "Now, let's hear Highlady Calder's testament: Please state why you believe your marriage to Corporal Ethenn Loxley will be in his best interest as well as the interest of Allund."

Ilain hesitated, playing with the ruby ring on her index finger. At last, she rested her hands in her lap and sat up straight. "I'll be as straightforward as I can," she said. "You heard Ethenn—he loves me. What better interest could there be than returning his love with my undying dedication and affection? Our marriage will give me the opportunity to love him the same way he loves me."

Deckard wet his bottom lip, recognizing the truth Ilain had skirted with her words.

"And you know perfectly well, Edmaund, that my Bonding is what the Administration has wanted for nearly thirty years. Allund's best interest is my appointment as the head of the Order of the Flame." The light caught Ilain's hair, making it glow brightly as she leaned forward in her seat. "You've prepared me for this since I was sixteen. All you required of me was to find a Warrior to whom I'd pledge my troth. Well—" She motioned toward Ethenn. "I've found him."

Her face grew serious. "This marriage isn't for me, and it isn't for Ethenn," she said flatly. "It's for the Allund we've all sacrificed to build."

Drawing back, Deckard frowned. No one in the room showed surprise—not even

Ethenn. They'd all known this marriage was political from the start. Deckard should have known it himself. More than a month ago, Auden had told Deckard about the Alliance's plan to use eight Bonded couples to carry the Relics. Though he was sure the Alliance would request that he and Evylin be one of those pairs, he had little interest in the position. They would deny it unless Evylin surprised him by wishing to take the job.

But Ilain wanted this. She'd been preparing her entire life to Bond and carry a Relic. Auden told him that she'd unlocked the secrets of Bonding herself, making her the foremost expert on the subject. Of course, the Alliance would want her to carry a Relic and take her rightful place.

As Ethenn didn't protest at Ilain's statement, it appeared he wanted that too.

Archminister Fishere drew a hand along his clean-shaven jaw, and his eyes narrowed on Ilain. "You left out the part about loving him," he noted.

Ilain flinched, but Ethenn spoke in her stead. "I know she doesn't love me," he said.

The man pursed his lips. "Yet, you wish to marry her?"

Ethenn gave a firm nod. "I do."

"And you have no problem with her using you and your love as a means to an end?" Fishere pressed.

Ilain's chin dipped as Ethenn replied. "I was aware of that reality when I requested to marry her."

A corner of Deckard's heart ached, pulsing with feeling for the young man. He knew very well what it was like to be married to a woman who didn't return his affections. But he also knew how wonderful it felt once she finally did. Their relationship might start with a one-sided love, but it could grow into something much purer and mutual over time.

"Hm." Fishere shook his head as though bemused. "It sounds as though you've made up your minds. We can commence with the advocacy."

Sweeping his gaze over Deckard, Auden, and Vayden, the archminister addressed them. "As the advocates for Highlady Calder and Corporal Loxley, it is your place to offer what you wish on behalf of or against the marriage. We'll start with Mr. Calder. What is your view on this marriage?"

Vayden stood tall on the far side of the small room, his blond hair golden in the early morning light. "What can I say?" he asked with a chuckle. "My sister isn't a child. She knows the wishes of her own mind and heart, and if this young man is the one she desires to spend the rest of her life with . . . I can't stand in her way. However, as her brother, I will admit to feeling hesitant."

"Vayd!"

He met Ilain's agitated glare steadily. "I'm not suggesting it shouldn't happen,

Lainy," he said soothingly. "I'm simply stating my reservations. You've known this young man for all of two months. Moreover, he's twenty years your junior."

"Says the man whose wife is twenty-five years older than he."

"I knew Isla for five years before pursuing her."

Ilain rolled her eyes but made no argument.

Vayden turned back to the archminister. "I'm not against the marriage," he restated. "I simply question the validity of their immediate nuptials."

Fishere raised his hand to appease him. "This would be a betrothal, Vayden. Breakable if deemed necessary by either party. A marriage ceremony would not take place until the end of a year or the establishment of Allund, whichever comes first."

That appeared to satisfy Vayden. "In that case," he said. "I can offer my support."

Ilain released a relieved breath.

Fishere turned to Auden. "Highlord Calder, what is your view of this marriage?"

Auden set a hand on Ilain's shoulder. "I'm in full favor of it. If Ilain is to marry a Warrior, then by all means, let it be Ethenn. He's respectable, competent, and dutiful. I could not ask for a better man to love my sister or stand at her side as the head of the Order of the Flame."

Though Deckard wasn't sure what heading the Order would entail, he couldn't fault Auden's statement. Ethenn was a trustworthy, hardworking soldier. He'd proven himself to Deckard many times over. He was a good man and would no doubt be a tender, faithful husband. But despite the young man's affections, Deckard wasn't sure that Ilain Calder was the right woman for him. She was brash, overzealous, and intense. He was reserved, contained, and stoic. They seemed to be opposites. And though some might see the stark variances between Deckard and Evylin, at the core of their beings, they were quite a bit alike. They valued the same things and dreamed of the same future. Did Ilain and Ethenn share anything in common?

"Thank you, Highlord Calder," Fishere said, then looked at Deckard. "Colonel Deckard, as the corporal's only advocate, I am anxious to hear your opinion on the matter. What is your view of this marriage?"

Even given the flurry of his thoughts, Deckard didn't feel decided on an answer. "I fear I am not qualified to share my opinion, sir," he admitted. "But as Ethenn has requested, I will do my best to remain an objective adviser."

Deckard looked at the young man—standing at his side, listening raptly—and then at Ilain—sitting with her usual proud posture. Were they a viable pair? Was this all a mistake? Surely, that's what others would have said of his and Evylin's union, and yet he wouldn't go back to alter his choice even if he could.

With a sigh, Deckard made his decision. "I married Evylin after three days of knowing her. We were strangers, we weren't in love, and she didn't even know my given name." He found himself laughing derisively at the fact. "And it is the best thing that ever happened to me."

He met Ethenn and Ilain's eyes with intention. "It is also the hardest experience of my life," he said. "I can't tell you if this marriage is the right choice or if it is a grave mistake. What I can tell you is that it will be difficult. You know one another better than Evylin and I did, but you are also very different people from either one of us. From each other.

"Ethenn," he set a hand on the young man's shoulder, "I do not doubt your regard and admiration for Ilain. She is a woman worthy of love. However, I do question if you understand the strain that a one-sided affection places on a marriage. It is not easily forgotten nor easily borne. Moreover, you and Ilain . . . There's a discrepancy between you two beyond your age."

Deckard faced Ilain then. "You are strong, my lady. You are impassioned, driven, and immensely powerful. I hardly comprehend your intelligence at times. But I fear you lack the tenderness and attachment to be the wife Ethenn deserves, as I fear he lacks the intensity and shrewdness that you require."

A slow, wry grin spread over Ilain's face even as Ethenn dipped his head, considering Deckard's words.

Deckard turned back to the archminister. "My final view, sir, is this: I do not know that Ethenn and Ilain are ideal partners nor that they will truly make one another happy. What I don't doubt is that they will give their all to their marriage and their country, and despite whatever trials they face, they will face them together. So if this is the path they wish to take . . . I will do my best to support them in whatever way I can."

At Deckard's conclusion, Ethenn raised his chin as though accepting his officer's orders. Vayden wore an impressed expression, while Auden's brows were drawn together in thought. Ilain's grin was still in place, though her steady gaze made it clear she took Deckard's charge seriously.

And the archminister let out a meager "hm" before drawing a deep breath. "Thank you, Colonel," he said. "With each of your inputs, I believe I have the means to make my decision."

He picked up a pen from the desk and dipped it into an inkwell. "As Archminister of Wauld's Administration, I am happy to approve the betrothal of Highlady Calder and Corporal Loxley, the ceremony of their marriage deferred a year's time or until the establishment of Allund, whichever comes first." He paused to scratch a few words across the paper before him. Then he looked up at Ethenn and Ilain. "Shall we commence with the rite of betrothal?"

"The . . . what?" Ethenn asked.

Fishere repeated himself.

"I'm sorry, sir," Ethenn said. "Are we not just . . . engaged?"

The archminister and the Calders all looked confused, so Deckard spoke. "In Ephria, once the proposal is accepted and approved, the couple is simply promised to be married until such a time that the ceremony can be performed," he explained.

"Ah." Fishere made another note on the page. "Well, in Wauld, we have betrothals. It's a long-maintained tradition, as Wauld no longer holds any Allorian kirks, and the traveling clergy are often unable to marry couples until such a time as they arrive. Due to this, marriages in Wauld are less . . . formal due to the lack of monotheism."

"Most simply put forth their request to their liege lord," Vayden added, "who then approves or denies the appeal, and the marriage is considered legal."

"Being Allorians," Fishere said, "we in the Alliance maintain the rite of betrothal."

Deckard and Ethenn shared a look but stayed silent with no reason to object to this country's foreign traditions.

Fishere turned the page and pushed it to the other side of the desk. "Corporal," he said, holding out the pen. "If you would come sign here. . . ."

Ethenn stepped forward and did as he requested. Then Ilain joined him and did the same. The uncanny resemblance to his marriage mere months ago played tricks on Deckard's mind. He felt as though he were experiencing what must have been their witnesses' perspectives.

Vayden and Deckard were each called upon as the principal advocates to sign as witnesses next. Then Fishere signed at the bottom. He read off the details of Ethenn and Ilain's betrothal contract, citing their personal details, the exchange of goods (in this case, the only amendment was that their individual finances would be joined), and a few menial legal particulars.

The archminister rose and stood before the couple at the front of the desk. "Join right hands, please," he requested, and they obeyed. With a rope braided of many-colored cloth, he bound their wrists and said a prayer of blessing, the uncanny similarities to Deckard and Evylin's wedding beginning to compound.

Fishere led Ethenn and Ilain in a short pledge to one another, murmuring the words "To my last breath, I shall serve, honor, and love thee," and then unbound their hands. He lifted a goblet and a small blade from the table, offering the first to Ilain and the second to Ethenn. Once they had them in hand, Fishere instructed Ethenn, "Prick your left ring finger, please."

Ethenn and Deckard furrowed their brows simultaneously, but the young man did as ordered, squeezing a bit of his blood into the goblet. When the archminister further requested that Ethenn prick Ilain's finger as well, he balked. But Ilain's hand was already out, waiting.

Hesitantly, Ethenn pressed the blade into the pad of her finger, and she accepted the cut without flinching before dripping her blood in the cup as well.

Then Fishere lifted a decanter of red wine from the desk, filled the goblet, and, just as Deckard was putting the shocking scene together, the older man ordered Ethenn and Ilain to drink the blood and wine infusion.

"What?" Deckard and Ethenn said at the same time.

None of the Calders showed the same alarm.

"It's a blood oath," Ilain explained. "We share our blood as the start of our own bloodline."

Ethenn stared at the goblet warily but drank his half before offering the rest to Ilain.

Deckard felt the ritual was rather pagan, no matter their country's traditions. However, he concluded that two small drops of blood in a glass full of wine weren't so unsavory that they couldn't be tolerated.

Taking back the empty goblet, Fishere smiled. "In the mighty name of Allore, I declare thee betrothed," he said, then turned to Ethenn, adding, "You may seal your oath with a kiss."

"Oh." Ethenn blanched and turned to Ilain, blinking like she was a mirage on the horizon. When she tipped her head forward encouragingly, the young man swallowed, leaned forward, and, with ears as red as the ruby on the Fire Relic, kissed her.

Generally, Deckard looked away from other people's public affections out of respect. In this case, he was captivated, realizing this was how he must have looked, kissing Evylin for the first time. Cautious, anxious, and awed.

However, Ethenn lingered far longer than Deckard had had the guts for on his wedding day.

Deckard thought to turn away just as the kiss ended. Ethenn turned back to the archminister even as Ilain swayed slightly. She let out a small hum before blinking away her apparent daze. The Calder brothers watched her reaction with dry humor. Vayden even muttered something to Auden under his breath, at which the younger Calder chuckled.

"Excellent," Archminister Fishere said. "With these our witnesses, I pronounce you man and wife. May Allore bless you both."

The words took a moment to settle. Then Deckard frowned, and Ethenn gaped.

"Wait," Ethenn said. "I thought this was a betrothal."

"It is," Fishere said.

"But you just called us man and—and wife."

"Because you are."

Ethenn shook his head, fumbling for words. "You said the wedding wouldn't be for a year."

"Or until Allund is established, yes," Fishere confirmed patiently.

"Then what was this?" Ethenn exclaimed, gesturing between him and Ilain.

Fishere and the Calders looked as baffled as Deckard felt, though he suspected it was for very different reasons.

Ilain set a hand on Ethenn's arm. "We're betrothed," she said. "In Wauld, that makes us probationary husband and wife until such a time as we can be properly married by the clergy."

Ethenn's face had turned more red than tan now. "I didn't know that!"

"You can nullify the betrothal at any point before the ceremony," Archminister Fishere offered. "As there is no loss on either side, there will be no ill will from a contract broken. That is so long as you don't consummate the marriage in the meantime."

Ethenn's eyes widened, and Deckard's narrowed.

"Is that allowed for a betrothed couple?" Deckard asked.

"Encouraged, actually," Vayden said.

"I beg your pardon?"

Ilain rolled her eyes and muttered something about prudish Ephrians before facing Ethenn and Deckard. "In Wauld, we don't have the luxury of pietism. Betrothals are oaths of intent, and the consummation of them, while not always enacted, is regularly viewed as the appropriate means of proving your dedication to the oath. From the time of betrothal, our tradition allows the man and woman to live together. Otherwise, they could be waiting years before the clergy arrived to perform the proper ceremony."

"But we're not in that situation," Ethenn protested.

"No," Ilain allowed. "But my culture's traditions remain."

Fishere interjected with a fatherly tone. "The consummation isn't required," he said. "In fact, in this situation, I'd advise against it per Mr. Calder and Colonel Deckard's advice. Take the betrothal as a chance to test your marriage and ensure a future together is what you truly want." Then he sent Ilain a knowing look. "Just don't go trying things you can't un-try, eh?"

Ilain gave him a pleased smirk. "After forty-three years, you don't think I can handle a few months, Edmaund?"

"My child," Fishere said fondly, "you are known for a great many virtues. Restraint isn't one of them."

With Ilain's silent acceptance, Fishere clasped his hands behind his back. "With that taken care of . . ." He turned to Deckard. "Last night, Highlady Freye put forth the request for your meeting with Lord Obel. He has agreed to receive you at his home here in Mouroc. You are expected . . ." He glanced at the clock and then grimaced. "In five minutes."

"We'll be late," Vayden said.

"Yes," Fishere sighed. "As Obel considers Vayden a friend, he will escort you along with Highlord Calder as your current tutor. However, with Blount's writ, you'll need to shroud Auden as you move through the city."

Deckard nodded, then put forth the request he'd been waiting to make. "Sir, I would like Evylin to join me as well."

"I'm afraid that's out of the question," Fishere said instantly. "We're putting you in enough danger with Auden's presence. Until the Bonding ceremony tonight, Private Deckard must remain in the protection of our compound here."

Disappointed but dedicated to Evylin's safety, Deckard accepted the denial. "Thank you for arranging the meeting, sir," he said.

"Yes, yes." Fishere waved his hand at them. "You're already late, and I have work to do."

Dismissed, Deckard exited the office with the Calders and Ethenn. Vayden and Auden kissed Ilain on the cheek and shook Ethenn's hand in congratulations, then stepped toward the hotel's front door. Deckard offered the couple a smile and his own salutations.

"Colonel," Ethenn called before he could turn away. He glanced at Ilain, then faced Deckard again. "Thank you—for your advice."

"Of course," Deckard said. "Thank you for requesting it."

Ilain took a step back, understanding in her gaze. "If you'll excuse me," she said, "I'd like to share the news with Isla and Reyana."

Deckard dipped his chin in farewell as Ethenn nodded awkwardly.

Ilain rolled her eyes. "Oh, come here," she said, then pressed a fierce kiss to Ethenn's cheek. His temples went pink, and she winked at him. "I'll see you later, husband."

Decidedly bemused, Ethenn watched her walk away, lips parted. Then he looked up at Deckard. "What the hell am I supposed to do with her?" he asked, desperation thinning his deep voice.

Working to hold back a laugh, Deckard couldn't help smiling at the young man. "You're the one who proposed," he said.

"Actually," Ethenn sighed, "she did the proposing."

"Of course she did." Now, Deckard did chuckle. "Loxley, as a man who went through a similar predicament only three and a half months ago, may I give you a suggestion?"

"Please do, sir."

Deckard held his gaze, impressing the significance of the lessons he'd learned over the last one hundred forty-five days. "Be honest," he said. "You've already told her you love her, which is a good start. Continue to be open with her. If you have expectations for your relationship, tell her. If you feel you're failing her, tell her. If you have questions or reservations, *tell* her."

Deckard tapped Ethenn's chest. "Such honesty will save your heart in the end."

Ethenn took the wisdom with his usual steadiness, though the corner of his mouth quirked. "I didn't exactly expect to come out of that room married," he said.

"Technically, you aren't, if that helps."

Ethenn gave a wry scoff. "She's my wife, though."

"Evidently."

"I'm not sure how to feel about that."

"You said you love her," Deckard prompted.

"I do," Ethenn assured him.

Deckard smiled. "Then love her," he said, knowing that was the advice he would have given himself all those months ago. "Whether she returns your feelings or not, love her with your whole soul. In the end, it'll turn out just fine."

CHAPTER NINE

After parting with Deckard, Evylin and Thom found Rafferty lingering in the dining hall. He was piling a plate full of the last bits of breakfast while the cook, Mrs. Howerth, glared at him.

"Eve!" Rafferty called as they walked in. "I've got your breakfast. No thanks to this old bag."

Hastily, Evylin apologized to Mrs. Howerth and then pulled Rafferty to a table in the far corner. Thom managed to patch up relations with the cook and procured cups of tea for them as Evylin tucked into her meal.

Once they were all seated, Rafferty leaned forward, brows raised. "Did you hear the news?" he asked.

"What news?" Evylin asked around a bite of browned bread.

"Little Loxley's done got himself into Highlady Calder's knickers."

Evylin choked on the bread at the same time Thom choked on a sip of tea. "I beg your pardon—*what*?" she asked.

Rafferty's eyes glimmered as he reached across the table to nudge Thom's arm. "You know how Lox decided to get chatty with her earlier?" At Thom's hesitant nod, he continued, "Well, I tried to listen in, but with you prattling on about the beguiling lieutenant, I had a hard time getting all the details."

"You're the one who asked about Brea," Thom protested.

Rafferty ignored him. "But then Lox stepped out on his own while Ilain spoke with her brothers. Shortly after, the three of them disappeared, leaving Isla and her daughter behind, and that Graicelle girl came to get Thommy. So I did what any sane man would—I eavesdropped."

Though Evylin felt she was missing a few key details to fully understand Rafferty's story, she smirked and said, "Naturally, of course."

Rafferty winked at her. "And wouldn't you know it," he said, "the Calder girl was all enthusiasm over the news that her aunt was going to be married."

"Married?" Evylin and Thom said in unison, then shared a look.

"Isn't it bloody ridiculous?" Rafferty laughed uproariously. "The kid's too young. He's got so much life to live! He's wasting his best years."

Evylin frowned. "I will admit I think it hasty, but I fail to understand how he's wasting his life by marrying," she said.

Thom set a hand on Evylin's arm. "Don't ask questions you don't want the answers to, Evie," he advised, then turned back to Rafferty. "You're sure you didn't misunderstand?"

Rafferty set a hand to his chest in offense. "*I* never misunderstand, Thommy. It's my job to procure information."

"Technically, that's not your job," Thom said. "It doesn't make sense, though. Why would Deckard be included in a meeting like that?"

"Maybe he's not," Evylin offered. "Perhaps it's a completely separate meeting."

"Then where are Ethenn and the rest of the Calders?"

Evylin shrugged. "Either way, I don't think we should discuss it until we have more information. You two are as bad as my aunt, Serene."

"Your aunt sounds like a splendid woman," Rafferty mocked, then scooted his chair back to prop his feet on the table. "Very well, we'll allow Loxley his privacy for Evylin's sensibilities. And you, Thommy-boy, can regale me with tales of that lieutenant again. I wasn't listening the first time."

Thom rolled his eyes. "There isn't much to tell," he said. "Honestly, I learned more about Vayden and Isla than I did about Brea."

"Brea?" Evylin prompted. "You're on a first-name basis."

Thom looked at her blandly. "Don't make something out of it, Evie. She's an interesting woman, but she's too old and too magical for me. Besides, the Alliance wants her to Bond with one of their Mages."

Suddenly, Evylin remembered Auden's special attention to Lieutenant Lohen the previous night. "Ah. She and Auden have a thing, then?" she asked.

Thom snorted. "Auden wishes. It's his life's goal to Bond with a Warrior, but she's not interested in him."

"It seems the Calder siblings share that goal," Evylin remarked.

"Do you really think it makes people better in bed?" Rafferty asked abruptly, and Evylin kicked his shin. "Ow! It was Ilain who said it."

"It isn't polite conversation," Evylin returned.

"Says you." Rafferty turned back to Thom. "So who does the lovely lieutenant have a thing for?"

Thom lifted his teacup. "I couldn't say. We didn't discuss her love life, only that she's thoroughly disinterested in being Auden's last resort."

Rafferty sighed. "Then what *did* you learn about her?"

After a moment of thought, the corner of Thom's mouth lifted. "She's fun," he reported.

"Fun, eh?" Rafferty's eyes danced. "Do tell."

Thom settled back in his seat, considering. "Flirting with her is like playing with a knife," he said. "You're pretty sure you're gonna get nicked, but it'll be damn thrilling in the meantime."

Rafferty howled with laughter, and Evylin couldn't help smiling. "You like her," she noted.

Thom tipped his head to the side. "I'll admit I admire her more than most women," he said plainly. "She's quick-witted, frighteningly beautiful, and I'm convinced she'd gut any man who tried to touch her. It's an attractive quality, knowing you could die at a woman's hand."

Evylin elbowed him. "You're ridiculous."

"I am." Thom set his empty cup on the table. "But I'm not fool enough to think anything will come of it. Lieutenant Breata Lohen is a daunting woman of impressive caliber. Even if she *was* interested in me, I'm not of value to her or the Alliance. I'll happily find myself a woman of less repute to prove my worth to. Maybe your little sister."

Evylin scoffed at the quip. "Oh, now you want Calyn? All it took was a near-death experience?"

Thom gave her a teasing look. "Well, she is prettier than you, even if she isn't as . . . muscular."

She threw a bite of egg at him, thankful to have her friend back. After his foolish confession a week ago, Evylin worried that she'd lost her best friend, her brother. That's what Thom had become to her over the last three and a half months of traveling and fighting side by side. She'd trusted him and relied on him. When he'd professed his love for her, her anger came not only from the sense of betrayal of Deckard but also from the loss of the friend she'd gained.

But Thom had rectified his mistakes. He apologized and admitted to his jealousy.

On their journey to Mouroc, he'd ridden at her side, explaining everything. He'd begged her forgiveness and told her he would spend the rest of his life making up for the idiocy of his actions.

Evylin hadn't hesitated to forgive him.

"You two," Rafferty said with a proud gleam. "It's good to see you back to normal."

Smiling, Evylin threw another bit of egg at him for good measure. "What about you, Raff?" she asked. "If Thom isn't interested in pursuing the lieutenant—Breata, was it? Well then, the path is wide open for you. Sounds as though you'd find her a splendid challenge."

Rafferty sniggered. "Oh, I'd certainly give it a go. As Thommy said, she's right stunning with her fierce look. Though she's a bit skinny for my tastes."

"I'd imagine that's muscle under those clothes," Thom said.

With a sly look, Rafferty twirled a teaspoon between his fingers. "I'd be happy to do some reconnaissance to find out," he said.

"I bet you would."

Evylin huffed at their innuendos. But then she suddenly wondered about Rafferty's true interest. She remembered, at the start of their appointment to the Order of the King, Rafferty had mentioned an attraction to Ilain, though he'd never pursued her. It was possible his restraint was because he knew of Ethenn's more genuine interest. However, Rafferty always showed interest in others' love affairs, so it seemed only natural that he should want one too.

"Raff," she found herself asking, "have you ever had a sweetheart?"

Rafferty's chin tipped up, his wily eyes glimmering wickedly. "Depends on your definition of the term," he said.

"Don't ask, Evie," Thom cautioned.

"What?" Evylin asked, gesturing to Rafferty. "I just want to know if Raff has ever been in love."

"Depends on your definition. . . ." Rafferty said in a singsong cadence.

The mischievous glint in his eye gave Evylin the answer. Her nose scrunched in disbelief. "Rafferty! Are you a philanderer?"

The weasel sniggered. "That's a fancy term. Not sure I quite warrant it, but I have been known to . . . dally with fine ladies here and there. Can't say I'd consider it love, though. I'd be happy to regale you with stories of my conquests if you'd like."

Evylin grimaced, pushing her plate away. "No, thank you."

Thom chuckled. "I told you not to ask," he said.

"Forgive me if I thought my friends to be gentlemen," she returned.

Rafferty snorted. "We can't all be your incorruptible colonel, Eve. We men have needs. Just because he's a masochist doesn't mean the rest of us men have to suffer."

"You're deplorable."

"I'm realistic," Rafferty said, sitting forward. "Should you have married any other man, you wouldn't have had three and a half months to make up your ruddy mind."

"I should hope that's not true," Evylin said. "If so, I'm sorely disappointed in the quality of men in this world."

Thom shook his head. "It isn't as bad as all that," he said lightheartedly. "But yeah, Jonn is the exception. Should I have been put in his situation—with any attractive woman, mind you—my patience would have run out at around a month."

"A month?" Evylin exclaimed. "That's hardly enough time to get to know a stranger, let alone to—to . . ."

"Evylin, men don't need a month. We need about ten minutes. Maybe less if she's charming enough."

"You're deplorable too."

"I'm not saying it makes it right," Thom said casually. "Nor that we act on it most times. All I'm saying is that Jonn is a better man than the rest of us. And you're lucky to have him."

Evylin had no doubt of that. She'd grown up with Hewitt teaching her to be wary of men's baser instincts as well as novels declaiming the sordid ways of the world. But they were always stories to her, figments that didn't have faces. After marriage to Deckard, she struggled to imagine life with a man of lesser morals. A fact for which she found herself infinitely thankful.

At the far side of the room, Ethenn appeared in the kitchen doorway. His shoulders visibly relaxed when he saw them.

"Tallyho, little Loxley," Rafferty called derisively. "You catch your quarry?"

Ethenn eyed him with his usual reserved demeanor. "What are you talking about?" he asked.

"A redhead about my height with an ample undercarriage from all accounts."

Jaw tight and ears pink, Ethenn glared at him. Then he turned to Evylin. "Morning," he said calmly. "Deckard wanted me to tell you that he's gone to visit with Lord Obel. He's running late, or he would have said goodbye himself."

"Oh." Evylin tried to quell her disappointment. "Well, thank you, Ethenn. I believe his appropriate address is highlord, though."

"No, he's a duke, and apparently that outranks his magical status," Ethenn noted. "Also, we're supposed to meet in The Rook this afternoon. Lieutenant Lohen is returning then, so we can discuss our plans."

"Hey!" Thom said, slapping Rafferty's boot, his heels still resting on the table. "You'll get to try your charms on her."

"Bloody fantastic," Rafferty agreed, hopping up. "In that case, why don't we head over to The Rook now?"

"It'll be at least an hour before we meet, won't it?" Evylin asked.

"Probably more like three from the sounds of the colonel's meeting," Ethenn confirmed.

Rafferty brushed a hand through the air. "The tavern won't even be open until this evening."

Evylin raised her brow. "If it isn't open, how are we going to get in?"

With a wink, Rafferty produced a small iron key. "I'd say this'll do the trick."

"Did you steal that?" she reprimanded.

"No." He gave her a snide grin. "The lovely Madam Imelda gave it to me."

"Imelda?" Thom scoffed. "She's got to be twice your age."

"She's thirty-eight and a widow," Rafferty said matter-of-factly. "Giving her a good time's the least I can do."

As Thom laughed and Ethenn failed to contain a smirk, Evylin blew out a perturbed breath. "I don't like you anymore," she lamented.

Rafferty headed for the door, grinning broadly over his shoulder. "As I'm not interested in your knickers, Eve, I don't rightly care."

Unable to hold her laughter at bay, Evylin followed the men out the back door to the courtyard. Rafferty led them to the tavern, key ready in hand. A soft wind blew into the open space, nipping at their noses in the late morning. The horses nickered in their stalls, and the stable boy, Coalum, waved as they passed by.

"Do you know," Thom began as they waited for Rafferty to open the door, "this is the first time it's just been the four of us since we made it to Loclight."

Looking over the men, Evylin realized it was true. Since she'd left Whickam Village, these soldiers had become her brothers, her dearest friends. In only three and a half short months, she'd formed a whole new family. They each possessed qualities she loved: Thom, with his passion and tenderness, Rafferty, with his good humor and cunning, and Ethenn, with his level head and fierceness.

Evylin smiled, joining them in the cozy tavern. Despite everything she'd lost, somehow, she'd found even more. Deckard. These men. Even the Calders meant more to her than she'd ever expected.

Playing with her rings as Rafferty tried to coax information about his morning activities out of Ethenn, Evylin brushed her fingers along the ivy etching. Hewitt had given her this family, who understood, accepted, and loved her. How she missed him, but how grateful she was to him too. He'd always known just what she needed, and he'd always provided it to her. And with him in her memory, she promised to accept his gift without allowing a trace of fear to taint it.

CHAPTER TEN

A carriage awaited Deckard, Vayden, and a shrouded Auden outside the Crimson Clover. Fine silken flags hung by the driver's perch, and the carriage's body was shiny black wood. A footman held the door for them before hopping on the back. Then the carriage rumbled down the cobbled streets of Mouroc and deeper into its heart.

After passing through another gate and winding through the streets, they finally stopped before a grand townhome with a white stone façade, copper gutters, and well-maintained shrubbery. Despite being squeezed in between numerous other houses, each building on the stretch was three times as wide as Deckard's home back in Loclight.

"I take it being a Mage is a lucrative profession," Deckard said, taking in the intricate architecture.

"It isn't bad," Auden said, keeping his voice low. His edges were fuzzy, confirming Deckard's shroud, but his invisibility didn't keep him from being heard. "But Lord Obel is the Duke of Flamesend Crest, making him a true nobleman and wealthy by birth rather than circumstance."

Deckard nodded as the footman opened the door. They stepped out, taking care to distract from Auden's exit before heading up the staircase to the front door, where a butler waited. The foyer's elegant design reminded Deckard too much of Renaul's palatial mansion for comfort. Paintings in golden frames adorned the walls, and a large, marble staircase spiraled to the top of the four-story building.

The tan and black tiles echoed under their boots as the butler led them to a drawing room. The butler offered them tea while they waited for their host, then left them alone in the grand space. A massive window filled the back wall with heavy, black velvet draperies drawn back on each side. Another wall bore mahogany bookcases full to bursting with leather volumes of all shapes and sizes. A pianoforte rested along the far end, and an oversized granite fireplace heated the room with its crackling fire.

While Vayden readily sat on one of the luxurious couches and Auden waited to the side, Deckard marveled at the fifteen-foot ceilings. An ornate mural spanned the room's length, and an opulent chandelier hung from the center. The painting on the vaulted ceiling depicted eight individuals in various poses, with variegated colors around them.

Deckard's eyes looped around the painting, entranced by the personification of what he understood to be the resources of life. First, a woman shockingly similar in appearance to Ilain stood wrapped in ruby-red flames that licked at the world around her. Fire's charred remains bled out toward the next image of a man who looked like pure gold, light reflecting off everything surrounding him. Day radiated a yellow pulse that shone onto the surface of a lake before rippling into the deepest sapphire blue. Another woman stood ankle-deep on the bank of the pool as streams of sparkling Water swirled around her. Shadows met the edge of the lake, turning an ominous shade of amethyst. A man shrouded in darkness stared down at Deckard with a hooded countenance he recognized from the antechamber of Renaul's family crypt. Night's darkness beamed with glimmering, metallic stars around him.

Deckard had to turn around to follow the shadows before they were whisked away by the soft gray streams of a gale, swathing another man in its tumultuous coils. The Wind blew away as stark white bleached an interpretation of all four seasons, an ageless woman sitting on an ivory throne, her face expressionless. Time bled into the roots of a tree, wrapping around the form of a man with the richest emerald green vines across his shoulders as a mantle. The Terrae grew lush and full around the man before being swallowed up in a void of eternal black. A woman hung suspended in the glittering nothingness of Space, palms up and face lifted to the darkness around her.

Deckard narrowed his gaze, studying the woman as a door opened at the back of the room. He jerked his eyes away from the mural, turning to see their host's arrival. Dressed in a black and brown jacquard coat, Lord Obel held his head high and his shoulders back with a regal bearing. Jet-black hair brushed his collar, silver streaks cutting into a beard of the same darkness.

With a steady stride, Lord Obel approached, eyeing Deckard with severe green eyes. Surprisingly, his face bore the weathering of age, light wrinkles etching his pale skin, unlike every other Mage he'd met thus far. However, he still looked barely beyond his prime, whatever his years.

Vayden rose as Lord Obel came to a stop in front of Deckard. "You're sloppy with your magic, young man," the nobleman said, his voice as dark as his hair.

It had been so long since anyone referred to Deckard as young that it took him a second to respond. The soldier in him took over, and he snapped to attention. "I do apologize, my lord," he said, keeping his tone respectful. "But I don't understand."

Obel blinked as though bored. "My appropriate address is 'Your Grace.' I may be a Mage, but my title as a duke ranks above that," he said flatly. "And as to your magic, any Night Mage could see the shroud you've got up around Highlord Calder. It's thin, at best, but I'd go so far as to call it visible. I can see the shadow around him attempting to mask his form. Who taught you?"

Deckard glanced at Auden, still standing shrouded beside his brother, before replying, "Highlord Calder."

Obel scoffed. "That explains it," he said, then waved a hand at Auden. "You can remove the shroud."

Deckard did as commanded, allowing the shroud to fade with a mental release, and Auden's figure sharpened.

Lord Obel ignored them both, moving for Vayden. "Welcome back, my boy," he said, patting the man's arm. "I still think they retired you too soon. You could be giving Blount more trouble yet."

"I'm an old man like you now, Sirraus," Vayden replied with a fond smile. "And I've found other work to suit me."

"So I hear," Obel said, then instructed them all to take a seat. He settled across from the Calder brothers on the second couch, so Deckard took one of the chairs nearer the hearth.

The duke surveyed Deckard thoughtfully. "Well, you're Colonel Deckard?" he asked, his Waulden accent finer than any he'd yet heard. "I thought you were Ephrian."

"So did I," Deckard replied.

"Life is full of surprises, I suppose." Obel rested his hands on his legs. "Fishere said you wanted to speak with me, Colonel, but as you're leaving in the morning, I'm afraid I don't know how much help I can be."

Deckard kept his gaze slightly averted from the duke's, uncertain how such high-ranking noblemen preferred to be treated. In Ephria, he'd only ever met magistrates and the occasional baron. A duke was a formidable ally indeed.

"Your Grace," he began, but Obel interrupted.

"Look at me when you're speaking, boy," he said. "I'm not going to chop off your head for insubordination."

Vayden chuckled as Deckard corrected his posture. "My apologies, Your Grace," he said, then started over. "I'm not entirely certain what help you might offer either. However, my magic is both inexpert and seemingly . . . dangerous. I would appreciate any help you can give me, even if it's just to control it better."

Obel huffed. "Fishere said you are a Night Mage, which strikes me as odd since you're not very good at it. I can understand that Highlord Calder isn't the best teacher for the craft, but if Night is your primary, why are you so damned pitiful at it?"

Deckard met Auden's gaze. The Day Mage's brows were drawn low in irritation and confusion, but he offered no assistance.

Angling toward the duke, Deckard worked to control his frown. "I'm not sure I understand, Your Grace."

Expression impassive, Obel looked from Deckard to Auden, over to Vayden, and back. "Why do you believe you're a Night Mage?" he asked.

Deckard took a deep breath before explaining. "A month ago, I discovered my magic when I held the Night Relic for the first time. From there, Auden and Ilain tested me, discovering that I'm an Existential Mage. Aside from that . . . the first time I unknowingly accessed magic, it was Night magic."

"Unknowingly?" Obel prompted.

"Yes, Your Grace," Deckard said. "Before I was aware of my power, I . . . accidentally summoned a ghost."

The duke's expression pinched. "You summoned a ghost *accidentally*?"

"Yes, Your Grace."

"Mm." Obel sat back in his seat, his hand stroking his silvering beard. He didn't speak, studying Deckard slowly. His eyes began at his face, then scanned down as though looking for traces of magic itself.

Finally, the duke let his hand fall away. "Well, I don't perceive death on you," he announced. "Usually, when the Deep is growing in a Night Mage, often spurred on by the summoning of a ghost or some other necromantic work, it hangs around them like a cloud. But you're clear as Day. When was the last time you summoned this ghost of yours?"

Deckard spared a glance at the Calder brothers. Vayden watched with amused interest while Auden pursed his lips in agitation.

Sitting up straighter, Deckard cleared his throat. "Two days ago," he answered.

Obel turned to Auden. "Have you seen this ghost?"

"I have," Auden said tersely.

"Did he look natural?"

Auden frowned. "He was a ghost. That's not natural."

Obel raised his eyes toward the mural. "Radia's light, you're dull," he muttered, then raised his voice as though speaking to a child. "What I mean, Highlord, is: Did the ghost resemble a living human rather than a deteriorating corpse?"

Vayden pressed his lips together as though suppressing a laugh while Auden ground his teeth. "Yes," the Mage said. "He looked exactly like he did in the moments before he died."

"Ah," Obel said, something like excitement injecting itself into his tone. "Then you knew this fellow?"

"He was a member of our party."

"Excellent." Obel turned back to Deckard. "I will admit your ability to summon a ghost unintentionally *and* make it visible to others is surprising. There's strength in you, even if your technique is lacking. Though I question if that might of yours has more to do with that thing around your neck rather than innate power."

Both Calder men shifted in their seats warily.

Deckard frowned, the Night Relic's chain suddenly heavy. "How did you—?"

"I sensed it the second I walked into the room," Obel said. "That's another issue we'll discuss in a moment. Are there any other reasons you believe you're a Night Mage?"

Deckard faltered, turning to Auden for support.

Auden took over readily. "I've seen his magic, Your Grace," he said decisively. "It's colored by Night. What's more, he shrouded the Night Relic, disguising it from Renaul's hired men."

Lord Obel tipped his head to the side curiously. "Is that so?" he said, then faced Deckard. "You disguised the Relic?"

"I did," Deckard replied, then added, "Your Grace."

"Interesting."

As Obel didn't expound on his statement, Deckard sat forward. "Your Grace, I would appreciate whatever training you could give me, even if it's just for the afternoon," he said. "But more specifically, I'd like you to teach me how to release the ghost."

"I can do that," Obel said with a singular nod. "But first, we need some answers."

"Answers to what?" Deckard asked.

Obel smiled. "Let's have a look at your magic, Colonel."

Deckard's brow pinched together. "I'm sorry, Your Grace, I'm not sure how to . . . show it off."

Lifting a palm, Obel summoned a dark amethyst shadow to hover over it. The small cloud twisted in a merry dance, gloomy and charming all at once. "You do it the way you do any magic," he said, then closed his hand, snuffing the shadow. "By focus and thought."

Drawing in a breath, Deckard adjusted in his seat. He set his gaze on the beige and brown carpet beneath his feet, working to find his center. Focus was rarely a problem for him. Deckard had managed to hold fast to his ideals and goals due to his unwavering dedication to them throughout his life. Ever since he'd begun training with the Calders, he'd managed to tap into his magic more quickly than they'd expected. And with his strong grip on the ability to focus, that magic always came roaring in with nearly unbridled force.

The Night Relic's setting felt like ice against Deckard's chest as the heat of his magic rippled through his veins. His heartbeat rose, pulse quickening, and the room was tinged in darkness as the edges of his vision blackened. He'd not yet harnessed his magic, but he could feel it roiling inside as though in anticipation.

Holding his hands in front of him, Deckard stared at his palms, willing the crystalline shadows to appear. Black shards erupted around his hands, twisting and shimmering in the late morning light. Comparing his magic to Obel's, he wondered if it could rightly be called shadows. The tiny, glass-like shards that coalesced together to form the larger mass looked very little like the cloud of Obel's power.

A scoff came from Deckard's left, and he released the magic, looking up to find Obel sneering at Auden. "You thought he was a Night Mage?" the duke asked.

Auden looked hesitant despite his evident offense at Obel's tone. "I—yes," he said. "Yes, his magic is shadows and darkness and—"

"What color are his shadows, Highlord Calder?" Obel interrupted.

Auden scratched his head as though trying to come to grips with an impossibility. "They're black," he murmured, studying Deckard for a moment, then meeting Obel's gaze again. "They looked purple, but . . . I was always distracted, fighting in the Keeps, or it was dark, and I couldn't see plainly. But . . . They're *black*."

Obel nodded knowingly. "And they're not shadows," he said. "They're silhouettes—the outline of darkness against a bright world."

Auden began muttering under his breath as Vayden watched with something like growing awe.

Deckard didn't understand. "Pardon me," he said, "but are you saying that I'm *not* a Night Mage?"

Obel met his stare. "That's exactly what I'm saying."

A wave of emotion hit Deckard, driving him to lean back in his seat. Amid confusion, elation, disbelief, wariness, and awe, one feeling rose to the surface: relief. After a month of worrying that he would be plunged into the Deep, his fears turned out to be unfounded.

Deckard let out a grateful laugh. "I'm not a Night Mage?" he asked again, desperate for confirmation.

"No," Obel said.

"You're sure?"

"You're not a Night Mage, Jonn," Auden said apologetically. "I misread your magic because—I saw what I expected to see. You were using Night Magic in Dunneshead, but . . . rarely again. It isn't your primary."

Deckard sat up, intrigued. "What kind of Mage am I, then?" he asked.

"Isn't it obvious?" Obel said, gesturing to the mural above them and the woman surrounded by the void of black.

Deckard gaped at her, the sight of the glittering oblivion hitting him with its resemblance to the shard of magic he'd summoned a moment before. *Space.* He was a Space Mage.

He was a Space Mage?

He knew so little about the resource that he hardly knew how to feel about the revelation.

"I will grant Highlord Calder the allowance that Night and Space are strikingly similar at times," Obel said, drawing Deckard's eyes back to him. "Dark, cold, and mysterious. It's easy to connect with Night when you meant to find Space. But you're no Night Mage, Colonel. Trust me, I've been one for nearly two centuries."

Deckard brushed a hand over his jaw, attempting to understand. "How is it I summoned Hewitt before I knew I was a Mage, then?" he asked.

"I take it Hewitt's your ghost?" Obel asked but didn't wait for confirmation. "There are a couple of possibilities, and being a Space Mage grants you some assistance in that matter. They are a rare breed for a reason."

"They're dangerous," Auden said.

Deckard frowned. "You said that about Night Mages."

Surprisingly, Auden smiled. "It's a different kind of danger. Night is dangerous because it's dark and can bring the Deep upon its wielder. Space is dangerous because it's . . . vast."

"By vast," Obel said, "he means it's limitless."

The concept was impossible to fathom. "Meaning what?" Deckard asked. "That I have unlimited power and can't deplete my energy?"

"Galatae's Heavens, no," Obel said with a chuckle. "The *resource* is limitless. *You* are not. You very much have limits, as every Mage does, and I'd be careful about pushing them. But," he angled toward Deckard, "it does translate to the way you use your magic. You see, all Space Mages are predisposed to focus. How are your abilities to draw on your concentration, Colonel?"

"Excellent," Deckard admitted. "I thought that was why my abilities with Night manifested so easily. I've always been able to focus intently on whatever I turn my thoughts to."

"Ah, so exactly as I said, then. It's a quality all Space Mages share." Obel nodded. "It has to do with the ability to open their minds to the boundless nature of the resource. Because of this, they are generally more apt to connect with all the resources, not just their primary."

"Which explains why you were so quick to pick up your magic," Auden added.

"And why you were able to summon a ghost without intending to," Obel concluded.

Vayden, lounging on the far side of the couch, began to laugh. "Oh, Fishere is going to lose his bloody mind," he said.

"Why?" Deckard asked, growing uneasy with the news.

The question seemed to catch Vayden off guard. He stared back blankly before finding his voice. "Well," he glanced at Auden, "like Sirraus said, your kind are quite rare. There are only two known Space Mages in the world—now three with you—and while the Alliance managed to pull Lord Grenwoode from retirement, he's over two centuries old. They don't expect him to live more than a few more decades at the most."

Deckard raised his chin in understanding. "And they need someone to carry the Relic," he surmised.

Vayden shrugged as Auden watched Deckard carefully.

Deciding this was a fight for another time, Deckard turned back to Obel. "How do I release Hewitt?" he asked.

"First," Obel said, "I need to know how you summoned him."

A blend of irritation and anxiety tensed Deckard's shoulders. He wanted to go back to the hotel, get Evylin, and leave Mouroc before the Alliance could stop them. Their situation was growing perilous. As a Bonded couple, he already knew the Alliance would desire their appointment as Relic bearers. Now that he was named a Space Mage . . .

Outwardly, Deckard controlled his fearful impulse, knowing more was at stake than their personal desires. He took a steadying breath and replied, "I don't know how I summoned him. He was just . . . there."

Obel regarded him with an unexpected patience. "Walk me through when he first appeared to you."

Running a hand over his mouth, Deckard thought back. He furrowed his brow, remembering the shovel in his hands, the frozen terrae that fought against him, the tears that blinded him, and the voice that rang in his mind: *Don't take my choices from me.*

Deckard couldn't help his sad smile. "It was at his grave," he said. "I was digging after his death, thinking of him . . . thinking of how I still needed him, how Evylin needed him. And then . . . he was there."

"You were digging his grave?" Obel asked.

"Yes," he said. "I didn't realize he was anything more than a figment—a vision brought on due to my grief. It wasn't until weeks later that I realized he was a true ghost, and I was the one who summoned him."

After Deckard concluded his explanation, Obel nodded sagely. The corner of his mouth twitched, and his severe stare twinkled like stars. "This," he said, "is nothing."

Deckard blinked, uncomprehending.

Auden sat up. "Summoning a ghost is not nothing. It's the start of the Deep. And just because Jonn is not a Night Mage doesn't mean the Deep can't come upon him should he continue to meddle in death itself."

Obel drew in an annoyed breath. "Highlord Calder, if you're going to discuss Night magic, I'd recommend you study it further." He turned back to Deckard then, emphasizing each word as he repeated, "This is *nothing*."

"I'd beg you to explain, Your Grace," Deckard said, leaning forward.

Obel met his desperation with a grin. "When you summon a ghost, you have to enter into their death mind, body, and spirit," he said casually. "As you were digging his grave, and due to your travels, presumably near the scene of his death and within hours of it, that makes the summoning of his ghost rather mundane. You aren't some Night magic prodigy, Colonel. You were simply in the right place at the right time, feeling the right thing to channel him. What's more, it sounds like he was a willing soul since he came to your call without a fight."

Deckard's brow pinched. "So this isn't a shock?"

"No."

"And I shouldn't be concerned?"

"No."

"And I'm not a Night Mage?"

Obel raised his brow. "If you were, it wouldn't be such a bad thing. But you're not. While it's clear Night is your second resource, I'm certain you're a Space Mage." He gave a slow shake of his head. "No, Colonel, this is nothing to concern yourself with. The danger in summoning a ghost is entering the essence of their death and violating the laws of life. *That* is what drives Mages to insanity."

A small grumble came from Auden, but he remained otherwise silent.

The relief returned to Deckard, but he pressed on. "How do I release Hewitt, then?" he asked.

"The same way you summoned him," Obel said. "The only way to release a ghost is to return it to the place of its death. You've summoned a soul from its body before it entered the afterlife. You must give it back to him so he can resume his journey to the Heavens."

Deckard frowned. "I have to return to his grave?"

"Yes," Obel said with a single nod. "Go back to his grave and let him go. Treat it like all magic: Tap into your focus and use the power of your thought."

"It's that simple?"

"For you," Obel grinned, "it's that simple. In other cases, with other Mages, this would be another conversation. But—" He raised his hand then, pointing at Deckard, "you have to mean to release him in all truth. It sounds as though this man meant something to you and this Evylin—your wife, I presume. You cannot harbor within you an ounce of desire to hold him here. The release won't take otherwise."

Deckard drew in a long breath. That was easier said than done. Even though he no longer needed Hewitt to earn Evylin's love, he didn't want to release the man, ghost or not. He didn't want to lose him. He'd become a mentor, a father-like figure, a friend— the thought of letting him go forever broke Deckard's heart.

"Now," Obel said, moving on, "I have a final question."

Deckard nodded, prompting him to ask.

Obel pointed to his chest. "The Night Relic," he said, sharp gaze piercing. "Why do you wear it?"

With a cautious glance at Auden, Deckard shifted in his seat. "After our encounter with Renaul, we agreed it would be best to keep the Relics more closely guarded. And as I was able to disguise it before, I could do so again should the need arise."

"Hm." Obel's brow quirked up. "Do you not feel a pull to use it? Does it not weigh on you like a cloak of sorrow or somberness? Is there no grand urge within you for rest and tranquility?"

Though Deckard knew he *should* feel those things—any Mage or Warrior not Bonded should feel the individual effects of the Relics upon their emotions by all accounts—he shrugged. "I do not," he admitted.

"It doesn't bother you at all?"

"No more than any other necklace might."

Obel frowned. "And the other Relics, what experience do you have with them?"

Pausing, Deckard found himself surprised. "I don't," he said. "I've never used any of the other Relics because we assumed I was a Night Mage, and therefore, the Night Relic would best benefit my powers. But I've not had the occasion to test the other Relics."

"Hm," Obel said again.

"Hm?" Deckard urged.

The duke's grin grew sly. "Bloody Space Mages," he said, then tipped his chin toward Deckard. "Bonded or not, you are not a Night Mage. That thing should be crushing you, demanding that you use it. The fact that it doesn't have that effect on you leads me to only one conclusion: the vastness of Space grants you a focus of mind, a willpower of infinite proportion beyond even what the Relics can demand. You managed to disguise that Relic with Space magic. You managed to carry it unhindered with Space magic."

Lord Obel's green stare bored into Deckard, penetrating to his core. "Highlord Calder is right, Colonel," he said ominously. "Your magic *is* dangerous. You are a young Mage, both in age and in experience. Yet, you've managed to carry a weight of power not even I could bear. It's good—for now. But as you learn to harness the vastness of Space, you will become even stronger and more capable of far more dangerous things."

His voice dipped low as he edged forward in his seat. "Yes, Colonel, if you wanted to, I believe you could take all eight of those Relics and destroy this whole damn world."

CHAPTER ELEVEN

The amber light of late afternoon flooded into the empty main room of The Rook. After hours of drinking ale and telling jokes, Rafferty stood behind the counter, juggling four wine glasses as Evylin finally got Ethenn to admit to his new relationship with Ilain. When he explained the unique tradition of a Waulden betrothal, they all gaped at him in shock.

"You're married to her?" Thom asked.

"On a trial basis," Ethenn confirmed.

"Wow," Rafferty said, having caught the wine glasses with expert precision. "Does that mean you can boff her on a trial basis?"

All three of his companions sent him a scathing look.

"Just asking," Rafferty said, then returned to his juggling.

Though Evylin didn't approve of the lascivious manner in which the question was asked, she couldn't deny her own curiosity. Knowing of Wauld's more open culture and scandalous fashion, she leaned closer to Ethenn. "Does it?" she whispered.

"No," he said immediately. Then he blushed. "Sort of—I mean, no, but we can . . . you know. If we decide to finalize it, I mean."

"Curious," Thom muttered, then emptied his ale. "Well, congratulations, Loxley. She's a wonderful woman, and you'll be happy, I'm sure."

Ethenn eyed him warily. "Thanks."

Sitting between them, Evylin wondered at their newly patched-up friendship. Thom was working to right his wrongs, but she didn't know if that included informing Ethenn of Ilain's true feelings. She thought it must since Ethenn and Ilain were engaged—or rather, wedded on a probationary basis.

What a confusing tradition.

"So," Rafferty said, eyes on his wine glasses, "Eve and Ethenn are about to be two Bonded Warriors while you and I remain ever ordinary, Thommy. How do you like that?"

"Can't say I care for it much," Thom replied good-naturedly.

Rafferty caught the glasses again, setting them on the counter one at a time. "How do you think it works?"

"Not liking something?" Evylin asked.

Rafferty smirked. "Bonding," he said, then pointed at her nose. "You're about, oh—four hours away from it, tops. What d'ya think it'll be like?"

"Bonding? Or the ceremony?"

"Both."

Evylin shrugged. "I truly don't know," she admitted, her previous worries resurfacing. She really should have gotten more information before agreeing to go through with it. "But I'm sure it'll be good. I believe Ilain knows quite a lot about it, and she wouldn't recommend it if it were going to be unpleasant or problematic."

"Mm." Rafferty tapped the rim of a glass. "I hope it isn't too boring. I hate tedious ceremonies."

While Evylin, Thom, and Ethenn laughed at their friend, a door opened in the back. They turned as the storeroom door swung wide. Lieutenant Lohen stood there, her petite, athletic frame appearing from the shadows. She wore an ivory blouse under a dark brown vest that matched her skirt, giving her outfit a masculine edge. She'd coiled her braided black hair into a low bun, and dainty gemstones dangled from her ears, catching the light.

"I thought we'd find you here," she said, then stepped aside. "After you, Deckard."

"Thank you, Lieutenant," Deckard said. Evylin's heart pattered happily at seeing her husband stride into the room.

Vayden appeared next, tapping Deckard's arm. "Call her Brea," he instructed. "Unlike Fishere, we don't do formalities."

The rest of their team entered the room. Vayden led Isla to a table, and they settled into the long booth against the wall. Brea took a seat across from them, positioning herself to face the others. Auden sat next to Vayden, while Ilain headed directly to Ethenn at the bar.

"Hello, husband," Ilain said, planting a kiss on his cheek.

Ethenn pressed his lips together and murmured, "Ilain," by way of greeting.

She grabbed his arm, tugging him toward the tables with her, leaving behind Thom and Rafferty, who sniggered like fools.

But Evylin was only interested in the charming smile Deckard turned her way. He stepped to her side, dipping his head for a quick kiss.

"Hello again," Evylin whispered as he pulled back.

Deckard's smile grew, though she saw something like hesitation in his eyes. The worry struck her that it had something to do with his meeting with Obel. "Hello," he replied. "I hope your morning wasn't as . . . dramatic as mine."

"Lucky you," Evylin teased. "My morning was as dull as can be."

"Not for lack of trying," Rafferty interjected, then motioned to the others gathering around the room. "Are we having a party?"

"Not exactly," Deckard replied. "We're discussing our mission."

"In that case," Rafferty flipped two glasses in the air, "I'd better get us drinks."

Deckard gave him a disapproving look. "It's half past two."

Rafferty raised his brow. "But Colonel, they've got wine."

After opening his mouth in rebuttal, Deckard paused. "What kind of wine?"

"It's a Schonese *rojal*," Brea said, reclining leisurely in her chair. "Smooth but acidic. It's from my cousin's vineyard in Nemos."

"Your cousin lives in Schon?" Thom asked, brow raised.

"I grew up in Schon," she replied.

"It's why she's the only one who gets Isla's jokes," Vayden said.

"You always said you liked my jokes," Isla said.

Vayden smirked suggestively at his wife. "I love your jokes."

She patted his knee as Rafferty said, "I'm still waiting to hear if the colonel wants some wine."

Deckard pursed his lips, tapped the bar, and sighed. "Give me a glass," he said.

"Atta boy!" Rafferty rubbed his hands together, then went to work. "Anyone else care to put in an order? It's on the house."

"It's not, though," Auden objected.

"I'll take a glass," Ilain said, seated next to her brother on the leather bench across from Ethenn.

While others put in their requests and Rafferty gathered their drinks, Deckard began the meeting. "As we have some important decisions to make and a limited amount of time in which to make them," he said, "I think we should get started. However, there are a couple of announcements to be given first."

"Announcements?" Thom asked, still seated on Evylin's other side.

Deckard nodded, thanking Rafferty when he handed him a wine glass. "Yes, perhaps some of you know by now, but congratulations are in order, as Ethenn and Ilain were betrothed this morning."

A chorus of "congratulations" rang out amongst the group.

"Betrothed, eh?" Brea said, propping her boots on the chair next to her. She eyed Ethenn slyly. "Good luck, kid. She's gonna burn you alive."

While Ethenn sucked in a perturbed breath, Ilain sent Brea a fiery glare. "Flames only burn those who mishandle them," she retorted.

"As I was saying," Deckard said, redirecting the conversation. "We are, of course, happy for Ethenn and Ilain and wish them all the best."

"Does this mean you're Bonding tonight too?" Rafferty asked, delivering Ilain's glass to her.

"No," she replied. "We'll wait until after the establishment of Allund."

"Why not?" Thom asked. "Wouldn't it be better for us to have two Bonded couples?"

Ilain took a sip of her wine, glancing at Ethenn before explaining. "While yes, it would give us more strength, the Alliance wants to ensure that should one of us die on our mission, the other will still be eligible for remarriage and Bonding to aid the governmental regime."

"Huh." Rafferty hopped up on the counter, turning back to Deckard. "What was the other announcement?"

Deckard opened his mouth, but nothing came out. He tried again. "Well, it appears . . ." He hesitated. "I met with Lord Obel this morning, and he informed me of not only how to release Hewitt's ghost but also that . . . I am not a Night Mage."

Silence met his statement.

Evylin looked up at him, not understanding.

"Jarrad was right, then?" Isla asked, then sighed. "He'll never shut up about it."

Brea snorted.

"What kind of Mage are you?" Ilain asked.

Deckard shuffled his feet, shifting away from Evylin. "It seems," he said cautiously, "that I'm a Space Mage."

"*Mal'iferno*," Brea cursed, mouth dropping ajar.

Thom's gaze shifted from her to Deckard and back. "Is that a good thing?" he asked, sounding as confused as Evylin felt.

"It's not a bad thing," Brea replied.

Deckard didn't voice his opinion, making Evylin regard him warily.

"It's a good thing," Auden said. "The powers carry with them volatile but also beneficial potential."

"How did we miss that you're a Space Mage?" Ilain asked, baffled. "We should have caught it right away."

"We weren't exactly looking for it," Auden replied. "And Obel confirmed that Night is his secondary resource. Beyond that, we were under duress when he accessed his powers most prominently. It's an easy thing to miss." He frowned, then added, "Particularly for me."

Though Evylin wasn't sure what he meant by that, she focused on Deckard. She wanted to ask how he felt about this monumental revelation and to hear what Obel had indicated it truly meant for him. But as she didn't want to put him on the spot, instead, she said, "I don't see how it changes much moving forward. You're still a Mage, and if anything, you're safer from the Deep than we anticipated, right?"

Deckard tipped his head to the side. "Yes, but this is . . ."

When it appeared that he wouldn't be finishing his statement, Vayden did it for him. "Unprecedented."

"Space is the most powerful resource," Isla clarified. "Few amongst us know much about it because of how rare Space Mages are. There are hardly any texts teaching how to employ the magic due to their rarity throughout the centuries. And even though some Night Mages find Space easier to connect with than others, even they struggle to control it. For it to be discovered that Colonel Deckard is one . . . well, we don't even fully know yet what this means for our mission." The hushed tone of her voice conveyed a sense of awe.

"And you're about to be a *Bonded* Space Mage," Brea said, resting her arm over the back of her chair. "Which means the chaos is just beginning. This ought to be fun."

Thom huffed out a laugh and looked over at Deckard. "Do you have to be the best at everything?" he asked, attempting to lighten the mood.

A small smile lifted Deckard's lips, and Evylin caught on, nudging Thom. "He isn't the best at *everything*," she said proudly. "I can still beat him in a sword fight."

Thom blew a raspberry. "Everyone can beat Jonn in a sword fight."

Deckard sent them both an annoyed, though grateful, glare. "Thank you for that," he muttered amusedly, then turned back to the group at large. "This discovery changes nothing about my commitment to protecting our group and completing our mission. Lord Obel granted me what texts he had for my study of this unexpected power, and I am ready to submit myself to further tutelage to ensure complete control." He clasped his hands together as if to conclude the subject before continuing, "And with our announcements out of the way, we can move on to planning. Firstly, I'd like to welcome our new members to the team. Mr. Calder, Highlady Freye, and Lieutenant Lohen, we're happy to have you with us."

The trio gave him appreciative nods, and he went on, "Given the Alliance's report on Blount and the fact that we have two more Relics to recover, we will leave first thing in the morning. As the Calders have been our navigators, I'll allow Auden to explain our route."

Auden drew his shoulders back under their sudden attention. "Well, our journey is rather simple," he said. "Our first stop is the Terrae Keep in Estshire. As speed is paramount, we'll return to Verlund Reach at the top of Wauld and cross over to Norhels through the Night and Day Keeps, cutting off days of travel."

"Damn it," Thom grumbled. "Do we really have to go back through that hellhole?"

Rafferty pointed toward Thom. "I'm with him! Can't we just cross the border? Surely, it won't take that much longer."

"We don't have time for that," Auden insisted. "Blount is already a day ahead of us. The gate from Night into Day cuts two days off our journey. If we leave in the morning, we'll only just beat him to Olbury."

"There's got to be another way," Thom said desperately.

"What's got you so riled, *mi'caro*?" Brea asked with a smirk.

"Breata," Isla said in a warning tone.

In reply, Brea rattled something in Schonese that sounded something like "*Es bromé*," then turned back to Thom in expectation.

"Uh . . ." Thom stared between her and Isla for an extended moment before replying. "It's black as pitch inside," he explained. "Neither Raff nor I could see a damn thing."

Brea pressed her lips together around a smile, but Vayden didn't look amused. "Just you two?" he asked.

"Us non-magical folk, yeah," Rafferty confirmed.

Vayden nodded slowly. "So I'll be blind in there too."

"Something to learn, mate," Rafferty said, tipping his white-blond brows up. "Being non-magical makes this journey a whole lot more difficult. This lot may appear more impressive on the surface," he brushed his hand toward the majority of the group, then slapped it to his chest, "but *we're* the ones who survive without a lick of magic helping us along."

"Fantastic," Vayden replied sourly.

Brea's amusement grew. "So we go through the Night Keep, pass through the gate into Day, and then we're in Ephria. Which, I suppose, puts you back at the helm, Colonel."

"I suppose it does," Deckard said, setting his half-empty wine glass on the counter. "The journey from Norhels to Olbury will take roughly nine days. Since we'll be in

Ephria and we have King Ephren's authority, we'll have the freedom to enter and stay in settlements, which will also aid our speed."

Evylin looked forward to the return to Ephria for numerous reasons, their ability to join civilization once more chief among them.

"After we've obtained the Terrae Relic," Deckard continued, "we'll travel back up through the countryside and onto Ephria City. There, in Loclight, we'll retrieve the Space Relic. That should take us about thirteen days . . ." He paused, glancing at Evylin. "The length due in part to the detour we need to make in order for me to release Hewitt."

Pulling in a sharp breath, Evylin's heart constricted. Though she knew it was the right thing, allowing Hewitt the chance to move on to the afterlife with his wife and son, she didn't want to let him go. She'd just gotten him back.

"This Hewitt—" Brea said. "He's your ghost?"

Deckard nodded, then explained Obel's instructions on how to free his spirit.

"If we're on such a short timeline," Rafferty said, "shouldn't we take care of Hewitt after we've got the Relics and Allund's all set?"

"It has to be done as soon as possible," Deckard insisted. "When I summoned Hewitt, I stole his soul from his body. Obel said that if a Mage dies before releasing any ghost that they've summoned, those souls are locked in the ethereal plane until another Mage comes along to summon them, which isn't recommended. If I die before releasing him, Hewitt could be trapped there forever with no way to find rest."

Evylin's breath caught at the thought of Deckard's death and Hewitt's perpetual unrest, but she forced her mind to focus on the matter at hand. "Then we have to release him," she agreed. "Immediately."

Deckard nodded. "As soon as humanly possible," he promised.

Turning back to the troop, Deckard raised his chin. "Once we've made it to Loclight, we'll have to meet with King Ephren, I'm sure."

"Weren't we supposed to be communicating with the old sot along the way?" Rafferty asked.

"I've kept in contact with him via Lord Carlile," Auden explained. "Our time in Wauld has forestalled our communications, but Carlile's taking care of it. I planned to send him an update once we've arrived in Ephria."

"That's good," Deckard said. "We need to retain his favor. And we'll have to formulate a story as to why we have so few Relics in our possession when we return. You three won't be able to join us either," he said to Vayden, Isla, and Brea. "Your presence will be too difficult to explain."

"Pity," Vayden said lightheartedly.

"With luck," Deckard continued, "we'll manage to find the Space Keep without any interference from King Ephren. Once we have the Relic, we will have control of half of them. From there . . ." He turned to Auden and Ilain. "I'd imagine our next step will be awaiting Blount's arrival in the capital. If we can stay ahead of him, then we can ambush him as he tried to do to us and take back the Relics he stole."

Around the room, the team members shared looks, each nodding and taking in the plan. Evylin couldn't quite fathom the idea of completing their assignment. They'd been traveling for so long that she hardly remembered what it was like to have a home.

"Is it just me," Brea said, hands folded in her lap, "or does it seem we're overlooking the glaringly obvious facts?"

Everyone turned to her, expectant and silent.

"Just me, then. Great." Brea sat up straight. "Here's the thing: We have no idea what Blount is going to do. The Alliance's intelligence says that he'll be heading for the Terrae Relic in . . . Estshire, is it? Reaching it will take him a vastly long time to get there. However, we don't truly know what plans he has or what he's capable of.

"Just the other night, Auden informed the whole of the Alliance that Blount not only ambushed you before the Water Keep, but he followed you into the Day Keep under a shroud and stole the Day Relic out from under your noses." She scanned them all. "Then he had the Night Mages waiting for you outside the Night Keep. He couldn't have known when you'd arrive. That means he told them to patrol outside the Keep until you came through. They were waiting for weeks. Same with the Order of the Wind. And then again with Renaul's liege officers at the Time Keep. Beyond that, he put out a writ on you."

Brea took a breath, letting the facts settle in. "Blount is cunning, he's manipulative, and he's unpredictable. We can't risk doing what's expected because he won't do what's expected. And we'll be putting our mission in danger if we behave exactly as he predicts."

"What are you suggesting, Lieutenant?" Deckard asked.

She met his gaze. "We have to assume that Blount is going to outsmart us again."

"We'll be in Ephria," Thom returned. "It isn't like he has a mistress there who can send her lackeys after us."

Brea raised her brow. "Do you know that for sure, *mi'caro*? Do you have spies among his men who are telling you of his plans?"

He blinked. "No."

She smiled dryly. "No. And we can't make plans based on information we don't have."

"How are we to compensate for that lack of knowledge, then?" Deckard prompted.

Brea turned her wry grin on him. "We're working off assumptions," she said. "But so is Blount."

Clarity hit Evylin all at once, and she nodded. "We have the chance to outplay him," she said. "Blount is notorious for outmaneuvering us and letting us do the work for him. If we want to beat him, we have to do something he won't expect."

"Won't you and Jonn going through the Bonding ceremony already cover that?" Thom asked.

"It's good," Evylin said. "But it isn't enough. Blount knows our goal is to retrieve the Relics. He'll make his plans according to those facts."

"And what?" Auden asked. "You want to subvert his expectations by letting him recover them?"

"It isn't about our plans," Brea said. "It's about understanding *his*."

"Something you said we *can't* do," Ilain retorted.

Brea didn't appear offended by her caustic tone. "True. But we can take what we know about him and ask the question: How might he try to subvert us?"

Silence filled the tavern.

Evylin and Deckard shared a worried look. This was a question they hadn't even considered, but it was a necessary, frightful one. Blount was good at crafting plans with devastating endings. They'd lost the Fire, Day, and Time Relics to his cunning. They'd lost Hewitt to his attacks. They couldn't afford to lose anything more.

In their hesitation, Brea continued, "We are assuming that Blount will go for the Terrae Relic. But he's assuming the same about us. All this time, he's used you. He'll do it again. He'll let you retrieve the Terrae Relic for him while he goes and enacts his own cunning plan."

"Like what?" Rafferty asked. "We'll already be expecting an ambush."

"And he'll know that," Brea said. Then she held up a finger. "So he'll do something you aren't expecting. Like going for the Space Relic."

Auden sat up straighter. "Going out of order is suicide. Blount knows this."

"Does he?" she asked.

"The prince did study the Relics for decades," Vayden cut in. "But Obel intentionally worked to keep his learning stunted—not that he had to work that hard."

"How does Obel play into this?" Deckard asked.

"He's Blount's godfather," Vayden explained. "That's why he and I are friends. He trained me to pose as the prince. And he taught me all that Blount knew about the Relics, which was very little. Blount didn't even know the locations of the Relics, which leads me to doubt he knew the order in which to obtain them."

"I *gave* him the locations," Auden said. "I told him to go in the order of creation."

"And you think he'll listen?" Brea returned. "We can't afford to lose the Space Relic to him."

"We can't afford to lose *any* Relics to him," Auden argued.

Brea shook her head dismissively. "That's where you're wrong, Auden. We have a Space Mage now, who will be Bonded in a matter of hours. With the Night and Space Relics in his hands and the Wind Relic in Ilain's hands—she is the most powerful Mage in two centuries, after all—along with the support of a Wind Mage in Isla and a Day Mage such as yourself, plus three Warriors fighting for you, do you have any doubt that we can beat Blount, who only obtained his rank as ViceMage in the Order of the Night by means of bribery and murder?"

In their stunned silence, she scoffed, brushing a hand through the air. "Let him have the Terrae Relic. He will burn himself out using five Relics while we divide our own, giving us control over his most powerful connections and the strength to defeat him."

"Don't underestimate Blount because he's a selfish bastard," Ilain said tersely. "He's studied under the best Night Mages for decades. He was capable of shrouding himself, following us around Ephria, and moving through the entirety of the Day Keep undetected. He has the Orders on his side—there are *hundreds* of Mages he can charge to fight us. Even if he isn't well informed about the Relics, his power is great. And if we hand him a fifth Relic, we may as well offer him the whole continent to go along with it."

"You're blinded by your fear," Brea said. "Blount knows that you will follow the order of recovery. He knows you will go for the Terrae Relic, and he will make his plans accordingly. So we must change our tactic to beat him at his own game."

"By getting ourselves killed in the Space Keep?" Auden said bitterly.

Ethenn angled forward, interrupting. "What if the lieutenant's right, though?" he asked. "What if Blount does go for the Space Relic? What would that mean for us if he gets hold of it?"

There was a long pause in which Brea glared at Auden and Ilain, demanding they answer honestly.

Auden clenched his jaw, chin dipped. "It would mean our defeat," he admitted. "If Blount obtains possession of the Space Relic . . . there's no taking it from him."

Evylin jumped in as he paused, asking the question she knew the Calders didn't want to hear. "And if we get the Space Relic, regardless of whether or not Blount has the Terrae Relic, what would *that* mean for us?"

After a long inhale and glance at his sister, Auden shrugged dejectedly. "Likely? It would mean our victory, even if it was hard fought."

"So," Evylin concluded, "we have no choice. We *have* to get the Space Relic, even if that means risking the loss of the Terrae Relic."

There was no response from any of the Alliance members, so Evylin pressed on.

"Because Blount doesn't know about Jonn. He doesn't know that he's a Mage, let alone a Space Mage, which means he can't know that we'll be Bonded when we do confront him again. And if we have the Space Relic, his demise is secured no matter what."

Reluctantly, Auden nodded. "Yes."

"Then we have our answer," she said. "We go to Loclight, retrieve the Space Relic, and hope we can beat him to the Terrae Keep."

"If we do that," Auden said in a last-ditch effort to convince them, "we risk our lives. The Space Keep is the most dangerous, the most difficult. With only two Relics in our possession . . . success is nearly impossible."

A weighted silence hung in the room.

Then Thom spoke. "What's our timeline looking like?"

When everyone stared at him in confusion, he continued, "I mean, say Blount *is* headed for the Terrae Relic first: How long would it take him to get there?"

Deckard shifted beside Evylin, his hand rubbing his jaw in thought. "The Alliance's spies reported that he was headed to Carrickbrack to rally with his new men," he reminded them. "How long would it take him to get there from Keale?"

Auden screwed up his face in thought. "Probably . . . five or six days, depending on his speed."

"We should assume five, then," Deckard said. "And what about the Mages coming to join him? How long will it take for them to arrive?"

"If he sent out letters yesterday after arriving at Renaul's estate, then . . ." Auden's lips moved as he calculated the time on his fingers.

Ilain reached over, setting her hand upon his. "If they're coming from the Doorstunds, Sutterlund, and Verlund Reaches, they'll be in Carrickbrack within a minimum of a week."

"A week?" Thom huffed. "We can be back in Loclight in a week, right?"

Deckard pursed his lips. "Eh, that's a bit generous. I'd say closer to nine or ten days."

"Which is essentially a week," Thom returned. "At which point, we'll head down to Estshire, and we could make it there in twelve days tops."

"But," Deckard added, "we have to account for the days we'll lose releasing Hewitt and any wasted time in Loclight."

"Why would we spend any longer than a day in the city?" Vayden asked.

"Like I said, Ephren will want to meet with us. We *may* be able to get out in two days, but what if he requires a longer debriefing or wants us to linger for some other reason? He could potentially cause us a serious delay."

"We just tell him we've got to get a move on to get the rest of the Relics," Rafferty offered.

"But he isn't aware of any pressing timeline," Deckard said. "And we can't exactly tell him that we're in a race with the Waulden heir when we've been lying, saying that everything is fine for the past two months."

They all nodded.

"To be safe," Deckard concluded, "we should allot two or three days in Loclight. Which puts us at an arrival in Olbury after an additional thirteen days of travel."

"Which means," Evylin realized, "three weeks and two days at the worst for us to retrieve both the Space and Terrae Relics."

"Assuming we can even cross the border," Deckard said. "Blount still has his writ out, remember? The Waulden border will be crawling with guards looking for us."

"That's not an issue," Brea said suddenly.

The Ephrians looked at her, confused.

She smirked and glanced at the Calders. "We have a secret passage through the mountains, which is how we got our lovely friends into Ephria in the first place."

"Right," Deckard said.

Thom jumped back in without lingering on this revelation. "And how long will it take for Blount to get to Olbury from Carrickbrack?"

Auden turned to Ilain. "He'll go to Virwoud first," he said thoughtfully. "It'll be the safest place in Ephria to restock before going into the countryside. And that will take him . . ."

"Nine days," Ilain supplied.

"And then from there, it will only be—"

"Four days."

"So all said and done, he is likely to arrive—"

"If Blount leaves for Carrickbrack today," Ilain said, "he'll arrive on the third of Radia. After waiting a week for his relief troop to arrive, he'll leave for Olbury on the eleventh. From there, he'll have to travel for a minimum of nine days, putting him in Virwoud on the twentieth. At which point, he won't arrive in Olbury until the twenty-fourth." She paused, brushing a few waves of hair over her shoulder. "If we leave tomorrow morning and head to Loclight, we should arrive on the ninth, possibly the eighth if we ride fast. Allowing for the worst case and two extra days for Ephren's leisure, say we leave on the eleventh—when Blount himself leaves for Olbury. After thirteen days of travel, that puts us in Olbury on the twenty-fourth as well."

Evylin's lips parted in shock.

Ilain hesitated only a second before adding, "But that's the worst case. In my personal opinion, removing the additional three or so days for error is quite feasible, which would put us at the Terrae Keep on the twenty-first, three days prior to Blount's arrival."

A sharp breath puffed out of Evylin as a flare of hope lit her chest. She set her hand on Deckard's arm, looking up at him. "We can beat him there," she said in an awed whisper.

Deckard's brow was crimped tight, unconvinced. While his eyes searched her face, she gripped his arm more firmly. "Jonn," she said, "we can *beat* him."

"Three days isn't enough room for error," he said worriedly.

"Either way," Brea interjected once more, "it's worth it. Three days early or right on time, we'd still have the Space Relic. We could still beat him."

"And what if you're right?" Deckard asked. "What if Blount's entire plan is to go for the Space Relic first while we head for the Terrae Keep?"

Brea turned to Ilain. "How long would it take for Blount to arrive in Ephria City from Carrickbrack?"

Ilain's brow furrowed in surprise, but it only took her a moment to calculate. "Oh . . . About eight days."

"Thank you," Brea said, turning back to Deckard. "So if he left for Carrickbrack today, arriving there on the third of next month, then he wouldn't arrive in Ephria City until the eleventh, which is when we would be heading for Olbury."

"At the worst," Thom added.

She smirked at him and repeated, "At the worst."

"What if he doesn't go to Carrickbrack at all?" Ethenn asked.

They all looked at him in shock.

Flushing, Ethenn ducked his head but kept speaking. "He knows he's being watched now," he explained. "With Highlady Freye's betrayal, he's aware that he has spies amongst his ranks. What if this is all a lie, another of his schemes? What if this supposed regrouping in Carrickbrack is a trick, and he's actually going straight to Loclight from Keale?"

Instantly, everyone turned to Ilain for an updated timeline. She stared at Ethenn even as everyone stared at her. Tugging on the collar of her dress, she fumbled only for a second. "Keale to Loclight would be roughly a ten-day journey. Meaning that if he left this morning, he'd arrive on the eighth. Which puts him either at the same time or . . . possibly a day ahead of us."

"So our true worst-case scenario," Ethenn said, "is that Blount gets both Relics before us."

The tavern fell silent as the facts weighed on them all. There were too many variables, too many potential pitfalls, and too many risks. Whatever choice they made could end in victory or defeat. They either obtained the Relics in order, risking the loss of the Space Relic and their inevitable defeat, or they went out of order, hoping to gain their ultimate victory through the Space Relic while risking Blount's complete subversion.

Yet, despite all the variables, Evylin thought the choice was clear.

She took Deckard's hand, drawing his attention. His green-blue gaze met hers with an uncertainty that pinched in her chest. "Brea's right," she said. "Blount isn't going to follow the rules. Thus, we can't either. We have to go for the Space Relic."

"We can't be sure it will work," he argued. "And we'll be risking our lives."

"We can't be sure any of this will work," she returned. "And we're risking our lives either way."

He continued to hesitate.

"Jonn," she slipped her fingers through his, "we need that Relic. Our odds of defeating him with Terrae alone are minimal. Our odds with Space are great."

Deckard continued to frown. "And if Blount is headed for Loclight as we speak?" he asked. "If he beats us there and takes the Space Relic? What then?"

"Then we would have lost either way."

His thumb brushed along the back of her hand. A moment later, he sighed. "I don't think it's a good idea," he said. "I'm sorry, but we should stick to the original plan."

"I disagree," Evylin insisted.

"We're doing this for the Alliance, right?" Rafferty said, an impish glint in his eyes. "Why don't we do this their way?"

"What way is that?" Thom asked.

"With a vote."

Vayden, Isla, and Brea chuckled lightly while the rest remained stoic.

"There are ten of us," Ethenn said. "What happens if there's a tie?"

"Same thing that happens during the ministers' votes," Isla said. "Tie goes to those opposed. Just make sure you phrase the question correctly."

Rafferty swung his legs up and hopped to stand on the bar. "A vote, then!" he exclaimed, clapping his hands as though to call them to order. "All right, the stunning Lieutenant Lohen proposes we skip the tedious Highlord Calder's plans—"

Brea snorted while Auden's face scrunched in disapproval.

"Saving our lives from the horrors of the Night Keep and going straight for the Space Relic before scurrying on down to retrieve the Terrae Relic. All those in favor of subverting Blount by being clever, please raise your hand."

"That's a rather manipulative way to phrase the proposition," Deckard remarked.

Rafferty ignored him, one hand in the air while he counted the others. "Brea, Vayden, Isla, Thommy, Eve, Ilain, Ethenn, and I stand in favor," he said, and then they all dropped their hands. "All those opposed?"

Evylin gave Deckard an apologetic look while he raised his hand along with Auden.

"Ministers Colonel and Audy stand opposed," Rafferty announced. "That's eight in favor, two opposed. The motion passes!"

"Very well," Deckard said with good-natured acceptance of his defeat. Then he gave Rafferty a pointed look. "Get down off the bar."

Rafferty jumped down, and Deckard turned back to the group. "So the new plan is this: We leave tomorrow morning at first light and, using the Alliance's secret mountain pass across the border, head to Ephria City, where we'll meet with Ephren and retrieve the Space Relic." He leaned against the counter, his arm brushing Evylin's. "From there, we'll continue to Olbury and the Terrae Keep, taking a short detour to release Hewitt near Virwoud. We'll be moving fast, so let's keep the load light. Essentials only. Are there any questions?"

Evylin scanned the room with Deckard. Rafferty sipped his ale, resting against the counter placidly. Ethenn glanced at Ilain, who sat with her chin raised with its usual cavalier tilt. Auden shifted in his seat, sending surreptitious looks toward Brea—either in vexation or hope. Crossing her legs, the lieutenant sat back casually while Isla and Vayden smiled at each other.

Last, Evylin met Thom's gaze a second before he looked directly at Deckard. "We'll follow you to the end, brother," he said.

Deckard's expression pinched despite his appreciative smile. Evylin knew he felt the weight of command stronger than most. He was good at leading; he was meant for it. But he didn't trust himself to do it well. Something she thought she ought to reassure him of. Perhaps not here, not now. But later, when they were alone.

For now, she knew she needed to bring levity to the moment.

Smirking up at him, Evylin said, "I have a question."

Hearing the sarcasm in her tone, Deckard's face relaxed. "How may I be of assistance?" he asked.

"I'd like to know when we can eat?" she teased. "I'm starving."

CHAPTER TWELVE

Ten, Evylin decided, was an ideal number of people.

When they returned to the Crimson Clover for an early dinner, it was with great laughter and easy conversation. The Bonding ceremony wouldn't take place for another few hours, so she put off her nerves as the group settled into the dining room, pulling tables together to make space for their large number. Vayden had to soothe Mrs. Howerth, who was busy making the suppertime meal, with promises to right the space before they left, but it seemed only Deckard's charm was enough to allow them access to her larder for their bountiful meal.

Soon, the table was filled with dried venison, sliced sausages, manifold cheeses, fruit spreads, and loaves of fresh bread.

As they clustered around the table, Evylin made sure to sit near Brea, eager to get to know the woman. Positioning herself thus wound up splitting her away from Deckard, who was seated at the head of the table with Vayden on one side and Ethenn on the other. Though Auden seemed intent on taking the seat on Brea's other side, Thom got there first, drawing a smirk from the lieutenant.

They all fell into small conversations, getting to know their new team members better. Evylin determined that, while she wasn't entirely convinced of the suitability of training with Brea, she did like the woman. The lieutenant was witty and companionable without being gregarious or overly enthusiastic, which made for amusing conversation, often filled with blunt statements and biting retorts.

When Auden was distracted by a conversation with Isla, Rafferty leaned across the table to surreptitiously remark, "So my lovely lieutenant," his brows lifted in a conspiratorial expression, "you don't seem all that keen on the two younger Calders. Or am I mistaken?"

Brea's mouth quirked in the corner. "They're perfectly honorable individuals," she replied.

"But . . . ?"

She popped a small morsel of cheese into her mouth. "Call it a difference of opinion," she said. "One wants something I cannot give, while the other blindly supports his pursuits. We look at life differently."

Based on Thom's explanation earlier, Evylin knew Brea was referring to Auden's wish to Bond with her. After Ilain's declaration that Bonding was the pinnacle achievement of any Warrior or Mage's life, she was curious to know why Brea wouldn't want that as well. But then, she supposed the lieutenant could love another Mage, and that's why she had rejected Auden.

"I do have a question," Thom said.

"Yes, *mi'caro*?" Brea replied casually.

Thom hesitated, then asked, "How long have you known the Calders?"

Brea paused, considering. "I met Vayden first, through Isla, of course. When my family and I came to Wauld fifteen years ago, I was sent to Sutterlund Reach to meet with Isla so she could teach me the Allundan language. As a cover, I was hired by the Order of the Wind as her lady's maid. We grew close due to our shared Schonese heritage. After a time, I met Vayden, and later, when I went on to join the Alliance's militia, I also met Auden and Ilain."

"Huh." Thom leaned forward then, eyes narrowed. "So your first language is Schonese?"

"Obviously."

"And what," he raised his brow, "does '*meekarow*' mean?"

Brea's dark eyes twinkled. "Wouldn't you like to know, *mi'caro*?" she said, emphasizing the correct pronunciation of the term.

"*Me care-o*?" Thom repeated.

"Roll the R," she corrected.

He attempted it and fell frightfully short.

Brea laughed, then reached over to pinch his cheeks between two fingers. "Try again," she instructed.

Even with her help, he still failed, mostly due to his smile.

Evylin watched them with fascination, bemused by their quick camaraderie. She'd never seen Thom take to anyone so fast. He'd not even been this comfortable and friendly with her in the early stages of their friendship. It was odd and potentially worrisome.

Deciding she should mention the peculiar relationship to Deckard later, Evylin was startled by Ilain's sudden grip on her hand. She turned to the woman on her other side. "Yes?" she said.

"It's time for us to leave," Ilain said.

Evylin frowned, noting that everyone else was still seated, looking perfectly languorous.

"Not them," Ilain said, reading her hesitation. "Just the two of us."

"Why just us?" Evylin asked.

"Have you forgotten you have an important ceremony this evening? We have to prepare."

Evylin blanched, her stomach suddenly knotting. The evening light had begun to fade, leaving the sky glowing a rusty orange as the shadows lengthened around the dining room. A few other guests started to arrive for their meals. The day was growing late, and the Bonding ceremony would begin in two short hours.

Glancing toward the end of the table, Evylin looked at Deckard. He listened intently to Vayden, his gaze steady and his smile attentive, completely unaware of her sudden unease.

"What about Jonn?" Evylin asked, turning back to Ilain.

With a sweep of her hand, Ilain pushed back from the table. "He can prepare in my room," she said. "You and I are going to need the larger space."

Seeing them rise, Vayden halted his story. "Off to get ready?" he asked.

"Yes," Ilain confirmed, then turned to Deckard. "Maurus has a parcel for you at the front desk. Take it and my room key from him so you can get ready. You'll need roughly thirty minutes."

"And Evie needs two hours?" Thom teased.

Ilain passed him a haughty smile. "Women are more important." She set her hand on Ethenn's shoulder then. "A package also awaits you at the desk," she said, "as does one for Auden, Thom, Brea, and Isla."

"What about Vaydy-boy and me?" Rafferty asked with a wily grin.

"Neither of you is invited."

"What?" Rafferty demanded, incredulous.

"It's a sacred ceremony," Ilain returned, "not meant for prying eyes. If you aren't part of the ceremony, you aren't welcome."

While Rafferty worked out a rebuttal, Ilain grabbed Evylin's arm and, without another word, began to drag her away from the table. Impressed by the woman's grip,

Evylin could do little else but follow. She gave one last glance at Deckard, meeting his gaze for all of two seconds before Ilain had her out the door and in the hall.

With purpose, Ilain led her into the foyer, stopping to accept two parcels from Maurus before heading up the stairs. "We'll have to hurry if we want to make it on time," she instructed as they walked to Deckard and Evylin's room.

"Exactly how involved a process is this?" Evylin asked.

"Not very," she replied. "And it isn't precisely necessary, just enjoyable. While you can Bond without the additional flair, this makes it all much more exciting. And the pomp and ceremony feels more official, wouldn't you say?"

"I haven't a clue what we're doing, so no, I wouldn't."

Ilain chuckled, then unlocked the suite's door and led Evylin in. She settled the parcels on the bed before charging about the space, preparing for whatever rigors she intended to put Evylin through. With a flick of her wrist, Ilain lit the stove in the corner. Then she found the bathing supplies in the wardrobe where Deckard had organized them.

"Ah." Ilain shoved them into Evylin's arms. "Here. Take your time, scrub every inch, and use this when you're done."

Evylin cautiously took the amber bottle, staring at the liquid inside. "What is this?" she asked.

Ilain smiled. "It's perfumed oil. It'll make you smoother than silk, and you'll smell like a whole garden of primroses and Tanemisian cypresses for a week."

Though she wasn't sure what a cypress was, Evylin didn't bother asking. "I bathed yesterday," she said.

"So did I," Ilain said. "That doesn't mean I won't be taking another."

Shoved into the hall, Evylin had no choice but to listen to the woman's instructions. She carefully swept her hair on top of her head, not bothering to wash it as she bathed. Once she dried off, she applied the oil, finding the scent light, like springtime. It reminded her of running through the forest or tumbling down the hills of Whickam Village with Ryen as a child. Smiling as she tied off her robe, she decided to ask Ilain if she could keep it.

The second Evylin returned to the room, Ilain swooped over like a mother hen. "Sit there," she instructed, pointing at the table by the stove, then taking the towel and other bathing supplies. "The tea is ready, and there's a book on Bonding. Read it. I'm going to bathe."

And with that, the door latched behind Ilain, leaving Evylin alone. She scanned the room. Draped across the bed were various garments, most in black but a few in white. She thought of perusing them but didn't want to face Ilain's wrath if she disturbed anything.

Taking her seat at the table, Evylin poured herself a cup of tea, then took up the book awaiting her. *Attachments of the Soul*, the leather cover read. The book was thin, no more than a hundred pages or so, and seemingly very old.

Opening the book, Evylin settled in. This was exactly what she'd been hoping for: a chance to learn about Bonding, to know what she and Deckard had agreed to. She turned to the first page, finding the lines tight and the writing cramped. A thin book it might be, but short it was not. That didn't matter; Evylin loved to read. She often read novels five times this length. This should only take her a matter of a few hours at most.

Evylin read the first paragraph. Then she read it again. And again.

Frowning, Evylin narrowed her eyes on the text and tried to focus.

> *"In attaching the souls and creating a Bond of their hearts, we find Allore's reflection in creation. The Children of the Creator were charged to bring his balance, to embody his power and beauty, to create as he created, and to reflect the resources of life, his holy frame. Upon the Bonding, we find strength and unity unlike any other. The Creation divinely wrought is brought into ultimate sanctification, a portrait of our holy father and his majesty. It is not without a fully completed crown of unified bodies that we can see the purest image of his might."*

Evylin set the book down, the ponderous text swirling in her head. She took a sip of tea, then picked the book up again, fighting to remain attentive and comprehend even a fraction of what she read. She'd only made it three pages by the time Ilain returned, and she thought she understood perhaps a handful of lines at best.

As Ilain entered, Evylin closed the book. She watched as her friend moved through the space, putting away the toiletries. "Ilain," she called as the woman began to rummage around in one of the parcels, "why are we doing this?"

"Doing what?" Ilain asked distractedly.

"This," Evylin said, gesturing to the room. "We're leaving in the morning. We're pressed for time. And yet, we're taking hours to prepare for this ceremony as though . . . as though it's a wedding."

Ilain crossed the room, a brush in her hand. "Look forward," she said, guiding Evylin's gaze toward the wall. Then she took up a small section of hair, swiping the brush across it as she began to reply. "We are doing this, Evylin, because Bonding is sacred. It is a hallowed act in which few Mages or Warriors ever have the chance to partake."

Evylin picked at the cover of the book, uncomfortable with all the religion associated with the ceremony.

"In fact," Ilain continued, "you and Jonn are the first to Bond in well over five centuries."

That caused Evylin to freeze. "How is that possible?" she asked.

"Bonding was lost to us," Ilain said. "As is much about our history. The Mages of Auld wiped out the Warriors, making Bonding impossible for a time. Further, they destroyed much of the texts regarding it out of spite, and while some have been recovered through the years, many of the core tenets of its tradition remain a mystery. Even that," Ilain motioned to the book, "we only have because the Alliance found it in the rubble of the old palace in Aulton. Thankfully, I was able to convince them to give it to me, helping me become the foremost expert in Bonding in this era."

"You've read it, then?"

"Many times."

"Really?"

Ilain chuckled. "It isn't the easiest to read, is it? But it is important, so I'd suggest you and Jonn make time for it."

"Tonight?" Evylin asked with worry.

"Of course not tonight," Ilain said, amused. "But soon. Hand me that oil, would you?"

Evylin did as requested. "Ilain . . ."

"Yes?"

Playing with the tie of her robe, Evylin stared at the wall while Ilain ran her fingers through her hair. "You're married to Ethenn," she noted.

Ilain paused, then resumed her work. "I am betrothed to Ethenn, which is a provisional marriage in Wauld."

Evylin smiled. "I'm happy for you."

After another pause, Ilain thanked her softly.

"Last we spoke," Evylin continued, "you thought you loved him. I take it that you've determined you do?"

Ilain picked the brush back up, working silently for a time. "As I said before, I'm not altogether certain what love feels like," she admitted quietly. "But . . . yes, I think . . . I think I'm starting to understand it enough to say definitively that I do love him."

"That's wonderful!" Evylin turned and took Ilain's hand. "And he admitted his love for you?"

"He did," Ilain said as though in awe.

"Then you're getting everything you ever wanted," Evylin said. "A Warrior whom you love and the chance to Bond."

Ilain's small smile grew, a light pink wash coming over her cheeks. She looked younger than Evylin had ever seen her, bashful like a teen in the midst of her first crush. "It seems too good to be true," she said softly. "I can't help fearing that it is."

Seeing the sudden well of tears in Ilain's eyes, Evylin gripped her hand more tightly. "Ilain, what's wrong?" she asked.

With a sweep of her free hand, Ilain waved her concern away. "Nothing," she said. "I'm just emotional. After all these years . . . I've wanted to be Bonded since I was sixteen. Now, nearly thirty years later, it's finally going to happen. I'm betrothed to a man who loves me—whom I love and will Bond with in a year's time. Or sooner if we can get Allund in order. Yet, all I can think is . . . What if something happens? We still have a month of travel to get the rest of the Relics. We have fights and trials to face. We will have to come against Blount himself, whether with three Relics or four. And through it all . . . What if we die? Worse, what if, in that time, Ethenn realizes that he doesn't love me? I'll lose everything."

Evylin rose, knowing those exact fears intimately. She'd faced them herself only days ago.

Setting her hands on Ilain's arms, Evylin leaned close. "Ethenn loves you, Ilain. Nothing will change that."

"How can you be sure?"

"Because he's a good man. And you make him feel alive, in a way nothing else in this world can." Evylin smiled brightly at her. "Trust me. As a Warrior, I know what it's like to love a Mage. It's not something you simply change your mind about. We feel it, here—" She set a hand on her stomach. "The magic draws us. It calls us to you. We couldn't ignore it if we tried."

Uncertain, Ilain nodded. Then she let out a low huff. "Enough," she said, drawing back. "This night is about you, not me."

"It is your wedding night," Evylin teased.

Ilain winked. "Oh, I won't forget that. But it's *your* Bonding night," she said. "And we have to get you ready."

Ilain helped Evylin into her dress, a complex piece of layers and buttons. First came an elegant black silk slip dress (in place of a chemise) with a matching silk scarf draped over her neck to hang until it brushed the ground. After that came a thick wool coat that buttoned over the scarf with black metal clasps. While the sleeves and bodice hugged her torso, the skirts flowed like ripples on a pond. Finally, Ilain attached a draping silk cape to the epaulets on the shoulders to trail out behind Evylin.

Clothed in such finery for the second time in a week, Evylin paused in front of the looking glass, curious at the transformation. This gown was far more modest than the one Renaul had forced her to wear, but it still spoke of a military precision and regality that seemed befitting of a Warrior. Though she would never prefer to fight in such a piece, she thought she could, if needed, in the adequately roomy skirts. She suddenly thought she understood how Ilain managed to run around in her own elegant dresses, fighting Shades with obvious ease. It was evident that the dress had been made for her.

Ilain helped her into a pair of shiny leather boots, and Evylin habitually slipped her small dagger into the ankle. Then she returned the favor, assisting Ilain as she dressed. The Mage's outfit wasn't nearly as complex, only a simple white silk sheath that shimmered like a star.

"Is there a reason you're in white, and I'm in black?" Evylin asked as she slid the fabric buttons through their loops along the back of Ilain's dress.

Holding her fire-bright hair out of the way, Ilain's voice belied her smile. "There's a reason for everything tonight, Evylin."

"I see." Evylin glanced at her in the mirror. The white silk made the Waulden woman's pale skin seem pink in contrast. "And what is the reason for these colors?"

"It's tradition," Ilain said, "though a forgotten one. We're working to resurrect it."

Evylin fastened the last button and stepped back. Ilain's dress was more demure than the scarlet gown she'd worn the previous night, though the neckline still displayed her decolletage with impunity. Small freckles dotted her skin like jewels, her only embellishment aside from the rings on her fingers.

"Bonding is about balance, remember?" Ilain said. "Mages wear white. Warriors wear black. Any non-magical members in attendance wear gray, though that will only be Thom and the archminister."

"Why only the two of them?" Evylin asked.

"Because Thom is part of the ceremony, and the archminister will be a witness."

Evylin nodded in understanding, their reflections catching her attention. They were in high contrast: her ensemble dark and mysterious, Ilain's bright and captivating—near opposites in every way.

"So," Evylin said, continuing to study their reflections, "Jonn will be in white too?"

"He and all the other Mages in attendance." Ilain tugged on her slippers, then straightened. "Come on then," she said with a glance out the window at the dark sky. "It's time for the ceremony."

The mention of leaving sent a jolt of anxiety through Evylin. She knew this was what she wanted. She loved Deckard, and Bonding with him, uniting their souls and hearts, was something she greatly desired. But there was still so much unknown. With

Deckard now revealed as a Space Mage, their overall ignorance of all manner of things magical, and the uncertainty of the Alliance's plans, it felt as though they were binding themselves to a future they weren't sure they wanted.

The whole ceremony to come was a mystery as well. The book Ilain had given her was full of laborious rhetoric. How was Evylin supposed to feel confident about pursuing this course? Too many questions remained to commit to this fate.

But as Ilain led her into the hall and down the stairs, Evylin drew in a steadying breath. This wasn't a foolhardy decision. It was a choice to Bond with the man she loved. Besides, the last hasty choice she'd made wound up granting her a husband more wonderful than she ever could have fathomed. This would turn out no differently . . . she hoped.

CHAPTER THIRTEEN

Through the courtyard behind the Crimson Clover, Evylin and Ilain returned to the event hall where the Alliance had met the previous night. This time, they went into a separate, smaller room intended for more intimate gatherings. Heat rushed out to encase them as Ilain unceremoniously opened the door. The tiled floors were cleared of furnishings, stretching the length of the narrow room to lead to the massive fireplace. The singular, simple golden chandelier cast the room in a dim, amber glow. Dark draperies hung open by the windows, looking out onto the courtyard, allowing the moonlight to gild the room in its silver light.

A cluster of people stood in the assembly hall. Nearest to the door, Thom and Archminister Fishere waited in coats of gray, flanking the path to the center of the room where two pillars of marble stood, one black with a silver box on its top and another white and topped with a golden box. Ethenn and Brea, dressed in black, stood on either side of the pillars.

Behind them was a coterie of men and women in white. Mages. And there, in their midst, stood Deckard.

Evylin's heart thumped giddily, and a sudden lightness swept through her thoughts. Deckard was, in a word, regal. He stood with his shoulders back, taking her in as she studied him. The cut of his white coat and trousers reminded her of his officer's uniform, though the coat was made of fine wool with intricate braiding and white metal buttons. A cravat peeked through the high collar of his coat, only his black boots breaking the starkness of his dress. His reddish-brown hair, freshly cropped short, was swept back with polished refinement, only a hint of stubble along his jawline—a concession she was sure he'd made for her.

The breathless feeling inside her lungs was the way Evylin knew she should have felt on their wedding day three months ago. On that occasion, she'd only felt bewilderment and unease. If only she had known then what she knew now. . . .

Impatient to be at his side, Evylin lifted her skirts and darted forward to Deckard. The train of her dress hissed, and her boots pattered loudly against the tiles. Deckard met her halfway, taking her hands to draw her close.

"You'd think I hadn't seen you in days," he whispered, his eyes twinkling, "with how my heart reacted just now."

Evylin grinned, rolling onto the balls of her feet to kiss his cheek. "Sometimes," she said, "hours can feel like days."

Deckard cupped her cheek then, his thumb tracing her skin.

The sound of the door closing drew them back to the room. Evylin turned to see Ilain, Thom, and Fishere approaching. "You look fancy," Thom remarked.

Evylin reached over to straighten his silken, silver cravat. "As do you," she teased. "You don't look half bad in gray."

"I think the term you're searching for is 'devastatingly dull,'" he replied self-derisively.

Unaffected by their banter, Fishere spoke. "Now that we're all here, shall we begin?"

"Indeed," Ilain said, hands clasped before her. "The Alliance has given me permission to officiate this ceremony, so allow me to explain a few things first, hm?"

Stepping back, Deckard offered his arm to Evylin. She slipped her hand into the crook of his elbow, enjoying his closeness. They followed Ilain to the pillars in the center of the room, her hair catching in the soft light. "Now," she said as they walked, "let me remind you that magic is balance, and Bonding is that balance perfected. Therefore, everything we do tonight is to represent that balance. Black and white, Warrior and Mage, female and male."

She turned around, jade green eyes landing on them with seriousness. "Next, it is important for you to understand that this is not a physical bond," she said. "That is what a marriage is—a binding of the body. This is a Bond of the soul. It is beyond the tangible, so it is only accessible through magic. Thus, we require attendants of a magical nature. Aside from Archminister Fishere, everyone is here to participate in some fashion."

Curiosity drove Evylin's brows to rise.

Ilain noticed and prompted, "Yes, dear?"

Evylin glanced over her shoulder at Thom. He shifted from foot to foot behind them. She turned back to Ilain. "What role does Thom play, then?" she asked.

"I'll get to that in a moment," Ilain said, then continued, "First, allow me to walk you through the ceremony and introduce you to all our attendants."

Ilain gestured to Ethenn and Brea on either side of the pillars. "Throughout the ceremony, we will utilize magic to seal the Bond, but during the process of the Bonding, our Warriors will assist each of you. In balance, Breata will assist Jonn—"

Brea's black-brown eyes glimmered in the low light, dipping her chin in an amused nod.

"And Ethenn will assist Evylin," Ilain concluded, motioning to the young man, who stood with hands clasped behind his back like a soldier at ease. Then her hands settled on the silver and gold boxes. "Black and silver for Warrior, white and gold for Mage, these boxes contain an individual moonstone to represent each of you and our dual moons, symbolizing the perfect balance Allore created for our universe. While the stones aren't magical in and of themselves, it is possible to infuse them with magic, as I've done with my own rings." She brandished her hands, the four gemstones flashing in their settings. It gave Evylin the sudden curiosity to know if she could do the same with her wedding rings, though she chose to ask that question at a later date.

"You'll do the same here," Ilain instructed. "Evylin, you'll infuse your magic into the black moonstone, and Jonn, you'll do the same with the white. Once completed, Ethenn and Breata will use their own magic to break the stones. Which is where our Mages come in . . ."

Ilain beckoned them to follow, leading them to the seven Mages awaiting them. "For the ceremony, we have one Mage to embody each resource. I will represent Fire, of course, and Auden will channel Day—" Auden smiled at them in greeting while his sister spoke on. "Next is our Water Mage, Ivry Doyle—" The golden-haired woman gave a gentle curtsy, a friendly expression on her face. "Grey Trumane is our Night Mage—" The man's head dipped in a bow, his dark eyes a curious contrast to his white-blond hair. "Isla is our Wind Mage, naturally." A kind, reserved greeting came from Isla. "And representing Time is Valiana Mourant." Another stunning blonde with crystal-blue eyes smiled softly, her beauty almost distracting. "Jarrad is our Terrae Mage—" The man smirked at them but remained silent. "And finally, Lord Obel will represent Space, as our only other Space Mage is currently on the other side of the country."

Evylin glanced at Deckard before returning the older Night Mage's reserved greeting.

"Upon the breaking of the moonstones," Ilain continued, "we will use the resources of life to fuse the halves together—white and black, Warrior and Mage in perfect balance. These reforged moonstones will symbolize your Bond, serving as reminders for you to carry with you for the rest of your days. These talismans will be tied to you as you will be tied to one another. You cannot lose them or misplace them, for they will always return to you."

Evylin thought to ask how that worked but assumed the book Ilain had given her explained the phenomenon.

"So long as you two live," Ilain said, reverence in her tone, "you will carry a piece of each other in your souls. It's what makes your magic and connection stronger. Half Warrior, half Mage, living within each of you."

"And . . ." Evylin took a deep breath. "How do we do that? Infuse our souls into moonstones."

"Like you would accomplish any magic," Ilain said simply, as though it should be obvious.

"By focus and thought," Deckard surmised.

"Exactly." Ilain smiled cheerfully at him. "Now, one last thing. As your magic takes hold, it will consume you. Don't fear that experience—it's necessary for the Bonding to unite. You'll be so caught up in the magic that you will lose control of your mind and body. That's meant to happen."

Evylin shifted uncomfortably, and Deckard's brow pinched. The idea of losing control of their faculties wasn't appealing. But Evylin supposed she already knew what it was like to let her magic consume her. She'd experienced a similar sensation in the Time Keep and Dunneshead, her magic and Deckard's working as one.

"And," Ilain added, "don't worry if you pass out."

Evylin blanched.

"That happens sometimes."

"Pass out?" Deckard repeated in concern.

Ilain waved a hand through the air. "Apparently, it's a common occurrence with these ceremonies. The senses become overwhelmed, and the magic locks you into a bit of a stasis. And that—" she smirked, motioning behind them, "is why Thom is here."

Perking up, Thom drew his shoulders back under their inspection.

"It's fortunate that your brother is present, Jonn," Ilain said. "You see, a non-magical individual is necessary during the ceremony to bring the Bonded pair out of that consumed state. The duty can be performed by any non-magical person, but having a blood relation present improves the chances of success."

Deckard frowned. "You mean there's a chance of failure?"

Ilain shrugged. "There's a chance of failure in everything."

Before Evylin or Deckard could voice any further concern, Ilain clapped her hands.

"All right, enough of the introductions," she said, guiding them to stand before the pillars. "Time to begin."

Evylin thought to protest, but with her heart lodged in her throat, she couldn't form the words.

Thankfully, Deckard managed to find his voice. "One moment," he said, then pulled Evylin to the side.

As he drew her to stand by the windows, Evylin looked over her shoulder. Most of the attendants began to talk amongst themselves, but a few watched the couple with interest, Lord Obel being one of them. His gaze was calculating rather than voyeuristic, as though he was trying to work out the sum of their strength.

The light weight of her husband's hands on her shoulders drew Evylin's attention back to him. His green-blue eyes held hers, the same intensity in them as they'd carried the night of their agreed-upon marriage. "Is this what you want?" he asked gently. "Now that we know, now that we have information about what this entails that we didn't have this morning, do you still want to do this?"

Evylin pulled in a breath to reply, then paused. A cool tingle raced across her skin as his thumbs brushed against her shoulders, his touch stirring her magic even through her clothes. If he already had this effect on her, what would it be like after they Bonded? Marvelous. Unbelievable. *More.*

Adoration welled in Evylin as she reached up to touch his cheek. "Yes," she whispered back. "Three months ago, I chose you without understanding my heart. Today, I choose you again, this time giving you all my heart and my very soul."

A slow, relieved smile softened Deckard's features. "In a thousand lifetimes," he said, "I could never choose another. I love you."

"I love you."

Deckard closed the distance, pressing two short but ardent kisses to her lips. Then he drew back, took her hand, and guided her back to Ilain. "We're ready," he announced.

Standing at Ethenn's side, Ilain's nose wrinkled happily with her bright smile. "Wonderful," she said, instructing them to take their places. She patted Ethenn's shoulder affectionately before joining them. She had them clasp each other's right hands, facing one another. "We'll start with the oath."

Gazes locked, Evylin and Deckard drew in breaths to steady themselves simultaneously. His thumb brushed along the back of her wrist, sending a flurry of tingles across her skin.

"Listen to my words," Ilain began, her voice serene, "and let them guide you into your magic."

The shadows in the room seemed to press in around them, heightening the intimacy of the moment. The amber glow of fire and chandelier blended with the silver moonlight. With the cool light of night at his back, Deckard's face was radiant in warmth.

"Fire, Day, Water, Night, Wind, Time, Terrae, and Space," Ilain recited. "This is the foundation of Terraeus, the resources of life. From the dawn of creation, Allore formed Warriors and Mages from his very soul, setting them as gatekeepers and anchors of his power, charging them to be caregivers and servants to all. The union of a Bond between Warrior and Mage is the perfection of that charge."

As Ilain's words echoed in the room around them, Evylin held Deckard's gaze, secure in his steadiness. His temperate smile soothed her, and her breathing slowed in response. A faint shiver spread up her arm from where Deckard clasped her wrist. She wished to hold him closer, to fall into his embrace and tuck her head beneath his chin. She wanted to feel the fullness of comfort and care that his arms always provided.

"The Bond is a responsibility to uphold the natural order of Allore," Ilain continued. "As he granted us power, so we honor him by reflecting his essence: creation, devotion, and life. To Bond is to release who you are alone and fasten to who you are together."

Deckard's grip tightened incrementally, sending a fresh spike of tingles into her skin. Her magic was rising slowly in response to him and the urging of Ilain's voice.

"Warriors are the champions, the guardians, the advocates, and the shields of Terraeus. They are justice and equity. They are strength and stability."

A stillness worked its way into Evylin's mind and body, whisking away all extraneous thoughts like a sweep of wind. Tranquility trickled down from her scalp, along her neck, and across her shoulders. Gooseflesh spread along her skin as the coolness of magic rose from the depths. Her thoughts calmed, though her heart remained passionate with longing for Deckard. The magic clarified and sharpened her senses as it settled into her core.

The burning firewood singed the air, popping with sharp snaps. Silver moonlight beamed through the windows with a blazing shine, chilling the air around the panes. The tiles beneath her pressed against the soles of her boots. Wax dripped from the candles like teardrops along their tapers. Ilain's voice took on a purity of sound, allowing Evylin to hear every nuance within, feminine and genteel in tone but deep and raspy at its core.

"Mages are the creators, the scholars, the philosophers, and the visionaries of Terraeus. They are intellect and wisdom. They are insight and inspiration."

As if manipulated by her words, Evylin watched Deckard's eyes shift to a rich green. His hair, which always appeared more brown than red when cut short, took on a copper tinge in the dim light. A vein pulsed on his neck when he flexed his jaw. Though the corner of his mouth still tilted up pleasantly, his expression took on a more serious, focused manner. Impassioned yet sober, intense yet contained.

In stark contrast to the chill that permeated Evylin's veins, heat began to flow through Deckard's touch. It seeped from his palm, through her sleeves, numbing her wrist before spreading up her arm.

"As individuals," Ilain continued, "Warriors and Mages are two halves of a whole. Bonded, they are no longer two souls but one, inseparable and complete. No more are they for themselves. They are a weapon, a tool created to serve the people, perfected in the balance of their magic. Not double-sided but never-ending—both singular and whole."

Ilain paused, shifting in Evylin's peripheral. "I ask you both: Do you accept the responsibility of this union?"

"Yes," Evylin and Deckard said in unison, their voices blending as they spoke.

The smolder of his magic pulsed again into her arm, drawing her a step closer.

"Do you release the hold of who you were alone?"

"Yes."

The heat traveled into her chest, weaving with the cold to create an impossible sensation of freezing and burning simultaneously.

"Do you accept one another in the Bond of Warrior and Mage?"

"Yes."

That last word was a gasp of breath from each of them. Deckard's brows tugged low in concentration as a sense of vertigo wound through Evylin's body. The cold grew ruthless as the heat seared white hot. She shivered even as sweat beaded along her spine.

Evylin couldn't tear her eyes from Deckard's, locked in a trance-like state. Yet, her magic revealed the whole of the room to her as though she no longer resided in her own form but in the very air around them. She watched as Ilain turned to face the Warriors. Brea moved first, Ethenn following her lead. They opened the boxes, the gold and silver filigree on them a scrollwork of flora. The Warriors reached in to take the moonstones from monochromatic velvet cushions.

"Raise your left hands," Ilain instructed. "Palms up." It took a moment for Evylin to realize she'd meant the words for *them*.

Lightheaded and her heart beating at a strange pace, Evylin and Deckard did as directed. It felt like moving through the deepest ocean.

Ethenn and Brea stepped forward under Ilain's guidance and placed the moonstones on their palms: white for Deckard and black for Evylin. The stone felt like glass to the touch. Silver filaments diffracted the light across the semi-opaque obsidian-colored gem. Deckard's moonstone bore the same variegation but in gold.

"Now," Ilain said gently, "let your magic overtake you, drawing your souls together, and channel it into the moonstone."

While Ilain, Ethenn, and Brea stepped away, a fleeting concern niggled at the back of Evylin's mind. How was she going to accomplish such a feat? Ilain hadn't taught them how to infuse a gemstone with their magic. How could they ever manage it in this strange, altered state of consciousness?

Then the worries floated away. Deckard's grip on her was firm and bracing. The Warrior's magic pulsed inside her like a heartbeat all its own. Without effort, her focus narrowed in, shutting out the rest of the world as her senses sharpened and refined their attention on Deckard alone. The room faded to black, her vision absorbed by her husband.

She saw every detail of his being: the fibers on his coat, the light patches of hair on his hands, the blend of red and brown in his stubble and brows, the seams in his clothes, the ridges on his lips, the lines around his mouth and eyes, and the thin sliver of blue that remained in his ever-deepening green irises.

She heard everything he was: the rhythmic pumping of his heart, the blood flowing through his veins, the brush of his thumb over the fabric of her sleeve, and the steady catch and release of his breath.

She smelled the very atmosphere of his presence: the fresh scent of new clothes, the tallow soap on his skin, the leather of his boots, the hint of perspiration in his grasp, and the intrinsic fragrance of him—warm and natural.

She tasted the essence of him on her tongue: the salt of his sweat, the metallic make of the buttons on his coat, the dry threads that stitched together his clothes, and the faint traces of wine that lingered on his breath.

She felt everything, down to his soul: the weight of the white moonstone on his palm, the tight sleeves that pressed into his arms, the instinctive tension of his muscles, the pressure of the dagger he wore in his right boot, the callouses on his hands, and the heat emanating from his body.

Evylin was alive with adrenaline and desire, fixated wholly on the man before her. She was so caught up in the rapture of everything he was that she nearly missed the black haze materializing around their clasped hands. A swirling, slow dance of glittering onyx crystals gathered to create an iridescent shadow. It grew to an inky mist, undulating like waves.

Deckard's eyes transformed under her gaze, shifting to a gradient of icy blue, vibrant emerald, and fierce black that faded into the pupils. His gaze turned severe and wild, powerful and passionate. The magic surged, rolling down their arms as he dipped his head toward hers. The onyx twisted and coalesced with rising speed, the unfamiliar fire under her skin spiking with its intensity.

Drifting up, the magic covered their shoulders and heads, running down to their feet. They were wholly encased in the crystalline shards of Deckard's power. She could feel him trembling and realized suddenly that she was too. The heat of his power seared her flesh, while the cool of her own cut deep to the bone. A gasp escaped them both as the fury of magic swept through them. Their foreheads tipped forward to rest against one another.

At the point of contact, a new feeling overtook them.

Tranquility slowed the frantic beat of Evylin's heart and evened the exhalations of her lungs. The fight between hot and cold ceased, and a subdued peace now ruled her like a gentle breeze on a summer's day. She'd never felt so open and alert, so aware and unlimited. Her mind was calm and her body serene.

Deckard's cheek pressed against Evylin's temple, the relaxed cadence of his breath tickling her ear. His hand was still on her wrist, and she felt the tingle of his touch through her sleeve. An urge for more goaded her. She wanted to lift her face and kiss him, to release his hand and drop the moonstone so she could enfold him in her embrace. But she was as marble carved into a statue, locked in time and place.

Her mind crystal clear, Evylin watched the room with an almost omniscient gaze. She was strangely detached from the sight of her and Deckard resting together in the storm of their intertwined magic. The moonstones glowed, continuing to shimmer as Ethenn and Brea lifted them away from their upturned palms. In turn, Brea took Deckard's now-empty hand and turned its palm over to rest on the couple's clasped hold, and Ethenn did the same for Evylin.

The Warriors stepped between the pillars. They extended their hands over the boxes and crushed the moonstones in their grasp, twin cracks splitting the air. Evylin felt a vague twinge constrict in her chest. Two perfect halves dropped from the Warriors' hands, landing to rest heavily on the velvet pillows.

The Mages came forward then; Fire, Day, Water, Night, Wind, Time, Terrae, and Space circled the pillars. The Existential Mages lifted their hands first, a halo of color emitting from them: golden yellow, vibrant purple, searing white, and smoky black. The four shards of moonstone rose, glowing from within.

Guided by magic, white and black fragments of moonstone met their opposite, creating two new stones of contrasting color. They flared brighter as the Mages flexed their hands. The contrasting halves fused into one, their cracks disappearing as though they'd never been.

The Elemental Mages raised their hands then. Chunks of metal materialized from Jarrad's palms, hovering in the air. Ilain sent roaring flames to envelop them, burning them to molten white ore. Together, they formed the metal into shapes around the moonstones. With a flourish, Isla sent a gale to cool it as the Water Mage washed over them with a gentle stream. Still luminous with light, the newly encased moonstones glittered in settings of silver and gold.

A sudden swell of magic surged through the room, strong and overwhelming. Evylin lost her breath as fresh power coursed through her, rattling her bones and sparking in her fingertips. Deckard's strangled breath told her he'd felt the same power slam into him like a tidal wave.

Profound desire and joy welled up within her, sending her into a delirium. The sensation rocked through her from head to toe and back up in such a violent ricochet of feeling that she lost all sense of where or who she was. Involuntarily, her eyes rolled back, and her vision went black, embracing her in a waking sleep. The feelings raged on—the burgeoning and confounding power filling her to bursting—but her mind had found rest. Oblivion gave her peace, cradling her as the shock of magic reformed her soul around Deckard's and his around hers. She fell into a void at the fusion of their beings.

Time became meaningless. A century could have elapsed, and it would have seemed to be the blink of an eye. A second might have gone by, and it would have felt like an eon.

Evylin was weightless and eternal, lost in the beauty of this forging.

A sound emerged from the darkness, familiar yet not quite recognizable. Steady, warm, and full but detached. It called to her, but she couldn't answer. The call wasn't right—too rigid and coarse to summon her soul into waking.

The void surrounded her in its emptiness, allowing her to rest in its hush. Eternity passed, gentle and serene. She floated unfeelingly in the vacancy around her. The overwhelming power was now subdued. Her body no longer swelled with furor but relaxed with absolute serenity.

A new sound arose, akin to the previous one, pulsing with the same tone and resonance but infused with an intrinsic difference.

This sound . . .

It pulled at her core, still steady, warm, and full but also more refined, poignant, and earnest.

This sound belonged to her. A voice as common to her as her own. And she couldn't help but heed its call.

Evylin gasped awake, eyes wide as they stared into Deckard's. His hand was on her neck, thumb brushing her jaw as he continued to grasp her wrist with the other. A look of pure astonishment and eager joy filled his face as he smiled down at her.

The shock of seeing his eyes returned to nearly full blue once more roused Evylin from her stupor. A thrill bubbled up inside of her, escaping in a laugh. It was different now between them. She could feel it in her core. The same respect, adoration, and devotion remained, but an increased attachment had formed itself, permeating deep within her.

This was what it felt like to be Bonded: a total connection, a complete sense of belonging, and a full understanding of how much she loved the man before her and how much he loved her.

Evylin wanted to express this sentiment, to tell him how happy it made her. But she couldn't find her voice. So she pulled her hand from his—the muscles aching in protest at the sudden movement—and wrapped her arms around his neck. She would have kissed

him, but it felt too brazen for the moment, too carnal for the magnitude of what they'd experienced, of what they'd become. Instead, she closed her eyes and leaned into him, basking in his nearness as he enfolded her in his embrace.

Slowly, reality came back to Evylin and Deckard. The crackling fire rumbled heartily, and its smoke filled the room with a comforting reminder of the mundane. The world had remained the same while they dissolved and came together as a new creation.

Deckard kissed Evylin's temple in a tender, cherishing touch. His fingers traced circles on her back before gliding up to settle on her arm as if telling her it was time— time to let go and face corporeality again. They'd experienced something of pure bliss and profound change, but the rest of life moved on unaware of the monumental moment that had just occurred.

Regretfully, Evylin drew back, but Deckard's smile was filled with such joy and contentment that she found she didn't mind the temporary break from his touch.

"One final thing," Ilain broke the silence reverently, "and then we're done, I promise. Your talismans await."

Deckard took a single step back, his hands drifting down her arms before pulling away completely. They turned to see Ethenn and Brea standing near, holding the silver and gold boxes out to them. On the velvet cushions lay the talismans the Mages had made for them.

Evylin reached out, taking the dagger from the silver and black box. Its golden handle fit perfectly in her palm, and the pommel contained a black and white moonstone. The narrow and deathly sharp silver blade was fitted into a sheath of gold and silver scrollwork. The dagger was small but ideal for concealing.

Smiling, Evylin turned to see Deckard's talisman. Between his fingers, he held a ring—a band of silver with a gold setting around the dual-colored moonstone. Simple but elegant, like the man himself.

Deckard looked up at Ilain, brow raised. "She gets a knife, and I get jewelry?" he asked good-naturedly.

Ilain grinned dryly, tipping her shoulder up in a shrug. "She's a Warrior, and you're a Mage," she said. "You get what you get."

Deckard chuckled as he placed the ring on his right hand.

With a lift of her chin, Ilain regarded them both like a proud mother. "Let it be known, Jonn and Evylin Deckard are officially and eternally Bonded, an embodiment of our Creator Divine, Allore, and his vast might."

Suddenly, Ilain, Brea, the archminister, and the remaining Mages bent their knees, bowing their heads. "It is our honor to be your friends and allies," they said in unison. "You have our vow to serve with you and for you until our last breaths."

At this pledge of fealty, Evylin gaped, and Deckard tensed.

Ilain looked up at them, her verdant gaze glimmering with excitement. "Now, my Highlord Chancellor and Highlady Commander, you are Bonded in the sight of Allore and the Alliance. May you live long and reign justly."

CHAPTER FOURTEEN

"You said nothing about reigning, Ilain," Evylin declared in a voice far more commanding than Ethenn was used to hearing from her.

Deckard appeared strangely stoic, with an energy like a storm threatening on the horizon. Yet, he set a hand on Evylin's shoulder, stilling her instantly. "We can discuss this later," he said calmly, then turned to the archminister. "But I'm not pleased with this trickery."

Ethenn watched warily as Archminister Fishere stepped forward, expression serious. "There has been no trickery, Colonel," he promised with soothing candor. "You asked to Bond, and we assented. Assuming your role in the leadership of our government is not mandatory, though we would kindly ask you to consider it."

A long silence passed as Deckard and Evylin exchanged a look that spoke volumes. It was obvious they understood one another and were in agreement—whatever conclusion they'd come to. The sight intrigued Ethenn, but it confused him as well. He'd thought he understood what Bonding meant, but watching the two of them now. . . .

He was just as startled as they were about this suggestion of reigning like monarchs. But even more shocking was the shift he could sense between the husband and wife. There was something new between them—and a closeness he'd never witnessed in any couple.

"Consider it we shall," Deckard said, tone still gruff. He took Evylin's hand. "Is that all, then? The Bonding is concluded?"

"It is," Ilain replied haughtily.

Ethenn frowned, wondering if her tone revealed her true feelings. He certainly didn't begrudge Evylin and Deckard their discomfort. He was rather uncomfortable himself. The ceremony had been awkward enough to begin with, standing by watching two people be joined together like that. Despite the complete lack of sensuality, somehow, it felt more intimate than sex. If Ethenn was honest, the ceremony was beautiful and alluring—it made his magic rise and his pulse race. Watching it, he found himself anticipating his future union with Ilain. But it was also odd and disquieting, something he felt he should not have witnessed.

Now, with this talk of governing, responsibility, and reflecting the image of Allore, Ethenn thought perhaps he was the wrong man for the job. He wasn't exactly pious, though he did have more faith than Rafferty.

"You're a disgraceful heathen."

Deckard and Evylin said hasty goodnights—though the ones they gave to Thom and Ethenn were far more cordial—and exited the room. Casually, the remaining Mages conversed among each other, seemingly unbothered by the ceremony or the Deckards' displeasure. Archminister Fishere began to speak with Ilain in hushed, almost reproachful tones, so Ethenn just stood in place, unsure of what to do.

At his side, Brea nudged his arm. "You still want this?" she asked.

"Oh, uh—" Ethenn scratched his brow.

Thom stepped over then, looking as bemused as Ethenn felt and saving him from having to reply. "Well, that was weird," he remarked. "Are all Bonding ceremonies like that?"

Brea grinned dryly. "I wouldn't know. That's the first Bonding ceremony the world has seen since . . . Well, you'd have to ask Ilain for the specific date, but I know it was centuries ago."

"Huh." Thom released an overwhelmed breath. "I guess we're not needed anymore?"

"No."

"In that case—" Thom motioned toward the door. "Raff said he'd meet us at The Rook for drinks. Care to join?"

Brea lifted her shoulder in a shrug, then called to Isla. They exchanged some words in Schonese before she turned back to the two of them. "Sounds like fun," she said. "Vayden and Isla are spending the night with Reyana since they won't see her until the end of this mission, so I'm bereft of company anyway."

"Oh, I wouldn't say that." Thom tipped his head toward the Calders. "I'm sure Auden would love to be your companion."

Brea rolled her eyes and muttered something caustic in Schonese. "Let's get out of here before he gets any ideas, shall we?" she said.

Thom laughed, and Ethenn found himself smiling too. Though he hadn't spent much time with the Alliance lieutenant, he found himself anticipating their training together. Her dry wit and blunt remarks reminded him of the best parts of Hewitt, while her ready smile and personable nature contrasted with the gruff man. Ethenn thought it boded well for the role of mentor.

As they turned to leave, Thom tapped Ethenn's shoulder. "You comin', kid—Loxley?" he asked, correcting himself yet again.

Appreciative of the sentiment, though still wary of his friend's repentance, Ethenn gave him a small, grateful smile. "No, I, uh—" He paused, glancing toward Ilain, where she stood with Fishere and Auden. "After that, I need some time to . . . think."

Brea smirked while Thom snorted in wry humor. "Yes," he said. "I'm sure you do. I can't promise that Raff won't be pounding on your door once he finds out you're not coming, though."

Ethenn grimaced. "Tell him I'm busy."

"With what?"

Ethenn didn't say anything, only giving a pointed look toward Ilain.

Thom raised his brow. "Eh? You planning to take your husbandly advantages?"

"No," Ethenn said. "But Raff doesn't need to know that."

"Fair enough." Thom gave his shoulder another slap. "Don't think too hard."

With a final farewell, Thom and Brea left.

In a room full of mostly strangers, Ethenn shuffled his feet nervously. He wanted to return to his room and consider the implications Bonding might have on his future. For that matter, he wanted a quiet moment to consider the fact that he was engaged—no, he was *betrothed* to Ilain. After that astonishing ceremony in Fishere's office earlier, he hadn't had time to process the change in his marital status or what it would mean for their relationship. He needed to be alone and ponder it all.

But he lingered, waiting for Ilain to finish her conversation with Fishere and Auden to say a proper goodnight as he assumed a husband should.

During that time, Isla stepped over to exchange short pleasantries, welcoming him to their family and wishing him a happy marriage before leaving to join her husband and daughter. Jarrad and one of the other Mages—Grey, the Night Mage presently betrothed to the third female Warrior in the Alliance, Alma—joined him to offer their own teasing congratulations. Evidently, Ilain's betrothal was exciting gossip within the Alliance. What's more, Ethenn learned that *he* was now the center of great envy among the other male Warriors.

"Haadge is going to have a conniption when he finds out," Grey remarked with a friendly laugh. "That man has been obsessed with Ilain for the last twenty-two years."

After learning of Major Olsen's affection for Ilain last night and now hearing about Haadge's fixation, Ethenn was starting to question why on Terraeus the woman would select *him*.

"You filthy gutter rat."

The moment that Fishere concluded with the Calders, Ethenn excused himself from Jarrad and Grey's company before anyone else could approach Ilain. Though Auden remained at her side, Ethenn was grateful for his presence. He didn't know the proper way to treat Ilain in their new relationship . . . if it could be called a relationship. Despite their betrothal, they weren't exactly lovers. They couldn't rightly be called friends either. Yes, they got along and had pleasant conversations during their travels, but Ethenn often relegated that to her niceness. Whatever "relationship" they currently had, it was more like acquaintances-turned-spouses than anything.

And that left him in a profoundly uncertain state.

Ilain and Auden turned to Ethenn upon his arrival. She smiled welcomingly, and Auden began to excuse himself. "Don't go," he said a bit too hastily, then added, "I won't be long" to cover for it.

Auden stayed, though he turned his head as though to give them a moment of privacy.

"I just wanted to say goodnight," Ethenn said.

"You're leaving?" Ilain said, sounding surprisingly disappointed.

"Um, yes," Ethenn replied. "We have an early morning, so . . . ."

"Right." Ilain clasped her hands in front of her, glancing sidelong at Auden.

Ethenn cleared his throat, unsure of what else to say.

Ilain continued to stare at him, her bright eyes unnervingly steady. She was stunning in her silky white dress. It draped loosely about her waist, though the square-cut bodice fit her snugly. The sleeves made him think of the whipped cream his aunt used to put on his cousin's birthday pies, rippling softly to her wrists.

Under other circumstances, Ethenn might have considered telling her how beautiful she looked in that dress. Should their betrothal have been one born out of mutual love, he might have admitted how he wished to hold her close, to feel the soft fabric under his hands as he kissed her. As such was not the case, he stayed his tongue.

"Well," he said with a forced smile, "goodnight."

Ilain's smirk wasn't as confident as usual. "Goodnight, Ethenn."

Taking his chance, Ethenn turned to leave, offering Auden a singular nod in farewell. Auden's expression was unexpectedly confused, but Ethenn didn't let himself ponder it as he strode from the room.

He hurried out of the assembly hall, through the courtyard, and back to the Crimson Clover. The truth was dreadfully clear. He knew he was too infatuated with Ilain, too desperate for her. It was problematic in ways he hadn't anticipated. She didn't feel a thing in return for him—not romantically, at least—and he'd allowed himself to be entrapped by her. What had he gotten himself into?

That ceremony . . . It was baffling. The intensity of it, the gravity of it—was he ready for that?

Yes, he loved Ilain. He felt all the things a man should feel for his wife. He would live and die for her. But could he Bond with her? Could he go through that terrifyingly intimate exchange of his inmost self and accept the role of . . . what exactly? Ruler of a country that didn't yet exist?

Ethenn shut himself in his room, the darkness pressing into him. The cold air nipped at his face and hands, the only parts of him exposed. Though his ceremonial uniform wasn't as elaborate as Deckard's or Evylin's, it was on the stuffy side. He undid the cravat, ready to be free of its choking grip. It was only the second one he'd worn in his life—the first being at Renaul's.

Of what use were cravats to Ethenn? He was a hunter, a fighter, not suited for society's frippery.

So how could he be what Ilain needed him to be?

Ethenn was a fool—a blind, wishful, idealistic fool. This was why he'd never said anything about his potential powers. He knew he wasn't made for this life, so why pretend? Why act like a Warrior when all he'd ever be was a town boy with broken dreams and blood on his hands?

Ethenn tossed the cravat angrily at the open wardrobe. It hit the back wall, right where he'd aimed. Then he wrestled off his coat, throwing it in next. Everything he'd been given to wear tonight was black—the garb of a Warrior, he'd come to understand. It all felt wrong.

He couldn't become the leader she'd want him to be.

After lighting the corner stove to heat the room, Ethenn went to the bedside. He turned on the oil lamp and sat down to pull off his boots. And then he stayed there, staring into the darkness for untold minutes, trying to puzzle out just what he was supposed to do.

Should he break off the betrothal just as it began? That's what an honorable man would do, wasn't it? It's what Colonel Deckard would do. He would let her be with a man who loved her *and* was the leader she desired, not some damaged brute who burned with an inner rage.

But then again, Deckard had advised Ethenn to be honest, to love Ilain with his whole soul. Could that be his redemption, loving her? And wasn't that what Bonding was intended to be? Loving someone so much that you gave them a piece of your soul.

Ethenn blew out a heavy breath. He was too tired for these thoughts, too confused to adequately weigh the right and wrong of them. So he stood, kicked his boots out of the way, and untucked his shirt when a knock sounded at his door.

Pausing, Ethenn stared at the door, sure he'd misheard.

A second, more insistent knock came.

Ethenn lifted his eyes to the ceiling, realizing that Thom hadn't been successful, and Rafferty was here to collect him. Well, he wasn't interested in getting plastered a second night.

Letting his shirt hang loosely about his waist, Ethenn crossed the room, preparing to tell Rafferty to go away. But when he opened the door, it wasn't Rafferty on the other side.

In shock, Ethenn couldn't quite process her presence until she was already pushing her way into his room. "Ilain?" he said, bewildered. "What are you doing here?"

"Shut the door, would you?" Ilain said. "It's letting in a draft."

Dumbfounded, Ethenn did as requested. Ilain strode into the room, a small carpetbag in hand. The moonlight caught on her white dress, making her look like a beam of light herself. She turned in a circle, surveying the small space, before looking at him. "Our rooms are identical," she noted.

Not sure what else to do, Ethenn just gaped at her.

"You look like a fish," she said.

He shut his mouth. "What are you doing here?" he asked again.

Ilain gave him a look that said it should be obvious. "Well, it's night, darling. And as you said a short while ago, we have an early morning." She dropped her bag onto the foot of the bed. "I'm going to sleep."

"Sleep?" Ethenn repeated. "In here?"

"Yes, of course."

"This is my room."

"If you want to be technical about it."

Ethenn shook his head frantically. "You can't—Ilain, you need to go."

"Don't be ridiculous."

"We aren't sleeping together."

She regarded him thoughtfully for several seconds before crossing her arms. "Ethenn, I told you this morning that this is expected. Husbands and wives share a bed, so we will too."

"We aren't married," he argued.

"We're betrothed," she returned. "Which means we're in a trial marriage, which further means we ought to *try* and give this our best shot, hm?"

Ethenn stared at her, incredulous.

Ilain muttered something under her breath, then gave him a placating look. "Don't worry, dearest. I'll keep your honor intact."

"It's not my honor I'm worried about," he admitted.

She laughed and turned to her bag. "In Wauld," she said, pulling out a small pile of items, "you have every right to my womanly virtue, Ethenn. Should anyone question our liaisons, my reputation would remain beyond reproach regardless."

Though Ethenn wanted to tell her that she was missing the point, the words escaped him when she promptly sat down and lifted her skirts. "Ilain!" he exclaimed, whirling around to avert his gaze. "You can't just undress in front of men like that."

"I'm removing my stockings, you prude," she said with laughter in her voice. "Besides, I'm not undressing in front of *men*. I'm undressing in front of my husband."

"In *Ephria*," he said, glaring at the wall, "women don't undress in front of *any* man unless they are intending on . . ." He cut off, his imagination rampant with images of that white dress pooling on the floor.

"On what?" Ilain prompted.

"Seducing him," Ethenn said through clenched teeth.

She let out a feminine chuckle. "Perhaps I am intending to seduce you."

He scoffed.

"You think it impossible?" she noted.

"I think it improbable," he said. "There's a difference."

"Mm." The bed creaked as she rose behind him. "Well, I need you to get over your puritanical Ephrian notions and help me."

Cautiously, Ethenn began to look over his shoulder. Seeing that she was still fully dressed, he felt safe to turn around. "Help with what?" he asked.

She angled so he could see the back of her dress, lined with buttons. "I can't reach."

Ethenn blushed. "You want me to undress you?"

She smirked. "I want you to unbutton my dress," she said, then mockingly added, "There's a difference."

"Oh."

"Unless, of course," she added, raising her brow, "you want to undress me."

Unsure if she was jesting or not, Ethenn shook his head. "Do I just—?" He stepped closer, inspecting the small buttons. He didn't quite have the confidence to touch her yet, so he merely stared. "Unhook them?"

"That's usually how you undo buttons, yes."

Ethenn met her gaze. "Don't make fun of me," he said flatly.

Her grin slipped for a second. "I'm not."

"You just did."

Taking a deep breath, Ilain shifted to face him. "Ethenn, I'm not making fun of you," she said. "Though I understand how it might have sounded that way. Believe it or not, I'm rather nervous too. However, I believe getting comfortable together is the best course, as we've promised our lives to one another after all. And I can't get out of this dress by myself. So it's either having you help me, or I interrupt Isla, Vayden, and Reyana's last night together to have my sister-in-law spare us this little moment of awkwardness."

She turned away, her back angling toward him.

A twinge of guilt went through Ethenn. He hadn't considered the possibility of Ilain feeling nervous. He'd never known her to be anything but unerringly confident. But she was right; if they were going to be together, he had to learn the signs of her true feelings, especially in moments like these.

Cautiously lifting a hand, Ethenn reached for the top button. "I'm sorry," he said. "I—sometimes, I have a hard time reading people."

Ilain pulled her hair out of the way, making the work easier for him. "That's all right," she said softly. "I'm known for being hard to read."

Ethenn kept talking to distract himself from the thin line of ivory skin and gauzy chemise revealed by the unhooked buttons. "You always seemed open about your feelings to me," he said.

"Oh, no," Ilain said, a hint of humor in her lilting tone. "I've always been quite the skilled liar."

Ethenn grinned wryly as he struggled with the tiny buttons. "You admit to being a liar?"

"The best liars are always honest."

"That makes no sense."

"It makes perfect sense if you're dishonest." She glanced over her shoulder at him. "Just ask Rafferty."

"If you're saying that I've gotten myself attached to the female version of Rafferty, then I'm afraid this union is at its end."

"Nonsense. I'm vastly superior to the female version of Rafferty. For one thing, I have scruples."

"And," Ethenn added, undoing the last button at the base of her spine, "you can't do sleight of hand."

She shot a suggestive look over her shoulder. "Oh, I have my own ways of making things disappear."

The innuendo slammed into Ethenn like a ram, knocking the wind out of him. He was certain his whole body had flushed red at the thoughts her words conjured. "Who the hell taught you to say things like that?" he asked.

"No one," she said. "I'm just a desperately lonely forty-three-year-old woman."

Ethenn grimaced. "I don't like it when you say stuff like that, Ilain."

"Self-deprecating comments?"

"That you're forty-three."

She smiled. "But I am forty-three."

"And I'm twenty-one," he replied. "It makes me uncomfortable knowing that you're—you're . . ."

"Older than your mother?"

His jaw clenched. "Yes."

Ilain faced him fully, adjusting the shoulder of her dress when it tried to slip down. "Ethenn, I understand that you're still new to the concept of living for centuries," she said. "But try to fathom this: The age difference between you and me . . . It's a fragment. I don't see you as a child because of your youth any more than you see me as an old maid. Yes, I have lived longer than you. And yet, I'd wager that you've lived more life—more real *life*—than I because I was stuck in Doorstunds Reach training for over twenty years."

"That's the whole of my lifetime."

"Believe me," she said, holding his gaze steadily, "it's made me no more experienced than you—not in the ways that matter."

Though Ethenn wasn't altogether sure she was correct, he recognized that he wasn't an authority on romantic relationships and the effects of age disparities within them. He'd never had a serious romance in his life, and while Ilain was twenty-two years his senior, she neither acted nor looked like it.

At his lack of response, Ilain straightened her shoulders, her grin turning sly once more. "Now, do you want to watch me get changed or not?" she asked bluntly.

Ethenn blinked, caught off guard by the offer. His initial reaction was to be a gentleman, to turn away and give her privacy. But then he thought of her pronouncement that this was a marriage—though it be probationary—and they ought to treat it like one.

"Honestly?" Ethenn said, then shrugged. "Yes."

Ilain's confidence slipped. "You do?"

"Yes."

Her face scrunched in dramatic shock. "No!"

"Then why did you ask?"

"Because I wanted to see you blush."

Surprisingly, Ethenn found himself laughing. "I hate to inform you, Ilain, but I'm not that innocent."

Ilain narrowed her eyes, inspecting him as though he were wholly incomprehensible. "Have you seen a naked woman before?" she asked, a hint of incredulity in her tone.

Ethenn pressed his lips together, trying to determine how honest to be. The shoulder of her dress slipped again, revealing the thin strap of her chemise, and she shimmied it back up. He tipped his chin toward her hand, still holding the sleeve in place. "Are you going to change or not?" he challenged.

After several seconds of hesitation, a slow, bashful grin worked its way over Ilain's face. And without any more ceremony, she tugged her arms free of the sleeves to work the dress down and over her hips. Its silky fabric puddled on the floor around her feet, leaving her standing only in her cotton undergarments.

Ethenn drew in a deep breath. The chemise's hem ended just below her knees. Her arms, decolletage, and lower legs were bare, displaying just how creamy white her skin really was. She looked like porcelain compared to his naturally deep tan complexion, her delicacy like a fragile doll or elegant statue. Even more alluring, the moonlight streaming through the window beamed through the chemise like it was gossamer, silhouetting her lithe, feminine figure perfectly. Ilain didn't exactly meet the Ephrian ideal image of a woman with her trim, narrow frame, long limbs, and angular shape. But somehow, that made her even more attractive to Ethenn.

His jaw twitched, and he realized he'd clamped it shut as he stared at her.

Ilain shifted uncomfortably on her dainty feet. "I need to put on my nightdress," she said, motioning toward the bed.

Ethenn nodded but didn't move. "Yes," he said, answering her previous question. "I've seen naked women before."

Ilain flinched. "*Women*?" she repeated, emphasizing the plural nature of the word.

Choosing to set her at ease, Ethenn moved to shut the curtains. "Not many, but I didn't exactly spend my time in Trollenston's most reputable establishments."

"And where did you spend your time?"

"In a shady tavern and fighting clubs." He turned back to see her sliding her nightdress, a simple, sleeveless thing made of a far thicker cotton, over the chemise. "Granted, I was there to fight or drink, not to see the women. They were just sort of . . . there."

Sneakily working the undergarment off under the nightdress, Ilain kept her eyes on her task, ensuring she maintained what little sense of modesty she had left. "I had no idea Ephria could be so debauched," she said with amusement.

"We're not all Jonn Deckard," Ethenn said, smiling at her strange blend of decorum and brashness.

"Evidently not." Ilain lifted the chemise from the floor with her foot before straightening abruptly. She stared at Ethenn with something like worry. "Have you . . . made love to a woman?"

An instant, nervous laugh worked out of him. "No."

She gave a steady, relieved nod and began folding the chemise.

A strange compulsion to be brutally honest drove Ethenn to add, "But I did get close once."

Ilain paused. "You did?"

He shrugged.

"Hm." Ilain turned to stare at the wall in thought. "I don't like that."

"And I don't like that you wear provocative gowns that other men purchase to win your affection," he returned. "We're all hypocrites."

She gave him a decidedly unamused smirk. "She must have been quite special, this one woman."

Ethenn couldn't decide if she sounded jealous or just disappointed in his impurity. "Not special, just . . . willing."

"I see." Ilain tucked the chemise and a few other items back into the bag before setting it on the floor next to his boots.

Hearing the accusatory nature of her words, Ethenn couldn't help his smile. "I'm telling you these things, Ilain, because I want you to understand," he said. "I'm not your knight in shining armor. I'm not Deckard, and I'm not particularly honorable. But . . ."

Ethenn paused, considering whether revealing these parts of himself was the right choice. If he didn't want to be the man she desired—if he *couldn't* be that man—then he ought to save himself the heartache of growing even more attached to her, of pretending that she could ever love him the way he loved her.

"But . . . ?" Ilain prompted him softly. She stood beside the bed, looking small and lovely in the dim light. Her hair shone like the brightest fire. And his breath caught, recognizing that she was there; she'd come to him, chosen him, even if it wasn't out of the same regard he carried for her.

Choosing to take Deckard's advice, Ethenn came to stand an arm's length away, the bedside rug bristling against his bare feet. "But I love you," he said. "I pledged my life to you. And no matter what you think of me, no matter what you wish I could be that I'm not . . . I will do what I can to make you happy, even if I'm not the one you truly want."

Ilain stood there for several long seconds, playing with the tie on the collar of her nightdress absentmindedly. Ethenn's gaze dipped, catching the smallest glimpse of the creamy skin beneath, feeling the heat rising in his back. He imagined tugging that ribbon free, loosening the collar, and kissing every inch of flesh, every freckle along her sharp collarbone.

His throat went dry, and he met her eyes again.

"I think," Ilain finally said, "we should go to bed."

"Go to bed?" Ethenn asked. "Or go to sleep?"

The faintest pink tinged her cheeks, and he was pleased to find that he could make her blush too. "To sleep," she clarified.

Though Ethenn wasn't entirely sure what he would have said if she'd chosen the other option, he nodded. "I agree." He glanced at the mattress. "There's just one problem."

"What's that?"

"This bed is made for only one person."

Her signature grin lifted the edge of her lips. "I guess we'll just have to cuddle then," she said.

While Ethenn's imagination conjured less than chaste thoughts of such behavior, Ilain left him standing there and climbed under the blankets. Since the bed was pushed into the corner of the room, she lay with her back against the wall, providing ample room for him on the outer edge.

Ethenn hesitated, unsure of what to do. Usually, he slept in his shirt alone, as was the habit of most Ephrian men. But with Ilain next to him, he wasn't sure he cared to be so . . . free. So he kept his trousers on, not bothering to remove his shirt either.

With a deep breath of courage, Ethenn joined Ilain under the blankets. It took a good deal of shifting to get comfortable, and he wasn't sure whether he should be elated or uncomfortable with the way her body pressed into his side. He kept his arms and hands to himself, but still, she snuggled against him as though this was perfectly normal behavior for them.

Ethenn stared at the crimson canopy over their heads, Ilain's breath heating his collar as his neck burned with a blush. Her feet first only brushed his, then stayed tucked against his soles. It was difficult sharing a pillow, but somehow, they managed. Her hair tickled his cheek.

"This isn't exactly cuddling," Ilain whispered, the words overly loud right next to his ear.

"I'm not very good at that," he admitted.

"What is there to be good at? You just do it."

"I don't."

"You live a sad life."

That he did.

"And who have you been cuddling with?" he asked in a manner somewhere between agitated and playful. "I thought you were beyond reproach."

"I am," she returned. "My family is very affectionate."

Ethenn snorted. "No, that doesn't make sense."

"What do you mean?"

"I'm trying to picture Auden cuddling with anyone, and it just doesn't work."

She poked his side, and he jerked, turning into her involuntarily. "My brother may be an academic bore, but he has the most loving heart you'll ever know."

"I'll take your word for it." Ethenn shifted, trying not to notice the press of her chest against his arm.

She set her chin on his shoulder. "You're supposed to put your arm around me, you know."

Ethenn shook his head. "That's not a good idea."

"Why not?"

"Do you remember me saying I'm not very honorable?"

"And what? You're going to force yourself on me?" She scoffed. "Trust me, if you try to take too many liberties, I'm perfectly capable of punishing you."

"Of that, I have no doubt." He grinned up at the canopy, unwilling to look at her, their faces disconcertingly close. "But it isn't your modesty I'm trying to protect."

"You saw me in my chemise. What modesty do I have left?"

"Very little," he said, proud of himself for being brave enough to tease her. "I'm not concerned about you, Ilain. I'm protecting myself."

"Oh," she murmured, seeming to understand.

Over their travels, Ethenn's attraction to Ilain had grown from infatuation to an unrequited love. Now, it burned with a full desire that was growing difficult to contain. Sleeping next to her was one thing. Embracing her, touching her, kissing her—those were cruel taunts on his psyche that he couldn't withstand.

Gently, cautiously, Ilain rested her hand on his chest. Even with the fabric between them, the touch sent spirals of energy coursing through him, tugging on the magic that rested beneath his skin. "Ethenn," she whispered.

"Hm?"

"If you love me . . . why do you tense when I touch you?"

Ethenn closed his eyes. How honest could he be with her? He settled for the most palatable truth. "Because I'm not used to being touched."

Ilain was quiet and very, very still. Then she asked, "Would you rather I not touch you?"

"That'd be rather difficult to accomplish in this bed."

"I meant as a point of habit."

Shifting, Ethenn finally gathered the courage to look at her. Their noses were almost brushing, and he edged slightly back to see her more clearly. Allowing himself one grace, he reached up and wrapped his fingers around hers where they rested on his chest. "As we've promised to spend our not-quite-eternal lives together—"

She smiled, bringing a wrinkle to her nose.

"I'd imagine that will be rather difficult to accomplish as well," he concluded.

"Ethenn . . ."

"Yes?"

Her eyes searched his. He was fairly certain he could feel her heart beating against his arm. Its pace was unexpectedly fast. "I think," she said so quietly he almost couldn't hear her breathy voice, "that I—" She cut herself off, her lips still parted around her unsaid words.

Heat built in Ethenn's chest as he held her gaze. The blankets grew stifling. "You, what?"

She was silent, her brow pinched. He couldn't tell what made her so hesitant. What could she possibly say that would make this situation any more awkward?

Ilain blinked as though clearing her thoughts. Then she said, "I don't know how Evylin and Jonn do this."

Ethenn frowned in confusion.

"It's so bloody hot," she clarified.

Ethenn laughed. She was right. Sweat beaded along his back, and their body heat made it sweltering under the blankets. "It really is," he said.

"And they always sleep like this," she said incredulously. "With even more clothing than we have now."

"It's baffling," he agreed.

"I don't think I can sleep this way."

He narrowed his eyes. "Do you want me to sleep on the floor?"

"No," she said, disappointment evident. "If we're not going to sleep together, I have an empty bed in my own room. I could just go back there."

Hearing the reluctance in her tone, Ethenn knew she didn't want to leave. For some reason, even if it were only to test the validity of their marriage, she wanted to stay with him. And he wouldn't deny her or himself that.

"Hold on," he said, pulling free to rise. First, he removed the comforter from the bed, leaving only the sheet behind. Ilain shivered from the sudden rush of cold air, but he knew it would only be temporary. Then he reached up and pulled his shirt over his head, forcing himself not to consider that he was half-naked in front of her.

When he turned back, Ilain lay there, staring at him, wide-eyed. "Wow," she said, the word drawn out. "You're very . . . muscular."

Ethenn glanced down at his chest. "Yes." He lifted the sheet to join her, then paused. "Is this all right?"

She nodded with a little too much enthusiasm.

Cautiously, he lay back down, feeling the surge of magic rise suddenly wherever their skin made contact. It took some time for them to adjust, their mingling breath slightly uneven amidst the renewed tension. However, the temperature felt more comfortable, and Ethenn assured himself it was the right decision.

Ilain's fingers brushed his arm, which was draped over his chest on top of the sheet. "What are these?" she asked.

Ethenn flinched, having forgotten about the marks on his forearm. "Oh, uh—" He tried to think of a way to downplay them. "They're scars."

"They look old." She traced the edge of one of the burned stripes. "How did you get them?"

Ethenn shrugged half-heartedly. "Working in my uncle's forge."

"That doesn't make sense."

"Well, hunting was just my primary job. I worked with my uncle when I was in town for extended periods."

"No, not that." Ilain propped herself on her elbow to look down into his face. "You're not clumsy, Ethenn. In fact, you're decidedly known for being the opposite. How did you accidentally burn yourself dozens of times?"

Though Ethenn had said nothing about the scars being accidental, he didn't bother to correct her. "I'm not a very good smith," he deflected.

She rolled her eyes at the noncommittal answer. "Fine," she said, sinking into the mattress again. "I'll let you keep your secrets for now. But know this, Ethenn Loxley: I'm your wife, and that means I'm entitled to know every last detail about your life, even if I have to pry the information out of you."

Closing his eyes, Ethenn forced himself to relax. "I'll look forward to your interrogation," he said.

There was a moment of silence before Ilain nudged him.

His neck turned, peering over at her through half-closed lids.

"Aren't you going to kiss me goodnight?" she asked.

Ethenn smirked, turning back to the canopy. "No."

"Why not?"

"Goodnight, Ilain."

After several seconds, she laid her head next to his, grumbling, "Goodnight, you bloody prude."

Part II: From the Heavens to the Terrae

When I look to the Heavens, I see the complete complexity of the resources spread like a canvas above me.
**Excerpt from Comprehending the Vast Expanse of Infinity
by Highlord Hyraum Grenwoode, Magister of the Order of the Heavens**

It is exceptionally difficult to train a man in magic. Once the wonder and pliability of youth have gone from him, the man gets in his own way. We liken the magic of an adult Mage to the sprout of a tree through rock; the magic will make its emergence, but it will fracture the man in the process.
Highlord Althur Elgur, Magister of the Order of the Age, circa 441

PYRALUNDLIGHT
DEPFAULT
SEVIN
MOUROC
KERAUN
KEALE
NIRAUS
DROUMING
RHUNAUR
COLLOONEY
BROUNES
HARMOUTH
NORSWITCH
MAASTERS
DUNBRIAR
TINDON
LOCLIGHT
EPHRIA CITY

CHAPTER FIFTEEN

39TH OF CHRONOS, 1574

The wan morning light drifted over the rooftops, pale in Deckard's eyes as he stared out the window at the overcast sky. He pressed against the band of his new ring with the pad of his thumb. Ever since the ceremony's end and Ilain's declaration, he'd wanted to remove the talisman. The cold metal stung his skin, irritating him with the reminder that he wasn't just a soldier anymore; he was a Mage. And worse, it meant that they'd been manipulated once again.

Despite his better judgment, Deckard believed Archminister Fishere's sincerity when he said their appointment in the government was a choice of their own. It had been plain in the old man's stern gaze that Ilain had chosen to add that final pronouncement of her own accord at the last second. But that didn't mean he trusted the aims of the Alliance either.

Time and again, the Alliance had twisted and exploited the Ephrian soldiers' dedication. They'd used them. They'd lied to them. And their troop continued to go along with it because they believed that a future free of Blount and Ephren was a better one for their people.

But would the Alliance prove to truly be any better?

After waking an hour earlier, Deckard had risen, his mind too full to remain still. In the darkness, he'd dressed and begun to repack their saddlebags. Now, the bags waited by the door, an outfit sat folded and ready for Evylin on the settee, the room was set to rights, and a pot of tea was steeping on the table.

And through all his tasks, Deckard ruminated.

It wasn't right. This wasn't how things were supposed to be.

The Bonding ceremony had gone well, though the experience left him feeling off-kilter. Already, he sensed and enjoyed the amplified connection to Evylin, though he was still uncertain as to what all it would prove to entail. But what really bothered him was that damn pledge.

Deckard didn't mind commitment to service. Being responsible for others wasn't a problem. From his youth, he'd determined to become an honorable soldier and gentleman who put others before himself. He would happily give his life to make the world a better place.

No, what irked him so much was the suggestion that simply by Bonding, they had somehow become an authority now and, as such, had an obligation to rule and lead because of their power.

The ring chafed on Deckard's finger, and he nudged it again. He didn't want to rule or lead the developing country any more than he wanted to be a Mage. He was a soldier, not a king. He and Evylin weren't superior because of their magic or their Bond. Those qualities didn't give them any divine authority from Allore. This dogma, this rhetoric that the Alliance believed—it didn't line up with the Allorian church in which he'd been raised.

Service, duty, and humility were rewarded. Pride, ambition, and selfishness were folly.

On a matter of principle, Deckard wanted to be a servant, not a sovereign. And this suggestion that Allore created him to be the head of his people as an inevitable matter of course, a politician who governed, a monarch who dictated—he rejected it.

Deckard heard Evylin shifting in the bed. He glanced over his shoulder to see her disappear deeper beneath the blankets. His thumb brushed the ring's band again. It rested snugly on his right ring finger, perfectly made for him.

When they returned to their room the previous night, Evylin had brought his hand to her lips, kissing the moonstone before meeting his gaze. *"No matter what they say,"* she'd whispered. *"No matter what they want. We are one soul now. And in a thousand lifetimes, that is what I'd choose."*

A reluctant smile came to Deckard's lips as he remembered that moment. If given the opportunity to go back, to reject the Bond, he wouldn't take it, even if it meant they'd be forced into leadership. Because now, he knew . . . He understood what it was about the Bond that so enraptured Ilain.

Stepping away from the window, Deckard let the pale, gray light fill the room. The blankets cut a softened silhouette of Evylin's sleeping figure. Only the mussed top of her brown hair peeked from under their folds. He couldn't help smiling as he took a seat on the edge of the bed.

Memories of her, of their Bonding, stirred in his heart. He wasn't sure what he'd expected of the night, but the experience shattered every preconceived notion. First, she'd stunned him in the fierce black gown, her beauty almost too exquisite for him to bear. But more striking was the strength of power he felt radiating off her.

Though it was still new to him, Deckard was slowly growing used to his magic, to the feel of it. He'd discovered it was hot and pulsing, enlivening and urging. It drove him to action, filling him with grandiose desires and compelling him with its might.

Evylin's magic felt nothing like that. Instead, hers was refreshing, the sensation akin to a soft breeze. During the ceremony, he could feel it providing stability, heightening his senses, and offering a startling clarity of the world. He felt more balanced—still motivated to act but with a reduced sense of attachment. Her power didn't drive him with its strength; rather, it enhanced him.

As the sensation of fire and ice had filled Deckard's core, he began to see the assembly hall with overwhelming detail. It gave him a sense of control that he'd never before experienced. And with it, he'd seen Evylin in ways he'd never been able to without the aid of her magic. As the Bonding took hold, he'd taken her in with all his senses, coming to know her like new. It granted him the profound understanding that her physical abilities far exceeded his; her lean muscles and honed skills providing prowess he doubted he'd ever obtain. She smelled like flowers and warmth, like joy and hope. Her cool brown hair refused to be tamed, drifting around her face in little wisps. So many small pieces of her gathered to form a new and complete image of the woman he loved.

As the ceremony concluded, the strength of the power was too much, causing Deckard to lose consciousness, as Ilain had warned. Thom had woken him then by resting a hand on his shoulder. He'd tried to wake Evylin, too, while Deckard recovered from the tremulous hold the magic had over him. But she was too deep in the rapture of its embrace, and it was Deckard who had to wake her.

After the ceremony, the senses that had been sharply heightened had faded just as his magic came to rest, untouched, in his core. But when they'd returned to the privacy of their room, he'd allowed himself to shunt aside the frustration and disappointment of the Alliance's presumptions and admire those details of Evylin's he'd come to discover. As he'd tipped his wife's chin up to kiss the small scar that hid under her jaw, she'd asked through a small laugh what he was doing. He told her without hesitation: He wanted to make amends for missing so much about her.

Now, in the freshness of morning, Deckard reached across to tuck the blanket back.

He leaned down and whispered, "Evie," just before pressing a kiss to her temple. "It's time to wake up."

Evylin stirred but lingered under the blankets. He ran his fingers through her hair over and over, patiently waiting for her to rouse. Finally, her arms slipped free of the blankets as she stretched, yawning.

"Good morning, my love," Deckard said as she squinted up at him.

Evylin grunted in reply, a grimace contorting her face. She closed her eyes and began to retreat again under the covers.

Chuckling, Deckard halted her escape. "We need to leave," he reminded her.

"I'm staying here," she grumbled sleepily.

"I'll miss you, then."

Her hand snuck out to latch onto his wrist, tugging him closer. "Oh, no. You're staying with me."

"Now, that's an idea I quite like," he said with a smile. "Unfortunately, there are eight people who require our company downstairs."

"Tell them to go without us," Evylin insisted. One eye cracked open to peek at him.

At Deckard's patient grin, she huffed. "I don't want to go," she said.

"Why not?" he asked.

Shifting to lie on her stomach, Evylin propped herself onto her forearms. "Because I like sleeping in a bed," she complained. "I like eating good food. I like being with you." She drew her fingers along his wrist. "Only you."

Deckard laced their fingers together. "I like that too."

"So we stay."

He sighed, leaning forward to rest his forehead against hers. "I wish we could."

Evylin leaned into him. "Me too," she whispered.

Knowing they didn't have time for a delay, Deckard allowed himself to give her one gentle kiss. He really did wish they could stay. He wished they could hide away in this safehouse of the Crimson Clover Hotel forever, letting others care for the troubles of the world. This mission of theirs had already asked too much of them. He didn't want to let it take any more of their lives.

At the thought, Deckard clenched his hand, the Bonding ring feeling like a vise on his finger.

"What is it?" Evylin asked.

Deckard averted his gaze, not wanting to admit his selfish thoughts. "Nothing."

Evylin watched him knowingly. "You're worried," she said. "I can *feel* it now."

His throat went dry. *That* awareness was a revelation he hadn't anticipated. Ever since the Bonding ceremony ended, he'd had the uncanny sense that he could feel what

Evylin was feeling. Similar to the way her power heightened her senses in the physical world, this was a heightened awareness that gave her emotions a tangible essence. And while he'd already experienced how the new ability was beneficial, knowing just how she felt, the reverse effect was also a nuisance, revealing *him* to her as well.

Deckard forced a smile to his lips, deflecting. "And I can feel that you're tired."

"Any idiot could tell that I'm tired," she teased, then took his right hand in both of hers. She ran her fingers along the back, lightly tugging on the moonstone ring. "What *is* it?"

Seeing no point in lying, Deckard set his worries free. "This isn't what we agreed to," he said.

Evylin's touch stilled, and a subtle spike of anxiety reached him.

"I'm not disappointed in the Bond, Evylin," he promised. "I'm happy with that. But . . . I feel like Ilain and the Alliance tricked us. Once again."

Staring at their hands, Evylin considered her words before speaking. "I'm not exactly thrilled with them myself," she admitted. "However, I will say . . . I don't think they meant it that way. And I think the pledge might have been more Ilain's doing than the Administration's. Fishere seemed sufficiently uncomfortable when he learned we didn't want it."

Deckard nodded, glad to hear she was as against assuming a leadership position as he was. "He did seem repentant. But that doesn't ease my concern."

Evylin met his stare, listening.

"We are highly valuable to the Alliance's aims," he explained. "You, as a female Warrior, and, to my great shock, me as a Space Mage. It's no secret that we are extremely rare. In order to achieve their goals, they need a Bonded couple of each resource, and they only have one other Space Mage, who is also a male. As we also learned, the last remaining female Warrior unspoken for in the Alliance is Brea. If she isn't willing to Bond with that Space Mage, what then? Do we truly believe their goodness will extend to the collapse of their plans?"

Chewing on the inside of her lip, Evylin's apprehension leeched through her touch. "You think they'll press us into service at the end of this?" she asked.

"They're a government," he replied. "Why wouldn't they?"

"They're a *religiously motivated* government," Evylin corrected. "If they believe their tenets, they are morally obligated not to use force."

"Religion rarely overcomes necessity."

She raised her brow in surprise. "You're sounding rather cynical. That's not like the man I married."

He drew away, not wanting to face that accusation, no matter how lighthearted its intent. "After everything we've been through," he muttered, "I find I'm unrecognizable to myself these days."

Evylin sat up to scoot closer. She set a hand on his cheek, drawing his gaze to her tender smile. "Don't be so dramatic," she said softly. "You're you. You're just an unmatched magical being now too."

Taking heart in her comfort, Deckard leaned into her hand. "And I have you."

The dimples in Evylin's cheeks appeared. "You always had me."

He kissed her palm. "It's a little different now."

"It is," she agreed.

He leaned closer. "It's good," he whispered, "this Bond between us."

"Very."

"I just don't want them to use it against us."

"They can't."

Deckard fixed her with a serious stare. "They *can*," he said, imploring her to caution. "At the end of this, if they truly succeed in bringing down two countries, two monarchies—if they have all eight Relics at their disposal, who is going to stop these people from doing whatever they choose?"

A small smile quirked up the corner of Evylin's mouth. "You?" she suggested.

He gave her a flat stare.

She chuckled. "Jonn, if they're a tyrannical government bent on controlling the world, why would they want two individuals opposed to their schemes set in a place of leadership, holding an all-powerful Relic? You made your position quite clear at the meeting two nights ago. We distrust them. So even if they are tyrants, why would they press us into service?"

Deckard's brow pinched in thought. He tried to work out an argument. If they were tyrants, they'd do whatever it took to reach their own ends. They could threaten Deckard's or Evylin's families or split them up. But in his heart, he knew that wasn't who the Calders were, and they wouldn't support a government that used such means of coercion.

With a sigh, Deckard said, "I don't like it when you're logical."

Evylin's grin grew sly. "Would you like me to be illogical? Very well." She slid closer, draping her arms around his neck, and whispered, "Let's run away together."

"Where shall we go?" he asked, encircling her waist.

She made a grand show of consideration. "Mm. Perhaps we could visit Schon." Her eyes crinkled. "Then you could get drunk on Schonese wine each night, and we'd dance until morning."

"Sounds delightful. But what would we do about the hangovers?"

Evylin shrugged merrily. "Then we'll go to the southern continent, Matra-something."

"Matteire," Deckard corrected, rather proud of his appropriately airy pronunciation of the continent's name.

"Know-it-all."

"I was a good student."

"Of course you were."

Deckard laughed. "And what would we do there?"

"I don't know," she admitted. "I *wasn't* a good student."

His smile grew. "I hear they have lovely beaches with white sand."

"White sand?" Her eyes grew wide then. "Like in the Time Keep?"

"I suppose. The descriptions I've read say that it isn't like our sand, not so coarse and gray but white and powder-like."

"Sounds lovely," Evylin said wistfully. "What else do you know about this place?"

A bashful smile came to Deckard's lips, and he looked down. Her nightdress had slid up, pooling around her legs carelessly. "Well, I once read that the women of Audis, the capital of the southern country in Matteire, swim the southernmost beaches entirely naked."

Evylin immediately guffawed. "My, my, Colonel Deckard!" she exclaimed amusedly. "How scandalous. Are you suggesting you'd like me to swim naked in the company of others?"

"I said no such thing," Deckard replied. "You asked what I know, and I told you."

"And this was part of your studies as a good student, was it?"

"It was extracurricular."

"Mm-hm." She drew herself closer until she was seated on his lap. "Well, if you want to take me to these beaches, you'll have to teach me how to swim."

"I'm not interested in visiting those beaches," he said. "But I'll still teach you how to swim."

"Is that a promise?"

"It is." Deckard set his hand on her thigh, brushing his thumb across her skin. "My life is yours, Evylin. Anything you ask of me, I'll do it. Anywhere you want to go, I'll go. Whatever will make you happy, say the word, and I will give it to you. Three months ago, I promised to serve you until my last breath. Today, knowing our lives will last centuries, I promise you that again. If you said the word, I would leave with you right now—I would take you to the vineyards of Schon, to the beaches of Audis, even to the frozen mountains of Estenoye in the far west."

Her happy smile twitched at the last one, betraying her lack of education about their surrounding continents.

Deckard took her face in his hands then. "Say the word, Evylin," he whispered. "And I will abandon this mission; I will cast aside everything for you."

Drawing in a long breath, Evylin's head tipped forward to rest against his. A full, heart-deep emotion pulsed in the air between them, revealing her joy to Deckard. Her lips parted, brushing his as she replied softly, "Liar."

Abruptly pulling back from her kiss, Deckard stared at her. "What was that?" he asked incredulously.

Unabashed, Evylin smirked. "You are a liar," she said, pronouncing the words with deliberate enunciation.

Hurt by the allegation, Deckard felt his brows draw low. "I am not."

She shook her head derisively. "Don't be upset," she said. "I know you love me, and I know you'd do whatever you could for me, but you're not that selfish. You care about people too much and are too noble to abandon your duty. Even for me."

Gently, Deckard pushed Evylin off him, pulling free of her touch. He didn't want to be reminded of his duty. Nor did he care to be touted as some altruistic paragon of virtue. "We should go," he said flatly and rose from the bed.

"Jonn, don't pout," she said with good-natured humor.

"I'm not pouting," he insisted.

Evylin's mouth lifted in a smirk. "I can feel what you're feeling, remember?"

Deckard sighed. "Yes, all right, I am pouting," he admitted. "But it isn't exactly pleasant to learn your wife views you as a liar."

Her smile softened, and she held out her hands. "Come here."

He did.

Threading their fingers, Evylin knelt on the bed, pulling their hands to her chest. Her amber eyes searched his knowingly. "None of that matters to me," she said. "What I once wanted—the life of adventure you promised to give me—it doesn't matter anymore. Whatever comes, whatever our Bond brings, I am yours, and you are mine. Who cares what life looks like so long as we're together?"

"I care," Deckard said, leaning closer. "I made a promise to you, Evylin. I made a promise to your uncle too. I care because I want you to be happy and to have the life you've always deserved."

The air seemed to dance between them. "I am happy," she promised.

"Are you?" he asked, searching her gaze for the truth. "Or are you just content because we're in love, we've Bonded, and you don't have to worry about losing me?"

"I'm under no illusions that I may not lose you still." Her grip tightened. "But I have chosen to love you and leave behind that fear."

A determined emotion thickened the air as she continued, "There have been too many times in the past that misunderstandings have come between us, when we've let them draw us apart. So let me be perfectly clear: Yes, Jonn, I am happy. Truly and deeply happy."

Struggling to believe her despite the ring of truth in her voice, Deckard nodded, accepting her words despite his reservations.

She tipped her brow up, pressing him. "Are *you* happy?"

Deckard blinked at the unexpected question.

"Or are you angry?" she asked at his hesitation.

That caused his mouth to gape. "Why would I be angry?"

"You seem angry," she said. "I'll admit I'm still new to this 'feeling what you feel' thing, but there is a decided irritation in your . . . aura at the moment."

Deckard sighed. "I'm just concerned."

"About what the Alliance will require of us?"

"Yes."

"Because you promised Auden you'd do whatever they asked?"

He gritted his teeth. "Yes."

"And you think they'll ask us to rule their new country."

"I do."

"And you don't want to rule?"

"Do you?" he asked, certain that she didn't.

Evylin grimaced. "I don't think I'd be very good at it."

"Neither would I."

The look she gave him was hard to read.

"But this is what I do know—" He brushed his thumbs along hers. "We will choose our own destiny, not the Alliance. And if that means I have to go back on my word to Auden, I will because I made a promise to you first. I will do everything in my power to make you happy, no matter what that looks like."

Evylin remained motionless beneath his touch, her gaze softening. A tangle of emotions emanated from her, yet Deckard struggled to decipher them. It was as if several feelings were intertwined, each vying for prominence. He guessed that interpreting the genuine range of a partner's emotions after Bonding required practice.

While he was preoccupied with sorting out her reaction, Evylin didn't wait. She leaned in and kissed him, the motion wild and dangerous. Her hands jerked free of his to clamp onto his neck, her fingers tangling in his hair.

A jolt of energy spiked through Deckard's chest, his magic lurching in reaction. He gripped her hips, trying to push her back. "Evie," he gasped around her amorous kisses. Rejecting her desires was the last thing he wanted to do, but they didn't have time for such exploits. "Evie, as—" He slipped free of her kiss only for her to begin accosting his jaw, cheek, and neck with her affection.

"As much as I'd love to continue this—" He gave a final shove, pushing her back to a seat on the bed while darting away from her touch. "We really have to leave."

Her gaze was fierce. "They'll wait."

Deckard couldn't stop the tremble that went through him as he finally recognized the emotion coursing in the air between them as *desire*. "I'm sure they would," he said weakly. "As I'm sure Rafferty would have a pleasant time guessing at the reason for our tardiness."

Evylin slunk forward on the bed. "Are we late yet?" she asked seductively.

"Not quite."

She smirked. "But we will be."

Deckard wet his bottom lip. "Only if you don't get moving."

"What if I move . . . *slowly*?"

His next words caught at the intonation of her tone. "Then we would be late."

"In that case," Evylin's fingers caught the waistband of his trousers and tugged, "we may as well be a bit later."

CHAPTER SIXTEEN

Evylin was right. It didn't matter that they were late, and Rafferty wasn't even present to notice. In fact, only Thom, Brea, and Auden were on time. His brother and the Warrior were seated by the fireplace playing a seemingly rousing game of chess while they baited one another with clever quips. Auden spoke with the clerk, Maurus, at the desk.

After exchanging their greetings, Deckard set a hand on Thom's shoulder. "I'm going to need the Relic back," he said quietly.

Before the Bonding ceremony, Auden suggested Deckard give the Night Relic to Thom, warning that it could impede the magic needed to solidify the Bond. Not wanting to risk something so important, Deckard hadn't hesitated, knowing his brother would be with them should danger arise. And though Deckard didn't feel the same oppressive weight of the Relic's pull as he'd come to learn any other magical individual would, after wearing it for so long, he was beginning to feel its effects on his emotions. Subtle as it might have been, there was an immediate sense of lightening when he removed it, as though he'd been wearing a heavy cloak over his heart and hadn't even been aware of it. He was grateful for the chance of a break from the pressure, even for one night. But now, it was time to assume the responsibility for it once again.

Readily, Thom tugged open the top buttons of his coat. "I must say, I'm happy to get rid of it," he said, lifting it over his head. "I don't know how you wear this thing all the time. It's a bloody nuisance. I could hardly sleep with it around my neck. Felt like it was choking me."

Across the small chess table, Brea propped her chin on her hand. "Tell me more about how you sleep, *mi'caro*," she teased.

"Perhaps another time," Thom returned casually.

Brea slid a wooden figure forward on the checkered board. "Checkmate."

Thom toppled his king. "And you said you'd win in four moves."

"Seven is acceptable," she returned. "I had to adjust to your chaotic strategy."

"Joke's on you." Thom stood and straightened his collar. "I had no strategy."

Watching their exchange with a level of bemusement, Deckard ensured the Night Relic was well hidden under his clothes. Evylin began asking about the game, never having played chess, as Ethenn and Ilain appeared together. The couple split off; Ilain greeted her brother at the desk while Ethenn joined their group, carrying both his and her saddlebags. Shortly after, Vayden and Isla joined them, having already said their farewells to their daughter in private. Rafferty was the last to make his appearance, yawning and grumbling about their early departure.

Once fully assembled, they went through the back courtyard to the stables, where Coalum had their horses waiting and ready. They loaded up and mounted. Then Deckard covered Auden, Ilain, and Evylin in a shroud, taking extra care to place it more securely around them based on the training he'd received from Lord Obel. After offering tips on improving his connection to Night, making his work less "sloppy," Obel gave Deckard three books on Space magic and one thin volume on the particulars of ghosts and related issues regarding Night magic. While the reading didn't excite Deckard, he was pleased to know there was a hope of mastering his powers.

With no further ado, they made their way out of Mouroc, leaving behind the city. Deckard had almost anticipated a send-off from the Alliance but realized that any grand affairs might attract unwanted attention. They were in the capital city of Wauld after all. He felt a twinge of guilt at not properly expressing his thanks to Emmaas, Jarrad, and all the Mages who'd assisted in their Bonding ceremony last night. But then he thought that the success of their mission might be gratitude enough.

The overcast Waulden sky lent a gray haze to the city's crowded streets. Merchants prepared their wares while men, women, and children ambled or hurried through the cobbled and dirt pathways. After nearly an hour of working their way through the gates and sectors of Mouroc, they finally made it free of the city walls, exchanging its buzzing hubbub for the silence of the road.

After a mile of travel, they slowed their pace, and Deckard released the shroud. They adjusted their ranks, Deckard and Auden taking the front to guide their journey east. It was odd seeing three additional members amongst their ranks. Some of the troop remained quiet during the early morning, the cold nip of rain on the wind. They'd all drawn their hoods up, obscuring their faces from the view of oncoming riders. While only Deckard, Rafferty, and Ilain were much for morning conversation in the past, it seemed that Brea and Vayden shared their chipper mood. The pair rode together, talking comfortably while Isla slumped in her saddle, evidently still shaking off the night's sleep.

The split in moods didn't do much to divide the group, however. Just behind Deckard and Auden, Evylin and Thom rode—infrequently exchanging quiet words—followed by Brea and Vayden, then Ilain, Isla, Ethenn, and Rafferty. But as the hours passed, spirits lifted, and conversation became far steadier amongst the whole of the troop.

His demeanor more wakeful, Auden turned to Deckard as they rode. As they'd only shared conversation to determine their direction up until that point, Deckard expected the highlord to offer some advice or suggestion for their continuation on the road. However, the Mage surprised him by saying, "I wanted to offer an apology to you, Jonn."

Startled, Deckard's head whipped over to see Auden's serious green stare under the shadow of his hood. "A twofold apology," the highlord continued. "First, on behalf of my sister for last night's . . . misunderstanding."

Though he bristled at the memory, Deckard dipped his chin in acknowledgment.

"Ilain's impetuosity has gotten her into trouble more times than I can count," Auden said with a good-humored lilt that didn't quite ease his nervous expression. "After forty-three years, you'd think she'd have learned to hold her tongue, but Fire has its way of relaxing one's sense of subtlety."

"If you're concerned that her presumptions will alter our dedication to this mission, you needn't be," Deckard promised. "While neither Evylin nor I care to become monarchs, we consider this present duty to be ours just as much as you do."

Auden paused before speaking again with a careful inflection. "You would not be monarchs, but that's beside the point. As Archminister Fishere said, while those of us in the Alliance would greatly appreciate your consideration of the offices of chancellor and commander, it is not required of you. Ilain is just under the assumption that anyone would want the honor of the position."

Though Deckard was ready to accept the apology, Auden cleared his throat, stalling his reply. "Additionally," the Mage added, "it brings a worry to my mind that I feel I must address with you."

Caught further off guard, Deckard listened as the man turned toward the road with a lowered chin. The drizzle of raindrops collected on his wool hood before slowly beginning their descent down to his back. "Several weeks back, I coerced you into an unjust promise in exchange for Evylin's accompanying me on our trip into Dunneshead," he admitted. "Frankly, I was annoyed that you were averse to my teaching and that both of you were so against Bonding. Furthermore, I'd become rather agitated with our situation in Wauld and the immature relations amongst our troop."

Auden looked up at him again with something like wry amusement. "It may be easy to forget with my youthful appearance, but I am nearly forty-five. Watching others blunder through romantic entanglements and illogical bouts of emotion is quite draining to my sensibilities. And though I love my sister dearly, she is prone to exacerbating such situations.

"I'd grown tired of seeing your relationship with Evylin struggle unnecessarily under the weight of her grief," the highlord explained. "I was perturbed with my sister's and your brother's childish repartee as a means of discouraging poor Ethenn's affection. I subscribe to the belief that one should be open with others when it comes to matters of moral or human concern. Yet, in finding myself surrounded by those who seemed determined to ignore the basic principle of communication, I was put out."

Pressing his lips together, Deckard fought the urge to defend his and Evylin's situation. She'd been grieving. While he would have been more than happy to have open communication about their feelings and her struggles, it would have been callous of him to pressure her into such a vulnerable conversation before she was ready. And while it would have been preferable for her to be open with him, he couldn't blame her for her fear when she'd lost so much.

With a sigh, Auden concluded, "With that understanding of my mental state at the time, I hope you can better appreciate the frustration that drove me to my fallacy. I should not have pressed you to promise your life to the Alliance. It was wrong of me, and I hope that you can forgive me for it."

Though Deckard knew he shouldn't be surprised by the request, he found himself staring blankly at the man in shock.

To which Auden appended, "Please know that I wholly release you from my unreasonable request."

An unexpected relief filled Deckard's lungs. Auden was freeing him from his promise. He was no longer beholden to joining the Alliance or their aims for him.

"Thank you," Deckard said with a new appreciation for the man who rode beside him. "And I do forgive you. I recognize the frustrations you felt, and while I never approved of your cajoling, I do understand the urge. We were all under a great deal of stress during those days."

Auden nodded. "That we were."

The men shared a compassionate smile, and Deckard thought he could sense a weight being lifted between them. It was as though that promise had enacted a barrier, causing the pair to hold equal distrust and dislike for the past three and a half weeks. And now, at last, they were free to be comrades again.

The troop rode on through the dreary afternoon. Over the course of the day, their chatter grew so loud that Deckard found himself overwhelmed by their numbers. At any given time, he overheard five separate conversations happening. Each drew his attention away from the person before him. After two months of growing accustomed to their much more subdued party, the cacophony felt outrageous.

At last, they set up camp a mile outside a village, the early spring sun that had emerged in the late afternoon still bright in the sky. The Ephrians and Calders readily began their old routine of setting up camp, but Vayden, Isla, and Brea looked to Deckard for direction, which suddenly made him realize that he didn't have jobs for them. Everyone else had created a pattern over the last few months, knowing exactly where their roles lay. Now, the seven original members of their party fell back into the rhythm of traveling together, which left the three newcomers decidedly on the outside.

Still, Deckard needed to assign them something to contribute to the evening's preparations. So he requested that Isla assist Ilain with gathering supplies for a fire, directed Vayden to assist Rafferty with seeing to the horses, and sent Brea with Ethenn and Evylin.

"A Warrior hunting party, eh?" Rafferty said with a smirk. "You lot had better bring us a banquet."

With her new bow in hand, courtesy of the Alliance, Evylin smirked. "We'll see what we can do," she said, then followed Ethenn and Brea into the woods.

The rest of the men set up the five two-person tents around the camp. As the weather was improving, they didn't need to be right next to the heat of the fire, so they were able to space the tents out nicely, giving privacy to the two married couples.

When their task was done, they readily accepted their break to sit by the now-merrily burning fire and rest.

"So," Rafferty said, dropping down beside Thom as he winked at Ilain, "what's it like being with a man half your age?"

"Rafferty," Deckard warned, but Ilain waved him off.

"When I'm with him in the way you mean," she said with airy haughtiness, "I'll be sure to let you know."

Rafferty leaned over to nudge Thom. "You said they were canoodling last night," he said as though in accusation.

Thom shrugged. "I simply said he was too busy to drink with us."

"You made other implications."

"You heard what you wanted to hear."

Deckard moved the conversation to a more appropriate subject and turned to Isla and Vayden. "Did I hear correctly that your daughter is returning to stay with her grandparents?"

"Yes, Reyana will stay one more night in Mouroc under the care of the Alliance before traveling south with some of our friends," Isla said.

"How do you do that?" Thom asked, then clarified, "Part with your daughter for so long."

Vayden and Isla exchanged a weighty look. "With great difficulty," he replied. "But we know that what we're doing is providing a better future for her and—one day—for her own children. So we do it trusting that Allore will grant us and her grace to fulfill his purposes."

Deckard sat across from Vayden, curious about the man's seemingly deep faith. He'd always been taught that Wauldeners were heathens, piteous and villainous wretches who worshipped false gods. But during all their time with the Calders, they'd come to discover that Ephren had contorted the truth. While there were a great deal of Waulden people who worshipped the Mages as deities themselves, not an insignificant few still held to the founding religion of their world. And Deckard was discovering with some discomfort that they held these beliefs with even more piety than most Ephrians.

Such faith confused Deckard in light of other things he'd witnessed. While the members of the Alliance proclaimed their dedication to Allore and seemed quite passionate in their professions, he struggled to accept it as truth. Not when they were wholly bent on conquering the nations and willing to do whatever it took to secure their new reign. How far would the Alliance go to secure their aims?

"I've got a question," Rafferty said, and they all gave him a wary look. "Perfectly innocent, I swear."

"Go on," Isla said.

"Your daughter," he said, motioning between the couple. "She's three-quarters Waulden, right?"

"Correct."

He pointed straight at Isla. "And you're a Mage."

"I am."

"So your daughter could be, too, right?"

Isla shrugged. "Technically, she could. However, she's been tested many times with no sign of magic. And it isn't likely, anyway."

"Why not?" Thom asked.

"Magic isn't necessarily genetic," Ilain clarified. "There are records that indicate the first Mages and Warriors bore exclusively magical children, but that was likely to ensure the continuation of the population."

"Some theorize," Auden added, "that it was possible to guarantee magical offspring due to the marital rite that Allore himself enacted over them."

"Yes," Ilain confirmed. "Though the more I study Bonding, the more I'm convinced that *it* was the marital rite Allore instituted. If that's the case, then there's a chance any children born out of a Bonded union would be sure to be magical, but it's been so long since any couple has Bonded, we can't be sure."

Deckard frowned. "So you're saying that a Bonded couple might only have magical children?" he asked, unsure whether or not that was a better outcome. He'd considered the implications of a magic-prolonged life on his dreams of fatherhood. It would be difficult to outlive your children, watching them grow old and die while you remain young and virile. But it would be equally difficult watching them carry the same burden of responsibility that came with magic, the same knowledge that they, too, were destined to watch those they loved fade long before them.

"Maybe," Ilain said. "But it doesn't seem likely. Think about the implications of that: If Bonded couples only had magical children, they would have centuries to reproduce, potentially birthing dozens of children. Eventually, that would overwhelm the populace with magic."

While Deckard was uncomfortably intrigued at the prospect of continuing the conversation, the Warriors returned from their hunting trip, each with a brace of birds. With Ethenn's hunting skills, Brea's keen eyes, and Evylin's quick ability to learn, it had only taken them a short time to secure enough meat for the next few days of travel. While Ilain, Auden, and Vayden helped the Warriors with the butchering, Rafferty praised their efforts.

"No one else is allowed to hunt for us again," he proclaimed.

When Deckard took the seat next to Evylin as she plucked the feathers from one of the fowls, she gave him a self-mocking grin. "I've never felt so useless in my life," she said. "Those two are scary with a bow."

Across from them, Brea split open a carcass. "Every Warrior has their individual strengths," she said with an instructor's tone. "And as you were not trained in archery, it seems it's taking you longer to get acquainted with the skill. Though, you may never take to it. I hear you are very impressive with a sword, which is a skill I have always been lacking in."

"Really?" Evylin asked. "I thought Warriors were predisposed to be good at fighting."

Brea smiled. "I'm not saying that I couldn't beat every single man in this camp in a duel," she said. "However, should I come upon a highly trained Warrior who is more proficient in swordplay than I, I would assuredly struggle. I'm not built for it. I'm too short and scrawny."

"You're anything but scrawny," Vayden said.

"I am trim; I have muscle, yes." Brea pointed her blade at him. "But . . . muscle alone does not equal strength. My figure is too slim and too small to add mass adequately. No matter what I do, I will never be built like Evylin. She is tall and agile, and you can see the roundness of her musculature, indicating the strength she carries."

"That you can," Rafferty said slyly.

Deckard gave him a withering glare.

Rafferty snickered. "Just complimenting your wife's figure, Colonel."

"I'd rather you keep your eyes off her figure, Corporal."

Evylin traded a plucked bird for a feathered one, beginning her task yet again. "Are you an archer, then?" she asked Brea.

"I am proficient in many styles of combat," Brea said. "I often carry a bow on my horse, and I always carry a short sword for close combat. However, my preferred weapon is a staff."

Ethenn looked up, curious. "I've never seen anyone fight with a staff before," he remarked.

"I'd be happy to teach you," Brea said. "It can be quite fun, though rarely as deadly. It is a more common practice in Tanemisa, the free states below Schon. I trained with one of their best staff masters when I was a young woman. He wasn't a Warrior, but he was impressive all the same."

"Could you teach the rest of us?" Thom asked.

"Maybe," she said, giving him a snide grin. "If I have the time, *mi'caro*."

"*Te'á envela, Breata,*" Isla said in a singsong tone.

"*Ai'á virtida, Islaren,*" Brea returned.

"That's going to get annoying," Thom said, and Deckard couldn't help smiling. Though he didn't begrudge the women the use of their native language, he also found it frustrating not to know what they were saying.

Brea filleted a pigeon's breast from its ribs in one steady slash. "If you want to learn Schonese, I'll teach you," she said.

"Really?" Thom asked.

"Would you teach all of us?" Evylin added.

Brea smiled. "I don't have the time to teach all of you. Though I'm sure you'll all pick something up here or there." She shook her head. "In the morning, we will begin our training—you, Ethenn, and I."

"We have to leave early each morning," Auden interrupted, "to ensure we make it to our next stop quickly."

Brea sent him a bland stare. "We will wake at first light—"

Evylin and Ethenn both frowned.

"For exercise," she explained. "Then, when we make our stop each evening, we will get to the real work."

Thom nodded. "That's when we normally train."

Brea gave him an amused look. "You won't be joining us."

"What?" Thom and Rafferty said together.

"Warriors need special training with those who challenge them," Brea said. "If they aren't constantly challenged, they stagnate. Since Ethenn, Evylin, and I possess the advantage of magic, we can push one another no matter what. As no one else in the camp is a Warrior, no one else is invited to our training."

"Well, that's—" Thom cut himself off, grumbling under his breath.

"Who are we supposed to train with, then?" Rafferty asked.

"Relax, Rafferty," Deckard said. "You'll train with me. And Hewitt."

"Eh!" Rafferty said happily as Evylin exclaimed, "What?"

Deckard brushed a comforting hand over her back. "Speaking of," he said, rising, "Evylin and I need to speak with him. We'll be back shortly."

Readily, Evylin hopped up at his side while the rest of the group turned away, and Rafferty immediately began pestering Brea with questions about her life in Schon.

As they walked into the trees, Evylin wove her fingers through his. The sunset peeked through the clouds, filtering through the thick canopy above their head. Though the air had smelled of rain all day, it had yet to fall. Still, the perpetual chill led them to keep their cloaks on their shoulders, though with their hoods down.

"I still can't believe I get to see him again," Evylin said, her voice tremulous. "There's so much to tell him and so little time. . . ."

Knowing she wasn't referring to the shortness of their evening, Deckard drew her closer to his side. "We'll make the most of what time we have left," he promised. "I can't keep him around at every moment, but I can make him part of most things. I have the strength for that now, especially with the Night Relic."

"Do you think it's wise, though?" she asked as if nervous to hear the true answer. "We know now that Night isn't your first resource, but . . . Isn't it still dangerous, connecting with it too much?"

"Despite Auden's concerns, the use of Night magic does not ensure a descent into madness." He squeezed her hand in reassurance. "Trust me. I can summon Hewitt without risking my sanity."

Visibly, Evylin relaxed, and the air around her eased. "He'll be happy for us," she said. "And I think he'll approve of our Bonding, even if it takes some convincing."

Deckard smiled. "I think you're right. If nothing else, he'll be glad to know it makes you happy and keeps you safe."

She nudged his side. "It keeps you safe too."

"And it makes me happy," he agreed. "But Hewitt won't care about that. He only cares about you."

"Don't say that."

He glanced at her, bemused by the flare of some sharp emotion emanating from her. Thinking it likely from embarrassment, he continued to tease her. "It's true. He's told me many times that he doesn't care what happens so long as you're taken care of. I'm just the best way to accomplish that."

Evylin came to an abrupt halt, expression serious. "Don't say that," she repeated.

Trying to determine her true feelings, Deckard studied her carefully. "Evylin, it doesn't bother me," he said, wondering if she was concerned for him. "He's your uncle. You two were closer than I've been with . . . Well, with anyone but you. My relationship with Hewitt has always been tied to you—it's always been about you."

Evylin pulled away from him. "Why does everything have to be about me?"

"What are you talking about?"

"Everything is always about me," she said with a huff. "Your relationship with Hewitt. Our future. According to Isla, even Blount is obsessed with me, no matter if he is mentally unstable. Why can't things ever be about someone else?"

Deckard couldn't help smiling. "Because we love you."

Evylin shook her head. "Blount doesn't love me. He wants to use me."

"What do you want me to say?" He shrugged. "Hewitt and I both have one aim: making you happy. Why is that a bad thing?"

She met his gaze with a strange adamance. "Maybe I don't want to be the one everyone sacrifices for. Maybe, for once, I want to be the one taking care of you."

Deckard frowned, confused by the sentiment. "So long as you're happy, I have no needs."

Slowly, a bewildered smile came to her lips. "You selfless idiot," she whispered fondly. Then she stepped forward, rolled onto the balls of her feet, and kissed him. "I love you."

"I love you," he replied, slightly perplexed by her behavior. "Now, do you want to see your uncle or not?"

Her smile grew brighter. "I do," she said.

"Come with me, then."

Deckard led her a short distance forward until he found a good, secluded spot. They walked together to a giant, overgrown tree with dry roots where they could sit. The light was growing dimmer, but they were less than five minutes from the camp. Even if they stayed out for an hour, they'd easily find their way back.

Summoning Hewitt's ghost took minimal effort. Deckard had grown so used to it over the past month that it was nearly second nature. He merely willed it, and the man was before them with his unruly beard, leather armor, and crossed arms.

"About bloody time," Hewitt said, standing at the base of the tree across from them.

"Sorry," Deckard replied. "Things got . . . messy."

At his side, Evylin stared at her uncle, joy, sorrow, and longing all wrapped around her like thread around a spool. "You're here," she breathed.

Hewitt's steely gaze landed on her, a soft smile on his lips. "And you're here," he said, gravelly tone softened. "I'm glad for that."

Catching the shimmer of tears in Evylin's eyes, Deckard took the initiative for her. "We have quite a lot to tell you," he said.

Hewitt studied them, taking in their closeness. "You're staying together," he said more than asked.

Evylin let out something between a sob and a laugh.

"We are," Deckard confirmed.

"While I hate to second-guess you," Hewitt raised his brow, giving Evylin a pointed stare, "you have fooled me once. There's no backing out, is there?"

This seemed to dry up Evylin's tears. She straightened her shoulders. "Not that it's any of your business," she said sharply, "but no, there's not."

Hewitt turned to Deckard, brow raised. "No?"

Deckard chuckled nervously. "Certainly not."

"Good." Hewitt drew up then, giving them each a firm nod. "I'm glad to hear you've gotten your affairs in order. Now, tell me about this mess you've gotten yourselves into and why it's taken you so damn long to talk to me again."

Over the next long while, Deckard and Evylin explained the past several days. The sun set, casting the sky in a deep purple blue. The forest grew colder, and Deckard wrapped his arm around Evylin to keep her warm. They talked through their time as Renaul's captives, their escape, their time with the Alliance, and their Bonding. Hewitt was wary of the concept of the Bond but accepted it readily enough. He wanted to meet Brea to ensure she was fit to train Evylin and Ethenn. He found Deckard's revealed classification as a Space Mage uninteresting so long as it didn't affect his ability to release him. When Deckard assured him that it would not, he went on to explain the process of summoning and releasing ghosts.

"I want to keep you around in the meantime, though," Deckard said. "I'd like you to train Thom, Rafferty, and myself. Maybe Vayden, too, if he'd like to join. And I want you to spend as much time with Evylin as you can. I'll have to be there, or at least nearby, but we only have a few weeks left, and I want to make the most of our time with you."

Hewitt nodded, a rare smile coming to his lips. "I'm proud of you," he said. "Of both of you."

Deckard was surprised at how much the praise made his heart swell.

"I shouldn't have this extra time," Hewitt said. "I know that. The dead are supposed to be dead. But I am thankful for it, if only because I get to see you happy, my Evie. I get to see you live the dream you and Ryen shared. And to me . . ." He shrugged. "That's worth everything."

Evylin cried then, and Deckard held her since Hewitt couldn't.

Once her tears dried, Deckard looked up at the ghost. "Would you like to come back with us?" he asked.

Hewitt nodded slowly, a strange softness in his steely gaze. "I would."

CHAPTER SEVENTEEN

In Deckard and Evylin's absence, the troop ate dinner and relaxed around the camp. Thom found the additional company of the Alliance members to be highly welcome. He'd not expected to like them so much. Though he supposed that after months of travel with Auden and Ilain, he ought to have anticipated enjoying the company of their older brother as well.

The newcomers fit in easily with the troop. Vayden and Auden sat to the side, talking about Alliance happenings over the last two months. Isla spoke comfortably with Ilain and Ethenn as the couple sat awkwardly next to one another. Ilain pressed so close to the young man's side that her leg regularly brushed against his, and his jaw kept flexing as though he were fighting the urge to run into the woods, which was one of the subjects that Thom, Rafferty, and Brea discussed with great mirth on their side of the fire.

"I have to tell you, my lovely lieutenant," Rafferty said, leaning against his saddle, which was propped behind him on the ground, "I hadn't expected you to be quite so companionable."

"No?" Brea said.

"No," Rafferty confirmed. "What with your logical speech the other night, I thought you'd be a right stick in the mud like Audy over there."

At the nickname, Auden paused mid-sentence to glare in Rafferty's direction before returning to his conversation.

Brea twirled her fork between her fingers. "When it comes to the craft of war, I am a stick in the mud," she said. "But I'm a Warrior as well. Life gets boring when I'm not working, so that means I have to make my own entertainment."

Thom expected Rafferty to make a lewd comment about the sorts of entertainment she might enjoy, but the weasel was already distracted by something else. "Oy," he called, gaze directed to the far side of the camp. Everyone looked up at his exclamation, but his focus was wholly on where Ethenn had rested his arm behind Ilain's back. The posture wasn't exactly affectionate, but it was certainly more familiar than the young man had been in the past.

"Getting rather cozy, aren't we?" Rafferty teased.

Ethenn's neck began to flush red, while Ilain showed no signs of discomfort. "It behooves a husband and wife to get comfortable with one another," she said, amused.

"This is Loxley we're discussing, my fine lady," Rafferty noted. "Women are a frightening mystery to his fragile sensibilities."

"Clearly," Ilain said with haughty indifference, "you don't know him very well."

The insinuation caused Thom to smirk while Rafferty sniggered and Ethenn blushed a deeper shade.

"She didn't mean it like that," the young man asserted.

"How did she mean it?" Rafferty asked.

Thom shoved the man's shoulder. "Leave them alone," he said. "It's bad enough we have to watch them snuggle. I don't want to hear about Loxley's conquests."

Rafferty rolled his eyes but turned back to Brea, content to find a new distraction.

Ethenn held Thom's stare for an extended second, an understanding passing between them. Perhaps Thom had progress to make, but their friendship was on its way to being mended.

Turning back to the fire, Thom smiled to himself. After all this time, he was finally improving. Becoming a better man was hard. Forgiving himself for his mistakes was even harder. But he thought he was getting the hang of it at last.

A few moments later, Deckard and Evylin returned to camp with Hewitt's ghost in tow. Deckard explained his plan to keep the ghost around in the evenings. Thom was grateful for that. Between their months in the Ephrian Army and traveling with the Calders, he'd come to see Hewitt as a mentor, just as they all had. The ex-general's gruff demeanor and blunt conversation were often abrasive, but Thom found his manner strangely reassuring. He had never questioned where he stood with Hewitt. From the start, he'd always known that they were soldiers, not equals but like-minded men all the same. And that made Thom feel understood in a way he rarely had in life.

After introducing Hewitt to Vayden, Isla, and Brea, the ghost proceeded to accost their new Warrior with questions. He wanted to ensure she was fit for training his niece and his men. Brea answered with confidence, unfazed by the intensity of Hewitt's gaze.

Thom hadn't realized how much he missed Hewitt until that moment. Even when he'd been tough on Thom, even when he'd said things Thom hadn't wanted to hear, Hewitt had made him a better man. And in his desperation to prove himself, Thom felt he needed his mentor all the more.

When Deckard announced he was going to release Hewitt for the night, Thom quickly spoke up. "Wait. Could I—?" He hesitated as everyone looked at him. "Sorry, I was just wondering," he met Deckard's gaze with a pleading expression, "if I could speak with Hewitt alone for a moment?"

Deckard and Hewitt exchanged a look. "I don't see why not," the ghost said.

"I can only send you so far away from me with my power's strength," Deckard warned.

"You can accompany us," Thom offered.

Deckard shook his head. "That's not necessary." He pointed to the trees where he and Evylin had walked earlier. "I'll send him just behind that oak tree."

With that, Hewitt disappeared from sight, and Thom rose. "Thank you," he muttered as he hurried past Deckard.

Ducking into the trees, Thom found Hewitt exactly where Deckard had said he'd be. The burly man stood in the shadows, looking the same as he always had. It made Thom's heart swell and break all at once.

"Well?" Hewitt said impatiently. "What did you need?"

Thom smirked. "You never change, do you?"

"Not if I can help it."

He laughed, then sobered immediately. "I wanted to apologize," he said. "You were right the other day. I betrayed your trust—and Evie's and Deckard's. I was foolish and arrogant, and if I could take it all back . . ."

Hewitt watched him coldly, his eyes like steel. "You always were too conceited to see past your own nose." He sighed then. "Just like I was."

Thom looked up at him, confused.

"I'm the second son, too, remember?" Hewitt said. "I spent my life as the lesser. All you lot like me now, but you didn't know me back then. It's a wonder I ever convinced Irena to give me a chance. I was foolhardy, arrogant, and violent. And I made even more mistakes than you in my day."

Thom shifted on his feet, wondering how that was possible. Since the day he joined the army, all he'd ever heard about General Hewitt Glaas was that he was a military master, a veritable legend. And then he was gone, leaving a gaping hole in the army's command. Imagining such a man to be a screwup like him. . . .

"What changed?" Thom asked. "If you were really as bad as all that, how did you become . . . *this*? How did you stop making mistakes and become a legend?"

Hewitt frowned as though he'd never considered it. "There was a draft," he said. "I was conscripted, and for once in my life, I had a purpose, somewhere I could put the aggression I felt and turn it into something good."

Nodding, Thom took in his words. *A purpose.* He couldn't say he'd ever felt he had a purpose either. He'd always just lived, never thinking of how he might do more. Deckard had a purpose. Since birth, it seemed that Deckard sought out ways to serve, to be of use to the world around him. All the while, Thom looked for ways that others could serve him.

Perhaps that was the key. If Thom could discover a purpose and a means to impact those around him, he might finally have a chance to become a man of value.

"Could you help me?" Thom asked the ghost. "I want to do that—find my purpose and do something good in this world. But the army didn't do that for me. Even this mission hasn't done that for me. And if saving our country isn't enough to give me that . . . I don't know what will."

Hewitt tugged at his beard. "I can try to help you," he said. "But in the end, you're the only one who can answer that question. What is more and what is less to *you*? That's the answer you'll have to find. Because it's different for us all."

The charge was weighty. It felt impossible. If almost twenty-eight years hadn't given Thom a direction, how was he supposed to suddenly figure it out for himself?

"Can't you just . . . *tell* me what I should do?" Thom asked, knowing the answer.

Hewitt didn't bother to reply, raising a bushy eyebrow instead.

Thom sighed. "Yeah, I get it." He gave a sour smile. "Thanks. It's nice having you around again."

"I'd say the same, but then I'd be a liar."

A deep laugh burst from Thom's core. "You always were a blighter. Don't know why anyone likes you."

The smallest grin tugged at the corner of Hewitt's mouth. "Me neither."

"All right, old man," Thom said. "I'll leave you alone."

"Thom."

He stopped in his tracks, turning back.

Hewitt stared at him, something like pride in his gaze. "She chose you too," he said. "And so did I."

The comment warmed Thom from the inside out. And he knew it was true. Perhaps Evylin had chosen Deckard as a husband, but she'd chosen Thom as a brother. Perhaps Hewitt had chosen Deckard to care for his girl, but he'd chosen Thom as well, albeit in a different way. The truth was that he'd never been rejected. He'd simply failed to see the value in the role he'd been offered.

Walking back into the camp, Thom's eyes immediately found Deckard and Evylin sitting together by the fire. They were eating their dinner, lukewarm from their late arrival, both of them smiling as though they weren't fighting to end a war. Deckard kept putting his slice of bread in Evylin's bowl, and she kept returning it to him in some secret battle of goodwill.

A pleased smile came to Thom's lips. Perhaps they were where he'd find his purpose—not in securing a future for himself or in pleasing his own personal designs but in protecting his family. A little over three months ago, Evylin had brought an opportunity into his life: the chance to care for his brother in a way he never had before. If there was one purpose, one goal he could accept without hesitation, it was ensuring the happiness of Deckard and Evylin. He could keep them safe and help secure their future. Their mission was fraught with danger. But Thom would readily accept the role as their protector. He would see them through this, no matter what.

Thom resumed his seat near Rafferty and Brea. While Rafferty was busy chattering to Evylin, Brea sat with her legs crossed, balancing a blade on the tip of her finger, a contemplative expression on her face. Thinking he shouldn't distract her, Thom turned, intending to join Rafferty's conversation, but then she spoke.

"Your ghost friend is strangely revered," Brea remarked quietly, eyes still on the dagger.

"Hewitt has a way of demanding people's respect." Thom motioned to the blade. "That's a neat trick."

Brea let it tip forward, then caught the handle in midair. "It's easy when you're a Warrior."

Thom huffed. "Seems most things are easy when you're a magical being."

She gave him a flat look, but Deckard spoke before she could respond. "We should keep watch while we're still in Wauld. There are two per tent, so we can sit up in pairs. If we split the night into quarters, one pair can skip a night, giving us all the opportunity for a solid night of sleep at least once every few days."

"Isla and I can take the first watch," Vayden offered.

"That's very sacrificial of you," Rafferty said snidely. "Seeing as that's the best shift."

Isla raised her brow. "We'll take the third shift, then," she replied.

"We'll take the second," Deckard said.

"Guess I'll take fourth," Thom said. "You with me, Raff?"

"Sounds delightful, Thommy-boy."

"I hate to break up the boy's club," Brea interrupted. "But I'll be staying with you, *mi'caro*."

"What?" Thom and Deckard asked together.

Almost everyone in the camp looked at Brea in question. Ilain muttered something under her breath, and Auden sighed.

"I'm not going to accost you, Breata," he said in irritation.

"Forgive me if I don't want to give you more opportunities to try to convince me to Bond with you," Brea remarked flatly.

Auden turned to Vayden as though his brother could resolve the issue.

Vayden laughed. "You've done this to yourself," he said unmercifully.

"I fail to see the problem," Thom said. "We have an even number here. Raff and I will share a tent, Auden can go with Ethenn, and—"

"You're forgetting," Ilain interjected, "that Ethenn and I are betrothed."

Thom blinked, then chuckled nervously. "You're not seriously going to sleep together, are you?"

"You Ephrians." Ilain rolled her eyes. "We already *have*."

"You said—"

Ilain cut off Rafferty's accusation. "We've shared a bed," she corrected. "Like any husband and wife would."

Rafferty's white-blond brow rose. "A husband and wife would shag," he said. "Unless you're the Colonel and Eve."

Deckard and Evylin sent the weasel a withering look while Thom wiped a hand over his smirk.

"Shut up, Rafferty," Ethenn said tersely. His eyes kept darting toward Vayden and Auden, a clear streak of red creeping above his collar. "Ilain and I are sharing a tent. That's the end of it." Then he turned to Deckard. "We'll take the first watch."

Reticent to agree, Deckard glanced between the couple and Thom and Brea. "I'm not sure . . ." He paused, seeking Evylin's advice with a single look.

She shrugged dramatically. "Don't ask me."

"Look," Brea spoke up again, "this isn't an issue. I'm a soldier. I've shared *closed* tents with men before. It isn't as though my virtue is at stake here."

"Because it's already been compromised?" Rafferty asked slyly.

Brea shot him a fierce look. "Why don't you try something and find out?"

Rafferty glanced down at the dagger she still twirled between her fingers. "I'll pass."

Thom snorted, then lifted a hand placatingly to the rest of the troop. "I'm not sleeping with you," he said to Brea.

"Sharing a tent is not the same thing as sharing a bed," she countered. "We will be on separate bedrolls and in full view of the rest of the camp. And should there be any attempts on my person," she gave Thom a teasing look, "I'll have you know that I sleep with five knives at all times."

Rafferty pulled an intrigued face and nudged Thom's side. "Not gonna lie," he murmured, "that's arousing."

Thom tried not to imagine being at the end of one of Brea's knives and turned to Deckard. "It's fine," he said. "We either split a couple, or it's uneven."

"It isn't appropriate," Deckard protested. "You three could share and give her a private tent."

"*Mírce d'Alle*," Brea exclaimed, her accent thick with agitation. "This argument is over. I will share a tent with Thom, or I will sleep under the stars. *Conte?*"

Gathering the context of her final word, Thom nodded. "Got it."

"*Béne.*" She stood then and moved for the tent on the far side of the camp.

Thom pressed his lips together, feeling rather awkward. He glanced across at Auden, the Mage watching Brea's departure with something like frustration on his face. And for the first time, Thom felt sorry for the man's plight. While he couldn't blame Brea for not wanting to live her life knowing she'd been a means to an end, he also couldn't blame Auden for hoping.

While the rest of the troop began preparing for bed, Thom crossed to where Auden crouched, cleaning the cooking pot. He dropped into a squat beside him. "Just so you know," he said, "I didn't mean to make this—"

"You're not to blame," Auden interrupted with a sigh. "I've been trying to get Breata to work with me for the last decade. But I know . . ." A sad smile came to the Mage's lips. He looked down at his hands. "Ilain confessed," he said. "We don't keep secrets from one another, and she told me that you know about Maura."

"I do," Thom admitted.

Auden's vibrant eyes lifted to pierce Thom with determination. "I won't let her languish in the Deep," he said. "Not even if saving her kills me. Can you understand that?"

Though Thom had never been in love—not truly—he nodded. He could understand because he knew without a shadow of a doubt that he would do the same for his brother. "I can."

"Breata won't work with me. I've . . ." A vein flexed in his jaw as he paused. "I've come to accept that. But that doesn't mean I've given up hope."

Thom frowned. "You intend to . . . force her hand?"

"No," Auden said immediately. "If she were to change her mind of her own accord,

I would accept. But I don't hold out hope for that. No, I intend to find another female Warrior, one who is compassionate to my cause rather than hard-hearted."

The bitterness in Auden's words struck Thom with force. The man was dejected and hurting. He wanted to save the woman he loved, though it would mean he could never be with her. And it seemed Allore was conspiring against him, taunting him with the means of her salvation in a Warrior who refused to comply.

Thom patted the man's shoulder once. "Not that I'm much of a help, but. . . ."

Auden nodded at the unfinished sentiment.

Thom began to rise, but Auden caught his elbow. "I've not forgotten," he said.

"Pardon—"

"Ilain tells me everything, remember?" His eyes narrowed. "You helped her. You made her believe you were her friend. Then you betrayed her. If you do it again, it'll be your ghost that Jonn needs to summon."

Thom didn't know how to feel at the threat. It was amusing, startling, and impressive all at once. As an older brother, he could relate to the protective action. As the one being threatened, he didn't appreciate it. And as a man who was working to be better, he accepted it.

With a dry smile, Thom said, "I know." Then he got up and left the Day Mage behind.

Nearly everyone was in their tent, ready for sleep. Ethenn and Ilain sat by the fire still, fixed on their watch. When he passed, Rafferty grumbled that he couldn't believe Thom was leaving him to share a tent with the dreariest member of their troop.

"It isn't as though I had much say in the matter," Thom commented.

"You could have let me sleep with her."

"I wonder why she didn't think of that herself."

Leaving Rafferty to his plight, Thom walked up to the tent where Brea sat, draping her coat over her boots. She'd taken to wearing trousers for their journey, her tucked shirt now hanging loose around her torso. With her short, trim figure, she looked even smaller under the canvas tent. It was hard to remember that she was twice his age. She didn't look a day older than thirty. Though her cutting brown stare bespoke a maturity Thom doubted he'd ever understand.

"I pushed the bedrolls apart," Brea said, a tinge of humor in her tone. "I wouldn't want anyone thinking I intended to have my way with you."

Thom took a seat at the foot of his mattress. "My chastity isn't the one in need of protection," he teased.

She eyed him knowingly. "If ever I find my womanly virtue threatened, I'll be sure to defend it myself."

"I don't doubt that." As he removed his boots, Thom glanced at the camp. No one was paying attention to them, but he lowered his voice anyway. "Can I ask you something?"

"Yes."

"It's . . . indelicate."

"My favorite kind of question."

Thom smirked but kept his gaze averted as he asked, "You're fifty-five?"

"That's a stupid question when I already gave you the answer."

"No," Thom laughed. "That's not the question."

"Then what is?"

He hesitated, grimaced, and forced himself to ask what he wanted to know. "I don't know the Schonese culture, but I'm aware that Wauld is less . . . conservative when it comes to . . . intimate relations."

Brea lifted her chin and scoffed. "You want to know if I've been with a man?"

"You make it sound as though I'm a deviant." Thom ran a hand over his face. "It's just—I can't fathom going fifty-five years without . . ."

"How old are you, Thom? Thirty?" Brea asked, her soft smile taunting.

"Twenty-eight," he said, not bothering to inform her he was technically still a day shy of the age.

She scowled as though disappointed in the truth. "Then you and I are on roughly equal terms in our lifespans," she said. "I am only a quarter Ephrian. This means that, at most, magic will take me to one hundred fifty years. If I'm lucky, I'll only have another sixty."

Thom frowned. "You don't want to live as long as you can?"

"Why should I?" Brea asked and moved on before he could answer. "No, I've not been with a man. Because fifty-five years is nothing when I'm faced with likely a hundred more."

Though it was hard to fathom, Thom thought he understood. Brea was just now in the prime of her life. Perhaps she was lonely, perhaps she wished for love, but she wasn't running out of time, and neither was Thom. They both had at least another decade before the dream of a family was out of the picture.

Which brought up another question . . .

"Can you still have children?" Thom asked.

Brea chuckled. "Magic keeps us young, *mi'caro*. That means I can have children likely into my eighties or nineties."

"Wow." Thom blew a raspberry. "This magic stuff is weird."

"Mm-hm." Brea slipped under the blankets atop her bedroll. "By your previous question, I take it you *have* been with a woman?"

Thom blanched. "I don't want to talk about this anymore."

Her laugh was soft and far more feminine than he would have expected from such a direct woman. "Very well." She leaned back, resting on an elbow as he stretched out a few feet away from her. "Then you can answer a different question for me."

"With pleasure." Thom kept his eyes on the canvas above their heads, unwilling to look at her while they lay so near one another—even if their bedrolls were on opposite sides of the tent. No matter her assertions and comfort, the idea of sleeping next to a woman with whom he wasn't romantically involved made his insides squirm.

"How did you betray your brother and his wife?"

Thom blanched. His gaze darted in her direction, but he remained facing the tent overhead. "What do you—?"

"I listened to your conversation with the ghost," she confessed.

Thom didn't need to ask how. "You Warriors and your eavesdropping," he grumbled.

"It is a fault of mine," she said. "I have this compulsion—this need to know the facts so that I can ensure no one in my company is in danger or a danger. And magic gives me excellent hearing."

"That's a poor excuse for bad behavior."

"Yes. But I don't apologize for it as it's saved my life three times now."

Thom grunted in acceptance. "I told you from the start: I'm known for being a shit. I grew up feeling inferior to my brother, and I let it control my actions many times over. It led me to make a mistake I regret wholeheartedly. Now, I'm trying to make up for it."

"By finding your purpose?"

She really had listened to the whole conversation.

Thom's lips twisted in a self-derisive grin. "Yeah."

Brea was quiet for several seconds, and Thom shifted under the blankets. The dark canvas stretched to blot out most of the sky. Only a sliver of the silver-shot deep purple night was revealed to his gaze. The stars twinkled like beacons of hope, and Thom tried to believe this newfound goal of his wouldn't fail him.

"Purpose can be delusive," Brea finally whispered.

Without meaning to, Thom found himself turning to frown at her. She lay on her side, facing him, with one arm tucked under her head. The barest glow of the fire reached to cast dark brown shadows on her face.

"What do you mean by that?" he asked.

Brea studied his face, her expression flat and unreadable. "Auden has a purpose," she said. "One that drives him wholly and has twisted him into a lonely wretch. If he could let go of Maura, he could find true love and perhaps *still* save her. Ilain has a purpose as well. She is solely focused on Bonding and becoming the Highlady Chancellor of Doorstunds Reach."

Thom's brows drew together at the term, but he didn't interrupt as she continued, "It has filled her with selfish ambition, and now she is betrothed to a man she does not love."

Though Thom knew Ilain did have feelings for Ethenn, he also knew that Brea was right: She didn't love him. She only hoped to love him.

"*I* have a purpose," Brea said coldly. "I have dedicated my life to the Alliance and the cause of Allund because I believe it to be righteous and just. And because of that purpose, I will eventually marry whichever man they tell me to—I will Bond with whichever Mage they choose for me, be it Auden or another I've yet to meet. Because I am dedicated to the Alliance, I will become what I have no desire to be. I will live for extended centuries. I will be a commander, a ruler. And one day, I will come to love the Mage despite myself. All because I have a purpose."

The emotionless manner in which Brea spoke confused Thom. He was so used to hearing Ilain and Auden speak of Bonding with reverence and, as they'd grown closer, so used to seeing Deckard and Evylin together—a perfect depiction of what Mages and Warriors should be—that he couldn't comprehend this distaste for the institution.

But that's when Thom realized the truth. Brea wasn't against Bonding in general. She'd readily supported Deckard and Evylin's Bond. She believed in the Alliance's plans to place Bonded couples into positions of authority—of whatever level that might be. She wasn't opposed to it as a matter of principle.

She was against it for herself.

"You're already in love," Thom realized, and she blinked in surprise. "There's someone else you want to be with, but because you're a Warrior—because of your dedication to the Alliance—you can't be."

Brea didn't answer, but the truth was clear enough in the set of her jaw.

Thom sighed, rolling onto his back to rest an arm over his eyes. "This is shit," he mumbled.

A humorless laugh puffed out of her. "It is."

He looked back at her. "Why don't you just tell them you want to be with someone else?"

"It's what we do in the Alliance," she said, repeating Isla's words in Mouroc. "We sacrifice everything for the sake of a better future."

The sentiment was profoundly heartbreaking. But having Deckard as his brother, Thom understood. Altruism, nobility, sacrifice—those were honorable things. And in war, they were necessary.

"I'm sorry, Brea."

She watched him in her steady, impassive way. "Thank you," she whispered, then added, "Don't tell anyone."

"They don't know?"

"Only Isla and Vayden. And they wouldn't dare betray me."

Thom frowned. "Would you be in trouble if they found out? Would the Alliance retaliate?"

She immediately shook her head. "No, they would never punish love. I simply don't care to have my heart inspected. This is personal, not political. I wish to keep it that way."

"I understand," Thom said. "And I wouldn't betray you either."

"Good," Brea said softly, though a cunning smile came to her lips. "Because if you do, I'll gut you with my dullest knife."

An amused snort burst out of Thom. "Dearest Lieutenant Lohen, you and your dullest knife will haunt my dreams for eternity."

CHAPTER EIGHTEEN

40TH OF CHRONOS, 1547

After their second day of travel, Brea took Evylin and Ethenn a short distance from camp to train. Their exercise that morning had thoroughly worn Evylin out, Ethenn not far behind her. Somehow, Brea had managed to make Hewitt's workout regimen seem light. The lieutenant had started them with a short jog before pushing them to their limits with calisthenics. Evylin wasn't so sure she looked forward to the combat training.

Walking through the trees, Brea quizzed them on their training history. "What weapons do you have the most experience with?" she asked.

Ethenn deferred to Evylin. "Most of my training was in swordplay," she said. "Though I'm also good with a dagger and basic hand-to-hand for self-defense."

Brea looked at Ethenn expectantly.

"I grew up as a hunter," he said. "So I'm trained in archery and skilled with a hatchet and dagger, but it wasn't until I joined the army that I had any training with a sword." He paused, then added, "I'm also good in a fistfight."

A dry grin pulled at Brea's lips. "So I've heard." She surveyed him. "You have a well-rounded background, even if it isn't highly trained for combat. How long were you in the Ephrian Army?"

Ethenn considered it. "I joined somewhere around four months ago, I think."

"So short a time?" Brea asked with evident surprise.

Evylin's thoughts went in the entirely opposite direction.

Four months. Had she and Deckard really been married for half a year? That didn't seem possible. Though she supposed it was the end of Chronos, so it hadn't *quite* been four months since they'd left Whickam Village.

"And how long have you been training?" Brea asked her.

Evylin blinked away her thoughts, trying to mentally calculate. "Well, Hewitt started training Ry—" Her voice caught over the name, then she forced herself to regroup. This was what caused her so many problems with Deckard. If she'd opened up about Ryen from the start, she might have been able to let go of her fear.

Clearing her throat, Evylin started again. "Hewitt started training Ryen and me when we were seven," she explained. "Though it was the basics, and only when he was on leave. My true training didn't start until I was thirteen. So I suppose it's been almost fourteen years."

Brea nodded while Ethenn watched Evylin with interest.

"That's a good long time," Brea noted. "And if your uncle's interrogation of me last night was any indication, he was an impressive trainer as well."

"He was exceptional," Evylin said, and Ethenn agreed.

Finding a small clearing in the woods, Brea brought them to a halt. She bore a formidable figure with her staff hanging from her back, a hunting knife strapped to her thigh, and her short sword hanging on her hip. Despite her lack of height, she was not diminutive, and her fierce stare made her all the more intimidating.

Unhooking the staff, Brea let it drop to the forest floor. "Though I'm not much of a swordsman, I'd like to get the measure of each of your skills." She held her hand out toward Ethenn, who carried the training swords. "We'll start with Evylin, shall we?"

"You can call me Evie if you'd like," she said, taking the second blunted sword from Ethenn.

Brea backed away. "I think Evylin is pretty. I shouldn't care to shorten it."

Stepping onto the sparring ground, Evylin smiled. It had been so long since she'd held a weapon in her hands. Her fingers wrapped affectionately around the hilt. "Do you prefer to be called Breata?" she asked.

"No," the woman said with a dry grin. "It is not nearly so elegant."

"I think it's lovely."

Brea let out an amused hum, then settled into a strange fighting stance. She held the hilt angled forward, the blade's tip pointing over her shoulder, and her feet staggered in a wider fashion than Evylin was used to seeing. "Shall we begin?" she asked.

Excited to test her skills against another Warrior, Evylin's heartbeat rose. She took her own stance, feet just outside the hips with knees bent to balance her weight and sword primed before her. "With pleasure," she said.

At first, they took it slow, moving with measured steps. Evylin's instinct was to leap forward, attacking quickly in anticipation of action. But she knew that was the wrong approach. Hewitt had taught her to fight with proficiency. While she enjoyed flair and tactical risks, he preached a level head and technical adherence. She couldn't let herself show off—not if she wanted to win.

The moment Brea lunged, Evylin moved too. Their blades met with a sharp snap. Though Brea was almost a head shorter than Evylin, she struck with equal power, alerting Evylin of the need to increase the strength of her blows.

After three more hits, they both pushed away, readjusting to their new understanding of each other. Evylin didn't give Brea much time to recover. She corrected her posture and lunged back into the fray. A strike up, then a feint down, before striking upward again. Brea blocked seamlessly, rolling with the hits.

Despite her smaller frame and claim of inferior swordsmanship, Brea managed all of Evylin's attacks with ease. They ranged across the clearing, attempting to break the other's defense. Evylin was surprised to find they were more easily matched than she expected.

That is, until Brea drove in with greater strength than before, her sword scraping against Evylin's as she angled it upward. Seeing her loss close at hand, Evylin took a risk. With their swords locked in a battle of strength, Evylin chose to lose that battle, releasing the blade altogether and spinning away from the Warrior.

Surprised by the abandonment of her weapon, Brea hesitated, giving Evylin the time to complete her turn, brandishing the long-bladed dagger she carried on the back of her belt. She'd intended to simply press the tip of the blade at the base of Brea's spine, winning the bout, but Brea moved with unprecedented speed, kicking out and catching Evylin's ankle.

Evylin hit the ground with a thump, and the air burst out of her lungs. When she caught her breath, Brea was standing over her, the tip of her sword grazing Evylin's chest.

"I concede," Evylin said self-mockingly.

Brea smiled and reached out to give her a hand. "That was good," she said with a pleased tone in her voice. "You're fast. And cunning."

"She's a show-off too," Ethenn said from the sidelines.

"I didn't show off that time," Evylin said, brushing the dirt from her pants.

"That's what you think."

Evylin tossed the practice sword to him. "I've warmed her up for you," she teased.

"Great," Ethenn returned. "Now, I'll look like an even bigger failure."

"Stop being modest." Evylin punched his shoulder as he approached, then turned to Brea. "He's beaten me many times."

"Has he?" Brea gave the young man an appraising glance. "That's surprising."

Ethenn huffed. "The only reason I've ever won is because I'm stronger than her, and she can't bear up under that forever. Especially not when she shows off."

Evylin shoved his head as she walked to his vacated observation spot. She took a seat on the grass as he and Brea prepared to spar. The woman took in his stance and noted how Ethenn absentmindedly favored his left hand. "You're left-handed?" she asked.

"I can use both," Ethenn said, adjusting his grip. "But yes, I prefer the left."

The idea seemed to please Brea. "That's a handy trick *if* you can learn to compensate for the openings it invites."

"Hewitt told me the same thing."

"And did he teach you how to change your footing and to adjust the binds to ensure your opponent can't get through your guard?"

"He did."

Brea tipped her chin up with approval. "Then, by all means, fight me left-handed," she invited.

Though Ethenn hesitated, he reset his grip. He adopted the steady expression he usually wore during combat, a flat, almost-bored look that Evylin had learned meant he was concentrating. Though it seemed laughable that Ethenn's four months of training could hold up against Brea's untold years as a soldier, Evylin couldn't help wondering if he could beat her. The hunter's strength and natural skill gave him enough of an edge that he just might outfight the lieutenant.

Ethenn moved first. He swung his sword to arc under Brea's blade, but he'd been too slow to bring up the strike, showing his hand early. The swords clanged together, and Brea adjusted appropriately to bear the brunt of its force. Another four connections rang through the air. Brea was fast and controlled, even more so than Evylin, and the young man struggled to keep up with her steady ripostes. Her feet shuffled lightly, her small stature keeping her agile as she moved around Ethenn's attacks. And in the end, it took only thirty seconds for Brea to find the opening in his defense. With lightning speed, she slapped the inside of his wrist with her blade, lunged forward, and drove one of her triceps up into his right forearm to knock it back, leaving his chest wide open to the tip of her sword.

Staggering to a stop, Ethenn grunted as the blunted tip dug into his stomach.

Evylin slapped a hand over her mouth, unable to hold in her amazed laughter. Ethenn sent her a sour stare. "I'm sorry," she said. "It was just over so quickly."

Letting down her defense, Brea pointed the sword into the dirt, leaning on the hilt. "Four months of training in swordplay seems about right," she remarked. "You're good, but it's clear that you're a hunter and not a true soldier. You'll need several more years of practice to truly become a master."

A beleaguered expression came to Ethenn's face. "I know."

Brea noticed the shift in his demeanor too. "And yet, the truth troubles you?" she noted.

Ethenn hesitated, glancing at Evylin. "It's only . . ." He sighed and shook his head. "Nothing. It's just daunting, knowing I have so much work ahead of me."

Watching the exchange, Evylin frowned. After their time training in the moors of Wauld, she knew Ethenn well enough now to know he wasn't telling the whole truth. Only just overcoming her own tendency to distrust others, she allowed him to withhold his private thoughts.

"Don't worry," Brea said, unaware. "Your inexperience won't damn our mission. Together, you've both done well over the last two months. You'll do even better with my training."

Ethenn gave her a half-smile.

Resuming their lesson, Brea talked with them about the individual strengths and weaknesses that she noticed and how she intended to improve them. Many of the things she'd told Ethenn were the same areas that Evylin had pointed out to him during their one-on-one sessions the last few weeks, which was gratifying. She'd never imagined herself to be a teacher, but it felt good knowing she was better than she'd expected.

However, Evylin didn't appreciate it when Brea directly contradicted Hewitt's training by correcting her grip.

"That's not how Hewitt taught me," Evylin protested.

"Perhaps not," she replied, unbothered. "But this is a better way. It's how the Schonese Imperial Guard are trained."

Evylin gave her a flat glare. "We're not in Schon."

Brea raised a brow but didn't reply.

Pressing down her defensive reaction, Evylin pursed her lips. "I understand that there are different ways to do things," she said. "But this worked for Hewitt his entire life, and it works for me. There's no reason to change it."

"I would not tell you to do something without reason, Evylin. The grip I've shown you is better because you are a woman. It allows you to take less brunt of the blow with your wrists, prolonging your strength." Brea tapped Evylin's current grip. "The way you have it now, you don't have the same mobility. While I'm sure that it worked just fine for your six-and-a-half-foot beast of an uncle, it is not sustainable for your build nor your quick, springy fighting style."

Feeling as though she were betraying her uncle, Evylin accepted the critique and adjusted her grip. It felt wrong, and she dropped the sword several times during her training bouts with Ethenn, but that was to be expected. Every new skill took time and patience to master. Something she'd learned with Hewitt more than a decade ago.

Brea assigned each of them skills to practice when they weren't training. She wanted Evylin to work on her dexterity by learning small tricks with knives, as well as improve her accuracy by throwing them. Ethenn's tasks were to refine his finesse and control. She demonstrated numerous exercises to help tighten his range of motion and make him more aware of his body movements. One of the practice assignments surprised both of her students.

"You want me to do what?" Ethenn asked.

"Dance," Brea said. "Dancing requires grace, stability, and control. It will sharpen your skills faster than most things. And it's far more enjoyable than simply standing there, thrusting and brandishing a stick."

Ethenn grimaced in doubt. "It isn't like I have an opportunity for dancing."

Evylin smirked at his discomfort. "We can make an opportunity. I'm sure Ilain would be thrilled."

He pursed his lips, but Brea nodded. "That's a good idea, Evylin," she said. "Perhaps you could start tonight."

"One problem," Ethenn said. "I don't know how to dance."

"Oh, that's not true," Evylin returned. "You danced with me after we saved Prince Ephren."

"You were drunk."

"So were you."

"Exactly." Ethenn shook his head. "I'm not good at it."

"So there's your first assignment," Brea said. "Get good at it."

"It isn't like we have music."

Brea brushed her hand through the air. "Just ask Vayden to sing. He has a splendid baritone."

Though Ethenn didn't look inclined to listen, Evylin patted his shoulder placatingly. "If it helps, I'll make Jonn dance with me too," she offered.

Shortly after, Brea concluded their training for the evening, and they began to make their way back to the camp. As they neared the mountains close to the Wauld-Ephria border, the terrain was growing rockier. Evylin remembered being taught that the giant mountain range was named Allmar, or Allore's Arm, its grandest peak known as Heavenscrest. But after being in Wauld for more than a month, she wondered if the Westerners had a different name for the range and peak.

Evylin's contemplation of the manifold differences between the nations was halted when Ethenn tapped her arm and whispered her name. She turned to him in expectation.

"Can I ask you something?" he said in a hushed tone.

Evylin glanced ahead of them. Brea was several strides away, though there was little doubt she could still hear them. "Of course," she said, turning back to Ethenn.

Stepping over a gnarled root, Ethenn kept his gaze on his boots. "What is it like? To be Bonded."

"Oh." Evylin blinked, surprised by the question. She scratched her head in thought. "Well . . . It's nice. I'm still getting used to it and what all it means, but it's—it's been good so far."

Though she knew that was an understatement—being Bonded to Deckard was incredible, life-altering, and wholly enlivening—she didn't know how to explain that. And she wasn't entirely certain she cared to bare her soul quite that much.

"So," Ethenn prompted, "it's worth it?"

Evylin smiled at him. "It's definitely worth it."

"Not if you don't love the person you're Bonded with," Brea said.

Evylin and Ethenn stopped in their tracks, caught off guard by her blunt interjection.

Hearing that they'd stopped, Brea turned around to face them but didn't add anything to her statement.

"But . . ." Ethenn settled a hand on his sword pommel. "Ilain said that even if the individuals weren't in love when they Bonded, they would fall in love eventually *because* of the Bond."

"It *encourages* love," Brea corrected. "But love takes many forms: parent and child, siblings, friends, lovers. Bonding cannot make you fall in love with your partner. It can only help you see their soul the way no other can. You may come to love them, but that doesn't mean you will be *in love* with them."

Having the fresh experience of a Bond with Deckard, Evylin could rightly say that the link did indeed encourage the feeling within her. But she'd already been in love with him. Was it possible that if she had Bonded with another Mage, like Auden or Blount, she never would have felt anything more than platonic admiration for them?

"That's not what Ilain told us," Evylin said, remembering the way Ilain had described Bonding to them the night they discovered Deckard's magic. "She said that even if the couple wasn't in love, they would be shortly after the Bond."

Brea's expression turned bitterly cynical. "Ilain Calder is a narrow-minded *elgotrá*," she said tersely, then glanced at Ethenn. "No offense."

He only stared at her, too taken aback to respond.

"I've known the Calders for over a decade," she continued. "They are powerful and intelligent, yes. But they are also stubborn and blinded by their own desires. Ilain has been set up to rule since she was sixteen years old. She began studying Bonding a year later. After centuries of failed study, *she* was the one who finally discovered the key. For more than twenty years, she has been planning her union with a Warrior, wholly focused on this idealized version of who she's supposed to become. No matter the reality, she'd convince herself that she would fall in love with the Warrior she chose because it's too devastating for her to believe otherwise."

Ethenn shifted uncomfortably, and Evylin glanced at him. Even though she assumed he knew the truth of Ilain's mutual affection for him, she felt sure that Ilain hadn't told him of her love. After all, Ilain was just discovering that for herself. But Evylin wasn't the person to tell Ethenn of those feelings.

After a short breath, Brea shook her head dejectedly. "I don't mean to be callous or belittling," she said. "It is simply hard for me to support Ilain's cause when I know she is wrong."

"How do you know?" Ethenn asked flatly. "If Evie and Deckard are the first to Bond in centuries, how can you be sure?"

"I think she's right," Evylin said with a sigh. "Being Bonded . . . It isn't that I feel more in love with Jonn. My regard for him, my dedication to him, my urge to see him happy—those have all grown. But the depth of my romantic love for him has stayed the same. I feel no more compulsion to be *in love* with him than I did before."

"Exactly," Brea said. "Magic doesn't induce romance. It spurs true connection. That is all. You may love the person, but that does not mean you will love them the way a spouse should."

Ethenn picked at the leather on his hilt, considering their words. He cleared his throat. "That doesn't affect me," he said. "I love Ilain."

"But does she love you?" Brea countered.

And though Evylin knew she did—or at least, Ilain thought she did—it appeared that Ethenn wasn't aware of that because he said, "No."

Brea raised her brow. "Can you live with that?"

Though he hesitated, Ethenn nodded. "I can."

"*Bénediáso.* May you be happy in your choices." Brea shrugged. "I know I will not be."

Evylin looked between the two of them, growing more bemused. Brea didn't want to be Bonded, yet it sounded as though she intended to be. Still newly acquainted with the woman, Evylin chose not to pursue her curiosity. If Brea wanted to explain, she would. But the other issue she could address.

Ethenn thought Ilain didn't love him. Whether he accepted that life or not, he needed to know the truth. And Evylin *was* close enough to Ilain to advise her on the subject.

Reaching over, Evylin tugged on Ethenn's arm. "Come on," she encouraged. "Let's get back to camp. We can talk more about this later."

They trudged back through the forest, coming upon their troop in mere minutes. A soft fire was burning in the evening light. They still had to be careful on their journey out of Wauld, but due to the extended hours of sunlight in the heart of spring, they were able to heat their meals without worry.

At the firepit, Vayden and Auden prepared the stew with a degree of comfort only siblings could display. Isla and Ilain sat near the brothers, the first conversing with the men while the second sketched in her notebook. Though Ethenn glanced their way, he drifted toward where Rafferty and Thom were snickering about some inside joke, and Brea followed.

Evylin searched for Deckard, finding him seated on their bedroll with a book spread over his lap. Their tent was the farthest from the campfire, offering them as much privacy as they would get in the presence of the troop. And after the conversation with Brea and Ethenn, she felt a strange need for her husband's presence.

Yet, though she took one step in his direction, she corrected her course at the last second.

Stepping over to the firepit, Evylin crouched down next to Ilain, who immediately covered her sketchbook. "Yes, Evie?" she said.

Though she had a purpose for speaking with the highlady, Evylin couldn't help her wry grin. "You presume I need something?" she quipped.

Ilain smirked. "You have a distinct manner in your stride when you're on a mission."

"Mm." Evylin lowered her voice so only the woman could hear. "I don't wish to push in where I'm not wanted, but as you've sought my romantic advice in the past, may I offer some more?"

The Mage's eyes glimmered brightly. "Please do."

"You should tell Ethenn of your true feelings for him," she suggested without any further preamble. "I don't think he understands."

Something like sadness flittered across Ilain's expression before it returned to its usual gaiety. Her lips curled with a knowing amusement. "I will take that into the most serious consideration," she replied.

Evylin tipped her chin down teasingly. "I'm glad to hear it," she said, then left the highlady to her sketches.

Upon her approach to their tent, Deckard looked up. "How was your training?" he asked.

"Hard," Evylin admitted, but instead of taking the seat next to him, she gestured to the forest. "Would you join me for a minute?"

With a glance toward the trees and the troop, he shut his book. "Of course."

Deckard took a moment to inform Thom of their departure, placing the camp under his charge. Then they made their way out of sight. "Did you have a particular purpose for this walk?" he asked. "Or are you just desperate to get me alone?"

Evylin grinned at his teasing question. "When am I not desperate for you?"

A bashful smile played at his mouth. He caught her hand, drawing her closer. "What is it?" he asked, surely sensing her unsteady feelings.

"Nothing is wrong, precisely," she began even as she worked to understand the emotions shifting inside her. "It's more that I feel . . . unsettled. We've just undertaken a magical bond that grants us vast power and responsibility, and yet we know little to nothing about it. Ethenn was asking me questions, and do you know all I could think to say?"

Deckard waited patiently for her to continue.

"'It's nice,'" she said self-derisively.

He stopped, an amused quirk on his lips as he stared down at her. "It is nice," he replied with his usual goodness.

Evylin shook her head. "No, Jonn, it isn't *nice*. It's magnificent!" She gripped his hand tighter. "It's incredible. It's life-changing. Nonetheless, I have no idea what it's done to us."

His brow furrowed. "It hasn't *done* anything to us," he objected. "We are the same people we were before."

"But we have a magical tie between our souls that offers untold power and benefit," she returned. "We had no idea that we would be able to sense one another's emotions, yet I feel your concern as plainly as my own. We are too uneducated in this."

Deckard nodded with reluctant acceptance. "I see your meaning, and I agree. We should learn what we can about all the Bond offers, and I'm fairly certain the Calders would happily comply. However, we've only shared this Bond for two days." His expression softened, easing her heart with its gentle affection. "We've only shared our love for *five* days."

A small shiver raced across her skin, remembering her confession of love at Renaul's and the ensuing romance between them.

Deckard's hand slid up her wrist and to her arm. She glanced down, seeing the evening light catch in the dual-colored moonstone of his ring. "While our mission won't wait for us to enjoy these early days fully," his voice was deep and filled with tenderness, "I think we should take what joy in them we can and be grateful that Allore has granted us the chance to love one another in this magnificent, incredible, life-changing way."

Chewing on her bottom lip, Evylin stared up into his green-blue gaze. Though the idea held a certain appeal, she hadn't brought him out into the forest to have her way with him. She rather thought they could use some time alone to *be* together, taking enjoyment in one another's presence and conversation. And perhaps they could learn something about their Bond that might ease her mind.

Sensing her apprehension, Deckard's expression grew sly. He pressed a kiss to her temple. "You Warriors and your need for action," he teased. "Very well. Is there something in particular about our Bond that you want to study?"

Grateful for his understanding, Evylin stepped out of his touch. She considered the offer with uncertainty. She had wanted to explore the possibilities of their Bond, yet she knew so little of its potential benefits that she didn't know where to begin.

As Deckard crossed his arms, her eyes found his ring again, and an idea sparked.

Reaching for her gold and silver dagger, Evylin pulled it from its small scabbard. "Ilain said that our talismans were tied to us, that we can't lose them because they will always return."

Deckard nodded along with her reminder. "So what do we expect that to mean? We can take them off. Your dagger is proof of that."

"Right." Evylin shifted the blade in her hand, its scrollwork hilt a comforting weight in her palm. A curious grin lifted her lips. Then she whirled and flung the dagger into the depths of the forest.

The rustle of Deckard's footsteps against the grass and twigs marked his approach at her side. "Do you know how hard that's going to be to find out there?" he asked.

Evylin didn't reply but searched inwardly, seeking a pull like the one she'd begun to sense toward Deckard. It wasn't exactly a compulsion to find him, but more of a direction, alerting her to his presence. With Ilain's pronouncement that they couldn't lose their talismans, she'd thought that surely, she'd sense the same sort of location of the dagger.

However, she felt nothing.

With a sigh, Evylin took a step in the direction she'd thrown the blade. "It was a foolish guess," she admitted. "I suppose when Ilain said we can't misplace them, she didn't mean literally."

Deckard walked alongside her, his brow furrowed. Then he caught her arm, pulling her to a stop. "Perhaps she did," he said and motioned to the scabbard at her side. "Call it back."

"What?"

"If you can't lose it or misplace it, then it must be by *some* magical design," he insisted. "Try calling it back to you—" he tapped his sternum near his heart, "in here."

Curious, Evylin did as he suggested. She turned her thoughts inward once more, requesting the dagger's return. Not a second later, she felt its weight again in the sheath.

Evylin gasped with excitement, drawing the blade once more. "It worked!"

Deckard eyed the talisman with interest. "That could be a handy trick," he noted.

"It certainly could," she agreed, another thought surfacing. "Hm."

He raised his brow in expectation.

Evylin smirked, flipped the dagger over, then flung it into a nearby tree trunk. It was firmly embedded with expert precision. Then she called it back, specifically to her hand this time.

In a blink, the scrollwork hilt was in her palm again.

Laughter flowed out of her. "This is incredible," she exclaimed.

"It truly is," Deckard agreed.

"Try yours."

He gave her an amused frown. "Why? It isn't like a returning ring is much of a trick."

"It could be," she argued. "Remember what Ilain said about her rings, how she imbues them with magic? You could do the same with this one. Then it's practically a weapon all its own. And should you need to fool someone like Blount into thinking you aren't a Bonded Mage, you could leave it off, only to recall it in a time of great need."

With a considering quirk to his brow, Deckard acquiesced. He slipped the ring off, then set it on the ground.

Evylin scoffed. "Oh, you're no fun at all," she teased. "You can't just set it down. Throw it."

"And what if it doesn't work for me, eh? Are *you* going to search for it in the underbrush?"

Without reply, Evylin reached down and scooped the ring from the terrae. Deckard tried to stop her, but she was too quick for him. With a rapid overhand, she thrust the ring out into the forest. It flew so far out of sight that they didn't even hear when it landed.

Deckard leveled her with a flat look.

Evylin just smiled. "Call it back," she snarked.

He shook his head at her derision but straightened his shoulders. He stared in the direction in which the ring had disappeared. His hand flexed, and suddenly, the ring was back.

"Hm," he hummed thoughtfully. "I suppose that could be useful when fighting Blount."

"And I'm sure many other times," she said, then furrowed her brow as a new idea struck her. "I wonder if I could change my dagger's shape."

"What do you mean?"

"You know," she looked up at him, "like the Relics. I can make them into whatever sort of weapon I want. Maybe I can do the same with this talisman."

He shrugged with curiosity in his gaze. "Worth a shot."

Holding the gold and silver dagger in the air before her, facing the forest rather than her husband, Evylin imagined the blade as a sword in the same manner she did with the Relics. It took almost no effort to change the Relics' shapes. It was as though they *wanted* to morph to her will. However, the dagger remained unchanged in her grip.

With a disappointed sigh, Evylin returned the blade to its sheath. "I guess not."

"It makes sense, I suppose," Deckard remarked. "The Relics are imbued with the resources, which are fragments of Allore himself. While they aren't exactly alive, they are sentient, so they can respond to your will. This talisman cannot."

"There you go again," Evylin teased, "being a good student."

Deckard smiled at her. "Sentient or not, I still say I got the short end of the deal," he joked.

With a nudge to his side, Evylin turned back toward the camp. "Your magic is a weapon in and of itself. You don't need a dagger when you can summon one of those shards out of thin air."

He chuckled but caught her arm. "Where are you going?"

"Back. Dinner should be ready by now, and I'm hungry."

"Oh, no." He wrapped his arm around her waist. "I followed my wife out here under the suggestion that she desired my private company."

"I said no such thing," she countered through her laughter.

"We're Bonded, remember?" Deckard returned, tugging her closer. "I don't need words when our very souls are entwined."

CHAPTER NINETEEN

Sitting by the fire, Ethenn palmed his small dagger, attempting to perfect the trick Brea had taught him. When she'd shown Ethenn and Evylin how she always kept a blade hidden in the sleeve of her coat, he'd decided he wanted to learn to do the same. So she'd sat down with him, helping him learn the secret of easily concealing and retrieving the blade without cutting yourself. Thus far, he'd determined it was nearly impossible.

Still, Ethenn sat, working on the skill while everyone else lounged after dinner. He'd nicked himself half a dozen times already.

When he hissed at the seventh prick, Ilain looked over at him. "Do you have a particular penchant for pain?" she teased. "Or are you just too stubborn to quit while you still have a hand?"

On Ethenn's other side, Rafferty sniggered.

"Skills like this take practice," Ethenn said. "Sometimes, that means getting hurt in the process."

Ilain's eyes twinkled in the firelight. "And what happens if you pass out from blood loss?"

"Then I'll try again when I wake up."

Her quick chortle made Ethenn feel inordinately proud.

Ilain patted his knee. "I'll leave you to it, then," she said and turned away.

Smiling to himself, Ethenn continued his practice. He hadn't been fully honest with Ilain. Yes, sleight of hand like this took practice, but that wasn't the only reason he was so doggedly trying to learn.

Brea's words stuck in Ethenn's head. *"You'll need several years more practice to truly become a master."*

It wasn't that Ethenn minded being a subpar Warrior. It was expected. He was young and inexperienced. Until four months ago, he'd never been trained in combat. All his experience came from hunting and the instincts that had helped him win brawls in Trollenston's fighting ring. He *shouldn't* be as proficient as Evylin or Brea.

Yet, he was disappointed in himself. And worse, he was confused.

Why would Ilain choose him to be her husband? If she was determined to be a ruler, if this had been her desired destiny since youth, why would she choose him? Several other male Warriors, who were undoubtedly more impressive and mature options, were available, so why would she choose *him*?

Ethenn flicked his wrist, but the dagger stuck in his sleeve again, its point sharp as it pricked him. He grimaced but kept silent.

He'd been told time and time again that Ilain Calder was the most powerful Mage in two centuries. Why choose a man half her age with abilities that couldn't even begin to compare to those she displayed naturally? It didn't make sense.

While conversation rolled around him, Ethenn kept his eyes on his task until Brea spoke up.

"Vayden," she said casually, "sing something for us."

Ethenn looked up, knowing the woman's schemes. Though Vayden shrugged, unbothered with performing in front of their troop, Ethenn didn't have any interest in dancing in front of the camp. "No," he said sharply.

Everyone looked at him in confusion.

Heat crept up Ethenn's neck in time with his rising agitation. "Not here."

Brea ignored him. "I think the 'Ol' Barrow's Reel' would be a good start," she said to Vayden. "It's got an easy rhythm. Not too slow."

"I don't know how to dance, Brea," Ethenn protested.

Rafferty started laughing. "Are we having a party?" he asked.

"Ethenn is learning control," Brea corrected, then gave the Warrior a flat look. "If I am going to train you, you will do as I say, whether you want to or not. If you refuse, I will no longer offer my assistance."

Ethenn clenched his fists, the dagger in his sleeve slipping down to embed itself into the heel of his hand. "Bloody hell," he exclaimed, then fiercely pulled the blade free. A hot trickle of blood welled out of the cut, filling his palm.

"Heavens," Ilain muttered, then grabbed his wrist. "Let me see."

While she ministered to the cut with a warming burst of magic, Brea waited for Ethenn's submission. He ground his teeth against the pain in his hand, the embarrassment of the moment, and the fact that no matter how much he didn't want to dance in front of everyone, he couldn't afford to lose his trainer.

"Fine," Ethenn said bitterly. "I'll do it."

Brea nodded and turned back to Vayden. "'Ol' Barrow's Reel,'" she repeated.

Vayden smirked. "Is this dance a free-for-all? Or is it only Lainy who gets to join the corporal?" he asked.

"He's my husband," Ilain said.

"Doesn't mean he has to dance with you."

The skin on his hand now healed, Ethenn stood and held it out to Ilain even as he addressed her brother. "I won't be dancing with anyone else," he said.

"Pity," Vayden said. "Isla's a right fine dancer."

"Why don't you ever dance with me, then, love?" Isla replied.

"Because I've two left feet, dearest, as you well know."

Letting Ilain lead him over to more open ground, Ethenn tried to forget the presence of the others in the camp around them. A particularly hard feat when Rafferty was making snide remarks to Thom, who was failing to hold in his laughter. Evylin slapped Thom on the back of the head, then turned to Deckard. "Help Ethenn," she said.

Deckard frowned. "What do you mean?"

"He doesn't know how to dance," she said. "Teach him."

"I can teach him," Ilain said.

"It is the man who leads," Brea interjected. "Let a man teach him."

Though Ilain pursed her lips at the lieutenant's orders, she stepped back nonetheless.

With a sigh, Deckard rose. He came over, offered an apologetic look to Ethenn, and then walked him through the proper form and steps of the most common Ephrian dances. Deckard demonstrated with Ilain so that Ethenn could watch before attempting it himself. Then Deckard guided the couple into the proper positioning.

Once Ethenn clasped Ilain's hand in his and set the other on her waist, Vayden asked, "Ready?"

Ethenn took a deep breath. His palms and fingers burned where they touched Ilain, but he refused to let his nervousness show. "Yes," he said.

In a steady, rich baritone, Vayden began to sing.

Ethenn didn't move.

"You're supposed to move your feet," Ilain advised quietly.

"I'm getting a feel for the rhythm," he said.

"Oh."

After several more beats, Ethenn took the first step . . . and promptly landed on

Ilain's toes. She grimaced, and he apologized, but she pressed him to keep moving even as several in the group fought off laughter.

Evylin shushed Rafferty and Thom, then grabbed Deckard's hand, taking the opportunity to dance with him as well. Ethenn appreciated her attempt to make the moment less awkward, though it didn't help much.

He glanced down, eyes on the ground. Carefully, he stepped to the rhythm, the toe of his boots brushing against Ilain's dark skirt.

"Look up," Ilain instructed.

"If I do that, I'll step on you."

"You can't lead the dance if you're looking at your feet."

He scoffed. "I can't lead the dance if I injure my partner either."

A gentle laugh filled her voice as she said, "Look at me, Ethenn."

Afraid he'd crush her toes, Ethenn lifted his eyes cautiously. The night had come, casting heavy shadows through the camp and across her face. However, her vibrant hair glimmered in the firelight.

"That's better," Ilain said, even as he stumbled through the next few steps. "So why does Brea have us dancing again?"

"Evidently, it helps a fighter gain finesse," he explained.

"And you're lacking that?"

Thinking she should already be aware of his failings, Ethenn nodded. "I'm lacking a lot of things," he said.

Her lips twisted up in a wry grin. "Oh, I wouldn't say that." Her hand squeezed his shoulder. "You have strength, intelligence, and me. What else could you need?"

Unsure if she was poking fun at him or not, Ethenn pressed his lips together in a false smile. He focused on the steps, carrying them over the grass in a box-like pattern. Ilain was a graceful dancer, as he would have expected. It was as if her lithe figure was made for it. She moved like a flame over a candlewick, seamless and graceful, her body seeming to float.

Vayden completed the "Ol' Barrow's Reel" and began a second, slower song before Ethenn could suggest stopping. He sang in Schonese, the words flowing with a languid poignancy. Isla joined in with harmonies, her voice smooth and sultry, perfectly complementing his deep, steady timbre.

Ethenn kept his eyes on Ilain, working to ignore the more romantic lilt of the ballad. A gentle breeze swept some of her fire-bright hair across her cheek, but she didn't bother to fix it. To his searching gaze, her expression remained unreadable, the sharp planes of her face almost ethereal in their exquisite refinement. His heartbeat ticked up as the cool of magic niggled at his mind. Being this close to her, touching her, always brought out the Warrior in him. And that worried him. If he was already attached to her now, what would happen once they Bonded? Would his magic overtake him completely? Would he become a brute he didn't even recognize in his pursuit of her? Was he willing to accept that possibility?

"You're staring at me very intently," Ilain said, breaking Ethenn's concentration.

He stumbled over the next step but managed to gain his footing once more. "I'm trying to focus," he said.

"By using magic?" she asked.

"No," he replied. "Just, you know, on the dance."

"You could use magic," she suggested. "It'd make it easier."

"Wouldn't that be cheating?"

Her nose wrinkled as she smiled. "When given the opportunity, I always cheat."

"That's not very honorable of you." Ethenn couldn't decide if her admission was a character flaw or not.

Her hand shifted higher on his shoulder, sending a short burst of chills through his coat and underneath his tunic. "Perhaps not. But it's made me very successful, and I find I've yet to regret it."

The corner of his mouth lifted in amusement. "You're a very strange woman, Ilain," he said.

"Only to those who don't understand me," she returned.

Ethenn tipped his head in an acquiescent motion. "I suppose you're right. I don't understand you."

Her smile didn't falter, but something in her eyes flashed darkly. "You haven't taken the opportunity to know me in such a manner," she said.

Knowing that she was right, he averted his gaze. The rest of the troop had moved on from their dance, enjoying Vayden and Isla's singing while they relaxed around the campfire. Deckard and Evylin swayed slowly, enjoying the ballad in each other's arms. Thom, Rafferty, Auden, and Brea played a game of Crooks and Crowns.

Feeling somewhat comfortable given their distractions, Ethenn turned back to Ilain. "I haven't," he admitted quietly. "But it isn't because I don't want to."

Ilain's jade green eyes drifted over his face. "Then why haven't you?"

"Because I've been afraid to," he said without guile.

Her lips parted slightly, but he continued before she could interrupt. "You're impossible, Ilain," he said. "You're a stunning, clever, all-powerful Mage. The moment I saw you, I knew I could never have you. So I didn't bother trying to get to know you because why torture myself?"

She stared at him with something like awe, which didn't make much sense to him.

He'd already told her that he loved her. She'd married him. Why should this truth surprise her?

"I didn't want to understand you," he said. "But I fell in love with you anyway."

Ilain sucked in her bottom lip and let out a small hum of thought.

Unsure what that meant, Ethenn raised his brow. "Hm?" he repeated.

Blinking as though drawing herself out of a stupor, Ilain blew out a scoff. He didn't know if it was in derision of him or herself. "Well," she said, tone falsely lighthearted. "It seems you ought to come to understand me, then."

"Probably," he agreed.

"And I should come to understand you."

Ethenn hesitated, then reluctantly said, "Yes."

"Which," she continued, unaware of his reservations, "leads me to think we should spend more time together."

"We spend every day together, Ilain."

"I mean, just the two of us."

"Privately?"

She nodded.

He drew his brows together, doubtful of the idea. "We don't exactly have the luxury of privacy."

Brea accused Rafferty of cheating just then, as though to prove his point.

"No?" Ilain asked slyly. She drew their dance to a halt, then looked over her shoulder at Vayden. He met her gaze and gave her a knowing nod.

While Vayden kept singing, Ilain adjusted her hold on Ethenn's hand and pulled him into the forest to their left. Though Ethenn was sure someone would see and stop them, no one did.

Under the heavy cover of trees, the world was a thick shadow. Carefully, they moved through the roots and underbrush. The chirrup of crickets filled the cool air. And though the foliage was still foreign to him, Ethenn could almost imagine he was back home in Estshire, stalking his prey through the forest with his father at his side.

"This will do," Ilain said when they came upon a willow tree by a creek that wound through the hillside from a mountain river somewhere ahead. She pulled him under the drooping branches. The world was even darker beneath the leaves. He could barely see her as she sat at the base of the trunk.

But then a small orb of flickering ruby and golden light floated before her. It played off her pale skin, revealing her bright smile. Now that they were traveling again, she wore a simple, dark brown dress. Its large skirt billowed around her, making her appear like a flower that had bloomed from the tree itself.

Ethenn sat across from her, drawing his knees up. Being here with her felt like he was in a dream. The orb floating above their heads almost made him worry that it was one.

"Now," Ilain said, placing her hands in her lap, "tell me about yourself."

Ethenn raised his brow. "This was supposed to be about me understanding you."

"And about me understanding you," she reminded him. "Besides, I know far less about you than you know about me."

Though he didn't doubt the truth of that, Ethenn wasn't ready to be open with her. "A question for a question, then," he suggested.

Her smile grew. "Very well," she said, playing with a pleat on her skirt. "Shall I go first?"

He gave a nod, preparing himself to lie.

"When did you first realize that you loved me?" she asked.

Ethenn let out a relieved huff. *That* he could answer. "Well, I always liked you," he said. "But I didn't realize quite how much until you told me in the Wind Keep that if I fell one more time, you'd let me go."

Her face scrunched in disbelief. "*That* convinced you that you love me?"

"When I thought about you letting me go," he shrugged, "I didn't fear dying. I feared being apart from you."

Ilain let out a strange humming sound but didn't speak.

"My turn," Ethenn said, distracting them from what might otherwise have been an awkward moment. "Why do you let people think you're vapid and brash?"

She didn't even hesitate. "Because it makes them underestimate me. And it keeps them at a distance."

Ethenn raised his brow, understanding but surprised that she felt the need to distance herself from people too.

She smirked at him, taking her turn at a question. "What made you decide I'm not vapid and brash?"

"You're smart," he said. "But not just normally smart. You're cunning and manipulative. I saw that from the moment we met—the way you played King Ephren, Thom, all of us. You're far too clever to be so ridiculous."

Now, it was her turn to look surprised. "You've always been more attentive than others," she mused.

"I'm a hunter," he replied. "It's our job to be keen-sighted."

Ethenn rested his arms on top of his knees, leaning forward. "How many men have you turned down in your lifetime?"

A wan smile crossed her face. "Not as many as you'd think, perhaps," she said self-mockingly. "Three? Maybe four."

"All Warriors?"

"No." She angled forward, a sly glint in her eyes. "Now, you asked a question out of turn, so I get two. Why didn't you want to be a Warrior at first?"

Ethenn averted his gaze, staring at the tall grass around him. This was the first question where he had to lie, even if only by omission. Once he'd decided on the selective truth, he met her gaze again. "Because it's not the life I imagined for myself."

"Be more specific."

"You weren't specific when I asked why you put on a façade or if all the men who've propositioned you were Warriors."

She gave him a perturbed look but conceded. "All right, then here's my second question: You told me you have an uncle, but do you have any other family?"

Ethenn stretched his back, shifting on the ground. "No," he lied.

Ilain's gaze narrowed. "You're an orphan?"

"It's my turn to ask a question," he countered. He watched her closely as he asked, "Do you really want to rule Allund, or is it just what's expected of you?"

Her expression remained unaffected. "I won't rule Allund," she said matter-of-factly. "I, along with my husband—that's you, by the way—will govern Doorstunds Reach, which is only a small portion of Allund. And yes, it's what I want even as it's what is expected of me."

Ethenn gave an understanding nod, accepting her answer.

Ilain's head tipped to the side, a cunning glint in her gaze. "How did you really get those burns on your arms?" she asked.

The urge to rub the scars tingled in his fingers, but he managed to quell it. "I told you. I got them working in my uncle's smithy."

"Tell me the truth."

"I am," he said, and he was, though it wasn't the whole truth.

"I can tell when you're lying," she said.

He forced himself to hold her gaze. "Can you?"

She smirked and reached forward to brush the hair off his forehead. Her touch sent a wash of cold magic across his scalp. "You maintain eye contact when you lie," she said. "As though you're trying to prove your innocence. But the thing is, I can see it in the hardness of your gaze, Ethenn. You shut off when you lie. Like a doused flame, all emotion fades from your eyes."

Wary of her insight, Ethenn refused to look away. *"Only cowards shrink in the face of adversity."*

Ilain tipped her brow up, hands back in her lap. "You lied for the last three answers you gave me. Why?"

Jaw tightening, Ethenn sniffed in the cold night air. "It's not your turn to ask a question," he said.

"You'll get two next time."

Knowing she wouldn't let it go, Ethenn shook his head, dropping her gaze at last. "Because I don't want to tell you the truth," he said flatly. He stared at her hands, the jewels of her rings glittering in the golden-red light of the orb. "And before you press me, know that I won't give you any more insight than this: I don't want to be a Warrior because I don't want the life it brings, but I've chosen to accept it anyway. Yes, I have family other than my uncle, but I won't be telling you about them. And regardless of whether you believe me or not—"

He met her stare once more then, glaring at her with his final response. "I did receive these burns while working in my uncle's smithy. And that's the end of it."

Ilain watched him with a knowing, determined look. "You're a damaged man, aren't you?" she asked softly.

"More than most," he admitted freely. "That's three questions I get now."

She dipped her chin in assent.

Agitated by her ability to see through him, Ethenn asked the question that he most wanted the answer to. "Why did you choose me?"

She had the audacity to smile sweetly at him. "Because I like you."

Unsure how to take that simple answer, he said, "I'm not good enough."

"That's a matter of opinion. Next question."

"Do you really believe Bonding makes people fall in love?"

"I do."

Ethenn nodded, assured of no falsehood in her tone. He knew that she genuinely thought that once they were Bonded, she'd come to love him. The problem was, he wasn't sure she was right anymore. And he didn't know if he could stand two centuries of unrequited love.

But he had one question left to ask.

"What if you're wrong?"

Ilain drew back, her gaze shuttered, and her lips pressed into a flat line. The light of the orb now made her appear menacing and dangerous, her pale skin flickering with ruby and gilded shadows.

"I am the foremost expert on Bonding," she said sharply. "I have studied the institution for nearly three decades. If people have questions, they come to me for answers. I'm not wrong."

Ethenn wasn't deterred. "What if you are?"

She tossed a hand flippantly. "Say I am. Why should it matter? Being in love isn't some fluke of fate, Ethenn. I could love you or Thom or even bloody Rafferty, should I choose to. And I would have potentially more than two hundred years to perfect that love. So why should it bother either one of us if I'm wrong?"

Ilain reached forward, taking hold of his hands, which hung between his knees. "I *chose* you, Ethenn," she said fiercely. "Out of eleven Warriors in the Alliance, out of hundreds of Mages, out of a thousand men. I chose you. And I will continue to make that choice every day for the rest of our lives."

At her words, something within Ethenn twisted. His body thrummed as the pulse of magic rose in his veins. His senses clarified, bringing the world into sharper focus under her touch. The faintest scent of perfumed oil drifted across the breeze. He wanted to take hold of her, to pull her onto his lap, and bury his face in her hair. He wanted to enfold himself in the whole of her being.

But he didn't believe her.

No matter what she thought, no matter what she said, she was forcing herself to feel something for him. And that could never last.

"Do we understand one another now?" Ilain asked, the soft glow of the orb glimmering in her hair.

Ethenn nodded, though he was sure she could never understand him. Nor did he want her to.

"Good." Ilain's eyes gleamed wildly. "Then I want you to kiss me."

His stomach pinched. "No," he said immediately.

"Why not?" she demanded.

He shook his head, pulling out of her touch. "It's not a good idea."

"Because you can't control yourself?"

He didn't reply, which he knew would be plenty of confirmation.

"You did just fine at our betrothal," she noted.

"There were people around," he said dully.

Ilain smirked. "I don't know if you know this, Ethenn, but I'm not Evylin." She leaned forward, inching closer across the grass on her hands. "I'm not looking for a knight in shining armor. I don't desire Jonn Deckard, and I'm not particularly keen on honorable men."

Their faces were within inches as she murmured, "What I do want is for my bloody husband to kiss me."

Tension squirmed inside Ethenn's chest. The heat was like a brand, burning all over his body, flushing him with desire. But that was the thing: Anger felt awfully close to desire at times. And anger had driven him to kill nearly three times now. He was afraid to find out what the rage of full-blown desire would do to him.

His skin burned under the flame of Ilain's proximity, her lips only a breath away. He swallowed down the longing, hardening himself against the urge within. And his words were a terse whisper between them.

"Then you'll just have to be patient."

CHAPTER TWENTY

1ST OF RADIA, 1574

Already, Evylin was growing weary of the crowd at the camp. Returning to the road was exhausting on its own. Coupled with their urgent quest for the Relics, the demanding training Brea put them through, the sensation of overwhelming emotions from Deckard, and the countdown of her last days with Hewitt, the continual presence of others became increasingly frustrating.

Dropping to a seat on the grass, Evylin heaved for breath after Brea's latest training session. After years of training with Hewitt, she'd thought herself in peak condition. Now, Brea's regimen had her second-guessing herself.

It appeared that Ethenn was of the same mind. "How is it that she is harder on us than Hewitt?" he asked, sweat dripping off his nose.

"It's because I don't have a soft spot for you," Brea said, surveying their exhaustion from the side. She'd worked up a sweat as well, though she wasn't nearly as worn out as the two of them.

Ethenn blew out a puff of air. "Hewitt only ever cared about Evie. He pushed me as hard as anyone else."

Evylin reached over to shove his shoulder. "Hewitt was hard on me too."

"If a mother hen is hard on her chicks, then sure."

She threw a clump of grass at him. Then she heaved a breath and stared at the thick curtain of trees above them. "Shouldn't being Bonded make this easier?" she lamented. "I thought I was supposed to be stronger."

"You are stronger," Brea said. "That doesn't mean you get to stop working."

Evylin grumbled her discontentment at hearing the truth.

Ethenn brushed the grass off his damp shirt. "How does that work?" he asked. "I mean, in terms of Bonding. How does it affect your magic? Can you . . . *feel* that it's different?"

Worn out, Evylin didn't want to think about the complexities she now felt inside of her. "Maybe?" she sighed.

His frown made it clear that her short reply wasn't a good enough answer.

"I don't know, Ethenn," she managed through a chuckle. "Jonn and I have been Bonded for three days. I knew nothing about it before, and all I know now is that I hardly feel different at all, and yet . . ."

He waited with expectation as she smiled and thought about the constant sense of a familiar presence in her chest. "And yet," she continued, "it feels unlike anything else I've experienced."

"How so?" Ethenn prompted.

Finding the words felt impossible. "It's just . . . On the surface, I feel the same as ever. Our relationship feels the same. Nothing seems to have changed." Evylin paused and set a hand on her chest. "But underneath all that, something has happened. And now . . . I can feel him."

Ethenn's brow rose.

Evylin tapped her sternum. "Right here. Even though we're nearly a mile out of camp, I can feel him like he's right here beside me."

"Isn't that . . ." Ethenn fumbled for words. "Odd?" he concluded.

She let out a breathy laugh. "It is," she admitted readily. "But it's also comforting, being able to sense every bit of my husband at every second. Somehow, I know exactly where he is." She pointed toward the camp, letting her internal compass guide her to Deckard's precise location. "There. If you were to draw a straight line from the tip of my finger, somehow, I know it would end right at his heart."

Ethenn and Brea listened with varying degrees of interest. While Ethenn was rapt, taking in all the information for himself, the other woman stood dispassionately nearby.

Letting her hand fall, Evylin sighed. "Ilain gave me a book," she said. "It's all about Bonding and what it is and does, and I imagine it explains all this better than I ever could. She told me that Jonn and I need to read it, so I assume she'll tell you to read it too."

"*Attachments of the Soul?*" Brea asked, a knowing look on her face.

"Yes."

She nodded. "I tried to read that once. Couldn't make it through the first five pages."

Evylin frowned with a self-mocking grimace. "Glad to know it doesn't get any better."

"Is it that bad?" Ethenn asked nervously.

"It's hard to understand," Evylin said.

"But Ilain has read it, right?" he asked.

"Six times, apparently."

"Then can't she just tell us what's in it?"

"I don't recommend making that request," Brea said. "Not unless you want to hear her lecture from night until morning, waxing poetic about the beauty and bliss of Bonding, conveniently forgetting to leave out the unpleasant parts."

"What unpleasant parts?" Evylin and Ethenn asked in unison.

Brea brushed back one of the braids that had loosened from her bun during their training. "I'm not the most knowledgeable on the subject, so don't think I have all the answers," she said. "Bad or good. But as the Alliance desires me to Bond, they've given me a reasonable education on the subject, and there's one great con that no one likes to discuss. In fact, I'm sure it's why Fishere wouldn't have approved you and Ilain Bonding before we left even if it would aid our mission," she told Ethenn.

Evylin and Ethenn listened with bated breath.

"When one member of the Bonded couple dies," she explained, "their counterpart experiences the death within themselves too. Depending on the length of the Bond, the living partner goes into a catatonic state while the soul heals. The longer the Bond, the longer the recovery needed. The hope is to last a century together. At that point, the death of one will kill the other outright. But if it's before that . . ."

Brea shook her head while her companions stared at her in abject horror. "If it's before the century mark," she concluded, "the living partner will fall into the stasis for an unknown period of time solely to provide the soul time to heal. When they finally wake, they will never be the same, and they will have to grieve in a world they don't know."

Evylin clamped her gaping mouth shut enough to ask, "Are you saying that if Jonn or I die, the other will lose their mind in grief?"

"Essentially," Brea said with a lazy shrug. "Though with the short length of your Bond, it isn't likely that it'd be any longer than a year of stasis. And you *could* attempt to Bond again, though it isn't recommended."

"I thought Ilain said you could only Bond once," Evylin said.

"You can only have one Bond at a time," Brea clarified. "Should your Bond break, you are able to pursue a second if you wish to risk it. It's only been done once, according to what Ilain said, and it didn't end well."

Evylin chewed on her bottom lip while Ethenn grimaced.

Brea looked adequately reassured by their somber moods. "So you can see why some wouldn't wish to risk such a thing, particularly not when you aren't decidedly in love with your partner."

"Yes," Evylin muttered. "I can."

The problem was, now, she worried that she'd trapped herself and Deckard into something they shouldn't have agreed to. Already, losing Deckard would have been devastating to her. She still struggled to let go of Ryen and Hewitt's loss. This . . .

The death of a Bond was a depth of depression that Evylin didn't think she'd survive.

Now, having a constant sense of Deckard's presence—feeling him within her very soul—how could she live without it? Their Bond was strange, uncomfortable, and unknown, but it was also wonderful, fascinating, and reassuring. To have this connection ripped away from her would hurt far worse than anything she'd yet to experience.

Each second that passed spread more regret into Evylin's veins. They'd faced so much danger already, and they were pressing even deeper into the heart of peril. What would happen if one of them died during this mission? Could Evylin handle waking after potentially years of unconsciousness only to discover herself devoid of her husband? And what of Deckard himself? She'd pressed him into their Bond. What if she died and left him to endure that broken desolation alone?

What a foolish, impulsive decision she'd made.

Evylin thought she should confess this revelation to Deckard. He deserved to know what they faced. And he deserved an apology.

From the start of their relationship, Deckard had made sacrifice after sacrifice for her. He'd married a stranger, promised to provide a happy life for her, and proceeded to grant her the adventure she sought despite his clear desire for a simpler life. Had she ever asked him what he wanted? Never once had she taken the time to discover *his* desires.

She knew Deckard well enough to know that he wanted more from life. He'd left Stocburrough because it wasn't enough. He'd remained single for far longer than his peers because no woman was enough for his high standards. He'd dedicated every second of his existence to bettering himself because *he* wasn't enough.

Just as she'd desired "more," he had too. It was part of what drew her to him. Unlike most men she'd met, he aspired to grander things.

What she didn't know was what "more" looked like for him.

Then again, she still didn't know what it looked like for herself either.

"There has to be something else out there. Some other reason to live." She'd said that to Hewitt once, more than three months ago now.

"What would be reason enough to live?" he'd asked.

Evylin needed to talk with her uncle. She needed direction. Her whole life, she'd longed for "more," imagining that achieving such lofty aspirations would mean a life of adventure. But when faced with the realities of her dreams—the truth that adventure was little more than constant travel and near-death experiences—she wasn't so sure it was the "more" she sought.

"What would be reason enough to live?"

After months of waiting for the answer to come to her, Evylin decided it was time to go find it herself.

The three Warriors returned to camp from their training, exhausted and contemplative. The smell of roasted goose and vegetable stew greeted them. In the rusty glow of sunset, the rest of their troop lounged around the camp. Thom sat next to Ilain, talking in low, amused tones. Their friendship had survived his mistakes, and Evylin smiled, knowing that it meant more to him than he'd ever say.

Nearby, Auden tended the meal, talking with Deckard, who pointed to a passage in a rather thick book. Vayden and Isla sat across from them, but Rafferty stood to the side, chatting merrily with Hewitt.

Instantly, Evylin's heart filled at the sight.

Splitting off from Brea, she and Ethenn hurried over to the pair.

"That's because you're cocky," Hewitt was telling Rafferty. "You pay too much attention to how you can outsmart your opponent, and you miss your opportunity to defeat him with simple skill."

"Simple," Rafferty said in a snarky tone, "is boring."

"Simple is effective," Hewitt returned. "And if you don't accept that, then you're an idiot."

With that, Hewitt turned to face Evylin. "Hello, Evie," he said, his words immediately becoming gentle.

Evylin crossed her arms to keep from reaching out for him. "I like seeing you around camp," she remarked.

"I like being around camp," he admitted, then greeted Ethenn. "Has your training been effective?"

"In a manner of speaking," Ethenn said sourly.

Evylin grimaced in agreement. "Brea is a fan of torture, it seems."

Hewitt nodded. "Good. You were getting sloppy."

"I was not!"

"You were grieving," he said casually. "It's to be expected. However, you three—" Hewitt motioned toward Ethenn, Rafferty, and then Thom by the fire, "were not, so you have no excuse for your regression."

Ethenn and Rafferty shared a look that said they disagreed.

Upon Auden's announcement that dinner was ready, they made their way to the fireside. However, Evylin lingered behind for a moment longer, looking up at Hewitt. "I want to talk with you," she whispered. "After dinner."

"Without Deckard?" he asked, a single bushy eyebrow raised.

She nodded.

Hewit returned the gesture, then motioned for her to precede him to the fire. Deckard had risen, returning his book to his saddlebag, so Evylin sat next to the empty spot he'd vacated. As had become the standard in the past three days of travel, Hewitt sat at her side. Though he had no need for food as a ghost, he took every opportunity to stay with her.

Auden handed out bowls to everyone. The hearty meal was made of the last of the meager supplies they'd brought for the beginning of their journey. Once they were back in Ephria, where they could move freely, they would replenish their food stores.

The conversation grew happily chaotic, filling the camp like an overstuffed turkey. It was strange to Evylin how only three more people could add so much more noise.

Deckard returned to the campfire, calling, "Thom." His brother looked up, and Deckard tossed something to him before taking his seat again next to Evylin.

Across the fire, Thom caught the small, cloth-and-twine-wrapped object. "Of course you remembered," he muttered sardonically.

"Remembered what?" Ilain asked from her seat at his side.

Deckard remained silent, a wry grin on his face as he spooned his dinner.

Thom clucked his tongue, unwrapped the object, and blinked. "Are you serious?" he asked.

"Don't lose it this time," Deckard said in a kindly manner.

Evylin peered across, trying to get a view of what Thom held. Given the shadows, she couldn't be sure, but she thought it was a wooden horse.

Thom tapped the toy's back. "I didn't lose it," he said good-naturedly. "Meria broke it, and she made me promise not to tell you because she was terrified that you'd be angry with her."

"She was right to be terrified," Deckard said. "I spent weeks making that bloody thing for you, and I was furious you'd lost it. I'm surprised it took you twenty years to rat her out."

Understanding dawned on Evylin at that moment, the unexplained pieces of the strange scene coming together. "It's your birthday?" she asked Thom.

Everyone stared at him, and Thom let out an embarrassed chuckle. "Uh, yeah," he said, holding the toy fondly. "It is."

A chorus of well-wishes was instantly passed around, and Thom graciously received them. Though he ducked his head bashfully, his side grin spoke of his happiness at being recognized. Evylin immediately saw why Deckard had made a spectacle of giving his gift.

Turning to her husband, Evylin whispered, "You did that on purpose."

"Did what?" he replied with false modesty.

She eyed him knowingly. "You can't fool me." She poked him in the chest. "I can feel what you're feeling, remember? And you're decidedly smug."

"I'm never smug," he said with a smile. "I'm simply glad to know that my brother feels loved and celebrated on his birthday."

Evylin nodded but didn't press him. Instead, she kissed his shoulder. "You're a good brother, Jonn Deckard," she said.

His expression softened, and he shifted closer to her.

The dinner fell to discussing Thom and the topic of birthdays after that. He recounted his favorite birthday: The day Deckard gave him the first iteration of the carved horse named Valor. Then he told them about his least favorite: The day he dislocated his pinky finger after punching the side of the house because he lost a sword fight with Deckard.

And while the conversation was charming and chipper, Evylin found herself frowning internally. This was her first time hearing these stories, just like the rest of the troop. She hadn't even known that Deckard did woodworking. And while she was rather certain that he was thirty-two at the time of their marriage, she suddenly realized that she'd never learned the date of his birthday. They'd been married for almost half a year. Had it already passed?

Once again, Evylin was faced with the reality that she didn't know her husband. It was disheartening. How could she make him happy when she didn't know what he wanted out of life? How was she supposed to love him—well and with care—when she couldn't even think of an appropriate gift to give him once she did learn the date of his birth?

And for Allore's sake, she couldn't even recall their anniversary!

While the conversation around them continued, Deckard leaned close to her. "Are you all right?" he whispered.

Blinking herself out of her worried thoughts, Evylin forced herself to nod. "Yes," she assured him. "Yes, I'm just thinking."

"I guessed that," he said lightly. "But it felt like you were . . . frustrated, maybe? I'm not sure. I can't quite tell the emotions apart sometimes."

Evylin couldn't help smirking. "I'm glad I'm not the only one who struggles to interpret them."

"Most certainly not." He brushed his hand comfortingly across her back. "Sometimes, I can't even tell whether they're yours or mine."

"I've been doing that too," she said, pressing into his side. "Do you think it's normal?"

"I have no idea." He dipped his chin, giving her a determined look. "But back to what you were feeling. Was it frustration?"

Uncertain if she should reveal her true thoughts here in the presence of others—be their conversation overheard or not—Evylin hesitated. She wanted to be honest with Deckard. They'd had too many misunderstandings in the past because of her withholding. But she didn't want to discuss the subject here.

"Not now," she said quietly. "I promise I'll tell you another time, but . . ."

When she glanced toward the others, he nodded, understanding. "Another time," he agreed.

Setting her empty bowl on the ground, Evylin glanced at Hewitt. "Could I talk with Hewitt?" she asked.

Deckard didn't hesitate. "Of course."

With his direction, Evylin rose and hurried into the trees where Deckard said the ghost would be. Sure enough, he was waiting readily. His scruffy beard and unruly hair didn't ruffle in the cold evening breeze. His military coat stretched across his broad shoulders yet showed no more wear than on the day he'd died.

"Now," Hewitt said, voice a soothing rumble, "what's bothering you?"

Evylin smiled forlornly. "Many things," she admitted.

He waited patiently.

With a sigh, Evylin leaned against an elm. "I don't know what to do," she whispered.

"In regard to what?"

"Life." She scoffed at the grandiosity of that sentiment. "If we make it through this, I'm going to live for roughly two hundred years, maybe more. I love Jonn, I'm happy being with him, and I know those two hundred years are going to be . . . so full. Full of everything good."

Evylin paused, scanning her uncle's face. "And yet, I don't know what I want any more now than I did three months ago."

Hewitt gave her a dry smile. "Adventure isn't what the storybooks say, is it?"

"Not even a little."

He dipped his chin, compassion in his gaze even as he fell silent.

Evylin sighed. "When we were children," she murmured, almost afraid to speak the words, "Ryen and I made all these grand plans. We were going to travel the world. And after he died, I thought that dream was lost even as I clung to it."

"It's why I got you out," Hewitt said.

"I know." She smiled sadly. "I knew even then—when you convinced Jonn and me to marry. All of this was meant to give me our dream. To give Ryen our dream, even if he couldn't be here with me."

Hewitt's silence was confirmation.

"But the problem is, Uncle," she said. "I don't think I want it anymore. I don't think I wanted it even then. Because I didn't know what it was. Instead, I blindly followed our plans, thinking that even without Ryen, adventure was still what I desired."

"You find that it isn't?"

She tipped her head in thought. "No, I—I do desire it. But I think I've discovered that it isn't enough. It isn't *all* that I want—traveling the world, going from one adventure to the next. I want more."

"And what is that more?" Hewitt asked.

"I don't know." Evylin let out a low hum of bemusement. "Isn't that awful? I want more, but I don't know why what I have isn't good enough."

"Then you should ask yourself why," he advised.

Evylin frowned into the darkness of the night, attempting to do as he said. Why wasn't what she already had enough? After years of pining and hoping, she had the adventure for which she'd longed. She lived like the heroes in her novels, like the legends she and Ryen swore to become one day themselves. To make it even better, she was married to a man she loved, one who was determined to give her a life full of the adventure she craved.

So why wasn't it enough?

"I don't like this game," Evylin said in good-natured agitation. "It confuses me."

Hewitt chuckled. "You don't have to figure it out in one moment, Evie. Most people don't figure it out in their entire lifetime. As you have two to three times that ahead of you, don't worry so much. You have time."

"Do I, though?" Evylin shook her head. "We are assisting the Alliance's overthrow of two monarchies. If we are successful, they hope to place us in a role as part of their governing leadership. I'll admit I'm not entirely certain what that might look like, but I don't doubt they'll require us to make a choice the instant Allund is reestablished. But if I don't know what I want before that day, how am I supposed to make that choice?"

Hewitt considered her, tugging on his beard. "They want you to lead?"

"As a Bonded couple, yes," she confirmed. "They want us to carry the Space Relic and take on a role in the newly formed government."

"Interesting," he muttered. Then he gave her an inquisitive look. "What is Deckard's take on this?"

"He doesn't want any part in it."

"Fool," Hewitt said through a scoff. "The man is offered what he bloody desires, and he rejects it."

Evylin tugged on her rings. "Being royalty is not what he desires."

"No, I suppose you're right," he admitted. "He aspires to become a legend, someone this world cannot forget. But the role of governing royalty would almost certainly ensure that."

She felt her brow draw low in thought. "So you think he really does want the role, but is, what? Too afraid to admit it?"

Hewitt's steely gaze was contemplative as he stared unseeingly toward the camp. "Perhaps his fear isn't so different from your own," he said. "You were afraid of losing him, so you convinced yourself you couldn't love him even though you already did."

Hewitt met her stare. "Thom told us from the start, Evie: Every choice Deckard has ever made is in pursuit of being perfect. His mind is set on morality and humility, determined to become a paragon of ideal virtues. Therefore, his personal aspirations—his desire to become someone of importance and ultimate worth—are seen as selfish flaws. I've spoken to him about those ends, and he blatantly rejects them on principle. Yet, it doesn't change the fact that he holds out hope that he may someday be as important to the history of Terraeus as Euon Sergus. He just wants to work toward that goal in such a way that he cannot be seen as self-seeking."

Evylin crossed her arms against the cold breeze, listening intently as Hewitt continued, "Deckard is afraid of his ambitions, of giving into his baser self. So, like you, he's convinced himself he doesn't want it even though he longs for it more than anything in this world."

The truth was clear, though Evylin had a hard time relegating such motivations to her husband. Deckard was always so considerate and honorable. Every day of his life, he lived with unflagging nobility, denying himself for the sake of others. He'd even deferred their entire future to her whims, proclaiming he'd abandon their responsibilities to make her happy.

"My life is yours, Evylin."

But Deckard's life couldn't be hers. Not when it belonged to so many other people too. Jonn Deckard had always been a servant—to Thom, their parents, their sister and her family, the Ephrian Army, his ideals, and now, to the coming Allundan nation. No matter what he said, he could never be happy following her from one adventure to the next. It wouldn't be enough for him, just as it wasn't enough for her.

Evylin dropped her face into her hands and let out an exasperated sigh. "Why is this so difficult?" she complained, letting her arms flop down to her sides. "Uncle, tell me what to do. Tell me how to make him happy."

Hewitt scowled. "How should I know what will make him happy? He's your husband."

"And yet, you know him better than I," Evylin said as if the words were an accusation. "How is it that you know his heart's deepest desires, and I don't even know his birthday?"

"You don't know his birthday?"

"Don't start with me."

Hewitt gave her a knowing smirk. "I listen to people, Evylin. Not to what they say but to what they mean. I've always been able to discern a lie, manipulation, or pretense from reality because I'm not interested in the surface. I aim to know the truth, ugly as it may prove to be."

Evylin pursed her lips. "And I'm content to take what people say at face value," she realized. "Which is probably why I didn't see Thom's jealous attentions for what they were."

"It isn't a fault," Hewitt said. "You and I are different people. We always have been. It's what made us such a good team."

The deepest urge welled inside of Evylin, her arms aching to hug her uncle just once more. As she could never wrap her arms around him again, her eyes filled with tears instead. "I want you back," she murmured.

Hewitt's expression softened. "You can't have me back. That's the way of life."

"Life is unfair."

"As unfair as it ever was."

Evylin sighed. "I still don't know what to do," she said with good-natured bitterness.

Hewitt smiled, taking a step closer. His dark gray eyes bored into hers with all the affection and warmth he held back from everyone else. "You'll figure it out," he promised, then tipped his head toward camp. "Together."

The deepest gratitude filled her. "Thank you," she whispered. "For him. For everything. Even if this journey has brought me a broken heart, even if it took you from me . . . I don't think I'd go back."

"I wouldn't let you."

Evylin took a deep breath, the heartbreak of losing him remaining but easing slightly. "We never said it very much, but I love you, Uncle, just as I loved Ryen. He was my everything, and so were you."

Hewitt dipped his chin, notably and surprisingly bashful. "I never deserved such admiration," he said. Then he smiled, large and full, for the first time in what might have been thirteen years. "But even in death," he spoke through a growl choked with emotion, "I will endeavor to deserve it."

CHAPTER TWENTY-ONE

Ilain

2ND OF RADIA, 1574

In an ideal world, Ilain would never have left her parents' home in Faurna. She would have grown up among the rolling moors, riding horses through the heather, and enjoying a small life.

Instead, her skin itched, and her hair was greasy. She'd been traveling so long that she should have become used to dirt under her nails and the constant ache in her limbs. It wasn't her age that made the journey difficult. Being a forty-three-year-old Mage was not the same as being a regular human in their forties. Magic kept her from feeling the natural weakening of age. Her muscles were still strong, her body in its prime.

No, the bone weariness within came from a distinct incongruity to who Ilain really was at her core.

Using the back of her wrist, Ilain brushed the hair from her eyes. Her fingers were caked with spices as she seasoned the rabbits. As she finished her task, she handed them over to Auden—some for drying, others for dinner that night. The meat sizzled in the pot, letting the scent of robust coriander and sharp rosesprig drift through the air.

Tucked between her brother and her betrothed, Ilain glanced longingly at Brea and Isla, lounging a few feet away and teaching Thom the rudiments of the Schonese language. She didn't particularly care for their company—though she loved her sister-in-law and did miss Thom's regular conversation, oddly enough—but she envied their freedom from the slime and sinew of raw rabbit.

Ilain was a woman who *liked* being a woman. She enjoyed the finer, more feminine things life offered—dresses, of course, and regular bathing being chief among them. But she also loved embroidery, poetry, music, drawing, and dancing. She liked grand parties, palatial luxury, and overindulgent food. Her life as a Mage granted her access to many of those things. Yet, it also came with the weight of injustice.

If Ilain could have chosen any life for herself, she would have remained in Faurna, non-magical and insignificant. She would have still worn many beautiful dresses, danced at all the local parties, and maintained the freedom of the tranquil life she truly preferred.

No one would guess that Ilain desired such a menial life. She'd worked hard to ensure it. Why should she—the ostentatious, flippant, reactive flirt—care to live a life of tedium?

Don't let people know what you value, and they can't take it away from you.

That was Ilain's guiding principle in the thirty-two years she'd lived in the Order of the Flame's tower. It was the only thing that kept her safe, kept her sane. The mantra and Auden.

Handing another fillet to her brother, Ilain smiled to herself. Auden had always been there for her. Even when he traveled for his work as a magister, he sent her constant notes to keep her company. And he had never been gone for long.

As a viceMage, Ilain's duties kept her bound to the Order's tower continually. When the breadth of her magic had been discovered, she quickly became a political figurehead, a symbol of power, both for the Order and for the Alliance. The people began to recognize her as Pyra reincarnated, and she'd climbed ranks quickly throughout her youth, moving from probate to aterian within ten years, a pace unheard of amongst the Orders. Yet, she'd never spent her time hired out as a regular aterian would.

Not with the power she wielded.

The Order of the Flame's archMage, Hybold Daleran, saw Ilain's potential from the start and wanted to ensure she never got away. Unlike the other aterians produced by the Order, he wasn't willing to sell Ilain off to the nobility's highest bidder. She was more than a simple guard, he'd professed. She was an asset to the whole of the Order. And so, he set her up to become his right hand, training her in politics and nurturing her mind as well as her power.

"It will be good for you, Lainy," Auden had told her. *"These are the skills you'll need when things change—when* you *run Doorstunds Reach."*

They'd always been careful when discussing the Alliance within the Order's walls. No one would be shocked to hear that Ilain aimed to take ArchMage Daleran's place. But they needed everyone to believe it would be upon his retirement and not through a coup that overthrew all the Orders and the monarchy itself.

"Do you really want to rule . . . or is it just what's expected of you?"

Ilain glanced at Ethenn on her other side. He was almost finished butchering the rabbits while she and Auden prepared and preserved them. How had Ethenn known her doubts? After all these years of preparing to become the Highlady Chancellor of Doorstunds Reach, Ilain harbored her uncertainty deep within. She hadn't even voiced her hesitation to Auden—and she told Auden *everything*.

Yet, somehow, Ethenn suspected the truth.

Perhaps that's why she liked the young man so much. He was vastly observant and keenly alert. He knew her and her heart without needing a word to be spoken between them, which was strangely touching. It made her feel seen in a way she had never been in her entire life.

Vayden dropped down beside the campfire. His tunic collar was rimmed with sweat from training. On the far side of camp, Hewitt's ghost stood with Deckard, Evylin, and Rafferty. Ilain was glad for their final days with the man, even if she still found his ghostly presence unsettling. It wasn't natural, no matter how safe Lord Obel claimed. And she knew that it made Auden uncomfortable as well.

"That's exhausting," Vayden said with a huff. "I haven't trained so hard in years."

Auden and Ilain shared a grin. "You are quite old," she teased. Though Vayden was only four years older than her, his non-magical body *had* experienced the rigors of age. And despite his lifetime as a spy impersonating Prince Rouland Blount II, he'd been out of the service for the past seven years.

"So are you, Lain," he returned good-naturedly.

Ethenn shifted uncomfortably beside her but kept his eyes down.

However, Vayden caught the movement. Ilain saw the shift in her eldest brother's demeanor. He remained playful, but his eyes studied the young Warrior with pointed interest.

Casually, Vayden cleared his throat, gaze locked on Ethenn. "While the others are distracted," he said, a light tilt to his voice, "I think it's the perfect time for me to do a little brotherly bonding."

Ilain snorted, hearing the truth behind his words. "You mean brotherly interrogating," she said.

"Not at all," he argued. "I've hardly gotten to know my little sister's betrothed. Seems an error of my judgment, and I'd like to rectify it."

Ethenn hardly looked up from his work, his hands preoccupied with skinning the last of the rabbits. "What would you like to know?" he asked, sounding neither forthcoming nor perturbed.

Ilain smirked. This was the same Ethenn who sat across from her beneath the willow two nights ago: reserved and guarded but smart enough to know he couldn't completely ignore the questions in front of him. *Why is he so closed off?* she wondered. *What has caused him to cling this tightly to self-preservation?*

Ilain knew why she protected her innermost self. She hid her truest values so others couldn't exploit or take them from her. But what caused Ethenn to defend his secrets so fiercely?

"Well," Vayden began, "you're a soldier now, but I know that's a recent development. What were you before?"

"I was a hunter," Ethenn said flatly. "But when I wasn't in the woods, I also worked in my uncle's smithy to pick up the slack."

"Sounds like you were busy."

"I was."

"And where did you live?"

"A small town in Estshire," he explained. "I believe we'll pass by on our way to the Terrae Keep."

Ilain perked up. "We will? Does that mean I'll get to see your hometown?"

Ethenn shrugged. "I'm not sure if we'll actually ride through Trollenston, but perhaps. Though it isn't much to see."

"Does your family still live there?" Vayden asked, and Ilain tried not to flinch. It was clear by Ethenn's avoidance of her own questions about his family that there was something damning he didn't want to say.

Ethenn's jaw tightened, but he replied, "Some."

"Do you have any siblings?" Vayden asked, either unaware of Ethenn's discomfort or not caring to acknowledge it.

With a final flick of his knife, Ethenn ripped the hide from the rabbit's muscle. He deftly slit it from neck to bottom and began to flay it from the bone. "A sister," he said.

Ilain blinked in surprise.

"I didn't know you had a sister," Auden said.

Ethenn shrugged. "It never came up, I suppose."

Vayden smiled brightly. "Older or younger? No, let me guess." He held up a hand, considering. "You've got a protective 'weight-of-the-world' sort of manner. The kind that demands you take care of those you love, even to your own detriment. You're the eldest, aren't you?"

Ethenn made his final slits to deconstruct the mammal, then handed it over to Ilain for seasoning. "Yes," he said without emotion, then stood. "Excuse me, I need to wash up."

And with that, Ethenn walked away.

Ilain and her brothers watched him thoughtfully.

"Is he usually so withholding?" Vayden asked quietly.

Ilain turned back to him with a pointed stare.

"I'm just curious, Lainy," Vayden said. "He's your betrothed, which makes him my brother. It makes him family. Yet, neither Auden nor you knew he had a sister?"

"Like he said," Ilain replied, shaking the jar of spices over the fillets of deep pink meat. "It never came up."

Auden nodded. "We don't exactly sit around telling childhood stories."

"And Ethenn is reserved," Ilain added. "He doesn't tell you things if you don't specifically ask about them."

"I know you, Lain," Vayden said. "Family is important to you. You asked, and he lied."

"He didn't lie," she said. "He simply didn't tell the full truth."

"Why not?"

Ilain met Vayden's gaze. "How should I know? We've been together less than a week, Vayd. He's had no reason to tell me these things, no reason to trust me with them."

"He's your husband."

Keeping her voice low, Ilain said, "He's been hurt."

Vayden and Auden's brows dipped in a nearly identical fashion. It reminded Ilain of their da. Despite the fact that Vayden didn't share their Calder blood, he'd adopted their da's mannerisms too. A testament that love and not genetics made family.

Ilain's gaze shifted between her brothers. "I don't know how, and I don't know by whom," she confessed. "But somehow, someone has hurt him—deeply. And he doesn't trust people anymore."

Auden dropped his eyes to his work while Vayden pursed his lips. His gaze flickered toward the Warrior in question, who was now talking with Hewitt and the others.

"I intend to fix that," Ilain said with determination. "No matter how long it takes."

Auden nudged her shoulder with his. His expression was soft as he smiled at her. "If anyone can do it," he whispered, "it's you."

"Because he loves me?"

"Because you are the most trustworthy woman Terraeus has ever known."

Ilain's heart pinched with affection and guilt. She leaned over, pressing a kiss to Auden's shoulder, and then rested her head there. He pressed his temple against hers before returning to his task.

Then Ilain rose to rid her hands of the rabbit and spices.

Using a bar of lye soap, Ilain kept her gaze on her hands in the wooden bucket.

Auden was wrong, of course. He'd always been too quick to believe in her. Perhaps it was because she usually shared her true heart with him. He knew her, even when no one else did. But she was a liar, as she'd told Ethenn. She wasn't trustworthy. She was a fraud.

If she'd been truly honest, she would have told Ethenn everything about the moment she'd realized her affection for him and the fear that accompanied it, as well as her hopes for their future. She would tell him that she didn't just like him; she loved him. But she feared his derision.

After Thom's assertion that Ilain didn't want Ethenn—could *never* want him—she worried that Ethenn wouldn't believe her when she spoke of her love. She needed to ensure his trust in her before admitting such a profound truth. Liar that she was, proving her honesty was a feat she wasn't sure even she had the power to accomplish.

Hands refreshed and clean, Ilain returned to Auden's side. Isla had joined Vayden, the two of them speaking in hushed Schonese. Ilain understood most of the language, but she didn't bother listening. Instead, she picked up her sketchbook and enjoyed her brother's steady company as he tended the evening meal.

With rote familiarity, Ilain's fingers began to sketch, finding the sharp angles of Auden's face easily. She'd drawn her whole family time and time again. They filled most of her sketchbooks with mixtures of strangers and acquaintances scattered throughout. It was rare that she'd repeated any but her family's images until she'd met their troop. Then she found the newcomers to be a unique case study.

Ephrians bore a fuller softness in their features. Of course, Jonn and Thom shared some of the Waulden sharpness, though they still bore a gentler tilt in their mouths and noses. With his paleness and broad forehead, Rafferty carried a Zemordian flair (he claimed a tale about an albino great-grandmother on his mother's side; however, at the mention of her notably violet eyes, Ilain determined she was, in fact, from the northwestern continent of Zemord), but even he was a true Ephrian despite his ghostly complexion.

As for Hewitt, Evylin, and Ethenn . . . They were true Shiremen. And she loved to draw them all.

Though she'd met several Ephrians through her work with the Alliance, she'd never spent longer than a few days around them due to her position as viceMage. This mission granted her an opportunity unlike any she'd ever had before to study the people of eastern Allund.

But after months together, Ilain found herself returning to the practice of sketching her family. Her parents, Daultun and Rowana. Her brothers, Vayden and Auden. Isla. Reyana. And Maura.

Ilain had only ever met Maura a few times, but she'd been sure to sketch the woman carefully, capturing each angle. She found herself draping the starting lines on the page alongside her brother's image.

Maura was a beautiful woman. Soft blonde hair curled freely around her shoulders. Striking blue-green eyes twinkled intelligently. She was trim, demure, and tall. In their first meeting, Maura had worn a dark purple coat with a high collar and golden embroidery. Despite her position in the Order of the Night, the woman maintained an air of gentility and grace. She wasn't brutish or malevolent. She wasn't egotistical or self-seeking.

Maura had been a magister like Auden, desiring only knowledge and the excitement of discovery.

Until her brother's death.

Then Maura lost herself, and Auden lost her.

Angling in his seat next to her, Auden's jaw tightened. "You got her nose wrong," he commented quietly.

"I got nothing wrong," Ilain replied.

"It's too long."

"You always did idealize her," she returned kindly. "Her nose was her one flaw. Hooked and far too long for her face."

"You take that back."

"I will not."

Dryly, Auden grinned, leaning against the saddles behind their backs. His demeanor became melancholy, as it always did when he thought of Maura, but despite his somberness, he also bore an air of contentment.

Ilain could read her brother's moods without fail. Auden was like the other half of her heart, the steady and even-tempered part. He wasn't over Maura—he never would be. Yet, with more than two decades removed from her descent into the Deep, he'd found a means of survival, even if that was through compartmentalizing his heartbreak by means of dedicating his life to healing her.

"I miss her," Ilain whispered.

"You didn't know her," Auden replied, staring at the fire.

Ilain rested her charcoal on the sketchbook's page and turned to him. "I knew her through you," she said. "And I miss who you were when she was in your life."

Auden offered her a weak smile. "I do too," he admitted.

Ilain took his hand on the terrae between them. "You don't have to sacrifice yourself to save her," she insisted for the hundredth time. "I can find a way."

"There's no guarantee," Auden said. "Even if you convince the Day Chancellor to help you, whoever it might be, they will not work endlessly to ensure her salvation. Only I will."

"Do not forget *me*," Ilain countered sharply. "You are not alone in this mission, Auden. And as the most powerful Mage in two centuries," she raised her brow, "I will *make* the Day Chancellor find a cure for Maura."

Auden's expression grew hesitant, so Ilain tightened her grip. "Then you could be with her," she whispered. "You've no chance with Brea, that we know. And while you may find another Warrior before the Administration demands a pair be Bonded, the odds of you loving her . . ."

He dipped his chin. "I will come to love her," he said dully.

"And Maura will wake to find that she cannot be with you." Ilain seared him with her glare. "She will have lost her entire family *and* the man she loves."

Auden swallowed, drawing his hand away from hers. "We've had this argument many times, Ilain."

"And you know I'm right."

"I do. It will hurt to let Maura go, but she will be healed and free, and that is what matters. She can find another husband, and I will be glad knowing I gave her a good life." He gave her a pointed stare then. "But if I give up—if I put all my hope in you promising to convince another Day Mage to shunt all responsibility until they find a cure for the woman I love, it may be too late.

"Her body is aging," he reminded Ilain. "Her mind is decaying. When she comes out of the Deep, she will need great care until she is whole again. If we wait much longer, it will be *too* late. Her body will deteriorate, and her mind will be wholly gone. Twenty-two years in stasis . . . She's already dying. And I will lose her wholly if I don't save her now."

Ilain held his fierce gaze. Auden was never as passionate as when he spoke of Maura. "Do you think I would let that happen?" she asked.

"I don't think you would have much choice," Auden said. His even-tempered mood returned, and he gave her a sad smile. "I will find another Warrior. We will marry and Bond, and I will save Maura and every other Mage locked in the Deep. That's *my* sacrifice for a better future. And it isn't such a bad one."

Ilain dipped her chin. She didn't want to accept his resignation. She wanted to see him happy with the woman he loved. But she either believed what she professed, or she didn't.

If Auden Bonded with a Warrior, he would come to love her. Perhaps it wouldn't be the same love he harbored for Maura, but eventually, their romance would be filled with passion and joy too. He was right. It wasn't such a bad sacrifice to make. Love, power, influence, and the chance to save the life of someone he cared for. Who could reject such a future?

Ilain's gaze drifted across the camp to where Ethenn sat with Evylin, laughing at something Hewitt had said. *Love, power, and influence.* That was the future ahead of her too. Marriage to a man she loved, the great power of Bonded magic, and a governing influence over a restored nation.

So why did it feel as though the slightest breeze would snuff out the flame of her happiness?

Ilain's grip felt loose on her fleeting future. If she didn't secure their marriage, Ethenn could take it away. He claimed to love her, yet still, he lied to her and rejected her. Why?

Ilain glanced over at Ethenn, her heart squeezing with fear.

This Warrior—observant, keen-eyed hunter that he was—saw through her better than anyone else. From the start, he'd seen her for who she really was: a fearful, lonely woman whose entire future was founded on the dreams of others. Ilain acknowledged that she was two-faced and two-hearted. Half of her longed for the chancellorship. Half of her wished she could be normal. Simple. Mundane. *Loved.*

Don't let people know what you value, and they can't take it away from you.

Maybe Ethenn had thought he loved her before he truly knew her but was realizing upon closer inspection that she wasn't what he'd desired after all. Maybe he recognized the brutal truth of Ilain Calder: She was a fraud and an actress, a fragile doll dressed in gilded gowns and sparkling jewels, who had no more substance than a child's plaything.

And maybe soon he'd take his love away from her, leaving her with a broken heart.

CHAPTER TWENTY-TWO

3RD OF RADIA, 1574

The Allmar mountains towered overhead, resembling a surge of ocean waves turned to stone. Their horses moved anxiously along the narrow switchbacks, the pebbles crunching beneath their hooves. The troop had dismounted to navigate to the Alliance's hidden passage, making the journey slow and challenging. The terrain was not just perilous; wild animals lurked within the caves and forests of the ridge, necessitating constant vigilance.

"You and Auden traveled this path alone?" Evylin asked Ilain when the path widened enough for them to walk two by two.

Ilain nodded, keeping her voice hushed as she replied, "It was no more fun than it is now." The corner of her mouth lifted. "It was easier, though, being just the two of us. We didn't even have horses."

At the start of their journey, the Calders had told the troop of their travels from Wauld to Ephria, but now Evylin realized they must have lied about most of it. After all, they hadn't told them they'd taken a secret path through the mountains. Instead, they'd reported that they used magic to sneak across the border. She wondered what else they'd altered to create a suitable tale.

To make the journey worse, the rain had returned. In the mountain's shadow, the cold wind splattered them across the face, biting into their cheeks and noses despite their hoods. Evylin was more than ready to quit Wauld and exchange the dampness for sunshine. Even if it was spring, the weather in Ephria was never as wet and dreary as its western counterpart.

After hours of travel, Auden finally stopped them at the entrance of a cave. He conjured an orb, its butter-yellow glow illuminating their path and ensuring there weren't any animals lurking inside. The horses were uneasy in the confined space, needing considerable coaxing to press forward in the darkness.

"Shouldn't there be magic that helps animals to cooperate?" Thom grumbled.

"There is," Ilain said casually.

Thom paused on the path, his face filling with awe. "Really? Which one?"

"Well, Terrae Mages are typically reasonable at it. But as Day magic speaks to life itself, it can also reach past the psyche and touch the soul."

"Then why doesn't Auden—"

Auden interrupted before the full question could be posed. "Because it takes a great deal of power, and I'm not particularly keen on wasting my energy talking to a horse."

So on through the darkness they progressed. Auden's orb of light hung over their heads, casting strange shadows on the stone walls, which were slick with condensation. The air grew continually colder until it settled at a frigid temperature that sent gooseflesh across Evylin's skin. The horses snorted their discontent but continued at a steady clop.

Eventually, the terrae began to decline beneath their feet. Auden had informed them that the passage would take them beneath the mountains themselves through an underground cavern. It would take a full day to cross. When they'd asked if any dangers prowled within the cavern, Ilain had replied, "No more than in the mountains above." None of them felt much better about the trek after that.

Evylin decided she didn't like caves. It reminded her of the Night Keep, closed off and full of shadows. And she'd read enough novels to know paths through underground caverns were usually an invitation to death. The closed-in spaces made her feel like the world was pressing in. It was too still, too quiet within these stone walls. When a sound did occur, she jumped, fearing that a monstrous creature was coming from the depths to eat them whole.

In the cavern's wide halls, Deckard found his way to Evylin's side. "Is my mind deceiving me?" he asked lightheartedly. "Or are you afraid?"

The aura of emotion radiating off him said he was just as uncomfortable as she was. Evylin smirked, grateful for his distracting company. "Warriors don't get scared," she said. "We simply have a healthy respect for the unknown."

"Ah, yes, I should have assumed that." In the glow of the orb, Deckard raised his brow. "I must have mistaken your feelings for mine, then."

She nudged his arm teasingly. "If you need comfort, I'm sure Thom would be willing to hold your hand."

"I believe he's a bit too preoccupied with his horse at the moment."

Evylin glanced over her shoulder, seeing Thom struggling yet again with his horse. Brea stepped up to him, exchanged her horse's reins with his, and moved on, the mare following her willingly, no longer protesting. Thom gaped after her like she'd tamed a wolf.

Chuckling, Evylin turned back to Deckard. "Seems he's free now," she said.

"Seems you're right," Deckard said, his gaze lingering on the scene. A slight tinge of emotion muddled his aspect for only a moment before he returned his coy grin to her. "But you see, I find the presence of a Warrior far more soothing to my sensibilities."

"Is that so?"

"Mm-hm." He dipped his chin. In the shadows, his hair turned a deep brown, and his scruff appeared thicker. Still, his eyes shone with a bright blue in the radiant light of Auden's orb. "They're immensely safer to be around, being that they can kill anything they put their mind to."

Evylin snorted despite her attempt to remain stoic in their banter. "Then perhaps you'd find Ethenn to be a superior comfort. After all, he's far stronger than I. Or Brea would be a fantastic savior. She's had decades of practice and is vastly more skilled than both of us."

"You know," Deckard said, giving her a wide-eyed look as though that thought were greatly appealing, "I'd not considered that perspective."

"Shall I call her over for you?"

Deckard pressed his lips together around a dubious hum. "Alas, no, I think not."

"No?"

"I believe my wife might become jealous as I'm a Mage, and she might think a Warrior would have designs on me."

"Oh, yes, I can see how that might be a problem." She forced down a smirk to sigh dramatically. "Well, I'm afraid that means you'll have to leave me too."

"Truly?"

"Indeed. After all, I, too, am a Warrior," she said, then let her gaze turn sultry, "and I have *great* designs upon you."

A soft affection came to Deckard's face, his feelings shifting to something between tenderness and want. "Well, I have good news," he said, voice hushed as if in a conspiratorial whisper. "The wife of whom I spoke? She's you."

Evylin gasped in mock awe. "Well, then, perhaps I'll take you behind the nearest rock pillar and have my way with you."

His eyes twinkled with mirth. "They're called stalagmites."

"I don't care what they're called."

"Hm." He gave her a cunning stare before turning away. His hand found hers beneath the folds of her cloak, and their fingers entwined.

They walked in silence then, taking quiet comfort in the other's presence. Dreadful creatures of the depths or not, they would be safe together.

After hours of traversing the darkness, the troop stopped to camp in another grand cavern. They hobbled the horses and placed them in a small alcove to ensure they wouldn't wander away. A stream trickled through the main hall, giving them the ability to refill their waterskins after Isla treated it with Water magic to ensure its purity. They didn't bother with a campfire, letting Auden's light orb glow, giving them just enough light to see without attracting any lurking creatures (hopefully).

Pressed against the damp rock walls, they didn't put up the tents or spread out the bedrolls but huddled close and doubled blankets to keep warm. The stalagmites loomed around them, and the orb light turned their long shadows into claws, as though they were sitting in the giant paw of a dragon.

It seemed their surroundings got the others to thinking about terrifying creatures as well because Thom said, "I've been thinking. The Keeps' Guardians? They were a dragon, a bloodwolf, and a flying bear-bird—"

"A *vængebjörn*," Ilain corrected.

"Right," Thom said dryly. "But they're all magical constructs, aren't they? Like the Shades."

"Well, yes, technically," Auden said. "But the ancient Mages did base them on real creatures. Why do you think we have tales of dragons, bloodwolves, and *vængebjörn*?"

"Because people like to make stuff up," Thom replied defensively. "We have all kinds of fairytales and implausible stories that some bloke randomly imagined."

Evylin cocked her head to the side, thinking of all the fantastic novels she'd read in her life. Stories filled with daring feats of courage, wild tests of strength, and mythical creatures of imagination. Only a few months ago, Evylin would have agreed with Thom, denying that any of the magical things she'd read were true. But now she was a Warrior, Bonded to a Mage. Perhaps the impossible was possible after all.

She turned to Thom with a smirk and asked, "Implausible stories like the existence of Mages?"

His face scrunched in distaste as a few around the camp chuckled softly.

"Bloodwolves are real," Brea said suddenly. "I've fought one before."

"Really?" Evylin gasped, her memory conjuring the hound they'd fought in the Night Keep with its violet veins and giant girth. The creature was frightening and deadly. She couldn't fathom facing one of true flesh.

Brea nodded. "We call them *demolobis* in Schon—demonwolves. The few remaining live in the Doraespin Mountains, though they aren't what they once were."

"Their magic is gone," Isla added. "Though they say the *Madraloba* sleeps in the darkest caverns, waiting for her power to return so she can restore her children's power and drink the blood of Mages."

Uncomfortably, Deckard shifted beside Evylin. "Do you really believe these creatures exist?" he asked.

"I just told you I fought one," Brea said. "Of course, I believe they exist."

He gave a faint, placating smile. "Yes, but I mean, the real creatures of myth. These demonwolves of Schon are clearly what inspired the tales. That doesn't mean that their magical counterparts were real too."

Brea said something in Schonese to Isla, who grinned dryly. But it was Auden who spoke. "The creatures of myth are real, Jonn," he said calmly. "Dragons, *demolobis*, *vængebjörn*. The flamehorn Ilain, Brea, and I fought in the Fire Keep. The wyrm in the Time Keep. They were all once great beasts that filled Terraeus. Until the ancient Mages locked the Relics away. Then magic ebbed, waning away until only the smallest number of Mages and Warriors survived."

Evylin could feel the unrest in Deckard's energy. He didn't like this suggestion that the mythical creatures had once been alive. However, she couldn't help feeling a bit of awe. What if dragons *had* been real? Was it possible that all the other tales were true too? The ones about men and women of old who tamed the creatures of myth, living in harmony with them, and riding them into battle. She'd not read many stories about such feats—Ephren had banned them with mostly great success—but enough to find the notion intriguing.

"What about the one in the Water Keep?" Rafferty asked. "We never did find out what that one was."

Auden answered him readily. "Well, there are eight great mythical creatures, as there are eight resources of life. Though I can't say for certain, not having been there when Blount and his men fought the beast, I'd guess it was a *dieumer*."

"*Dieumer*?" Deckard repeated his pronunciation of the Matteirean word with a far more natural-sounding accent. "What is that?"

"Sea god," Ilain translated. "Also known as a kraken."

"Wonderful," Thom grumbled while Rafferty sat forward in excitement, exclaiming, "I've heard stories about kraken. Growing up in Rasnaack, we heard lots of weird tales, being a waypoint of a sort. But it wasn't until I started going to Bridgewater for business that I got firsthand accounts of such sightings, what with all the sailors coming in and out from the Veridus Sea. One even said there's this pirate down near the

Illes who can control a kraken. But I always thought the story was him showing off. Kraken, eh? They're real?"

"As real as dragons," Ilain said. "Though far more populous near Matteire and lower Giyda than Allund."

"So," Ethenn interjected, brow furrowed in thought, "if there are eight creatures of myth for the eight resources of life . . . What two creatures are left for the Terrae and Space Keeps?"

Evylin ran through the creatures and myths she knew in her head. Auden and Ilain had mentioned six of the eight: flamehorns, dragons, *dieumer* (or krakens), bloodwolves (or *demolobis*, demonwolves), *vængebjörns*, and wyrms. In all her reading and hearing of legends passed down, she'd only known of dragons, bloodwolves, and kraken. Now, she could only think of one other.

"The Living Land," Evylin said quietly. "It was a creature in *The Traveler and the Rook* who spoke with Iona the Worthy, teaching her to care for Terraeus properly."

Auden nodded. "Likely our Terrae Guardian, yes."

"Wasn't that just a great clump of dirt?" Rafferty asked.

"Living dirt," Thom confirmed.

"That doesn't sound too bad."

Evylin doubted it would be easy to defeat, even if it did sound simple. "And what about the Space Guardian?" she asked, looking up at Deckard. "I can't think of an eighth creature."

"I wasn't known to study myth," he said good-naturedly, though she could still feel the unease pulsing through him.

"No one remembers the eighth creature," Ilain said, her raspy voice haunting in the shadows of the cavern. "When the ancient Mages locked the Relics away, the creatures of myth disappeared too. They faded from memory, and only a few were immortalized in literature through the millennium. We only remember the names of the seven because of folk tales and the uncovered texts from the Alliance's research."

"So we have no idea what we're facing in the Space Keep?" Thom asked.

She gave him a flat look. "We didn't have any idea what we were facing in the others either. Auden and I knew some of the possibilities, but we didn't know in what order we'd face them." She paused, then added, "Though we were pretty sure about the sea god being in the Water Keep."

"But," Ethenn said worriedly from his place pressed against her side, "they're all gone now, right? These creatures don't exist anymore because they died when the Relics were taken away."

Ilain shrugged, and Auden's expression pinched in uncertainty.

Vayden smirked. "For all their genius, my siblings don't know everything," he remarked. "However, it is presumed that the creatures have either gone extinct or that the loss of magic mutated their forms. As Brea said, *demolobis* no longer appear as the stories say. They aren't the size of buildings, they don't hunger for blood, and they aren't afraid of sunlight."

"So," Rafferty said wryly, "we aren't concerned that by bringing back these Relics, we're bringing back these creatures as well?"

Auden shook his head. "It's highly improbable. And even if we did, the stories suggest that they *could* work in harmony with the Mages and Warriors if given the right incentive."

Evylin pursed her lips at the uncertain statement. She couldn't decide whether the potential of these mythical creatures' return was horrifying or thrilling. Perhaps a little of both.

"On that pleasant note," Thom said. He shifted, settling himself on the ground between Deckard and Rafferty. "Brea and I've got the second shift, so excuse me while I try to forget this whole conversation in pursuit of two minutes of sleep."

Evylin chuckled, though she understood the sentiment. In the wide-open cavern with the hulking shadows around them, it was too easy to let visions of sneaking bloodwolves fray your nerves.

As much of the camp followed Thom's lead, Evylin huddled closer to Deckard, resting her head on his shoulder. They sat against the back wall, safe in one another's presence and in no hurry to sleep. The watch rotation had continued, and this was their night off. All around them, their friends lay down, clustered together like a flock of sheep. Auden's orb dimmed.

On the other side of the camp, Vayden and Isla sat up to take the first watch. The couple spoke quietly to one another in Schonese. Only the faintest threads of their speech echoed across the cavern to Evylin. Deckard's fingers grazed her arm, sending a current of magic snapping under her skin.

"Do you believe them?" she whispered so faintly she wondered if he heard.

Deckard adjusted his seating, bringing his lips down to press against her temple. "About what?" he murmured.

"About the creatures," she said. "Do you think the Alliance expects them to return?"

He was silent for several seconds, and she could feel the conflict within him, though she couldn't name all the emotions within it. Hesitation, worry, and . . . anger?

"I don't know what to think," he replied at last, voice low in her ear. "But I'm beginning to doubt this mission of ours."

Evylin tensed. "Why?"

"At every turn, we learn of another secret they're keeping," he whispered. "I don't trust the Alliance. I don't trust their aims."

Unsure how much trust she placed in the organization herself, Evylin scanned the camp as she reflected on Deckard's cynicism. Near her, Ethenn lay beside Ilain, their backs pressed against one another. It was an odd sort of intimacy, different from the way she and Deckard were, but still affectionate. And it tugged at Evylin in the strangest way.

These people had become part of their lives. After their months of travel, Ilain felt like a sister to her as surely as Ethenn had become a brother. Even Auden held a place in her heart. They'd fought together, survived together. They'd shared their knowledge and trained them as best they could. Everything the pair did was in pursuit of a better world, spurred on by the love of their brother, who sat in their camp now, sacrificing his own life along with his wife to see that future come to pass for their daughter.

Whatever the Alliance's aims, Evylin had to trust in the goodness of the Calders. Because if people as loving and loyal as the family existed, she wanted to stand by their side.

Evylin looked up at Deckard, softening her gaze. She set a hand on the side of his face, keeping him near. "I think you're wrong," she whispered. "They do not maliciously keep secrets. Whenever we ask, they're forthcoming. It's just that we haven't thought to ask these questions until now."

His demeanor didn't ease, and she could see he didn't believe in the Calders' goodness in the same way.

Remembering Hewitt's advice, Evylin gave him a tender smile. "Do you truly not trust the Alliance? Or is this just your frustration with their hopes for us?"

Deckard flinched, and his emotion flared, but he took a deep breath, steadying himself before responding. "Can not both reasons be true?" he asked.

"Of course they can," she said. "But as I can sense your feelings on this topic, I have a strong suspicion that it's not the case."

With a sigh, he brought his forehead to hers. He didn't bother speaking. Not now, when his emotions did that for him. His very essence was heavy, weighted down with concern, disappointment, and frustration. Evylin didn't know what caused this exact turmoil within him, but she wanted to soothe it away.

She whispered his name, brushing her thumb along his jaw. "Once, you told me not to worry about the future, to focus on our mission, and then we'd figure it out—together. Now, I'm telling you to do the same. Think about the Relics. Think about saving our country. Whatever comes after, we'll be together. And that's all that matters."

Deckard drew her closer. He took solace in her, his mood tempering as she held him.

The soft snorts of sleeping horses and the gentle trickle of the stream echoed in the cavern. Vayden hummed a low, soothing tune. The cold, damp air pricked their skin. And Evylin forced herself to believe her own words. Deckard couldn't know her doubts; he couldn't feel that she was as uncertain as he. She trusted the Calders, but that didn't make her any happier about the expectations of the Alliance.

Whatever came, yes, they would be together. But that *wasn't* all that mattered. And the future wasn't guaranteed.

Once Deckard and Evylin lay down for the night, she stayed awake in his arms for far longer than usual, wondering: Between Relics and thrones, politics and magic, wars and rebellions, would they have any future at all?

CHAPTER TWENTY-THREE

4TH OF RADIA, 1574

After spending the night in the caverns, the troop entered Ephria at last. Deckard was thrilled to be back on their half of the continent. Not only were the Ephrians home again, but their nights under the stars were also almost entirely behind them. There would be times here and there through the rest of their journey that they'd stop at settlements that had no inns or rooms for rent, and they'd still need to keep a keen eye out for Blount and his men. But now that they were back in Ephria and on friendly ground, the group could move with far more freedom.

However, that fact didn't make Deckard any more relaxed. Constantly, his mind pestered him with the reminder that they were in a race against time. Blount's determination to retrieve the Relics put undue pressure on their mission. If the cruel prince wasn't involved, they would have no cause for such expediency. They could take their time, determining whether the Alliance was worthy of service or if they should leave them behind as soon as possible.

Instead, Deckard was forced to make a rash decision, supporting this organization regardless of his lack of understanding of their true aims. He didn't like that. The mounting questions about the organization caused him greater worry with each passing day. He feared toppling the sum of everything he knew and the country he'd sworn to serve in exchange for a questionable government.

After their conversation the previous night, it was now clear to Deckard that he couldn't discuss the topic with Evylin. She wasn't worried about their circumstances.

Deckard couldn't help thinking sourly that it was just like her, being carefree and unconcerned about the intricacies of politics. She'd never been interested in those things; instead, she trusted others to guide her.

Though to be fair, she wasn't letting Deckard determine her opinion on this. She'd made her own choice to trust the Alliance based on her relationship with the Calders.

The problem was that Deckard didn't trust the Calders all that much either. They were fine people and a dedicated family, but with only three months of acquaintance during which they'd lied and duped them into service, there wasn't much to recommend their honorability in his mind. Yes, he liked Auden and Ilain. Yes, he found Vayden and Isla companionable. No, he didn't trust a single one of them.

Under the cheery morning sun, Deckard scanned the rocky, tree-studded terrain of the foothills ahead. After a full day of travel, the mountain range would be behind them, though it would take the rest of their day's travel to get truly free of its rugged grasp upon the land. Then they would return to the lush grasses and open plains of Ephria's heartland.

Tugging back on his reins, Deckard diverted his horse's path. He excused himself from Evylin's side and drifted next to where Thom rode with Vayden. They were discussing the Keeps and Thom's experience as a non-magical individual.

Apologizing for interrupting, Deckard requested that Thom scout ahead with him. Though Vayden immediately acquiesced, Thom gave him a skeptical look. Still, he listened, guiding his horse away from the troop's line to gallop ahead with Deckard.

They rode half a mile ahead before slowing to a trot.

"So," Thom said with amusement. "What did you want to talk about?"

Deckard didn't bother asking how he knew. They rarely bothered with scouting ahead; it'd been too dangerous in Wauld, and it would be altogether unnecessary in Ephria. The request had been a ploy, and there was no reason to deny it.

"Several things," Deckard admitted. "Starting with how you're doing. We haven't had much conversation since our escape and your promise to stop trying to be me."

Thom gave him a wry look.

"You seem to be doing better," Deckard said. "But do you feel you are?"

With a deep inhale, Thom considered the question. Then he shrugged. "Yeah, I suppose I do," he said. "It seems that after royally screwing things up, I'm not so afraid to make mistakes anymore because how could I ever top what I've already done? So being better isn't quite so hard. I *can't* compete with you. Why try? And surprisingly . . ." He smiled. "I don't mind."

Thom let out a self-derisive chuckle then. "It's like I can be myself now because I find, after all, it's impossible to be you. And when I try, I don't like who I am. So why not be myself? Even if I'm not as good as you, I can't be any worse than the man I am when I compete with my own brother."

"You are neither better nor worse than I, Thom," Deckard countered.

"But I am less than you."

When Deckard began to protest, Thom lifted a hand. "I don't mind, now that I've accepted reality," he said genuinely. "You're meant to change this world, Jonn. Men like you—they're different. Small lives aren't enough for them."

Deckard felt his brow pinch, uncomfortable with the statement.

"But small has always been enough for me," Thom continued. "I like being a soldier. I like the routine of it—the order of it. I like being given commands and following through on them. And I don't mind being a lackey for my officers so long as they respect me and I can respect them. I only ever reached for more because I thought you'd never see me as a man of worth if I accepted life as a menial foot soldier."

Steadily, Thom's gaze held his, reassuring Deckard as he said, "I know better now. And I'm beginning to find that I can accept a life of less because I'm not made to save the world. I'm not a Mage or a Warrior. I'm only a man. And men like me aren't meant for greatness."

That sentiment Deckard couldn't disagree with more. "Magical or not, you are no less capable of greatness than anyone else, Thom." He paused, then realized by the look on his brother's face that this wasn't what he wanted to hear. Thom was through with aspiring to more; it had only led him to ruin. Now, he was only looking to redeem himself—not the world. Greatness couldn't factor in at this point. Not when he needed to learn how to be happy first.

Deckard sighed and clapped a hand on Thom's shoulder. "Ignore me," he said. "I just want you to feel important because you are. To me, to Evylin, and to so many other people."

"I don't care about other people," Thom said immediately, a smile on his face. "So long as you and Evie want me around, that'll be enough."

"I'm glad," Deckard said. "We want you around for good. And if it ever gets too hard, or you feel like you're slipping back to how things used to be—if *I* make you feel less than—just let me know. I'm here for you, always."

"I know."

"Good."

They rode in silence for a few moments, a strange comfort in the air between them. Their relationship had never felt like this. It had always been hard and fraught with challenges. Before, Deckard could only wish for casual and caring conversations, but now that they had them, it almost felt wrong to indulge in them while their mission loomed ahead.

Shifting in his saddle, Deckard decided to move on. "I was wondering," he began, eyes on the road. "What are your thoughts about the Alliance?"

Thom was quiet for a moment. "I mean, they seem like a fine organization. A bit zealous perhaps but noble in their own way."

Deckard turned to him. "But is that in a good way?"

"What do you mean?"

"I don't trust them, Thom."

His brother's brow rose, but he didn't say anything, so Deckard continued. "They say all the right things, proclaim all the right motives, profess the right faith. And yet, they've lied, manipulated, and even resorted to kidnapping to achieve their cause. How can those be the actions of a noble organization?"

Thom eyed him thoughtfully as their horses plodded onward. He tapped a finger on the saddle's front. "Is this a genuine concern of yours?" he asked. "Or are you just worried they'll press you into service as a king? Sorry—Highlord Chancellor, I believe Ilain called it."

Hearing the derision in his tone, Deckard pursed his lips and turned away. "If you aren't going to take this seriously, then I'll keep my concerns to myself," he said.

"Don't be cross," Thom said lightly. "I'm not saying you're wrong. I'm just questioning your rationale."

Deckard tightened his grip on the reins. "My reasoning is this: If they kidnapped Prince Ephren, allowing the deaths of dozens of men in his capture and our rescue, all to determine if Evylin was a Warrior, why wouldn't they force us into service however they see fit? How can their intentions truly be honorable when they're willing to sacrifice their people so negligently?"

"Maybe it wasn't the *Alliance* doing the sacrificing," Thom offered.

Deckard stared at him, dumbfounded and confused.

Thom tipped his chin back toward the rest of the troop riding half a mile behind. "You heard Isla the other day," he said. "The people of the Alliance sacrifice willingly. That's part of what makes them so assured of their success. They are willing to do anything—absolutely *anything*—to ensure the establishment of their government. Even if that's at the cost of their individual lives."

"And what if that requires the murder of innocents?" Deckard demanded. "If they'd do *anything*, would they do that?"

Thom frowned. "Now, you're just being dramatic."

"This is important, Thom. What if the Alliance isn't what it seems? What if they trap us into a life of service to worse tyrants than are already on the thrones?"

That made Thom hesitate for a drawn-out moment. Then he shook his head vehemently, a dry scoff working out of him. "Have you met the Calders?" he said. "They may be odd, but they aren't cold-blooded murderers. And I think it's safe to say they certainly wouldn't support an organization made up of homicidal maniacs."

Deckard ran a hand over his face, sighing heavily. This was Evylin's exact argument. Why was he the only one willing to consider the Calders' additional duplicity? He wondered if Rafferty would be any more rational. After all, Evylin and Thom had built friendships with Ilain, and Ethenn was now betrothed to her. They would be incapable of seeing the woman's fraudulence until it was too late.

If Ilain was deceitful.

A tinge of doubt lingered in Deckard's mind as to that fact. No matter how much he questioned the Alliance and their people, he couldn't deny that Ilain and her family showed a level of loyalty, bravery, and piousness that he didn't think could be feigned for quite this long.

Maybe Evylin and Thom were right. Maybe Deckard was being overly cautious.

Repentant, Deckard faced Thom again. "I do fear that they'll force Evylin and me into a life we don't want," he admitted. "After all their lies in the past, I struggle to trust that they're as good as they claim."

Thom nodded in understanding. "I don't know that any government can be called 'good,' Jonn," he said thoughtfully. "There's better and worse, but goodness . . . That belongs to people."

"And people are what form a government," Deckard said.

"Yes," Thom agreed, then grinned. "So wouldn't you want to make sure the best people are at the head of it?"

"Of course."

"Right." Thom's grin turned sly. "Personally, I can't think of anyone better than you."

Immediately, Deckard scowled. "I'm not a ruler. I'm a soldier, and that's all I want to be."

Thom raised a pacifying hand. "Then don't become Highlord Chancellor," he said. "But perhaps you could help select the men and women who *are* going to rule. If the Alliance values you enough to let you lead, then surely, they'd value your opinion on who they set in your place."

Deckard considered that. The idea wasn't altogether abhorrent to him.

Rulership was out of the question. But advising? That he could do.

With a slow nod, Deckard surveyed his brother with interest. "When did you get so wise?" he asked companionably.

Thom scoffed. "I've been spending too much time with Ilain. That woman is downright insightful and frighteningly blunt. You've got her to thank for any improvements."

Deckard chuckled. "Remind me to do just that when we get back to camp."

"Nah, don't." Thom smirked. "It'll just go to her head."

They managed to make it to the large town of Gaatshead, deep in the foothills. Near the mountain range and one of the few towns in the area, the fiefdom was granted to a well-trusted Ephrian nobleman whose ancestor was one of the Shepherd King's closest friends. Deckard couldn't quite remember the name of the viscount, but he recognized the insignia of the green banners with the charging knight, his steed rearing, and his sword raised.

Watching those banners flap above the walls a mile away, Deckard gave his instructions. "We'll go into the town for the night," he said, then reached into his coat's interior pocket. "Thom, this is our letter of assignment. Take Rafferty and Vayden and get us rooms in the best inn you can find."

"Aye, sir." Thom took the folded letter, then winked at Evylin. "A bed'll do nicely."

"It certainly will," she agreed.

"I presume," Ilain interjected, "that the rest of us are meant to train?"

Deckard nodded. "Yes. Brea will continue her training with Evylin and Ethenn. And I need your help," he met the gazes of the other Mages in turn, "to understand these tomes Lord Obel gave me."

Though Auden and Isla showed approval, Ilain brushed a hand through the air. "I'll go with the boys," she said. "You don't need three tutors. And someone magical should stick close to the Relic that Rafferty's got up his sleeve."

"It's around my neck, actually," Rafferty corrected, then leaned toward Brea to add, "And it chafes like hell."

While Brea grinned, Deckard accepted Ilain's suggestion. The three groups split; four of their party headed for the town, while the other six rode into the trees. Deckard, Auden, and Isla didn't bother going as far into the rocky and overgrown brush. The sound of swords would draw more attention than their light conversation and attempts at magic. So while the Warriors headed deep into the forest, Deckard remained with the Mages.

They tied their horses to the low branch of a thistleberry tree, its brilliant blue flowers blooming in the springtime. The berries were still too small to eat; their bristly protective covering kept Deckard from bothering to pick any of them, but Isla studied their flowers curiously.

"These trees are lovely," she commented, looking around at the rest of the forest. Blossoming white pears and blush-colored myrtles brightened the greenery around them. "We don't have as many flowering varieties in Wauld."

"I noticed," Deckard replied. "This part of Ephria is known for its flora. We get most of our teas, spices, and perfumes from the side of the mountain."

"So the rest of your country isn't as beautiful?" she teased.

Realizing Isla had never been to Ephria, Deckard found himself smiling. "Actually," he said proudly, "the Shires are known to be the true beauty of our land. They're green and glorious."

Isla chuckled lightly. "Vayden would love to see it. Green is his favorite color."

"We're going there," he reminded her. "That's where the Terrae Relic is."

"Then he *will* love it." She patted Auden's arm and drew the men toward the center of the small clearing. "How shall we begin, Highlord Magister Calder?"

Auden clasped his hands before him, giving her a fond smile. "Well, Highlady Aterian Freye, I believe our pupil has aims of his own with this training," he returned.

Deckard watched their sibling-like exchange with interest. It was a marvel that no matter the difficulty or distance their work with the Alliance demanded of the Calder family, they still held such a strong regard for one another. Even as in-laws, Auden and Ilain acted no differently toward Isla than they did toward one another or Vayden. She was one of them, wholly adopted into the family, even if she hadn't taken their name.

Realizing that they were waiting for his reply, Deckard cleared his thoughts. He met Auden's verdant gaze and explained, "Much of our previous training focused on Day or Night magic. As we now know that I'm a Space Mage, it seems that we ought to change our course. I've begun reading the books Obel gave me, but we're pressed for time. In the short evenings and breaks that we have, I can only make it so far in my studies. So I think the best way to ensure our success is for you and Isla to train me to use Space magic more effectively."

Auden and Isla exchanged a look. Then Auden gave him a penitent frown. "We're not exactly experienced with Space magic, Jonn," he said. "Isla is an Elemental Mage. Accessing Space is nearly impossible for her. I myself have only accessed it a handful of times in my life. And my hold on it was tenuous at best."

At Deckard's evident disappointment, Isla spoke. "However, we can help you hone your ability to feel magic in general, which will make connecting to Space on your own easier for you."

"By all means," Deckard invited.

Auden gave Isla a nod, and she stepped forward. She wore a deep navy blue dress that caused her brown eyes and bronze skin to radiate warmth. Her expression was gentle, and her posture was relaxed as though to set him at ease. "The first lesson a Mage must learn is connection," she explained. "Our connection to the resources is the means of our power. If we cannot connect, we cannot act. When we're young Mages, often months are spent attuning ourselves to our primary resource, building such a strong relationship that we can feel it surrounding us with our every breath.

"I am a Wind Mage," she continued. "Therefore, I can feel the very air around me, always. It's like a constant companion. Even the air in your lungs is tangible to me. I can sense it—*everywhere*."

She gestured to her brother-in-law. "Auden can see with the light of Day in the darkest of nights. He can sense the light and the life force of those around him always. If you are in danger, if your heart is weak, he can feel it."

Deckard raised his chin in understanding. "When I come to my full power as a Space Mage, I'll feel the Heavens' presence in the same way?" He didn't bother waiting for confirmation but pressed, "What will that be like?"

"We can't tell you," Auden said. "There have been too few Space Mages, and even Highlord Grenwoode, who aligns with the Alliance, hasn't been able to answer for that. At two hundred and eight, he's aged a great deal and can't risk the other Mages discovering his allegiances. So he remains aloof while supplying what information he can."

Deckard recognized the name. "He's the author of one of the books Obel gave me."

Auden nodded. "I believe he translated an old manuscript from the Allminian Gaelic. We don't have many texts on Space magic because of its rarity."

Still unaccustomed to the oddity of being considered such a "rare" species, Deckard blew out an overwhelmed breath. "So what you're saying is, I'll have to learn to wield my magic for myself?"

They both gave him apologetic smiles.

"Excellent." Deckard forced himself not to be bitter. "Well, I'll thank you for whatever training you can give."

"I've already begun to teach you the meditations of a Mage," Auden said. "That's really the start."

Deckard frowned. "I don't remember that lesson."

"I told you when we were discussing the Path of Vieran, the first Mage who discovered how to distill magic into elixir, about his process of meditation. It's the beginning of all Mages' journeys."

Deckard blinked, the story completely gone from his memory. "I'm afraid I wasn't listening."

Isla set a hand on Auden's shoulder to soothe his abject disappointment. "It sounds as though it wasn't a very clear lesson anyway," she said reprovingly. "Really, Auden. You're a magister. It's your job to teach Mages."

"It's my job to study magic," Auden countered. "Teaching is secondary."

She brushed off his answer, turning back to Deckard. "The Path of Vieran *is* the start of each Mages' training," she confirmed. "He was an example of stillness and inner reflection. You see, the resource chooses the Mage. Wind chose me. Day chose Auden. *Space* chose you. So there is a fragment of Space inside of you.

"To access it, to *know* it, you must find that fragment," she pressed a hand to her sternum, "that connection deep in your soul through such means of stillness and inner reflection."

"And how do I do that?" Deckard asked.

Isla smiled knowingly. "You sit," she said with a gesture to the forest floor. "You think. You ruminate on the very essence of Space within you until you feel it surrounding you."

"That's not exactly a step-by-step rubric."

Isla's dark eyes glowed. "Magic isn't a rubric. It is creativity embodied."

"Mm." Deckard looked between them. "I take it I should sit and think now?"

"We all will," Auden suggested, lowering himself to the grass. He adjusted his long brown coat, crossing his legs beneath him. He settled his hands on his knees and held his chin high. Isla sat next to him, her full skirt billowing around her legs. She rested her hands demurely in her lap.

They both stared up at him, waiting.

With a sigh, Deckard took a seat. He emulated Auden's posture, though he kept his chin dipped.

"It will take time," Auden said, his red hair shining in the late afternoon sunlight. "You've accessed your magic enough now to know what it feels like. And with your Bond, it should be even easier. Focus but try not to conjure the magic itself. You'll get a stronger connection just by being with it rather than using it."

Deckard gave a hum of acknowledgment. "Shall we begin?"

"Yes." Auden shut his eyes then, and Isla followed suit.

With an internal grumble, Deckard closed his eyes too. The rusty light of sunset glowed behind his lids. The *pip* of robins echoed around them. Bees buzzed from flower to flower, and a soft breeze rustled the trees.

Deckard turned his attention inward, knowing just where to find the connection of his magic. It burned like an ember in his chest, right next to the tether that now tangibly bound his soul to Evylin's. The one that told him she walked roughly half a mile southwest of his location. He liked that sensation, that assurance that she was safe and well. Even from the distance, he could feel her, the gentle thrum of her soul within his. It was strained, informing him of her training, but it wasn't stressed by any form of danger.

Taking her safety as a gift, Deckard allowed himself to relax. He left their Bond alone, focusing on the spark of magic within. Its gentle heat flickered under his skin in response to his searching, almost like a greeting. Ilain had once mentioned that magic had a sentience. It wasn't alive, but it was aware. The relationship between Mage and resource was built on regard and cherishing the resource itself. And while Deckard couldn't say he cared deeply for the magic within him, he did respect it, and he was thankful for the link to Evylin that it granted him.

In response, the magic trilled within him like a playful coo. It seemed to appreciate his undivided attention. He murmured an inner *"hello,"* and it jumped, leaving his skin tingling. Somehow, it almost seemed to have emotions, rudimentary as they seemed. His magic was almost like a puppy, reacting instinctively and simply to its master's affections.

The thought made Deckard smile. *You're rather friendly when we're not fighting for our lives,* he thought.

The magic continued to tingle, curling down his spine and along his arms. Its heat filled him with a peaceful sense of control.

You chose me?

It brushed against his chest as though snuggling up to him.

Why?

There was no answer. The magic just continued to fill him with tingling warmth.

Deckard's head grew light, and the magic buzzed in his ears like a wordless whisper. A steady fullness settled into his core. The magic pulsed in rhythm with his heart, heating him from the inside out. His hands began to prickle as though they'd fallen asleep, yet the sensation was soothing and not painful.

With each moment that passed, a glimmering blackness emerged in Deckard's chest, building gradually. The feeling was refracted and absorbed at the same time. It felt like everything and nothing awakening within him. In his mind, it was vast and endless. It was empty and void. It called to him, the wordless whisper growing louder. And then he began to understand; this was Space. The infinity of the Heavens beckoned to him with its power.

Suddenly, Isla's voice broke through his concentration. "That's not good," she said dryly.

Deckard's eyes flew open to find Auden and Isla watching him in the deeply shadowed forest. She wore a bland, contemplative expression while Auden looked positively beside himself. "What?" Deckard asked.

Auden sighed. "You don't even realize you're doing it, do you?"

His lack of response was confirmation enough.

Auden gestured to Deckard. "Look around you," he said.

Turning his attention to himself, Deckard found his entire body encapsulated by a swirling spiral of crystalline shards. Like a dome, they arced above his head as though wrapping him in an embrace.

Deckard's lips parted in shock. "I didn't—"

"We didn't assume you did," Isla interrupted. "Drop the field."

Though he wasn't entirely certain how to follow her instructions, Deckard clamped his jaw shut. *Do you mind?* he thought to the magic.

Instantly, the onyx shards blipped out of existence. Though it still thrummed dully in his chest, the magic was gone. His vision cleared, and the darkness in the clearing lightened.

Deckard sighed and ran a hand over his face. "I don't know how I did that," he admitted.

"We do," Auden said matter-of-factly. Then he leveled him with a serious stare. "This is problematic, Jonn. Not like the Deep, but . . . it's almost worse in the immediate problem it presents."

Deckard narrowed his gaze, wary but listening.

"It seems that you're *too* connected to your resource," Auden explained. "You have a level of focus many Mages spend years developing. As Obel said, that seems to be a penchant of Space Mages. And while that can be a good thing, since you're undertrained, it puts us in a tight spot." Auden raised his brow. "Your magic is uncontrolled."

Deckard frowned. "It always does exactly what I tell it to do."

"And did you tell it to surround you just now?"

Deckard hadn't.

"It consumed you here," Auden said. "Like it did in Dunneshead. Like it has every time you've connected to it."

Realizing that he was right, Deckard frowned. "What does that mean?"

"It means you have a lot of training to do," Isla said. "The ease with which you access your magic is as problematic as it is beneficial. When you focus, you are connecting with *all* your magic. You aren't currently skilled enough to regulate the amount of magic you grasp; therefore, it controls you rather than you controlling it."

"When you connect," Auden clarified, "you are gone, and only Space is left."

Deckard shook his head. "I'm always aware of what I'm doing. I'm in control. It just . . ." He didn't have the words to explain what happened when he accessed his magic. But he didn't like this suggestion that it overcame him. He didn't want to think he had such little self-control.

Auden and Isla were unmoved by his weak defense.

"You have to be careful, Jonn," Auden said. "You have a limited supply of energy. And when you access your magic, you will have no means of managing your output. If you don't learn to control it, you'll blow through every ounce of strength you have until it's too late, and you collapse from overexertion."

Remembering how Ilain blacked out during the ambush in Sutterlund Reach, Deckard blanched. He remembered how close they came to death at that moment. If Evylin hadn't gotten him the Night Relic, they *would* have died.

"The good news," Isla said, breaking through his worries, "is that you've proven to be naturally strong, based on my siblings' accounts of your past experiences. And now, you're Bonded. Reaching the end of your energy stores isn't going to happen quickly. However, that doesn't negate the need to check the use of your magic."

Auden nodded in agreement. "For the rest of our journey, I'd advise you to take time each day to connect with Space while practicing keeping it outwardly dormant. Your relationship with your resource is important. But you need to learn how to calm down its excitement when you call to it."

"It's something all Mages have to learn," Isla added, then smirked. "And we are often given years to learn what you're attempting in a few weeks. So don't be hard on yourself if you fail."

"If I fail," Deckard returned morosely, "it could mean our deaths."

Isla's expression softened. "My dear Colonel, life is beyond our control. We will all die one day. If it is to be on this mission, we accept that. If it is to be when we're old and gray, we accept that. *Metá pe'la creá.*"

Deckard adjusted his Bonding ring. "What does that mean?"

"It's a Schonese proverb," Isla said. "Death for creation. For something to be created, something else must die. Even if that simply means the death of old ways and mindsets. But life cannot come from nothing. Love cannot come without sacrifice."

Sacrifice.

That was a common theme in the Alliance, it seemed.

The sun had completely set, leaving them sitting in darkness. A chill settled into Deckard's bones, and he felt Evylin's presence drawing nearer. The Warriors had finished their training.

Still, Deckard studied Auden and Isla's somber expressions. "And you're accepting of that fate?" he asked. "Giving your life for the Alliance's aims?"

Auden shared a smile with his sister-in-law. "We *are* the Alliance," he said, meeting Deckard's gaze. "We are not an organization born of overlords but of men and women who are dedicated to a cause. So, yes, we'll die if we must. For our cause and for the people we love."

The sentiment weighed heavily on Deckard. His gut twisted, finding himself inordinately worried about the Alliance members. Auden, Ilain, Isla, Vayden, and Brea. They were willing to die, to sacrifice it all. He'd known them for such a short time, and yet he felt an unexpected ache at the thought of their loss. Perhaps it was the simple sorrow at the thought of any life lost. But if he were honest, he thought it had more to do with the fact that he was getting to know these people. Despite his distrust, he was coming to know them, and he had to admit the value of their friendship. To lose any of them would hurt.

As though reading Deckard's mind, Isla leaned forward and caught his gaze. "We *are* willing," she said, then her brown eyes twinkled even in the dim lighting. "But we'd really rather not."

A light chuckle slipped out of Deckard. "I suppose I'd better learn to control my magic, then," he replied, not feeling the wry tone he adopted.

"And you shall," she promised.

But Deckard wondered if it would be in time.

CHAPTER TWENTY-FOUR

5TH OF RADIA, 1574

"Almighty, I love inns," Rafferty said brightly as they left Gaatshead the next morning. They'd left early, barely taking time for breakfast, planning to make up some of the time they'd lost going south to the mountain pass before traveling north to Ephria City.

They traversed the dirt road, heading deeper into the east. Thom positioned himself at the back, intending to avoid early morning conversation. Instead, Rafferty and Vayden chose to ride on either side of him.

"Feather mattresses are far superior to dirt," Vayden remarked through a sleepy yawn.

Thom slumped in his saddle, wishing they'd leave him alone.

"How much farther is it to Loclight?" Vayden asked.

"I haven't the foggiest," Rafferty replied. "I'm not much on timelines, myself. What do you say, Thommy-boy? About a week?"

Thom rolled his eyes. "Try half that," he grumbled.

"Only four days?" Vayden pursed his lips in approval. "That's nice. Though I suppose we won't have much of a break from travel. The hope is to stay only two days in the city, then on to the Shires, yes?"

Thom nodded, suppressing a yawn.

"You should let those out," Vayden commented. He settled his hands casually on the saddle before him. "So what should I expect?"

"From what?" Thom asked.

"The Keeps."

"Ah."

Thom and Rafferty exchanged a dry look.

"Well," Thom said, "they're always different."

"And they're always miserable," Rafferty added.

"Lots of running, lots of fighting, and lots of wishing you were anywhere else," Thom concluded.

Vayden smirked. "Sounds invigorating."

"Quite so," Thom muttered.

Rafferty sniggered at their sarcasm. "Your chances of dying—now, those are pretty high," he said. "With your sword fighting skills and the fact that you're non-magical, I'd give you a one in three odds against."

"Hm. Not as bad as I would've expected." Vayden stroked his jaw thoughtfully.

"I would've made them less, but I thought you could use the encouragement."

"You have my sincerest gratitude."

The smallest smile lifted the corner of Thom's lips. "We'll be all right," he said. "Yes, they're bad, but we've yet to lose anyone to them. Injuries are to be expected, but death . . . Our team has only increased in strength and numbers. We'll be fine."

Vayden gave an appreciative nod while Rafferty smirked. "That's rather optimistic of you, Thommy," he noted.

"I'm becoming a bloody fine man, and cynicism isn't becoming," Thom retorted. "Now, shut up or leave me alone. The mornings are meant for brooding, not conversation."

Vayden and Rafferty laughed, then nudged their horses forward, leaving Thom to his desired isolation.

As they momentarily left the mountains behind, the terrain sloped down into a valley. Above them, the sky was a grand blue, the sun shining behind the scant clouds that darted around its face. Already, springtime had given Ephria a bright, cheery atmosphere, a stark contrast to the gloom of Wauld. The grass was a vibrant green, the trees lush and full of leaves, and the woodland creatures were active as they rode. Flocks of birds sailed overhead, heading north again after the harsh winter.

Thom had been stationed in the arid mountains of Ephria in his earliest days as a soldier. The culture within them was far more archaic than the lowlands, lingering in the old ways. The bygone clans of Allund still wandered within the mountainous region. The greater Ephrian nation no longer recognized them, but the people still wore their ancestral plaids and crest pins in enduring respect.

It always struck Thom that even a continent as small as the Isle of Allund could hold great variance among its people. Now that he knew Brea and Isla and was learning the culture and language of Schon through them, he had to wonder what other wonders Terraeus held.

As the morning wound on, Evylin dropped back to ride with him. With the sun high in the sky and its warmth on his face, he was happy to accept her ready conversation. They shared anticipation of returning to Loclight and their home, and Evylin asked about his and Deckard's life there before she'd met them. Thom tried to give her what answers he could, but he couldn't speak much about Deckard's time in the city. While he knew his brother had been stationed in the capital on and off for several years, they'd never talked much about his assignments.

In fact, until just a few weeks ago, they hadn't talked much at all since Deckard's commission twelve years ago.

The revelation emphasized Thom's need to prove himself. He knew Deckard didn't require it. But *he* felt the need for it. His new purpose demanded that he rectify the mistakes of his past.

In the midst of their conversation, Ilain dropped back to join them. Her roan horse nickered softly on the other side of Evylin. "Might I interrupt?" she asked.

"You already have," Thom noted.

Ilain hummed in mock amusement. "Well, if you don't want me here, I can go. I just had a question, and you two are the only ones who can answer it."

"We'd be honored to be of service," Evylin said brightly.

"Don't patronize me, Evie." Ilain's eyes glimmered with good humor. "I'm a woman on a mission at the moment."

"And what mission is that?" Thom asked.

Ilain drew her shoulders back, looking straight at Evylin. "How did you get Jonn to kiss you?"

Evylin—and Thom—froze. "How did I—what?" she asked.

Ilain brushed her hand through the air flippantly. "Well, I know he's the prudish sort, so I was wondering: How did you get him to kiss you?"

Thom screwed up his face in disgust. "And *why* do *I* need to be here for this conversation?" he asked.

"It's the follow-up questions for which I require your masculine expertise."

Thom didn't know whether to be intrigued or terrified.

"So Evie . . . ?" Ilain prompted.

With an uncomfortable sigh, Evylin shrugged. "Well . . . I didn't really have to *get* him to do it. He just did."

"Hm." Ilain narrowed her gaze thoughtfully. "How long did it take?"

"About a month."

"Mm." Her hum sounded disgruntled this time. "I'm not that patient. Is it an Ephrian thing? Being slow to affection?"

Suddenly, Thom understood what was happening. "Ethenn hasn't kissed you?" he stated rather than asked.

Ilain scowled. "Not since our betrothal ceremony."

"Interesting," he muttered, then inquired, "And is this the area where my expertise comes in?"

"Something like that."

Thom chuckled in disbelief. He wasn't sure why Ethenn hadn't kissed Ilain yet; it might have been due to their discrepancy of feelings. But he wasn't entirely certain why that should stop him. The woman had quite literally offered herself to him. What man wouldn't take that as an invitation?

With a toss of his hand, Thom decided the young man was a fool. "Well, no, it's not an Ephrian thing," he said. "We *are* a more reserved culture, but not all men are so 'proper' as to remain so chaste. I'm actually rather surprised to hear that Ethenn is so reticent in that regard."

"That's the thing," Ilain said, eyes darting between Thom and Evylin, "I don't think he is. He told me that he's kissed dozens of women."

"Dozens?" Evylin exclaimed.

"He *told* you that?" Thom asked incredulously. "Why on Allore's green Terraeus would he tell you how many women he's been with?"

"He hasn't *been* with any women, thank you very much," Ilain said with a haughty thrust of her chin into the air. "He's simply kissed a handful of them . . . Amongst other activities as well, apparently."

Thom snorted, still bemused. "And he informed you of this when?"

"On our betrothal night."

"Huh." Thom raised his brows at Evylin. "The man's crazier than I thought."

Evylin shook her head despite the laugh that bubbled out of her. She turned to Ilain. "Was there a particular reason you discussed your past relationships on your first night together?" she asked.

Ilain shrugged. "No. And they weren't relationships from the sounds of it."

"Ah." Thom grimaced. "I never pegged Ethenn for a lecher."

"He *isn't*," Ilain objected vehemently. "As clearly evidenced by the fact that he refuses to touch me. And which," she swept a hand toward her lithe figure, "is profoundly confusing when I've practically thrown my barely clad body at him twice now."

Thom scanned her approvingly and spoke in a dry tone. "It is baffling. Should you throw yourself at me, you'd have no virtue left."

"What did I say about patronizing me?"

He grinned at her. "I'm just agreeing with you, Ilain. Something is wrong with Ethenn. Any other man, even bloody Jonn Deckard, would lose himself to a battle against the will of a wife such as you."

"Thank you," Ilain said while Evylin scoffed.

"Even if I stripped naked in front of Jonn that first night, he's such a gentleman that he would have simply asked if I needed to borrow a shirt," Evylin protested.

Though Thom would rather avoid thinking of his brother in such scenarios, he couldn't help embarrassing her by asking, "Does he do that now?"

Evylin blushed. "No," she said, letting the short reply hang suspended in the air.

"Mm-hm," Thom chuckled victoriously. Then he leaned forward to look at Ilain. "So what? Ethenn's not responding to your advances?"

"No—well . . ." Ilain scrunched her nose in self-derision. "I haven't exactly made advances, so much as asked him to kiss me while attempting to cuddle with him."

"Attempting?"

"He can't cuddle," she said in exasperation. "Isn't that bizarre?"

"Perhaps you'd like to cuddle with me?" Thom offered wryly.

"I'm a betrothed woman now, Thom. I have no further interest in your charms."

"I never realized I had charms."

"You don't," Evylin sniped and turned to the highlady. "I'm a little confused, Ilain. Are you saying you'd like to . . . consummate your betrothal?"

"No," Ilain said instantly, then winced. "Maybe. Probably."

Thom sniggered. "That progressed quickly."

"Oh, shut it." Ilain straightened in her saddle. "He's the man I always dreamed of. Why wouldn't I want to secure our future together?"

Thom eyed her dubiously. "You dreamed of a man twenty years your junior who's kissed dozens of other women but won't kiss you?"

Ilain glared at him.

"You're not helping," Evylin said.

"No," Thom agreed, grinning. "But I am having fun."

"This is pointless," Ilain grumbled. "If you're not going to help, then I'll just deal with it myself."

"Good," he said. "Yes, deal with it yourself. I'm certainly not interested in helping you boff the boy."

"Pardon me," Ilain glowered at him, "but I do believe I remember you saying that you'd fix that rather egregious mistake you made when you falsely told the man I love I wanted nothing to do with him."

Thom flinched. "The man you *love*?"

Ilain blanched and averted her gaze. "Yes," she whispered awkwardly. "I think so."

Growing more uncomfortable with the conversation by the second, Thom snarled. "Fine. I'll talk with him."

"You will?"

Thom shrugged. "I screwed up. It's my job to fix it."

"And just *how* do you intend to fix it?" Evylin asked suspiciously.

"I'll tell him that when a woman offers you her knickers, you take your shot."

She rolled her eyes, and Ilain huffed.

"I'm joking," Thom assured them. "I'll approach him as a friend, ask how married life is going, and subtly suggest he take his wife up on her offers of intimacy. Satisfied?"

Though Ilain seemed to be appeased, Evylin shook her head. "Ethenn won't respond to that," she warned.

"How do you know?" Thom asked.

"Because I understand Ethenn, believe it or not." She tipped her chin toward the others, who were several hundred feet ahead now that they'd unconsciously slowed their pace for their private conversation. "I guarantee you the reason he hasn't made a move is because he isn't ready to. He isn't the trusting sort. *And* he doesn't know of Ilain's feelings for him."

"Yes, he does," Ilain objected.

"He does?"

Ilain nodded vehemently. "I just told him the other night: I chose him because of my feelings for him."

Evylin eyed her. "Is there a chance he didn't believe you because of Thom's prior idiocy?"

"Thanks for that," Thom muttered, though it was a fair question.

Ilain considered, then sighed. "Yes, there's a great chance. He doesn't seem to believe anything I tell him."

"You are a notable liar," Thom offered.

"But I've been nothing but honest with him," Ilain countered, then picked at her skirt. "After the whole flirting-with-you fiasco."

Thom couldn't help smiling at her predicament. "That *was* your choice. You could have been honest with him from the start."

"That's very helpful," Ilain mocked.

He held her glare. "Do you want me to talk to him or not?"

"I don't advise it," Evylin remarked in a singsong tone.

Ilain stared between them, lips pressed together. At last, she heaved another sigh. "Yes, fine. Please *subtly* see if you can nudge him in the right direction. I'm not asking for anything so monumental as intercourse, but at least a kiss would be nice."

With a nod, Thom guided his horse forward. "I'll see what I can do."

And with that, he left the women behind. Cantering up the road, he caught the others shortly, finding Ethenn in the middle of the group talking with Brea. She was telling him something about her time in Schon but paused when Thom arrived.

"Pleasure to see you this morning, *mi'caro*," she teased.

Thom dipped his chin in a dramatic bow. "The pleasure is all mine, Lieutenant." He scanned her casually, noting that she'd twisted back her braided black hair along the sides. "You look particularly lovely. Add some myrtle blossoms to those twists, and you'd look like a veritable Ephrian dryad."

Her brow furrowed. "What is this 'dryad'?"

"They're woodland spirits," he explained. "Supposedly friends with The Living Land."

"And they wear flowers in their hair?"

"They're made of flowers, I believe."

"Ah. I look like a flower to you?"

Thom winked. "You look like a whole field of flowers, ma'am."

"This is awkward," Ethenn said flatly.

Remembering his reason for being there, Thom cleared his throat and forced himself to ignore Brea's playfully challenging stare. He turned to Ethenn. "Could I talk with you?"

Glancing between the Warrior and Thom, Ethenn shrugged. "Sure."

Guiding their horses away from the others, Thom and Ethenn dropped back on the road until even Evylin and Ilain passed them. Evylin eyed him dubiously while Ilain kept her gaze on the road ahead, pointedly ignoring the two men.

Thom shook his head at her obvious behavior.

"What did you need?" Ethenn asked once they were safely out of earshot.

"Oh, it isn't me who needs something," Thom replied.

Ethenn's expression pinched in confusion.

Thom grinned pleasantly. "Tonight, when we arrive at whatever inn we find along the road, go into your room, lock the door, and shag your wife."

"What?"

"You heard me." Turning his head, Thom held the Warrior's gaze unflinchingly. "You're married now, Ethenn. Or betrothed or whatever it's called. For all intents and purposes, you two have pledged your lives to each other, and the fact is, your wife thinks you don't love her because you won't bloody touch her. So get over whatever hang-ups you have and shag her. You'll both be happier for it, I promise."

Ethenn stared at him for several seconds, shoulders tense, back rigid, and eyes narrowed. Then he scoffed. "She put you up to this?" he asked.

Thom raised his brow. "Tells you something, doesn't it?"

Ethenn shifted awkwardly in his saddle. "Great. Consider your task fulfilled. I understand her request."

"And are you going to do it?"

The young man shot him a furious glare, a blush creeping up from his collar. "Not that it's any of your business, but no, I'm not," he said sharply.

"Why not?" Thom demanded in disbelief. "Come on, Corporal. You've got a bloody fine wife who wants you. Why hold out on her?"

Ethenn turned away in silence.

Thom shook his head. "Why am I constantly surrounded by idiots who don't know when to boff their spouses," he muttered to himself. Turning in his seat, he pressed a hand to his chest. "My whole life, I'd have killed for a woman who wanted me the way Ilain wants you. And yet, you don't appreciate it."

"Maybe I'm not a masochist like you."

"What the hell are you talking about?" Thom glared at him incredulously. "She *wants* you. What's so painful about that?"

Ethenn didn't respond.

Thom sighed in vexation. Here he was, trying to be helpful and make his friend happier, and somehow, he was failing again. He pinched the bridge of his nose. *Why is this so bloody hard?*

"Look, Ethenn," he said, attempting to be long-suffering. "I'm not sure why you aren't ready for that sort of relationship with Ilain, but . . . I guess I understand."

A contemptuous scoff slipped out of Ethenn.

"Okay, fine. I couldn't understand," Thom admitted. "Not really. But the point I'm trying to make is simply: You love her, right? If that's true, then shouldn't you make her feel loved? Even if that's just by holding her hand or bringing her gifts or—or—"

"By telling her she looks like a dryad?" Ethenn mocked.

Thom grimaced dramatically. "No, that's far too corny. She'll never believe you."

Ethenn laughed quietly. "You like her, don't you?"

"Ilain?"

"Brea."

Thom shrugged. "She's fun. But she's far too magical for my tastes." He tossed Ethenn a lazy grin. "I prefer a woman who doesn't make me feel quite so inferior."

"You're trying too hard."

Feeling caught, Thom adjusted in the saddle. He *was* trying hard, trying to be a better man, a better friend, and a better soldier. And he felt like he was failing at every turn.

With a sigh, Thom held Ethenn's stare. "Just give it some thought, all right? Ilain wouldn't ask for help if she weren't desperately lost."

Ethenn's jaw clenched, and his eyes fell to the road. "I can't be what she wants me to be," he said quietly.

"Are you sure you know what that is?" Thom asked.

He let out a thin huff. "Maybe not."

"Well," Thom began cautiously, "perhaps you should start by kissing her. She seems to want that."

Ethenn tipped his head back, glaring up at the sky as he sucked in a long breath. His face was growing so red that he looked as though he was about to burst. "Could you not give me advice anymore?"

Thom smiled ruefully. "Just one last thing," he said, then lifted his brow. "Do you really not know how to cuddle?"

"This conversation is over," the young man replied tersely.

"All right." Thom lifted his hands in surrender. "Just—if you need any pointers—"

"Shove your pointers."

"I'd rather not."

After several seconds of tense silence, Ethenn sighed. "I appreciate your attempt to help," he said, each word pronounced in an achingly flat tone as though he were forcing them out.

Thom failed to hold in his laughter. "Maybe next time I'll actually be successful."

Ethenn sent him a coldly amused look. "There's not going to be a next time. At least, not with this subject."

"Because you're going to take care of the issue tonight?" Thom asked suggestively.

"Because if Ilain comes to you again, you're going to tell her to talk to me herself."

"Right." Thom smirked. "*And* you're gonna take care of it tonight."

A faint grin tugged at Ethenn's lips, and he nudged his horse forward. "Right."

CHAPTER TWENTY-FIVE

The day's travel brought them to a village whose name Ethenn didn't catch. Due to its small population, there was no need for an inn, so while the Warriors and Mages trained separately, Thom led the others (including Ilain once more) to the tavern, seeking rooms for rent. When their training was completed, Ethenn and the rest of the troop entered the village too.

After days of exhaustive work and sweating through his clothes, Ethenn wanted nothing more than an opportunity to languish in a hot tub. It was a new experience for him: bathing in hot water. In Trollenston, he often spent weeks at a time in the forest hunting, and when he returned to his family's small cottage on the outskirts of town, his only option for bathing was water from the trough. Despite the fairly modern innovation of many houses in town being outfitted with pipes to draw the water inside, their old home had yet to see the innovation.

His sister, Terrina, often complained about the "incivility" of such primitive arrangements. But Ethenn hadn't minded. They were happy; they were together. That was all that mattered . . . until it was gone.

It wasn't until Ethenn's commission with the Ephrian Army and his short stay in the Loclight barracks that he experienced a hot bath for himself. Ever since then, he understood Terrina's desire for a proper bath.

Arriving in the backwater village, Ethenn began to debate his chances for a bath of any sort. Tucked within the mountains, the settlement solely survived on its mining exports. The likelihood of them having a proper bath setup (even without hot water) was slim.

Riding through the ramshackle buildings, it was easy to find the tavern. A rusty sign hung above the door, and a single oil lamp was mounted at its side, glowing yellow in the late evening. Voices thrummed from within its walls and out onto the dirt streets. There was an open stable to the side where they saw the rest of the troop's horses tied for the night. Ethenn's gut reaction was to distrust that the villagers wouldn't steal their mounts, but he followed Deckard's lead, tying his horse next to the rest. He knew he was more paranoid than the others. It came with the territory of having spent time with the rejects and refuse of Trollenston. Yet, as devout Allorians, the average Ephrian was too concerned with incurring the wrath of Allore to be dishonest. Still, he unstrapped both his saddlebags and Ilain's, bringing them into the tavern just to be safe.

The tavern was old and in great need of repair, though not dilapidated by any standard. An aged woman with gray hair piled atop her head played a zither by the hearth, her fingers deftly sweeping across the strings. It was "Draaw's Jig," a lively tune he'd often heard in Trollenston's taverns. Men and women filled the room, enjoying drinks and meals and singing along to the song.

And in the corner was a roped-off area that looked all too familiar to Ethenn. Instantly, he averted his gaze.

"Cheery place," Brea noted.

Near the middle of the tavern, they found their companions. Rafferty was eyeing a nearby party playing cards, his foot tapping merrily to the music, while Ilain picked at a clumpy-looking stew, and Vayden hummed with the patrons. Thom rose as they neared, immediately informing them that there weren't enough rooms for all of them in the tavern.

"How many rooms are there?" Deckard asked above the din.

Thom shrugged apologetically. "Two. They said they don't get travelers out this way often, so they've no need for so many spares. We can split six and four. Men and women?"

Somehow, the idea both appealed to and annoyed Ethenn. The chance to sleep away from Ilain would be a welcome reprieve, as it would also be a great disappointment.

Deckard wasn't pleased either. "How many beds in a room?" he asked, running a hand along his jaw.

Thom grimaced. "Two singles."

"Singles? What's the point of a room if most of us end up sleeping on the floor?"

"We could push them together," Thom suggested.

"Unless my bedmate's a lady," Rafferty piped up, white-blond brow raised, "I'm not sharing."

Evylin rolled her eyes. "What choice do we have?" she asked. "There are two rooms. We'll have to split and make the most of it."

A smattering of disgruntled looks spread through the troop, primarily among the married couples. But it was Ilain's downcast gaze that caught Ethenn's attention the most. From the moment he'd entered the tavern, she hadn't looked at him. He wondered if she regretted recruiting Thom's help.

At first, Thom's offered advice had greatly angered Ethenn. Who was he to tell him what to do with his wife? Not only was Thom a notable screwup, but he hadn't even had a single successful love affair. How would he know the appropriate manner in which to handle their situation?

Yet, Ethenn found himself considering his friend's words. *"Ilain wouldn't ask for help if she weren't desperately lost."*

Studying his wife in the dim tavern light, Ethenn wondered at that. Why was Ilain so desperate for his physical affection that she'd go to Thom for help? It didn't make sense.

"Shouldn't you make her feel loved?"

With a sigh, Ethenn set the saddlebags on the floor by their table and then stepped away from the group to head for the bar. Men lined the counter, tankards in hand, and spoke in grumbling and gruff tones. He pushed into a singular empty spot, flagging down the barkeep.

"Can I help ye?" the man asked in a clipped Ephrian accent. It seemed the mountain region had its own dialect.

Ethenn leaned in so he wouldn't have to yell. "Anyone in the village looking to make extra coin?"

The barkeep raised his bushy eyebrows. "That's everyone in the village, lad."

"Anyone with a spare room in their house?"

He gave a bored blink. "I already told yer friends; there's nothin' but my two rooms upstairs."

The zitherist finished her song and began packing away her things as a man stepped up. His dark-skinned, bald head shone amber in the firelight. He wore only a tunic tucked into his trousers, but a red and blue woven tartan draped across his chest like a sash. Ethenn knew his announcement before he made it.

"Thank ye, Laurey," he said to the elderly musician, then faced the crowd with outstretched arms. "The night's entertainment shall begin in twenty minutes."

The crowd cheered, stomping their feet under the tables. Ethenn clenched his jaw.

"Our champion is back again to defend his title," the man proclaimed, thrusting his hand toward the back of the room. "Aangus the Hammerfist!"

While the room roared with applause and excitement, a bull-like man with a green and yellow plaid raised his boulder-sized fist in the air. His scraggly bearded face split into a proud grin, and he let out a bellow of challenge.

Ethenn pressed his lips together. He'd fought many men like the Hammerfist. Men who were broad and muscle-bound with skulls thicker than a sheep's woolly pelt.

The announcer continued with his exuberant speech. "The Hammerfist told me this morning that he's ready for a challenge, so any man who wants to test his worth against our champion, come forward. We've a grand prize for the night: the title, three crowns, and as much ale as you can drink."

Laughter and chatter filled the room. A few men rose to put their names in the ring.

Ethenn turned back to the barkeep. "Surely, there's someone with a room," he said.

The barkeep shrugged lazily. "Sorry, lad, can't help ye."

Grinding his teeth, Ethenn's back grew warm. "You're telling me that out of an entire village, no one has a bed to spare?"

"We're small if'n ye didn't see, laddie." The barkeep's eyes were dark with agitation. "Everyone with rooms has got them filled with their own loved ones. We ain't got space to house travelers."

Unwilling to give up, Ethenn bristled at the idea forming in his mind. But he held the barkeep's gaze and asked, "And where do you sleep?"

The man's expression pinched angrily. "Ye threatening me, lad?"

With a dry grin, Ethenn shook his head. "No, old man, I'm offering you a deal." He gestured toward the patrons. "This fighting ring of yours brings in good profit, yes? You put on a show, garner a crowd, earn lots of coin. Yet, it costs you, doesn't it? Three gold crowns? And what's our ringleader there get to organize the event for you? At least a crown of his own, right? And I'm guessing the Hammerfist isn't a lightweight when it comes to ale. He probably drinks you just about dry."

The barkeep eyed him curiously, clearly unsure how Ethenn could know all this information.

"What I'm offering you is a chance to keep three crowns and a whole barrel of ale."

"How's that?"

"I'll fight him."

The barkeep didn't look impressed. "Ye'll lose," he said flatly. "Yer a strapping lad, but Aangus has got twice yer size. Perhaps ye'll beat two or three of the men on yer way to him, but he'll stop ye cold."

"Then you've got no reason not to take my deal," Ethenn argued. "If I win, I get your room for the night, and you get to keep the prize purse. If I lose, you're out nothing, *and* I'll pay the prize. Including the Hammerfist's ale."

"Yer daft," the barkeep laughed.

"I'm confident."

With a hearty guffaw, the barkeep held out a hand. "Pay the prize regardless, and ye've got a deal, laddie."

Though Ethenn didn't know where he was going to get three gold crowns, he accepted the handshake, nonetheless. He turned and headed for the announcer. After giving his name to the bald man and getting on the lineup, he returned to his troop. With the number of patrons in the tavern, they'd had to split themselves between three tables. Isla and Brea had broken off to sit at a two-person table on a raised section near the hearth while Evylin, Deckard, and Auden sat nearby, leaving Thom, Vayden, and Ilain at their original spot. Rafferty had weaseled his way into the card game a few tables over, and Ethenn took his vacated seat across from Ilain. She eyed him upon his approach but turned back to her meal.

They hadn't spoken all day, and this moment of avoidance confirmed his earlier suspicions: She was nervous now that Thom had approached him, and yet still, Ethenn hadn't sought her out.

Choosing to ignore her discomfort for the time being, Ethenn settled into his chair.

"You forgot your ale," Thom remarked.

Ethenn looked over at him, confused.

Thom gestured toward the bar. "You spoke with our host for quite a while, yet you've returned empty-handed."

"I was working out a deal," Ethenn said.

"Eh? Have anything to do with that chat you had with the blighter by the hearth?"

Ethenn shrugged. "Might've."

Thom smirked. "You gonna put on a show, Loxley?"

Vayden tipped his chin up, listening with interest. Ilain shifted awkwardly at his side.

Leaning back, Ethenn flashed a grin he didn't feel.

"Well, this ought to be fun," Thom remarked.

Ethenn disagreed. He'd win, of course. In Trollenston, he'd regularly fought in the underground fighting rings. One of his less reputable friends, Finn, whom his uncle called an uneducated lout, introduced Ethenn to the ring when he was only thirteen. Though it took some time, Ethenn quickly got the hang of the fights and found his way to victory in practically every bout. He'd won nearly two hundred crowns through the endeavor, managing to buy Terrina all the pretty fabric, quality threads, and sharp scissors she'd needed to become the best seamstress in town.

Then Uncle Vernon got greedy.

Despite his success, Ethenn didn't enjoy the fights. Winning didn't mean you came out unscathed. He often wound up with a split lip, black eyes, and bruised ribs. When he was only fifteen, Auchter MacGaans, the butcher's twenty-six-year-old son, had even broken Ethenn's right wrist during a particularly brutal fight. He'd missed a month of hunts to the injury, and since his uncle couldn't use him in the smithy either, he and Terrina had struggled through that blistering hot summer.

But now, he was a Warrior, and he wasn't afraid of what injuries the fight might bring, only of who he might become during it.

Ethenn stretched his shoulders, scanning the tavern around him. Several men were shaking out their arms or downing their ales in preparation for the fights to begin. None of them were as big as the Hammerfist, but they were burly and looked mean enough to fight dirty. They wouldn't go down easily.

Suddenly, a tingle shot up Ethenn's arm as Ilain took his hand. He looked up at her, finding her green eyes cutting into him sharply. "What are you up to?" she asked quietly.

Ethenn didn't pull away, but neither did he return her touch. "Taking a friend's advice," he said.

Ilain's expression turned confused just as the announcer called out the names of the first two fighters. "Bartras the Bludger and Eogahn the Axe."

Ilain scanned the two men walking toward the ring. "Why do they all have such ridiculous names?" she asked.

Rising, Ethenn withdrew his hand. "Because it's expected," he said flatly. "Excuse me, I need to see to something."

Without waiting for their approval, he slipped to Rafferty's side at the card table. Coins of copper, silver, and bronze were piled high in the center as the final cards were dealt. Ethenn glanced at Rafferty's hand and grimaced. "Bad luck," he said casually.

Rafferty pulled back his winning cards incredulously. "Don't tell them that," he whispered dramatically. Then he smiled at the men with a falsely nervous chuckle. "My friend doesn't understand Flock's Fleece. I'm not bluffing, of course."

Greedily, the men around the table smiled, thinking that Rafferty was, in fact, bluffing. They each added to the pot, sure of their success. When it came to Rafferty, he thumbed his cards anxiously, saying, "Time to reveal then?"

Across the table, the men laid down their hands.

Rafferty let out a low whistle, seeing one man's trio of kings, the figures holding a crook in one hand and a sword in the other, and a pair of princes. "That's a good one," he noted. Then he laid out his run of five with matching black ivy leaves under their numbers. "Unfortunately, I was telling the truth. I wasn't bluffing."

As one, the men blanched with disappointment.

"Pleasure doing business, chaps," Rafferty said, scooping up his winnings.

There were grumbles of discontentment, but as none of the men could accuse him of cheating, they let the pair go.

Once they'd found their way to the far side of the room, Rafferty slipped his winnings into his money pouch at his side. "You need something, little Lox?" he asked pleasantly.

"I need you to start some bets on the fight," Ethenn said.

Rafferty raised his brow. "Oh, yeah? I can do that. What's the take?"

"I want people betting against me," he said.

"Won't work."

"Why not?"

His light eyes flickered around the tavern. "These gents won't stand against you," he said quietly. "The first round, I *may* get some good bets against you, but you're going to win. And then, you'll win again. And I'm going to be stuck convincing a shepherd his prized ivory ewe has spots."

Ethenn didn't flinch. "I'll take some hits."

"*Some* won't cut it, Lox."

"I did this for eight years, Raff. Give me some credit."

Rafferty raised his brow. "You think you can fleece them?"

"If you want to convince a shepherd his ivory ewe has spots," Ethenn raised his brow, "throw dirt on her when he isn't looking."

Rafferty sniggered merrily. "You're a rotten scoundrel."

Having heard the exact sentiment from his uncle before, Ethenn said, "I know," then turned away.

Most of the tavern occupants had already risen from their seats to surround the ring in the corner. Men and women stood on chairs and stools to see over the crowd. Thom and Vayden peered over in interest but remained in their seats. Brea surveyed from her vantage on the raised platform, likely criticizing the fighting stances of the men in the ring. Meanwhile, the rest of the troop ignored the fight.

When the first pair concluded, the announcer called out the winner: the Bludger. Cheers and boos reverberated through the room. Ethenn stepped over to the table with Rafferty at his side. Thom looked up at their approach. "Should I be concerned?" he asked casually.

"No," Ethenn said.

Thom turned to Rafferty. The weasel gave a snide grin. "Certainly not."

"Now, *I'm* concerned," Vayden remarked. "What's happening?"

Before any of the men could respond, Ilain answered, "Ethenn is going to fight."

Vayden looked momentarily baffled, then amused. "Really? Why?"

"Because he's an idiot," she muttered, then pushed her wooden bowl of stew away from her.

Ethenn's neck warmed. Why was *she* upset? Why should she even care if he fought?

"Our next fighters," the announcer called as the Axe slumped at the bar to forget his loss, "are Vergus the Bloodwolf and Loxley the Slayer."

At his moniker, Ethenn readily unbuttoned his coat as his friends stared at him. Deckard, Evylin, and Auden rose from their table, a combination of curious and concerned, as Thom gaped at him.

"The *Slayer*?" he said wryly.

Ethenn tossed his coat over the back of his chair and began removing his weapons next. "I have a reputation," he said coldly. His knives *thunked* heavily against the tabletop.

"For killing?" Thom's laughter said he didn't believe it.

Ethenn simply continued to divest himself of the weapons hidden on his person. He didn't want to be accused of cheating or of the intent to pull a blade. Regardless, the weapons would inhibit his ability to move as freely as he liked.

Ethenn removed his boots, and Deckard came to his side. "Are you sure this is wise?" he asked.

Though he worried the colonel would disapprove, Ethenn held his ground. "I can get us a third room," he explained. "But only if I come out the champion."

The troop exchanged looks of understanding.

"Yeah, but that room's gonna be for you and your lady love, isn't it?" Rafferty said. "Why should the rest of us care?"

"It'll make it one less person to squeeze into a tiny room," Thom said. "I'm for it."

The rest nodded in agreement, but Ilain glared at Ethenn. When he caught her gaze, he held it, imparting the unspoken through one look—he was doing this for *her*.

The announcer appeared at their table. "Ready, Slayer?" he asked cheerfully.

Internally, Ethenn bristled at the name as he always had but, nevertheless, donned the persona he'd been given those years ago. With a sharp nod, he stepped toward the fighting ring. His opponent was already there, stretching an arm across his bare chest. Vergus the Bloodwolf was spry and lean, with black hair shaved close to his scalp. His dark skin almost glowed in the dim light. He had a scar running from his clavicle down to his pectoral, and he wore a bored expression that said he'd done this many times already.

Standing barefoot on the wooden floor planks, Ethenn tested their warp and spring. They were worn greatly with age, leaving them soft and pliable. Dark spots stained the wood. Ethenn wondered how many men had bled in this ring. Then he stopped thinking altogether and readied himself to fight.

As he faced off against the Bloodwolf, the crowd surrounded Ethenn. After weeks of training, his instinct was to tap into his magic, the cool tingle of it already bristling under his skin. But he tamped it down, knowing that he couldn't use the magic if he wanted to make it look like he could barely win these first couple of fights.

The announcer stood on a crate by the side of the ring. He raised a hand in the air, then brought it sailing down. "Fight!"

Ethenn and the Bloodwolf circled, sidestepping as they sized one another up. To ensure his opponent didn't have enough time to make a judgment, Ethenn charged the Bloodwolf. He didn't bother with slow jabs or feints; he thrust his fist forward and connected with the man's wrist as he brought it up to protect his face. Pain lanced through Ethenn's fingers at the hard hit. The Bloodwolf's eyes widened a fraction, evidently unaccustomed to such an aggressive fighting style. But this was how Ethenn won. He went in fiercely and without fear. More often than not, his tactics wound up ending the fight far faster but with far more personal liability.

The Bloodwolf was prepared now. He swung his fist, and Ethenn ducked. A swell of magic rushed through him, but he shoved it away, then landed another punch, this time to the Bloodwolf's side.

Angered, the man attacked with renewed intensity. He feinted right, then cut in with his left. Had Ethenn been using his magic, he would have been able to stop him. Instead, he caught the blow on his chin, turning with the hit to lessen the damage.

Ethenn heard a feminine gasp come from somewhere behind him. He didn't have to look to know who it was. *Ilain.* He ground his teeth against the distraction, but in the split-second diversion, the Bloodwolf hit him again. His sternum erupted with pain. It ricocheted through his ribcage, causing his lungs to wheeze.

Focus.

Ethenn knocked the Bloodwolf's arm back and followed it up with a punch. He connected with the man's chest, right where the scar began. The Bloodwolf snarled, then attacked. In a flurry, he landed three more hits to Ethenn's chest and one to his face. If Ethenn hadn't been defending so well, the man would have broken his nose. Still, blood trickled from his nostril.

He didn't bother to wipe it away but decided he'd allowed enough hits to justify the fight's end.

With a careful weight shift, Ethenn leaned back and then struck out with his foot. He connected with the Bloodwolf's calf, sending him to a knee, and followed it up with three successive hits: one to his arm, one to his clavicle, one to his jaw.

The Bloodwolf's spittle and blood dripped to the floor. He stared dazedly but managed to hold his arms back in front of him. Ethenn leaped to one foot and brought his other up in a sweeping kick, completely subverting the Bloodwolf's attempt at defense and connecting with the side of his head.

The man crumpled.

"We have our winner!" the announcer yelled.

Ethenn wiped at his nose, his hand coming away bloody. While the announcer continued to talk, Ethenn left the Bloodwolf to pick himself up, exiting the ring. From their positions mixed in with the crowd, the troop watched him. Ilain stood among them, wide-eyed, with her brothers at her side. He couldn't read the expression on her face but decided he didn't care. He diverted his path to where Thom and Brea stood.

"That was sloppy," Brea commented.

"It was intentional," Ethenn replied quietly.

"Hm. You're more like her than I thought."

He met her knowing gaze in surprise.

"Ilain likes people to underestimate her, too, *Slayer*," she said slyly.

Ethenn huffed and pressed his fingers beneath his nose to stop the bleeding. Two more fights passed. The Hammerfist and another man named Morgaan the Thunder won their separate bouts. The troop, sans Rafferty, who was managing bets, gathered around Ethenn. However, Ilain remained distant, her expression cold.

"You fight the Bludger next," Brea coached as the first round ended. "He lacks skill, but he's much larger than you. Taking hits from him will be more damaging than from the Bloodwolf."

Ilain flinched, but Ethenn said, "I've had worse."

"He fights dirty too," Brea added. "I noticed he'll try to choke his opponent if you let him get too close."

"As I said," Ethenn stepped forward as his name was called again, "I've had worse."

Shaking out his arms, he prepared for the next fight. The Bludger stepped onto the floor to hooting cheers and chants of "Bludge him, Bludger." The man's burly arms and meaty fists were flexed for a fight. He eyed Ethenn disdainfully.

"Ye think ye can best me, boy?" he growled.

Ethenn didn't reply. He darted forward, slipped under the Bludger's grasp, and landed a hit under his sternum. It felt like hitting rock, but he heard the Bludger grunt anyway.

"Ye little scum." He lunged forward, swiping with one hand and punching with the other.

Ethenn avoided the grab but caught the punch on the shoulder. He dodged another hit, then spun around the Bludger. He kicked the man's ankle, causing minimal damage but agitating him greatly.

Ducking, Ethenn evaded the Bludger as he whirled around. He blocked a hit and struck the Bludger in the jaw. With a roar of fury, the man jabbed wildly enough to connect with Ethenn's temple. The crowd erupted in excitement, but Ethenn only heard Ilain's dismayed cry as his face burned. Heat rose along his back and collar, searing his insides. His vision was spotty, and he'd certainly have a black eye in the morning. Brea had been right; the Bludger hit far harder than the Bloodwolf.

But he wasn't out of the fight yet.

Fire burning in his core, Ethenn dodged the Bludger's next strike. He slammed his fist into the man's inner arm as he swung again. Then he followed it up with an elbow to his jaw, the same side he'd hit before.

The Bludger roared with anger, and immediately, he went for his throat as Brea had warned.

Prepared, Ethenn pulled back, yet the Bludger caught the collar of his tunic. Violently, it ripped open in his vise-like grasp. Ethenn grimaced internally at the thought of those fingers around his throat. Killing wasn't permissible in a brawl like this, but that didn't mean you couldn't choke someone into unconsciousness.

Nor did it mean that deaths didn't occur.

Backing away, Ethenn's head was slow to recover from the Bludger's temple blow. He blinked away the floaters, then charged before his opponent could. The tingle of magic cooled his core, reminding him of its presence, and this time, he reached for it. With impossible speed, he knocked the Bludger's fist aside and struck with his own magic-strengthened punch. He felt the man's nose crack as his knuckles connected, tearing the skin. Then he punched him again. And again.

The Bludger dropped to the floor, his face contorted and disfigured. With proper attention, the nose could be reset, but it would never look the same again.

An improvement, Ethenn thought coldly.

He flexed his bloodied fingers and stepped from the ring as the crowd gasped in shock. The announcer seemed startled as well but called the victory in Ethenn's favor. He could feel the splatter of the Bludger's blood on his cheek and chest. It had been a quick and brutal takedown. Murmurs passed through the room as he walked back to his group. He tugged free his torn shirt, discarding it on the floor.

Those last blows had been a mistake. The crowd now knew he was stronger than he appeared. And they wouldn't bet so freely against him. Granted, Rafferty had almost certainly obtained the three crowns he needed to pay for his victory. He decided not to let it worry him.

When Brea moved to advise him again, Ilain pushed in front of her. "Are you bloody insane?" she hissed, her eyes blazing like fire.

With his magic alight inside of him, he took an instinctive step toward her. "I know what I'm doing, Ilain," he said.

"Do you? Because it seems to me that man almost killed you."

Ethenn's hand shot out to grip her arm, and she flinched. He pulled her closer. "I *know* what I'm doing," he snapped. Her eyes darted between his as he continued, "This is who I am, Ilain. This is what I'm good at. Now, I can either get you a private room for the cost of a handful of crowns and some bruises, or I can let you sleep alone on the floor. Which would you prefer?"

Her lips parted in shock at his harsh tone.

In the background, the Hammerfist started fighting the Thunder. It was quickly clear who would win.

Ethenn leaned in closer so that only she could hear him. "Why did you send Thom earlier?" he demanded. She tried to tug free of his grasp, but he held her steady. "If you want to talk about our intimate life, Ilain, you talk to *me*. Not to my friends."

"We don't have an intimate life," she returned. "That's the point."

"*We* didn't have anything until less than a week ago," he shot back. "You do remember that, don't you? We're not lovers, Ilain. We're betrothed because I love you, and you need me. That's it. It isn't fair of you to demand something of me that I'm not ready to give."

Applause erupted as the Hammerfist won, raising his giant fists in the air. A short break was called for the victor's recovery, and Ethenn tugged Ilain farther away from the crowd, which headed for refills of their tankards at the bar. Standing before the fireplace, he felt as though his whole body was on fire despite the smallest prickle of cold magic lingering at his core.

Ilain stared at him, silent and oddly reserved.

With a sigh, Ethenn released her but remained close. "We were advised to wait," he whispered. "By your brother, the colonel, and the bloody leader of your government. Do you not understand?"

"Of course I understand," Ilain said sharply. "I'm a woman trained in politics. *That* is who *I* am. I understand that our marriage is a beneficial arrangement, as I understand that the Alliance worries that if we consummate our marriage, I'll be too heartbroken if you die to marry another. I understand that my brother is protective and that Jonn presumes to know us based on the personas we've provided him. I fully comprehend the nuances of our relationship. What I don't understand is your utterly baffling behavior."

His brow furrowed, but she kept going. "You tell me you love me, and yet you don't want to touch me even though *I* ask you to?" she said the words like an accusation.

"How am I supposed to interpret that? What understanding would you like me to have of your feelings toward me, *husband*?"

Blood thrummed through Ethenn's veins, pumping loudly in his ears. He stepped forward until their faces were inches from one another. "I *can't* touch you," he hissed. "Not when I don't know what it will do to me."

Ilain blinked rapidly. "What do you mean?"

"Magic does things to me—it changes me. And when we touch, it gets worse."

She sucked in a sharp breath but didn't speak under his intense stare, so he continued, "Haven't you learned by now, Ilain? I'm a killer," he said softly so only she could hear his words. "Magic heightens that part of me. *You* heighten that. Sleeping beside you is torture. Kissing you, touching you . . . I can't trust myself with it."

"We're husband and wife," she said matter-of-factly.

He dipped his chin.

"You'll have to touch me eventually."

"Not until I've figured out how to control what magic does to me."

She scoffed nervously. "You aren't afraid you'll kill me, are you?"

"No," he assured her quickly. "No, I just—I don't know what magic will drive me to do."

A look of clarity crossed her face, and Ilain drew back in understanding. "It's why you didn't want to be a Warrior," she realized.

The announcer called for the Hammerfist and the Slayer to begin the last fight. Unsteadily, Ethenn pulled in a breath. Then he reached up and cupped Ilain's face in both of his hands. He brushed his thumbs across her knife-sharp cheekbones, pulling her closer. Her bright green eyes flickered between his expectantly.

"I'm going to win a damn bed for you to sleep in tonight," he said, and then he kissed her. Sharp, deep, and passionate. He heard catcalls from the crowd awaiting his entrance to the ring, but he ignored them.

Ilain melted under his caress. Shivers spiraled across his skin, his magic soaring at the feel of her. His muscles trembled with anticipation. His split lip stung against hers, but he refused to pull away, soaking up as much of her magical influence as possible. The room burned to life; light, color, sound, taste, and smell intensified. He could feel the very wood grain beneath his feet. Every sense snapped like overheated firewood. A coolness settled over his mind, priming him for action.

Ethenn released Ilain, barely ensuring that she was stable before striding to the fighting ring. At the side, Rafferty and Thom watched them and sniggered together. Brea pursed her lips, watching with amusement. Deckard kept his gaze averted while

Evylin smirked. The Calder brothers pointedly avoided looking at them, but Isla gave him an encouraging nod.

Ethenn ignored them all. He stepped in front of Aangus the Hammerfist. He was tall, and his bare chest rippled with muscle. One blow from him would hurt twice as much as the Bludger's. If Ethenn wasn't quick, he'd wind up with more than bruises and a split lip.

"Ready?" the announcer asked. At Ethenn and the Hammerfist's nods, he proclaimed, "Fight!"

With magic pounding in his veins, Ethenn charged. He knocked back the Hammerfist's defense, dodged a sly punch, then threw his fist into his opponent's jaw.

The Hammerfist spun, jaw slack, and fell face-first to the floor.

Ethenn looked straight at the barkeep. "About that room?"

CHAPTER TWENTY-SIX

It turned out that the barkeep was also the tavern owner. His small home abutted the back of the building, where he lived with his wife, a sweet lady with graying black hair and crooked teeth, their two teen sons, and their three cats, Vergal, Stergal, and Clide. Clide took a particular fancy to Ilain the moment she walked into the house. The brown tabby even slipped into the bedroom before they could shut the door. It was to be expected. Cats loved Ilain.

"Sit," Ilain ordered Ethenn, pointing to the old bed.

While he did as instructed, Ilain took quick stock of the room. Cramped, with a bed, wardrobe, vanity, and dresser—all of simple wooden make—there was hardly enough space to move around. Lorn and Nance, the tavern owner and his wife, would sleep in their sons' room while the boys sprawled in the parlor, thanks to Ethenn's deal. Nance was understanding and even approving once she heard the conditions. Ethenn paid more than handsomely for a straw-stuffed mattress and threadbare blankets.

Once she'd completed her inspection, Ilain sat next to Ethenn, and Clide the cat jumped onto the blue and yellow quilt at her side. Jaw tight, Ethenn kept his gaze averted even as she took his face in her hands to examine his injuries. He'd donned one of his spare shirts, leaving it hanging loose over his trousers.

"Well," she said tersely, "beyond the split lip, bloodied nose, extensive bruising, bloodshot left eye, and mental psychosis, nothing much seems to be the matter with you."

Ethenn flinched as she prodded his bruised temple. "What's a psychosis?" he asked.

A short chuckle slipped out of her. "I always forget you grew up in a small town." She reset her hands over his injuries and then closed her eyes, preparing to summon Day. It was harder at night to find that deep connection inside of her. Most Elemental Mages wouldn't be able to do it at all. But by Allore's design, she'd been born stronger than any Mage since before Ephren split their countries. And she had Auden as a brother.

"It's gentle," Auden had taught her. *"So many people think Fire and Day are similar because they're both bright. But Fire is intense, fierce, and powerful—like you. Day is a quiet warmth, like Mum's fresh bread or the sun on a misty morning. It calms and soothes. It gives you life."*

Reaching into her core, Ilain found the gentle part of herself. It was small, fragile, and rarely seen. She'd locked it away when she was only ten, taken from her mum and da for the Order of the Flame's tower in Doorstunds Reach. The Fire Mages didn't prize gentility. Being a soft woman was a fault in those halls. So she'd become strong, unyielding, and proud. And it had earned her the second-highest rank in the Order.

Ethenn gasped as the Day magic flared, easing the internal pressure surrounding his brain. When she opened her eyes, the rest of his wounds were gone, too, but his expression radiated agitation.

"I may be a town boy," he said tightly, "but that doesn't mean I'm uneducated."

Ilain raised her brow. "Did I say you were?"

He turned away, but she caught his jaw in her hand and forced him to face her. "You got to say your piece before," she said in a fierce, hushed tone. "Now, I get to say mine."

She could feel the tension of his clenched teeth in her grip, but he gave a permissible nod.

"First," Ilain released him and let Clide climb onto her lap, "a psychosis is a mental condition that drives people to behave in unnatural ways."

Ethenn huffed in self-derision. "So it's magic," he concluded.

She smirked without humor. "Not in the slightest."

Weaving her fingers into Clide's soft brown fur, Ilain held Ethenn's stare. "What did Thom tell you this morning?"

Ethenn's jaw flexed. "To bed you."

Ilain blew out an annoyed breath. "Well, I certainly didn't ask for that."

"What did you ask for?"

"A kiss," she said quietly. "That's all. And now, you've provided that, so I suppose I can accept it as enough."

A long silence passed between them as Ilain studied his impassive expression. She was angry with him. Not because he'd stupidly let himself get beaten up for a bed or because he'd kissed her so abruptly as he sought to stir his magic for the fight. Because he was baffling.

For Ilain's whole life, she'd dreamed of finding a Warrior like him. One who could match her in heart, power, and will. Ethenn might be young, and he might be less educated, but he was clever. He was stubborn. He was strong. And he was far more passionate than the people around him realized.

She'd seen it the first day they met. She saw it in the intensity of his deep brown stare, a stirring heating the depths of his soul. He was like a fire in a hearth: contained yet waiting to be unleashed. And she'd known then that she would have to be very careful with her heart around this handsome young man, lest she lose herself to a man without magic.

Ilain couldn't be with a non-magical man. She'd prepared too long and worked too hard to become the Highlady Chancellor of Doorstunds Reach. It was her responsibility. The Alliance was counting on her and her power to help guide their nation into what it should be. She had to marry a Warrior. That was that.

She'd initially protected her heart from Ethenn despite her growing attraction to him. And then he'd proved to be the bloody Warrior of her dreams. It'd been too late to explain her heart to him at that point, not after all her foolish choices. But when she'd seen him with Ivry Doyle, the Water Mage, and he'd admitted wanting to Bond, she couldn't refrain from acting. He'd admitted his love for Ilain. Perhaps she couldn't explain herself, but she could have him, she reasoned. And eventually, he would see her heart through her actions.

Yet, still, he held her at arm's length, refusing to know her or to let her know him.

Well, she'd bare her soul now whether he wanted her to or not.

"I'm scared, Ethenn," Ilain whispered.

He looked up at her admission, brow furrowed.

She held his dark gaze unflinchingly. "I'm afraid that you're going to do to me what Evylin did to Jonn," she confessed. "That you're holding yourself back from me because you don't trust me. I'm afraid you'll realize I'm not what you want and leave me because of it. I'm not asking you to bed me. But I am asking that you consider treating me like your wife—*loving* me like your wife rather than just as a woman for whom you harbor an infatuation."

Ethenn sucked in a sharp breath, and his features pinched in confusion. "Ilain—" He paused, wet his lips, and began again. "I'm not sure how to do that."

"You could start by being a little sweeter to me," she said with a playful grin. "Maybe telling me how pretty I am."

"You're not pretty," he said, and his expression softened. "You're stunning."

Ilain's smile grew bashful, but she forced herself to hold his stare. "And I know touching is difficult for you, but . . . perhaps you could hold me sometime?"

Without hesitation, Ethenn reached over and scooped Clide off her lap. The cat let out a disgruntled "mew" when he plopped on the ground. Then Ethenn wrapped his arm around her waist and startled her by pulling her onto his lap.

Ilain's breath caught. She wasn't altogether sure what to do with her hands, so she clasped them on her skirts, which bunched around her legs. "And not tonight," she murmured, their faces mere inches from one another, "but eventually, you should probably make love to me."

Ethenn's lips twitched with a smirk. "Would you like to schedule it?" he offered.

"I'd prefer spontaneity."

"Mm." He brushed his thumb along the base of her spine, sending a flare of warm magic up her back. His gaze shifted to the room beyond her, a blush spreading at his collar. "Well, to be honest," he whispered tensely, "I imagined our first time together being a bit more romantic than in a random inn or barkeep's house along our journey."

Ilain knew there were more important things to discuss, but she tilted her head, stuck on the thought. "You've imagined our first time?" she asked.

He chuckled nervously. "I'm a man, Ilain. I've imagined our first hundred times."

"I see." Somehow emboldened by his bashfulness, she draped her arms around his neck. "And where have you imagined this union taking place?"

A small smile softened his whole demeanor, though his muscles were tight, and he still wouldn't look at her. "In Estshire, there's a forest with a hidden glen that's filled with gilda lilies. Their petals are white with golden dots all over them. They're graceful, beautiful, and rare." He traced her freckled cheek with one finger. "They're like you."

His eyes met hers then, and he whispered roughly, "I'd like to take you there."

A thin, untimely laugh slipped out of Ilain at the unintended double entendre. "You want to *take* me in the forest."

Timidly, his chin dipped. "Yes."

"That's rather wild, even for you."

"I *am* a hunter."

"Oh, and all hunters take their wives into the forest to copulate?"

"Only the smart ones."

Ilain laughed fully then, though she tried to stifle it so as not to disturb the barkeep and his family. She let her fingers run through the outgrown waves that brushed his collar. "We are going to Estshire soon," she reminded.

"I thought you didn't want to schedule it."

She lifted a shoulder in feigned casualness. "Just presenting the opportunity."

Ethenn took a steadying breath, his arms loosening around her. "Ilain," the way he whispered her name was gentle but full of serious intensity, "it's been less than a week. Even in Estshire, it will have been less than a month."

"I know." She tightened her arms around his neck, leaning closer to impress her heart. "But Ethenn, I'm not undecided about us. I see no reason to wait untold months to commit to what we already know we want."

His gaze darkened only long enough for Ilain to wonder at its cause before he slipped an arm under her legs and stood, lifting her. He showed no signs of difficulty in the exertion, turning casually to lay her on the bed. Then he settled next to her. Their heads rested on the pillows as he stared into her eyes. "I'm not rushing this, Ilain," he said in a hushed voice. "It isn't because I don't trust you. It's because I love you, and I want to do this the right way."

"You won't leave me?" she asked, her heart stuttering.

He shook his head. "Not unless you tell me to."

"That's not going to happen."

Ethenn ran a finger along her cheek, gently pushing back the stray hairs there. Her skin prickled with heat. The fire within her leaped, begging to be unleashed.

"It happens for me, too, you know," Ilain whispered. His thick eyebrows pulled together, and she explained. "When we touch, my magic responds."

His chin rose. "Is that why you want me to kiss you?"

"Among other reasons."

"Such as?"

"I told you," Ilain smiled shyly, "I like you."

His rich brown eyes darted between hers as though trying to understand her meaning. Then he swallowed roughly. "We should get some sleep," he whispered.

"We're still dressed," she reminded him.

"True," he smirked, "but as I don't care to sleep between the same sheets as Lorn and Nance, I think it'd be rather cold otherwise."

"You intend to sleep on top of the blankets?"

He shrugged.

"What if *I* still get cold?" she said flirtatiously.

Ethenn's lips lifted knowingly. "Are you asking to cuddle with me?"

"It seems appropriate, given the circumstances."

"I suppose I'll have to learn at some point," he said with dry humor.

Clide leaped onto the bed just then, nuzzling his way between them. Disdainfully, Ethenn eyed the cat, but Ilain merely prodded him enough times to force him to the foot of the bed. Then she slid across the mattress to press herself into Ethenn's chest.

He rested his arm loosely around her, and his chin pressed into her temple. Despite his protests, he proved rather adequate at the task. His breath heated her face, and her magic flickered happily inside of her.

"Ethenn," she whispered.

"Yes?"

"I'm sorry."

He shifted to look down at her. "Why?"

"I didn't mean to push you," she said. "I didn't know how this—how *I* made you feel."

"It's not just you, Ilain. I've felt this way my whole life. It's just heightened with you."

"So you don't feel like killing something now?"

He laughed nervously. "No. I feel on the verge of losing control, but . . . I'm all right. For the moment, at least."

"When you say, 'losing control,' you mean . . . ?"

His hand twitched on her back. "I mean, as you said, I have a psychosis. It must have always been there, lingering below the surface. Magic drives me to do things I wouldn't normally do. It makes me more aggressive, more reactive, more . . . desirous."

Ilain pulled back to look up at him. "That's it?" she said blandly.

Ethenn frowned. "Isn't that enough?"

"You bloody prude," she muttered, rolling her eyes. Then she slugged him playfully in the chest. "That's how I feel every day of my life. It's what being connected to Fire does to you. I'm impulsive, reckless, and overly eager. It's why I'm ready to consummate our relationship after seven days while you're over here debating its wisdom. It isn't a psychosis. It's the resource."

"Oh," he said with obvious uncertainty. "But I'm not a Mage. I can't connect to the resource, can I?"

"Not in the same manner, no," she confirmed. "I'm simply saying that these inclinations of yours don't bother me, as I have them too."

"Oh."

Ilain sighed, then settled her head back on the pillow. "We're going to have to work on your priggish tendencies. In the meantime, cuddling will do."

After several seconds of silence, Ethenn whispered her name.

"Hm?"

"I still don't understand you."

"I'm a complex woman. It will take time."

She could feel him smile against her hair. "I think we should make more time."

Her heart warmed, and she snuggled closer. "Any particular reason?"

"We were advised to test the validity of our marriage," he murmured. His fingers trailed across her lower back. "And cuddling is likely to lead to solidifying it sooner rather than later."

Ilain grinned, though she knew he couldn't see her delight. Then she pressed a kiss to his neck, and he sucked in a sharp breath. "I think that's a splendid idea, husband."

CHAPTER TWENTY-SEVEN

9TH OF RADIA, 1574

Cresting the top of the hill, Deckard surveyed his home. Ephria City sprawled across the valley by the sea, looking just as they'd left it eighty-six days ago. The early evening sun glittered across the water. Farmsteads dotted the land in small pockets around the city like the sheep of Estshire, while tightly packed buildings filled the walls' interior to overflowing.

"I guess you were right," Thom admitted somberly, pulling up beside Deckard on the hilltop. "It took us eleven days to get here."

"This is one time I don't welcome congratulations," Deckard said with a sigh. "We didn't account for the divergence of the tunnel. If we could have cut straight across the border—"

"We couldn't." Thom met his gaze. "You know that, right? This isn't a failure on your part. If we had tried the more direct route, we would have wound up dying at the border."

Deckard nodded but couldn't accept that truth. "What if Blount has already come and gone?" he asked quietly.

"Then we'll find another way," Thom said confidently.

Appreciative of his brother's encouragement, Deckard clapped him on the shoulder, then spurred his horse into a gentle trot. At the head of their troop, he and Thom guided them toward the city's gates far below. He kept his back straight, working not to betray his worries.

Over the past eleven days of travel, Deckard's apprehension of their plan hadn't waned. It was clever, and it was potentially perfect. But there were too many opportunities for failure; too much could go wrong. One slipup, and they handed yet another Relic over to Blount.

Nudging the band of his moonstone ring, Deckard worked to maintain his casual manner. He'd gotten better at controlling his emotions, keeping them subdued enough not to disturb Evylin. It wasn't that he intended to keep things from her. It was simply frustrating, having her deduce his feelings before he'd even had the chance to process them himself. And he had lots to process these days. His opinion on the Alliance, his fears over their mission, and the development of his powers. All of them scratched at the back of his brain like a hound seeking its bone.

As if Auden and Isla's concerns about his ability to control his magic weren't enough, Deckard was struggling to find time for the books Obel had sent with him too. Of the four, he'd only had the time to truly study one. Granted, that one had already taught him a great deal about the basics of Space magic, giving him a rudimentary understanding of the resource he wielded.

Space was beyond anything Deckard had anticipated. The magic could create and destroy. It could alter the very fabric of the world, should a Mage connect with it deeply enough. However, the practical applications of those things were still a mystery to him.

Obel had insisted Deckard start with the book, *The Immense and Infinitesimal Expanse of the Heavens*, as it was a primer of a sort—if you could consider a seven-hundred-page tome a primer. While the other two books on Space magic appeared more useful at a glance—their pages filled with discussions of magical application and use— Deckard stuck to Obel's instruction, learning about the foundation for his connection to Space and building his relationship with the resource through the Path of Vieran.

But the fourth book haunted Deckard's thoughts the most.

The thin text provided a basic education on the appropriate methods for summoning and releasing ghosts. When Deckard had asked if there was a chance he might fail in releasing Hewitt's ghost, Obel laughed as though he'd asked the most ignorant question in Terraeus.

"Of course," he said. "You're not good at Night magic, to begin with, and if you don't read that book, there's a chance you'll wind up tethering him to the grave or the forest around it rather than his body and leave him to wander aimlessly for eternity."

The suggestion left Deckard anxious. There were too many chances for Hewitt's release to go wrong. Obel made it clear that if Deckard harbored any hesitancy about releasing the ghost, then the attempt was likely to fail. And Deckard could readily admit that he felt more than a little hesitation. He didn't want to release Hewitt for his own sake, having grown close to the man over the past few months. But more than that, he knew truly losing her uncle once and for all would cause Evylin further pain.

Their shared reluctance lingering in the back of his mind, Deckard grew increasingly worried that his attempt wouldn't work. He feared that he'd end up locking Hewitt in limbo, his soul trapped in a state of perpetual wandering. That thought was nearly as frightening as the idea that they'd fail to defeat Blount.

As they neared Ephria City's gates, Vayden, Isla, and Brea split away from the rest of the troop, as they'd discussed the previous evening. Since they needed to maintain their cover with King Ephren, they had to return as they'd left, sans Hewitt. It wouldn't do for the king to become suspicious of them or question their extra party members. So the Alliance trio would ride into the city on their own and meet the troop at Deckard and Evylin's house.

Meanwhile, as Order of the King members, the seven of them would report to the barracks as would be expected.

The towering gray stone walls of Ephria City loomed above them, and Deckard straightened as they approached the expansive, open gate. Guards were positioned at the entrance, casually observing the activity around them, a stark contrast to their time in Wauld. They felt no fear in approaching the guards, nor did they hesitate as they clomped onto the city streets.

Evylin pulled up alongside Deckard, a bright smile on her lips. "The last time we arrived," she said merrily, "you made sure to be at my side. This time, I won't miss the chance to be by yours."

Deckard's taut muscles eased at the cascade of warm feelings emanating from her. "How different things were then," he said and reached over to take her hand. "We're wholly new people."

"And yet," she squeezed his fingers in hers, "we are the same as ever. Just together."

"Together," he confirmed.

Under the massive gate, they passed into Ephria City. Its bustling interior was just as he'd remembered. People hurried through the streets, the clatter of hooves and cart wheels ricocheting off the stone buildings. Street merchants hawked their wares while clerks hurried to and fro with their missives and paperwork. Here, by the entrance to the city, the houses were smaller and more spaced out. As they neared the heart, they'd grow closer together, often interconnected, like a dense forest of stone.

Deckard had been raised as a farm boy, but he'd never felt quite at home in the countryside. It was beautiful, and he'd loved his childhood. But it wasn't until he came to Loclight as a soldier that he truly found his home.

Though his assignments often kept him from the city, Deckard had jumped at every opportunity to be stationed there. When he was a sergeant, he'd had his longest stint within Loclight, as the locals called it. A few years later, he'd earned the rank of lieutenant and a house to go with it. To his great disappointment, he spent far less time in the city than he liked, and the house had remained practically vacant throughout his entire ownership.

Taking the familiar path to the barracks, Deckard's thoughts drifted. Could his wandering lifestyle change after they completed their mission for the Alliance? If Evylin and Thom were right and his fears were unfounded, could he and Evylin retire to Loclight and live out their days in their home the way he'd always hoped? Would she be happy with such a meager existence? Would he?

Through the cobbled streets of the Military District, the troop returned to the very spot they'd departed from more than two months ago. They passed through the gate to the barracks and into its large courtyard. A smattering of soldiers trained on the far side, while others strode about their work. The stable hands and soldiers manning the gates all gaped at them, recognizing the Calder siblings with hair like fire and the first female soldier, Private Evylin Deckard, who was now evidently a legend among the ranks.

Suppressing his amused smile, Deckard dismounted and took charge as a good officer should. He ordered their horses to be cared for and sent Thom, Ethenn, and Rafferty with them to gather their saddlebags and supplies. Then he scanned the courtyard, finding the nearest officer.

"Lieutenant," he called, stepping forward.

The man, on course for the barracks stairs, came to a stuttering stop. Short and stocky with deep brown skin and thick curly hair, he was no doubt from the lower Shires. He scanned Deckard upon his approach, likely looking for an insignia of rank. "May I help you, sir?" he asked, not finding one.

Deckard pulled their folded orders from his inner coat pocket and held them out to the lieutenant. "Good afternoon, I'm Colonel Deckard of the Order of the King," he explained, doing his best not to take undue pride in the officious title.

The man blanched, his eyes flickering from the page to Deckard's face and back. "Blimey," he muttered, then cleared his throat. He bowed and offered the orders back. "Lieutenant Silvaa at your service, Colonel. How may I help?"

"Thank you, Lieutenant," Deckard said. "My troop and I have returned to the city for a short reprieve from our mission for the king. We can't stay long, but I need to get word to His Majesty so that we may debrief with him during our short stay. Could you see to it that a page is sent with word to the palace?"

Lieutenant Silvaa's lips parted, though his reply was hesitant. "Well, Colonel, I—" He glanced back toward the barracks. "I'm sure the general will want to speak with you.

You know, to debrief and such. And he'd be better qualified to ensure your message to the king is received anyway."

Deckard grimaced internally but maintained a stoic façade. He was uninterested in conversing with General Rand, who had assigned him an impossible task and subsequently attempted to send him to his death.

"I understand, Lieutenant," he said calmly. "But we don't have time for such additional meetings, I'm afraid. His Majesty will require our full attention before we resupply and depart once again."

Though the lieutenant nodded vehemently at the second mention of the king, his gaze drifted to the side as Evylin approached. Then he did a double take, and his jaw went slack.

Expecting that the officer was awed to see the legendary female private in person, Deckard was surprised when Lieutenant Silvaa burst out with a laugh. "Evie?" he gasped. "Is that really you?"

Deckard furrowed his brow just before Evylin leaped forward, startling him by hugging the lieutenant. "Druan!" she exclaimed through her own laughter. "I can't believe it."

Unsure of what to make of this unexpected exchange, Deckard held up a hand. "Excuse me," he interrupted, and Lieutenant Silvaa jerked away from Evylin as though realizing how untoward he'd been. He snapped to attention as Deckard asked, "Evylin, how do you know the lieutenant?"

"My apologies, Colonel," Silvaa broke in before she could reply, a nervous tremor in his voice. "I forgot myself. Evie—she's my sister-in-law."

Deckard raised his chin as Evylin jumped in to add, "Druan is married to my eldest sister, Euna. We thought—well, last I heard," she turned to the lieutenant, "we thought he was dead."

Druan Silvaa's expression pinched. "You thought I was dead?"

Evylin shrugged. "Euna hadn't heard from you in more than half a year. Which," she adopted a scolding look, "you'd better rectify immediately."

"Oh!" Druan sighed. "No, no, I know. I tried to write, but I was stationed in Tesscomb, and they didn't care much about the post down there."

Deckard raised his brow at the mention of Tesscomb. Like Ostwatch, it was on the border of Wauld and Ephria, though not as dangerous as the notorious post he'd served. But that didn't make it any less daunting an assignment. The lieutenant had seen many hard days, to be sure.

"We have exchanged letters since my reassignment here in Loclight, though," Druan assured Evylin. "Euna knows I'm alive, and I'm happy to say she and the girls are doing well too." His dark eyes flickered to Deckard for only a second. "I also heard all about your marriage. Euna was right peeved you didn't bother inviting her to your wedding."

Evylin's chin dipped bashfully. "Oh, I—it was rather unexpected."

"You're telling me," Druan said with a twinkle in his gaze. "Never thought I'd see the day you'd settle down."

"Neither did I," Evylin said dryly.

With a smile, Deckard held out his hand. "It's a pleasure to meet you, Lieutenant," he said as they shook. "I hope to further our acquaintance in the future and to make amends to your wife for our poor manners. I regret that I never got to meet her or your children."

Druan smirked and turned to Evylin. "How'd you get such a proper gentleman to stoop to your squalor?" he teased.

"I tricked him," Evylin said flatly.

Druan snorted. "Well, it's a pleasure to meet you, too, Colonel," he said. "I'm sure Magistrate Glaas was right proud to make this match. A gentleman and a high-ranking officer working on the king's commission to boot." He let out a low whistle. "The brownnoser must be beside himself."

Finding that Druan was no more a fan of their father-in-law than Deckard, he couldn't help his amused grin. "We haven't spoken in some time, but I don't think he'd be glad to know that I've helped his daughter become a soldier," he said.

While Druan laughed, Evylin set a hand on Deckard's arm. "Looks like the welcome party has arrived," she murmured.

Deckard and Druan both followed her gaze, turning to see General Rand descending the staircase, two other officers in tow. A young private hurried behind, carrying a ledger and pen. The double gold braids on Rand's right shoulder gleamed in the sunlight, his hooked nose and sharp eyes giving him the cunning look of a hawk about to swoop down on its prey. He walked in strides filled with superiority.

"Colonel Deckard," the general said brusquely. He came to a stop before the trio, his eyes scanning them haughtily. "I'm surprised to see you. You've been gone so long that I thought you might have died."

Having spent far too much time with Hewitt to cow to the general's aggression, Deckard adjusted his posture to that of an officer at ease. "Gratefully not, sir," he said with a light tone. "My men and I have returned for a short resupply before continuing on with the king's mission. It's good of you to greet us."

General Rand didn't give him the satisfaction of a response. Instead, he turned to look beyond him. "Lord and Lady Calder," he greeted indifferently, drawing Deckard's attention to their arrival at his back along with the rest of his men. "As the king's guests, I hope you've had a pleasant journey. While there isn't much to entertain the likes of nobility such as yourselves in the barracks, I'm afraid I must beg you to wait here while I speak with Colonel Deckard and the rest of my men."

"My apologies, General," Auden said, stepping up. "But why would they need to meet with you?"

Rand arched an eyebrow. "Because they are my soldiers, and I require them to debrief me on their mission."

"Pardon me, sir," Evylin said sweetly, drawing Rand's scorn. "But I don't work for you."

Rand's haughty scowl spoke for him. Still, he added, "Despite your appointment to His Majesty's services, I would have to agree, madam, you are *not* a soldier."

Deckard's jaw tightened, but Evylin's lips lifted in a sly smirk. Behind them, Thom scoffed as though aware of the mistake Rand had made.

"Oh, I understand, General," Evylin said cordially. "You don't agree with King Ephren's decision to appoint me as one of his *chosen* soldiers for this classified mission of ours. Perfectly understandable. I am, after all, a woman with such little understanding of military proceedings and swordplay. Perhaps you could teach me. Then maybe the king's choice won't be so erroneous in your mind."

"I take no issue with King Ephren's choices, madam," Rand said, his dark voice thick with agitation. "His Majesty is perfectly within his rights to commission whomever he likes into his services. I wouldn't begin to question his wisdom."

"Then you won't question our refusal to meet with you," Deckard said. "Our mission is, as Private Deckard said, classified and only for the king's ears. You'll forgive us for leaving you in the dark."

Rand took a threatening step forward, flat gray eyes boring into Deckard. "I am the king's head of the military in Loclight," he hissed. "That means that I am in charge of all assignments and proceedings regarding my men. Therefore, Colonel, there is no such thing as a mission above my classification. You will report to me as your commanding officer."

"Actually," Deckard replied calmly and lifted the orders between him and Rand, "if you read this, sir, you'll note that it clearly states we are to report to King Ephren alone. It further states that no one in the Ephrian Army is to detain us or impede our mission. As such, I'd be happy to acquiesce to your command, General, should His Majesty wish to induct you into our mission. Until such a time, I'm afraid we must be going. The king will expect our report."

Rand ripped the orders from Deckard's hand and began perusing them. Fiercely, his eyes scanned the lines.

"Unless," Evylin chimed in as he read, "you'd care to test His Majesty's leniency. I'll admit—" Her brow lifted with a menacing tilt, "I have wished for your demise after your attempted murder of my husband."

Rand unfolded the orders with a dismissive glare in her direction. At their side, Druan pursed his lips, staying silent to avoid incurring Rand's wrath. And behind them, their friends bore up, hands on their weapons and shoulders drawn back. A display of force with the king's blessing upon them.

A low growl rumbled in the general's throat as he read the orders. Deckard knew those pages were the only thing keeping Rand from finding some horrendous punishment for them all. These were his barracks. And they were insulting him in front of his men. After all his time under Rand's command and with Hewitt's insight, Deckard had come to understand that Rand only prized one thing in this world: respect. He mostly demanded it through fear, making him almost universally disliked. But he came from wealth and status that made him impossible to depose . . . for now.

Deckard couldn't help thinking that one of the better changes the Alliance could make was replacing General Rand as the head of the military. Though Commander Estham, whom they'd met at King Ephren's Annaltide celebration, was the official military leader, he dealt with the administrative and political aspects of the job. It was Rand who oversaw the day-to-day activities and the actual training of the soldiers. He was the one who truly *ran* the Ephrian Army.

One day soon, that would change.

Snarling, Rand shoved the orders back at Deckard. "Go then," he said.

Deckard gave him a polite bow, tucked the orders into his coat, and turned away. Evylin smiled at Druan and tossed General Rand a mocking salute. After taking his and Evylin's saddlebags from Thom, Deckard led his troop to the main gate, leaving the general and his lackeys behind. He once belonged to this barracks. It had been his duty to serve men like General Rand unquestioningly. Last time, he'd allowed that duty to bully him into blindly accepting a reassignment to Ostwatch just before the king saved him from that fate.

Now, he walked from the courtyard into Loclight proper, knowing that he was no longer a true soldier of the Ephrian Army. Though he remained undecided about his place among the Alliance, he refused to serve men like Rand anymore. Nor would he support men like King Ephren as his monarch. He was tired of watching the world fall into the hands of corrupt and ignoble men. They were the sort that knights like Sergus fought to unseat a millennium ago.

Perhaps Deckard could never be Sergus, but he'd be damned if he didn't do what he could to uphold the principles he knew to be right.

"Is the general always so pleasant?" Ilain asked suddenly. "Or are you just special?"

Exchanging a look with Thom while they made their way down the street, Deckard fought down a scoff. "General Rand doesn't like most people," he explained. "I don't think I'm a special case."

"He was always pleasant to me," Thom said. He nudged Evylin's side. "I like to think I impressed him."

"Or he saw himself in you," Ethenn remarked dryly.

The unexpected snark drew laughter out of them all. Even Thom grinned despite himself.

"Particularly cutting remark, kid," Rafferty said, patting him on the back. "I feel like a proud father."

Ethenn eyed him dubiously. "I'd be profoundly embarrassed to be your son."

"Oh-ho!" he sniggered. "I think your time with the Lady Flame has been a bad influence."

Thom tossed a smirk over his shoulder. "Ilain does have a way of corrupting people," he sniped.

Ilain's gaze flickered dangerously. "You had your shot at my corruption," she said. "It isn't my fault you weren't magical enough to tempt me."

"Magic had nothing to do with it," Auden said lightly. "I seem to remember some clandestine comment of yours about the impeccable shape of Corporal Loxley's—"

"If you utter one more syllable," Ilain interjected, "I will burn every inch of your body and make you heal the scars yourself."

Auden frowned playfully. "It's my birthday tomorrow," he lamented. "I get a free pass just this once."

As laughter filled the air again and the Day Mage received warm wishes, Deckard couldn't help but smile. He'd come to cherish the camaraderie among their group. Their prolonged stay in Wauld had been filled with grief, hurt, and anger, making these fleeting moments of joy and togetherness feel hard-won. But they'd become a family in their time traveling with the Calders. It was strange and unexpected. From the moment he'd met the Mages, Deckard had been wary of them. And yet, now he thought he understood why Evylin and Thom were so trusting of them. The Calders were more than their traveling companions. They'd become friends and mentors. In Ethenn's case, one became a lover. They belonged now as surely as any of the Ephrians.

Nearing their home, Deckard felt a buzz of happiness coming from Evylin. Her hand slipped into the crook of his elbow. She drifted closer, eyes on the buildings around them. Just over two months ago, they'd walked this very path. So much had changed. So much remained the same. And while Deckard wished they hadn't had to undergo all the trials they faced, he wouldn't exchange their lives for any other.

Three-story, stone-faced townhomes lined the streets as they made their way to number thirty-two. Though the interior would be austere and dusty, Deckard's heart filled with anticipation. His muscles eased, and his heart warmed. He was home with his wife and his brother at his side.

It could only be better if Hewitt were with them, hale and whole.

As they strode to the door, their trio of Alliance comrades hurried over from the tavern across the street. In the heart of the city where the majority of the officers lived, there were abundant taverns to frequent, kick back, and forget the rigors of army life.

"This is your house?" Brea asked Thom, a hint of wonder in her tone as she surveyed the façade.

"It's Jonn and Evie's," Thom said. "But I do live with them. At least, for now."

Vayden pursed his lips. "It's nice," he said, then looked at Deckard. "I didn't realize you were so well off."

Unlocking the door, Deckard chuckled. "I'm not. Though officers are given reasonable compensation and a housing stipend, I wouldn't be considered wealthy." Deckard stepped back, leaving the door open for their guests.

"In Wauld," Vayden said, following his wife into the house, "this would cost at least three years of the average living wage."

"Another reason to thank Allore we don't live in Wauld," Thom commented. He slapped Deckard's shoulder. "Though I don't think they'll be so impressed with what we've got inside."

While Thom hurried in to give their guests a rough tour of the downstairs, explaining that they'd lived in the house as two bachelors traveling too often to furnish the place appropriately, Deckard turned to Evylin.

He held out his hand. "Welcome home, my love."

He could feel Evylin's smile thrumming through the air around them as her fingers slipped between his. "I'm so happy to be home," she replied, voice a gentle rasp.

Two months of dust and cobwebs greeted them in the sparse townhome. A sofa and a wingback chair with a tea table were all that awaited them in the parlor. The hearth was cold, with only a smattering of coals in it. Though the house boasted four rooms, only two of them were outfitted for residents, while a third held a meager bed. Most of their troop would have to sleep on their bedrolls on the floor.

"Where should we put our things?" Vayden asked, glancing toward the staircase.

While Deckard scanned the group, Thom didn't hesitate. "You and Isla can have my room," he said. "It's at the top of the stairs, the door on the left. I should probably clean up, though. Can't promise it's in any state for company."

"We won't put you out like that," Isla said.

"Nonsense," Thom said with a wave of his hand. "There's another room across the hall with a bed, but it's only big enough for one."

"We'll take that," Ilain said with a grin. "We've made a single-person bed work just fine before."

Rafferty immediately began to chortle while Ethenn's neck turned pink.

Thom smirked. "Right," he said, then moved on. "Well, then there's just one more room on the top floor, but it's completely empty. Brea, you can have it. Us three," he motioned to Rafferty, Auden, and himself, "can share the living room."

"I'll take the sofa," Rafferty volunteered magnanimously.

"You're a saint," Evylin noted. Then she tugged on Deckard's arm. "Well, I hope you all settle in nicely. In the meantime, I'm going to take a nap."

"And what's the colonel gonna do?" Rafferty asked wryly as they reached the base of the stairs.

"Jonn," Evylin said teasingly, "will unpack."

CHAPTER TWENTY-EIGHT

As soon as they entered their bedroom, Evylin glided across the floor and threw herself onto the bed. "Oh, the comforts of home," she exclaimed, sprawling on the blankets. "Why do we ever leave?"

Deckard laughed, shutting the door behind him. He crossed to set their saddlebags on the end of the bed. "I'm afraid my wife only married me on the promise of adventure," he teased. "And lounging about in bed all day doesn't make it into the great epics."

Evylin let out a grunt of discontentment. "Your wife is a fool."

"I wholeheartedly disagree."

She rolled onto her side, propping a hand under her head to watch him as he began to unpack. Still dressed in his travel clothes, he looked far less like a soldier and more like a mercenary with his scruffy beard. She smiled at the image. "Even if it's only for a day," she said softly, "I'm glad we're here."

Pausing, Deckard leaned forward, pressing a hand to the bed in order to kiss Evylin on the forehead. "I'm glad too," he whispered.

"I know," she replied teasingly. "I can feel it."

Deckard chuckled, then straightened to return to his work. Though they'd be leaving in the morning, he emptied their saddlebags entirely, one object at a time. She presumed he'd wash the clothes, repack their other goods, replenish some of the papers, and remove other extraneous items from his stores.

After kicking off her boots, Evylin sat cross-legged on the bed. She grabbed her remaining saddlebag before he could and unceremoniously dumped her belongings in a pile. She rummaged through the disorganized stack, separating the dirty and used up goods from the rest.

Deckard raised a brow at her haphazard rifling. "I thought you were going to take a nap," he remarked.

"I will," Evylin said, focused on her task. "I just want to find something first."

"What?" he asked, gathering her dirty clothes along with his. As he lifted one of her tunics, it unfurled, something small and hard tumbling out.

"Aha!" Evylin reached out to claim the object. "There it is!"

As Deckard began to ask what it was, he paused when Evylin opened the leather pouch. She pulled out the oval vignette, which was no larger than the palm of her hand. It was the painting he'd given her for her birthday, a nearly perfect replica of the Wayford countryside where they'd celebrated one month of marriage and he'd made his promises to her, the place where they'd shared their first real kiss.

"You still have it," Deckard murmured in awe, a softness in the air around him.

Evylin smiled up at him. "I found it in my bag after we escaped Renaul," she explained. "Thanks to Emmaas, we didn't lose everything after all."

Though they'd had to leave behind the Fire, Day, and Time Relics, the retrieval of her painting was a reminder: They hadn't lost what truly mattered. They'd all made it out with their lives, and that was enough.

"Where should we put it?" Evylin asked, holding the painting with reverence.

Deckard shook his head. "Wherever you like, I suppose."

"Hm." Evylin looked around the room, gaze lingering on her nightstand. She already had a picture there—a painting from Dolia depicting the rolling, ivy-covered hills of Whickam Village—along with her jewelry box, its lid open to reveal an unruly stack of small slips of paper.

Evylin retrieved another slip from the leather pouch. "This," she proclaimed dramatically, "will go in here." She placed the note in the jewelry box on top of all the others. "For safekeeping."

Deckard pressed his lips around a broad smile, and she knew he recognized the papers. They were all the notes he'd left her through their earliest days of marriage. Most of those letters were menial at best; their contents ran along the same lines: *He was sorry to miss her; he'd be gone, but he hoped to be back soon.* Yet, she'd kept them all because she couldn't bear to part with them.

Deckard's gaze turned desirous as his mood shifted, and Evylin bit her lip slyly. She could tell he wanted to kiss her. So she slipped demurely off the bed and made her way toward him. His hand reached out to grip her arm and pull her close just as a knock came at their door.

They both halted and stared at the door.

Deckard sighed, releasing her.

Evylin smirked, rolled onto her toes to kiss his cheek, then resumed her pursuit of a new home for the vignette.

When Deckard opened the door, Rafferty was on the other side. "Am I interrupting?" he asked, peeking around Deckard.

"We were just unpacking," Deckard said. "What do you need?"

He raised his white-blond brow. "You do realize we'll be leaving on the morrow, should all go well, don't you?"

Deckard gave him a dull stare. "And in the meantime, we'll be more comfortable in our home. What did you need?"

"It isn't what *I* need, Your Magefulness," he said, thumping a hand to his chest. Then he waved toward the stairs. "Lord Carlile's here, and he'd like to talk to you."

Instantly, Evylin and Deckard abandoned their unpacking and followed Rafferty out the door. They wound down the three flights of stairs, finding the king's advisor waiting in the parlor with the rest of the troop standing around awkwardly. Only Ilain and Auden appeared at ease, talking casually with Carlile.

The old nobleman's white hair fluffed around his head with untamable whimsy. Otherwise, he was the perfect image of a gentleman. He wore a navy coat with a patterned blue waistcoat, as was the current fashion. His silk cravat mimicked his stark hair, though crisply tied with a pleasant drape. Hands clasped behind his back, he stood with unexpected comfort in their meagerly furnished home.

Upon Deckard and Evylin's arrival, the parlor's occupants turned to them. "Ah, Colonel Deckard," Carlile said merrily. "Pleasure to see you again. And Private Deckard," he winked at Evylin in a conspiratory manner, "as impressive as ever."

"Milord," Evylin greeted with a curtsy that felt strange in her trousers.

Deckard suggested they take a seat, though there weren't enough available in the room. They made do, letting Evylin, Ilain, and Isla take the sofa while Brea perched on the arm and Carlile took the wingback chair. The rest of the men stood around the room, listening expectantly.

"Well," Carlile said, inspecting them each in turn, "I am here to extend an invitation on King Ephren's behalf. He requests you join him for dinner, where you may debrief him on the status of your mission."

"Dinner, eh?" Rafferty asked, leaning against the stair railing. "Count me in. What time shall we arrive to dine with his royal fatness?"

Carlile gave the weasel a quick, appraising glance. Though they hadn't known of Carlile's place in the Alliance upon their first meeting, Ilain and Auden had assured them that he had no more affinity for King Ephren than the rest of them. However, Evylin wondered if the advisor disapproved of the disrespect to their sovereign.

"Seven," Carlile answered, ignoring the quip. "There will be two carriages sent for you, though—" He looked at Vayden, Isla, and Brea as he said, "I'm afraid the invitation is only extended to the Order of the King."

"I can't say I'll miss meeting His Majesty," Brea said flippantly.

"It bodes well that you'll be staying here," Carlile continued, "as we'll require Mr. Calder to carry the Relics while Highlady Freye and Lieutenant Lohen act as his guard."

Evylin glanced over her shoulder at Deckard with wary apprehension. Being in Ephria once again, where magic's very existence was touted as a heretical legend, the Relics were far safer than before. But leaving them with only two guards made her uneasy.

Deckard cleared his throat and asked, "His Majesty didn't consider delivering this message to be a waste of your time?"

Carlile's eyes glimmered with humor. "Not when I suggested I should bring his most honored guard a few gifts." He gestured to a medium-sized trunk that could be seen in the entry. "After so long on the road, His Majesty thought you'd appreciate some grander clothes for the occasion."

Ilain brightened. "You brought me a gown?" she asked excitedly.

"I did, Highlady."

She failed to contain a squeal, pressing a hand to her lips and looking very much like she was ready to bolt off the sofa to peruse the trunk.

"But my real reason for coming," Carlile said, "was, of course, on behalf of the Alliance. I'd like to hear your plans and offer what advice I can. About this evening and beyond."

He looked at Rafferty then. "My first bit of advice is to keep that tongue in check. King Ephren is fond of jokes but not at his expense. We don't need to offend the king or alert him to our cause."

The setting sun cast shadows across the wooden floor, marking the short period remaining between the present and their dinner. Deckard spoke again, hastily suggesting, "Perhaps we'd better inform you of our plans quickly, as it will take some time to make ourselves presentable for His Majesty's company."

"Certainly," Carlile said, prompting Deckard to begin his explanation.

With steady progress, Deckard went through the plans. They would seek out the Space Keep in the morning, retrieve the Relic, and begin their journey to Estshire posthaste. He explained how they hoped to subvert Blount by obtaining both Relics before him, even at the risk of going out of order. Once they accomplished that phase of the mission, they didn't have much of a plan in place, hoping the Alliance would give them directions on the best way to recover the remaining four Relics from Blount himself.

Carlile tapped a finger on the chair arm in thought. "It's certainly daring," he noted. "I am awaiting an update from the Waulden Administration on Blount's movements, but last we knew, your plan is viable. The prince was in Carrickbrack, waiting for his allies to join him. Where he is at present, I cannot say until I receive further updates. Birds can only fly so quickly."

Evylin wasn't sure if Carlile meant actual birds like carrier pigeons or if he was using a code.

Behind her, she could feel Deckard's discomfort as he continued, "Even with our delay, if our calculations are correct and Blount does go for the Terrae Relic first, he should arrive in Olbury shortly after us," he said. "Which would mean we could wait for him there and hope to ambush him as he's done to us. With the Night, Wind, Terrae, and Space Relics, we should be able to accomplish that, yes?"

"Oh, yes, I should hope so," Carlile said, though his expression belied uncertainty. He hesitated, then sighed. "It is hard to know how to proceed in matters such as this when men like Blount are involved. He's dangerous. He's cunning. He's been trained under the most powerful and cruel Night Mages for over four decades. Underestimating him and his abilities is a mistake."

Ilain glanced at Brea as though to impress the statement on her.

Brea ignored the woman.

"However," Carlile continued, "with four Relics, a Bonded couple, the highest trained soldiers in Ephria, the Alliance's most impressive spy, two additional Warriors, and three Mages, including the most powerful to be born in the last two centuries who is also a purported goddess—" He grinned, scanning the whole of the troop before turning back to Deckard. "I have little doubt that you will succeed, Colonel."

Evylin shared a hopeful look with Deckard, feeling his anxiety diminish in the air around him. Brea's plan *would* work, and they would win this war once and for all.

Yet, she felt a sudden shift in Deckard's emotions once more, the worry returning. "We'll plan for that then and pray to Allore that Blount is days behind us," he said in a tense tone. "Do you have any other advice?"

"I do," Carlile said. "Though more in line with the evening's festivities. First, don't mention the Space Relic. Remember, Ephren doesn't know it exists, believing there are seven Relics. In fact, should he mention magic of any sort, it'd be best to keep your conversation vague. Ephren is a distractible man. If you bore him, he'll move on to something more diverting."

"We'll just let Audy handle the magic talk then," Rafferty said. "Anytime he gets going, people are bound to be bored."

Brea snorted while Auden glowered at the man.

"Speaking of the Calders," Carlile said, turning to Ilain. "Congratulations on your betrothal, Highlady. And to you, Corporal Loxley."

Standing at the far end of the couch, Ethenn dipped his chin in thanks, his expression tightening at the room's attention. At his side, Ilain patted his arm placatingly as she replied, "Our thanks, my lord."

He raised a knowing brow. "That said, I'm afraid it would be best if His Majesty doesn't discover your relationship. Ephren won't take well to one of his soldiers falling in love with a Waulden Mage. It doesn't make for a good story on his part, his personal guard switching loyalty to a dangerously suspect ally. It'd be best if you didn't show preference to one another tonight."

"We can do that," Ethenn said readily.

Carlile addressed the rest of them. "As a matter of fact, I'd suggest none of you be overly friendly with the Calders. His Majesty might get suspicious."

"We've traveled together for two months now," Evylin said. "Isn't it expected that we've grown close?"

"As the Order of the King, your troop has been given two assignments," Carlile reminded. "To help recover the Relics and to keep an eye on the untrustworthy Wauldeners."

The truth filled the room awkwardly. It was a strange reminder that in Ephria, Auden and Ilain were considered the enemy. Even the king's trust was conditional.

"Your friendship," Carlile continued, "would suggest that you have lost your sense of caution. Ephren may be easy to manipulate, but he is no fool. He will question your allegiance if he thinks you are complicit with the Calders."

Evylin chewed on her lip, growing uncomfortable about the dinner. She wasn't much for stately pretense or politicking. And she worried that she'd slip up, revealing their hand to the king.

But ever gracious, Deckard accepted Carlile's task before asking if there was anything more.

"Yes." Carlile gestured to the trunk again. "Inside, you will find a box with replicas of the Day, Water, Night, Wind, and Time Relics. The king will want to see them and hear your tales. Feel free to embellish them as much as you wish. However, keep Blount from the accounting."

Rafferty perked up, his silvery eyes gleaming. "These replicas of the Relics," he said, "are they as gold and encrusted with gems as the real things?"

"Indeed," Carlile said. "But you aren't to touch them, Corporal. Only Colonel and Captain Deckard will be given charge of them as the highest-ranking officers. Though, Highlord Calder—"

Auden looked up, attentive.

"It'd behoove us if you'd give them some extra luster when the king holds them, hm?" Carlile's eyes glimmered merrily. "Make him believe they hold magic."

Auden grinned. "I'll do what I can."

"Excellent." Carlile stood then. "I'll leave you to your preparations. It will be a private affair tonight, just you and the king's family. Be prepared for some preening, but don't worry, this won't be an ostentatious affair. You'll all do just fine."

After Carlile's departure, they perused the trunk, finding individual packages awaiting them. Once they'd been handed out, the group dispersed to prepare. The men all shaved, and Brea offered to trim their hair should they wish.

"You can cut hair?" Thom asked, incredulous at the discovery.

"Well enough to make even *you* look presentable, *mi'caro*," she teased, beginning to work on Ethenn's hair. It had grown so long that it regularly hung in the young man's eyes, a less than presentable appearance to go before the king.

Brea did an excellent job. Rafferty no longer looked quite so scraggly with his close crop, and she even trimmed Auden's hair to make it easier to manage.

Carlile had chosen to outfit the soldiers in uniforms with regal cuts and luxurious finishes. Each of the men wore the dark green of Ephria's standard, their high collars trimmed with silver braiding, black silk cravats, and white trousers tucked into shiny black riding boots. Deckard's uniform bore the single gold braid of a colonel strapped to the right epaulet. As a sign of her unique station, Evylin was given a similar coat made in silk and cut short to emphasize her waistline, where her emerald skirt flared dramatically.

Evylin thought they all looked like quite a respectable set of soldiers.

The Calders, however, were placed in much finer garb. They were dressed like royalty with elaborate embellishments that created a clear distinction between soldiers and Mages. Evylin assumed it was a deliberate choice on Carlile's part.

Auden wore a long, burgundy coat with a capelet embroidered with golden leaves and flourishes and a yellow topaz brooch clasped beneath the high collar. With his clean-shaven jaw and slicked-back copper locks, he looked like a prince from one of the tales of old. Or perhaps more correctly, one of the Mages who'd ruled Auld two centuries ago.

Ilain was even more striking. Carlile had chosen to put her in an ivory gown of gauzy fabrics. The massive skirt floated around her hips and legs, though the bodice hugged her torso tighter than Ephrian society would often deem appropriate. Small appliqués of flowers in pastel pinks, yellows, and blues covered the low-dipping bodice. Its straps hung off her shoulders, baring her shoulders and décolletage with impunity. She wore her fiery red hair pinned back to display the dress even more effectively.

Evylin wondered at the bodice's rigid construction, and Ilain mentioned something about boning, which kept its shape. "It's nearly impossible to breathe, but at least I look splendid," the highlady proclaimed.

Ethenn stood to the side, pointedly avoiding looking at his wife.

When Deckard returned downstairs, freshly dressed in his regalia, Evylin smiled brightly. "Look at you." She greeted him at the bottom of the stairs. "It's like stepping back in time."

"You mean back to when we first met the king?" Deckard asked, brushing down the front of his coat. His right hand looked odd without the moonstone ring. They'd decided to leave behind the tokens of their Bond, leaving her dagger and his ring in their room. Though they'd proven that the objects would return to their side at a moment's thought, they lingered so long as the couple willed it. "I must say," he continued, "I don't believe I'm any less nervous this time."

Evylin chuckled, adjusting the braid on his right shoulder. They were mostly alone in the parlor as the rest of the men were preparing in the rooms upstairs. Vayden, Isla, and Brea were whipping together their own meals in the kitchen while Ilain and Ethenn sat in the dining room, sipping tea and talking in hushed tones.

Looking up at Deckard's clean-cut appearance, Evylin narrowed her eyes thoughtfully.

"What?" he asked.

"I'm trying to decide," she said, crossing her arms.

"Decide on what?"

"On which way I like you better." She raised her brow in appraisal. "As an officer, clean-cut and trimmed. Or as a Mage, wild with curls and an unruly beard."

Deckard scoffed out a laugh. "Why would you ever prefer me unruly?"

She fixed him with a flirtatious smirk. "It is awfully masculine," she noted. "And mysterious. Which is a particularly potent combination."

He huffed even as she draped her arms around his neck. "However," she continued, "I did fall in love with you when you were an officer. And that . . ." She scanned his face fondly. "I think that's the real you. It may not be so fearsome, but it is quite attractive—and refined and caring. Just like you."

A gentle wash of joy swept through the air, and Deckard dipped his head. "You're too kind," he whispered, his lips a breath away from hers.

Their lips didn't quite meet before footsteps pounded on the stairs, and Thom's call for Deckard reverberated down to them.

Deckard pursed his lips in agitation at the second interrupted kiss of the day while Evylin pulled away, amused.

Thom appeared on the staircase behind his brother, eyes fixed on the breast of his coat. "I can't figure out how to put this bloody thing on," he lamented, struggling with his captain's insignia.

"Give it here," Deckard said, then turned to help him affix the silver metal pin to his coat.

Evylin took a seat on the sofa, surveying them with amusement. "You've been a soldier for how long, and you don't know how to apply your insignia?" she teased.

"It's different once you become a captain," Thom defended. "They switch from patches already attached to the coats to these—" He waved a hand at the metal pin. "*Things*."

"They are somewhat intricate," Deckard said, fastening the last clip. "There. I'll teach you properly when we have more time."

"Thanks," Thom said, and then a knock came on the front door. "Sounds like our ride is here. I'll get the others."

While Ilain and Ethenn rose from the table, Thom bounded back up the stairs, calling for Rafferty and Auden.

Deckard turned to Evylin, his happy air blurred into a tangled flurry of concern. "Are you ready?" he asked, his demeanor tense and constrained.

Evylin watched him cautiously for only a moment. Whatever was causing his concern, she wouldn't let him wallow. Not when they were headed into a dinner where confidence would count.

She slipped her hand around Deckard's arm, tugging him close. "We're about to dine with the king we're working to overthrow," she remarked dryly. "This is what I live for."

CHAPTER TWENTY-NINE

The carriages pulled up to the palace just as the sun was setting, casting the white stone edifice in a rosy, orange glow. The lush gardens were lit by strung-up lanterns, with men and women of the court strolling through the hedges on pebbled paths. Evylin took it all in through the window. Her eyes flitted from one place to the next. Though it hadn't changed much from their last visit, the springtime had filled the grounds with verdant life, and she was as in awe of the grandiosity as ever.

Evylin sat back, smiling over at Ilain and Auden, who were seated across from her and Deckard. "What was it like?" she asked. "Living in the palace."

Ilain lifted her shoulder in a shrug. "Boring."

"When we first came to Ephria, we lived on Carlile's small estate the majority of the time," Auden added. "It wasn't until we'd met King Ephren that he offered to have us stay with him, though it was more to keep an eye on us than out of true hospitality. We weren't allowed out of the northern wing unless specifically ordered by the king himself."

Evylin saw why that would lead to a dull residency. Though she imagined a palace as grand as this would still hold wonder after wonder, even in its guest rooms.

The carriage clattered to a stop, and the footman opened the door for them. Auden exited first, helping his sister down before Deckard did the same for Evylin. Behind them, Thom, Rafferty, and Ethenn disembarked from their carriage. They all met at the foot of the stairs before being greeted by a servant at the opulent entrance.

The servant led them through the halls, informing them that they'd dine with His

Majesty in his private apartments. They passed hall after hall of rooms, painting after painting of landscapes and royalty. Vaulted ceilings towered above them. Evylin remembered attending the Annaltide Ball in awe of the beauty. Now, she wondered how the Shepherd King justified his indulgent life when he came to power in a coup against the Mages' immoderation.

Of course, Evylin hadn't realized the tyrants the first Ephren overthrew were truly magical. She'd always been taught they were heretics who believed in a false theology and claimed powers that weren't real. Ephren had done his work, effectively controlling his people's knowledge. The present King Ephren was no different.

At last, they came to the dining hall. The vaulted ceiling there was painted with a landscape of the rolling hills of Estshire. The richly carpeted floor, a reflection of the green countryside, stretched beneath a large table. Fine porcelain plates and silverware gleamed along its mahogany length. Candlelight flickered dully under the immense glow of the crystal chandelier overhead.

And at the head of the table, King Willem Ephren sat with the shining, platinum crown of the Shepherd King on his white hair. The banner of the Shepherd hung behind him, the crook and sword crossed on the verdant silk.

"My Order," Ephren exclaimed, rising. He chuckled excitedly. "Come in, come in. Take your seats. You won't mind that I've invited my family to join us. My son, Caspar, you know."

At the foot of the table, Prince Caspar regarded Evylin and Ilain with thoughtful consideration, likely pondering whether either was worth his efforts at seduction. He remained as handsome as ever, featuring curly brown hair and appealing looks. However, Evylin steadfastly avoided his gaze and his unwelcome attention.

The king went on to introduce the rest of his dinner guests. "The lovely lady at his side is my daughter-in-law, Henriette." The woman in question was rather plain with her dull brown hair and round features, but she had a beautiful, genuine smile. "This is my brother, Grayham, Duke of Loclight province," he said, clapping the shoulder of the man on his right. "And my niece, Seretta. She's quite taken with the daring story of Caspar's rescue." He chuckled and sent a wink to the soldiers. "Might even grace one of you with her company if you please her enough. They're all wildly excited to hear your extravagant stories, though we'll save the most important bits for after dinner, shall we?"

Once the king had introduced the troop to his family, he instructed Deckard to sit on his left but stopped Evylin from following him. "I apologize, dear woman," Ephren said, not sounding apologetic in the least. "But my daughter-in-law has requested your presence at her side."

Not at all interested in sitting so near Prince Ephren, Evylin forced her smile. At least the man's wife would be between her and him. Perhaps she wouldn't have to speak with him at all.

The seating arrangement was quickly decided after that. Auden was to sit beside Deckard while Ilain took the place across from him next to Duke Grayham Ephren. Thom readily took the seat between Evylin and Ilain, dodging the advancement of Seretta, presumably the duke's daughter, by their shared sharp jawlines, though the young woman had a far deeper complexion than any others at the table.

Seretta didn't seem to mind this loss as she went right for Ethenn, slipping her hand under his arm and guiding him to the seat next to hers. Ilain watched keenly but stayed silent, and Rafferty wound up next to the prince.

Once the king took his seat, so did the rest of them, the servants pushing in their chairs readily. He started up a conversation with Deckard, the duke, and the Calders, capturing the far side of the table's attention.

Henriette turned to Evylin immediately, her friendly smile infectious. "I couldn't believe it when His Majesty told me I could join tonight," she said with gleeful excitement. "Ever since I heard of your commission, I knew I had to meet you. Just think of it: the first female soldier."

While Evylin knew she was far from the *first* in all of Terraeus, she kept the information to herself. "It's a great honor," she said. "I'm indebted to His Majesty."

"Aren't we all?" Prince Ephren grumbled at the end of the table.

His wife, who looked a decade younger than her husband, didn't heed his sour remark. "However did you learn swordplay?" she asked, her guileless demeanor reminding Evylin of her youngest sister, Dolia.

"My uncle taught me," Evylin said. "He was a general and a very great soldier."

"He was the one in your party who died, wasn't he?" Seretta asked from across the table. Her words weren't venomous or cruelly intended. Instead, they sounded ignorant.

Evylin glanced up the table's length to catch Deckard's compassionate gaze. Despite the way her heart squeezed, she gave him a nod, promising that she was fine. Then she turned back to Seretta. "He was," she said. "It was a dreadful experience, losing him. But he died in battle protecting me, and I know he wouldn't have wanted it any other way."

Seretta pursed her lips. She was pretty, her tight black curls and hazel-brown skin tone suggesting her mother's southern ancestry. "Were you close with your uncle?" she asked as though she couldn't fathom the concept.

With an uncle such as King Ephren, Evylin didn't doubt the struggle the young woman faced. However, she replied readily. "I was. Hewitt was a wonderful and attentive, if gruff, uncle. I adored him."

"How darling," Henriette said, then her expression pinched. "Or, I suppose, horrible. It's a terrible thing—you having to watch him die like that."

"It was terrible," Evylin agreed.

Taking pity on her, Rafferty jumped into the conversation. "If you ladies like terrible stories," he said dryly, "you should ask Ethenn to tell you about the time I slipped a frog into his trousers."

"You just told the story, Raff," Ethenn said flatly while the women tittered.

"Nah, I left out the bit about how you screeched like a goose in a fox's maw."

"Is this the sort of work the king's highly specialized Order does?" Prince Caspar asked, a snide grin on his lips. "Pranking one another."

"That was before we were in the Order, Your Highness," Rafferty said with mocking respect. "While we were mere foot soldiers. We wouldn't dream of behaving so unbecomingly now."

Seretta set her hand on Ethenn's arm, her expression taunting. "What else have you had in your trousers?" she teased under her breath.

A flash of red covered his neck while Evylin choked on her wine, Henriette flushed, and Caspar burst into laughter. Rafferty merely sniggered into his napkin.

But the comment had obtained both Thom and Ilain's attention now, the pair of them thoroughly drawn in.

Though his ears were as red as his neck, Ethenn replied steadily, "Only my wife, ma'am."

Evylin and Thom shared an amused glance. Seretta frowned in disbelief while Ilain turned back to the other side of the table, satisfied.

"You're married?" Seretta asked.

"I am," Ethenn confirmed.

"You're not wearing a wedding band."

"I can't," he said, lifting a forkful of turnip and yam. "It inhibits my fighting."

Seretta clearly didn't believe him. Her eyes narrowed as though pleased with the challenge. "What's her name?"

Evylin blanched, but Ethenn answered without hesitation, "Eina."

Ilain glanced over again, a small smile on her lips as she sipped her wine.

"It's easy enough to invent a name, Serrie," Prince Caspar chimed in amusedly. "Laurette. Mina. Eileen. See? If you want to discover the man's honesty, you have to ask more pointed questions."

"Why should I lie?" Ethenn asked with blunt calmness.

"Because, as I'm sure you know, my good man," Caspar tipped his wine glass in Ethenn's direction, "it's more fun to play games than to give in too easily."

"Do aid me in my investigation, cousin," Seretta said pleasantly.

Caspar leaned forward. "Tell us: What's your Eina's deepest fear?"

Evylin frowned, sure that Ethenn would flounder under their questioning. Not even she could provide an answer regarding Deckard's deepest fear.

But Ethenn said, "Sea travel. And abandonment, but that's less tangible." He raised his brow then. "Would you like me to tell you the number of freckles on her nose? It's forty-seven. I've counted them many times."

Thom, Rafferty, and Caspar laughed at the quip, while Seretta pursed her lips.

At Evylin's side, Henriette set a hand to her chest. "I don't think we can doubt him any longer," she remarked merrily. She smiled brightly at Ethenn. "You must love her very much."

"I do," he said without hesitation.

"Sap," Caspar muttered into his wine glass.

Henriette ignored her husband. "It must be quite difficult, being parted from her for so long," she said.

Ethenn shifted to reach for his wine. "It is."

"And you," Henriette said, turning to Evylin. "You must be so happy to have your husband with you on your journey."

"Oh, yes," Evylin confirmed. "I wouldn't want to be without him. Not even for a day."

Evidently bored, Caspar turned to Rafferty. "You're not married, are you?"

"No," Rafferty said in blatant confusion.

"And you're not in love?"

"No."

"Excellent." Caspar tossed back the rest of his wine before holding it up for the servants to refill. "Tell me about Wauld. Are the women as shapeless and foul-tempered as the one traveling with you?"

Pitying Henriette more and more, Evylin smiled at her gently.

Upon the encouragement, the woman continued. "Your husband," she said. "How long has he been a soldier?"

Evylin paused, searching her mind for the number. She turned to Thom on her other side, who was clearly listening in as the king, Deckard, Auden, and the duke discussed dull politics. "Twelve years?" she asked, and Thom nodded.

She turned back to Henriette. "Twelve years."

"So long! Have you traveled with him for much of it?" the princess asked.

"No, Your Highness, we only married four months ago, so I just began to travel with him then."

"Oh, you must have missed him terribly during your courtship."

Evylin didn't bother to correct her assumption.

"I heard about his station when you saved Caspar," Henriette said. "But what did he do prior?"

Evylin couldn't answer.

Thom leaned forward and offered, "He worked in Colonel Caarter's regiment for roughly five years. They traveled most of the border, ensuring the officers there had enough supplies and followed protocol."

"That sounds awfully important," Henriette remarked.

Thom shrugged. "He was a glorified courier."

Evylin struggled to contain her snort and took a bite to cover it.

"Ah," Henriette said, seeming oblivious to the snide statement. "Now, I'm not familiar with the details, Private Deckard, but as a soldier, how long does your commission last?"

"Well, I'm not sure," Evylin said. "The traditional soldier has a ten-year contract. But I'm not officially a soldier, you see. I never signed a commission, so I believe that I simply work at the king's leisure."

"Oh." The princess sounded disappointed. Her brown eyes shone sadly. "Couldn't that last forever?"

"I suppose it could." Though not once Allund was raised.

"Don't you want to have children?"

Evylin blinked, and Thom shifted uncomfortably at her side. "Yes," she murmured uncertainly. "One day."

"And your husband? He seems like such an honorable man. I'm sure he would make an excellent father."

"He would," Evylin agreed, though she and Deckard had never outright discussed children. She assumed he wanted them, but she couldn't say for sure, especially not now that they were a Bonded Mage and Warrior, certain to live for another century or more. Did that change his feelings about having a family? Did it change hers?

Henriette patted Evylin's hand, a happy smile on her face. "I'm sure His Majesty would excuse you once you chose to start a family. Won't that be wonderful? You and your husband could retire to the countryside. I've heard it's beautiful. Maybe you could live in a cottage, like in the storybooks."

Evylin didn't feel the smile she gave the woman. "Perhaps," she said, then turned to her plate. She stabbed a large chunk of roasted beef and shoved it into her mouth to avoid any more conversation.

Chewing slowly, Evylin glanced at Deckard. He thanked the servant who'd just refilled his wine glass, and she furrowed her brow, studying him discreetly. Who was her husband? Did he want children? Would he like a cottage in the countryside? All this time, he was so good and giving, promising to supply *her* dreams, and yet he'd never once stated what *he* dreamed of. Did he even like adventure? Would he be happy to settle in Loclight, filling their house with furniture and children, turning it into a home? Would there even be a Loclight when the Alliance was through?

"He won't want that," Thom whispered at Evylin's side. She met his sharp gaze, and he smiled. "He doesn't approve of the mundane."

"Are you sure?" Evylin whispered back.

"He married you, didn't he?"

She chuckled softly. "I mean, are you sure he wouldn't want to live in the countryside?"

"Why would he?"

Evylin shrugged. "It's beautiful, restful, away from danger. It could be a good place to raise a family." She furrowed her brow. "Does he want a family?"

Thom's eyes widened. "Shouldn't you know the answer to that yourself?"

She pursed her lips. "I *should* know a lot of things. But I'm stuck here wondering how it is that Ethenn knows Ilain better than I know Jonn."

Thom blew a silent raspberry. "He made all that stuff up."

"Are you sure?"

"Well, he made Eina up."

"No, he didn't," Ilain whispered, leaning in on Thom's other side.

"What?" they both asked in hushed tones.

Ilain's green eyes glimmered slyly. "Eina is my middle name. Sea travel *is* my worst fear, though he gleaned the abandonment bit for himself. And he did, in fact, count the freckles on my nose just last night. Forty-seven."

"Please, don't inform us about anything else that happened last night," Thom muttered ruefully. "Now, we're not supposed to be friendly, so turn away and act like you hate us."

Ilain chuckled in a snide manner, then did as ordered.

Thom offered Evylin an apologetic shrug. "So it seems Ethenn knows random, odd facts about his wife. That doesn't mean he knows her better than you know Deckard."

Tugging on her wedding rings, Evylin glanced at her husband. Her heart thudded with agitation. Deckard looked up then, a curiosity in his air. He'd felt her frustration.

With an appeasing grin, Evylin dismissed his concern. Then she turned back to her meal. It didn't matter what Thom said. Evylin *should* know those random, odd facts about Deckard. She should know his greatest fear and his deepest desire. She should know if he wanted children.

For how else was she going to love him with the same dedication and care with which he loved her?

CHAPTER THIRTY

The dinner proved to be miserable. Entertaining the king's whims was worse than appeasing all the egos of the magistrates in the Shires combined. Ephren was a lazy monarch, a frivolous man, and blatantly prejudiced against the Waulden people. Yet, Deckard had to smile and nod, partaking in the conversation with faux enthusiasm.

The meeting that followed was no better. With the influence of Auden's magic, they more than adequately convinced the king that the Relic replicas were real. Then Deckard had to lie carefully, explaining the last two months of their lives, Hewitt's death, and their continued mission.

"We'll leave in the morning," he said in conclusion. "And hopefully, we will return within a month with the final two in our hands."

King Ephren believed the story but pulled Deckard aside before they left. "There are spies in my court," he said in a hushed tone.

Deckard frowned, shock rolling through him. "Your Majesty?"

"The captain of my guard has discovered strange inconsistencies in—oh, I don't remember the exact details." Ephren waved his hand in agitation. "But there are spies in my court, that's what he said. And I'm starting to suspect the Calders aren't who they appear to be."

Deckard lifted his chin. "I see," he replied thoughtfully. "If I may, Your Majesty?"
Ephren beckoned for his response.

"I've been questioning the siblings myself. I have yet to see true signs of duplicity, but one can never be too careful. Especially when it comes to Wauldeners."

"Mm," Ephren agreed.

Playing on his prejudice and paranoia, Deckard dropped his voice a decibel lower. "I will continue to keep an eye on them, Your Majesty. If they're up to no good, I will discern it, and my men and I will stop them."

King Ephren gripped his shoulder, gave a firm nod, and dismissed him.

Deckard had a headache from the pressure of maintaining such duplicity when they arrived back at the house, but he was relieved that Ephren had bought his lies. Vayden, Isla, and Brea sat in the parlor, greeting them happily on their arrival. "We found a few bottles of *cairen* in your cellar," Vayden said, holding up a glass of the red wine. "I hope you don't mind that we opened two."

"We'll replace them," Brea added, then frowned at the bottles. "Not that they're very good."

"No, it's all right," Deckard assured, then moved for the kitchen to retrieve a glass. "I'll join you."

Once they were all gathered, Deckard accepted the Night Relic back from Vayden, feeling a dampening sensation washing over his emotions at its touch. After weeks of wearing the Relic, at last, he was beginning to experience its true effects. He was unusually tired, worn down from the dinner, from their travels, and from the weight of all that was still to come.

While Rafferty exuberantly filled the Alliance members in on the laborious affair of maintaining their cover during dinner, the group began to split. Ilain grabbed Ethenn's arm, tugging him toward the stairs.

"I need to get out of this dress," she proclaimed with exasperation. Though Ethenn blushed and Rafferty sniggered, it seemed she hadn't meant it nearly as provocatively as it sounded.

When they disappeared, Auden sat beside his brother. Thom pulled a chair in from the dining room, settling next to Brea to add his own snide remarks about the meal. Deckard intended to stay to inform them of his plans for the Space Relic's retrieval in the morning, but Evylin excused herself, ascending the stairs quietly.

Deckard frowned, watching her go. Ever since the dinner, she'd carried a sense of uncertainty around her. He couldn't quite name the full emotion—perhaps it was disappointment or worry—but he could tell she needed reassurance. She needed him.

"Pardon the interruption," Deckard said, stopping Rafferty mid-sentence. "We should set out at first light tomorrow. We'll have to seek out the Keep first, and it will likely take hours to recover the Relic once we're inside. I'd like to ensure plenty of time for travel later in the day."

"Won't we need to recover for a time after battling the Keep?" Vayden asked.

"We can't afford to," Deckard said. "Not if we want to stay ahead of Blount."

The group nodded with disappointment, and Deckard said his goodnights, then followed after Evylin. When he approached the second floor, Ethenn stepped out of the bedroom alone. Deckard moved out of the young man's way, exchanging a nod and discovering the door to his study propped open. He glanced inside, finding Evylin standing behind the desk, running her fingers over its clean surface.

He leaned against the doorframe, wine glass still in hand, watching her. Her dark hair framed her face as she looked down. With the moonlight from the window at her back, she was enshrouded in light. Her unbuttoned coat hung open to reveal her white blouse. She lifted the cover of the singular book on the desk's surface.

"What are you doing in here?" he asked softly.

Evylin jumped, setting a hand to her chest. "You startled me," she said through a nervous chuckle.

"My sincerest apologies," he said, moving into the room. "I didn't intend to sneak up on you."

She shook her head. "I was deep in thought."

"I could tell." He stood on the other side of the desk and grinned. "However, unless you're concerned about my financial status, you won't find the answers in that ledger."

She tapped the book. "This is your financial record?"

He nodded. "Do you intend to audit me?"

Her nose scrunched playfully. "No, that's far too dull."

Deckard sipped his wine. "What *are* you doing in here?"

"I just . . ." She scanned the room, and he followed her gaze. There wasn't much to see. A desk, a chair, and a meager collection of books on the built-in shelves, plus an inkwell, sheaves of paper, and a cold oil lamp.

Evylin met his gaze, brow furrowed. "Do you really work in here?" she asked.

"No," he admitted. "Aside from doing my finances, that is. Though I'd like to do more, I'm not home often enough."

Her expression shifted, and he caught that strange emotion again. Concern? Confusion? He couldn't be sure. "What work would you do?" she asked.

The laughter of their friends echoed up the staircase as he said, "Read and write, I suppose."

"What would you write?"

Deckard shrugged. "Letters. Records. Maybe I'd take notes on my studies. I'm not sure; I've just always imagined that I'd write something."

"I didn't know that," Evylin whispered, studying him as though seeing him for the first time.

Now, the emotion came through clearer, and Deckard frowned. Evylin was apprehensive. Nervous. Why?

"What's wrong?" he asked.

"Nothing."

Deckard set the wine glass on the desk and reached across for her hand. "Evie," he held her gaze, "tell me."

Evylin pulled in a shallow breath. In the unlit room, her skin appeared darker, the hollows of her cheeks deeply shadowed. She averted her gaze and pulled away. "Over the past weeks, I've realized something," she said.

"And what's that?" he asked.

Her eyes met his. "I don't know you."

At the intensity of her gaze, Deckard felt a cold shiver, and his brows pinched together. "I can assure you," he said gently, "you know me better than anyone else in this world."

Evylin shook her head vehemently. "I don't know anything about you, Jonn. I don't know your birthday or our anniversary. I don't know your favorite book or if you have hobbies. I wasn't aware of your desire to write anything. How long have you lived in this house? Would you prefer to live in the country?"

Deckard took in her distress with confusion. "Those things don't matter," he promised. "You'll learn them over time, or they'll prove their pointlessness. But that doesn't mean you don't know me."

Evylin pressed her lips together. Worry radiated out of her, fuzzing the atmosphere with her doubt. Whatever had prompted these questions, Deckard realized this wasn't a mere curiosity. She was deeply bothered by this lack of knowledge.

Another burst of laughter reverberated up the stairwell, and Deckard sighed.

He reached out a hand. "Come on," he whispered. "Let's go upstairs where we can talk."

Together, they walked out of the study, Deckard stopping only to retrieve his wine glass and shut the door behind them. The stairs were cold, the dim oil lamp sconce on the wall flickering with a gentle yellow flame. Once on the third floor, he led her to their bedroom. They took the time to light the lamps inside, casting the space in a warm glow. It was no warmer within, but Deckard drew the curtains and grabbed one of Evylin's shawls from the wardrobe.

Securing the wrap around her shoulders, Deckard smiled gently down at her. "What do you want to know?" he asked.

"When is your birthday?" she asked quietly.

Such a rudimentary question. He decided to offer her more than the simple facts.

"It's the seventh of Pyra," he said. "I'll be thirty-three, and I don't like celebrating. I never have."

The ready information relaxed Evylin. She took a seat on the bed and pulled him down beside her. "Why don't you like celebrating?"

Deckard shrugged. "I don't need people to celebrate me to make me feel special. It feels vain."

She pierced him with a pointed look. "But you celebrate others," she argued. "Why wouldn't they want to do the same for you?"

"I see your point, but I don't care to be the center of attention."

Her smile twitched down in the corner.

"Now, our anniversary," Deckard entwined their fingers on the bed between them, "is the thirteenth of Terraen, and I will *always* want to celebrate it."

"How do you remember it?"

"What do you mean?"

She raised her brow. "We didn't choose the date, as normal couples would. It just happened to us."

"That doesn't make it any less important to me."

She deflated, so he tightened his grip, shifting closer. "Evie, I don't care that you didn't know the date. You don't need to remember it. I'll do that for us."

"Did you mark it down or something?"

"No."

"Then how do you remember?"

He dismissed the question with a smile. "I've always had a memory for that sort of thing."

Evylin huffed self-derisively. "I haven't. I didn't even remember my own birthday last month. I think I've forgotten yours already, and you've just told me."

Deckard laughed. "Good. That means you won't try to do anything when it comes around."

"I *want* to do something, Jonn," she insisted. "I want to give you a gift as thoughtful as the one you gave me. But I don't have the first idea of what to get you."

"Nothing," he said comfortingly. "I don't want anything."

"If you had asked me, I would have said the same thing for my birthday. But then you gave me that," she said, gesturing toward the vignette still awaiting its proper home on her nightstand. "Somehow, it was exactly what I didn't know was missing from my life."

Deckard smiled, proud of his gift. The moment he'd seen it in the small shop in Blacklion, he would have sold the very clothes off his back to have it.

Evylin tightened her grip on his hand. "I want to know you, Jonn," she whispered, "in the same way you know me."

Appreciative of the sentiment, Deckard dipped down to kiss her. "I'll tell you anything you want to know," he promised.

Drawing back in thought, Evylin took his offer seriously. It was charming to see her work so hard to understand him, even if he didn't feel the necessity of it. Their souls were Bonded, and she could sense his every emotion. How much more understanding did she need?

Evylin took a deep breath, then asked her first question. "Is Jonn short for Jonnathan?"

An abrupt laugh burst out of him. "No. It's just Jonn."

"Just Jonn?" She smiled. "So your parents weren't pretentious like mine, then?"

"What do you mean?"

"They didn't give you a middle name."

"Ah. They did, actually."

She waited expectantly.

"It's Marc."

Evylin pursed her lips in consideration. "Jonn Marc Deckard," she said and tipped her head. "That's rather . . . boring."

He grinned dryly. "We can't all have names as elegant as yours."

She let out a mocking guffaw. "You don't know my middle name."

"Don't I?" he said, reaching out one finger to brush the silver pendant hanging over her open collar. Its rosette design matched her middle name. Evylin Rosette. Such a feminine name for such a fierce woman.

Evylin's lips parted in surprise. "How do you—?"

"The same way I know your birthday," he interrupted. "It's on our marriage contract."

"And you remember it?"

"I have a copy of it."

"Oh. Right."

Though it was standard practice for two contracts to be designed—one for the magistrate's records and one for the groom—there was no reason Evylin would have thought about the document. Deckard had kept it stored in his trunk for the entirety of their travels with the Third Volunteer Company, and as she'd never had a use for it, she'd not seen it after their ceremony.

"Where is it?" Evylin asked.

"In the study," he said. "Once we arrived, I put it with other important documents, like my contract and past orders."

"*Past* orders? Why keep those?"

"I like to be prepared should anyone ever question my work."

Evylin hummed in thought, pulling away from him. He could tell she was working up another question, and he reached for his wine glass waiting on the nightstand. Evylin eyed him as he took a sip.

Suddenly, she asked another question. "Why can't you say no to wine?"

Deckard forced himself to swallow rather than scoff. "I can say no."

"You never do."

"I have," he defended. "Perhaps I'm not in the practice of rejecting it, but I enjoy it. Is there a reason I shouldn't?"

"It just doesn't match the man I know," she said. "You're so proper and straitlaced all the time. And you're religious—which is another topic we need to discuss. Yet, you don't seem to worry about overindulging when it comes to wine." She shook her head. "It doesn't match your impeccable reputation."

A flicker of agitation twisted Deckard's stomach. "I don't overindulge," he defended.

"You regularly drink two to three glasses in an evening, should they be offered. While it isn't exactly excessive, it is beyond what polite society would deem appropriate."

Shifting uncomfortably, Deckard set the wine aside, suddenly put off by the alcohol. "I have no explanation to offer," he said, keeping his tone light.

"You're always beyond reproach in every area except this." Her eyes widened in revelation. "Is that it? You hold yourself to such a high standard, and wine is the one vice you allow yourself?"

He chuckled nervously. "What do you mean?"

"You told me once that I'm the only woman you've kissed." She raised her brow. "Thirty-two years is a long time to wait for such a simple affection. You keep your bloody orders as proof you've done your job, and I've never once seen you lose your temper. Yet, you let yourself drink, even to mild inebriation."

Deckard cleared his throat, shifting away from her. He'd never considered his behavior, never thinking to question it. But her suggestion made him uneasy, like he was a fraud or a drunkard.

Evylin caught his wrist, stilling him. "Jonn, it isn't a problem," she said. "If anything, it makes me love you more."

His eyes flashed to hers. "A flaw makes you love me more?"

"Yes," she laughed. "Because, for once, I don't feel completely inferior to you."

"You've never been inferior to anyone."

Despite his darkening mood, joy hummed into the air around Evylin. She scooted closer, resting a hand on his leg. "I have my next question," she said.

Though hesitant to discover any more startling revelations about himself, Deckard nodded.

Evylin's smile turned tender. "When did you first know that you loved me?"

Deckard instantly relaxed. "Two months ago," he said. "Here."

"What, in this room?" she asked, beaming at him.

"No, here in Loclight," he corrected. He reached over to brush her hair behind her ear, then cupped her cheek. "At the ocean."

Deckard could remember the exact moment as they stood beside the sea, the wind sweeping up her hair wildly. Her expression softened at the memory, and contentment pulsed between them.

"I've loved you longer than that," he admitted. "But that was the first moment I *knew* that I loved you."

The softest flush of pink tinged her face. "I'm sorry it took me so long to figure it out myself," she whispered.

"Don't be sorry."

"But I *am*," she insisted, holding his gaze adamantly. "We could have had so much more time together if I had just been honest with myself . . . and you."

Deckard ran his finger across her jaw, resting his forehead against hers.

"I think I knew then too," Evylin admitted. "It's why I unpacked the way I did. Even if you were sent to Ostwatch, I refused to leave you. I couldn't fathom losing you for a second, even then. I just wasn't brave enough to say it."

For a brief moment, Deckard grieved what could have been. If Evylin had opened up and trusted him, they might have enjoyed two additional months of love like this. Her fears had cost them eighty days of happiness.

"We have a hundred years ahead of us," Deckard reminded them both. "What are mere days?"

He tipped her chin up and kissed her. The heat of magic thrummed gently in his chest. He left it dormant but leaned in to deepen the kiss. He slipped Evylin's coat from her shoulders, preparing to draw her close, but she set a hand on his chest to stop him.

"I have another question," she whispered against his lips.

"It can wait," he murmured, wrapping his arm around her.

She pulled back, her brows lifting dramatically. "You won't distract me from my mission," she said. "I have too much to learn."

Deckard tightened his jaw, pulling in a halting breath. "It's getting late, Evie."

"Then we'd better talk quickly," she teased.

Though he didn't care to answer more questions, he would accept their closeness in exchange. He pulled her over his lap, her legs straddling him, and tightened his grip around her waist. "Ask away," he said.

Evylin settled her arms on his shoulders, smiling with happiness. "What do you want to do with your life?" she asked.

Deckard tensed. "I've already given you that answer."

"When?"

"In Mouroc," he said, the words coming out more sharply than he intended. "I told you: Whatever you want, I'll give it to you."

"That's not an answer," Evylin argued.

"It's the only one I have."

Her jaw set with determination, and he could feel her agitation as if it were within himself. "What about what *you* want, Jonn?"

Suddenly, holding her felt wrong. But as she didn't seem inclined to move, he simply loosened his grip. "I don't want anything."

"That's ridiculous," she said tersely. "Everyone wants *something*, Jonn. Even martyrs like you."

Deckard had the urge to shove her off his lap. But he held back his baser instincts and took a deep breath instead.

"What do you want?" Evylin pressed.

"You," he said automatically.

"You have me," she replied. "What else?"

"Nothing."

She ignored his protest. "Do you want a family?"

"Evie—"

"Do you want children?" she demanded.

Deckard couldn't take their closeness anymore. He pushed her aside as gently as he could, his agitation brewing, and rose from the bed.

"Jonn."

"I don't know," he said sharply. "Yes, I suppose I do, but—"

"Then we'll have children."

"No!" He whirled, glaring at her. "That's not how we make decisions, Evylin. I want children, yes, but if you don't—"

"I do," she interrupted.

He stared at her, disbelieving. He didn't know why, but he'd never expected her to want to be a mother. She was independent, adventurous, and sometimes selfish. She didn't trust people easily, and she feared losing those she loved. He doubted motherhood would appeal to someone like her.

Deckard forced himself to calm down, relaxing his shoulders. "It's all right if you don't," he promised. "We're going to live up to two centuries. Children will just add to the list of those we'll lose. I don't mind giving that up."

With a cold look across her face, Evylin stared at him. "What else are you willing to give up for me?" she asked. "Everything?"

"Yes."

"That's not fair."

Deckard smiled gently. "I don't mind making sacrifices for you."

"No," she returned sharply. "It's not fair to *me*."

He blinked, confused.

"Why are you the only one who gets to prove their love through sacrifice?" she demanded.

Deckard gaped at her, unsure of what to say.

"I love you too," she continued. "And I'd like the chance to show you that. Yet, not only do you refuse to let me make a choice for *your* betterment over mine, but you're also so busy loving me well that you won't let me know who you truly are. You withhold yourself to let me be happy. That isn't fair."

Deckard stared at her. Emotions churned through the room like the sea, heightening the tension in his chest. He couldn't even tell whose feelings were whose as frustration, resentment, admiration, impatience, anxiety, and desire spun through the room. The feelings were potent and intense. And he couldn't keep his head above their swelling depths.

"What do you want me to do?" he whispered weakly.

"Tell me about yourself," she pleaded. "That is what I want. That's what will make me happy."

He ran a hand through his hair. "I don't know what to say."

"Tell me what you *want*."

He shook his head, unable to find the answer. "I don't like talking about myself, Evylin."

"But I like knowing about you," she pressed.

He fell silent, staring at the rug beneath their feet.

Evylin took a single step toward him. "Why does it bother you so much?" she whispered gently.

Despite the soothing emotion she emitted, Deckard's frustration couldn't be calmed. "Because it's not worth discussing," he said flatly.

Her nose scrunched. "It's *you* we're discussing."

With no reply inside him, he simply turned away with a sigh.

"Why do you think it's not worth it?" she asked, a deep sympathy drifting through the air. "That *you're* not worth it?"

The comment struck Deckard, its truth unadorned. A nervous laugh slipped out of him. "It's not like that," he lied. "I just don't want people paying attention to me."

Evylin stared at him for a single heartbeat before scoffing. "You do remember the job you had when we met, don't you?" He frowned, but she kept on. "You spoke in front of hundreds of people, over and over again, giving a bloody fantastic speech. In each settlement in the Shire, you stood before every last citizen, and they *all* paid attention to you. And do you remember what you told them?"

"Evie—"

"You said you wanted to be the man who made the difference." She smiled widely as though the answer should be blatant to him. "How much more attention could you ask for, Jonn?"

Deckard ground his teeth. He'd heard this argument; he'd been charged with this delusion of grandeur before. "Did Hewitt tell you this?" he asked coldly. "Has he convinced you that I want to be Euon Sergus? Or perhaps a living legend like he was? He's wrong. I have no interest in being so important."

Evylin's brow tipped up knowingly. "What's so wrong with being important? Why can't you admit that you like admiration?"

Her blatant disregard for his denial grated against his scruples. His hands trembled at his sides, and the Night Relic weighed heavily around his neck. Certain that it was affecting his unruly emotions, Deckard quickly removed it from beneath his collar and pulled it over his head. He thrust it onto the nightstand, yet his irritation did not settle.

With his back to Evylin, he squeezed his eyes shut. Why couldn't she let it go? His wants, his dreams, his desires—they were meaningless. They were wrong. He would happily let her have the future she'd promised to Ryen and ignore the selfish urges of his heart.

"Jonn," her voice was loving but adamant, "you're *worth* admiring."

The sentiment pierced his gut like a blade. He clenched his jaw, trying to control his anger and the fear that her statement had awakened.

"Do you know what that would mean?" he asked, his voice low and rough. He turned slowly to face her, settling a demanding glare on her. "Do you realize what that sort of life would look like? I wouldn't belong to you, Evylin. I would belong to everyone else. The entire nation would rely on *me*."

Her expression slackened as he took a step closer. "Do you understand the sort of weight that entails?" he demanded, his voice rising uncontrollably. "The kind of work and sacrifice that takes from a person. Life stops for you. It isn't about what you want or what you desire; it's about what's best for everyone else. I don't want that responsibility. I can't carry it!"

Deckard's throat was raw from the fury of those last words ripping out of him.

Evylin stared at him, wide-eyed and jaw slack. He didn't need the Bond to reveal her shock. However, the magical link sent a cold wave of fear crashing into him. *Her* fear.

Evylin was afraid of him.

"Oh, Allore," Deckard muttered, guilt instantly rising in his gut. He never yelled, not at anyone, not even his soldiers. She stood frozen, staring up at him. Desperately, anxiously, he raised his trembling hands to her arms, deeply grateful that she didn't flinch away but rather leaned into his touch. "Evylin," her name rushed out of him, "I'm so sorry. I—I didn't mean . . ."

"No," she whispered fiercely, her amber eyes glassy with unshed tears. "It's all right. I didn't realize . . ." An air of heavy compassion pressed through the air around them. "Do you always feel this way?" she asked tenderly, her hands coming to rest on his arms too. "That everything comes down to your perfection, to your actions."

He had no answer.

Evylin sighed somberly. "We don't have to talk about this," she promised. "I understand now."

"Evie—"

She shushed him, pressing into his chest as her arms went around him. "It doesn't matter," she muttered against him. "I understand."

Deckard closed his eyes, resting his cheek on top of her head. "I'm sorry," he said again, holding her close. "I'm so sorry."

"It doesn't matter," she repeated. "I love you. I won't push you like this again."

Tears burned in his eyes. He hated himself for making her feel this fearful guilt. "No," he whispered into her hair. "I'll tell you anything you want to know."

But Evylin didn't ask anything more. Instead, she leaned back, tipping her face up to kiss him. Deckard knew he should pull back and bare his whole soul to her. He should tell her the truth, trusting her as he'd once wished she'd do with him. Yet, her touch was absolving, her kisses comforting. His heart was heavy, and his responsibilities weighed too much. He hadn't lied. He couldn't carry it.

So he gave in to the distraction of his wife's touch. He let her tenderness assuage his conscience. He kissed her fiercely, deeply, and with intense need. Instinctually, their hands started pulling at the other's clothes, desperate for the soothing connection of flesh upon flesh. They lost themselves in the vulnerable, physical assurance of their love and care. And it wasn't until they lay beneath the blankets with her curled into his side and her head on his shoulder that he admitted his weakness to them both.

"I'm sorry, Evylin," he whispered.

Somehow, she managed to roll even farther into him, cheek pressing against his chest. "I'm sorry too."

A hollow sigh seeped out of him. "You have no reason to apologize. I'm the one who . . ." The truth tasted bitter on his tongue. "I shouldn't have yelled at you. I shouldn't have lost control like that. I'm sorry I frightened you."

"You didn't frighten me."

While he knew it was a lie—he had *felt* the surge of her fear—he didn't contradict her but wrapped the arm tucked beneath her neck more securely around her.

"Well," Evylin said with a tinge of playfulness, "you did, but it wasn't because I was frightened of *you*." She lifted her head to meet his gaze. "I was frightened because I realized what I'd done to us."

"What you've—" Deckard shook his head. "You haven't done anything."

"I made us Bond," she said, the words emerging halted and broken. "And now we face the Alliance's hopes for us, and . . . I'm afraid that you're right, and I've gotten us stuck in a role we don't want."

Deckard shifted onto his side, resting a hand on her cheek. He wiped away the single tear that slipped free. "Listen to me," he charged. "I'm not sorry that we Bonded. I could never regret that. No matter what it brings."

More tears fell, but she listened as he'd asked.

"You were right," he said. "We needed to Bond so you could safely continue this mission. But more than that, I'm grateful to now be fully one with you, to have my soul bound to yours."

Evylin's fingers grazed his, tugging lightly on the moonstone ring. "Are you really?" she whispered. "Or are you just saying that to make me feel better?"

He smiled gently to encourage her. "Are you calling me a liar?"

A reluctant grin pulled at her lips. "I already have once."

"My second vice, I suppose."

"And I love you all the more for it."

Deckard pressed his lips to her forehead, then pulled her back into his arms once again. "I truly mean it," he promised. "Even if it means a future we never desired, I would do it all again."

She relaxed into him, and a renewed peace radiated into his skin. They lay there for several long minutes, silently resting in each other's embrace. He drew his fingers along her back in circles, thoughts drifting.

"You're still worried about something," Evylin prompted.

Deckard smirked ruefully. "This Bond doesn't allow you to hide anything, does it?"

"Not at all."

He twisted his fingers into her hair. "I'm concerned about what we'll face in the Space Keep," he said.

"Why in there more than the others?"

"I have this sense . . ." He paused, staring at the wall beyond the bed. "This Keep was designed to be last, only entered with all seven other Relics in hand. I fear that we won't be strong enough."

Evylin was silent for several seconds. "You're a Space Mage," she whispered. "This is the Keep you were born to succeed in."

He tightened his jaw, uncomfortable with the responsibility that was set to fall on him. "*I'm* not strong enough," he confessed. He could tell she was about to protest, so he hastened to add, "Auden and Isla confirmed it. I can't control my power; it controls me. Even with our Bond, even with the strength you provide me, it may not be enough."

Evylin pulled back to meet his gaze. "Whatever it takes," she vowed, "I will not let you fail."

He smiled gently at her, then drew her close once again. After several silent minutes, he felt a contentment settle into his wife. He'd come to recognize this emotion. It was the easing of her body, the moment just before sleep.

"Jonn," she said, a gentle slur in her voice.

"Yes, my love?"

"I don't want you to be Euon Sergus."

A soft laugh slipped from him. "I thought every woman dreamed of Sergus."

She shook her head sleepily, her hair rubbing against his chin. "Not me," she murmured. "I just want you."

Deckard held her tighter. "You have me, body and soul."

CHAPTER THIRTY-ONE

10TH OF RADIA, 1574

They rose before the sun to prepare for their journey through the Keep. With so many people in the house, the space felt cramped. Several members of their party ate breakfast while Deckard stood at the head of the table, discussing the plan with Auden and Ilain.

"How do we intend to find it?" Deckard asked. "Usually, we simply travel the region until either of you feels the location, but we can't do that in the city. If Ephren hears reports that we're wandering the streets, he'll wonder why."

Ilain shook her head, setting her spoon into her bowl of porridge. "That's not necessary," she said calmly. "I know where it is."

Many of the table's occupants paused to stare at her. Deckard blinked curiously. "And you're just informing us of it now?" he asked dryly.

"Mm-hm."

"But you're an Elemental Mage; I would have thought—"

"I don't need to be an Existential Mage when I lived on top of it for over two weeks." Ilain took a sip of her tea. "We learned of the Keep's location quite by accident, honestly."

"Wait," Ethenn said at her side. "Are you saying that the Space Keep is *in* the palace?"

"Under, more precisely," Ilain replied.

Deckard blanched. "How are we supposed to get *under* the palace without the king noticing?"

"Carlile," Ilain said.

Auden nodded. "When we told him about the Space Keep's location, he informed us of a secret access to the palace grounds. He knows we'll be there and will do his best to keep all eyes off our path."

"It's awfully nice," Rafferty noted, "having a man on the inside."

"Indeed," Deckard replied, feeling uncertain. It was good to know they shouldn't have trouble accessing the Keep. If necessary, he could even use a shroud to cover them. But his stomach still roiled with unease at what was to come.

"I have a suggestion," Rafferty said then.

"What's that?" Deckard asked.

Rafferty's dry expression tightened. "When we enter the Chamber, let's not take our merry time as usual. Instead, we get Deckard to the Relic pronto and let him take down the Guardian using it, rather than risking our necks while the Mages try to focus."

Though Deckard's insides pinched at the responsibility being thrust on him, he nodded. Rafferty had proposed a valid plan. If they threw all their magical force at the Guardian while he ran for the Relic, they could save themselves a great deal of energy. And that could be the difference between success and failure.

Scanning the table to gauge the opinions of his team, Deckard surveyed each member. Evylin and Thom sat at the far side, large plates of food before them. They both paused in eating to give him approving looks. Brea stood behind them, slowly nibbling on a piece of venison jerky, her expression casually bland. Vayden and Isla had chosen to eat in the kitchen, determining to let the others make their more informed plans. Auden pursed his lips as though doubtful of the success of the plan but offered no rebuttal. Ilain ate her porridge with disinterest, and Ethenn tapped his fork on his plate, the expression on his face indicating his deep thought.

As no one offered any argument, Deckard met Rafferty's keen stare once more. "All right," he said. "Once we get to the Chamber, I'll keep my head down and sprint for the Relic without delay."

With their plans in place, the troop finished their meals, gathered their weapons, and prepared to depart. Deckard had already given the Night Relic to Evylin that morning. As a Warrior could turn the Relics into weapons that dealt true damage to the Guardians, it was decided that she would carry Night while Ethenn carried Wind. Though the young man had suggested they give the Relic to Brea, as she was the more experienced Warrior, the lieutenant insisted he carry it.

"I may have lived longer, but I've never fought with a Relic," she said. "It will be of more use in your hands."

As Evylin and Ethenn could also siphon some of the Relics' powers to Deckard and Ilain, the decision was made.

When they slipped out of the house, the sun was just beginning to peek over the rooftops. The sky was a rusty brown, and only a few people milled about the morning streets. Still, they exited through the back door, keeping to the alleys to avoid prying eyes. While they weren't overly concerned about stealth, thanks to Carlile's interference and King Ephren's trust in them, they didn't care to explain their detour to the monarch should he hear of their continued presence in the city.

It took them nearly an hour to reach the outskirts of the palace grounds. The large white stone and wrought iron walls only showed the top of the palace's second story and its slate roof.

The rising sun glared off the windows, and Deckard squinted as they wound around the perimeter. The gentle rush of the ocean lapping against the shore echoed to them through the streets. Auden and Ilain led the way, bringing them to a row of shops across from the palace walls. They snuck into the alley, and then Auden knocked in a rapid pattern upon a side door.

A young woman answered almost immediately, her dark brown hair twisted into a bun at the nape of her neck. She wore the simple dress of a scullery maid, and the moment she saw Auden's bright hair, she ushered them into the building with frantic urgency. Deckard presumed she was a member of the Alliance, alerted to their coming by Carlile.

"You're late," she whispered as they entered what appeared to be a storeroom. "My master will be here any moment."

"Then we'd better move quickly," Ilain said.

The maid guided them to the far wall and pressed against the wooden planks. Suddenly, a door revealed itself, opening into a dark corridor. Ilain darted in first with Ethenn on her heels. Deckard thanked the maid before following with Evylin. Soon, they were all inside, and the door was shut behind them, sealing them into darkness.

At the head of the group, Ilain summoned a flickering ruby and golden orb of light to guide their way. The corridor was narrow and made of stone. A staircase led them farther into the depths of the terrae. Auden informed them that, according to Carlile, the passage's origin was an escape route for the royal family. As there was presently no danger of attack, the king's advisor had talked him into leaving it unguarded, posting his soldiers at more "pressing" locations throughout the city.

They passed a handful of staircases leading upward, but Ilain led them past each one. Then they reached a dead end, where a wooden ladder reached far above their heads. Evylin stared up with a crease in her brow. A soft wave of annoyance filled the air around her. "That's troubling," she murmured.

"Why so?" Deckard asked.

She gave him a self-deprecating smirk. "I don't like heights."

"Says the woman who fought on top of a wyrm's head," Ethenn quipped.

Evylin gave him a flat look. "I was using my magic then. All sense of self-preservation is rather lost when it takes hold."

With a knowing chuckle, Ethenn ascended the ladder first, Ilain following on his heels. Deckard suggested that Evylin go next, teasingly promising to catch her if she fell. The others funneled up behind. The climb was slow, but the ladder was solid. Deckard supposed that if it was meant to provide safety to the monarchy, they'd check it regularly enough to ensure there was no decay on the rungs.

It was when Deckard neared the top that he first felt a heat race along his spine. He gasped at the unexpected rush of his magic.

With Ethenn's help, Ilain stepped off the ladder onto the ground above. She looked down, meeting Deckard's gaze. "You feel it, don't you?" she said.

"Feel what?" Deckard replied distractedly.

"The Keep. It's tugging at your magic."

Deckard paused, staring at the last set of rungs as Evylin climbed free. "Yes," he realized. "Why have I never sensed it before? Last night or with the other Keeps."

"Probably because you weren't looking," Ilain said. "You weren't even aware of its presence last night, and you let Auden and me seek out the pull of the previous Keeps. But now, you're Bonded. And this is Space, which you are inextricably connected to. When you intentionally look for it, it's ready to be found."

Deckard could only hope the connection would bode well for their time within the Keep.

The top of the ladder opened into what appeared to be a garden shed. Ethenn snuck out first, checking the perimeter to ensure their safety. At his signal, they emerged. Together, they darted carefully through the gardens. While Deckard suggested shrouding the troop, Auden warned against it, reminding him not to drain his magic until absolutely necessary.

Sneaking through the hedgerows and shrubbery was no easy feat. Guards patrolled in the distance, but Carlile had done his work, clearing their path. Still, they had to keep their heads down and eyes alert to ensure no one spotted them. The Keep pulled on Deckard with its call. As they drew nearer to it, the heat became a blanket over his back, urging him onward.

Out of nowhere, he noticed a shadow cast on the rear palace wall. But upon squinting, he realized that it wasn't a wall at all but rather an illusion concealing the entrance to a slender passageway.

"There," he whispered to Auden, directing him toward the shadow.

With a final scan of the grounds, they darted forward, hurrying into the passage. Darkness met them within, and they rushed down the staircase one by one.

"How is it," Rafferty asked as they descended, "that no one's found this before now?"

"The ancient Mages made the Keeps' entrances impossible to see unless you are also a Mage, or it's directly pointed out to you," Auden explained.

"Yes, but—" Rafferty's voice rose when they reached the antechamber, "this place is a thousand years old, right? How'd Ephren build his palace on top of it and the entrance remain so accessible if he couldn't see it? It isn't as if he'd knowingly harbor a Relic, right?"

"Magic would never allow the entrance to be truly blocked," Auden said. "If you were to place a boulder over the entrance, it would simply turn the rock into its new entrance. If you were to seal it with plaster, it would create another opening."

"How does it do that?" Thom asked. "I didn't think it was sentient."

"It isn't," Ilain said. "But it is alive."

"That's confusing," Thom noted.

As he ignored their banter, Deckard's blood now pulsed erratically. His skin was covered in gooseflesh despite the heat coiling within. An unknown tug drew him a step forward, and a strange black light flooded the hall before him. Somehow, the blackness refracted in such a way that it gave off the brightest brilliance, almost like the light of the moons on a cloudless night.

"Wow," Rafferty said dryly, stepping up to his side. "That's creepy."

A smattering of nervous laughter filled the antechamber, yet Deckard was silent, staring down the arched hallway. The iron door to the Keep lay ahead, and his magic eagerly anticipated his touch. It buzzed under his skin. Desperately, he reminded himself that whatever lay beyond that door, he couldn't lose control.

Evylin's hand brushed his arm. He looked down at her, catching the wave of encouragement she sent his way. When their eyes met, she smiled, the Night sword already glowing violet in her hand. Its purple beam almost looked dull next to the black light of the windows. "Together," she whispered.

Deckard dipped his chin in gratitude, his heart swelling with a sudden assurance. He could do this. With Evylin at his side, there was nothing to fear.

Auden moved for the door, but Ilain caught his sleeve. Then she looked at Deckard. "Jonn," she said, nodding to the hall, "this is your Keep. You should do the honors."

Though his throat went dry at the thought, Deckard gathered every last ounce of courage and began walking down the hall. The arched windows depicted swirling cosmoses, planets, and small stars. Through the light, he could almost see a rainbow of colors glittering at him.

Deckard stopped before the large iron door, its face etched with the same designs. His hand trembled at his side. He wasn't sure whether it was from anxiety or anticipation.

"What is it you say?" Deckard asked, looking over his shoulder at the Calders. "Into the fray?"

Auden and Ilain smiled slyly.

"It's the 'Psalm of Sigrid,'" the highlord said. "She was a Warrior Bonded to a Day Mage. The psalm was her mantra before a battle: 'Into the fray, into the fight; With goodness and honor, with Allore's might.'"

"We say it to remember why we fight," Ilain said, a fire igniting in her eyes.

The sentiment settled into Deckard, and he found his lips turning up. He could do this. For Allore. For the people of Allund. For Evylin.

Turning back to the door, Deckard raised his hand. "Into the fray, then."

The moment his hand pressed against the cold metal, a loud *hiss* erupted. The lock popped free, and a *thunk* resounded as the door began to slide open. On the other side was blackness.

Cautiously, Deckard and Evylin took the first steps into the infinity of the Space Keep.

The sky was black—pure, deep, rich black. So dark and whole that Deckard felt as though it might swallow him, like it could collapse and consume him into its nothingness. It stretched forever, so far ahead that Deckard didn't think it could end. Only the faintest glimmer of refraction marked the division of floor and ceiling. Far in the distance, a glossy black obelisk loomed.

Deckard took one step down the staircase, and everything changed.

The Keep became alight with life. A vibrant green and blue nebula shattered the sky. Flashes of gold and ivory starlight tore into the blackness. The ground spun with a vortex of crimson and violet clouds, colors twisting into one another. It was startling. It was terrifying. It was mesmerizing.

And it all reflected under Deckard's skin.

"Evylin," he gasped so quietly he didn't think she heard him.

His heart began to pound. His muscles trembled. His breath caught.

The vastness of Space, the boundless energy it possessed, the colossal magnitude of its form—it settled into his core, filling him with infinite power.

Deckard took another unintentional step forward, unaware of anything but the eruption of light, nebula, and life around him. Wordless whispers filled his ears. His heartbeat calmed, his muscles relaxed, and his lungs eased. He felt weightless and unworried.

Magic pressed in on him, collapsing into his form. It pulled at him, twisting and tearing through his body like those clouds and starlight. It demanded everything he was, down to the most infinitesimal part of himself. The infinity of Space wanted it all.

"Evylin," he murmured again, fumbling for her hand this time. He made contact but couldn't control his limbs enough to grab hold. He was too consumed, too overcome by the sights around him and the feelings within.

He heard Evylin curse under her breath and knew she was likely feeling the overwhelming sensations radiating out of him as well. Then she was there before him, taking hold of his face. "Jonn," she called, but he couldn't look at her. He was too overcome by the Space Keep's grandiosity, by its beauty. "Jonn, what's going on?"

Deckard felt his brows pinch together. "I can feel it," he whispered.

"Feel what?"

"What's wrong?" Thom asked at their side.

Deckard could sense the presence of their team, but he was too distracted to pay attention. More nebulae, more stars, more clouds, more infinity erupted before his eyes. A blend of awe and indifference filled him. He couldn't find the ability to move.

"I can't tell," Evylin was saying to Thom, her grip tightening on Deckard as she worked to get his attention. "He's feeling something—something intensely powerful—but . . . I can't tell what it is."

Hearing the worry in her tone, Deckard's heart managed to overpower the compulsion within him. He met her amber-brown eyes. They reminded him of the shadows cast from the green and blue nebulae above them. He smiled and brushed a tender hand along her cheek. "Everything," he said.

She gaped up at him, confused. "What?"

"I feel everything."

Auden swore and rushed forward, pushing Thom out of the way. He grabbed Deckard's collar to get his attention, but Deckard could only stare at the sky around him. "Jonn, listen to me," the Day Mage ordered. "You can't give in to it. If you access your magic now, it's going to take over, and you can't sustain that. Not in here."

A chorus of concerned questions filled the air like the stars that pieced the sky around them. Deckard couldn't understand their worry. Why weren't they as mesmerized as he was? The sky was overwhelmed with galaxies, the power within compelling him. He couldn't stop what was happening to him any more than he could act. He was locked in a stalemate of everything and nothing.

While the others pressed Auden for answers, Evylin yanked Deckard's collar, forcing him to look at her. "I need you to focus, Jonn," she whispered. "I don't know what's going on in your head right now, but you need to clear it and focus on me, understand? Don't think about the Keep. Think about me."

Deckard blinked. Flares of starlight reflected in her eyes. He cupped her face, grasping for the clarity she offered. It was easy to think about Evylin. She was all he wanted to think about anyway. Her cleverness, her beauty, her smile, her strength, her perfection: She was everything. What else could he think about?

A calm descended over Deckard with a renewed weight. It slid like a lock into his mind, shutting out all other thoughts or worries. The bar slid down so tightly he couldn't feel anything but the love he had for Evylin, its assurance whole and serene. Fondly, he ran his thumb across her cheek.

Evylin smiled, and a wash of relief filled her. "That's it," she said. The others were talking over one another, but he could only hear her voice. "Just focus on me."

A hum started in the distance, an echo of emptiness that couldn't be defined.

"They're coming," Deckard told her.

Her expression tightened. "The Shades?" she asked, but Auden called out before Deckard could answer.

"The Shades are coming," Auden cried. "Get ready."

Brea, Isla, Ilain, and Auden rushed to the front. Thom, Rafferty, and Vayden raised their weapons, following behind. Ethenn lifted the Wind bow, ready but waiting near Deckard and Evylin's side. Only the couple remained still, gazes locked on one another.

"Jonn," she said, holding the Night sword at her side. "Stay focused on me, all right? Don't use your magic until absolutely necessary."

The humming of the Shades grew louder, joining the whispering in his head. Their combined refrain was like the drone of the ocean, but one where the waves never crashed. It stayed constant and endless, urging him to think about Evylin. Only Evylin.

She took his hand, guiding him down the stairs. He watched her every move. Why had he been so worried about losing control? He had control. He had *her*.

Before them, the Shades formed from clay and crystalline shards. Their shapes were familiar. Those reflective black prisms looked like Deckard's magic. Transformative and sharp. Deadly.

"Don't let them touch you," he warned Evylin.

She gave him a playful grin. "Wouldn't dream of it."

A soft yellow and light blue explosion broke out behind the glassy obelisk in the distance. Deckard looked up to appraise it. It reminded him of the frosted countryside of Wayford under the winter sky. His body warmed, a burning sensation rising in his veins. His heart leaped.

"Jonn," Evylin said with obvious worry, "focus on me."

With a gentle smile, Deckard met her gaze once more. "I am," he promised.

And then the never-ending sky crashed down on him with its power, and his vision narrowed to black. Ethenn let off a single arrow as the Shades took a step forward, but no one else had the chance to attack.

A sense of total focus overcame Deckard. His mind became a vacuum of thought, focused only on the woman at his side. Her strength. Her goodness. Her safety. The silhouette of space erupted around him, black shards glittering in the vibrancy of infinity. Everything and nothing ruled his mind, and his emotions leveled with a singular aim. He heard Evylin's voice call out to him, but her words were unclear as the voice of magic filled his ears.

Evylin.

Deckard didn't bother to raise his hands. With a single thought, the crystalline shards erupted behind him like a supernova, flashing through the air to crash into the first wave of Shades. He was solely focused on defending his love. And he would stop at nothing until she was safe.

CHAPTER THIRTY-TWO

Evylin forgot to breathe.

Her whole being was locked in shock and awe as Deckard's magic exploded around him. The onyx cloud of crystals glittered with shards of vibrant ruby, topaz, sapphire, amethyst, silver, opal, and emerald, reflecting as they spun. Deckard's eyes had become so dark they could no longer be called green, yet the expression on his face radiated peace, and she could feel the utter calm within him. It was as though he no longer exuded any emotion. His aura was a void, cold and dark like the Space around them.

While his magic tore through the first wave of Shades, Deckard began a slow, calculated walk down the onyx stairs, moving deeper into the Keep. The shards emitting from him hit the creatures dead on, shadows separating into dozens of sections to pierce through their clay forms. Evylin watched as the Shades burst apart, their own shimmering fragments launching forward. If anyone had been standing nearby, those shards would have ripped through flesh easily.

Then a single note vibrated through the air around each Shade that had been struck. It was a hum so deep and low that it echoed in her chest as the shards halted their spinning explosion. A twisting black hole formed at each Shade's core. The vacuum of space caused the crystalline pieces to rotate back in on themselves and into the center of the creatures' beings, where they were swallowed up into the darkness.

"Don't get near them," Brea ordered at the front, seeing the destruction the Shades' deaths brought. "They'll suck you in."

Evylin's stomach sank as she looked around the group. The rest of the troop had blanched, their defensive postures slackening in horror at the scene before them.

Deckard stepped off the stairs, and Evylin was woken from her stupor. She darted down after him, grabbing his sleeve. "Jonn, stop!" she called.

But only for a moment did he pause, looking back at her with those dark black-green eyes. A small smile lifted the corners of his mouth. He set his hand atop hers, then removed himself from her grip.

Deckard turned and continued on the path.

Evylin gaped after his unimpassioned march away. Every time she'd seen a Mage use magic, they'd always guided their power with their hands. But Deckard's still hung loosely at his sides while the magic did the work for him.

Once the first wave of Shades was gone, the crystalline shards returned to hover around his body, twisting and refracting like the nebulae around them.

A tremor worked through Evylin's hand, and she felt the Night sword slip. She tightened her grip but couldn't move. She'd never seen Deckard so void of emotion like this, so consumed by the resource that gave him power. In their life together, he was so controlled, so reserved. Now, he'd lost himself to the magic in a way she couldn't fathom. It struck her like a devastating blow to the heart.

Auden grabbed Evylin's arm, worry creasing his brow. "We have to go," he said. "If Jonn gets too far ahead of us, the Shades will cut us off."

"He can't sustain this," Evylin muttered, eyes locked on Deckard as he continued across the Keep.

"It's too late," Auden said apologetically. "He's gone to the magic. We must go with him if we want to ensure his survival and ours."

Evylin caught Thom's worried gaze as they hurried down the staircase after Deckard. But the moment her feet touched level ground, her stomach leaped into her throat. Her head spun. The world swirled around her, nebulae and starlight beaming with blinding intensity. The infinite black sky surrounded her, and the world lost its center. She floated in nothing, and she was overwhelmed by the *everything* of it all.

Evylin curled in on herself, unable to tell if she'd fallen to her knees or was free-floating in the Heavens. Her head reeled. She could see no up and no down. There was only everywhere in every direction.

Through the haze, a powerful tug began to pull at Evylin's core. Peace thrummed within her. Total, unhindered, and restful peace.

Deckard.

Somehow, he was able to walk through this terror of chaos like it was nothing. She knew the pulse calling to her was his way of caring for her, telling her to relax and surrender to the everything and nothing surrounding her.

Evylin closed her eyes against the maelstrom. There was no calm in that expanse. So she turned inward—giving in to the part of herself that felt his gentle, soothing presence.

And there, at the very center of her being, Evylin could sense Deckard—fifty yards ahead of her and a little to the right. He was moving at a slow but steady pace. His heart rate was elevated slightly, and his whole body was alight with the heat of his magic. His vision was tinged black, casting the world in a shadowed hue. Magic rolled through him, but serenity ruled his thoughts.

No. Not serenity. Focus on one thing to the isolation of all else.

It was devotion. Loyalty. Love.

Evylin pressed into that feeling, letting it seep into her soul and overtake her body. Heat seared her chest, followed by a sudden sting of cold. Her heartbeat rose in time with his, and her blood pumped in a rush. The hair on her arms lifted as her body acclimated. The Keep took on a new form in her mind, the sights, sounds, smells, tastes, and touch shaping its every inch. It was everything and nothing.

And she was one with it.

With a deep breath, calm settled Evylin's mind. She opened her eyes to see the world in that black tinge she now knew Deckard was also experiencing. Her thoughts were open and clear. The infinity of Space no longer swirled around her. Rather than floating in nothingness, she stood on solid ground, body primed for fighting. Her heart lurched, seeing Deckard in the distance fighting the second wave of Shades. She needed to be at his side.

Tightening her grip on the Night sword, Evylin sprinted across the Space Keep. Midstride, the sword transformed into a bow. Evylin raised it, pulled back the string, and let an iridescent amethyst arrow fly.

She caught up to Deckard's casual gait easily, coming to a stop before him, sending off arrow after arrow, ensuring no Shade got too close. His magic took care of the rest.

As they cleared out the second wave, Evylin became vaguely aware of Auden helping the rest of the troop behind them. Her focus was on the Shades and Deckard, but her Warrior magic sharpened to take in the rest of the Keep as well. Auden moved from member to member, setting his hands on their heads for several seconds. They'd all fallen to the Keep's chaos as she had. After Auden's ministrations, they would rise, and he'd move on. Soon, everyone was standing and hurrying up behind Evylin and Deckard.

Another Shade collapsed in on itself, sucking in its glittering fragments before disappearing with a pop of silence. It was the last one. Deckard met Evylin's gaze. With excitement, her magic surged, and she took an unconscious step forward. She could feel his gentle pride swell in her own chest. They'd taken on an entire wave of Shades themselves and defeated them all.

Deckard held out his hand as the obsidian silhouette of space coiled around his arm. He didn't say anything, but the offer was clear. He wanted to walk through this Keep with her, just the two of them.

Evylin's lips lifted in a smirk. She liked that idea very much.

She raised her hand, ready to take his. Then Auden called out, "Wait!"

Evylin hesitated just long enough for the Day Mage to make it to her side.

"You can't go with him," Auden said in a panic. "You'll die."

With the magic rushing through her veins, Evylin struggled to comprehend the danger in his warning. Her hand twitched to take Deckard's. But a glance at the troop now gathered around them made her pause.

Thom's gray-blue eyes were frightened, his jaw tight. Brea stood at his side, bow in hand and ever watchful, while Rafferty palmed his short swords nervously. Even Ethenn and Ilain watched warily.

Isla stepped around Vayden, her expression serious. "He's lost himself to Space," she said. "If you take his hand, if you go with him, you'll lose yourself to it too."

Evylin frowned. "But he isn't lost."

"The magic is controlling him," Isla said. "Your husband is gone."

Deckard's confession from the previous night filled her mind. *I can't control my power; it controls me.*

Evylin wanted to deny it. Her magic urged her to give in to the surging pulse of Space. But she knew it was true.

Seeing her hesitation, Auden pressed. "He's using too much magic. It's only a matter of time before he blacks out."

"But we're Bonded," Evylin said.

"That's the worst part." Auden's gaze was soft and mournful. "If he begins to tap into your energy, he can take you down with him. Then you'll both pass out, and we'll have to carry the two of you out of here."

She turned to look up at Deckard. In his altered state, he acted as though he couldn't hear them. He simply watched Evylin, hand extended.

"Come with me," he offered, his voice both empty and deep all at once.

Painfully, Evylin's heart squeezed. "I will not let you fail," she whispered, then took a step back.

Understanding, Deckard let his hand drop. He showed no signs of disappointment or frustration. He merely turned around dispassionately and continued on his path toward the obelisk.

The troop hurried after him.

"What's happened to him?" Thom asked, watching his brother's departure, his expression filled with worry.

The hum of the Shades returned—the singular combined note an eerie drone.

"Tapping into focus is like a gate for Mages," Auden explained. "Once the gate is open, the magic can flow out. But Jonn doesn't have the training he needs to regulate how much power comes at once. He has a particularly strong focus, so when he accesses magic, it's like opening the floodgates. The magic flows into him with such a force that the gates can't be shut until it's all used up."

"But he's stopped before," Rafferty said, eyeing Deckard curiously.

"He's not been inside the Space Keep before," Isla said.

Auden scanned the swirling expanse around them, flares of vibrant color tearing through the darkness. "The Keeps are magic in its purest form," he explained. "When we entered, it pressed in on Jonn, urging him to access it. Once he gave in to that call to focus, it was too late."

The Shades arrived then, twisting and coalescing, those black shards glittering in a circle around them, and Evylin realized the mistake she'd made. "I did this," she gasped, realizing that it had been *she* who had urged him to find his focus.

Ahead, Deckard's magic burst into life, cutting through the air. Ethenn, Brea, and Evylin began picking off the Shades one by one as they tried to surround them. Ilain, Isla, and Auden used their magic to take down the rest; ruby flames, golden flares, and steely gales burst through the infinity of blackness.

"What do we do?" Thom asked, standing with Vayden and Rafferty in the center, their weapons raised uselessly. "If we attack at close range, we'll die, right?"

"It appears that way," Auden called, then sent off another burst of Day.

"But we need to fight," Thom said. "If we want to keep Jonn from using too much magic, then we have to make it to the obelisk as fast as possible."

"It would help if you could, yes," Isla shouted.

"I don't fancy getting close to those things," Rafferty said. "Not even for the colonel's sake."

However, Thom reset his grip on his sword and began to step forward.

Brea swept in front of him, then drew another arrow from the quiver on her back. "Don't even think about it, *mi'caro*," she said sharply. "Thom, Vayd, and Raff, you three *do not* fight. Stay in the middle. You'll be our support. If Deckard goes down, we'll need you to carry him."

Though Thom ground his teeth, neither Vayden nor Rafferty seemed inclined to argue about their removal from the battle.

"We need to get to the Chamber," Ilain ordered.

"Jonn doesn't seem too concerned about speed," Evylin noted.

"If you go," Ilain said, "he'll follow."

Though she didn't relish getting any closer to the Shades, Evylin began a steady walk toward the obelisk. Deckard waited until she closed the distance and stepped with her. He had already made good work of the Shades. The rest of them hardly had to fight at all. Flashes of Day, columns of Fire, and rushes of Wind tore through the Keep as silver, amethyst, and wooden arrows launched through the air with perfect precision.

"If you start to feel him draw on your energy," Auden called, "shut him out. We can't lose both of you in here."

"I don't know how to do that," Evylin called back. A blast of shadow erupted to her right where Deckard walked, drawing her gaze to him. But he wasn't there anymore. "What—?"

In the split second since she'd turned, another black cloud appeared in the center of the Shades up ahead, driving their numbers back.

"Holy hell!" Vayden exclaimed behind her.

"He can teleport?" Rafferty asked in wild awe.

Evylin's fingers slipped on the bowstring as she watched Deckard standing amidst the Shades where the shadows appeared. Her throat tightened at the thought of him surrounded in their midst as they exploded into black, yawning holes. Yet, she couldn't deny how impressed she was by the feat of power her husband displayed. She didn't know how much magic it took to accomplish such a thing, but she imagined it was far more than he should be using so early in the fight.

"Evie?" Ethenn called from far to her right. "What is he doing?"

Evylin lifted her bow again, forcing herself back to action. "I don't know."

"Should he be doing that?" Vayden asked.

"No," Auden answered tightly. "He's going to get us killed."

But as Evylin let loose another arrow, she wondered if Auden was right. With her steady press forward, they were already within a hundred yards of the Chamber's entrance. They'd never moved through a Keep this quickly. Even if Deckard was using too much magic, they might move fast enough for it not to matter.

The third wave dwindled to the final few Shades, and the troop bolted for the obelisk's black door. Though Deckard didn't seem to be in a hurry, when Evylin made it inside, he moved with purpose to join her. They piled into the spiral stairwell, and Thom closed the door with a firm snap.

"Are we safe in here?" Vayden asked.

No one replied. Thom leaned against the wall, running a hand over his face. Evylin chewed on her lip in shared concern. They weren't nearly as physically spent as they usually were when they reached the Chamber stairs. Yet, their worry for Deckard was proving just as exhausting.

Unaware of their need to rest, Deckard began down the stairs, his stride casual. Evylin caught his sleeve, pulling him to a stop. Two steps below, his eyes leveled with hers. His magic still glittered around him, and his gaze was cruelly soft in its blankness.

"Jonn," she said gently, "I need you to listen to me. Let your magic go."

Deckard's brow pinched together. He reached up to cup her cheek, the shards shifting down his arm as he moved. "Evie," he said tenderly, "it's all right."

"You can't sustain this," she warned.

"I can," he promised. "I have you."

"You can't use me," she insisted. "Do you understand that? I can't carry us both."

"You won't have to."

"Jonn," she said sharply, "do *not* use my strength. You mustn't."

The lines in his brow deepened, but he nodded.

Evylin's heart felt as though it would split in two. She wanted to believe that Deckard was right; together, they were strong enough to sustain whatever magic they needed to carry to fulfill their mission. But she was afraid. Terribly, awfully afraid.

Taking hold of his hand, Evylin whispered, "I can't lose you."

"You won't." His thumb brushed across her cheekbone, sending a line of tingles across her skin. "Trust me."

Evylin pressed into his touch. "Always," she promised, then kissed his palm. She released him, strengthened her gaze, and ordered, "Wait here."

He dipped his chin in acceptance.

Then Evylin turned back to the others. They all watched with uncertainty, a strange blend of curiosity and fear in their gazes. "We can still do this," she told them. "We've made it through this far faster than ever before. Not one of us has grown tired yet. Even if Jonn goes down, we *can* make it out. Once we defeat the Guardian, we'll have the Space Relic. Auden, you can take it. I fear it will be too much of a temptation for Jonn to channel my power if I have it."

Auden nodded.

"We can do this," Evylin repeated. "We *will*. Together."

A smattering of nods and bolstering smiles were passed around the troop. They all trusted her. They believed in her. And in that moment with their fates in her hands, Evylin thought she understood the weight of responsibility Deckard so feared.

At her side, Auden's fierce green eyes met hers. "We'll get out of here," he promised, voice low. "We'll get *him* out of here."

With an appreciative smile, Evylin turned to the others. "Are we ready?"

Their renewed courage emboldened her. They *would* do this. Together.

At the head of the troop, Evylin and Deckard descended. Even with his strange attitude, her heart began to fill with hope. No matter what happened, no matter how quickly Deckard's strength waned, the rest of them could make it. And they would *all* survive this Keep.

They stepped into the vast expanse of the Chamber, a replica of all the others. Across its grand length, the dais awaited them. Black marble with luminous, ever-changing veins covered the floors, walls, columns, and ceiling. The rainbow of gemlike colors still shifted within, fading away into black as though the nebulae above were captured in these stones.

Deckard paused at the entrance. "I'll get the Relic," he said quietly.

The team edged into the room behind him, weapons at the ready. "How fast are you?" Rafferty asked him.

"Reasonably."

Rafferty looked at Thom.

"I mean, he's not you. But yeah," Thom shrugged, "he's pretty fast."

The weasel's silver eyes flickered to the dais. "Should I go with him?"

"Couldn't hurt," Evylin said, wanting someone's eyes on Deckard while she focused on the Guardian. "Eight will be enough to distract whatever creature awaits us here."

Rafferty danced on the balls of his feet. He looked up at Deckard slyly. "Ready, old man?"

A strangely emotionless grin came to Deckard's lips. "We'll wait for the Guardian to show itself," he said.

"Why?"

"Do you want to run straight into its path?"

Rafferty pursed his lips. "Fair point."

They didn't have to wait long as the ground beneath their feet began to shiver. From the right side of the room, a giant beast came into view. The Guardian's feathered head nearly grazed the ceiling. Long black talons clicked along the floor as it strode with graceful but deadly steps. Scaly wings unfolded from its back, a long and muscular tail whipping behind its powerful form. The point of the tail reminded Evylin of the crystalline shards of Deckard's magic, jagged and fierce. Its black beak snapped as glittering eyes surveyed them. Somehow, Evylin could pick out bits of the dragon, bloodwolf, *vængebjörn*, and wyrm in the shape of the wings, furred hide, beak, and tail. While she'd never seen the *lehavran* or *dieumer*, she wondered if there were pieces of their construction in this creature as well.

Deckard and Rafferty took off to the left. The remaining eight charged forward.

From a distance, Auden, Ilain, and Isla attacked along with Ethenn and Vayden. Brea, who had given Vayden her bow and arrow, ran beside Evylin and Thom, her short sword lifted.

The creature made no sound. It didn't appraise them with rage or anger. Instead, it moved with swiftly refined flicks of its tail, claws, and wings. Each strike was purposeful and sure. It wasn't afraid of them. It had no reason to be.

Sticking close to Evylin's side, Thom was able to slip past the creature's defense with her. However, in ensuring his safety, she was distracted enough to let a swipe from the Guardian catch her on the arm. A gush of blood warmed her sleeve, leaking down her bicep. She ignored the sharp pain and slashed with the Night sword.

Fire and Day erupted across the creature's hide. Silver arrows peppered its flesh. And Evylin's blade drew a line down its foreleg. But instead of blood, it wept onyx shards, razor sharp and glittering.

Evylin and Thom leaped back, but not before obtaining several scrapes along their coats and hands. "That's not ideal," he muttered, then called a warning to Brea.

"Doesn't matter," she replied from beneath the beast's stomach. "I can't penetrate the hide."

"It's because you don't have a Relic," Evylin said. "It takes twice the effort, but as a Warrior, you *can* do it."

"Splendid." Brea ground her teeth, then stabbed upward with all her might, letting out a fierce growl. Her sword chipped the Guardian's stomach as though it were glass. A single shard dropped free, and she slid out of its path. "Better than nothing," she said dryly.

Evylin readied herself to strike again. They weren't intending to kill the creature but were simply keeping it distracted from Deckard's charge. But as she reared back to thrust the Night sword into the Guardian's hide, a sudden inferno lit a fire in her core.

Gasping, Evylin stumbled backward a step. Shivers raced along her body, and her muscles trembled. Only once before had she experienced such a feeling. Power radiated through her as her senses absorbed every detail of the room. Brea and Thom still slashed at the Guardian. Vayden and Ethenn held their bows aloft, arrows flying. Flames, flares, and wind coursed through the air. And on the dais, Rafferty watched as Deckard lifted the onyx Space Relic, raising the object aloft in his hand. His magic glimmered like the Relic.

The Guardian paused and looked back to the dais. Frozen, it stared toward the Relic for a drawn-out moment. Then it began to collapse in on itself.

Glittering shards pulled the Guardian apart, sucking it into the black hole that twisted around its center. Evylin yanked Thom away, though she felt no tug toward that black hole.

And in the blink of an eye, the Guardian was gone.

CHAPTER THIRTY-THREE

Thom stumbled and would have fallen if Evylin hadn't held him so securely. He gaped in awe at the empty space where the Guardian had been only moments before. They'd never killed one so quickly. Never.

A collective shock seemed to roll through the room. Deckard and Rafferty approached from the dais as the rest joined them from the back.

Brea stepped over, checking to be sure Thom and Evylin were all right before saying, "It wasn't that easy in the Fire Keep."

"It's never been that easy for us either," Evylin said, her eyes on Deckard.

Thom didn't like the tense expression on her face. Nor did he like the placid one on Deckard's. It startled him, seeing his brother so completely vacant of his humanity. He was empty. Void. Infinite. They'd feared the Deep. But whatever this was . . .

Thom worried the consequences of this vacantly terrifying display would be much worse.

As their troop huddled together, Auden held his hand out toward Deckard, who stared at it blankly. "The Relic," Auden prompted.

Deckard didn't move, allowing the Space Relic to hang at his side. He turned to Evylin, practically dismissing the Day Mage. "It will be more powerful in my hands," he said matter-of-factly.

Distress flashed across Evylin's face. "You've already used too much power, Jonn. We can't risk you blacking out."

Deckard's expression remained eerily unmoved. "Remember the Day Keep?" he asked.

They all paused, exchanging curious looks.

"What does that—?"

Deckard cut Thom off. "In the Day Keep, when Auden wore the Day Relic, he was able to control the Shades." Understanding passed through the troop while Deckard concluded, "When the Mage and Relic match, they can control the Keep."

"We don't know that to be true," Auden objected. "We are attempting to take the Relic *from* the Keep, not returning with it. The Shades will likely still try to stop us, and we have no way of knowing how much of your energy remains."

Though Deckard showed no outward signs of irritation, Thom frowned. Those magical shards still hovered around his brother's form, undulating gently as though waiting on his command. No other Mage had behaved that way in Thom's experience. Not even Ilain—the strongest Mage in two centuries—wore her magic like a cape. Deckard had truly lost himself to his power, and he was bleeding magic every second he left it alive around him like that. How long could he keep that up?

Deckard didn't bother fighting a battle of wills with Auden. He turned back to Evylin, waiting for her command. She blinked and glanced at Thom. He knew she felt the same concern as he. But she also trusted Deckard. She *wanted* him to keep the Relic, to test the theory and see if they could simply walk out of here unchallenged.

Thom held no such quandary. He knew the danger. They'd seen Ilain lose consciousness after similar grand displays of power. Though Deckard wasn't showing signs of fatigue, letting him access the power of the Relic would only speed his exhaustion.

"No," Thom said suddenly, the word emerging with powerful force.

Everyone looked at him, but he didn't flinch. This was his moment to prove himself, to show his dedication to his new purpose. He'd get Deckard and Evylin through this Keep; he would protect them, even from themselves.

Thom turned to his brother. "Jonn, give Auden the Relic," he ordered. "Now."

A curious expression drew Deckard's brow down, but he didn't act.

Thom sent Evylin a commanding look. She raised her chin in understanding, then reached across and took the Relic from Deckard's hand. Immediately, she placed it in Auden's.

The corners of Deckard's lips twitched downward, but he didn't argue.

"All right," Thom said, wasting no time in taking control of the potentially perilous situation. "We've got a Keep to fight our way back through. Vayd, Raff, and I can't do much, but we can keep an eye on the group. If anyone starts to falter or is in danger, we'll intervene. Otherwise, we'll remain in the center.

"Auden, Isla, you two take the front with Brea," he instructed. "The Shades will await us at the top, so we'll need you to knock them back initially. Ethenn, Ilain, you take the left flank. Evie and Jonn, you've got the right. Keep the attacks ranged unless otherwise necessary. Agreed?"

Each of them nodded except for Deckard, who merely stared down at Evylin stolidly.

"Great." Thom curled his fingers tighter around his sword, his heart thumping with nerves. "Let's go."

The others moved into formation, with Auden, Isla, and Brea leading the charge, but Deckard and Evylin remained frozen.

Thom skidded to a halt, wary of their exchange.

Deckard angled down toward Evylin, speaking with a flat, lifeless tone. "I could have carried it."

"Maybe," Evylin admitted, though Thom could see she held no more hope than him.

"Evie," Deckard said, his voice taut, "I *could* have."

"*Maybe,*" she returned.

His brow pinched together in that telling way of his. "Why don't you trust me?"

Though Thom felt he was intruding on a private moment, he couldn't look away. Not when he had to ensure Evylin didn't give in to whatever hold Deckard's magic might have on her. He'd seen her expression when Deckard offered his hand in the Keep above. She was ready to let the magic consume her, too, and Thom wouldn't lose them both to this strange, enthralling force.

Evylin took what appeared to be a breath to steady herself. "I do trust you," she reassured, then gestured to the roiling cloud of crystalline shards around him. "But *this* isn't you."

Deckard looked disappointed, his brow furrowing deeper.

Evylin reached across, grabbed his collar, and pulled him down so their foreheads touched. Thom averted his gaze, listening only to ensure their safety. "I trust you, Jonn," she said fiercely. "I love you."

Through his peripheral vision, Thom saw Deckard lean in for a kiss, but Evylin pulled back. She held his gaze, piercing him with a sharp stare. "Which is why I need you to get this under control," she charged.

Thom grinned to himself, proud of her fierceness.

Not a second later, Evylin was at Thom's side, Deckard trailing behind. "Let's get out of here," she said.

Thom sent her a smirk. "With pleasure."

The three Deckards hurried across the black marble tiles to meet their troop in the stairwell. Thom kept an eye on Deckard's magic, which still drifted around his form. However, something in his brother's eyes had lightened, which gave him hope. And if nothing else, Deckard didn't *appear* tired. At this point, Ilain had needed assistance before she blacked out.

Maybe Deckard really had the strength to see this through.

At the top of the staircase, they readied themselves to continue the fight. Brea had a hand on the door; Auden and Isla prepared to summon their magic. "On your word, *mi'caro*," she called lightly, though even across the distance, Thom could see the respect in her gaze. She was a lieutenant, and he was a captain. In the army, he would be her superior, Warrior or not. And she was demonstrating that she honored his authority despite her experience over his.

Thom gave her an appreciative nod, then checked the troop once more. Assured they were all prepared, he met her gaze again and ordered, "Now."

At his command, Brea yanked the door open. Auden and Isla's magic leaped forward, a torrent of wind and a strange shard-like flare—his Day magic altered by the influence of the Space Relic. The first several rows of Shades flew back in the combined explosion of element and existent. Auden's power was much more potent than usual, and it replicated Deckard's in its new glittering form.

Brea's arrows covered the pair as they pushed out into the Keep. Vayden went next, sword at the ready, followed by Ethenn and Ilain. Rafferty and Thom plunged forward after them, with Deckard and Evylin at the rear. Everyone sprang into action, moving into the formation Thom had instructed.

At the front, Isla and Auden cleared swathes of Shades while Brea laid down cover with her arrows, keeping them safe as they pushed their attackers back. Together, Ethenn, Ilain, Deckard, and Evylin watched their rear and flank, preventing the Shades from surrounding them. The non-magical members jogged in the center, watching keenly, calling out warnings when Shades came too close or were attempting to outmaneuver them.

At first, it seemed they were doing well. The Shades were dwindling in number, and they were making steady progress.

Then a fresh wave of Shades joined the fray.

Their clay and onyx forms twisted to life like the nebulae above their heads. Desperately, they charged, pressing toward the front where Auden carried the Space Relic. Thom heard Deckard tell Evylin, "I can stop them."

"It isn't worth the risk," Evylin replied.

He scowled, and Thom knew it was a sign that his brother was weakening. His emotions were growing less stoic, his posture more rigid. Though he could kill the

Shades in great strikes of magic, it seemed he'd chosen to pull their impact, perhaps a response to Evylin's plea for his control.

The Space Keep was alive with whole new stars, clouds, and nebulae. The colors flashed rust, turquoise, magenta, honey, and cobalt. If they weren't fighting for their lives, Thom would have stood in awe, surrounded by the stunning expanse.

But they *were* fighting, and he was incapable of doing anything while watching his friends grow tired from the extended battle.

Their progress slowed as the Shades pressed in. The Warriors couldn't use their bows anymore, as too many creatures managed to slip through the ranks. Evylin's bow flashed amethyst and switched to a sword. Ethenn did the same with the Wind Relic. And at the front, Brea swore, then tossed her bow to Vayden and drew her staff in one swift movement.

As Evylin swiped down one Shade, its shard spray sliced her across the cheek. Almost instantly, it began to swirl from the interior, sucking in everything around it. Evylin slid forward just as Deckard grabbed her arm, keeping her from falling into the black hole. Thom's heart hammered as he watched several surrounding Shades get pulled into the void, ripping and tearing apart. Then it blipped out of existence.

Thom sucked in a sharp breath but knew there was nothing to do but join the fray. "Raff," he called.

"Thommy?"

"Let's end this."

Rafferty twirled his short swords excitedly. "Try not to get yourself killed, eh?"

Without another word, the two of them slipped among the ranks of their comrades. Wherever holes appeared, they slid in, slicing and knocking back the Shades. The blowback of the shards ripped through the group, leaving slashes on everyone's arms, faces, and bodies. Together, they relied on one another to steer clear of the black holes. It was a constant battle of wounds and retreats.

The volume of the hum announced another wave of Shades.

Drenched in sweat, Thom checked his troop. The attack had forced them to a crawl, and they were only halfway back to the entrance. Already, his muscles felt fatigued as he brushed a trickle of blood away from his eyes. Rafferty still fought eagerly, but Vayden had run out of arrows. With the pressure intensifying on all sides, the troop had scrunched together in a strange huddle. It was getting harder and harder to avoid the black holes each shattered Shade created.

Thom's stomach sank, and the terrifying truth settled: If they didn't do something soon, they were going to die.

"Auden," Deckard's voice commanded across the top of the group, "give me the Relic."

Thom blanched but kept fighting.

"No!" Auden yelled back.

While attempting to dodge the blowback of a dying Shade, Isla slipped. Vayden caught her, but they had to scramble frantically backward to avoid the black hole, nearly tripping Ilain in the process.

"Damn it, Auden," Deckard yelled. "Give me the Relic!"

"You'll black out!"

"We're about to die!"

Thom yanked Ethenn back as a black hole nearly sucked him in.

A shard embedded into Brea's arm.

Rafferty lost a sword to a void, the weapon disintegrating as the gravitational pull tore it to pieces.

"Auden!"

"Fine!"

Deckard and Auden angled toward the center, arms outstretched. Cautiously, Auden tossed the Space Relic across the twelve-inch gap. Thom watched with fear as the golden and onyx necklace spun, glittering across the darkness. It landed in Deckard's palm, the precious metals springing to life with an additional, iridescent glow.

Within an instant, the Shades went still.

The creatures straightened and turned to Deckard, awaiting his command.

The troop relaxed, their breaths puffing out in exhaustion and shock.

"Thank Allore," Rafferty wheezed.

Thom wiped the sweat from his brow. It seemed that Deckard had been right from the start. They should have allowed him to carry the Relic. They could have simply walked out of the Keep.

But then, Evylin gasped in frightful panic, and Thom whirled just as one desperate word burst from her lips. "No."

Deckard's knees buckled, and his eyes rolled back.

Thom's heart lurched. "Jonn!"

He hit the ground, unconscious, and the Shades surged forward once again.

The troop, worn out and ragged, jumped back into action. Thom's arms felt like lead, but he slashed, attempting to keep the charging Shades away from where the Relic lay beside his brother's crumpled form.

Evylin dove over Deckard, protecting him from the attack of the Shades. Thom could see the creatures cutting into her flesh as they fought to pry the Relic from beneath the couple. He took a step closer to help, but a swell of golden light knocked them back.

"Evylin," Auden called, "get up."

Evylin scrambled to her feet, now gripping a glittering black sword. Its onyx-colored metal gleamed like the Relic, and vibrant colors illuminated its edges. The sword was long, sleek, and deadly, and it fit perfectly in her hand.

"Vayd, Raff," Brea ordered. "Get Deckard."

With the Night sword still in her other hand, Evylin spun. "Brea, catch."

Though mid-attack, Brea lifted her hand and caught the Night Relic. It beamed a bright violet, then morphed into a sharp-ended staff, perfectly sized to the Warrior's height. She stashed her old weapon across her back and spun into action.

Thom's heart throbbed in his throat. While Rafferty and Vayden hoisted Deckard between them, the rest of the troop surrounded them like a guard. They still had a great expanse to cover. Now down to seven fighters, they were all running low on energy. But Thom wouldn't let them fail.

Tightening his grip on his sword, Thom fought with all the vigor he could muster. "Keep going," he called. "Whatever you do, keep moving forward."

Beside him, Ilain panted, but her jaw was tight with determination as she burned through a line of the Shades. Isla sent out a gale that knocked several creatures from their feet. Auden finished them with a burst of light. The three Warriors fought with their glowing swords, all of them slinking back to avoid the deathblows of the creatures.

And Thom fought, unaided by magic, as he struggled to defend his friends.

Beside him, a subtle glitter caught Thom's attention. He glanced just long enough to find a swirling cloud of onyx shards materializing out of the Space sword and descending over Evylin's arm. The magic rolled around her, covering her in a shield of protection that lashed out whenever a Shade got too near. The magic ignored Thom and Isla on her other side but defended Evylin effortlessly.

"How are you doing that?" Thom asked in awe, though he kept his attention on the fight.

"I don't know," Evylin admitted, casting a swift glance at him.

Thom grinned dryly. "Well, keep it up, eh? And if you've got some extra to spare, I wouldn't complain."

The magic moved like an extension of Evylin. It attacked the Shades with each thrust of her sword and protected her like armor. She was an unstoppable Bonded Warrior at the height of her power.

One step at a time, they worked their way back through the Keep.

Slowly.

Very slowly.

Defending Deckard, Rafferty, and Vayden made the fight even more difficult. The Shades were getting more furious and more numerous by the second. The seven fighters grew increasingly tired. Their breaths came out with ragged desperation, and Thom wondered if any of them felt the burn in their lungs like he did. Did magic help with that? Or were they all on the brink of collapse too?

Isla's gust of wind knocked a large portion of Shades from the front, providing a path. Auden, Brea, and the men carrying Deckard hurried through the line. Thom abandoned his post beside Evylin, desperate to stick by his brother's side. But then the Shades filled the gap he'd left behind, funneling through and cutting Evylin, Isla, Ethenn, and Ilain off from the rest of the party.

Thom's gut clenched. With swift precision, the Shades created a wall between them, attacking now on all sides. Three fighters defended Deckard, Rafferty, and Vayden. But three of their most powerful members were left behind. He could see that the four other members of the troop were struggling to thin out the Shades, but they couldn't work fast enough.

Thom muttered a curse but charged into the front, slashing and ducking, each kill bringing him perilously close to death. "Auden," he shouted, "you got any tricks up your sleeve?"

"I'm running out of energy," Auden called back.

"Would the Night Relic help?"

"It would only drain me faster. And we don't need two bodies to carry out of here."

"Damn." Thom cut down another Shade, narrowly missing its black hole when he heard Rafferty yelp.

"Thommy!" the weasel called.

Thom whirled, but Brea was already there. She slashed the Shades that drew too near the three men in the center, saving them from certain death.

Heaving a single relieved breath, Thom turned back to the front, determined to get them out of there. If they could get Deckard to safety first, then they could go back for the others. The Shades couldn't leave the Keep, could they? So all they needed to do was get Deckard into the antechamber, and then they could ensure the safety of the rest.

With a surge, Thom slashed and hacked and pushed ahead. His eyes stung with the sweat and blood that trickled into them. He couldn't see clearly, but it didn't matter. He had to keep pushing onward. He had to get them to safety. This was his one purpose. This was his redemption. If he could save Deckard and Evylin, everything else he'd screwed up in his life would be atoned for.

He had to get them out.

Thom cut down another Shade. It burst into a supernova of shards, slicing his arms and face. He barreled back to avoid the void twisting in its gut. And in doing so, turned himself straight into the path of a Shade.

The creature brought its knife-like arm down, and Thom tried to raise his sword, but he couldn't move fast enough.

A sharp, piercing sensation tore through his gut.

Thom gasped. Blood filled his mouth, coating his tongue in the taste of iron. He looked down to find his stomach ripped open by the Shade's attack. Stumbling, his body trembled. The Shade drove its foot into the side of his knee. He cried out as the joint shattered.

Thom fell to the floor, his head slamming against the glass-like infinity of the floor. His vision grew spotted. Nebulae swirled. Starlight blazed. Vortexes twisted.

Above him, the Shade reared back, and Thom knew he was about to die.

He'd failed his mission, his purpose, his family.

A vibrant violet light rammed into the Shade's head. It burst into a thousand shards. Then a pair of arms was around Thom's chest, pulling him back and away from the black hole that opened in the creature's core.

"You can't die yet, *mi'caro*," Brea said with a fierce growl as she dragged him away. She released him and sprang back into action. With a fury, she fought the Shades. The Warrior was a blur of speed, strength, and power.

But it wouldn't matter.

Thom lay on the ground, gasping and spluttering for breath. He couldn't move. He could hardly breathe.

With one hand on his splayed guts, Thom's body began to shake. He was dying. He knew it. No matter how staunchly Brea defended him, the world was growing ever darker as the battle raged around him.

Thom turned his head, the expansive floor cold against his temple. He saw the Keep's iron door waiting in the distance.

Fifty yards.

He'd gotten them fifty yards away.

Tears slipped out of Thom's eyes. They could do it. If Evylin and the others could make it to them, the group could cross the final distance. He might die, but they would live.

Thom turned back to look for Evylin. He couldn't see her through the fray. But he heard her voice. She was calling for him. He smiled sadly. His death in exchange for her life. It seemed fitting.

His eyes drifted to Deckard then, his brother hanging limply between Rafferty and Vayden. Desperately, Auden fought around them in weakening flares of golden light. Thom's brow furrowed. While Brea was defending him, she'd left Auden alone to protect the others. Rather than let him die, she'd risked their lives.

A blast of blinding light burst apart several Shades in front of Auden. The blowback sent hundreds of cuts across his body. He backed away to escape the reach of their inner collapse. Then he turned and sent another burst of light to the other side of the men. The Day magic flared, shielding them. But Auden was wearing down. His gestures were weak, and his reactions sluggish. Without a doubt, he was dangerously close to passing out.

Brea continued to defend Thom's slowly dying form. Auden whirled, prepared to strike at another group of Shades. And neither of them noticed the Shade that leaped forward from the creatures' ranks.

Thom opened his mouth, prepared to warn them, but only a gurgle of blood slipped free.

"Auden!" Ilain's scream ripped across the Keep just before the Shade wrapped its cutting arms around his waist, tackling him backward.

As if in slow motion, Thom watched as the weight of the Shade drove Auden back and into the collapsing Shades behind them. It bore him into the very enemy he'd killed to defend Deckard, Rafferty, and Vayden only a second before.

Auden's vibrant green eyes went wide, contrasting with the vivid crimson streaks of blood marring his face. His hands were still raised from his last strike, the glow of Day reflecting off his pale palms. Sweat matted his copper hair to his forehead, and he gasped as the Shade's arms sliced into his gut.

Ilain's scream burned like fire.

Thom watched in helpless horror while Vayden released Deckard to scramble toward his brother. But it was too late.

Trapped in the gravity of the black hole, Auden began to tremble, the edges of his body and the Shade that tackled him shivering violently. Then both were torn apart, instantly consumed by the blackness of the void.

A guttural cry of agony echoed through the Keep.

Ilain.

Thom's heart broke for his friend. He sobbed quietly, his own life bleeding out on the floor. They were so close. He'd gotten them so close. Yet, they'd still lost.

With a gut-wrenching scream of agony, a fierce gale slammed through the Keep, ripping through it with desperate fury. The gust of wind sent their whole troop and the remaining hundreds of Shades crashing to the floor. Narrowly, Brea avoided landing on top of Thom even as the torrent sent him skidding backward, leaving a streak of blood on the shiny black floor.

The only one left standing was Ilain.

Her arms were raised over her head, and a raging pillar of black fire burned around her, the inferno the color of the onyx infinity around them. In her hands, the Wind and Space Relics glowed with a blazing brightness. Thom imagined she must have torn them from Ethenn and Evylin in her grief-empowered fury.

The flaming pillar burned blisteringly hot as Ilain threw her arms to the side. Fire and Wind became a torrent in her hands, burning and slicing through every Shade that remained. They collapsed to ashes all around them.

Then, shaking violently, Ilain collapsed to her knees and screamed in bitter misery.

CHAPTER THIRTY-FOUR

The iron door of the Space Keep slid shut behind them with a rumbling *boom* that reverberated in Evylin's chest. Under the shared weight of Thom's mutilated body, Evylin and Brea rushed toward the arched windows of the antechamber. He was heavy, slowly turning to dead weight as the blood drained out of him.

Isla helped ease him to the ground, her face wet with tears. "We've got to stop the bleeding," she said, voice surprisingly even amidst the chaos.

Carefully, Rafferty and Vayden deposited Deckard's unconscious form beside them. Thom's wheezing rasped loudly in Evylin's ear. Her whole body trembled. Tears blurred her vision, but she focused on making her brother-in-law as comfortable as possible.

"It doesn't matter," Thom said weakly. His gray-blue eyes shifted around, ensuring everyone had made it out of the Keep. Rafferty hovered over Evylin's shoulder, wringing his hands. Off to the side, Vayden and Isla clung to one another, watching helplessly and openly weeping. And in the far corner, Ilain sobbed in Ethenn's arms.

Seeing that their remaining friends were safe, Thom met Evylin's gaze and offered a resigned smile. "Don't bother. I'm already dead."

Her breath caught. Losing Auden was horrible enough. Losing Thom too . . . Deckard would feel the weight of it when he woke. He would be crushed by it, sure that the losses were his fault.

Steadily, Brea checked Thom's pulse, squatting next to where he was propped upright against the stone wall. Her dark eyes blazed with fury even as she worked with a steady calm, surveying his stomach wound and broken knee. "As you just spoke, *mi'caro*," she said casually, "I'd say it's safe to assume you aren't dead yet."

Thom huffed with a straggly, viscous-sounding chuckle. "How much . . . blood . . . have I lost?" he gasped.

Brea gritted her teeth, removing her coat deftly. "Too much."

"So . . . I'm dead."

"No, you're not." Brea balled the coat and pressed it to the wound.

Thom grimaced at the pressure and the pain. "That's not . . . gonna work."

His words grew weaker by the second, and Evylin's heart stuttered with fright, pain, and dread. This whole time, she'd feared losing Deckard, and she'd never stopped to consider how heartbroken she'd be to lose Thom. Especially now that he'd grown so much as a person, righting his wrongs and proving his devotion as a brother. He was trying so hard. It wasn't fair to lose him this soon.

"What do we do?" Rafferty demanded. For the first time ever, he looked truly afraid. "How do we save him?"

Brea remained calm as she leaned heavily against the wound. But she also remained silent, which was its own damning reply.

"Evie." Thom's hand gripped her arm weakly. "Tell . . . Jonn . . ."

Evylin shook her head and clasped his bloody fingers. "No," she refused. "No, you are telling him yourself. You are not allowed to die."

A small, pained grin lifted his lips. "You don't . . . get that choice."

"You're going to live," she ordered.

Vayden stepped closer. "Is there *anything* we can do?" he asked through his tears.

Isla brushed a comforting hand along his arm, then turned to Brea. "The blood is soaking through on the right. You'll have to apply the pressure more evenly," she instructed.

Brea immediately straddled Thom, pushing down with all her might. She grinned teasingly at him, though Evylin could see a glimmer of tears in the woman's eyes. "Not how you imagined this moment, eh, *mi'caro*?"

He wheezed with a laugh that turned into a cough. Red coated his chin as he hacked up more blood.

Brea's face hardened. She muttered something fierce in Schonese, then glared at him and said, "I'm not letting you die."

But Evylin could feel Thom's pulse fading through his wrist. He began to choke, and her heart squeezed. "Thom," she gasped, seeing the light fade quickly from his eyes.

Then Ilain was there, shoving Brea aside. Her face was soaked in tears, and her expression was hollow. But she worked quickly, flinging Brea's bloodied coat aside and ripping open Thom's shirt. The deep, horrid gash spurted more blood, gurgling grotesquely. Evylin fought a gag and held Thom's gaze instead of staring at the open wound.

Reaching out to him, Ilain tugged Ethenn closer, then set one hand on the wound while the other gripped the Warrior's hand like a vise. A burnt orange light pulsed under her hand, and her shoulders notably slumped while Ethenn drew in a sharp inhale, and he wilted as well. As the light continued to burn, Evylin realized that Ilain was using his energy—energy that he hardly owned at the moment.

Leaning forward, Evylin set her hand on Ilain's shoulder to offer what little strength she had left as well. The orange light grew brighter as an immediate surge of power swept out of Evylin.

The magic burned across Thom's skin, cauterizing the wound and causing him to groan in pain. But his eyes grew wide again, and he sucked in a desperate, lung-filling breath.

At Thom's regeneration, Ilain immediately began to collapse, but Ethenn caught her. He pulled her close, keeping her upright. Though her lashes fluttered sleepily, she managed to retain consciousness.

Thom's breathing steadied, his torso now whole, though still slick with blood. He stared at Ilain in awe and gratitude, then squeezed Evylin's hand tighter, though the pressure was feeble.

"He's alive!" Rafferty exclaimed.

Thom grimaced. "Not so loud, please," he said, voice still weak. He met Ilain's gaze again and whispered, "Thank you."

Visibly drained and resting against Ethenn's shoulder, she nodded. "It will take time to heal," she murmured, tears still coursing down her cheeks. "I produced only enough blood to keep you alive. You'll be weak for several days, and the wound will ache."

Thom's chin dipped. "I'm so sorry, Ilain."

Ilain blinked but didn't respond.

Ethenn tugged her closer. "Is anyone going to set that leg?" he asked.

They all avoided looking at his shattered leg, bent unnaturally at the knee.

"I don't have the energy," Ilain admitted.

"Even with help?" Brea asked, offering her hand.

Ilain glared at her. "You've done enough, don't you think?"

Brea flinched.

"Ilain," Isla said gently, "she didn't mean—"

That furious jade green stare fell on her sister-in-law. "You dare to defend her?"

she spat. "She killed Auden, if not by her own hand, then by her negligence. Her *preference*."

Isla tightened her jaw, and Vayden's hand brushed comfortingly across her shoulder. He spoke calmly, though his voice was tight. "His death was an accident, Lainy," he said, and the words were broken and strained. "No one is at fault."

Rage seemed to fill Ilain with new life as she sat up, pulling out of Ethenn's arms. Her posture was rigid, her features taut with sorrow, and her fists curled with fury. "She made a *choice*," Ilain accused. "She abandoned Auden. She suggested this plan in the first place. If we had gone to Estshire first, if she had stayed at Auden's side—"

"If I had Bonded with him, you mean?" Brea interrupted coldly.

Evylin shifted uncomfortably beside the Warrior. Thom's hand was still limp in hers, though she could feel subtle signs of strength returning. "Ilain," he said gently, "if anyone is to blame, it's me. I was foolish. I thought I could get us out, but—"

"No, Thom," Brea interrupted. "She's right. I made a choice. I knew I could either save you or defend Auden. I did what I thought to be best."

Ilain let out a haughty scoff. "You did what you wanted to do," she accused. "You chose Thom because of your selfishness."

Evylin frowned, and Thom's hand twitched in hers.

Brea's brow lowered. "I may not have wanted to be your brother's sacrifice," she said with a tense fury, "but I did not abandon him out of any ill will."

"No," Ilain agreed. "You did it out of your own personal desires." Her voice rose as she held Brea's stare accusingly. "You did it because you're happy to let all of us sacrifice, but Allore forbid you have to make one of your own."

Behind Ilain, Ethenn's brow furrowed with the same confusion that Evylin felt. "What is—?" he began, but Isla interrupted.

"Ilain," she said, her accent thicker than usual, "stop."

She didn't listen. "You abandoned Auden to his death because of your love for Thom. *Te'caro*."

The allegation was so abrupt and so absurd that Evylin almost scoffed. But Brea sat rigid, her expression void of feeling even as her hand rested gently, caringly against Thom's broken leg.

Evylin's lips parted. *Te'caro*. She didn't know the translation of the Schonese term, but she recognized the adjusted form of the original *mi'caro*. She could readily divine the affectionate nature of the pet name.

But love . . . ?

They'd only known one another for a day before Brea began to use that term of endearment for Thom. Could she really have fallen in love with him so readily?

Thom shuddered, his broken body shivering with exhaustion, and Brea pulled her hand away from him. She rose to her feet, glaring at Ilain.

"You don't know what you're talking about," she said flatly. "Your grief is blinding you, Ilain. I made the choice I thought was best. It was not my intent to abandon Auden. I had hoped that I could return to his side to protect him too. I'm sorry that I was wrong."

With that, Brea turned and walked toward the far side of the entrance. She took a seat on the cold and shadowed staircase, staring at her hands. Isla squeezed Vayden's arm, then hurried after her friend. The two women sat on the staircase, whispering unheard words as they wrapped their arms around one another comfortingly.

Vayden stood in the hall, watching his sister with a compassionate but broken gaze. Ilain, however, shook with anger. She looked ready to burst forth in a rage of flames, but then suddenly she crumpled, sobbing pitifully.

Without hesitation, Ethenn cradled her close, burying her face in his chest. He rocked her slowly and gently as his hand glided across her back.

Tears slipped from Evylin's eyes at the sight. Deckard had held her that way after Hewitt's death. He'd held her close and let her expel her grief until she lay there, an empty shell of pain. She knew Ilain's sorrow, the gut-wrenching agony of knowing you'd never see your loved one again, knowing the world would never be right again—that you'd never again be whole.

A sudden urge swelled within Evylin. She needed Deckard; she needed the calm and comfort he provided to her. Yet, he lay unconscious a few feet away.

Evylin turned to see her sleeping husband. Rafferty and Vayden had laid him on his back so he could rest peacefully. With his eyes closed, breath steady, and body relaxed, he looked as though he'd simply chosen to nap. She reached out with her free hand, stiff with Thom's drying blood, and brushed her fingers along his jaw.

Was this how Deckard would look if he died? She would never see his lifeless form, she realized. When he died—and he *would* die, even if it were two centuries from now— she would either die with him or fall into a stasis to recover from the wound in her soul. When she awoke, he'd already be cold in his grave. It was somehow a bitterly sad and hopeful revelation.

The morbid thoughts drove Evylin to check Deckard's pulse just to ensure that his life remained. It was strong and steady. He was fine. He was alive. And her heart ached to hold him.

Instead, she turned back to Thom. He'd closed his eyes, scrunching them shut. He appeared to be in miserable pain.

Rafferty crouched down next to them. "Hey, Thommy-boy," he said. "Ready to set that leg?"

"Not if you're going to do it," Thom quipped, face still contorted.

Rafferty smirked. "Can't blame ya. Fact is, I don't even know how."

"Then I definitely don't want you attempting it."

Evylin squeezed Thom's hand. "I can do it."

His eyes opened, meeting hers with sorrow. "I'm not going to be able to walk on it," he said. "Probably not for a month or two at the least."

Though she understood his point—he would be no good to their mission any longer; he wouldn't be able to ride a horse, let alone walk if it wasn't healed by magic—she chose to tease him rather than placate his self-pity. "So," she raised her brow, "you don't want me to set it?"

Thom snorted humorlessly. "Of course I do."

Evylin offered a light smile and shifted toward his knee. "Then you'll need to tell me how."

"What?" he gasped, head shooting up. He groaned and leaned back against the wall once more. "You don't know how to set a bone?"

"I never needed to learn."

"And you're going to practice on me?"

"Do you want your leg repaired or not?"

Thom sent her a flat stare. "Yes, but it'd be nice if it were by someone who knew what they were doing."

Ethenn moved to sit next to Evylin by the mangled leg. On the far side of the room, Ilain now sat in Vayden's arms, the siblings crying silently together.

Ethenn set his hand on Evylin's arm. "I've got this," he said.

"You know how to set a broken limb?" she asked.

He nodded, sizing up the leg. "It's a rather necessary skill when you're out in the woods for weeks at a time. If you or your fellow hunters break something," he felt along the knee, causing Thom to grimace, "you need to be able to set it as you're likely to be days from the nearest healer."

Ethenn leaned back on his haunches, releasing the leg. "The good news is," he said to Thom, "this isn't as bad as it looks. The kneecap isn't fractured, just dislocated. However, there is a fracture on the bone beneath. That's what's causing the strange bend. I can set the break and shift the kneecap back into place." He paused and offered a frown. "But it's gonna hurt like hell."

"What's new?" Thom replied, lips still twisting from his current agony.

Ethenn shrugged. "The bad news is I don't have anything to use as a splint. I can't set it until there's something to hold it steady, so it'll heal properly."

Thom sighed. "So much for that."

"I can fuse it," Ilain murmured, kneeling next to Ethenn. Her cheeks looked sunken, her body worn ragged with exhaustion and grief.

"Ilain," Ethenn argued, "you don't have the strength."

She held his gaze steadily. "With you and Evylin helping me, I can manage a simple fusing," she said. "You do the hard work of setting and fixing it, then I'll channel Day to speed the recovery." She looked at Thom then. "You'll be able to walk just fine in the morning."

Thom eyed her warily. "You're sure?" he asked.

"Shocking as it may be, I'm not that fragile," she said, but the words were empty.

After a second of consideration, Ethenn turned back to the task at hand. "Raff, take off your belt," he instructed.

"You'll have to buy me a drink first," the weasel snarked.

Ethenn stared at him with dull annoyance. "It's for Thom to bite down on."

While Rafferty moved to follow orders, Thom raised his brow. "It's gonna be that bad?" he asked, worry pitching his voice higher.

"Sorry," Ethenn apologized. He turned to Vayden. "Could you hold his left leg down?"

"Seriously?" Thom said incredulously.

"I don't care to be kicked in the face," Ethenn returned.

Rafferty offered the leather belt. Thom rolled his eyes, then bit down. At Ethenn's continued instruction, Rafferty leaned against Thom's shoulder, carefully wrapping his arms over him to hold his torso down. Evylin continued to hold Thom's hand, fear causing the whites of his eyes to appear.

She squeezed his hand and smirked. "Don't be a baby," she teased. "You were just bleeding out a moment ago. This will be nothing."

He rolled his eyes at her sarcasm, then screamed through the belt when Ethenn set the broken bone unannounced. His body jolted from the pain, but Rafferty and Vayden held him steady.

"Hold still," Ethenn ordered.

Thom muttered muffled obscenities into the belt between his teeth.

Tenderly, Evylin brushed the dark hair off his forehead. "You have the lowest pain tolerance I've ever seen," she goaded.

Somehow, she understood when he mumbled, "Don't try to distract me, Evie. It's not going to—" He cried out again as Ethenn twisted the kneecap back in place.

Quickly, Ilain grabbed Evylin's hand while Ethenn gripped her shoulder. Then she rested her hand on the newly set leg. A flare of rusty light seared through as Evylin slumped against the archway, a deep exhaustion creeping into her bones.

Once Rafferty removed the belt from Thom's mouth, scowling at the bite marks left along the edge, Thom released a whole new slew of curses. "I'm gonna get you back, Loxley," he snarled even as his head fell back against the stones. "Just you wait. When you least expect it, I'm gonna break your leg, then set it with the exact same care you just gave me, and we'll see how you like it."

"I'd hate it," Ethenn returned, sinking next to Ilain. His features were shadowed with tiredness, but a small grin pulled at his lips, seeing his friend alive, whole, and spitting mad. "But I'd whine less about it, that's for sure."

Evylin grinned and patted Thom's shoulder. Then she looked over the others.

Thom was alive, and they had the Space Relic. But the victory had come at great cost.

In the shadowed stairwell, Brea and Isla watched sadly. Vayden helped Ilain hobble toward an arched window to slump against the stone. Ethenn barely made it to sprawl at their side. Rafferty plunked down next to Thom, leaning his head against the arched window. Everyone had sustained cuts and scrapes along their faces and bodies. Their clothing was ragged and torn. And each of them carried a soul-deep weariness.

Worst of all, they'd lost Auden.

Evylin's eyes filled with fresh tears. She whispered her thankfulness for Thom's safety to Allore, then released him and turned to Deckard. Grasping his limp hand, she pressed it to her lips. She wanted to curl into his side and take comfort in his nearness.

Instead, she sat there, fearing the guilt he'd face when he woke. He'd take Auden's death personally. He'd shoulder the weight of the responsibility like he carried everything else. She didn't want that for him. He was right; it was too heavy, even for the impeccable Jonn Deckard.

Evylin leaned against the archway as close to Deckard as she could. She held his hand to her heart and closed her eyes. Already, her soul felt heavy, anticipating what was to unfold. She couldn't fathom the added load this would place on Deckard's heart.

But whatever came, she'd help him carry it and every other burden to come.

CHAPTER THIRTY-FIVE

11TH OF RADIA, 1574

Infinity surrounded him, its vastness rippling through his core with unmitigated power. Deckard stood in the Space Keep, the beauty of the Heavens alight around him. Amber swirled with vivid green across the onyx depths of eternity. The Shades stood like soldiers, awaiting their officer's command.

Deckard surveyed them and, with a mere thought, released them to their charge. They barreled into him, giving him their strength as he absorbed each one. He closed his eyes to soak in the thrumming power in his chest. His body vibrated with intense vigor. He could hear the enthusiastic whisper of Space in his mind.

Upon opening his eyes, Deckard found himself in the Chamber, standing on the dais. The Relic rested on the pedestal before him, its gold setting almost glowing. He reached out eagerly, the magic in him quivering with anticipation. The tips of his fingers could feel the ricocheting energy that pulsed off its onyx stone even as they hovered above it. But the moment his touch met the amulet's golden ridges, a scream ripped through his ears, cutting through him like the shards of his own magic.

He recoiled from the Relic, stumbling back to fall off the raised dais. His form hit the marble with a body-numbing *thud.* Yet, the screaming didn't cease. It echoed in his mind, rocking through him like tremors until he lost all sense of himself or the world around him as it repeated one phrase over and over.

"Let me out!"

A gentle wash of cream light woke Deckard. His body was pleasantly warm, the soothing weight of blankets and the mattress's plush support embracing him. Stretching, he instinctively kept the movement contained to avoid disrupting Evylin. But then he realized she wasn't in his arms.

With a rush, the drowsiness of sleep evaporated, and Deckard opened his eyes, seeking his wife. He was in their bed, the morning sun filling their room. Evylin never rose before him. Why had she now?

His searching eyes cast about the room, and then he found her. Evylin stood at the window, fingers on her wedding rings. She turned at the sound of his movement. An air of worry radiated around her, but relief flared above the emotion as she hurried to his side.

She took a seat on the bed and smiled gently at him. "Welcome back," she said, her voice light. He sat up slowly to rest against the pillows, and she brushed her fingers along his jaw.

A wave of power surged from her fingertips and into Deckard's soul.

Space.

Deckard's heart jolted, and he jerked backward. His mind reeled, reminding him of all that had happened. The moment he'd stepped into the Space Keep, its magic had overwhelmed him. And then he lost control. . . .

Worse than in Dunneshead, worse than during the Wind Mages' ambush. He wholly lost himself to Space—mind, body, and soul.

"Oh, Evie." He lunged forward to pull her into his arms. The jarring surge of power went through him again, but he needed to hold her, to apologize to her, to know she was safe despite his horrible failure. "I'm sorry. I'm so sorry."

"Shh," Evylin whispered soothingly. She ran her hand through his hair, holding him close. "It's all right. We made it out."

Deckard refused to be absolved. "Forgive me," he pleaded, face pressed into her neck. "I lost control, and—"

"It's all right," she repeated, though he could feel the tension and pain in her heart. "We made it out."

For several minutes, they sat there, comforted by the physical assurance of their safety. He laced his fingers through her wavy hair. Her arms cradled him tenderly. His muscles relaxed as she nuzzled deeper into him. He wanted to stay wrapped up in her forever, on their bed, in their house, under the calming morning sunshine.

But Evylin pulled away, her mood still somber. Deckard sat back, studying her face even as she took his hands in hers. "What is it?" he asked.

Her brown eyes were locked on their entwined fingers. He could feel her reluctance as she took a steadying breath, and worry wrapped around his heart. "Evie," he pressed.

"We, uh . . ." She trailed off, adjusting his moonstone ring absentmindedly. "After you fell unconscious, things grew difficult."

Deckard wet his lips, preparing for what she was about to reveal.

"Thom," she began, and his heart stuttered, "fought valiantly and made sure we got out, but he was gravely injured in the process. He would have died if it weren't for Brea and Ilain."

Deckard didn't know whether to feel relief or guilt. His brother was alive. But he'd almost died because of Deckard's failure.

At Evylin's lingering solemnity, Deckard realized there was more. He tightened his grip on her. "What else?" he asked.

Evylin scooted closer again, her side pressing into his legs. She met his gaze, impressing him with her next words. "It isn't your fault," she insisted.

"What isn't?"

"You have to understand; you couldn't have stopped it."

"Evylin—"

"Tell me you understand," she demanded.

Deckard's brow pinched so tightly it ached. "What happened?" he asked in a determined but hushed tone.

A cloud of grief, worry, and compassion swelled between them. "We lost Auden," she whispered.

Deckard struggled to take in the revelation. Nothing about it made sense. Without seeing their friends, without the ability to visually comprehend the truth, he couldn't rectify it in his mind. Auden wasn't gone. He couldn't be. She'd merely meant that he'd been taken, stolen away by Blount and his men. They would rescue him, and all would be well.

Swallowing past the dryness in his throat, Deckard asked, "Where did they take him?"

Evylin's expression clouded with sorrow. "Jonn . . ."

Deckard shook his head, the awful truth dawning on him, but he refused to accept it. She didn't mean that Auden was dead. Deckard's mistake, his inability to control himself, hadn't gotten the man killed. "It was Blount, wasn't it?" he asked. "He took him, and now—"

"Jonn," she repeated his name again but said nothing more.

Deckard's eyes filled with tears. "He's gone?" he asked.

She nodded.

"Dead?"

Her gaze averted apologetically.

Guilt and despair slammed into Deckard's gut. He'd gotten Auden killed. "How, uh—" He fought back his tears, forcing himself to accept the responsibility for his actions. "How are Ilain and Vayden?"

"Coping," she said softly. Her own eyes brimmed with tears. "He's been quiet, relying on Isla."

Deckard grimaced. He hadn't considered Isla's grief as well.

"She's staying strong for him," Evylin continued. "But I can see it's hard on her. Ilain, though . . ."

Evylin glanced at the door, then turned to him again. "Ilain didn't take it well."

"I wouldn't expect her to."

"After Auden died, she took the Wind and Space Relics from Ethenn and me," she explained. "She unleashed a storm of black fire that killed hundreds of remaining Shades. It was . . . terrifyingly impressive."

Deckard gaped at her. "I left you to fight hundreds of them?"

Evylin leaned in at his desolate words. She took his face in her hands. "Stop," she ordered. "They would have come whether you remained conscious or not."

"But Auden wouldn't have—"

"You don't know that," she insisted. "None of us can know what would have happened."

Deckard's jaw tensed, but he let the argument go. "Does Ilain blame me?"

Evylin released him and sat back, sighing. "No," she said. "She blames Brea."

She explained the rest of it then, how Brea left Auden to defend Thom and relegated the Mage to his death. She told him of Ilain's accusation that Brea had feelings for Thom, which was why she'd chosen him over Auden.

Deckard's brow furrowed. "I wondered," he murmured.

Evylin cocked her head. "You did?"

He shrugged. "She's paid more attention to him than is strictly platonic, in my opinion."

"It could be cultural," Evylin offered with a wry smile. "Isla is also rather friendly."

He gave her a flat stare. "She gave him a pet name that's blatantly affectionate."

Evylin pressed her lips together as though she knew her amusement was ill-timed. "She denied it," she said.

"And we both denied our feelings for months," he reminded. "It doesn't mean they weren't real."

Evylin accepted the point. "Ilain isn't talking to Brea anymore," she warned. "She said she also won't work with her because she can't trust her."

Deckard drew in a long sigh, pinching the bridge of his nose. It was understandable. Ilain was reactionary and passionate. Her anger as a result of her grief was to be expected. But they couldn't have rifts that made their troop unstable. Not when they all depended on one another for survival.

"I'll handle it," he said.

"One other issue," Evylin said with a grimace. "Brea won't talk to Thom either."

"What?"

Evylin shrugged. "Evidently, she doesn't want him believing Ilain's accusation, so now, she's shut him out. Perhaps it will blow over, but in the last twenty-four hours, she's hardly looked in his direction, let alone spoken to him. But it doesn't bode well for our journey if she keeps it up."

Deckard tried to focus on the matter at hand, but he couldn't help latching onto the one fact she'd revealed. "I've been asleep for twenty-four hours?" he asked.

"Closer to twenty-six at this point," she confirmed.

Deckard's heart stuttered. They'd entered the Keep around seven the previous morning. They'd lost an entire day to his mistake. One full day, putting them even farther behind schedule.

Not wanting to face that particular consequence yet, Deckard asked, "How did you get back?"

"Carlile," Evylin said. "We rested in the antechamber until nightfall. Ilain gave Rafferty directions, and he snuck through the palace to find Carlile's office. He orchestrated our return without the king's knowledge."

"And how did I get all the way to the third floor?"

Evylin gave him a gentle grin. "You can thank Ethenn, Rafferty, Vayden, and me. Thom would have helped, but he's still recovering."

Deckard's heart squeezed at the thought of his brother. "How is he? Can I see him?"

"He's all right," she promised. "He'll have a scar and several days of recovery ahead of him, but he's just fine thanks to Ilain. Though walking is a bit of a struggle, so you'll have to visit him in the parlor. He's on the sofa."

"He can't walk?"

She shook her head comfortingly. "His leg is just tender," she corrected. "It will take several days for the swelling to go down, but Ilain managed to heal the break. She offered to heal it the rest of the way once she's better recovered. For the moment, he just needs support getting around."

Deckard took a restoring breath. His brother was safe and alive. He had to focus on that.

"And what does Thom think of Brea's potential . . . regard for him?" he asked.

Evylin wore a bemused smirk. "I really don't know," she admitted. "I haven't exactly gotten the chance to speak with him privately, but he hasn't appeared to notice Brea's avoidance. Neither has he acknowledged Ilain's accusation."

Deckard let out a disappointed huff. "Do you think he intends to ignore it?"

"Actually," Evylin's grin turned proud, "I think he's just giving them space. He was mortally wounded, so perhaps it's the result of blood loss, but he's kept a level head through it all. It seems he's simply trying to behave maturely about it all."

Despite the heartbreak and guilt in his chest, Deckard found himself smiling. "He's growing up," he said fondly.

Evylin nodded. "Seems that way."

"What now?" he asked. "Is everyone else well enough to travel?"

"Yes. Perhaps we're all emotionally fragile, but I think continuing our mission will give us purpose," she said. "Something to do other than wallow in our misery."

Knowing he'd need to apologize profoundly to Ilain, Vayden, and Isla, as well as to the rest of their troop, Deckard decided to start with the most important confession first.

Taking Evylin's hands in his once more, Deckard sat up straighter. Another well of power tugged at his core, but he focused on the task at hand. "Evylin, I'm sorry," he said.

"I already told you it isn't your fault."

"No, listen," he insisted. "I'm not apologizing for the consequences of my actions now. My apology is for leaving you."

A twist of dismay cinched the air around them. Evylin's eyes filled with tears again, and he drew closer. "I'm so sorry, Evie," he whispered. "I wanted to be stronger for you. I'm sorry I became someone you couldn't trust and that I abandoned you when you needed me most. Although unintentional, it was wrong. I don't know how, but I promise you, I will figure out how to control this. I will never leave you like that again."

The first of Evylin's tears slipped free, and she rested her forehead against his. He wrapped his arms around her, pulling her to his chest. She cried silently in his embrace. Love, sorrow, fear, and relief all fluttered around them, tugging on his soul.

"Please forgive me," he begged, the words a mere whisper.

"Always," Evylin said into his collar.

Deckard pressed a kiss to her temple and held her as her arms coiled around him. They were too overcome with emotion to move. Her tears soaked the shoulder of his tunic while his own fell into her hair. The anguish of his inadequacy and the damning weight of his lack of control cut through his stomach, leaving him raw and aching. He had failed them miserably. If only he hadn't given in to the magic, if only he could have waited until they made it to the Chamber. . . .

Evylin pulled back in his arms, a sad smile on her lips. "How long are you going to blame yourself?" she asked.

"Forever," he admitted.

She sighed. "Will you never accept absolution?"

"I can't," he whispered hollowly.

Evylin brushed her thumb along his cheek, sending an arc of magic under his skin. "You are a bloody martyr," she said with a mix of affection and vexation. "And I love you."

Deckard forced himself to return her tender smile, though he knew his expression fell woefully short. "I love you," he promised.

With a heavy sigh, Evylin pulled away. "We should get going," she said. "It's late, and if we want to make good time, we need to get out of Loclight as soon as possible."

Deckard nodded, then paused. "Evie," he murmured. "Are you wearing the Space Relic?"

Her chin raised in surprise. "Yes."

He pressed his lips together. "I can feel it," he admitted.

"Oh?"

"It's . . ." He ground his teeth. "It calls to me."

Evylin furrowed her brow. "What do you mean?"

He met her eyes. "It wants me to use it," he explained. "Every time you touch me, I feel it, here—" He pressed a hand to his sternum. "It tugs on my magic but not like your touch usually does. It isn't something I can easily ignore or let go."

Deckard stared at her collar, at the place where he knew the Relic hung. "It's a demand," he said tightly. "A compulsion."

The scream in his dream reverberated through his mind. *Let me out.*

Evylin watched him warily as he continued, "Even now, I can feel it, like a presence looming over my shoulder. It wants me to touch it, to wield it. It wants to consume me." He met her gaze, confessing his darkest truth. "And I want to let it."

Caution and worry glided around Evylin, muddling her lighthearted personality. "I don't understand," she said. "We're Bonded."

Deckard waited, unsure of her point in bringing that up.

She leaned closer. "Jonn, the Alliance wants Bonded couples to carry the Relics because they are the only ones who can carry them without being affected by their pull," she said. "You and I are Bonded. The Relic shouldn't affect you."

The damning fact became clear to Deckard then. "Perhaps I'm too weak," he said. "And perhaps that's all the evidence we need to reject the Alliance's desire for us."

Though Evylin didn't seem convinced, she didn't contradict him.

Rubbing his hands together, Deckard ignored the agitating weight of his moonstone ring. "I'd like you to give the Relic to Rafferty," he said. "We can't risk my error again should I prove too weak to resist."

Evylin began to nod, then paused as though in thought. "No," she said.

Deckard flinched at the unexpected refusal. "What?"

She held his gaze with determination. "Jonn, you need to learn to control your magic," she said with finality, "to control your impulse. You can't do that if you take the temptation away."

"Evylin, it's dangerous."

"Everything we're doing is dangerous," she said, a hint of playfulness back in her tone. Then she set her hand on his cheek, sending a jolt of power through him once more. "You *can* control it."

"I don't trust myself," he admitted.

"*I* trust you," she said. "Let that be enough."

Deckard tightened his jaw but saw that she wouldn't be convinced. So he dipped his head in acquiescence. Perhaps he could talk Ilain or Isla into forcing her to give it up. But for now, he'd have to be careful with how much he touched her, how close he let himself get.

Rising from the bed, Deckard offered her a doubtful grimace. "I hope I don't disappoint your trust," he said.

Evylin's expression was so full of love and affection that his heart almost broke at the thought of failing her. "You never have," she said.

But Deckard knew that wasn't true.

No matter what Evylin wanted to claim, he'd failed her too many times to count. He'd broken her trust on numerous occasions. The Space Keep was just the most damning among them.

And even as he prayed that it would be the last time, he was certain it would not.

CHAPTER THIRTY-SIX

Ilain was entirely numb.

She'd spent all her emotion in the Keep and its antechamber. Now, she had nothing left. Even the tears had been drained from her broken heart.

Throughout the night, she sat up, staring at the wall. Ethenn offered comfort. She'd rejected it. How could she rest in his arms while Auden was . . . ?

Ilain's eyes were perpetually hazy from her grief. Yet, she couldn't cry. She sat on the wooden floor in her chemise, too brokenhearted to do more than peel the dirty dress from her sweat-caked skin. Next to her, Ethenn sat silently, with enough distance between them not to touch. He seemed to understand her need for independent mourning. However, he didn't abandon her for the bed or leave her in isolation. Somehow, he knew exactly what she needed. Which almost made the pain worse.

Her body felt hollow, worn down from misery and overuse. Her magic had frayed, the Fire within burning dimmer than ever before. It would return, she knew, but in the meantime, the emptiness left her frame lifeless and limp.

During their perilous battle in the Space Keep, Ilain had used up every ounce of power she possessed. She'd already been weary, feeling herself weaken in the Keep, yet she knew she still harbored enough energy to save them. She knew that. She'd known it the whole time. From the moment Deckard lost himself to Space, she began to conserve her strength, knowing they'd have to rely on her to get them out.

Hours later, in the darkness of the room, Ilain stared at the four rings on her fingers: ruby for Fire, sapphire for Water, diamond for Wind, and emerald for Terrae. They'd always twinkled with an inner light, a barely perceptible reflection of the magic within. For thirty years, she'd slowly siphoned reserves of her power into those gemstones. Each day, she'd granted them a little more.

Today, they'd gone dull, their power fully expended.

Borrowed energy. That's what her rings were. Free magic, available to be used in the darkest hour, when all hope seemed lost. And they were the only reason their troop was alive, the only reason she'd remained conscious and able to heal Thom's mortal wounds.

For years, Ilain had been saving the magic, preparing to use it when, eventually, they entered the final battle with Blount. It was meant for the Alliance's success. That's the only reason she'd waited so long to use it. She didn't view it as her magic anymore; it belonged to the Alliance—*her* sacrifice for the country's rise to power.

A fresh tear escaped and slipped down Ilain's cheek. She didn't bother brushing it away, letting it burn across her skin.

It had been Auden's forty-fifth birthday. And she'd let him die.

The moment he'd fallen into that black hole, Ilain felt it in her heart. Her brother was gone. All because she hadn't acted sooner. She'd hesitated to use the power in her rings, believing they were strong enough to get through the Keep alive. She needn't consume even an ounce of their energy stores; they could all make it free.

She'd been wrong.

Tearing the Space and Wind Relics from Ethenn and Evylin had been an impulse— an internal fury driving her to do what she should have done long before. In the final moments of battle, she'd summoned all the power of the Relics and all the borrowed energy of her rings, expending them in one profound strike.

Thirty years of power. Gone.

And she still lost Auden.

When the morning came, a soft knock accompanied it.

Ethenn had fallen asleep sitting up, his head lolling toward the side of the bed. Not once had Ilain closed her eyes.

At the knock, Ethenn startled awake. He rose quickly, his steps unsteady. Evylin was on the other side. She brought the news that they were preparing to leave, her voice gentle.

Ilain stood, speaking before Ethenn could. "We'll be ready shortly," she told Evylin, her voice tight and scratchy.

Evylin dipped her chin, gaze wary. "If you need longer—"

"I don't," Ilain said firmly. She forced a smile across her face, knowing it was terse rather than friendly. "We'll be down shortly."

After Evylin departed and Ethenn shut the door, he turned to her, uncertainty written across his features.

"I'm not going to crumble into ash," she said with a lightness she didn't feel. "You can stop treating me like it."

Ethenn studied her for a moment longer. "When you need something from me," he began, "tell me. Otherwise, I'm going to leave you alone."

"That's not very chivalrous of you," she remarked snidely.

"You're strong, Ilain," he said, steady assurance punctuating each word. "You don't need chivalry. You need support. Now, do you need anything in this moment, or shall I leave you to get ready yourself?"

Standing there in her chemise and undergarments alone, Ilain should have felt embarrassed in front of him. They'd dressed in front of one another, though with their gazes averted, but there was more vulnerability in this moment than any they'd yet experienced.

Tears stung her eyes again, but Ilain took a deep breath. "I feel shaky," she admitted.

"Do you need something to eat?" he asked practically.

Realizing she hadn't eaten in over twenty-four hours, Ilain nodded. "But I need help dressing first."

Without a word, Ethenn moved for her clothes. Isla had taken their clothes from the day before to launder, so he brought her spare dress, a dark moss-green and brown brocade, along with her clean underclothes. Handing her the frock, he remained at her side, turning his back so she could replace her sweaty chemise with the fresh one and steadying her when needed. Otherwise, he didn't touch her or speak. It was strangely bolstering and irritating.

Ethenn had redressed the night before but only now tucked his shirt in before grabbing his coat and pulling on his boots. "Do you need anything else?" he asked.

Ilain shook her head. When he turned to go, she caught his hand. His dark eyes met hers, his expression placid.

"Thank you," she whispered, unable to muster the emotion the words required.

Ethenn gave a single nod, then left the room.

A moment later, Isla entered. "I was told not to leave you alone," her sister-in-law said kindly. Then she began helping Ilain pack their few things.

"Doesn't Vayden need you?" Ilain asked with dispassionate politeness.

Isla shook her head. "He has Rafferty to keep him distracted."

Ilain didn't feel the smile she forced, focusing on her task. With every movement, her eyes caught on her now-dull rings, and her heart squeezed, reminding her that *she* was Auden's real killer. She'd let him die.

Too soon, Ilain was packed, and the women left the room.

Emerging from the dark room, with its curtains drawn to cover the solitary window, the rest of the house felt unbearably bright. The troop waited in the parlor for their arrival, ready to continue their journey. Dejected, Vayden sat in the wingback chair, staring aimlessly at nothing while a cup of tea cooled on his lap. On the sofa, Deckard perched beside Thom, who sat with his left leg outstretched. She would need to heal that to speed his recovery. The brothers spoke in hushed tones until Ilain appeared, when everyone went silent.

In the dining room, Evylin ate her breakfast while Rafferty flipped a small dagger from hand to hand absentmindedly. Ethenn appeared from the kitchen, a small bowl in his hand. Spotting her, he stepped immediately to Ilain's side, and Isla went to Vayden.

Ilain accepted the meager breakfast. She scanned the room once more, noting their missing compatriot. "Where's Breata?" she asked coldly.

"She went to the stable to prepare," Vayden said.

More likely, it was to avoid Ilain.

Deckard stood, drawing everyone's attention as he cleared his throat. "We are running short on time," he said, "but before we go, I'd like to say something."

Ilain leaned against the stair rail, eating the porridge and nettleberries Ethenn had prepared for her to soothe her trembling limbs and queasy stomach.

Meeting first Vayden, then Ilain's gaze, Deckard said, "I'd like to offer my sincerest apology. What happened yesterday was due to my failure to control my magic. Should I have been stronger—"

"Auden still would have died," Ilain interrupted.

They all turned to her with visible shock.

Ilain scraped together another spoonful of the creamy oats. "The blame doesn't lie with you any more than it does me," she finally said, then met Deckard's gaze. "I'm the most powerful Mage in two centuries, remember? Should I have chosen to, I might have taken all three Relics and destroyed every last Shade that came across our path. So why didn't I, Jonn?"

He stared back at her, speechless as she shoved the bite of porridge into her mouth.

She could see in his haunted gaze and haggard features that, already, he carried this weight too heavily. He genuinely believed that he was to blame for the tragedy. And Ilain wouldn't have that.

"Because we were too far away," Ethenn answered for her.

Though he was wrong, Ilain nodded and turned back to her breakfast. "Exactly," she said. "Should I have used my magic too soon, I would have burned out. We weren't close enough to the exit. I had the means to save my brother's life, but I feared exhausting myself . . . until it was too late."

The room was silent while each person present took in the truth. Ilain could have saved Auden herself. Despite Brea's abandonment, Ilain had the power. She'd simply been too late to use it.

However, that didn't absolve Brea's guilt in her mind. The Warrior still made her choice: Thom over Auden. And Ilain could never forget that.

"I still put us in additional danger," Deckard said, then looked at each person in the room. "And I'm severely sorry for that." He faced Ilain, meeting her gaze with submission. "I'd ask that you help me never to make that mistake again."

Even in the light of morning, a bone-deep numbness swirled through Ilain's body, and she welcomed it. Her emotions were fighting to return—anger, bitterness, hurt, and sorrow. She smothered them, giving Deckard a final nod and refusing to look toward the rest of the room. She couldn't bear to see them gathered without Auden.

Her heart squeezed all the tighter at the thought. It was impossible. It was wrong. Her brother had always been there, his quiet presence constant and loyal, good and loving. Now, he was forever gone.

Ilain forced the rest of her meal down, the nettleberries' sweetness adding an unwelcome flavorous quality to the porridge. She didn't bother listening as the others made their final plans. They were leaving Loclight for Estshire, two days behind schedule. Departing immediately was essential. If they didn't leave today, they'd arrive after Blount, and everything they'd gone through would be for nothing.

When their travel plans were complete, Vayden came to Ilain's side, and Ethenn took her empty bowl to the kitchen, leaving the siblings alone.

Her brother's sharp blue eyes stared down at her, the barely restrained tears within them saying more than words ever could. He cupped her cheek, and his palm was cold against her clammy skin. "Lainy . . ." he whispered, but nothing else came out.

Ilain gripped his wrist, suddenly feeling like a little girl once again. She clenched her jaw, fighting off the tremor of emotion within. "We'll be fine," she said flatly. "We just have to keep going."

Vayden's brow furrowed sorrowfully, but Ilain impressed her will upon him with her glare. "Vayden, we must all make sacrifices," she reminded him, "for the sake of a better future. This was Auden's."

"He was our brother."

The words were gentle, yet they hit Ilain with more force than she thought possible. Their brother.

Auden.

Ilain closed her eyes against the sudden swell of tears. One slipped past her closed lids, nonetheless, dripping onto her cheek.

Auden was gone. Her confidant, her most trusted companion. The other half of her heart.

Her knees threatening to buckle, Ilain leaned into Vayden and let him embrace her. She knew the others were still present, but she also knew they wouldn't watch. Even Rafferty would turn away to honor the siblings' grief. They'd lost too much.

Resting her face on her only remaining brother's shoulder, Ilain hardened her jaw. Despite her words, this was no sacrifice. Auden hadn't given his life in the Space Keep. It had been taken from him, all because of one woman's selfish choice.

No matter what Brea wanted to claim, the Warrior had betrayed Auden. She'd chosen Thom on a whim of fancy. The soldier had been dead in point of fact if not reality, his wounds beyond recovery. Had Ilain not been magnanimous enough to care, he would have bled out in the antechamber. As it was, Ilain's strength had almost failed her, even then. If Evylin hadn't offered her own energy during the healing, Ilain would have passed out, and Thom would have breathed his last.

Brea's decision came from infatuation rather than logic. It was between Thom's life and Auden's. And she'd chosen Thom.

Ilain should have let him die. Then the woman might have seen her error.

But the bitter thought pricked Ilain's heart, starting a burn of guilt searing through her veins. Thom was her friend, albeit a miserable excuse for one at times. Yet, they'd genuinely come to care for one another. Had the choice been hers, she might have fought to save Thom too.

No. Ilain pulled away from Vayden. She wiped her wet cheeks dry and straightened her back. She never would have chosen anyone over Auden.

But Brea wasn't the only one to blame for his death. . . .

Finally, readied for travel, the troop left the Deckards' home. They took back streets in case anyone saw their late departure and alerted the king. Carlile had assured them he'd cover for their delay, but they did their best not to make extra work for the man.

Vayden and Isla broke off to meet Brea at the stable while the rest continued to the barracks. Deckard and Thom went in alone to recover their horses. They mounted up and headed for the main gate.

And Ilain's heart left a trail of blood through the streets of Loclight as she rode away from the site of her brother's demise.

CHAPTER THIRTY-SEVEN

Once they made it beyond the walls of the capital, they rode hard for the first several hours, hoping to make up time. Thom's wounds ached, his leg stretching uncomfortably over the saddle as every hoofbeat sent a jolt through his scarred stomach. However, with their late start, it would be a struggle to reach the nearest village before sunset. So despite his injuries and their collective sorrow, they galloped away from the city before slowing to a fast canter when the horses tired.

Tension filled the air even as they rode. Brea isolated herself, bringing up the rear of the group. Though Evylin and Isla each attempted to join her at separate times, she'd sent them away. At one point, Thom began to drop back, but the cutting glare the Warrior gave him was enough to return him to his place in line.

"Not sure why she's so pissed at you," Rafferty commented in a bemused manner once he was at his side again. "It's she who wanted in your trousers, not the other way around, eh?"

Thom tightened his jaw, unease building in his gut. "That isn't why she protected me," he said. "Ilain made her accusation out of grief, and Brea denied it."

"Yeah, well, she would, wouldn't she?"

Thom rolled his eyes. "She doesn't want me that way," he insisted, knowing the truth but unwilling to share it.

Though he didn't understand her avoidance, Thom knew Brea couldn't have an interest in him. She was in love with someone else. Moreover, she carried that bloody purpose of hers: She'd marry a Mage whether she loved him or not because she believed in the cause of the Alliance more than her personal desires. She would selflessly wed a man she didn't love rather than be with the man of her secret affection.

Though Thom couldn't deny the strange way Ilain had thrown that nickname back in Brea's face. *"Te'caro."*

Over the last two weeks, Brea and Isla had begun to teach Thom the basics of the Schonese language. While he would not become fluent anytime soon, he already understood the basic concepts of their foreign dialect. *Mi* was self-explanatory. "Me" or "my" when directly accompanying another word. *Te* came similarly. "You" or "yours." The second part of the endearment was more challenging to decipher. Schonese depended heavily on gender, altering words based on the subject. Therefore, if Thom were to introduce Deckard in Schonese, he would say *"mi'broso,"* while he would call their sister, Meria, *"mi'brosa."*

Mi'caro. Te'caro. The gender didn't change despite its possessive link to Brea because the subject remained the same: Thom.

Of course, Thom had asked Brea what *mi'caro* meant. She'd teased him with a Schonese explanation at first, but he pressed, "In Allundan, Brea."

She leveled him with her dark stare. "You won't like it," she said.

"Doesn't matter though, does it? You're going to call me by it anyway."

Brea shrugged. "True." She'd sat forward, smirking. "It means 'little dog.'"

Thom furrowed his brow. "What, like a small dog or like a puppy?"

"I don't know the Allundan word," she said. "It's the baby dogs."

"Puppies."

"What a ridiculous word," she laughed but nodded firmly. "Puppy it is."

"You're calling me 'your puppy.'"

"Yes, because you're cute and floppy." She reached across to flip the hair from his forehead backward at the last bit.

Thom frowned in disappointment. "I don't like that."

"I warned you that you wouldn't."

In the moment, Thom had accepted it. But then Isla pointed out one of the farm dogs they passed on their journey, using it as a point of teaching for him. "We don't have dogs in Schon, just wolves, and they're called *lobis.* If the gender is known, then they're *lobo* or *loba.*"

Thom frowned and asked, "And what do you call their pups?"

"Lobites."

From that moment on, Thom knew Brea had lied to him. But he couldn't figure out why.

Thom didn't believe Ilain's declaration. Even if Brea held a foolish infatuation with him, she wasn't in love with him. *Mi'caro* was always said in a joking manner anyway. She didn't mean it, whatever its translation. But perhaps it meant more than he'd once thought. . . .

Regardless, Thom wouldn't act upon whatever interest—or lack thereof—either one of them held because he couldn't imagine a life with a woman like Brea.

For Thom was tired. Tired of fighting and striving, tired of struggling and failing. He wasn't cut out for this life of glory and grandeur. He'd already known that. And yet, he'd practically gotten himself killed trying to be the hero—trying, once again, to be his brother.

He was done pursuing the reverence of others. And he wasn't about to chase after a Warrior who was intended to rule their nation either.

Thom liked Brea and was attracted to her, but that didn't mean he wanted to be with her.

Shrugging away the irritating thoughts, Thom glanced over his shoulder toward Ilain and Vayden, riding just behind him. *Another mistake to mend,* he thought. Whether the siblings blamed him or not, it was his fault Auden was dead. If he hadn't been foolish enough to think himself capable of heroism, imagining himself strong enough to break through the enemy and get the group to safety, he wouldn't have rushed forward in the fray. He wouldn't have given Brea a reason to abandon Auden.

Just then, Evylin appeared at Thom's side, breaking into his self-pitying reverie. "You're replacing me," she said with mock offense.

"Pardon?"

Evylin smirked. "Jonn requested that you join him up front."

Thom raised his chin. "Am I in trouble?" he teased.

"The worst." She nudged his arm. "He's worried about you, which means you'll have to deal with his pestering until you convince him you're fine."

"An impossible feat."

"Allore's grace go with you."

Thom chuckled and relinquished his spot beside Rafferty to her. He guided his horse forward until he rode beside Deckard at the head of the group.

"Afternoon," Deckard greeted casually.

Thom returned the greeting and asked, "Would you like to discuss the weather? Or are we to have a heart-to-heart?"

Deckard didn't bother beating around the bush. "Evylin told me what happened after the Keep."

"Which part?" Thom asked dryly. "The almost dying part or the revelation of my undeniable magnetism?"

"All of it. I'm sorry I put you in that position."

"It seems I put myself in that position. Me and my rugged good looks."

Deckard gave him a flat, if amused, stare.

"Genuinely, Jonn, it was my fault, not yours," he said. "I was stupid, thinking I could get us out of there. I charged to the front, knowing I wasn't strong enough. I'm not magical; I'm not special. I'm just a man. And apparently, I have an even bigger hero complex than you."

"It wasn't your fault."

"You weren't there."

"No, but Evylin was." Deckard raised his brow imperiously. "And evidently, her powers let her see everything that happened during that battle."

Thom grunted.

"She told me that if you hadn't rushed forward with Auden and Brea, they would have fallen defending Rafferty, Vayden, and me."

Thom shrugged, unsure if it was true or not. His leg ached, but he ignored the dull thrumming in his knee.

"I'm fine if that's what you're after," Thom said. "Yes, nearly dying wasn't pleasant, but I've found peace with knowing that I lived. Granted, I don't intend to lead the charge next time."

Deckard offered a wry smile. "And what about the situation with Brea?"

Thom shook his head. "What situation? Ilain was off base."

"Do you know that for sure?"

"Have you met Breata Lohen?" Thom scoffed. "She's twice my age, twice my worth, and more than twice my intelligence."

"Yet, you receive all her spare attention."

Thom rolled his eyes. "Jonn, she's bored. She likes to flirt and joke around, just like Evie. It isn't serious, any of it."

"How do you know?"

"Because she told me."

Deckard raised his brow. "Did she?"

Thom hesitated. He looked over his shoulder, catching sight of Brea riding far in the back. He didn't want to break her trust, but this was his brother. And Deckard wouldn't believe him if Thom didn't tell the truth.

With a sigh, Thom turned back. "She loves someone else," he whispered. "I'm just a fun distraction while we're on the road, and she's waiting for the Alliance to arrange her marriage to some Mage."

That caused Deckard to frown.

"That's her sacrifice," Thom said. "You know how these Alliance saps are. They rather remind me of you, actually, with that 'all for king and country' nonsense."

Deckard gave him a perturbed look.

Thom eased his humor to warn, "She told me in confidence, though, so maybe don't let her know I said anything."

Deckard's expression softened, understanding dawning in his eyes. "That's why she won't defend herself against Ilain's accusation. She doesn't want anyone to know."

Thom's lips lifted in a wry grin. "Fantastic, isn't it? I finally find a woman who actually enjoys my company, and she's already taken."

Deckard cast him a disapproving look. "She's twice your age," he reiterated.

"It's a joke, Jonn. I'm not interested in magical sorts. It's a recipe for heartbreak." Thom smirked, hoping to lighten the mood. "To be honest, I'm considering writing to Evie's sister. You know, the one with those curls and the pink dresses."

"Calyn?"

"That's the one. She was quite pretty."

"She was childish."

"No more than me."

Deckard shook his head. "You wouldn't be happy with her."

"Why not?"

"She's too . . ." Deckard paused, and Thom knew he was searching for a polite description. "She isn't serious enough for you. Besides, I don't think she'd want to leave her village."

Thom waggled his brow suggestively, giving his best Rafferty impression. "I bet I could convince her."

"Why would you want to?"

Thom sighed. "Because I'm tired, Jonn. I'm twenty-eight years old, and I'm alone. Our world is about to change, and if, by some miracle, I make it through alive, I don't want to return to who I was. I'm not a Mage or a Warrior. I'm a man. And I can accept that now."

Deckard studied him warily. "That doesn't mean you have to marry a woman you don't love."

"You married a woman you didn't love," Thom countered. "And look how well that turned out."

Deckard pressed his lips together, considering. "You're right."

"Of course I am. I'm bloody wise, I'll have you know."

"But," Deckard raised his brow, "you still shouldn't marry Calyn."

"Why shouldn't I?"

"Because I'm already your brother once," he teased. "I don't care to be your brother a second time."

Thom chuckled. "Maybe I'll seek out one of your old sweethearts, then. The last one was pretty and had a tolerable personality. Helena, right?"

"You wouldn't like her."

"No?"

"Too religious," he remarked. "Even if I'd *tried* to kiss her, she would have slapped me across the face."

Thom scowled dramatically. "No, that won't do at all. She'd never put up with my debauchery." He snapped his fingers then. "Say, I heard Ethenn mention a sister the other day. Maybe I'll see if she's available. Surely, with his pretty face, she's got to be a looker."

"Ah, yes, imagine the pleasant Annaltide feasts you'd share. You'd have to let Ethenn carve the roast, of course. He will be king, I hear."

"Highlord Commander, I believe," Thom corrected. "But no, you have a point. I don't think I'd like being related to Ilain, by marriage or not. Might make things awkward knowing I'd once flirted with my sister-in-law."

"You've already flirted with your sister-in-law."

Thom grimaced. "I'd rather not go for the set."

They rode in pleasant silence for a few moments. Then Deckard turned to him again. "You're worth more than that, Thom," he said.

Thom blinked, confused.

"You shouldn't seek marriage to quell your loneliness any more than you should seek obscurity to mask your fear of responsibility." Deckard held his gaze, brotherly affection bright within. "You are worth so much more."

Uncertain, Thom dipped his chin. He wanted to believe his brother, but he couldn't. Because if he *was* more, then that meant he had to *be* more. And he was growing weary of trying to measure up to the high expectations of himself and others.

"I don't want to be more, Jonn," he said. "I just want to be me."

Deckard's whole countenance softened. His eyes dimmed, and his lips turned down. "What if they're the same thing?" he asked.

That possibility Thom hadn't considered.

With a reluctant grin, he replied, "Then don't tell me. After nearly losing my guts and bleeding out on the Space Keep's floor, I'm about ready to live in blissful ignorance."

Deckard chuckled lightly and reached over to clasp his shoulder. They shared a smile and a long look before turning back to the road. A cool spring breeze swept through, rattling the lush tree branches. A hawk sailed overhead, seeking mice in the vast fields around them. To the west lay the mountains they left behind, and to the southeast awaited the forests and, beyond them, the Shires.

They were returning to the very beginning of their journey, and Thom couldn't help hoping it was symbolic.

After making so many mistakes and experiencing so much loss, he needed a fresh start. He wanted to begin again. And more than anything, he wished to be enough—not as a hero, not as a soldier. He simply desired to be a man. Whatever that meant for his purpose in life, he didn't know.

Thom turned to Deckard. "Do you think I could talk to Hewitt tonight?"

"Of course." Deckard smiled. "Though I'll need the Night Relic returned to manage it."

"With pleasure." Thom tugged at his collar, where the Relic hung concealed. "This bloody thing is rubbing my neck raw."

Though Thom wasn't sure what he hoped Hewitt would tell him, he needed the man's advice. Only days ago, he thought he could spend his life in service to Deckard and Evylin. Now, he worried that he'd never be enough for them. Deckard had fallen to Space, and Thom had been unable to do anything. He'd tried to get Evylin to safety, and he'd practically left her to die alongside himself.

Whatever his purpose, Thom needed help finding it. Because if it was left up to him, he feared that next time, his delusion would get them all killed.

CHAPTER THIRTY-EIGHT

Given how long it took to get to Bewold, there was no time for training that night.

Having lost two days due to their time in Loclight, the troop had to move with urgency to reach the Terrae Keep before Blount. However, they all agreed they couldn't push so hard as to wear down the horses, which they couldn't afford to replace regularly, nor themselves.

With the final Keep and the confrontation with Blount looming in their future, they need to arrive with full strength, prepared to take on the Night Mage. Even if Blount beat them to the Relic, they all needed to continue their training, magical and otherwise, to ensure their success against the prince. And if his dream and the constant luring pulse of Space from the Relic around Evylin's neck were any indication, Deckard needed that training more desperately than them all.

The village of Bewold was reasonably sized, larger than both Stocburrough and Whickam Village. As one of the few waypoints to and from the capital city, it boasted three separate taverns that doubled as inns. This provided them with the extra rooms they needed, and they reserved one for each couple, one for Thom and Rafferty, and one for Brea alone. She insisted on paying for her room, and Deckard allowed it, but he carefully observed the location of the room the barkeep assigned to her.

Despite the late hour, there were many patrons in the tavern. Ilain was clearly too emotionally run down to sit among the loud chatter, so she and Ethenn ordered their meals and left to eat in their room. Rafferty found a table big enough for the seven remaining members of their party near the back of the room, but Brea slipped away, choosing isolation as well.

Deckard watched her go but said nothing.

And thus it was that the four Ephrians and two Calders ate their hearty beef, potato, and rutabaga stew with a semblance of quiet comfort. Their corner table gave them distance from the rest of the patrons. An oil lamp flickered overhead, its flame glinting off their glazed ceramic tankards.

"How're you holding up there, Vaydy?" Rafferty asked, his signature flippancy softened by the genuine concern in his tone.

Vayden took a deep breath as he stared into his stew. "As well as can be expected when one loses their brother, I suppose," he said. "It's hard, but . . . I don't feel it the same way Ilain does. I'd rather be among people and remember what Auden died for than process my grief in solitude."

Deckard's stomach twisted, the beef sitting heavily. "If there's any way we can be of service, let us know," he offered.

Vayden gave an appreciative smile but said nothing more. At his side, Isla squeezed his forearm in support. The couple had always bemused Deckard. Despite Isla's youthful appearance, he couldn't fathom having a wife so much his senior. It rankled against his sensibilities. There was enough disparity between being a man and a woman; wouldn't a great gap in age make it even more difficult? Though he supposed many men married women twenty years their junior, and that didn't often bother him. To take issue with the woman's maturity was hypocritical.

"So," Rafferty said, turning to Deckard and breaking into his wandering thoughts, "how'd you manage to teleport?"

Everyone paused, spoons raised, looking at Deckard.

He shifted uncomfortably in his wooden chair. "I don't know," was his placid answer as he returned to his stew.

Evylin's hand brushed his under the table. It sent a thrill of magic through his veins, and he fought the urge to flinch as Space took the opportunity to whisper in his mind.

"Well, however you managed it," Rafferty continued, "it was bloody incredible."

Thom gave a wry grin while Evylin chuckled softly. Wishing to avoid the topic, Deckard shoveled another spoonful of meat and potato into his mouth.

Isla leaned forward with curiosity. Though it was clear that she, too, was mourning, her grief had proved far more tempered. It was almost as though her additional years had helped mature her control over her emotions. "You don't know how you did it?" she prompted.

Deckard gave her a quick, apologetic glance. "No."

Her dark eyes narrowed. "You just came up with it on your own?"

Realizing that she wouldn't let it go and, if nothing else, her question presented an opportunity to learn more control of his magic, Deckard replied, "No, I was flipping through one of Lord Obel's books, and I saw it referenced."

"You studied it?"

He shook his head. "I didn't have time."

"You didn't read it?"

"Only the header."

Isla's brow rose, and Vayden let out a low curse.

"What?" Evylin asked, concern clouding her energy. "Is that bad?"

After a mumbled string of Schonese, Isla said, "It is not bad. It is strange." She met Deckard's gaze. "Jonn, you managed to accomplish a magical feat that would take other Mages years of study to fully comprehend. Off a header."

Too afraid to do much else, Deckard stared back at her.

"You connected with Space in a way that is so intimate that it did exactly what you wanted without any effort on your part." Isla shrugged. "That's good. And it's bad. Your connection to Space is strong, but you've proved to have no control over the amount of power flowing through you."

The way each member of the group looked at Deckard made it clear they were either worried or mystified by him. He fought not to slump under the weight of their inspection. He was a danger to their party; it was becoming clearer by the day. Not only had he gotten Auden killed, but if he didn't get his magic under control, next time, he might kill them all too.

"Excellent choice of conversation, Raff," chided Thom lightly.

Rafferty huffed. "How was I supposed to know it was a touchy subject? I'm bored. While the interpersonal conflicts of the lot of you are generally entertaining, we're going through a bit of a crisis, if you hadn't noticed, Thommy. Who am I supposed to poke fun at when Loxley's off consoling his highlady, eh? Brea's not even here for me to tease about her love for you."

Isla and Vayden exchanged looks while Thom kicked Rafferty's shin under the table.

"I told you," Thom said sharply, "Ilain was mistaken."

While his brother took a long swig of ale, Deckard continued to study Isla and Vayden. They kept their attention conspicuously on their meals. He murmured something in Schonese, to which she snorted in quiet amusement.

"Fine, then. Here's a less touchy topic: What do you think?" Rafferty began. "Will Lox and Lain's wee bairns be dark like him, or will they come out freckle-faced and red as a tomato?"

Thom scowled dramatically. "I don't want to think about that."

Evylin propped her arms on the table, intrigued by the idea. "Actually, I know this answer. My eldest sister, Euna, looks most like my father, with a lighter complexion and bright green eyes. Even her hair is more of a golden brown than dark, like mine or the rest of my sisters. But her husband, Druan, is dark-skinned with black hair and deep brown eyes. They had four daughters, and Euna was with child before he was drafted; all their girls look far more like Druan with brown complexions and dark hair, despite Euna's fairness. My mother said that's because the darker colorings are the dominant trait," she said, then gestured to Vayden and Isla. "Think of Reyana. She's paler than Isla, but otherwise, she more closely resembles her mother."

"I am Schonese," Isla reminded. "Our features are more pronounced. However, it is unlikely that Ilain would have redheaded children due to the strength of Ethenn's complexion and coloring."

Evylin lifted her brows in Rafferty's direction to prove her point, and he rolled his eyes.

Deckard appreciated the weasel guiding the lighthearted conversation, letting it wind into silly debates about genealogy and questions about Isla's heritage and family in Schon. It allowed him to process his weighty thoughts while his comrades were distracted. Even when Rafferty made a point of teasing that Deckard's own children were bound to come out ruddy and paler than snow, he stuck to his wandering thoughts. He had too many things to figure out and too many responsibilities to ponder to engage in casual banter. And that ominous murmur of Space still thrummed in his ears, making every thought harder to control.

Let me out.

When they finished their meal, Vayden and Isla departed. Deckard rose as well, telling Thom to join Evylin and meet him back at their room in half an hour. Then they could talk with Hewitt. "I have to take care of something first," he said, excusing himself.

Though Evylin's gaze questioned him, she let him go, remaining at the table with Rafferty and Thom.

Climbing the rickety staircase and striding down the dimly lit halls, Deckard wound his way to the back of the second floor. He scanned the wooden doors, noting the numbered plaques hanging from each doorknob. When he reached room thirteen, he knocked.

The door opened a fraction before it swung wide. "I wondered when you'd come to see me," Brea said by way of greeting. She gestured for Deckard to enter, then shut the door behind him.

"You expected me?" he asked.

Taking a seat on one of the two single beds in the room, Brea crossed her arms. "I have no designs on your brother," she said flatly. "You need not worry."

A small smile lifted the corner of Deckard's lips. "You're rather blunt."

"I see no reason to mince words. It would be a waste of both our time."

Brea's dark gaze held his with a forthrightness, and he had to admit she was beautiful in an intimidating way. In addition, she had a confidence that few other women carried. Deckard could understand the appeal, though he couldn't help but notice the underlying hardness in the woman's bearing.

Deckard leaned against the footboard of the bed opposite Brea. "That's not why I'm here," he said.

A cynical smirk filled her expression. "No," she agreed. "You're here to do your duty as a commanding officer."

"I thought you'd understand."

"I'm a soldier, Colonel. I recognize a censure when I receive one."

Deckard cocked his head. "This isn't a censure," he said. "I merely wish to understand your side of the events in the Keep."

Brea lifted her chin, taking a slow inhale. "It's rather straightforward," she said. "I saw Captain Deckard fall with a mortal injury, and I did what any fellow soldier would: I went to his aid. I pulled him from danger as best I could, but he was worse off than anticipated. In defending him, I was forced to leave my other comrade unaided. Auden died because I was unable to be in two places at once. An unavoidable fault, not an intentional abandonment."

Deckard nodded. "As I thought."

"Ilain does not see it that way," Brea continued as though he hadn't spoken. "She will not accept it. No matter what I say, she will take this as an affront to her and her family. In her eyes, I betrayed Auden."

"She's grieving," Deckard said. "The wound is fresh, but Ilain is not unreasonable. She will come to understand the truth in time."

Her smile grew hard. "No, she won't," she said with surety. "But that's just fine. Ilain and I don't have to get along. We just have to work together. And you can trust that I will do my job, Colonel, no matter the personal conflicts I face."

Deckard believed her. Though he disagreed—he did think Ilain would come to see reason—he accepted that Brea would follow through with her job on this mission to the fullest extent of her ability.

However, there was one matter yet unresolved.

"Why are you avoiding Thom?" he asked.

Brea didn't so much as flinch. "Because it's better this way."

"I fail to see the logic in that."

"I don't need friendship to get a job done," Brea said. "And if I'm going to be accused of romantic inclinations every time that I save someone's life at the expense of another's, then I'd like to protect myself from foolish and petty accusations. Whatever Ilain or anyone else thinks of me, I do not love your brother. I chose to save his life because that is who I am—a protector. I would have done the same for you, for Vayden, for Ilain, and indeed for any of our party. It has nothing to do with emotion or infatuation. And I don't care to be condemned for my actions."

Deckard held Brea's stare through her explanation. He watched her, looking for any sign of emotion or falsehood. Yet, he found none.

"I appreciate your candor," Deckard said, straightening away from the footboard. "But I would request you find a way to be amicable at the very least. It makes life awkward otherwise."

Brea gave him a dutiful nod.

He moved for the door, placing his hand on the brass knob. "One more thing," he said.

She lifted her brow, attentively listening.

"I don't believe you," he said.

Brea's shoulders tensed, but it was the flicker of fear that passed through her dark eyes that truly gave her away. "Pardon?" she said, the mask of her typical stoicism slipping quickly into place.

Deckard pressed his lips together. "You watch him too carefully," he said. "You smile at him too easily. And you speak that pet name of yours too fondly."

Her fingers tightened on her arm, resting folded in her lap.

"You may not love my brother," Deckard concluded, "but you do have feelings for him. And I would advise you to quell them. For his sake."

Brea didn't reply. Instead, she sat upon the bed, fierce gaze locked with Deckard's. Her expression was stolid and unreadable. With her dark skin, dark hair, and dark clothing, she looked like a raven tucked among the mundanity of furnishings and linens.

"Goodnight, Lieutenant," Deckard said, then exited the room.

CHAPTER THIRTY-NINE

While her husband went off to handle whatever task was on his mind, Evylin and Thom remained at the table with Rafferty. The conversation remained casual, helping distract them from the weight of the past two days. Evylin felt strangely sensitive to Auden's death, having gone through a similar experience to Ilain and Vayden's grief two months ago.

The knowledge of Hewitt's impending release didn't help matters.

After some time, Thom nudged Evylin, informing her that the thirty minutes Deckard had asked them to wait had expired. Leaving Rafferty behind, they headed up the staircase and down the simple, clean hall to her and Deckard's room. He was already inside when they entered, reading one of the books Obel had given him.

"Were you just reading this whole time?" Thom asked.

Deckard shook his head. "I had a conversation with Brea first."

"Oh." Thom shut the door behind him, his movements suddenly stiff. "Did that, uh . . . go well?"

Evylin shared a knowing look with Deckard. She removed her coat while he replied, "It did. Now," he closed his book, "sit down, and we'll have a talk with Hewitt."

Doing as ordered, Thom sat in the upholstered chair tucked into the corner. Evylin perched next to Deckard on the edge of the mattress. And not a moment later, Hewitt was there, standing amidst the furnishings and papered walls.

His bushy eyebrows rose as he took in the three of them. "How long has it been this time?" he asked, voice a low rumble.

"What do you mean?" Deckard asked.

"Well, time's different over here," he explained. "I can't tell how many days it's been, but this stint was longer than the last."

"Over there?" Thom repeated curiously. "What exactly is it like . . . wherever you are?"

Hewitt looked to a vacant corner in thought. "Empty. It isn't a place so much as a shadow. There's no time, no use of the senses, no nothing. I'm just waiting."

"That sounds horrible," Evylin whispered. She couldn't fathom being left so isolated and cut off from the world. It made her want to cling to her uncle and never let him return to that awful place.

Casually, Hewitt shrugged. "It isn't so bad. It gives me space to rest and think. And as I said, I can't tell how many hours or days pass between our meetings, so I don't mind."

"I'm sorry to leave you there, in any case," Deckard said. "As it is, only three days have passed this time. However . . ."

Hewitt narrowed his eyes, catching the heavy tone. "I miss all the fun," he commented dryly. "What catastrophe are you to recount today?"

Evylin and Thom let Deckard explain while they each gave context or clarification to the moments he missed. He took the blame for Auden's death, to which Thom argued that *he* was truly at fault. Evylin reminded them both that no one was Auden's killer. He'd died because they were all risking their lives. Any one of them could have been sucked into that infinite void.

When Deckard insisted that improved control over his magic would have kept them from the predicament altogether, she had no logical arguments left.

Hewitt stroked his beard thoughtfully. "You can't control it at all?" he asked.

Deckard shrugged. "Sometimes, it seems that I can, but in that Keep . . ." He cast a sidelong glance at Evylin. "It drew on my power, just like the Relic she wears does now. I *want* to access it, to let it consume me again. And it takes great effort to resist."

"What do the Mages think of this?"

"They don't seem overly concerned. Though I don't understand why. I'm a danger," he said. "To all of us."

Evylin frowned, saddened to hear his true opinion of his power.

However, Hewitt only let out a grunt. "When will you learn to stop taking responsibility for all of Terraeus?" he said, and Thom smirked. "I told you at my grave: Stop blaming yourself for other people's choices."

"That isn't exactly relevant when it's *my* powers that are causing the problems," Deckard returned in agitation.

Knowing that arguing would resolve nothing, Evylin spoke up. "We have other issues to discuss," she said. The men acquiesced to her. "First, I believe Thom has something he wants to ask you."

Thom straightened then. "Yes," he said. "I was hoping . . . When we spoke before, you told me to find a purpose. I thought I had done so by protecting Deckard and Evie and helping them find happiness."

Evylin and Deckard shared a soft, bemused look.

"But now," Thom continued, "I realize I'm not qualified for the job. And I'm more likely to get myself killed trying." He took a deep breath. "So now I need a new purpose."

"And you want me to give one to you?" Hewitt surmised.

Thom ran a hand through his hair. "I want you to advise me. How do I find what I'm meant to do with my life?"

"Generally," Hewitt replied, "it finds you."

"That's not helpful."

Evylin chuckled as the slightest grin tugged on her uncle's lips. "What do you *want* to do, Thom?" he asked rhetorically. "How do you best want to serve this world? Answer *that* question, and you'll find your purpose."

Thom frowned, his thoughts visibly turning, but nodded. "Thanks," he murmured.

Hewitt returned the nod, then faced Evylin. "What else would you like to discuss?" he asked.

She took a deep breath. "We're on our way to Estshire," she said. "Which means we're less than a week from your graveside."

"Which means," he concluded, "that we have less than a week left together."

"Yes."

"We ought to make the most of it, then."

Deckard's hand brushed Evylin's arm, and she felt his fingers twitch, resting on her arm more loosely than normal. "As we'll be staying in inns along the way, I'll have to include you after dinner exclusively. I can't keep you summoned while I'm training, and keeping you visible during travel is too taxing. Which likely means you'll only be seeing the three of us most nights."

"You're the only ones I care to see anyway."

They fell into other, easier topics. They discussed Deckard's surprising new powers as well as Evylin's discovery in the Keep. "I don't know how," she said, "but I managed to tap into Jonn's power. With the Relic's help, I summoned the same onyx crystals to defend me. It wasn't quite the same, but . . ."

"It was Space magic," Thom confirmed.

"That's surprising," Hewitt remarked. "Though not unwelcome."

Deckard drew a hand along his jaw. "Is that supposed to happen?" he asked.

Evylin shrugged. "I know as much about Bonding as you," she said. But her thoughts drifted back to the book Ilain had given her about the union of Warrior and Mage. She wondered if it explained the phenomenon. Was accessing your partner's power expected of a Bonded couple? Suddenly, she felt careless for neglecting her studies.

After more than an hour of conversation, Thom departed. Hewitt said his goodnights, and Deckard released him back into the shadow wherein he would linger until summoned again. Suddenly, the room felt empty and quiet without the other men present. Deckard drifted across the room to where the saddlebags rested on the chest of drawers, his mood contemplative and somber.

Evylin knew he was uncomfortable with her choice to keep the Space Relic on her person. Ever since the morning, she'd noticed how he kept his distance. It felt wrong, this new chasm between them. She understood that it wasn't a rejection of her—he was afraid of giving in to the pull of Space. Yet, it *felt* like a rejection.

Evylin had chosen to keep the Relic because she knew it would be best for Deckard. He needed to face this fear, to come to a place of peace with his magic despite how much he wished to be rid of it. And she knew that no matter how subconscious it was, if Deckard kept pulling away from her because of the Relic, he would eventually grow to resent her choice to carry it.

They readied for bed in tense silence. Deckard was pointedly careful not to touch her as they stood side by side at the drawers, changing into their nightclothes. After brushing out her hair, Evylin replaced the brush in her saddlebag, her fingers brushing the leather spine of the thin Bonding book still within.

At her side, Deckard methodically set out his clothes for the morning. Evylin watched him in her peripheral vision and withdrew the book. She passed her fingers over the embossed title. Guilt gnawed at her, reminding her that they *all* had reason to blame themselves for a part in Auden's death. If she had studied this book, perhaps she could have helped prevent Deckard's lapse in control.

"Jonn?" she whispered, eyes on the cover.

He turned, folding his trousers. "Yes?"

Evylin moved to sit on the bed, letting a deep sigh escape her. "I have a confession."

He raised his brow.

Evylin bit her lip and held out the book. "Ilain gave this to me," she explained, "when we Bonded. She told me that it was important. Yet, I've not read it."

Carefully, Deckard stacked the trousers beneath his shirt and coat for the morning, then accepted the book. He examined its cover. *"Attachments of the Soul,"* he read aloud. "Why haven't you read it?"

Evylin grimaced. "It isn't my kind of book."

"It's nonfictional, then," he remarked with amusement, thumbing the pages. "The print is quite small."

"And it's laborious writing."

"Mm." He met her gaze. "Are you asking me to read it?"

"No—I mean—" Evylin sighed again. "Ilain told me we *both* need to read it, so yes, I suppose in a way I am, but . . . it's more that I'm asking that you *help* me read it. I struggle to pay attention, but I believe it could help us. So I want to give it a try."

Deckard smiled and handed the book back to her. "In that case," he turned to the bed, pulled back the covers, adjusted the pillow, and sat down, "come here."

Evylin raised her brow but obeyed, crawling over the blankets. "Are we to snuggle?" she teased.

"It will likely make the process easier," he said, settling against the pillows. However, when Evylin joined him beneath the covers, she noticed that his frame immediately tightened at her nearness.

Evylin tried not to be disheartened.

Deckard cleared his throat and held a hand out for the book once more. "Let's read it together," he suggested.

"Are you going to tutor me?"

He chuckled tightly. "Should you like me to?"

Evylin lifted his arm to drape over her shoulders. She kissed his jaw, noting how sternly it was clamped shut. "Help me understand, husband," she quipped.

Despite his tension, Deckard's smile was genuine. He shook his head in amusement and opened the book. "In attaching the souls and creating a Bond," he began, "we find Allore's reflection in creation."

Deckard's warm voice swept over Evylin, and contentment built within her. He read the first paragraph, then stopped to consider it before restating it in his own words. At first, Evylin thought he was just doing it for her, but when he lamented not having a notebook to write out his thoughts, she realized reiterating the text was a means of understanding it better himself.

They didn't read long, and Deckard remained tense for the entirety of it, but even as Evylin began to drift off while he read, she felt they'd made a reasonable effort. She already understood better than before. And together, she knew, they would glean all the information this burdensome book offered. Their Bond would be stronger than ever, and she would find a way to help Deckard control his magic.

And as they settled in to sleep in one another's arms, Evylin whispered her promise once more, "I will not let you fail, my love."

Deckard pressed his forehead against hers. His muscles were still tight and rigid, and she could tell he was fighting the urges within him. But a gentle wash of love swept between them as he replied, "I know."

CHAPTER FORTY

12TH OF RADIA, 1574

The past forty-eight hours had worn immensely on Ethenn. He was proud of himself for withholding his emotions. Through every moment, he'd been present for Ilain, offering her support no matter how ready he was to collapse and break apart himself.

Of course, he didn't grieve like she did. He'd hardly considered Auden a friend, let alone a brother. The Day Mage's missing presence was oddly draining, but he didn't *feel* the loss.

No, it wasn't mourning that caused Ethenn such internal discomfort. It was the memories that formed the agitation currently rising in his chest like a burr under a saddle.

Ethenn shut them out as best he could, only accessing what personal experience he possessed as a means of helping Ilain through these first unbearable days. He knew the pain of loss just as he knew that the best way to get through it was not to coddle or smother her with care. Ilain didn't need him to babysit her. She needed him to trust her, support her, and let her live.

As the sun faded to a yellow-orange glow on the horizon, they neared the town of Kesgrave. They pulled to an early stop by a grove of trees. The settlement's buildings awaited them down the road, shops and homes all clustered together. He eyed them longingly. Ethenn was weary of constant travel. He'd grown up going on long trips through the forest, but none of them had lasted for over three months. After his time with the Third Volunteer Company and then joining the mission for the Alliance, he was ready for an extended stay in one place.

"We'll stop here for training," Deckard announced, and Ilain shifted in her saddle beside Ethenn. "Thom, Rafferty, and Vayden, you can spar together, then go into town early to get us a place."

The three men nodded, dismounting to lead their horses into the trees.

Deckard continued giving his orders. "Ilain and Isla, I'll need your help while Brea continues to train Evylin and Ethenn."

"No," Ilain said flatly.

Everyone turned to her in surprise. At the edge of the woods, Vayden looked back, his brow furrowed. "Lainy—"

"No," she repeated, facing him this time.

"I'm sorry," Deckard said, leaning toward Ilain with a confused expression. "I don't understand what the problem is."

Ilain turned back to Deckard with an imperious stare, and Ethenn's jaw tensed, somehow already knowing what was coming. "Ethenn will not be training with Breata anymore," she stated firmly.

Grinding his teeth, Ethenn fought the urge to snap at her. It was ridiculous. It was childish. It was petty. Of course, he was going to train with Brea. He didn't have a choice. If he wanted to be a better Warrior—one who could defend Ilain and become the man that she needed by her side—then he *had* to train.

But he shoved down his rising anger, even as the heat crept along his spine. "Ilain," he said softly, "my training is necessary."

"I don't disagree," Ilain said. "That doesn't mean you have to train with her."

A scoff slipped out of him. "Who would you like to train me?"

"Evylin was doing a splendid job of it a few weeks ago."

"It wasn't enough."

The troop watched them, frozen in silence, eyes darting between the couple. Ethenn's neck grew hotter. Ilain's expression grew harder.

"We'll discuss this later," he said, preparing to dismount and follow Evylin and Brea into the woods.

Ilain's hand snapped out and clutched his wrist. "We'll discuss it now."

A long, painful silence stretched.

Thom cleared his throat and gave Deckard a pointed look. With a sigh, Deckard nodded, and Thom tugged Rafferty with him into the trees. Vayden met Isla's stare, looked between Ilain and Ethenn, and then he departed too.

"Evylin, Brea, go ahead," Deckard said. "Isla, if you don't mind. . . ."

"Not at all," Isla replied, but she urged her horse to Ilain's side. She whispered something in Schonese. Ilain pursed her lips, and then Isla followed Deckard farther down the road to where the trees thickened in the distance.

Effectively alone, Ethenn held Ilain's challenging gaze, fighting the anger rising within. She was no fool. She knew better than to set out ridiculous ultimatums like this. So why behave so irrationally? Mourning didn't excuse idiocy.

"Shall we take this somewhere more private?" Ilain asked. "Or are we to have this conversation by the road?"

Without a word, Ethenn turned his horse toward the town. If he was going to miss training, he may as well do something useful with his time.

Leading her into Kesgrave, they wound their way through the narrow streets in silence. A large market filled the town center. The populace was comprised mostly of women closing up shop for the day. It was easy to find the inn, a squat but large building with colorful bunting hanging around its entrance. They stabled their horses, paid an urchin to keep an eye out for their friends, and entered the inn.

Ethenn secured their rooms for the night and declined the dinner the barkeep offered, stating that they'd wait for the rest of their party's arrival. With that, he took Ilain's hand and pulled her to the back of the inn, where their room awaited.

Once they were inside, and the door was shut, Ethenn turned to glare at his wife. She wore an indifferent expression as she took in his tense demeanor.

"Are you going to chastise me, husband?" she asked with a snide tilt to her voice.

"Why do you do that?" he said bluntly.

Her brow furrowed, and for a moment, he saw her guard slip. "Do what?"

"Pretend to be petty and illogical," he said. "You're not an idiot, Ilain. You know I need to train, and you know Brea is the only one who can do it. So why act like an unreasonable child?"

Ilain's lips parted in shock. "You're rather testy today."

"And you're pushing my patience," he said. "Why?"

She crossed her arms, the fabric of her dress rustling with the movement. "I just lost my brother—my closest friend—if you've failed to remember."

"Of course I haven't."

"Yet, you ask me to be reasonable in my time of grief."

Ethenn pushed away from the door. His chest was beginning to burn, so he unbuttoned his coat, looking for some relief from the sensation. "You were reasonable the morning after his death," he said, keeping his gaze averted. "You were reasonable when you healed Thom. Why shouldn't I expect you to behave the same way now?"

"She's the reason he's dead," Ilain spat. "Why is it so much to ask that you reject her the same as I?"

"Because she didn't have a choice," Ethenn returned, fully shrugging off his coat. He turned back to her. "As *I* don't have a choice. I either train with Brea or I don't train at all. Do you want that?"

Ilain didn't hesitate. "Yes."

Ethenn gaped at her, incredulous. "How can you be so irrational?"

"How can *you* not see that I'm mourning?" Ilain demanded. "That this is my greatest fear come to life?"

Ethenn's shoulders slumped, and he pinched the bridge of his nose. The truth was, he did see those things. It hurt him to see her in such deep pain. But the world didn't stop, no matter how much life took from you. He'd learned that the hard way.

"What do you want me to do, Ethenn?" Ilain demanded in his silence. "I am working to hold it together. I am trying to be 'rational.' But when I look at her, I see my brother ripped apart in front of my eyes. How am I supposed to feel about that?"

Ethenn didn't have an answer.

Ilain took a step closer, pressing her hands to her chest. "I don't want you to be around her because I don't trust her. Can't you understand that?"

"No," Ethenn admitted. "No, I can't. She didn't intentionally kill him. You have to see that."

"I don't."

"You refuse to acknowledge it is what you mean," he corrected, the heat climbing up to the base of his skull. "Ilain, I understand that it's difficult for you. But you know— you *know* that I need training. You fear losing those you love, but what about me? What about what I fear?"

She stared at him, uncomprehending.

Ethenn grabbed her arms, holding her gaze. "If I don't get stronger—if I don't become a better Warrior—it might be me who fails next time. What if my lack of training causes Vayden to lose his life? Even worse, what if my failure costs me you?"

Her lips pressed together at his argument.

"I *have* to train, Ilain," he insisted. "And that means it has to be with Brea."

"No." She shoved his hands away, pulling out of his grip. "You can train with Evylin—with Thom and Rafferty. You don't have to work with her."

Ethenn's hands balled into fists. He fought back a growl of frustration, yet his next words slipped out unbidden. "Why are you being so deliberately illogical?"

The curl of Ilain's lips showed her building rage. "I'm sorry that my grief makes me so illogical, darling. Would you like me to pretend that everything is all just fine? Perhaps I should forget the heartache of my loss."

Ethenn threw his hands in the air, the heat blazing in his cheeks. "We've all lost someone, Ilain. Shall the rest of us join you in your madness? Or are you to be the only one who gets to fall into delusion while we poor saps are resigned to reality?"

Ilain froze, mouth agape at his outburst.

Realizing the harshness of his words and the aggression in his tone, Ethenn sighed. He'd gone too far, letting his emotions get the better of him. This was why he was so careful with his feelings. If his heart wasn't involved, if he locked it away, he couldn't get angry. He couldn't hurt someone.

Ethenn opened his mouth to apologize, but Ilain drew back, her composure regained as she studied him. Her jade green gaze bore a sly glint, and suddenly, he realized what he'd confessed.

"Who did you lose?" Ilain asked.

Ethenn's throat burned, and his heart stopped. "No one."

Ilain's eyes narrowed. "You just said you did."

"I meant—" Ethenn fumbled, working for an excuse. "That's not—"

He stepped back as Ilain moved in closer. "Who did you lose, Ethenn?" she demanded.

A tremble worked through his muscles. He didn't want to speak, didn't want to give voice to the memories. Yet, the determination in Ilain's gaze told him she wouldn't take no for an answer.

"Which time?" he said quietly.

Ilain's face fell. "Oh, Ethenn," she whispered.

He began to shake his head, backing away, but she reached out, grabbing the edge of his open collar. Her expression softened, and she stepped up before him, the nearness of her muddling his thoughts. "Tell me," she pleaded.

Rejecting the pain the memories of the past brought, Ethenn spoke with rote blandness, like he was giving directions rather than recounting the worst days of his life. "My father died when I was eleven in a hunting accident. Five months later, my mother grew ill. She passed while I was away on a hunting trip."

Ilain stared up at him. "You lost both your parents before you were twelve?"

"I turned twelve two months after my father's death, actually."

Compassion drew Ilain's features downward as she frowned. "Oh, Ethenn," she whispered again. Then she cupped his face. Her hands were cold on his cheeks, soothing the heat that burned under the surface. Gently, she pressed her lips to his. He leaned into the caress, the familiar magic spiking within him. Coolness tingled across his skin, causing the flames of his anger to recede as a swell of desire rose in its wake.

Ready to relinquish himself to the soothing torrent of her touch, Ethenn fought his disappointment when she pulled back before the kiss ever really began. His heart thrummed in his ears, whispering lies that his qualms didn't matter; he could lose his whole heart and soul to her. Why should he hold himself back when she was his wife?

After their kiss in the tavern, Ethenn hadn't had the gumption to take another. He knew it would exert this same insatiable effect on him. One caress wasn't enough. He craved her, his skin tingling under her touch. The heat rose along his scalp, urging him to kiss her again.

The reaction startled him, and yet he longed to give in to it.

Ilain brushed a few locks of hair from Ethenn's forehead, her verdant gaze searching his face. "What were they like?" she asked.

He fought the urge to clench his jaw against the memory of his parents. "Good," he said without emotion. Ilain was about to press for more, but he clutched onto her arms, stopping her. "And I don't want to talk about it."

He could read the disappointment on her face. "Why don't you trust me?" she asked.

"For the same reason you don't trust me," he replied.

She didn't bother denying it. A gentleness came into her gaze. "Could I persuade you to?" she asked, running her hands over his chest.

Ethenn's shoulders stiffened as she drew closer. "Not that way," he said.

A shadow crossed her expression for a moment. Then she chuckled. "I'm not trying to seduce you," she promised. "I'm merely comforting you."

"I'm not the one who needs comforting."

"You're a bloody orphan," she teased. "They always need comforting."

Ethenn couldn't help his amused grin. "That's quite insensitive."

"I'm not known for empathy."

Without his consent, his hands found their way to her waist. "And I'm not known for my openness."

"How's this, then?" She tugged on his shirt, pulling him toward the bed with her. She sat on the edge, gripping his hands. "You said to tell you when I needed something. Well, this is what I need, Ethenn. I want you to distract me."

Ethenn grimaced. "By telling you about my parents?"

She shook her head, staring up into his eyes. "By telling me about yourself," she said, patting the mattress beside her.

Ethenn stared at the pattern on the worn brown quilt. "Ilain—"

"Ethenn," she interrupted.

He met her gaze, seeing the mix of hope, fear, and sorrow within.

"Please."

Taking the seat she'd offered, Ethenn sucked in a deep breath. Could he do this? She needed help; that much was clear—a distraction to keep her mind off her loss. But if he opened up about his past, that would mean reliving everything, *revealing* everything. And he wasn't sure he could do that.

Ilain's fingers brushed his on the bed between them. She looped her forefinger around his, gently prodding him to speak.

Turning to her, Ethenn made his decision. "I'll make a deal with you, Ilain."

"What's that?"

"I'll answer one question with total honesty," he said. "Then you'll never ask about my past again."

Her eyes narrowed. "That's not much of a distraction."

"I wasn't finished."

She nodded for him to go on.

"One question, one honest answer," he said, then swallowed down the last of his fear and added, "And I'll kiss you."

Ilain blinked. "I don't—"

"As often as you want," he clarified. "Whenever you want, however long you want."

Her chin lifted in understanding. "You'll kiss me as a distraction?"

He shrugged in response.

Ilain pursed her lips, drawing back. "That doesn't seem . . . *rational*," she said, throwing the term back at him.

"It isn't," he confirmed. "But this is a deal, remember? I get something in exchange."

She smirked. "Oh, and the kissing is only for me?"

"No, that's for both of us. The question is for you, so I get something in return."

Ilain tapped a finger over her skirt. "Let's hear it, then I'll decide."

"I'm going to continue to train with Brea." Her expression tightened, but he went on. "I have to improve as a Warrior, Ilain. If I'm going to be your Warrior, I have to *be* better. And as much as it hurts you right now, that means I have to work with the one woman who can help me become that."

She hesitated, a wry smile tugging at her lips. "So I have to be rational about your training, but I get to be irrational by distracting myself with your kisses?" she surmised.

"Something like that."

A weak laugh slipped out of her. She stared across the room, a haunted expression on her face. Her vibrant curls drifted over her tense shoulders. It was plain to see that the request hurt her. She was so intelligent and cunning that sometimes Ethenn forgot how reactive and emotional she also was. Like the resource she connected with, Ilain was full of passion, violence, and insatiable need. And it drove her to these dramatic swings in reason, no matter how wise she might truly be.

Slowly, Ilain turned back to him. "Fine," she said softly.

"You'll accept the deal?" Ethenn wasn't sure whether he felt more excited or disappointed.

"Yes, I accept it." Her sharp eyebrows lifted slyly. "Do I get to ask my question now?"

He nodded.

Her fingers latched onto his forearm, tracing his sleeve. "How did you get your scars?"

Ethenn gritted his teeth but said, "In my uncle's smithy." Ilain's glare flashed, immediately incensed by his repeated answer, but he interrupted her sharp reply. "He gave them to me."

Her eyes widened. "Your uncle . . . *burned* you?"

"If I moved too slowly, messed something up, or talked back, he'd hit me with the poker straight from the forge," he said. "You have to work with your sleeves rolled back; otherwise, they can get caught in your work, plus it's blistering hot, so . . ."

When he didn't continue the thought, she concluded it for him. "He branded you by marking each of your mistakes."

An embittered grin came to his lips. "Good thing hunting took me away for weeks at a time, else I'd have more."

Ilain's fingers traced his sleeve. "How many—?"

"I haven't bothered to count."

The look on her face was so brokenhearted, so purely sorrowful, that a soft laugh escaped him. "I'm free of him, Ilain," he reminded her. "I left behind Trollenston and my uncle for good."

With a heavy sigh, Ilain scooted closer. "I want to ask more," she whispered. Her green eyes were lined with tears. "But I won't."

"Thank you," he said and brushed his fingers over her jaw. "Now, about that kiss. . . ."

Dry humor spread across her face, and she pulled back. She caught his hand, entwining their fingers. "Actually," she whispered with obvious reluctance, "I think your damned sense of 'reason' has caught up to me."

Ethenn frowned.

She squeezed his hand. "We shouldn't."

"Because it isn't what you want?" he asked, lingering close to her, their breath mingling. "Or because it's irrational?"

"Because," she said, swallowing back her disappointment, "magic makes you feel out of control. And I don't want to make this harder on you than it already is."

Ethenn lifted his chin in understanding. She was letting him back out for his own sake. He'd opened up to her, and she would let him train with Brea. There was no need for any physical distraction that might entangle his heart or stir up his desire.

"Hm," Ethenn hummed, considering the letdown he felt in his chest.

"Hm?" Ilain hummed back. She was so close, their faces within inches, that he could practically feel the energy of her magic tugging on his in the air around them.

With a singular nod, Ethenn made his decision. He turned to her again, took her face in his hands, and said, "I don't care about that."

Her eyes darted between his. "You don't?"

"No," he replied. Then he kissed her, distracting both of them for as long as she wanted.

CHAPTER FORTY-ONE

14TH OF RADIA, 1574

Over the next two days, a semblance of normalcy returned to the troop as they traveled. Through the morning and early afternoon, they rode hard, stopping only in the evenings to train and rest. Ilain joined Deckard and Isla in their training, allowing Ethenn to return to his work with Brea and Evylin, leaving Thom, Rafferty, and Vayden to spar together.

Despite the constant worry over Blount's location and the stress of what waited for them in the final Keep and the battle to come, the brief return to routine was enjoyable, though Thom was still uneasy around Vayden. Despite the man's good and temperate nature, Thom constantly felt the urge to apologize. To his surprise, Vayden lived with a calm, ready acceptance of his brother's fate. There was a harrowed, haunted look in his eyes at times—moments where he would stare out in the distance as though remembering the loss—but all in all, he seemed to choose to live unburdened by the grief.

Thom found it impressive and utterly baffling. How could someone be so levelheaded when faced with the death of someone they loved so dearly? But, as he witnessed Isla's similar reaction, Thom realized that the couple had already faced more than their fair share of heartache and sacrifice.

That night, after sparring for an hour, Thom, Rafferty, and Vayden began their trek into the next settlement to find an inn. They stabled the horses, procured rooms, and sat down at the tavern's bar to order tankards of ale.

"Ah!" Rafferty said as the barmaid set the tankard in front of him. "I've missed you, old friend."

"We drank at the inn last night," Thom said.

Rafferty swiped an affectionate hand over the tankard's handle. "One can never tire of their true love, Thommy."

Vayden eyed the weasel knowingly. "You had an unhappy childhood, didn't you?"

Furrowing his white-blond brows, Rafferty seemed truly confused. "My childhood was perfectly joyous. Rasnaack may have been a small, seedy village, but my pa and I were quite content in our drudgery, I'll have you know."

"You didn't mention your mother," Vayden noted.

Rafferty raised his tankard in a mock toast. "Didn't have one."

"That explains it," Vayden commented dryly, then turned to Thom. "What about you? Seems you and your brother are mostly well-adjusted. I take it you had a good homelife."

Thom swallowed down a gulp of the nutty brown ale and wiped his mouth with the back of his hand. "Oh, yes," he said readily. "The best in many ways. Though Father was gone, serving in the army for most of my earliest years. It was just Mother, Jonn, and me for a bit, but I don't really remember those days. Then Father finished his commission, came home, and our little sister was born. Anyway, my family is great. I was a shit, though."

"You still are," Rafferty quipped.

"Mostly," Thom agreed. "I'm trying to do better."

Vayden gave him an approving nod. "As far as I'm concerned, you're doing just fine."

Thom smiled with appreciation. He'd come to greatly enjoy Vayden's company. The man carried a maturity and self-sufficiency that he couldn't quite understand. It made him think that the man had somehow learned the secret to life—how to live happily despite your circumstances.

After taking another sip, Thom turned to Vayden. "Can I ask you something?" he said.

Vayden shrugged casually. "I don't see why not."

"Are you . . . all right?" Thom asked, broaching the subject with caution. He dropped his volume to ensure their conversation wasn't overheard by the few patrons and the barmaid. "Not only considering Auden's death but—the Keeps are harrowing. Especially for those of us without magic."

Vayden drew in a long, thoughtful breath. "That they are," he muttered.

"Yet, you seem to be handling all of this chaos and catastrophe rather well."

A forlorn tilt lifted Vayden's lips. "I lived as a spy for twenty years," he said matter-of-factly. "I've endured my share of harrowing experiences. During my career, I was also apart from my wife and daughter for months, if not years, at a time. I know the sting of separation better than most. Ilain . . . She and Auden were more than siblings. They were always together. Me? I'm the *other* Calder, the oldest, and yet the least notable. I'm not magical, and I have no claim to greatness."

Thom raised his chin, feeling keenly connected to Vayden's words.

"As much as I love my siblings," the man continued, "there has always been a distinction between us. Not one set in place by my parents or presumed by our neighbors. It's the simple fact that I'm not biologically a Calder. Nor am I a Mage. Auden and Ilain were taken to Doorstunds Reach when I was fifteen. I lost my siblings that day—my closest friends. While they went off to learn magic and become a magister and a goddess, I was left to muck stalls and train horses."

Vayden's smile turned self-mocking. "There was a time I felt bitterness toward them for it," he admitted. "And while those days are long past, I think it helped me gain a better understanding of what it truly means to love someone. I was forced to recognize that devotion doesn't always mean close proximity. You can love someone with your whole heart and not see them for weeks or years. That's faithfulness. It's a divine love."

He paused, staring at the barrels that lined the back of the bar. His dark blond brow drew low. "Ilain's grief is selfish," he said softly. "She's desperately mourning her loss of Auden because she never had to learn that love supersedes the physical. While she's brokenhearted without our brother, I am not. My heart is heavy; my sorrow is deep. But I mourn the loss of Auden, not because I won't see him again in this life. I mourn what he was never able to accomplish. Yet, I take comfort, knowing that he's in the peace of the Heavens, resting in Allore's arms."

A heavy silence passed as Thom gave Vayden a small, encouraging nod. He appreciated the vulnerability the man offered. It was another reason he was impressed with the eldest Calder brother. He wondered if he could ever be so open, so trusting, so wise with his heart.

Rafferty's empty tankard hit the bartop with a *plunk*. "You really believe in all that religious optimism, eh?" he asked, waving to get the barmaid's attention.

Vayden smiled at his irreverence. "I do."

"I don't," Rafferty said. "I think when you die, you're dead."

"That's bloody insensitive, Raff," Thom scolded.

Rafferty shrugged. "Why? It's not really that sad. You get one life to make as much money as you can, make as many people miss you as you can, and earn as much respect as you can. Then you get to sleep for eternity, never having to worry about anything ever again."

"And what's the point of all that?" Thom returned. "Why earn money and respect if you're just going to rot in a grave for eternity?"

"It's the impact you leave that matters, Thommy-boy." His eyes twinkled merrily. "If enough people care about you—whether 'cause you're rich or 'cause you're their friend—then they'll make a bloody big deal out of you, telling stories and writing songs that'll live on for generations."

"You'd rather have songs written about you than to live in eternal bliss in the Heavens?"

"I've told you before: Allore and I made a deal. When I die—which won't be until I'm fat with a head of white whiskers, mind you—Allore will forgive my predilections because I've done him more than one service."

"Such as?" Vayden asked in amusement.

Rafferty gave a wry grin. "That's between me and the big man now, isn't it?"

Thom and Vayden chuckled at the weasel's flippancy. The barmaid returned with a fresh pint, and Rafferty said, "Thanks, love," adding a wink for good measure.

When the pretty young woman blushed at his attention, he took it as encouragement to continue. "What's your name?" he asked.

"Tilda," she replied, playing with the end of one of her brown braids. She was a medium-skin-toned, curly-haired girl with a buxom figure. Despite her bashful countenance, her batting lashes made it clear she wasn't quite as coy as she seemed.

Rafferty's grin grew. "My, Tilda, that's a lovely name. Matches the face."

"I'm used to flatterers like you," Tilda replied. "But I'll warn you, my father runs this place, and he doesn't take kindly to dishonorable men chasing his daughter."

"Then maybe don't run," Rafferty quipped. At her look of confusion, he explained, "Then I won't have to chase you."

Tilda burst out with a girlish laugh but darted down the bar to clean up after a recently departed customer.

"Excuse me, gents," Rafferty said with a wily look in his eyes. "I've got an impact to make and a song to inspire."

And with that, Rafferty followed the young Tilda to the other side of the bar to continue flirting.

Together, Thom and Vayden shared a disapproving chuckle.

"Do you think that man has a single scruple?" Vayden asked.

"I've spent the last four months traveling with him," Thom replied. "And no, he doesn't even know what the word means."

"Pity." Vayden sighed, shrugging his shoulders in a resigned manner as though leaving Rafferty's incurable case of misbehavior in Allore's hands. "So you asked after me," he said. "Is it my turn to ask after you?"

Surprised, Thom settled his ale back on the counter. "What about me?"

"You nearly died," Vayden said knowingly. "That's typically a notable event in a person's life."

Thom nodded slowly, and his eyes drifted to the bartop. "I'm all right," he said, voice low and unfamiliar to himself. "I've been dreaming about it sometimes, but . . . I've dealt with that before. Not the dying part. However, I've been a soldier for almost six years now, and I've faced my fair share of trauma."

"I understand," Vayden said, and Thom knew he did.

Vayden was a retired spy. Thom was a defecting captain. And they were both the "runts" of their impressive families.

The metaphor caused Thom's brow to furrow. He glanced sidelong at Vayden, a sudden idea forming. "I have another question," he said, tone curious.

Vayden sipped his ale casually. "What's that?"

"You're fluent in Schonese, right?"

A knowing glimmer came to Vayden's eyes as he said, "My wife ensured it."

"What does *mi'caro* mean?"

Vayden set his tankard on the bar, adjusting it so the handle was at an exact angle. He cleared his throat, and for a moment, Thom thought he might actually provide the answer. Then he said, "You'll have to ask Brea about that."

Thom pursed his lips in agitation. "She won't talk to me."

"Tells you something, doesn't it?" Vayden said dryly.

"That she's upset with me," Thom concurred. "Though I don't understand why. I don't believe Ilain's accusation. Whatever Brea's feelings are toward me, they aren't romantic. I *know* that."

Vayden tapped his thumb against the rim of his tankard, studying Thom for several seconds. "My wife," he began at last, "has been best friends with Breata Lohen for over a decade now. By extension, I know many things about that woman that few others have had the privilege to learn. She is as wonderfully complicated as any other female. And she has a past just as complex. I would not advise assuming you understand her based on your limited acquaintance."

Thom held the man's gaze pointedly, leaning in to whisper, "She told me that she's in love with another man."

"Did she?" Vayden's eyes drifted away in thought before returning to meet his again. "What did she say exactly?"

Thom struggled to remember. "Not much, actually. I guessed it, and she asked me not to tell anyone because it was personal, and she didn't care to be that vulnerable with the others. Though she told me that you and Isla already knew."

Vayden nodded with understanding. "So she didn't mention anything about the man in question?"

A strange interest sprang up in Thom, his brow rising. "Are you going to tell me about him?"

Vayden laughed instantly. "Not if a *demolobis* dragged me to hell."

Thom's hope deflated. "Because if she found out, it'd be worse than the fiery pits?"

Vayden shook his head. "I'm allergic to dogs."

Thom's laugh rang out then, but his thoughts wouldn't be diverted from the information he sought. He took a swig of his ale, subduing his amusement with its robust malt. When he turned to Vayden again, the serious expression had returned to his face. "Why is she punishing me for something that isn't true?" he asked.

For several seconds, Vayden stared into his cup. He seemed to consider his words with extreme care, alerting Thom to his deep caution in handling the subject. Was it out of fear of betraying Brea's confidence? Or was the truth simply beyond what Thom could understand?

Either way, it made him profoundly uneasy.

Finally, Vayden spoke. "As one of the few who understands Brea's heart," he met Thom's gaze pointedly, "allow me to inform you that she doesn't behave illogically. She's not punishing you. She's protecting herself. And you should respect that even if you don't understand it."

Thom frowned, utterly bemused. Brea was protecting herself. From what?

Regardless of his confusion, Thom accepted the man's advice. "Thank you," he said. "I'll, uh . . . I'll take that into consideration."

Vayden dipped his head and turned back to his drink.

Thom ran a hand over his mouth. *Brea is protecting herself,* he thought again. He couldn't fathom why she'd need to protect herself from him. They were friends, or so he'd thought. He had imagined that he'd proved his loyalty to her by keeping her secret and through his general companionship. Yet, she still felt the need to push him away now.

Why?

Thom threw back the last of his ale. He thought to call Tilda to pour him another, but Rafferty seemed to be making good progress with the lass, so he left his friend to his wooing.

Whatever his bewilderment at Brea's rejection of him, he would accept it for now. As Vayden suggested, he would respect her decision. Though he wouldn't abandon their friendship for lost, he wouldn't push her or demand her attention either. He'd let time take its course, sorting out the awkward feelings of grief and guilt that currently stilted their camp.

In the meantime, he had bigger topics to ponder, like his own life purpose. *"How do you best want to serve this world?"* Hewitt had asked him. That was a question Thom had never considered.

Service was Deckard's territory. Thom spent his life wondering how the world could serve *him*.

Now, he was left with the sudden realization that taking from others wasn't enough. Rafferty wasn't entirely wrong in his earlier assessment of life. No, it wasn't about earning money, notoriety, or respect. But it was about leaving an impact.

"How do you best want to serve this world?"

Thom didn't know.

But he was determined to find out.

CHAPTER FORTY-TWO

15TH OF RADIA, 1574

The forests grew denser as the troop descended into the south of Ephria. Nearing the end of springtime, the trees were at their fullest. Their flowers had almost completely turned to berries or fruits, now ready for harvest. Woodland creatures roamed freely across their path, the deer and furbearers wandering with impunity. The skies were blue, and the air was warm.

They passed regular hunting parties on the road, always catching interested looks when their army coats were recognized. The troop bypassed all noble estates to ensure they wouldn't get caught up in the aristocrats' grasp, potentially delaying them due to whatever goodwill the men and women might hope to garner from the king by entertaining his special Order. Though Brea reminded them that several Ephrian noblemen were actually in service to the Alliance, she couldn't remember which ones.

"Our work kept us focused on the Waulden nobles far more than the Ephrian ones," she noted.

"It'd be best not to risk it if you're unsure," Deckard decided.

So they continued to stop in the settlements at night, renting rooms in the inns. Their coins were dwindling, though not by much. Most innkeepers granted them considerable discounts upon learning that they were the king's personal task force, and Ephren had sent them off with quite a large sum upon their stop in Loclight.

Once again, the troop fell into a rhythm. Waking, traveling, training, eating, sleeping. Every day felt wrong without Auden. Somehow, even though the man had been less talkative than others, his absence was felt more keenly than Deckard might have expected. In retrospect, the Day Mage's presence seemed to have had an unforeseen soothing effect that was only noticed when he wasn't there. His steady work and constant care, as well as his attentive and insightful demeanor, all lent a subtle ease to their travels. And now that it was gone, everything else felt off balance within the troop.

However, they were beginning to find their way into a new normalcy. Deckard discovered a natural split of trios amongst the group—Mages, Warriors, and non-magical individuals. This divide helped keep Ilain from Brea and Brea from Thom. After Deckard's conversation with the lieutenant, she readily complied with his request to behave amicably. While she didn't seek out Thom's attention, if he spoke to her, she would reply kindly, and she didn't intentionally leave a group to be removed from him.

As for Ilain and Brea's tenuous relationship, the women had settled into a mutually indifferent treatment of one another. Ilain was no longer reactively rude toward the lieutenant, and Brea graciously avoided placing herself in too close a proximity to the woman that it might make her uncomfortable.

Deckard was still agitated by it all. He knew Brea wasn't trying to be difficult. She genuinely appeared to be working to get along with everyone. But it seemed her decisive and frank nature lent itself to causticity. People either appreciated her direct mannerisms or they didn't. And she wouldn't change for them.

Her personality was a foreign concept to Deckard. He'd spent his life catering to the whims of others. It was his job. As a soldier, you did what you were told, bending to the will of your officers. As a recruiter, he'd had to draw on each volunteer's individual sense of duty, shifting his style of speech and demeanor to make the appropriate impact. Even as a boy, he learned that if you made people feel seen and respected, they would typically do whatever you asked.

But Brea didn't seem to care about that. She lived wholly to be herself, and she didn't mind if she was disliked. She simply accepted the individual's opinion and continued living.

Deckard couldn't understand it. Though he would admit that the quality intrigued him.

Especially as he continued to struggle to come to terms with his magic.

The compounding failures Deckard had experienced over the last four months of his life had driven him into a near-existential crisis. As a matter of principle, he worked endlessly to do the right thing, and no matter what, it seemed he was destined to fail. He had no idea how to control his magic, and, as a result, he'd brought Hewitt and Auden to their deaths.

Additionally, his promise to Auden all those months ago loomed in his conscience. *"I want your word that you'll join the Alliance in whatever capacity they ask of you."*

Though the Mage had released him from the promise, apologizing for his underhanded finagling, now that Auden had died as a direct result of Deckard's inabilities, his guilt made him feel as though he ought to follow through. Didn't he owe the Mage that much? Or would it only be a worse failure—accepting a position as a subpar, inept ruler as a Mage who couldn't even control his own power?

All those questions plagued Deckard, along with the recurrent whisper in his mind. *Let me out.*

The magic was getting more adamant and less controllable. Even as he trained with Isla and Ilain, improving his connection to Space, he was making too grand a leap in his capabilities. An unexpected danger, as these great feats of power took far more energy than an untested Mage should attempt, according to the women.

Over the past few days, Isla had suggested that Deckard specifically practice his teleportation. "It seems you have a penchant for it," the Wind Mage said. "If you could so naturally produce the reaction based on a header, we should see what you're truly capable of with it."

Initially, Deckard was only able to replicate the basic jump from one place to another. But over time and with Ilain's creative suggestions, he discovered that he could use the power to teleport more than just himself. If he focused enough, he could bring both women along with him or send objects through the space around him, shifting them from one location to the next. He didn't even have to see where he was teleporting himself or the objects to. All it required of him was the foreknowledge of the final location, and *poof*, the person or object would land there.

Quite a handy trick. But a costly one, if Deckard's exhaustion after each evening of training was complete. He was coming to have a better understanding of his limits and how these masterful expenditures of power truly cost a Mage.

"You're getting better," Isla said with thoughtful consideration as they finished their most recent training session. "Though it still seems to flare out of control when you get distracted."

"How do I fix that?" Deckard asked, determined to follow through with whatever she advised.

"With practice."

Deckard was tired of practicing. After months spent as Hewitt's student and now a month consumed with training to become proficient with magic, he was tired of the constant lessons.

But he also knew he needed the women's help.

"What if the practice isn't enough?" Deckard asked, the prolonged weight of his fears sitting like a rock in his stomach.

"What do you mean?" Isla asked.

Looking between the highladies, Deckard was determined to get the answers he'd so long put off. "Do either of you have dreams of the Relics after the Keeps?"

Ilain shared a look with her sister-in-law, who shook her head. "No," the Fire Mage said. "Do you?"

"After the existential ones," he admitted. Apologetically, he added, "Do you know if Auden had the same experience? I thought perhaps it was due to our resources."

Raising her chin, Ilain took a deep breath. "He never mentioned it to me, which makes it highly unlikely that he shared your experience." Her shrug failed to hide the sorrow in her posture. "We told one another everything."

Deckard couldn't help his frown. "What does it mean? Why am I dreaming of the Relics?"

"We don't know," Isla said. "It is possibly due to your connection to Space, especially as it is so powerful. However, we can't know for sure."

"Tell us about your dreams exactly," Ilain prompted.

With a sigh, Deckard recounted each experience, noting that they all had nearly the exact same format. He stood in the Keep, the Shades ran to him, and he absorbed their forms. Suddenly, he found himself in the Chamber, standing on the dais with the pedestal and the Relic before him. In each dream, he would pick up the Relic, feeling its power radiate through him. He hesitated before sharing the alteration that came from after the Space Keep.

"When I touched the Space Relic, I heard a scream so loud it knocked me off the dais," he said. "It was my magic; it echoed through my mind, crying the same thing over and over again."

The women listened intently, silently waiting for him to go on.

Deckard stared at his hands as though he could visualize the black crystalline shards he'd grown so used to summoning. "It was demanding that I let it out."

Isla set a hand to her mouth, a look of blatant worry across her face. However, Ilain let out an easy-sounding hum. She stood from where she'd slumped against a nearby tree. "Jonn," she said suddenly, "come with me."

Deckard glanced at Isla, whose expression had shifted with understanding. "I'll meet up with Vayden and the others," she said, then disappeared through the trees.

Left alone with the Calder sister, Deckard turned to her, confused as to her purpose in requesting his delay. A gentle breeze rustled the full leaves around them, the forest growing shadowed in the late spring sunset. Ilain gestured for Deckard to follow as she walked farther into the forest.

With little other choice, Deckard hurried after her. "Where are we going?" he asked.

"For a walk," she replied.

"Any particular reason?"

"You like to pace when you're working through a problem," she noted. "I thought a walk might aid your thoughts as I explain some things to you."

At Deckard's beckon, Ilain continued, "Did you know I went to Doorstunds Reach when I was only ten?"

"I did not. That's when you began your training?"

"Yes. It is the youngest age that magic presents itself, and in myself, it was rather strong. I nearly killed the Mage who administered my test because of the intensity of the flame I produced."

Deckard lifted his chin in surprise and understanding. "Your power was uncontrollable once too?"

"It was," she confirmed, the remaining shafts of sunlight causing her hair to shimmer. "And it took six years for me to master it."

Drawing back, Deckard gathered her point. He sighed and said, "We don't have six years."

"Don't we?"

His brow pinched. "I need to control my power now. I can't risk failing our troop again."

Ilain stopped suddenly, her verdant gaze meeting his. "Jonn, do you feel everything comes down to you?"

The words were too familiar to the question Evylin asked. *Do you always feel this way? That everything comes down to your perfection, to your actions.*

"Yes," Deckard confessed. "I know it's foolish. And selfish. Terraeus does not revolve around me. Yet . . ."

"Every failure is a reminder of your insignificance?"

He stared at her, baffled at her insight.

Ilain's cunning smirk glinted in her gaze. "As the most powerful Mage in two centuries, I know something about the weight of responsibility. For my whole life, my family has worked for the Alliance. They groomed Vayden, Auden, and me to become devotees to the cause. And we followed the path happily.

"The Alliance is good," she insisted. "They are just. They are noble. But when the height of my powers was discovered as a teen, I became something more than a mere foot soldier for their cause. I became a symbol of hope. My power makes me uniquely qualified to overthrow Blount and Ephren and to take up a place as the Alliance's greatest ruler. My time in the Order of the Flame made me into a goddess to the Waulden people. When the time comes, they will listen to me above any other because I was named as Pyra's Heiress."

Deckard frowned, unable to fully comprehend the title. "And what does that mean exactly?"

"In Wauld," she explained, "the Mages of Auld created the religion known as the Faith of Eight to make their right to rule absolute. They taught that the Mages are incarnations of the resources themselves, turning us into deities. However, most Mages are seen as demigods—reflections of the first gods. However, the eight rulers of Auld were purported to be reincarnations of the prime deities themselves. Now, every few centuries, there is *one* Mage believed to inherit the true power of the gods. Because of my strength, they believed me to be the heir of Pyra's power."

"Meaning . . . They really thought you were a god?" Deckard's mouth dropped open. The very idea was blasphemy. But he supposed that was the point. Turn yourself into a god, and who could deny you?

"Goddess," she corrected dryly. "And yes, the Waulden people think I'm Pyra reincarnated."

Deckard shook his head, unable to fathom the illogical heresy. "But Blount put out a writ on you. Surely, they wouldn't support a monarch over their goddess."

Ilain gave him an amused look. "The Faith of Eight does not hold the same weight as Allorianism. Gods are born through the generations. They are destructible. They are fallible. Allore is solitarily, infinitely divine, and righteous. Their faith is not like ours."

She resumed walking and added, "Besides, some think Blount is Obscura's Heir, though he hasn't been given the title officially. It's laughable, anyway. He isn't nearly as powerful as I am."

Following at her side, he asked, "Do you truly believe in the inheritance of their powers?"

"Hm? Oh, no. The paganism of the Eight didn't arise until after the ancient Mages locked away the Relics. Although, I do believe Allore himself grants some of us more vast wells of power than others to help point us to the natural leaders."

"And your great power qualifies you to lead?"

"It does," she said, somehow without a hint of pretension.

Deckard clasped his hands behind his back, the thought settling uneasily in his stomach. "You aren't bothered by that responsibility?" he asked.

Ilain was quiet for a moment, her gaze on the forest floor. She sidestepped a soft blue elderlily, lifting her skirt so as not to disturb the flower. "Sometimes I am," she said softly. "It's a burden to carry—knowing your actions will determine the fate of the world. But it's also an honor. And I'm grateful that Allore considered me trustworthy enough to bear it."

Deckard's throat grew tight. "Is this your way of telling me that I'm destined to rule?" he asked, fighting the bitterness that welled within him.

Ilain's smile was unaffected as she looked up at him. "No, Jonn," she said with earnestness. "This is my way of telling you that you need to stop being afraid of yourself."

He watched her warily. The setting sun's rays filtered through the treetops to cast a golden glow on her pale skin as they walked. "You carry a burden, yes," she continued. "But it is also an honor. Rather than fighting your magic, work with it. Stop trying to control it and start relating to it."

Deckard wet his bottom lip, nervous. "When I focus, it consumes me."

"Does Evylin consume you?"

Deckard's first instinct was to say yes, but then he reconsidered. "No. I love her; I put her first, but . . . She isn't my every waking thought."

Ilain nodded encouragingly. "So should you treat magic. Love it, cherish it, but let it be free. Let it live in the world around you unimpeded by your control. *Let it out.* Space already exists without you. Stop trying to bend it to your will and start getting to know it as it *is* rather than as you *want* it to be."

The sentiment was reasonable, but Deckard couldn't fathom the means to accomplish such a feat. "I don't know how to do that," he admitted.

Ilain grinned. "That's because it takes time. Six years for me, remember?"

Deckard came to a stop, and she halted with him. He looked down at her, determined to seek her serious advice. "And what if my lack causes our mission's failure?" he asked, knowing that it *was* his lack that had caused her brother's death.

Ilain didn't hesitate to reply, "It won't."

"What if it does?" he pressed.

"Then we die," she said flippantly. "But at least we'll have tried."

The plain, unembellished truth struck Deckard. They could try, or they could quit. Either way, misery awaited them. Or . . .

Quitting would secure failure. Trying *might* gain them success.

Why not try?

In the worst case, Deckard would get them all killed. But if they abandoned their mission of fighting Blount, the man would stop at nothing to gain power over the continent. Deckard didn't know the man's motives; he didn't know what drove him to this madness, but he'd seen the prince's cruelty in action more than enough times to know a life under Blount's rule would be filled with despair.

Death might be a mercy from that existence.

With a defeated sigh, Deckard scoffed at his own morbidity. "Thank you for the advice," he said.

"Anytime," Ilain said, setting a hand on his arm. "You're not to blame for your inability, Jonn. There's a reason the Mages don't seek out students among those above seventeen. The older you grow, the harder it is to learn."

Deckard held her adamant gaze, something like relief welling inside of him at her words.

"You're doing well," she promised. "I've seen great progress in you just in the short time we've trained together. It just takes time, and you weren't given any before being thrown into the fray."

Swallowing down his worry, Deckard dipped his chin. "I want to apologize to you, Ilain," he said. "Your brother didn't deserve to die. And I . . . It was my weakness that got him killed."

Ilain's gaze shuttered. She stepped away, walking forward again. Deckard didn't know whether to follow, so he stood there, watching as she drifted among the trees before she came to a stop next to a golden apple tree.

She lifted a hand, tracing one of the fruits that hung from the limbs. "No," she said so quietly he hardly heard her. "Auden didn't deserve to die."

Ilain turned to him then, a hardness in her vibrant green eyes as tears sparkled on her lashes. "But you are not the only one who failed him that day," she said, the words weak.

Something within the frailty of her voice confessed the truth to Deckard then: Ilain blamed herself. In all her anger toward Brea, in all her insistence that the Warrior had intentionally chosen to let Auden die . . . Ilain was merely attempting to absolve herself of the guilt.

Deckard didn't understand her reasons, but he felt it wasn't his right to ask. However, he'd come to know Ilain as a friend. He cared for her as he might his own sister. And he would be damned if he let her stand there, crying in the forest, blaming herself for her brother's death.

With a determined stride, Deckard stepped to Ilain's side. He set a hand on her shoulder, unflinchingly holding her watery gaze. "Whatever has caused you to believe this lie," he whispered, "banish it from thought."

A tear dropped onto her cheek, but Deckard didn't bother to brush it away. That wasn't his place. He could console and encourage her, but he would not comfort her with such affection. That was her husband's job.

"Have you spoken to Ethenn about this?" Deckard asked.

The subtle shake of her head was all the response she gave.

"I'd advise you to," he said. "In this life, Allore granted us a greater gift than magic: a spouse. Your husband is meant to be your closest confidant, your most trusted friend, and your dearest advisor. Speak to him about this. Let him know your heart and allow him to help you heal these wounds."

Drawing in a deep breath, Ilain stepped back, out of his reach. A gentle smile came to her lips as she brushed away the tear that clung to the edge of her jaw. The smallest, breathy chuckle escaped her. "You know," she said, "you're rather wise for a young man."

Deckard laughed at the dry compliment. "I haven't been called a young man in years."

"You're only thirty."

"Thirty-two."

"Eleven years younger than me," she quipped, then her brow raised with a pointed emphasis. "We're *both* young by magical standards. But age doesn't determine wisdom or maturity."

She reached over to give his hand a quick squeeze. "And I'm grateful to have friends like you and Evylin," she said passionately. "I'm impulsive and reckless at times. Despite my age, I can't quite seem to act it. I need people like you two. I need your steadiness to remind me that all my emotions, all my reactions—they aren't the truth."

Deckard gave her a smile, though he felt bashful under such kind words.

Ilain hummed with amusement at his reserved demeanor. "Come now," she said, moving back toward the path they'd taken. "We should return. I've got a husband to speak to."

CHAPTER FORTY-THREE

16TH OF RADIA, 1574

Evylin only had one more day with Hewitt.

As they cantered down the road that cut through the thick forests of central Ephria, Evylin's heart stuttered every few moments. They were within a day's travel from the site of Hewitt's grave. Tomorrow, they would arrive at the village of Acre, where their friends would settle in for the evening while she and Deckard made the short ride to the forest where they'd buried her uncle's body. Then Deckard would release him . . . forever.

Evylin didn't know if she could face the loss a second time.

With Deckard's power, she could keep Hewitt with her for the rest of her life. They could end the war, save their countries, and rebuild Allund as it was always meant to be. She and Jonn could live out their lives in the bliss of their Bond, traveling the world. And they could keep Hewitt at their side all the while.

But it wasn't what her uncle wanted.

Evylin had fallen back to ride at the rear of the troop, her thoughts muddled by the impending dawn of a new day. The Space Relic hung hidden under her coat, its thick golden chain accompanying the thin silver necklace Hewitt had made for her fifteenth birthday. The Alliance was right. As part of a Bonded pair, she felt no effects from this Relic. After her time with the Day, Fire, and Night Relics, she knew how their emotional manipulation tugged on your soul subtly. Yet, there was no urging of Space on her, no push and pull of everything and nothing like she'd felt in the Keep. It simply rested against her breastbone, pleasantly cool and content.

That was something unexpected. After wearing the Relic for a full day, she'd begun to receive near-sentient pulses from it. It didn't seem alive, exactly, but it still bore its own personality, its own emotions. And through her growing understanding of the Relic's magic, she could tell that it was happy to be with her.

With a deep breath, Evylin stared at the riders ahead. She didn't know how to handle that revelation. The Relic *liked* being with her. How would it feel if she gave it away? Did it matter?

Considering a magical necklace's feelings had never occurred to Evylin before. But now . . .

Deckard didn't want a future governing the country, which meant they'd hand the Relic over to another Bonded couple. She'd heard talk of another Space Mage, which meant the Alliance had a viable option other than themselves. While Deckard and she could safely carry the Relic during their mission, once Allund was settled, they would give it to its rightful caretakers.

Evylin glanced down as though she could see the Relic through her tunic. "What do you think of that?" she asked quietly. No one was near enough to hear her, but she didn't care for them to find out she was talking to the thing, even if it was just this once.

There was no response. Not a spike of energy or even a sense of emotion. The Relic just lay against her chest, unseen and steadily giving off the same feeling of contentment.

Evylin pursed her lips. Perhaps the Relic didn't care about *her* so much as knowing that it was out in the world again, free of its confines in the Keep. It probably wouldn't mind being given away to someone else.

But what if Evylin minded . . . ?

Looking ahead again, Evylin saw Deckard guide his horse away from where he led the troop with Thom. He dropped back to join her. His green-blue gaze studied her even as he offered a gentle smile.

"You've been back here for quite some time," he noted.

"I've been ruminating," she admitted.

"On what exactly?"

Evylin drew in a slow breath. "Many things," she said. She let her lips lift in a teasing grin. "You came back because you felt my worry, didn't you?"

"I did," he confessed.

"Mm-hm." Evylin nudged his arm and tried not to notice the way he flinched in reaction to the Relic's tug. Clinging to amusement rather than disappointment, she smirked. "Well, I must say I rather like this Bond of ours," she teased. "It's very handy. All I need is to feel the slightest concern, and you'll come running."

Deckard dipped his chin. "Anything to serve you."

That was part of the problem.

"What's bothering you?" Deckard asked.

Though there were many things causing Evylin's distress, she chose the most immediate concern. "I don't want to let him go," she confessed quietly. "I'm not ready to lose him again."

Deckard's head hung lower as though he bore the weight of her disappointment alone. "I know," he said.

"Having Hewitt with us these past weeks has been wonderful," she continued. "Being around him, speaking with him—it has made the pain easier in so many ways. But it's also made it harder, knowing that these are truly our last moments."

Deckard nodded. "I've felt the same. I know he and I haven't always gotten along, but he became very important to me. He gave me you, after all. Losing him will be like losing a part of who we are. I think that's why I summoned him in the first place. I needed him; *we* needed him."

Evylin grinned tenderly, knowing he was right.

Deckard's eyes fell to her hands, resting upon the saddle. Somehow, she knew he was staring at her rings. The ivy and onyx bands—representations of her past and their future, Hewitt and Deckard.

"Sometimes," Deckard whispered, "I think we still need him."

Evylin pressed her lips together, sadness rising with her. "I'll always need him," she agreed.

Deckard met her gaze, worry bleeding out of him. "No, I meant *we* need him. As a couple."

"In what way?"

The sunlight turned his gaze light blue as his expression grew adamant. "He's the only reason I have you, Evylin," he said softly. "And I'm afraid . . ." He paused, wet his bottom lip, and tried again. "I'm afraid that without him, I'll fail you. Without his knowledge and guidance, I fear that I can't be the man you need me to be."

"Jonn—"

Letting the others ride ahead, he pulled his horse to a stop. When she'd done the same, he took hold of her hand. "In order to release Hewitt, I have to *want* to let him go, Evylin. I have to mean it with everything inside me. Otherwise, it might not take effect."

Evylin stared at him with wary hesitation.

"I don't want to do it," he admitted. "Not only because I'll miss him, and not simply because it will break your heart a second time. I don't want to lose him because I'm afraid it will mean losing you."

Evylin leaned forward, tightening her grip on him. "You can't lose me, Jonn. We're Bonded, remember," she said with a smile. "You're stuck with me for good."

Though he tried to return the grin, it fell woefully short. "But I can disappoint you."

Evylin froze, eyes locked with her husband's as they bored into her. "I can fail you," he continued. "Everything I've done, every right choice I've made, I had Hewitt to help me make it. He's the reason we married, the reason you came to trust me, the very reason I ever knew how to care for you. Without him, how can I ever be the man you need?"

For the first time in her life, Evylin realized just how much Hewitt had held her back. Had anyone tried to tell her before this moment, she would have cursed them, rejecting the claim. But staring into Deckard's soft, concerned gaze, she finally knew the truth.

Pulling her hand from his, Evylin took hold of Deckard's face and kissed him. Their horses shied uncomfortably away from one another, keeping the caress light and quick.

"What was that for?" Deckard asked.

Evylin brushed her thumb across his stubbled jawline. "It was an apology." His brow pinched together, so she explained. "I'm sorry I ever let Hewitt stand between us."

Deckard's lips parted to contradict her, but she held up a hand to refuse his objection. "I loved my uncle more than anyone," she said. "Possibly more than life itself. And I'm only now realizing that if I hadn't idolized him the way I did, I would have loved you—trusted you—far sooner. We would have been happier. And you never would have cause to fear failing me."

"If you hadn't regarded him so highly," Deckard said determinedly, "you wouldn't have married me."

Evylin pressed her hand to his chest. "I already told you," she said. "Whether we married then or months later, we would have ended up together. Had you asked to write to me, I would have said yes, and our marriage would have followed."

"I would have failed my assignment and gone to Ostwatch," he said.

"You still would have saved the prince," she reminded.

"Carlile only selected us for the Alliance because of you."

She rolled her eyes. "Fine," she said. "Say you're right, and you were assigned to Ostwatch. I would have married you even then."

"I wouldn't have asked."

Evylin frowned. "Why not?"

His gaze was haunted as though envisioning that future. "I wouldn't have brought you into that horrible life only to make you a widow."

"You wouldn't have died," she said with a playful tug on his collar. "I would have demanded you let me come along, and I would have protected you. Then we both would have discovered our magic and made Ostwatch our kingdom."

Deckard raised a brow skeptically.

With fondness, Evylin rubbed the crease between his eyes. "With or without Hewitt," she said, "I would have married you. But if we must live within the parameters that necessitate our marriage in the same timeline, then so be it. Either way, I shouldn't have held onto him so tightly. I should have trusted you with my whole heart the moment I realized how wonderful you were. If I had, we would have been in love within weeks."

Though he didn't look convinced, Deckard didn't argue her claim.

"If I had loved him less," she whispered with new understanding, "I would have loved you more."

Disapprovingly, his eyes narrowed, and Evylin smirked, amused at his dedication to the surly veteran-turned-smith. Seeing that he didn't understand, she said, "Because of Hewitt, I never told you about Ryen."

Deckard's expression shifted then, and Evylin realized that he already knew. Somehow, he'd learned of her beloved cousin without her uttering a word.

"He told you?" she asked.

He dipped his chin in confirmation.

"Hewitt was my replacement for him," she explained. "He was the only thing that kept my broken heart beating. And as I grew older, I never let go. I never recovered from the loss of Ryen. I clung to him through Hewitt as though I could keep him alive by sheer will. And when you showed up, you threatened my love for him."

In surprise, Deckard drew his shoulders back.

"I was so afraid of you," Evylin whispered. "Of how much I liked you. My heart was ready to be yours—to let you mend the brokenness that kept me from loving others. And that frightened me. Even as I began to love you, I held myself back from you because I couldn't fathom letting Ryen go."

Evylin caught both of his hands in hers. "In another life," she whispered, "one where I wasn't so afraid, where Hewitt wasn't my everything—my heart would have been yours within weeks. Not because Hewitt stood in our way himself, but because I used him as a shield against you. I hid behind him because he was my memory of the boy I lost too soon. In that other life, I wouldn't have feared giving myself to you because I wouldn't have clung to the brokenness of my past.

"And now," Evylin sighed, shaking her head even as she held his gaze, "you think you can't make me happy without him. That our love is *because* of him." She squeezed his hands. "It's not true. I would have loved you with or without Hewitt's support. I will always love you—with or without him beside us. And you have made me happier than I ever imagined in only four months' time."

The moment the flow of her words came to an end, Deckard kissed her again. A shiver raced down her spine at his fervency. Bursts of joy and affection erupted between them. Heat coiled within her chest. She could feel every ounce of his love pulsating within her.

Evylin angled closer to him, but the horses snorted their complaints. Deckard pulled back, reaching for her waist even as she was preparing to swing her leg over the saddle so she could join him on his horse.

"Hey!" Thom's voice echoed through the trees.

They both froze in mid-motion. Far up the road, Thom waited, a sly grin on his lips. "You two mind finishing this up later?" he said. "We've got somewhere to be."

With a chuckle, Evylin settled back down on her own saddle. But Deckard waved his brother away. "We'll be right there," he promised.

Though he eyed them with dubious amusement, Thom guided his horse around and cantered away.

Evylin turned back to Deckard as he brushed her hair behind her ear. "Are you sure?" he asked.

"Am I sure of what?" she replied, mind still slightly muddled by their kisses.

"Are you sure that you're happy?" he said. "Are you sure that you'll be all right without him?"

Evylin took a deep breath, her heart squeezing at the thought. But she said, "Yes. I will miss him—desperately. But I have you, and I know I'll be more than all right with you by my side."

CHAPTER FORTY-FOUR

17TH OF RADIA, 1574

They reached the village of Acre in the early afternoon, finding an acceptable inn before Evylin and Deckard left for Hewitt's grave, which was a short ride away.

Uncharacteristically, Hewitt requested to say one last goodbye to the troop. So they gathered in Thom, Rafferty, and Brea's room (the inn didn't have enough rooms for Brea to sleep on her own), everyone cluttering up the small space. As Vayden, Isla, and Brea had never known Hewitt well, they excused themselves from the meeting, relaxing in the tavern on the main floor of the inn to provide a more private farewell for the troop.

Now, Rafferty sat on the footboard of one of the single beds, Thom at his side. Ethenn and Ilain stood together near the far wall. Evylin fought the rising tears in her throat while Deckard took the Night Relic from his brother.

Hewitt's ghost became visible, looking like the military legend he'd always been—broad shoulders bound in his Order of the King coat, beard growing scraggly after weeks of travel, and those steel-gray eyes that caught everything.

"All right," Hewitt said, his bushy brow raised as he surveyed the troop. "This isn't going to be an emotional farewell. I have a few things to say, and that will be that."

Hewitt turned to Ilain and Ethenn. "First," he said, gruff voice softening, "I'd like to offer my condolences to you, Highlady. As someone who lost their family, I'd advise you to take comfort in those around you. If I'd have allowed myself to do the same, I wouldn't have ended up a bitter old man."

He paused, then added, "I wish I'd had the chance to tell your brother myself, but

I appreciated his dedication to his craft. It was impressive, even if I don't care for magic."

An airy chuckle escaped Ilain, and her gaze grew glassy. "Thank you," she said.

"And take care of this one," Hewitt said, gesturing to Ethenn. "He seems docile, but he's even more dangerous than you. He needs your love, not your cunning. Remember that."

Hewitt turned from Ilain before she could reply. He faced his pupils—Ethenn, Rafferty, and Thom—with the steady stare of an officer. "You lot," he began, the growl back in his voice. "Remember what I taught you. You're my chosen team—not Deckard's, not the bloody King of Ephria's, not this damn Alliance's. *Mine.* You look out for one another and listen to Evylin and Deckard. Got it?"

The three men shared a proud look before saying together, "Yes, sir."

Hewitt turned to Thom alone then. "Remember," he said, "your purpose is whatever you make it; just make sure it's a worthy one."

Thom's shoulders drew back, accepting the charge. "I swear," he said, a slight tremble in his voice, "I will make you proud."

With a grunt and a small grin, Hewitt nodded. He scanned the gathered members of the troop once more, and though his expression remained as impassive as ever, Evylin could see the softness in his gaze. Then he turned to Evylin and Deckard. "Let's go," he said.

The ride to the site of the grave was quiet. They chose to take one horse to allow the others to rest as much as possible before another hard day's ride. Evylin sat behind Deckard, her arms around his waist. It wasn't the most comfortable ride, and she could still feel his tension at her touch, but the trip was short. Only an hour later, they slowed to take in the forest between Acre and Virwoud.

Evylin tapped into her magic, scanning the tree line. Despite knowing the general location of their old camp, the seasons had changed the landscape dramatically. Lush green leaves clung to the branches, dancing gently in the wind. The late afternoon sun was golden, casting languid shadows across the grass. Their memories could only serve them so much.

With the Space Relic around her neck, she found her focus easily. She worried she'd start relying on the Relic too much, but she was grateful for it as her hands trembled at the task before them. She meant what she'd told Deckard the previous day; she would be all right without Hewitt. But that didn't lessen her desire to keep him by her side.

"It's another fifty paces up," Evylin said, pointing toward the entrance to the woods.

Deckard guided the horse off the road. They dismounted and led the horse into the trees. Almost two months ago, they'd camped within these woods. Yet now, it looked like an entirely separate land. Bright green growth filled the terrae. Woodland creatures darted through the trees and underbrush. Birds called their songs to one another. If Evylin wasn't using her magic to guide them, she might have thought they were in the wrong place.

But she could also smell the subtlest decay of an old campfire and the charred remains of their attackers. It was a foul means of tracking, but it was all she had.

Her breath caught as they stepped into the clearing. The barren camp appeared haunted. One tent remained, almost entirely burned to ash. Burgeoning flora had already begun to reclaim it. The vacant firepit's rocks were scattered from her scuffle with one of the swordsmen who'd attacked them. What few camp supplies remained lay strewn across the dirt and grass. They'd scavenged what they needed but chose to leave behind the rest, as Hewitt's death tainted it all.

Evylin's memories plagued her. She chewed on her lip, fighting them back. She didn't want to remember Hewitt's broken body. Yet, her imagination assailed her with the vision of his dead form—cold, rigid, and swiftly turning a sickly green. Her knees weakened, but she remained staunchly upright.

Deckard stood at her side, his fingers finding hers. He didn't speak, but she could feel his sorrow wrapping around him like a wool cloak too.

"This is bloody depressing," Hewitt's ghost said, appearing suddenly.

An unbidden breathy laugh escaped Evylin.

"Come on," Hewitt said with an unusual gentleness. "You can mourn me on the way to my grave."

Deckard hobbled the horse, not wanting to lead it deeper through the thick trees. They began their trek, stepping over roots and rocks. Evylin's heart felt as tangled as the underbrush around them. She didn't bother stopping her tears or bearing up under her sorrow. She let herself mourn, knowing that this would truly be her final goodbye.

Shafts of yellow sunlight streamed through the treetops, creating a haven within the hollow of Hewitt's grave. The mound lay to the far side, covered in a thick coating of lush green and ivory everbloom ivy. Evylin gasped at the scene. It was beautiful and heartbreaking all at once.

"You did a good job," Hewitt said as they halted at the hollow's edge. "This is a peaceful place."

Pulling in a slow, staggered breath, Deckard muttered his response brokenly. "I'm glad you like it."

Evylin looked up to see his eyes rimmed in glassy tears, though he held them at bay. His jaw was hard, and his hands were fisted at his sides. She rubbed his arm, offering an encouraging smile, though she doubted its strength.

Deckard's eyes met hers, a sea of blue and green, blending and shifting together. "I'll give you a moment alone if you'd like."

Evylin shook her head. "Stay with me," she whispered.

Together, they walked to Hewitt's graveside.

The ghost took in the ivy patch. "Is this the Fire Mage's work?"

"Only in part," Evylin said. "I took an everbloom from Ryen's grave and laid it to rest here with you. It seems her magic brought it back to life."

"Mm." Hewitt drew in a long, emotion-filled breath. "That's good."

He turned to them. "This is it," he said with decided assurance. "I will sleep and find rest. Perhaps if the stories are right, I'll wake in the Heavens and be reunited with my family. Either way, I'll be at peace."

Evylin's throat grew painfully raw. Her chest tightened with a well of more tears.

Deckard kept his head high, but she could feel the tension leaking out of him as he fought his grief.

Hewitt's steely eyes swept over them fondly. "Don't miss me," he ordered. "Live your lives and know that I'm proud of you. Both of you."

They bore up under his charge.

"Evie," his lips lifted in the smile he only gave her, "if I couldn't have my son by my side in this life, there was none but you I'd ask to take his place. The woman you've become is more than I ever imagined. I will always be thankful you chose me. I only wish I could have deserved your love."

"You did," Evylin sobbed. "I couldn't have loved you more."

Flexing his hand as though wishing to wipe away her tears, Hewitt shared her sad smile. "But I could have been better to you. I *should* have been better."

"You were everything I wanted."

Hewitt dipped his head, accepting her words. He turned to Deckard. "She chose you, but so did I," he said. "Remember that. She's yours because she chose you. But I gave her to you because I knew you'd take care of her the way she needed—even more than I could. Never forget that."

"I swear to you," Deckard said thickly, "I will do whatever I must—whatever it takes—to be sure she has the life she deserves. Just as you charged."

With a step closer, Hewitt glared at him. "I chose you because of who you are," he growled. "If you sacrifice the man you truly desire to become, you *can't* be the man she needs. Do you understand?"

Deckard lifted his chin, expression pinched. But he gave a swift nod of acceptance.

Hewitt glanced at the grave. His lips pursed. "One more thing," he murmured as though convincing himself. He turned to Evylin. "He's yours. Don't take that lightly. I could never have entrusted you to someone less than him. Care for him the way he cares for you. He deserves that too."

"I know," Evylin promised, leaning into Deckard. "I will."

Hewitt smiled softly, then reluctantly said, "I'm ready."

Evylin could feel her husband holding his breath as he straightened. Her heart jolted with sudden panic. "Wait," she said, gripping his arm. "Wait, I—*I'm* not ready."

Both men looked at her with sadness.

"I have to go, my dear," Hewitt said. "Sooner or later."

Evylin nodded through her tears. She stepped up to him, holding his deep gray stare. "I have to know," she whispered.

"Know what?"

"I need your help," she confessed. "One last time, I need your advice."

Hewitt dipped his chin, listening.

"I've lost who I am," she said. "For so long, my life was Ryen's—living for the dream we'd promised to share. But now . . . I've done it. Yet, it doesn't feel anything like what I hoped it would. What do I do?"

Her uncle's gaze was gentle and affectionate. "I can't decide that for you."

"I'm not asking you to," she promised. "I just need to know: This life—this adventure—there are moments of joy and adrenaline and excitement. It's thrilling, and it makes me feel alive. But then there are *these* moments." The words caught with her tears. "Moments of pure *agony* and pain."

Evylin took a sharp breath in to get her last words out. "I can't stand it," she whispered. "There's too much death."

Hewitt sighed as he appraised her. He beckoned to Deckard, who readily slipped his arm around Evylin's shoulder, enfolding her into his comforting embrace.

"Listen to me, Evie," Hewitt said, the growl of his voice tender. "Death is everywhere. It's here in these woods, and it reaches back to Whickam Village. Ryen died at home in his own bed. Adventure no more guarantees death than mundanity guarantees safety. Nowhere is safe."

The unpleasant answer carved another layer of uncertainty within her. Wherever Evylin went, whatever she did, it didn't matter. Death was inevitable. Loss was inevitable. So was the choice truly up to her? Was "more" really whatever she wanted it to be?

Blinking away her tears, Evylin looked up at her uncle, memorizing each line in his face for the last time. "You once told me that everyone has their own definition of what is more and what is less. That the knowledge is innate within us."

"I remember," he said.

"What was your 'more'?"

Hewitt's eyes crinkled softly. A broad smile brightened his face. She hadn't seen him smile like that since Ryen's death. He reached out, his fingers grazing her cheek without touch. "You were," he said.

Evylin's breath caught. *She'd* been Hewitt's "more." Life was enough for him if she was in it. So simple.

"Are you ready now?" Hewitt asked.

Grimacing from the joy and sorrow twisting in her chest, Evylin nodded.

Hewitt took a step back, looking at Deckard. "So am I."

Arms tightening around her, Deckard's breath grew rapid as though with fear. "Thank you," he said, "for everything."

"Thank you," Hewitt replied. "You were more than I expected. Goodbye."

Deckard whispered his farewell, and Hewitt turned to Evylin. "Goodbye, my Evie."

Evylin's voice caught as she held Hewitt's steady stare. His unruly beard was no longer singed by the forge but scraggly from travel. His brawny arms hung at his sides, tight under his wool coat. He was now everything she would always remember him being.

"I will always love you," Evylin whispered.

Hewitt's eyes shone. "And I, you."

"Goodbye."

A wave of heat rolled through Evylin, a flash that coursed across her skin. Deckard's breath sharpened, then steadied. The Night Relic beamed its deep purple around his neck, his coat open to the warm spring evening.

While Evylin held her uncle's gaze, a shadow crossed over them, causing his form to thin. Hewitt's ghost faded, then dissipated altogether, the fading of his presence like the trailing off of a whisper.

Deckard pressed a kiss to the top of Evylin's head. "He's gone," he whispered, pulling her closer.

"I know," Evylin heard herself say.

Her whole body was numb, her heart too sore to feel anything but emptiness. In the midst of the hollow, staring at Hewitt's ivy-covered grave, she rested in her husband's embrace. Despite their sorrow, a gentle peace radiated through them. Despite the heartbreak of knowing she'd never see Hewitt again, Evylin knew she'd be all right.

And she knew, however the afterlife looked, Hewitt was now embracing his wife and son.

CHAPTER FORTY-FIVE

After Deckard and Evylin departed for Hewitt's grave, Thom, Rafferty, Ethenn, and Ilain joined the others in the tavern for dinner. Thom's heart was heavy, knowing his mentor was lost to him, but he took solace in the truth that Hewitt would finally be at peace.

Upon entering the tavern hall, Thom spotted the open seat next to Brea. He quickly and intentionally stepped forward to take it. She flinched, but neither of them said a word as he sat beside her.

The barmaid brought their meal and drinks, and the troop ate with somber moods and falsely casual conversation.

Thom's mind kept replaying Hewitt's final words to him. *"Your purpose is whatever you make it; just make sure it's a worthy one."*

He still didn't know how to do that, but he thought perhaps the best way to start was by getting his affairs in order.

During the meal, Thom and Brea didn't utter a word to one another. For the time being, he allowed her to maintain her ridiculous avoidance. Late in the evening, Deckard and Evylin returned but immediately went to their room, evidently still suffering the grief of Hewitt's secondary loss.

Night had long fallen before the rest of them departed. They said their goodnights and began climbing the stairs. Thom was careful to lean over to whisper to Rafferty before they left the noisy tavern, Brea striding well ahead of them. A sly grin crossed the weasel's face, but he accepted his task wordlessly.

Continuing up the stairs, the couples went to their rooms while Thom and Rafferty followed Brea to their shared space. She unlocked the door, slipped the key into her coat pocket, and moved to claim one of the two beds, since Thom had volunteered to sleep on the floor. Rafferty winked at Thom.

The space was small, so two grown men and a petite woman made it feel even more cramped. Brea stripped off her coat and draped it over the footboard.

"Raff," Thom said, "spare me a blanket, would you?"

"What? Your precious back can't handle the hardwood, Thommy-boy?"

The innkeeper had provided Thom with an extra blanket and pillow, but there weren't any spare mattresses to offer a more comfortable sleep. And while he'd laid out his bedroll, it would be of little comfort against the hard floor.

"Hard-packed dirt is softer than these planks," Thom complained. "You've got the inn's quilt plus your spare from camp."

"And you'd like me to freeze?" Rafferty said.

"It's practically balmy this far south. You'll be fine."

Rafferty waggled a finger at him. "I'm cold-natured."

Brea heaved a sigh at their banter. "Use mine," she said, gesturing toward her pack at the foot of the bed. Her camping blanket was rolled up with her own bedroll.

Thom took a step forward, but Rafferty held up a hand. "No, no," he said dramatically. "Allow me, Thommy. After all, I wouldn't want you to strain yourself."

With dramatic mockery, Rafferty lifted Brea's pack, unhooking the bedroll. It dropped unceremoniously onto the footboard, knocking down Brea's coat.

"Many apologies," Rafferty said, swiping it off the floor. He settled it back on the bed, then unfurled the blanket. With a lazy toss, he handed it over to Thom. "There. Be gratified."

Thom smirked. "I am."

"Good." Rafferty paced across the room. "Well," he said, letting the word drag out.

Brea looked up as she untied her boots.

Rafferty laced his fingers and stretched his arms before him. "I've got some patrons to fleece, so you two have a nice chat."

Brea's brow furrowed, but before she could say a word, Rafferty slipped back out the door. The immediate sharp scrape of the lock engaging from the key he'd stolen out of her pocket followed his departure.

Leaping to her feet, Brea's expression grew instantly hard. "Rafferty!" she called.

But he was gone.

Nonchalantly, Thom folded the wool blanket. "Guess we're stuck with each other," he observed.

Brea turned her flat glare his way.

Thom smiled pleasantly.

Kicking off her boots, Brea turned. Without a word, she began climbing into bed, fully clothed.

"Hey!" Thom lunged forward, catching her arm and jerking her back.

She whirled, slamming the heel of her hand down on his wrist fiercely. Thom yelped, his grip breaking readily. He cursed as the pain coiled up his arm, but he tried again. Using his other hand, he gripped Brea's sleeve, tugging her toward him.

With another jab, Brea hit a pressure point in his left arm, making it immediately numb.

"Stop it," he ordered.

"Then leave me alone," she returned.

Thom sucked in an angered breath as she turned her back on him again and adjusted her blanket, preparing to lie down. "You're going to have to talk to me eventually," he said.

She didn't reply, sinking onto the mattress and slipping her bare feet beneath the blankets.

"We work together," Thom pressed, refusing to feel awkward as he stood over her bed. "That means you and I need to get along."

"We can get along without talking to one another."

He scoffed. "You know, for an old woman, you're surprisingly immature."

Sitting on her bed, Brea lifted a brow threateningly.

Thom wouldn't be put off. "Why are you ignoring this?"

"Why shouldn't I?"

"Because it's ridiculous," he exclaimed. "Brea, you don't have to avoid me. Of all people, I know Ilain's accusation was false. Whatever your reasons for saving my life, it wasn't out of anything resembling romantic affection. I thought we were friends. And I'd still like to be that. So you don't have to avoid me."

She tossed him an irritated frown. Then she turned away, keeping her eyes on the far wall.

Thom scowled. "Dammit, Brea, I'm trying to be reasonable."

"Yelling does convey reason, after all," she mocked.

"Oh, sod off," he snapped.

Her gaze flashed to his, dark and cold.

Thom held it unflinchingly. "This isn't on me," he said. "We could be perfectly normal right now, but you're acting as though I've done something wrong. Which, unless you count nearly getting myself killed, I haven't."

Brea rolled her eyes. "Sit down," she said flatly.

"What?"

"I'm tired of craning my neck to look up at you. Sit down," she repeated and gestured to the other bed. "Over there."

"Are you going to talk to me?"

"Yes."

Thom took a seat on Rafferty's mattress.

Brea turned to face him, letting her legs slip from under the blankets and dangle off the edge. She was so short that her toes barely grazed the wooden planks. "Did you ever consider that I don't like being accused of murder?" she said.

"Of course," Thom said. "But I'm not the one accusing you."

She shook her head. "It's *because* of our friendship that I'm being accused. And Ilain is right: If I let feelings get in the way of doing my job, my decisions *should* be called into question." Her brows rose. "I'm distancing myself to ensure I can do my job correctly from here on out, Thom."

Thom stared at her. Dozens of thin, black braids hung around her shoulders, brushing them loosely. Her gray tunic caused her brown skin to appear slightly ashen in the dim room. And she looked startlingly small for such a fierce woman.

"You saved my life, Brea," he said quietly. "I don't give a damn what other people think."

She turned away, looking almost annoyed.

"Whatever anyone else says," he pressed, "your choice kept me alive. I owe you everything."

And even with her gaze averted, he could see that his words softened her.

"I'm not sure what changed, but I'd like my friend back so I can thank her for keeping me alive."

With a sigh, Brea pulled her feet onto the bed. "I'm not trying to punish you, Thom," she said.

"Then maybe talk to me."

"What do you want me to say?" she demanded, meeting his gaze at last. "Yes, I saved your life. You're welcome. But I also caused us to lose one of our most powerful members because I chose *your* life over his. If I can't act with indifference, I can't be sure that I'll save the ones who matter most."

Thom's eyes widened. "You regret saving me?"

Her face scrunched. "No, that's not—" She stopped and ran her hands over her face. "It was the right choice," she said, the words muted. "If I could go back, even now, I would still have chosen to save you."

"Thanks," he said with dry humor.

She gave a half-smirk. "Magical or not, these people need you. Deckard, Evylin—they would crumble without you. Rafferty and Ethenn? You're their leader, even if Deckard is their officer. The rest of us don't matter in the grand scheme of things. You Ephrians are the heart of this team."

"You're an Ephrian too," he reminded.

"Distantly." Brea leaned forward, holding his gaze with a serious look on her face. "Letting you die would have crippled us . . . permanently. I couldn't let that happen."

Thom dipped his head, uncertain how his presence could mean so much. He chose to ignore that statement and asked instead, "If you don't regret it, why are you treating me as though you do?"

Brea pressed her lips together. "Because I regret what happened after."

"Ilain's accusation?"

She gave a small nod.

"I told you I don't believe her."

Brea stared at her hands. From somewhere, she'd produced a knife. Likely one of the five he knew she slept with at all times.

Thom frowned at her dispirited mood. Her shoulders were uncharacteristically slumped. All her confidence seemed to have abandoned her in the shadowy room. And suddenly, Vayden's words came back to him.

"She's not punishing you. She's protecting herself."

Furrowing his brow, Thom decided to ask the question that had been foremost on his mind since the Space Keep.

"What does *mi'caro* mean?" he asked.

Brea twirled the knife, a humorless smile on her lips. "It doesn't matter."

"You wouldn't be avoiding the answer if that was true."

She scoffed in a self-deprecating manner. "It is a joke, that's all."

"Then we can laugh about it together when you tell me what it means."

A long silence stretched between them, and he could see she was working up courage. No matter what she claimed, the term was far more serious than a simple nickname.

Finally, Brea's eyes lingered on the blade in her hands as she whispered, "*Mi'caro.*" Her gaze met his. "My heart."

Thom's pulse stuttered.

Ilain was right.

Fighting to gain some semblance of understanding, Thom ran a hand through his hair. He grappled with the nickname's meaning. *My heart.* Such a tender endearment. And she'd given it to him after only a day.

"It was me?" Thom gasped, locking eyes with her again. "This whole time—the man you want to be with but can't—it was me?"

Brea shook her head furiously. "No!" she insisted, then grimaced. "Sort of. Listen—" She stashed the knife and held out her hands. "It's hard to explain, but . . . I was in love once, and the moment I saw you . . . You remind me of him."

Thom blanched. "So it isn't me personally? I'm just your chance of being with this man you can't have?" He wasn't sure if that situation was better or worse.

"Thom—"

"No, it's—that's great, actually," he said wryly. "Helps me feel a little less bad for you, knowing you're using me to reconnect with your past lover."

Brea scooted closer to the mattress's edge. "It isn't like that," she protested. "Yes, you look and act like Adie in many ways, but he wasn't—" She broke off, chewing on the inside of her cheek.

Adie. A moderately common pet form of Adem in Ephria. As a child, Thom had a friend they'd called Adie. He'd been drafted, too, and Thom had no idea where he was now, like so many of his childhood friends.

Carefully, kindly, Thom asked, "Do you want to tell me about him?"

She looked shockingly fragile as she sat there, the oil lamp's rusty glow casting stark shadows over her dark skin. "He was an Ephrian sailor," she said softly. "He came to Tanemisa on a merchant ship. I was training there, and we met at a tavern."

Thom quirked his brow, realizing they had met at a tavern too.

"We became friends," she continued. "He, uh—he was like you: dark hair, tall and muscular, bright, clever eyes. A total shit."

Thom couldn't help his grin. "You have terrible taste."

"And terrible luck," she said with false humor. "Despite myself, despite knowing he wasn't magical, and we couldn't have a future, we fell in love, and he . . . he asked me to marry him."

Knowing the story couldn't have a happy ending, Thom asked, "Did you say yes?"

"No."

Thom frowned. "You refused him?"

She merely nodded.

"Why?"

"He wasn't magical." At Thom's rueful look, she held up a hand. "Before you tell me what a horrible person I am, I know. I was young; the Alliance had just found me in Giyda, and I was scared. I'd made promises to the Alliance. I'd found a purpose for the first time in my life. And then Adie . . ."

Brea sighed. "If I could go back, I would change my answer. But I can't."

Thom cocked his head. "You could always find him again."

"It's too late for that."

"He's married?"

"He's dead."

"Oh."

Brea gave a forlorn smile. "A week after I refused him, his ship returned to Ephria. They hit a storm, and it ripped the ship apart. He drowned. His body washed ashore. He had no identification except for a letter from me in his pocket. They returned it to me, and that was it. I'd lost my chance."

They both stared at the floor after that. Thom didn't know what to say. It was a heartbreaking tale, yet she'd said she was young. It likely happened over twenty years ago, if not longer. She'd moved to Wauld, became a soldier for the Alliance, and lived an entire other life. The pain couldn't be as strong as it once was.

Yet, he knew it was devastating all the same.

"I called him *mi'caro*," Brea admitted hollowly.

Thom's gaze flashed up to find her watching him.

"When I met you," she continued quietly, "you reminded me of him. It slipped out, and I told myself it didn't matter because it was a joke."

Thom nodded, understanding.

Brea's expression tightened with pain. "But the more I got to know you, the more I saw your differences. And the thing is . . ." She stared at him, her eyes haunted. "The name became true."

Thom's blood ran cold.

"I'm not in love with you," Brea promised hurriedly. "But my heart . . . It does feel for you, as it did for him. And Ilain was right. I chose you over Auden because of my feelings for you."

Thom hung his head, eyes trained firmly on the floor. "Brea, I—"

"You don't have to let me down easily," she said. "I know it isn't mutual."

The bed creaked as she leaned forward. "And I don't want it to be, Thom," she swore. "I had love with Adie. I don't care to replace it. It is my burden to carry on with my promise to the Alliance. I will marry and Bond with a Mage, I will become Highlady Commander of whatever province they wish, and the rest of my days will be spent in service to my people."

It sounded so wrong to Thom. Such a dreadful sacrifice for such a noble cause.

"You shouldn't have to do that, Brea," he said.

"It's all I have left."

Several moments of silence passed between them.

"Where do we go from here?" he asked, looking up at her. "I want to be your friend, but if that's too hard for you—"

"It isn't," she said. "I didn't pull away because I can't handle your friendship."

"Then why did you pull away?"

She grimaced. "Because I didn't want others finding out the truth."

He nodded in understanding. "I'm sorry you lost him," he said.

A gentle smile came to her lips. "Thank you."

Thom studied her in the silence that followed. Somehow, she looked different to him. The sharpness of her gaze no longer bore hardness but rather sadness. Her confidence was gentler, her beauty softer. She was striking, strong, and powerful, but for a whole new reason. He saw her as she truly was. She'd lived through heartache, and while she hadn't quite yet overcome it, she was doing her best to live with purpose.

Just like him.

"Thank you," Brea said again.

Thom raised his brow.

"For this," she said, gesturing between them. "For listening. For being my friend."

He pressed his lips together in a smile. "Thank you for *wanting* to be my friend," he said.

"Only a fool wouldn't want your friendship, Thom," she assured. "You're far better and far more worthy than you think."

The affirmation hit Thom with a jolt. "I don't want to be," he said.

A sly, cunning grin lifted her countenance. "You don't get that choice," she said. Hopping to her feet, she reached across the short distance and slapped his shoulder. "Now, leave me alone so I can get some sleep."

Thom rose, too, shifting away to give her space. "We're friends again, right?"

"I doubt it." At his lifted brow, she teased, "You flirt with your friends, and I don't care to have my heart toyed with."

Thom eyed her. "It isn't my fault that I'm your exact type," he said. "Why punish me for what I can't control?"

Settling the blankets over her lap, Brea looked down at him as he lowered himself to the bedroll on the floor. "Allore gives us all an affliction to bear, I suppose."

"Then friends?"

"Friends," she confirmed.

With a satisfied nod, Thom lay down, rolling onto his side to face the wall. "Goodnight then, Brea."

Brea turned down the oil lamp, leaving the faintest orange glow for Rafferty's late arrival. The bed creaked as she shifted down, and the room fell silent.

"Goodnight, *mi'caro*," she called playfully.

Thom smiled, tucking one arm under his lumpy pillow. He might not have decided on his true purpose yet, but he had time. For tonight, at least, he'd set one thing right.

CHAPTER FORTY-SIX

20TH OF RADIA, 1574

Trollenston loomed in the distance like a bad dream.

Terraeus didn't seem to care about Ethenn's sour mood. The sun shone brightly. Birds sang merrily. His friends chatted casually.

Over the last couple of days, things had improved within the troop. Thom and Brea were back on speaking terms, though their banter was decidedly less flirtatious. All were somber after Hewitt's final release, but crossing over into Estshire seemed to return cheer to Evylin and Deckard, which helped the rest of them relax too. Ilain hadn't gotten over her dislike for Brea, but she'd allowed Ethenn to train with her and was agreeable enough in the lieutenant's presence. And in the evening, alone in their room, Ethenn and Ilain distracted themselves from their troubles with each other's kisses.

The diversion of Ilain's embrace hadn't been Ethenn's original intent with their first agreement. He'd thought they'd kiss that once and be done with it. But each night, Ilain pulled him down onto the bed beside her and pressed her lips to his. Inevitably, the activity devolved into them tangled under the blankets, though he was quite careful not to go *too* far.

A feat that proved nearly impossible with his head and body buzzing from her touch.

Somehow, Rafferty noticed their newfound comfort with each other. He'd begun pestering Ethenn about it, which made him incredibly uncomfortable, but he assumed that was likely the point.

Glancing up ahead, Ethenn caught sight of Ilain riding beside Evylin. The physical development in their relationship made things more complicated. While he'd tried to keep a level head and a tempered heart, he could feel himself growing dangerously attached to his wife. What if Ilain realized his faults? What if she found another Warrior she liked better? He wouldn't blame her if she threw him over, but he wasn't sure his heart would survive such a blow.

Maybe he should take her up on her offer and consummate the marriage. Then she couldn't leave him, even if she eventually realized what a terrible mistake she'd made. . . .

Ethenn's jaw tightened as his eyes drifted back to the buildings of Trollenston, drawing ever nearer in the distance. He hoped to get through the town unrecognized. Were they still looking for him? He'd have to be careful. They couldn't try him now that he was a soldier, but he didn't want Deckard or the others to find out about his violent indiscretions.

Four months. Would they still be looking for him after half a year had passed?

It was murder, he reminded himself. *Of course, they're still looking.*

"You vile heathen."

Ethenn blew a breath, forcing his uncle's voice out of his head. He would steer clear of Vernon Loxley's smithy, that was sure.

"What was that for?" Rafferty asked at Ethenn's side.

Ethenn furrowed his brow. "What?"

"You just sighed," Rafferty said, then mimicked the troubled exhale. "Like that. What's got your knickers knotted?"

He deflected with a shrug. "I joined the army to get out of this town. I didn't think I'd ever come back."

"I'm not entirely sure why you wanted to leave," Rafferty said. "From what your old pal, Carmichael, said, you were living it large—on quite the winning streak and with the prize purse to match, *Slayer*."

Ethenn leveled a flat glare at Rafferty. "You know, don't you?"

A sly lift came to Rafferty's lips. "The gruesome tale of your little stage name?" His silver-gray eyes twinkled. "I haven't an idea."

Hearing the lie, Ethenn nodded. "It was labeled an accident," he said emotionlessly.

"Was it honestly an accident, though?"

Ethenn shrugged. "Technically."

"Murder isn't a technicality, little Lox. You either meant to kill him, or you didn't."

Though he held in his anger, Ethenn knew his face was turning red. "Perhaps I don't know the answer."

"Huh." Rafferty grinned dryly. "Well, from the account I was given, it seemed involuntary manslaughter was the verdict. Though informally, of course. You can't go to the magistrate for justice when the death occurs in an illegal fighting ring, can ya?"

"It's a known risk you take," Ethenn admitted.

"Especially when you're fighting the Slayer."

Ethenn didn't bother replying.

"So," Rafferty continued, "you wanted to avoid a return because you don't like your reputation. That's understandable."

There was more to it, but Ethenn didn't care to explain.

"There isn't anything or anyone you're happy to visit while in town?" Rafferty pressed.

"No," Ethenn lied, then nudged his horse forward, avoiding any more conversation.

He came alongside Ilain, locked in conversation with Evylin about legendary magical artifacts that had gone missing shortly after the Relics were locked away. Since she'd already told Ethenn the story, he didn't bother to listen.

Instead, he watched Trollenston as it inched closer. The evening sky shone with a bronze cast, the sun disappearing behind the horizon. The forests grew thinner this close to the town, the hilly countryside pushing the trees aside. In the center of it all, homes and businesses twisted and wound together in a cluster, greenery growing along their fronts. But off in the distance, Ethenn could see a small, vacant cottage separated from the town. He intentionally kept his gaze away to ensure no one asked him about it.

Once they were within half a mile, Deckard dropped back to talk with their group. While the road wasn't technically wide enough for four riders, the countryside was open enough to allow for it. "Evylin, do you think your aunt and uncle will expect us to stay with them?" he asked.

"Yes," Evylin said without hesitation. "If Serene learns that we were in town, she'd be greatly offended if we stayed anywhere else."

"But there isn't enough room for the rest of our troop to stay with them?"

"Certainly not."

Deckard nodded. "I suppose we could send the others to that inn near their house."

"Which one?" Ethenn asked. "Felden's Inn, The Shepherd's Rest, or The Wanderer?"

Ilain, Evylin, and Deckard looked at him in surprise. "Right," Evylin said with a grin. "I forget you lived here sometimes. They live near The Shepherd's Rest."

"Ah," Ethenn said thoughtfully. The Shepherd's Rest was a good tavern and inn, but it was located too near Vernon's smithy for his liking. "Not as nice as Felden's Inn but better than the alternative. The Wanderer tends to attract people like Raff."

"What's that supposed to mean?" Rafferty asked in a bright tone, riding up just behind them with Thom.

"It means I've fought in their cellar," Ethenn said.

While Rafferty snickered, Deckard began to give his orders. Due to the presence of Evylin's relatives in town and the need to spend time with them, they'd skip training for the night.

"It'd be best to rest as much as possible before the final Keep anyway," Isla added.

The troop split up, the Deckards—sans Thom—heading to visit Evylin's family while the rest of them rode through the winding streets to the inn. Ethenn offered to lead the way, intentionally taking them on the long route so they wouldn't pass his uncle's smithy. Though it was evening and Vernon Loxley refused to work past sundown, there was a chance his son, Tylaar, was still there, cleaning up.

In fact, there was a chance Ethenn would run into his cousin at The Shepherd's Rest as well.

So he kept his head down the entire ride through the town, carefully avoiding eye contact. There were no true police in Trollenston, but the town watch occasionally patrolled near the taverns to keep the peace. And he didn't care to catch their attention.

Once they arrived at the inn and tavern, Ethenn let Thom take the lead in securing the rooms. He pulled Ilain to the side, still keeping his head down. "I'm going straight to our room," he said for her ears alone. Knowing she'd ask questions, he preemptively explained, "There are some people I wish to avoid who frequent this tavern."

Ilain raised her chin. "Are you in some kind of trouble?" she asked smartly.

"You caught my discomfort," he noted.

"I'm rather aware of your moods, yes."

Ethenn didn't know whether his wry grin was due to amusement or annoyance. "No," he lied. "I'm not in trouble. I just didn't like my life here and don't care to reminisce with old acquaintances."

"You're hiding on the off chance they'll show up?"

"I'd rather not tempt fate."

Ilain chuckled and patted his arm. "All right, darling. You go up, and I'll bring a meal up in two shakes of a lamb's tail." Her brow lifted as she asked, "That is what you Estshire lot say, right?"

Ethenn chuckled at the familiar colloquialism. "You catch on quick."

"I'm known for my wit, dearie." She kissed his cheek, then gave him a shove. "Get going. The men are starting to stare at me, and they'll notice you before too long, even if it is from jealousy. Then we'd defeat the whole point of you abandoning the party."

Taking his key from Thom, Ethenn hurried up the stairs and out of the tavern's main room. He ducked into their room and waited for Ilain to join him. When she came up, they enjoyed their meal—a hearty ale-braised lamb stew with peas and purple potatoes and a side of honeyed biscuits—and Ethenn began to enact his plan.

"I don't think I'm feeling so well," he said, rubbing his forehead, ensuring it was appropriately furrowed.

Ilain glanced up at him. "No? Do you think it's the stew?"

Nervously, he chuckled. "Not that kind of unwell," he replied. "I think I'm just tired."

The faintest blush crept along Ilain's cheeks as her gaze dropped to the dregs of her soup in the bottom of the bowl. "Is that your subtle way of telling me I've been keeping you up too late?" she asked, her tone somewhere between bashful and coquettish.

Ethenn massaged his temple, a faint smile coming to his lips. "You are a pleasant distraction from sleep," he admitted. "But no, I think . . ." He paused, grimacing. "I think all this travel is just catching up to me. I feel . . . weak."

Ilain eyed him, and he couldn't tell whether her close inspection was from worry or suspicion. "Do you think you ought to lie down?" she asked, and now he could hear her concern.

After a labored sigh, Ethenn finally dropped his hand. "Probably . . ." he said reluctantly. "I don't want you to feel as if you have to coddle me, though. You should spend the evening with everyone. I'm just going to turn in early, I think."

Ilain reached across to take his hand. "Would you like me to ask for some tea? I always find an illus flower infusion the best cure for a headache."

"No, I'd rather sleep," he said, then pulled a face. "My mother used to make me drink that stuff whenever I showed the slightest sign of a cold, and now I'm permanently averse to it."

While it wasn't a lie, Ethenn felt guilty as Ilain's expression showed genuine worry. "All right," she said, rising. "I won't stay up late, but I would like to spend more time with Vayden and Isla."

Nodding, Ethenn encouraged her out the door carefully. She left, taking the empty stew bowls with her after a quick peck on his lips.

His mouth still tingling from the mild kiss, Ethenn shut the door. Then he turned and walked straight for the window. He unlatched the lock and pushed lightly on the panes to open it. The sun had set, leaving only the faintest glow on the horizon. With a single glance around the empty street, he proceeded to climb out.

The house sat on the hilltop, newly built in the last decade. Its stone edifice was far more luxurious than any of the other houses in Trollenston. Even the magistrate didn't own such a home.

Ethenn climbed a nearby tree and hid, watching the building carefully. The house was still and quiet. Golden lamplight lit the windows. It appeared to be a quiet night in the household.

Finally catching sight of movement near the bedroom, Ethenn studied the shape that materialized. It was feminine in form.

He dropped from the tree, snuck across the lawn, and found the same ivy-covered trellis he'd already used once to break in. Then he hopped over the balcony rail, thinking what a useless construction the opulent overlook was in a place like Trollenston. The estate didn't even look out over a proper garden.

With ease, Ethenn picked the lock on the door. He opened it a fraction, peering into the room.

Luxurious furnishings—a bed, a vanity, a wardrobe, and a settee—filled the bedroom. A plush rug covered the wooden floor. Velvet draperies and thick wallpaper gave the room a rich air. Trollenston didn't have nobility, but the shrewd merchant empire of Bastien Muirren had made him wealthier than any other man in Estshire. He was as close to nobility as the province would ever get.

A young woman sat at the vanity on the far left side of the room. Dark brown curls tumbled around her shoulders. A light green robe with embroidered pink flowers draped around her figure, hanging down haphazardly over the back of the stool. He could see her face reflected in the mirror. Soft brown skin like his, a rounded jawline, a pert nose, and deep brown eyes. She was even more beautiful than he remembered.

Silently, Ethenn stepped over the threshold. The movement caught the woman's attention in the mirror, and her eyes darted to him. She did a double take, then gasped.

"Ethenn," she exclaimed in a low whisper, leaping from the seat. She whirled, rushing to him.

Ethenn couldn't help his smile, catching her in his embrace. She smelled like lilies and other rich scents he couldn't name. And something was decidedly different about her frame as he held her. She didn't feel right in his arms.

Pulling back, Ethenn looked at his sister's face. "Hi there, Rin," he said gently.

Terrina's expression was pinched with a smile even as tears filled her eyes. "I've missed you," she said. "I didn't know where you'd gone, and—and they said you joined the army, but . . . I couldn't believe you'd leave me like that."

"I didn't have a choice, Rin," he said sadly. "You know that."

She shook her head, hand absentmindedly drifting to her stomach.

That's when Ethenn realized what was so off about her figure.

"Rin," he gasped, eyes locked on the protruding roundness of her stomach. "Are you—?"

Terrina's smile softened. She used both hands to cup her pregnant belly, the flowing white cotton nightdress underneath her robe growing taut. "Only another couple of months, now," she said. "He's to be a Pyra baby like you."

Ethenn gaped at his sister. She was five months pregnant, with less than eighty days left before she gave birth.

"He?" Ethenn asked.

Terrina shrugged. "Well, obviously, I don't know, but . . . He feels like a boy."

Ethenn's stomach roiled. The bastard had gotten her pregnant. At least it wasn't out of wedlock, and Terrina had inherited the house and fortune. But still. . . .

Four months ago, Ethenn had returned from a three-week-long hunting trip. He always hated leaving his sister for such extended periods of time, but there was nothing he could do. He'd moved out of Vernon's home the moment he could afford it, providing a menial room for himself above the butcher's shop. But when their father died, guardianship of Terrina had legally passed to their uncle. Though Ethenn contested to have her moved under his headship, there was no precedent in Ephria for a brother to become a woman's authority. Magistrate Steevensun followed the law, which stated that a woman was under the headship of her father or her husband. As Terrina had neither, it fell to whomever her father deemed worthy in his will. In this case, that was Vernon Loxley.

Their father hadn't known how dreadfully his choice would turn out, of course. He could never have expected to die so early or that his brother would be so cruel to his children. But Vernon was interested in only one thing: his success. Upon the inheritance of two new wards, he only asked how his niece and nephew could benefit him.

Even at the age of twelve, Ethenn was required to work twice as hard to find ways to pay for their survival. Though he'd managed to escape from their uncle's household, Terrina was forced to stay under his roof. So Ethenn still had to pay for her livelihood. He hunted, he smithed, and he fought. During the few hours of the day he wasn't working, he was with Terrina or drinking in The Wanderer.

But when Ethenn returned from his hunt those fateful months ago, Terrina wasn't at home.

When he asked his aunt where she'd gone, the woman's lips turned up snidely. "With her husband," she said.

Ethenn had never been so angry. In his absence, his uncle had sold his sister off like chattel. Bastien Muirren, a thirty-eight-year-old merchant known for his cruelly cunning business deals, had spotted the then-seventeen-year-old Terrina Loxley at a town dance. Bastien had returned from his stint in the army six years prior and begun to build his empire through the funds and connections he'd made during his military career. A shrewd man with a penchant for good luck at cards, he'd managed to secure himself a hefty stipend to set up his business. And his profits only grew.

Evidently, Bastien Muirren's success in business instilled in him the belief that he could buy anything, including his wife.

Upon noticing Terrina's great beauty, Bastien approached Vernon Loxley and offered a hefty bridal price. Vernon hadn't hesitated to accept the deal, which was to excuse him from paying the dowry in exchange for thirty gold crowns. It was far too easy a price to accept.

And far too cheap by Ethenn's estimation.

His sister was worth far more than meager coins. And yet, she hadn't been given a choice.

Upon learning of Terrina's marriage, Ethenn hurried to the Muirren estate. He found his sister alone in this very room, just as he had tonight. And he'd begged her to leave with him. "I have enough money," he said. "We can go to Olbury, buy passage across the sea to Schon, and neither Uncle nor Muirren will be able to come for you. They wouldn't dare."

Yet, Terrina had rejected his rescue. "I have a duty to my husband," she told him.

"You don't love him," he objected.

"No, but . . . Bastien is a good man," Terrina said. "He's been kind, gentle, and affectionate. He knows I don't love him yet, but he said he hopes to earn it in time."

"Purchase it, you mean."

Terrina shook her head. "You know I'd never love a man for what he can give me."

"Muirren isn't a good man," he argued. "He's a snake. He makes underhanded deals, gambles, and cheats. The only reason he's good to you now is because he wants something from you. You're a toy to him, Rin. He'll grow bored with you, and all this goodness you believe he has will disappear. You'll be alone and mistreated. And I won't stand by while that happens."

But Terrina refused to see reason. She insisted that her husband was trustworthy. Ethenn hadn't understood why until now. She'd already been pregnant. Leaving with Muirren's heir would have ensured the man seeking them out. He wouldn't have let them escape with such a prized possession.

In the low lamplight of the present night, Ethenn gently took his sister's shoulders between his hands. "Rin, I'm so sorry," he said.

Terrina clutched his wrists. "You needn't be."

Before he could argue his case, she pulled him toward the bench at the foot of the bed. "Now, come, tell me: How are you? Has the army treated you well? You look good. This insignia looks important."

Ethenn glanced at the Order of the King patch on his coat and smirked. "Lots has happened," he said. "Too much to tell tonight."

"Are you happy?" she asked.

Ethenn opened his mouth to reply, but the words caught. Was he happy? He couldn't say he was. Despite his love for Ilain, their relationship was complicated. His feelings were deepening while hers were . . . Well, he didn't know what she felt for him. Perhaps something, but it wasn't yet love. That wouldn't come until after their Bonding.

Unable to explain such things to his sister but not wanting to disappoint her, he said, "I think I will be. Soon."

She squeezed his hand. "How long will you stay?"

"In town?"

She nodded.

"Just the night," he said. "But, Rin, I'm going to come back for you."

Terrina's brow furrowed.

"I'm in the middle of a mission now, and there are some things that need to be figured out. But as soon as it's all taken care of, I'm going to come back for you." He glanced at her growing stomach. "And the baby," he concluded.

Terrina's dark eyes clouded with something he couldn't read.

"I'm going to get a promotion of a sort soon," Ethenn explained. "I'll be able to provide for all of us. You can raise your child however you like—far away from here. We'll be together, and you won't have to worry about anyone making you do anything you don't want to do ever again."

"Ethenn—"

"Trust me, Rin," he pressed, tightening his grip on her. "We can be a family again."

His sister pressed her lips together, seeming to struggle for words.

Then the bedroom door opened.

Ethenn and Terrina shot out of their seats as a servant stepped in. And behind him came Bastien Muirren.

Ethenn's heart stopped beating. It was impossible.

The night he'd come to rescue Terrina four months ago, Bastien found them. He'd entered the room then, like he did now. He'd rushed in and, finding a strange man with his wife, flew into a rage, even as Terrina screamed that it was her brother. Ethenn and Bastien fought. They'd tumbled out onto the balcony. And as Ethenn's anger flashed hotter than ever before, he'd kicked Bastien over the rail to fall crashing to the stones below.

Ethenn had killed Bastien. That's why he joined the army. That's why he ran.

Yet, here his sister's husband was—fully alive.

However, tonight, Bastien didn't stride into the room. The servant wheeled him inside on a chair made with wheels like a wagon. His once proud and handsome face bore still-healing scars, soft red lines across his umber skin. Otherwise, he appeared hale and whole.

A tremble worked through Ethenn as his skin began to heat.

Bastien was supposed to be dead. His sister should have been free, a wealthy widow living a life of luxury, but instead, she remained shackled to the scoundrel who'd stolen her freedom.

Just as Bastien and his servant noticed Ethenn's presence, Terrina rushed forward. "Dear," she said, setting a hand on Bastien's rigid shoulder, "my brother has come to visit. Isn't that nice?"

A long, tense silence stretched. Terrina excused the servant, and he shut the door behind him. Her fingers massaged Bastien's shoulder, even as the man glared at Ethenn.

"Bas," Terrina whispered.

Ethenn bristled at the nickname.

But Bastien softened. "Welcome, Ethenn," he said tightly. "Let me apologize before anything else is said for our . . . misunderstanding when last we met."

And yet still, Ethenn couldn't breathe. He'd killed the man. He'd solved his sister's problem. And yet, the bloody man survived.

Terrina straightened. "Ethenn," she said, a strange authority entering her voice. She had one hand on her husband's shoulder and the other on her pregnant belly. "Bastien didn't realize who you were the last time you met. I explained everything to him, and he regrets his hasty actions. He recognizes that he was just as much to blame for his accident as you."

Ethenn held Bastien's coal-black gaze. "You should be dead," he said flatly.

A haughty expression lifted the older man's brow. "Some men have all the luck," he said.

Terrina's hand tightened on his shoulder.

Bastien adjusted in his seat. "I wasn't as gravely injured as you presumed," he explained. "While I am still recovering, the doctor assures me that I'll walk again. Though likely with a cane. I am an old man, after all." He said the last bit with a wry grin, glancing up at Terrina, who smiled fondly at him.

Terrina turned back to her brother. "Despite our strange start," she said, "Bas and I have come to an understanding over the last several months."

"Being at the mercy of others forces you to obtain perspective," Bastien said dryly. "At least, when your nurse is Rina."

Terrina giggled lightly. "I helped Bas see that his purchase of me was due to infatuation and not love," she said. "But together, we decided that we'd try to find love anyway. Especially for the sake of our little one."

A strange expression came over Bastien's face as he gripped Terrina's hand, which still rested on his shoulder. Ethenn couldn't determine whether it was regret, agitation, or hope.

Ethenn refused to believe any of it. "He bought you, Rin. You're just another of his acquisitions."

Bastien's jaw tightened. "I would request your respect while a guest in my house," he said threateningly. Though Ethenn didn't know what the cripple thought he could do to him in that chair. But then it wasn't Ethenn who was at the man's mercy.

It was Terrina.

The merchant might have duped his sweet sister with his lies, but Ethenn wouldn't be fooled. However, he wouldn't let his sister be punished for his actions either.

Bastien Muirren was a clever bastard. His manipulation and underhanded scheme were lauded in the shady corners of Trollenston. The man had shown up to some of Ethenn's fights in the past, spending illicit evenings in The Wanderer. He couldn't believe that the man had sought redemption. Not when he had possession of his beloved sister—his only remaining immediate family.

"What will it take?" Ethenn asked.

"Pardon?" Bastien replied, eyes narrowing.

Ethenn nodded to Terrina. "I want to purchase my sister back," he said. "What will it take to have you sign her under my headship?"

Terrina gasped in disbelief while Bastien blinked shrewdly.

"You want to purchase her from me?" he said.

Ethenn held his gaze with unfaltering intensity. "Name your price."

Bastien cocked his head. "It isn't just my wife you'd be taking. It'd be my child."

"So the price goes up." Ethenn shrugged, waving away the comment with flippant nonchalance. "What're they worth to you? You paid thirty gold for Terrina. Would you like to double it? And what about your child? We'll sign over any rights to inheritance so you can sire another heir and not have to worry about us coming for your money."

"Ethenn!" Terrina objected.

He ignored her. "Forsaken rights and, what? A hundred gold?"

"Two hundred," Bastien said. "Each."

Ethenn grinned. "Four hundred gold and a letter denying inheritance. Deal."

Terrina stared at him, dumbfounded.

Bastien narrowed his gaze again. "You don't have that sort of money."

"Don't I?"

"I know about you, Slayer," Bastien said. "I run the fighting pits as I run this whole town. You made a good profit, but not nearly that much."

Ethenn smirked. "I don't think you heard about my new job." He tapped the insignia on his coat. "I work for King Ephren now. I've got plenty of gold to spare."

It was a lie. In total, Ethenn had about two hundred and thirty gold stored in the Loclight royal bank thanks to the king's reward, his earnings from the fights, and his pay from the army. But he knew after his appointment as Highlord Commander at Ilain's side, he'd have more than enough to rescue his sister.

Bastien blinked, uncertain of how to respond. His eyes latched onto the patch. Terrina took a step away from his chair, but his hand shot out, capturing hers and pulling her back. "No," he said flatly.

"What?" Ethenn demanded.

"No, you cur," he hissed. "I'm not selling my wife and child to you or anyone else. Now, get out of my house."

Ethenn took a threatening step forward. "I'm not leaving without her," he said, though he knew it was a foolish demand.

Terrina couldn't join them on their journey, pregnant as she was. And without a formal letter granting him authority over her, Bastien could recall her at any time with the lawmen's help. Until Allund came to be, Ethenn was powerless.

His sister looked conflicted, her expression pinched as she stared between her husband and her brother.

"Get out," Bastien replied, the threat returning to his voice. "Or I'll call the guard."

Ethenn raised his brow. "Not if I kill you first."

Bastien scowled, but Terrina stepped in front of him. "Stop it," she ordered. Her fierce look reminded him of their mother, and his heart winced. Tears sparkled on her lashes, but her voice remained steady as she spoke. "I don't know why you've done this. Why would you want me to lose my husband?"

"Because he's a *liar*, Rin," he shouted.

The tears slipped down her cheeks. "But he's my husband," she said. "And I can either choose to be happy with him, or I can spend the rest of my life in misery. I'm sorry if you don't believe him, but I have to. I must believe that no matter what he's done or who he once was, he might love me enough to become a better man."

Ethenn shook his head, ready to fight her. But she cut across his words. "Leave."

The pressure of his anger flared. "What?" he gaped.

"Leave," Terrina repeated, silent tears staining her face. "And don't bother coming back until you can accept my husband as I have."

His heart stuttered, the anger receding under the shock of hurt. "Rin—"

"Goodbye, Ethenn," she said with finality. Then she turned back to her husband.

The merchant took his wife's hands, holding Ethenn's gaze with a triumphant expression. A slight smirk tugged at the corner of his mouth. But when he turned to Terrina, his gaze did soften. Could his feelings for her possibly be genuine?

Dismissed, Ethenn left. He climbed over the edge of the balcony, descending back down the trellis.

It wasn't possible. Bastien couldn't be a good man. He couldn't change that quickly.

Bastien had purchased Terrina; he'd used her. He didn't care about her love. Did he? But for Terrina's sake, Ethenn had to hope his claims were true. He had to hope they could find love.

Ethenn walked through the dark night as a light breeze swept through the hilly valley. He shivered. Could they grow to love one another? Or was Terrina destined for a loveless marriage, no matter how hard she tried to feel something for her husband? And even if she did, Bastien was still a scoundrel who worked underhanded deals to grow his empire in the small town.

How could Ethenn leave her to that fate?

He entered the town, taking the long way to the inn to avoid the smithy again. When he approached The Shepherd's Rest, he looked up at the second story. The window he'd climbed through an hour ago was glowing. He hadn't thought to light the lamp before he'd left.

Ilain was inside, then. She would have discovered that he was gone, and she would be waiting for an explanation.

Ethenn's heart squeezed with sudden understanding. Same as Bastien Muirren, he was trapping a woman into marriage with him simply because he wanted her. It didn't matter that Ilain didn't love him; he was allowing her to sell herself for the success of the Alliance's plans. She deserved so much more. A man she loved. A Warrior of value worthy of her. An honorable man who could lead justly beside her.

But Ethenn was a murderer. He was a wretch. And he was no better than Bastien.

CHAPTER FORTY-SEVEN

After joining her family and friends in the tavern, Ilain settled in the seat next to her brother. In her absence, the others had finished their dinner, and many young men had filtered into the tavern. Most of them were of a medium or dark complexion and quite short. They made her feel rather tall, since she was their height or more.

As she settled in, Vayden leaned over to Ilain and whispered, "Where's your husband?"

Ilain accepted the tankard of ale from the waitress, resigning herself to the simpler offerings of the countryside. "He isn't feeling well," she told him casually.

Vayden raised an eyebrow as Isla sat forward across the table from him. "Was it the stew?" she asked.

Ilain smirked. "No," she said in amusement. "It's a lie. He's up to something, but I'm allowing him to think he's gotten away with it."

The couple chuckled, sharing a look. "You're a good wife," Vayden said lightly, lifting his ale.

"I'm an inexperienced wife," Ilain replied. "But I have the age to offset my ignorance. Ethenn doesn't lie maliciously; whatever he's up to, I trust his heart."

"That is very good of you," Isla said. "Few women are so confident in their husband's intentions."

"The intentions of very few men are entirely pure," Vayden quipped.

"Though you are wholly virtuous, my love," Isla replied.

Vayden gave her a flirtatious grin. "Not wholly, *mi'amená.*"

Ilain mocked a gag at the suggestive nickname. "Anyway, I'll let him do whatever he thinks he's keeping secret, and since there is no doubt I'll catch him on his return, I'll find out what it was."

"Perhaps it is a surprise for you," Isla suggested. "This is his hometown, is it not? Maybe he hopes to introduce you to his family. Or to bring you a gift of significance."

"I had considered it," Ilain admitted.

However, she'd also considered that his lie was likely to pay his abusive uncle a visit. She rather hoped so. Ethenn deserved to shove his good fortune in the old blighter's face. Though Ilain somewhat wished he had taken her with him so she could give the man a piece of her mind. And perhaps a burn scar or two of his own.

Ilain smiled to herself at the thought. She sipped her ale—wincing at the malty taste—and let her thoughts drift as her brother and his wife returned to the conversation with their friends.

There was *one* alternative that Ilain had considered. One that made her heart dance and her stomach flutter.

"In Estshire, there's a forest with a hidden glen that's filled with gilda lilies."

Ilain felt her cheeks heat. It was possible that Ethenn had gone off to prepare a romantic escapade in the woods. She certainly wouldn't turn down such a gesture. And it would be the perfect setting for her to tell him the truth: She loved him.

Ilain had come to that definitive conclusion eight nights ago. When he'd told her the story behind his scars, something within her unlocked. Like the heavy lock within the Keeps' iron doors, it opened with a resounding *thunk*. While she had thought she *might* love him before, that story, along with the deepened understanding of him, made her heart squeeze and her lungs weaken. More than anything, she'd wanted to pull him into her arms and heal all his wounds, the ones she knew and the ones he'd yet to reveal. He'd lost so much. He'd been hurt so much. She wanted to care for him and love him—not for her sake but for his.

Ilain knew, at that moment, she would do anything for Ethenn. If his happiness meant vengeance on his uncle, she'd burn the man to ash. If it meant razing Trollenston to the ground, she'd find a way. If growing an entire garden of gilda lilies in memory of his lost parents would soothe his pain, she'd spend the next ten years of her life dedicated to the study of Terrae magic and sprout an entire, eternal mountain of the flowers (though he'd have to show her what they looked like first).

If Ethenn Loxley asked her to forsake the Alliance and give up the position of Highlady Chancellor to move to the forests of Estshire . . .

Ilain stared at the ruddy-colored ale in her tankard. Her heart stilled, knowing she would do it. She would leave behind everything she'd worked toward for the past thirty years because she loved him more than anything else in this world. And she would not sacrifice him on behalf of the Alliance.

While the others continued their evening revelry, Ilain excused herself at last. She climbed to the room they'd reserved on the second floor of The Shepherd's Rest, finding it empty, as expected. It was a simple room. The bed was narrow, though built for two, and covered with an ivy-patterned quilt. A threadbare rug was draped over the warped wooden floor. The only other furnishings were a singular nightstand, a large trunk for storage, and a small, upholstered chair.

Habitually, Ilain began preparing for bed. Though she had no way of knowing when Ethenn would return, she saw no reason to wait around for him. If he were preparing a tryst in the forest, it would be better to be in her nightclothes anyway. If he'd gone to deal with personal business, she might as well prepare for his arrival and welcome him back with open arms.

Once clothed in her nightdress, Ilain laid out her dress for the next morning. While traveling in Wauld, there had been no reason to change for the night. She'd worn the same clothing for weeks on end. An experience she never desired again.

Now that they were in Ephria, regularly able to stay in inns, she took the luxury of fresh clothes seriously.

Ilain grabbed a small woven bag from her saddlebag and began to slip off her rings, one at a time. The gemstones glinted with the faintest softness. She'd begun reinfusing them with magic slowly, but they wouldn't hold any real power for several months.

The oil lamp's light reflected in the ruby ring's facets. Thirty years of magic had been lost, and she still hadn't acted soon enough.

She pushed away the feeling of guilt that tugged at her again, tucking the last ring into the bag. She stared at her bare hands as she fixed the clasp, her gaze catching on her empty marital finger. In Wauld, they rarely exchanged rings upon marriage. It was an Ephrian tradition that had begun with the Shepherd King. Upon his coronation, he'd gifted his wife, Fionn, with an emerald and platinum band. From then on, the women of Ephria wanted wedding rings too. The men only began wearing them as a sign of returned fidelity, often matching their bands to their wives' rings.

When Ethenn insisted that he'd get her a wedding band once they were married, she reminded him that they would be Bonded that day. "I'll already be given a ring," she said.

He shook his head. "That won't be a wedding ring, though. I'll get you a separate one to represent us."

"Am I to wear six rings, then?" Ilain teased.

"You're to wear however many you'd like," he replied.

Staring at her hands now, Ilain smiled at the memory. *No,* she decided, *I'll just wear two.* After all, what use would she have for the extra stores of power once they'd Bonded? Her moonstone ring and wedding band were all she'd need.

A draft swept through the room, causing Ilain to shiver. She looked toward the door, finding it still shut.

"Ilain." Ethenn's voice drew her to whirl around. He stood there before the open window, expression strangely devoid of emotion.

Ilain set the ring pouch on the bed. "Did you climb in through the window?" she asked with an incredulous tone.

"I didn't care to explain myself to Thom and Raff," he said.

She lifted her chin in understanding. Cautiously, she asked, "Did you go visit your uncle?"

"No."

Ilain almost asked where he had gone but wondered if she had been right earlier. Maybe he was intending to surprise her. "Well," she said with a friendly smile, "clearly you're not ill."

Ethenn's jaw twitched. "No, I'm not."

"Would you like to tell me where you went? Or am I to guess?"

He didn't respond, shifting in obvious discomfort before her.

Noting that his manner was even more reserved than usual, Ilain wondered if this was typical of Ethenn on the verge of revealing a surprise. But by the tension in his expression, she thought it must be something far worse. "Ethenn—"

"Ilain, we need to talk."

Ilain blinked at his serious tone. "All right," she said. "Why don't you come sit next to me, and we'll talk?"

Though he hesitated, Ethenn slowly joined her on the bed, leaving a large gap between them. "I realized something tonight," he said, clasping his hands between his knees. He kept his eyes down, his jaw clamped tight.

Ilain narrowed her gaze on the space between them. "You aren't taking me to the forest, are you?"

Ethenn began to look at her but stopped himself. "No."

"Hm." Ilain took a deep breath and sighed. "Where did you go?"

"That doesn't matter," he said. "I've just learned that I can't do this."

While it certainly did matter, Ilain asked instead, "Do what?"

"This," he said, then gestured sloppily between them. "Us."

Ilain blanched.

"It was wrong of me to ever accept your offer," he said. "I knew how you saw me.

I knew we weren't meant to be together, but . . . I wanted to think I could be enough for you. I realize now that I can't."

"What are you talking about?" Ilain asked weakly.

His dark eyes met hers, and she saw they were filled with resignation. "I can't be the man you need, Ilain," he said. "I'm not fit to stand by your side. And I won't let you relegate yourself to a life with a husband you don't love."

Ilain gaped at him, the words caught in her throat. Was he serious? How could he be so blind? How could he think . . . ?

"Are you ending our betrothal?" Ilain blurted in shock.

Ethenn dipped his chin. "I am."

The truth slammed into her like a shadow of Night. Her limbs grew heavy, and her skin became cold. She could feel the sudden tears welling in her throat. "W—Why?" she whispered with a broken whimper. "Because you think I don't love you?"

Ethenn angled toward her, eyes down. "I know this is a disappointment," he said. "But, Ilain, you deserve so much more. I'm not the man you want. I never have been. And it would be a mistake to force yourself to feel something for me when you could find a man you *do* love and who can be the sort of man you truly need."

The tears burned up as indignation flared in her chest. "Are you bloody insane?" she said sharply. "Do you think I would ask to Bond with a man I couldn't love? Who wasn't enough for me?"

Ethenn's jaw tightened, but she continued before he could get a word in. "I've waited forty-three years—" With a flash, she grabbed his chin, turning him toward her so he didn't have a choice but to look at her. "Forty-three lonely, boring, self-sacrificing years, searching for a Warrior with whom I *wanted* to Bond. Do you think I would just give up and pick some random fool for whom I felt nothing?"

A flicker of confusion lit his eyes as she kept on, her voice rising with each word. "I didn't ask you to Bond with me because I was settling, Ethenn." She released him to toss her hands in the air, her frustration driving her to rise from the bed. "If I'd wanted a man's obsession alone, I could have chosen Major Olsen, who gave me that fantastically stunning dress you couldn't keep your eyes off of."

The base of Ethenn's neck turned red. He opened his mouth, but she refused to let him get a word in yet.

"But I didn't want him." She shoved her hands toward him. "I wanted *you*, you bloody prude. I don't care if you're not strong enough, old enough, wise enough, or whatever else you think you're lacking. I. Want. *You*. Don't you understand that?"

"No!" Ethenn jumped out of his seat, the singular word a fierce blow to her heart. The heated blush was spreading up to his jaw now, coating his entire neck. "No, I don't understand that. I'm not a ruler, Ilain. I'm not meant for your world. Whatever you think I can offer you, you're wrong. Perhaps you like me, but that's because you don't know me. You don't know the kind of man I really am."

"And what kind of man are you?" She raised her brow, throwing his previous assertion back to him. "A killer?" Caustically, she laughed and stepped up to meet him eye to eye. "I don't believe that for a second."

His cheeks were red now, his chest rising and falling sharply. His hands reached up to clamp onto her arms, his calloused palms rough against her bare skin. "Don't make me prove it to you," he growled.

"We are a balance, Ethenn," she said. "You say you fear what my magic will do to yours, but when we Bond, our magic will bring life, not death."

His eyes roved over her face, and she leaned in, knowing he wanted to kiss her. Their noses brushed, his breath catching. "We are *meant* for one another," she whispered.

Instantly, Ethenn released her with a slight shove. "This is pointless," he muttered, pacing away. He scraped his hands through his hair. With a deep breath, he straightened his shoulders and met her gaze. "We're done, Ilain. I'm sorry for the last several days. I—I let myself get carried away, and we did things we shouldn't have, but all in all, your virtue is still intact. Consider our betrothal ended, and when we return to the Alliance, you can find another Warrior if you wish. We'll part ways with no hard feelings."

Ilain stared at him, dumbfounded. Her heart ached in the strangest way. While she wanted to be angry, all she could feel was the greatest sorrow. She'd lost Auden; now, she was losing Ethenn.

The tears returned, blurring her vision. "You promised you wouldn't leave me," she whispered.

Ethenn's expression shifted for a second. His eyes held the greatest remorse, and his lips parted with a regretful intake. Then he blinked, and his resolve returned.

"I promised to make you happy too," he said. "And you won't be happy if you're married to me."

Ilain shivered as a breeze swept through the open window. "You don't know the first thing about making me happy," she said as a tear slipped free.

Ethenn swallowed roughly.

Ilain stepped forward, determined to get her confession out. She stopped short, holding his gaze adamantly. "I don't care about what the Alliance wants. I don't care if you're a worthy ruler," she said. She smiled in a way that conveyed the affection she felt looking into his eyes. "I only want you."

His expression pinched, and she knew he was wholly confused.

Ilain reached out to brush his cheek, whispering, "I love you."

Ethenn's entire demeanor changed with her confession. But instead of softening the way she expected, he closed off completely.

"Don't you dare," he said, his tone cold and hard. He knocked her hand away. "I'm not a flame you get to manipulate, Ilain. I was right in front of you, and you ignored me until you discovered I was of value to you."

"That wasn't—"

"You said your piece," he interrupted. "You want me. You *love* me." He said it with such derision that it was as if an arrow struck her heart. He shook his head, face burning fiery red. "You don't know what love is."

Ilain's tears seared across her skin. Her lips parted around unspoken words, her heart too torn between anguish and fury to find her voice.

A breath shuddered from his lungs, and Ethenn turned. He put his hands on the windowsill, preparing to leap back out into the night.

"Ethenn—" Ilain rushed forward, but he was gone.

When she made it to the window, he was already dropping from a beam, landing lightly on the ground below. Then he took off into the night.

The truth crushed her. He didn't believe her because he was right: Ilain hadn't known what love was. She'd dreamed of it, imagined it, hoped for it. But she'd not known it. She'd played games with him, attempting to manipulate him into accepting her without ever being honest with him. Why should he believe her now?

Don't let people know what you value, and they can't take it away from you.

Dejectedly, Ilain backed away from the window, sinking onto the mattress. She stared through the window into the dark sky, unseeing as tears slipped down her cheeks. No matter his faults and unwillingness to listen, Ethenn was right.

Now, Ilain had lost her one chance at happiness because she'd been too afraid to let him know her true heart. She'd refrained from letting him know she valued him, hoping it would protect her. Yet, her one guiding principle had failed her, and he'd taken his love away regardless, leaving her with a broken heart anyway.

CHAPTER FORTY-EIGHT

21ST OF RADIA, 1574

Evylin and Deckard joined the troop again early the next morning. Serene and Jorge had showered them with hospitality the night before, asking them dozens of questions about the past several months of their lives. Skillfully, Deckard answered, cleverly avoiding the topic of magic and the specifics of their mission.

Serene lamented that they hadn't known about their arrival earlier and, thus, were unable to have Evylin's cousin and her husband, Nelle and Nixon, join for dinner. Evylin was glad, knowing how many more questions there would have been to field with Serene's daughter in the mix. As it was, her aunt updated them on all the gossip of Trollenston and the Glaas family. Before the deluge of questions began, she and Jorge offered their sincere condolences on the loss of Hewitt. When Evylin asked how they'd heard, Serene said, "Your mother told me at Dolia's wedding."

Evylin furrowed her brow, baffled at how her mother had learned of the events. Seeing her confusion—or perhaps feeling it—Deckard leaned over and whispered, "I wrote to them after it happened."

"You did?" Evylin replied in shock.

He gave a soft nod. "I've been keeping them mostly informed since we left. Same as my family."

Evylin gaped at him then. He'd been writing to her family. She didn't know whether to find the diligence sweet or absolutely ridiculous. But after an appropriate shower of condolences, Serene carried the conversation on, eager to fill them in on Dolia's nuptials, so she and Deckard had not yet had the chance to discuss it further.

And in the bright, dawning morning, the troop left the town for Whickam Village.

It was half a day's journey between the settlements, and Evylin knew it well. The once-familiar twists and turns in the road held a sudden and curious unfamiliarity. Each season, she'd traveled this very road with Hewitt, headed to and from Trollenston's market. Every hillock and dale, every copse and glen—she knew them all. And yet, they seemed so foreign to her now.

Memories and distance caused a strange imbalance to unfurl within her. What had once been her homeland was now a novel sight. The sun crested over the eastern hills, gilding the emerald grasses, ivory sheep, ivy-covered trees, and the winding road. She'd forgotten how beautiful Estshire could be.

As the day wore on, Rafferty began asking Evylin about her old home. "When we passed through on our dear colonel's jaunt, I hardly got to enjoy it, what with the duties at camp," he lamented.

"What duties?" Thom sniped. "You never listened to a word I said."

Their banter turned to reminiscing on their time in the Third Volunteer Company. Rafferty enjoyed regaling the Alliance folk with tales, though in the morning light, Ilain seemed abnormally disinterested. She rode beside Isla, her gaze on the horizon while the others laughed. Dark circles shadowed her eyes, and she yawned regularly.

Evylin glanced back at where Ethenn's horse walked next to Thom and Rafferty's. Though he was often subdued in the mornings, the Warrior also looked abnormally tired.

Scrunching her nose, Evylin decided she didn't care to dwell on what might have occurred to make the couple's night particularly tiring.

Contenting herself with the distraction of Deckard's company, Evylin turned to him. "Do you remember the last time we took this journey?" she asked, then added, "Though it was in the opposite direction."

Deckard grinned at her. "Of course I do." His fingers twitched where they rested on his saddle, but he didn't reach across to touch her as she expected him to. "Things were quite different then."

"You have a gift for understatement."

He chuckled. "I remember being rather bemused at how I'd wound up winning so much as the loser of our bet." At her arched brow, he clarified, "I'd gained a beautiful, witty wife who was better versed in swordplay than any man I knew. And all I had to do was take her on an adventure. Seemed like a lopsided deal to me."

Evylin gave him a flirtatious smirk. "Yet, you didn't bother to capitalize on your winnings for three months."

"I didn't care to press my luck. I'd seen what you could do with a blade."

Her laugh danced among the hills.

The sun was hot overhead as Whickam Village came into view. The rolling hills of Estshire embraced the village with their vibrant greenery. Ivy crawled over the stone buildings and low fences, and the windows glinted in the noonday light. Gentle clouds drifted through the soft blue sky, reflecting the fluffy white herds that dotted the distant terrae.

"Welcome home," Deckard said gently.

Evylin continued to stare at the village, her heart strangely detached from the sight. Twenty-six years of her life had been spent there, and she remembered every moment. Her eyes caught on the stone fence around Mrs. Cohle's yard, where she and Ryen once watched the soldiers depart from their home. Within those buildings, her family awaited: her mother and father, her sisters and nieces. The Glaas smithy still stood with the stables next door.

Yet, this village wasn't her home.

Not anymore.

With a smile, Evylin turned back to Deckard. "This is my past," she said, then took his hand, forcing herself to ignore the pulse of discomfort that raced through him. "You're my home now."

Deckard's expression softened with joy and affection.

Leading the troop down the dirt streets of the village, Evylin scanned the buildings with fresh eyes. Everything was the same. Mrs. Lyvingston, the town healer and midwife, sat on her stoop, preparing bushels of herbs for drying. She looked up, doing a double take at the sight of the riders. Then she called a merry, surprised welcome to Evylin.

They entered the square where the Glaas family home awaited. Ivy covered the pale stone walls. Its slate roof and large windows were a luxury in the village, additions made only after her father's appointment as magistrate. While their family was by no means wealthy, they were granted the finest the small settlement could offer, thanks to the king's funding.

The smithy and stables greeted them to their right. A soft amber light glowed within. Upon Serene's information, Evylin knew it was Dolia's new husband, Devaan, who worked the forge. After their marriage, he'd moved to Whickam Village, taking up the position under Lawton's tutelage. Though Devaan had never trained formally, nor had Lawton practiced smithing for some years, the farming and shepherding village still relied upon Hewitt's old trade. As they couldn't afford to spend days traveling to Trollenston and waiting for repairs, even an inexperienced smith like Devaan was welcome.

They drew up before the stables and dismounted. Deckard ordered Thom, Rafferty, and Vayden to speak with the farrier and take care of the horses. "Then see about finding somewhere to stay," he instructed.

Evylin tore her gaze from the village hall, stained with soot from the fire of now fourteen years past. "There isn't anywhere," she said.

They all turned to her, expectant.

Evylin shrugged. "The village doesn't get travelers," she said. "All we have is the tavern, and it's got only one spare room. You *could* ask Mrs. Morgaan to rent it, but it likely only has one bed."

"I call dibs," Rafferty said.

Chuckling, Evylin shook her head. "Nonsense. My family will put us up," she said. "Some of us will stay with my parents, but my sisters have homes, too, so they can house a few of us. And worst case, Hewitt's old apartment above the smithy should be open. No need to spend our gold."

With the plan in place, Thom led Rafferty and Vayden toward the stables while the rest of them made their way to the Glaas residence.

Evylin paused at the dark oak door. Her instinct was to walk in, but she questioned her right to do so. Instead, she rang the bell.

Several seconds passed. The quick shuffle of feet sounded on the other side. The latch clicked free, and the door swung inward to reveal a young woman with dark brown waves, softly tanned skin, and a newfound sense of maturity in her once-rounded features. Her eyes went wide, and she gasped. "Evie!"

Evylin barely had a second to brace herself against Calyn's enthusiastic embrace. Unexpected delight welled in her, and she heartily returned the hug, giggling happily with her sister. "Oh, Caly," she said into her sister's wavy hair. "I missed you."

Abruptly, Calyn pulled back. She gripped Evylin's arms fiercely. "Well, I missed you, but why are you here?" Her gaze flittered to Deckard, and she gave a quick, sloppy curtsy. "Pleasure to see you, Cap—Colonel."

Deckard smiled dryly. "Pleasure to see you as well, Miss Glaas."

She scanned the crowd gathered behind them curiously, her eyes lingering on Ethenn. "Your last letter didn't mention you coming here."

"Our assignment took an unexpected turn," Deckard offered. "We're passing through for the night and hoped to visit with family while we have the chance."

"Oh, that's lovely!" Calyn said, her attention back on Deckard. "Please, come in. You'll stay with us, of course. And your friends," she added with another obvious glance at Ethenn.

Evylin fought down her amusement while Deckard gestured for the women to enter first. Evylin walked arm in arm with Calyn as Ilain, Isla, and Brea trailed them.

"Mother is in the drawing room," Calyn said. "And Father is in his office. But I'll ring for them."

While she stepped away to do that, she asked, "Did you come by way of Trollenston?"

"We did," Evylin confirmed distractedly. It felt so strange being a guest in the house she once called home. She'd grown up in these halls. This foyer was once a common pass-through in her day-to-day. She'd fallen from the banister of that dark wooden staircase as a youth. She'd painted the watercolor that hung on the wallpapered hallway that led to the dining room.

Calyn mentioned inviting their elder sisters for dinner, but Evylin hardly heard a word as her parents made their simultaneous appearances. Lawton stepped out of his office off the foyer first. He looked the same as ever, dressed in a dark blue waistcoat and trousers. His brown hair contrasted with his bright eyes, a gaze that widened ever so slightly as he caught sight of them.

"Oh!" Laurisa cried out from farther down the hall. Her cream dress rustled as she hurried across the wooden floors. Evylin had barely taken a step forward before her mother crashed into her, motherly sobs wracking her body. "Oh, Evie. My sweet Evie."

Evylin had forgotten the pleasure of a mother's hug. The embrace provided so much love, safety, reassurance, and devotion. Her muscles instinctively relaxed in her mother's arms, soaking in the woman's goodness and care.

Beside them, Lawton greeted Deckard. "This is a most welcome surprise," he said as they shook hands. Then he added teasingly, "So long as you aren't returning her."

Deckard chuckled with polite amusement. "Not for the world, sir," he said.

Laurisa finally released Evylin, forcing her to turn to her father. For her entire life, the relationship between Evylin and Lawton had been strained. She'd never really known him, as he was commissioned with the army for the first six years of her life. Even when he returned, it seemed they were destined to merely be acquaintances since he spent all his time working, and she spent all her time with Ryen. Due to their shared stubborn and independent personalities, father and daughter had never developed any real relationship.

Evylin had never minded until now.

Staring at her father, Evylin didn't know what to do. She didn't care to hug him, but it felt wrong not to greet him with the same warmth as her mother.

Lawton took a step forward, gently placing a hand on her shoulder and smiling. "I'm glad to see you, Evie," he said, his eyes glistening strangely. "So very glad."

Her breath caught. Evylin believed him, but still, she felt no more inclined to embrace him. Instead, she returned the smile and the salutation alone.

"What brings you to Whickam Village?" Lawton asked, stepping back to stand at his wife's side.

Deckard took the initiative. "We're on a mission for King Ephren," he said. "I believe I mentioned that in my last letter?" At Lawton's nod, he continued, "Well, it's taking us to Olbury, which led us here. We don't wish to impose on your hospitality, but—"

"Family is never an imposition," Laurisa pronounced brightly. Then her gaze drifted to the four behind them. "Or their friends. I'm not sure we'll have quite enough room though—"

The ringing of the doorbell interrupted her.

Calyn opened the door and froze. Her jaw dropped.

"Hello, Miss Glaas," Thom said, standing there as handsome and officious as ever in his Order of the King coat. His gray-blue eyes scanned Calyn with interest. "You're looking quite well."

Rafferty peeked around him. "Oh, you're right, Thommy," he said snidely. "She is prettier than Eve."

Calyn flushed brighter than Ethenn ever had, and Evylin sent the weasel a disapproving glare.

While Calyn backed away to let the remaining three men into the cramped foyer, Laurisa laughed, her nerves obvious. "As I was saying, I'm not sure we'll have quite enough room for *all* your friends. Though we'll do our best."

Deckard offered an apologetic look. "We are a large party, I know, and if you can't host us, we completely understand."

"Not at all," Laurisa insisted. She scanned the group once more. "Is there, uh . . . You travel with quite a mixed company, and I just wonder, are there couples other than yourselves among you?"

"Ah, yes." Deckard turned and gestured to the group. "Allow me to introduce our friends. You know my brother, Thom, of course."

Thom raised his chin toward Magistrate and Mrs. Glaas. "Pleasure," he said, then winked at Calyn.

Calyn blushed even deeper, and Evylin pursed her lips.

"Beside him is Corporal Rafferty—"

"Call me Raff."

"And on his other side are Mr. Vayden Calder and his wife . . ." Deckard hesitated, then said, "Isla."

The couple wore amused smiles as they bowed and curtsied.

Deckard gestured to Ethenn at his side. "This is Corporal Loxley and . . ." He paused again, tipping his head in consideration before adding, "his wife, Ilain."

Ethenn tightened his jaw while Ilain—standing by Isla's side—gave a small curtsy, her expression abnormally uncomfortable.

"Ilain is Mr. Calder's sister," Deckard explained, then motioned to Brea, standing next to Ethenn. "And this is *Miss* Lohen."

Rafferty leaned in and said, "*My* wife."

"I'd sooner eat a dagger," Brea quipped, then offered a friendly smile to the Glaas family. "This is a charming village."

Lawton, Laurisa, and Calyn smiled with curiosity in their gazes.

"Well," Lawton cleared his throat, "we will certainly have to be creative in finding rooms for you all. But be assured, we'll be happy to provide a hearty dinner. Colonel," he looked at Deckard, "I'd appreciate a word in my office if you don't mind."

Deckard drew his shoulders back, and Evylin felt her stomach twist. Her father knew. Somehow, he'd figured out that things weren't what they appeared to be. *Somehow?* she thought contemptuously. *You and Brea are wearing trousers, and you're both heavily armed. No Ephrian woman of repute would look as you two do.*

"Of course," Deckard said with charming ease. "Might Evylin join us?"

"No," Lawton said in a sharp tone despite his casual demeanor. "Let her and the womenfolk freshen up. I'm sure our talk would only bore her."

Deckard nodded and turned to Thom. "Once lodging is determined, get everyone settled," he said, dropping his voice. "This will take a while."

Laurisa and Calyn stepped forward to guide their guests toward the parlor, causing a flurry of motion around them. Evylin caught Deckard's hand, pulling him close. "Keep it simple," she whispered. "He won't understand."

Deckard dipped his chin reassuringly. Then he was gone, shut into her father's office.

"Come now," Laurisa said, setting a hand on Evylin's shoulder. "We'll get you all figured out and settled with rooms."

Ushered into the parlor with the others, Evylin forced herself not to worry about her husband. She helped her mother determine where to place all her guests. Calyn hurried off to make tea, returning shortly with all the teacups their family owned. It was decided that Evylin and Deckard would stay in her old room, Isla and Vayden would take the guest room, and Calyn graciously offered her room to Ethenn and Ilain.

"I'll go stay with Doli and Devaan," she said, then turned to Brea. "Miss Lohen, you may join me if you don't mind sharing a room."

"Oh, Brea is a splendid roommate," Thom teased. "She positively loves 'girl talk.'"

Brea passed him a bored look, stirring cream into her tea. "I'm rather an expert at feminine chatter, *mi'caro*," she said. "I grew up with a sister of my own." She turned to Calyn with a kind smile. "I'd be delighted, Miss Glaas."

"Please, call me Calyn," the girl said cheerily.

"Then you must call me Brea."

Thom leaned over to Brea then, whispering so only she and Evylin could hear when he said, "Put in a good word for me, eh?"

"There is only one word I'd use to describe you," Brea returned. "And it isn't good."

Thom chuckled, then turned back to Laurisa. "Evylin mentioned that Hewitt's old apartment is vacant," he said. "Rafferty and I can bunk there if that's all right with you."

"Hewitt's . . ." Laurisa's expression filled with momentary sorrow, but she recovered quickly. "Oh, I would hate to put you gentlemen there. It's awfully small and drafty. And there's only one small cot."

"That's all right," Thom replied. "Raff can sleep on the floor."

With the arrangements settled, the men left to retrieve their things. Evylin watched forlornly as they left. She didn't care to be stuck with the women sipping tea and sharing idle chatter. Not while she could feel Deckard's tension leaking toward her down the hall.

Setting her teacup down, Evylin turned to her mother. "I do apologize," she said, keeping her voice low as Calyn asked after the other three women's unique accents. "But might I be excused? We're only here for the night, and I'd like the chance to visit . . ."

Evylin didn't complete her thought, and Laurisa didn't need her to. "Yes, of course, dear." She squeezed her daughter's hand. "Go, and I'll prepare a bath for when you get back."

With a grateful smile, Evylin left the parlor. She slipped back through the hall and out the front door. Catching up to the men in the stables, she waved her hello to great-uncle Ned, the farrier. The wizened old man should have retired, but he'd lost his son in the war, and his grandson had been taken by the last draft.

"What are you doing out here?" Thom asked as Evylin approached.

Evylin joined in unlacing their bags from the saddles. "I wanted the chance to visit my and Hewitt's old haunts," she said. "Care to join me?"

Thom raised his brow. "I'm afraid my commanding officer ordered me to help get the troops settled."

"I believe I can persuade him to give you a pass."

With a smirk, Thom called to Ethenn. "Take Deckard and Evie's things, too, would you?"

"Sure," Ethenn said, his voice rougher than usual.

Thom turned to Evylin again. "Let me put our things up in Hewitt's old space, and we can be off."

"I'll come with you," Evylin offered.

While Vayden, Ethenn, and Rafferty carried the other bags to the Glaas house, Evylin led Thom up the back of the smithy to the apartment. It wasn't locked, as Hewitt hadn't left anything of value when he'd left, but the door stuck slightly when they opened it. Dark and dusty, the room was stuffy from the warm spring air. Evylin helped Thom open the windows to let the space air out. Then they retreated down to the paddock.

"Care to have a go?" Evylin asked, slipping over to the practice swords that Hewitt had left behind.

Thom eyed her curiously. "Looking to relive the glory days?"

"I'd hardly call them glorious." She tossed a sword to him. "But I do enjoy beating you."

Together, they stepped into the paddock. Evylin expected to feel something at being back in the place where she and Hewitt trained together—a thrill of sorrow or a nostalgic wistfulness. Yet, there was nothing—just a vague sense of peculiarity, as though she were walking through a dream.

Determined to clear her head, Evylin twirled the sword and set up to face Thom. He took a deep breath before dropping into his stance. "This isn't going to be fun," he quipped. "For you or for me."

"Why not?" she asked.

"We haven't sparred in almost a month, Evie. You're going to beat me in ten seconds flat."

She smirked. "That's a lot of confidence for a man going up against a Warrior."

He gave a mock laugh, then tightened his grip and attacked, slashing down with his sword. She defended with a resounding *clack*. The first strike settled her mind, proving that dueling was going to be the perfect distraction for her disjointed thoughts and feelings.

They ranged around the paddock. Though holding back a little to prolong the bout with Thom, Evylin channeled all her frustration into the practice. All the anxiety she felt for Deckard, currently dealing with her father's demands. All the grief from saying goodbye to Hewitt. The disappointment that still clung to her from Auden's death. The fear of what was to come. The concern toward Deckard's attachment to Space and his seeming discomfort with touching her.

The vibration of each hit charged through Evylin's arm and into her chest, shaking off every thought but the moment before her. Her focus narrowed on the blade in her hand and the one Thom held. At first, she won every fight with ease, just the way they'd expected. But soon, she eased her effort, allowing Thom to get in good practice of his own. It turned out to be a solid exercise for her as well, reining in her skills and increasing her endurance.

After a bout that lasted for a full, tiring five minutes, Thom backed away. "All right," he heaved. "I need a break."

Evylin grinned, sucking in a deep breath of her own. She'd only just begun to get winded, her body warm and her skin tingling. "You really are out of practice," she teased.

"It doesn't help that you're naturally better than me," Thom said, taking a seat on the paddock fence. He dropped his head back and took a labored breath.

Evylin hopped up next to him. The afternoon sun created a small flare against the window of the smithy. Metallic clanging rang through the open doors as Devaan worked inside. Evylin had yet to say hello, having only met her brother-in-law a handful of times in the past.

Evylin wondered if the rest of her in-laws would ever return. After seeing Druan in Loclight, she held a glimmer of hope that her sisters' husbands would find their way back to their wives. It made her realize just how important their mission was. The Centurial War would not end if they didn't end it themselves. Families would be torn apart for generations more until the entire countryside was left vacant.

But how many men would wish to return to their quaint lives after having explored the country? Would something so small and mundane be enough?

"Thom," Evylin said, staring at the smithy door, "do you think you'd ever want to move home?"

He looked down at her, brow furrowed. "Like to Stocburrough?"

"Yes."

"No."

She met his sharp eyes. "Why not?"

"It isn't my home anymore, Evie," he said. "It hasn't been for five years."

"But your family is there."

"No," he nudged her elbow with his, "my family is *here*, traveling with me."

She gave him an amused smile. "That's adorable."

"I was born to be a romantic."

With a chuckle, she nudged him back. "So you're going to follow Jonn and me around for the rest of your days."

"That's the plan."

"And what happens when you find a woman worth marrying?" she asked.

He gave her a sly grin. "I already have."

Her expression grew flat. "If you're referring to Calyn, you can stop right there."

"It's a joke," he said, then added, "Unless she'd actually have me."

"Stop that."

"Why?" Thom shrugged, turning to stare at the sky. "She's lovely, sweet, and pliable. I could be very happy with a wife so devoted to my whims. And it helps that she'd be more than willing to bear plenty of my children."

Evylin shook her head. "I don't like this version of you."

"What version?"

"The cynic."

"Cynicism is part of my charm."

Evylin pierced him with her glare. "You don't want a simple wife, Thom. Yes, Calyn is lovely. She would dote on you to distraction. You'd enjoy her company for a while, and you might even come to love her if you'd let yourself." She frowned then. "But you wouldn't be happy."

"Why not?" Thom asked sadly, almost as though desperate for her to be wrong. "Why couldn't I be happy with a normal life? Why should I pursue something that I may never find?"

"Because you want more," she said. "Just like Jonn. Just like me."

"Maybe I'm tired of wanting more." And Thom did look tired. His expression was almost harried, his eyes dulled. "Maybe I just want to be happy with who I am and what I already have."

Evylin offered him a soft smile. She took his hand. "You're a much different man than when we met four months ago," she noted. "I have a feeling that the same will be said four months from now too."

Thom's chin dipped, but he didn't reply.

Evylin let him hold onto his reluctant thoughts. She squeezed his hand, then released him. "So," she said, "you plan to follow Jonn and me wherever we go. What if we go to Stocburrough?"

His brows drew together. "What? To live?"

She nodded.

Thom scoffed derisively. "Sure, yeah. And Raff's going to find himself a pious woman who'll change him into the picture of an Allorian gentleman."

"I'm serious," Evylin said, even as she laughed with him. "What if we all moved to Stocburrough and built a life there with your family?"

Thom eyed her as though trying to puzzle her out. "You wouldn't want that."

Her shoulders lifted in a casual shrug. "But Jonn might."

A sharp laugh burst out of him. "Evie, you really are predictable," he said fondly. He gave her a pointed look. "Jonn does not want to live out his days in Stocburrough."

Ignoring his offensive comment, Evylin raised her brow. "You're sure?"

"Deckard can't shrink to that world again," he said with certainty. "It's too mundane for him. He's always been an idealist, and he likes to imagine that the world should measure up to the perfect standards he holds. It's why I was so determined to prove myself to him. I didn't want to disappoint him like everything else in his life."

Evylin nodded, understanding. "He wants to be Euon Sergus."

"Bloody Sergus," Thom agreed. "He just won't admit it because he doesn't want people finding out he's as selfish as the rest of us."

"Do you think he realizes it?"

"Realizes that he's in denial of harboring delusions of grandeur?" Thom scoffed. "Of course not."

Evylin tugged on her rings and sighed. "Then I'll have to help him figure it out."

"Good luck," Thom grumbled. "He's been lying to himself for at least thirty years."

Running her fingers along her wedding rings, Evylin scanned the empty paddock. She'd sat out here so many times as a child, watching the horses or playing with Ryen. This had been her refuge in the village. And now, it held only memories.

"By the way," Thom said lightly, "I meant it."

Evylin looked up at him.

"Wherever you and Jonn go," he smiled, "I'll follow."

They shared an affectionate look, and he hopped off the fence. "Ready to go back?"

Evylin shook her head. "I have somewhere to be, actually," she said, joining him as they walked out of the paddock. "If Jonn finds his way free of my father anytime soon, send him my way, would you?"

"And where shall I tell him you'll be?"

Evylin glanced toward the edge of the village. "At the kirk."

CHAPTER FORTY-NINE

The kirkyard was exactly as Evylin had left it. The gate rattled gently against its latch in the afternoon breeze. Ivy climbed the white fence, though Father Dover ensured it never grew too wild or invasive. Midday sunshine highlighted the light gray headstones of all the villagers lost amongst the creeping white and green everbloom ivy.

Evylin knelt next to Ryen's plot, a peculiar sense of contentment in her heart. She brushed her fingers across the weathered quartz, brushing back the ivy leaves.

"Hello again," she said with a smile. "Didn't expect me back so soon, did you?"

She traced his name.

"Neither did I. But I did as I promised—and more."

The breeze ruffled Evylin's hair, causing it to trail across her face. She reached up to push it back. "I've seen the sea," she told Ryen. "It's as beautiful as we imagined. It stretches on forever; though I know it ends, I can't fathom how. I explored the Shires. I won dozens—well, probably hundreds of duels. I rescued a prince, which is even better than a princess. I fought a dragon, *and* I found Mages."

Evylin paused, her smile turning wry. "I *married* a Mage."

The ivory flowers of the everbloom shivered in the wind.

"I know," Evylin said, amused. "I couldn't believe it either. But do you want to know what's even more amazing? It turns out that I'm magical too. Have you heard of Warriors? I hadn't. But I'm one of them, and together, Jonn and I are Bonded, our magic a perfect balance to help protect and serve Terraeus."

Evylin glanced down at her ring, the onyx gemstones glinting in the light. The elegant band represented Deckard and their future—that's what he'd told her when he gave it to her. He'd chosen this ring with its obsidian black stones because it felt right. And for the first time, Evylin realized *why*.

Eyes still on the ring, Evylin pulled the Space Relic out from beneath her collar. She compared the two. One setting was gold, the other silver, but their gemstones were identical.

Onyx. The blackness of Space. The infinity of the Heavens.

He'd known. Subconsciously, Deckard had known even then that Space was his resource. He was drawn to it, though he didn't feel it. It made her wonder how many times he'd connected with the resource without knowing it.

"I was told I'd find you here."

Deckard's voice soothed over Evylin, and she turned, greeting him with a dry grin. She studied her husband, understanding for the first time how deep his magic ran. It was always within him, always drawing on him. It was the thing that made his eyes shift green and his temperament unfathomably steady.

"I hope my father wasn't too unbearable," she said as he approached, sliding the Relic back beneath her collar. A gentle wash of pleasure swept into her palm from the gold and onyx pendant.

Deckard carefully walked through the kirkyard to kneel beside her. "He's fine," he said. "I showed him our orders and explained what I could, and he was quite gratified to learn that he'd married his daughter off to the king's most valued soldier."

They shared a sardonic grin. The sunlight caught in Deckard's hair, making it look redder than usual. He still wore his uniform, the gold braid of a colonel looped around his shoulder. His gaze softened with a somber respect as his eyes turned to the grave marker.

Evylin took his hand, ignoring the hesitation in his returned grip. "Thank you for joining me," she said as he knelt beside her. "I wanted to introduce you. Silly as that may be."

He squeezed her hand. "It isn't silly at all," he promised.

She returned his gentle smile, and they turned to face the headstone embedded into the terrae.

"Jonn, this is Ryen." Evylin drew a finger along the edge of the stone. "Ryen, this is my husband, Jonn."

Deckard bowed his head.

"I always came to visit Ryen when I needed to talk to someone," Evylin said, feeling the need to explain herself. "Of course, Hewitt was who I went to for advice, but . . . If I just needed someone to listen, Ryen was always there, before and after his death."

Deckard scooted closer but remained silent.

"I know Hewitt told you about him," Evylin looked up at him, "but I never did. I should have."

Deckard shook his head. "You were hurting."

"You're my husband. I should have trusted you with it."

"I never blamed you for it."

She rested her head on his shoulder. "You're too forgiving sometimes," she said softly. "But I love you for it."

He kissed the top of her head.

"Would you like to hear about him?" she asked, sitting up again. "From me?"

Though she could feel a growing tension in his body from their proximity, Deckard didn't pull away. "I would," he said. "Very much."

So Evylin told him all about Ryen. She told him about their promise to one another, their shared dream of adventure. "I haven't quite become a legend worth five hundred tales, but I'm not sure I'd like to anyway," she admitted.

Then she told him about their childhood. They'd spent whole days fishing by the river, pretending to be pirates, and taking turns reading aloud from their storybooks. When their mothers forced them to do schoolwork, they would only do it if they were together. Irena was a second parent to Evylin when her father was gone in the war. She felt her aunt's loss, too, but not nearly as keenly as Ryen's.

Ryen had been her everything.

"He was so clever, so good," she said. "He always made me feel so safe."

But then the fire came and took him away.

"I married you because of him," Evylin confessed at last. "If it weren't for my promise to Ryen—that I wouldn't let our dream die—I would never have agreed so soon."

"I have much to thank him for, then," Deckard said. "I only wish I could have met him."

A wistful sigh escaped Evylin, and she looked down at her cousin's name embedded in the headstone. "Well," she began, "I like to think that in another life, you did meet him."

"Oh?"

She nodded. "Yes. In a world where there was no fire—where no one was careless enough to leave a candle burning in the village hall and the houses behind it never burned—Ryen lived and grew to manhood with me. Hewitt stayed in the service, enjoying his commission and helping Ephria excel in the war. At seventeen, Ryen would have joined the army, as we'd agreed. He would have been gone for some time, and that would have been hard, but I would have known that it was in service to our future. I imagine he rose through the ranks, became an officer just as quickly as his father, and shortly after, returned on leave.

"I would have asked if he'd found a husband for me yet," she said, and Deckard grinned. "'No, but I have a plan. I'm going to talk to your father,' he would say. 'I'm going to convince him to let you come with me to Loclight, and we'll find you a husband together there.'"

"Would your father have agreed to something like that?"

Evylin nodded theatrically. "Oh, yes. Ryen was very persuasive."

They chuckled together, and she continued, "Then off to Loclight we would go. Months would pass, and I wouldn't find anyone who interested me. I'd be lonely, worried my father would recall me if I didn't find a husband soon enough for his liking. And then when all hope seemed lost, I would go to a dinner party and meet this handsome, young lieutenant—were you a lieutenant when you were first stationed in Loclight?"

His eyes twinkled merrily as he corrected, "I was a sergeant."

"Mm. Well, I would have met this lieutenant and realized he was stupid."

"Mm-hm."

"Then I would have been introduced to the most singular Sergeant Deckard, who would have inevitably swept me off my feet."

Deckard laughed gently. "I doubt that."

"No, it's quite true," she insisted. "This sergeant was ostensibly charming, unassumingly handsome, and excessively witty. I couldn't have found a better match."

"So I only *seem* charming?"

"You're perfectly charming," she said. "But I see through your charms to the depth in your heart."

His expression grew almost bashful.

"As I was saying," Evylin teased, continuing her tale. "In this other life, we would have met at a party in Loclight, and I would have fallen in love with you readily and easily. You would have courted me and become friends with Ryen, and together, the three of us would have gone on our adventure. Although I don't think you'd make a good pirate."

"This is your fantasy," Deckard noted. "I could be a fantastic pirate in this other life."

Evylin scrunched her nose. "Mm, no. I wouldn't change a thing about you."

His smile flattened slightly. "So I'd still be a Mage in this version of reality?"

"And I'd be a Warrior," she said. "So would Ryen, by the way. If this is my fantasy, the three of us live together forever."

Deckard chuckled. "Just the three of us? Shouldn't Ryen have his own love?"

Evylin pursed her lips and looked at the headstone. "What do you think? Do you find love?"

A gentle breeze rustled the everbloom flowers.

With a pert nod, Evylin turned back to Deckard. "Yes," she confirmed. "A beautiful Mage who works with the Alliance."

Deckard's eyes grew wider. "The Alliance exists in this other life?"

"Well, someone has to stop Blount. And it won't be Ephren."

"I suppose you have a point."

They were silent for a moment, and Deckard kissed her temple. "I like this story of yours," he said.

"So do I," Evylin said, a well of longing for the life that could never have been filling her chest.

Another long silence drifted between them as they sat there, the sun dipping lower in the sky. They stared at the headstone together, imagining what might have been. After a while, Deckard released her hand and adjusted to sit more comfortably beside her.

She could feel his unease, and it caused him to pull away from her. It bothered her that the Space Relic's presence did this to him. But he needed to learn to control it. She wouldn't allow him to take the easy path. Not when it could potentially mean their demise.

"Jonn," Evylin whispered, breaking the silence, "I need to ask you something."

"All right," he said softly.

"You won't like it."

His brow pinched, but he waited patiently.

Evylin took a deep breath. "When this is all over, if we could have any life, what would you want it to look like?"

Deckard pressed his lips together. A flutter of agitation and confusion melded around him, but resignation broke through a mere moment later. "I don't know," he said. "Whatever you wanted to do, wherever you wanted to go, I'd be happy."

Evylin bit her tongue and fought down her irritation at his overinflated sense of goodwill. "I appreciate the sentiment, Jonn, but that's not what I'm asking. I want to know what life *you* want. I want your answer, not mine."

"Why is it so wrong of me to want what you want?" he asked gently. "Why can't I wish to give you your dreams?"

"You *have* given me my dreams." She motioned to Ryen's headstone. "You've given me *our* dreams. Now, I'd like to give you yours."

"I don't have any," he said, and she knew it was a lie. But he held her gaze so adamantly she knew he must think it the truth. "Making you happy is all I desire."

Evylin didn't have a response. She felt the same. After living out her and Ryen's dream, after going on her grand adventure, she found herself decidedly underwhelmed by the reality of it. She'd kept her promise. Now, she was ready for something new. The problem was that she didn't know what she wanted. And she felt it was only right that Deckard be selfish for once in his life.

But Deckard would continue to be selfishly selfless. He wouldn't assert his desires because he felt it was wrong to do so. No matter how much she prodded or pleaded, he was rigid in his sacrificial stance.

So she'd have to push him.

"What if what makes me happy is accepting the position at the head of Allund's government?" she said in a calm tone.

A flare of worry he couldn't hide filled the air between them, and Deckard scanned her warily. "Is that what you want?" he asked.

Evylin shrugged. "I don't know," she said. "I don't have all the information. But what if, after this is over and they've explained the role, I decide it sounds fun? What if I request that you become ruler beside me? Would you be happy then?"

Deckard's jaw tightened as he turned away in thought. She studied his profile. His jawline was peppered with scruff. He'd begun shaving each morning again, returning to the routine of a soldier's life. He liked routines. He liked orderliness. He liked control.

Evylin smiled affectionately. She disrupted his life in so many ways. Perhaps that was necessary to force him to grow, just as he had forced her to grow. She trusted now because of his steadiness and stability. She wasn't afraid of loss because she knew that loving fully—loving sacrificially as he did—was the only way to truly be happy.

It was her turn to help him.

"Jonn," she whispered tenderly, "I want the truth. I want to know *your* heart."

Deckard closed his eyes, pulling in a deep breath. When he exhaled heavily, she felt his tense demeanor ease. His eyes met hers, and they were a cool blue with hardly any green left in them. "My heart only desires you," he said. "If you asked it of me, yes, I would become ruler beside you. But if it were my choice alone?" He shook his head gently. "I wouldn't take it."

Evylin cupped his cheek, leaning in close. "Then we won't take it."

Deckard's brow pinched. "What if they don't give us a choice?"

"What if we die in the Terrae Keep two days from now?" she returned. "What if we fail to defeat Blount? What if the Alliance isn't everything they pretend to be?"

She kissed the furrow between his brows. "Those questions don't matter, Jonn, because we can't know the answers until they come. And we'll figure it out together when they do."

"And what if they attempt to force us?" he asked tiredly. "Will we reject them, no matter the consequences?"

"I suppose so."

Deckard stared at her, a flitter of reluctance stirring the air.

Internally, Evylin took it as a confirmation of Thom's earlier words. Deckard *wasn't* as opposed to this appointment as he said. He wanted it, but he denied himself as a point of pride. Yet, the part of him who desired to be Sergus lurked beneath, itching to take the role. He wanted the responsibility he feared. He wanted to prove his worth. He was just too scared to admit it.

"All right," Deckard said, a heaviness in his posture. "We won't accept it."

Evylin nodded, but she knew within her heart that their future was still undecided. And her husband would not be happy until he let himself be loved, no matter how selfish it seemed.

CHAPTER FIFTY

Dinner with the Glaas family was insightful. Evylin's eldest sisters, Euna and Albina, arrived with their brood of daughters, seven between the pair, while Dolia and her young husband, Devaan, joined as well. The house was full of feminine chatter.

Euna was notably dubious of Deckard at first. She nearly glared at him with suspicion, making pointed remarks about his taking Evylin away without even bothering to meet the whole family first or inviting her sisters to their wedding. Swiftly, Deckard apologized, assuring her it was not meant as a slight. He lied mildly, swearing that his love for her sister drove him to forget his reason, determined to marry her regardless of the cost.

Under his manifold charms, Euna softened. From then on, she began to sing his praises to her daughters, aged twelve all the way to four, coaching them to find husbands so devoted.

The dining room was bursting with guests. There wasn't enough room for them all at the main table, so they squeezed a secondary table in from Devaan and Dolia's house just down the road. It made the room almost impossible to maneuver, but the splendid meal of mutton sausage, mashed potatoes, and roasted vegetables, smothered in butter and herbs and served with a fine vintage of Setshire wine, made it all worthwhile.

At the head table, Lawton insisted that Deckard take the seat of honor he'd been given last time, with Evylin sitting on his right and Thom on his left. They squeezed Laurisa, Euna, Albina, Vayden, and Isla into the remaining seats. At the other table, Ethenn, Ilain, Brea, Rafferty, Calyn, Dolia, and Devaan were clumped together, the children having been sent to the kitchen to share their meal.

Calyn had specially requested Brea's presence at her table, seeming to have decided she'd become her special friend, as they were to share a room together that night.

The meal was pleasant, and they readily found their way into the parlor for easier conversation. Card tables were drawn out for games of Crooks and Crowns, and tea was served. While Whickam Village was just as small as Deckard's home village of Stocburrough, with Lawton as a magistrate, their homelife was quite different from his family's. The house was finer, the manners more precise, and the overall air more refined. Deckard had little cause to wonder why Evylin liked the more extravagant, luxurious things in life. Her childhood home was a constant attempt at replicating those fancier indulgences.

As the night wore on, the party slowly began to split apart. Ilain excused herself early, stating that she wasn't feeling at her best. Ethenn remained to play cards with Rafferty and Brea at the far end of the room, but Calyn hopped up to usher Ilain to their lodging for the night.

"Right this way, Mrs. Loxley," she said cheerily.

Ilain's expression pinched in an odd manner, but she followed the girl with a gracious, "Thank you."

From there, the others slowly drifted off to their own rest. Euna and Albina took their daughters home, bidding Evylin a fond farewell as they would not likely see her the next day. Dolia also requested Devaan take her home.

"I'm always overtired these days," she said with a wink.

Evylin didn't appear to understand the pointed comment. "What do you mean?" she asked.

Dolia giggled, glanced at the far end of the room where the men were distracted by their cards, then lowered her voice to say, "I'm with child."

"Oh!" Evylin exclaimed, then laughed at her ignorance. "Congratulations to you both."

Dolia leaned in closer, her voice dipping even lower. "You've been married longer than I. Are you expecting too?"

Immediately, Deckard blanched, and Evylin's laugh grew nervous. "No," she said with definitive assurance.

Dolia glanced sidelong at Deckard, then tugged Evylin closer, not whispering quite quietly enough for him to avoid hearing as she said, "Try lifting your legs after next time. Mrs. Lyvingston advised me that it helps."

Evylin pressed her lips together, a blend of agitation and amusement shimmering around her at her sister's naively inappropriate suggestion. "Thank you, Doli," she said dryly.

And with that, Dolia and her husband departed with Calyn and Brea in tow.

Deckard and Evylin shared a wry glance. "Don't try that," he said.

"It's an old wives' tale," Evylin said. "It doesn't work."

"I don't wish to press our luck."

With a chuckle, Evylin went off to join the card games.

An hour later, the rest of them departed for the evening. Evylin led Deckard up the stairs, reminding him of his previous stay in the Glaas home. He smiled to himself, watching her skirt swirl around her feet as they ascended to the second floor. He'd been so enamored with her all those months ago. It wasn't love at first sight but perhaps could be considered interest at first conversation. She was attractive, but so were many other women. However, her wit and candor were what struck him, combined with her openness and authenticity.

Evylin was who she was—and she was charming.

Deckard supposed that was what had drawn him to her. While he worked hard to gain the good opinion of others, Evylin seemed to come by it naturally. He admired that.

Stepping into her old bedroom, Deckard did a quick scan over the space. He'd already visited it earlier when they changed for dinner. The room was simple but nice. The rich brown wooden furnishings were well-made and beautiful. A light blue patterned wallpaper covered the walls, and a medium-sized bed with a cream-colored quilt sat directly across from the door. He'd already perused her collection of novels on the far bookcase, unorganized and haphazardly put away. Many had stains on their cloth and leather bindings.

In fact, much of Evylin's belongings were in disarray. The wardrobe held many dresses, blouses, and skirts, all nearly falling off their hangers. The chest of drawers could hardly shut.

Sitting on the bed, Evylin kicked off her boots, letting them clatter to the floor. Deckard eyed the careless behavior but didn't say a word. They prepared for bed, and he intentionally—guiltily—kept his eyes away as she peeled off her chemise. He didn't think he would ever grow used to the delight of seeing her naked form, but recently, it'd become a less wholesome pleasure.

Evylin never took off the Space Relic anymore, and seeing the gold and onyx necklace draped openly across her bare chest gave him the unholiest of urges.

Since waking after the Space Keep, touching Evylin had grown increasingly difficult. Each time, he felt an immediate surge of magic—profound and provocative. Deckard had been careful not to reveal his discomfort, but it had made sleeping next to one another a struggle. He lay awake with her in his arms each night, fighting the whispers in his head.

Let me out.

Gratefully, Deckard had managed to avoid intercourse for the past thirteen days. He didn't know what such blatant and open intimacy would do to him. Remembering the surging power that swept through him since their Bonding, he feared losing control to the Space Relic—and he couldn't ask Evylin to remove it, knowing she'd only tell him that he needed to learn to ignore his impulses.

Pulling his nightshirt over his head, Deckard cautiously glanced toward Evylin. He found her in her nightdress, climbing under the blankets. He forced himself to relax. His muscles felt unendingly tight these days, his brow unceasingly pinched.

Deckard picked up *Attachments of the Soul* from his nightstand and joined Evylin on the bed. They'd made it through several pages over the last week and a half, discussing the archaic wording thoroughly to ensure they both understood. Despite their steady progress, he hardly felt more informed on Bonding, the earliest pages dealing primarily with the process and ceremony of the Bond and its significance.

As he settled against the pillows and lifted the book's cover, Evylin's hand stopped him. He looked over at her, confused. "Not tonight," she said.

"No?" he asked, even as she took the book from him.

Evylin leaned across him to set it back on the nightstand. He couldn't help but tense as she brushed against his chest, a current of magic slipping across his skin even through the fabric of their nightclothes. He forced his breath out, attempting to ease his taut muscles.

With a knowing smile, Evylin sat back down at his side. "I want to talk with you," she said.

"All right," Deckard said, thankful she hadn't tried to take his hand.

In the bronze lamplight, her amber eyes glowed. She tucked some of her waves behind her ear and settled on the bed beside him. "Jonn," she began, "you have to stop being afraid of me."

He frowned in confusion, so she clarified, "Afraid of touching me."

Deckard's body seized.

Evylin's lips lifted with dry humor. "You thought you'd hidden it from me?" she noted.

Clearing his throat awkwardly, he admitted, "I did."

"I noticed the first day," she said. "Ever since I started wearing the Relic, you've flinched every time I touch you."

Deckard pulled a tight smile. "I suppose it's a virtue, being a poor liar."

"We've already discussed your penchant for lying," she teased. "Now, tell me: What's wrong?"

Drawing in a deep breath, Deckard considered his words. "I can't control it," he said at last.

"Why not?"

"I don't know."

"So you're letting it control you?"

Deckard frowned, meeting her gaze.

Evylin grabbed his hand, and as expected, the touch sent a thrill of power through his arm. "You keep fighting it," she said. "But it's fighting back, isn't it? Every time you push it down, it grows stronger, making the urge to use it greater. And touching me draws on it."

Deckard gave a slow blink, knowing he didn't need to confirm it.

Her expression grew concerned. "You can't keep this up," she said. "Not only do you have to learn to control it, but you can't stay away from me forever. I need you."

He dropped his head. "I know," he said, aching to touch her, to hold her, to kiss her. "I need you too."

"Then have me."

"I *can't*," he insisted. "Every time we touch with that *thing* around your neck, I feel it—the magic, its power. It whispers in my ear." He wet his lips in agitation. "Do you have any idea how hard it is to touch you and not give in to it? Every moment, I'm fighting so hard, and I fear it will soon be too much. That we'll arrive at the Terrae Keep, and I'll lose myself to magic again. That I'll get us killed because I can't control it."

Evylin watched him, a worried and uncertain expression crossing her face.

Deckard longed to pull her into his arms, to assure her of his love. But he fisted his hands at his sides, determined not to lose himself. "I fear that if I touch you—with or without the Relic—my magic will implode," he confessed. "Because I can't control it."

"Training hasn't made it better?" she asked gently.

He shook his head. "I keep letting it consume me."

Evylin frowned in consideration. "Do you . . . feel better after it consumes you?"

"What do you mean?"

"When the power is released and you've 'imploded,' as you say," she cocked her head, "do you feel better? Is the urge quite as strong?"

Deckard hardly needed to think about it. After several days of experiencing the same sensation over and over, he knew the answer. "No. It's not."

Evylin nodded. "So use me."

Deckard's brow furrowed. "What?"

She grinned flirtatiously. "It isn't unheard of," she teased. "A man taking comfort in his wife's embrace."

As Deckard struggled to comprehend the illicit suggestion of her words, she shifted on the bed. Evylin knelt before him, moving to straddle his lap and looping her arms around his neck. The magic coiled violently through his body from each place she touched him, its demanding whisper filling his head.

"Use me," she repeated. "Touch me, love me. Learn to control it by letting yourself go with me."

Deckard stared at her, baffled. It couldn't be right, could it? Using one's spouse in such a manner was selfish.

"You need to stop being afraid of yourself," Ilain reminded him.

Deckard ground his teeth, not caring to remember the Fire Mage's voice at such a time. Yet, her advice kept ringing through his head. *"Stop trying to control it and start relating to it . . . Let it live in the world around you unimpeded by your control . . . Stop trying to bend it to your will and start getting to know it as it is rather than as you want it to be."*

But to do that in the context of making love to his wife. . . .

It felt practically sacrilegious.

Another spike of power spiraled through Deckard as Evylin wove her fingers in his hair. "Jonn," she whispered, inching closer to him, "let me help you."

His heart lurched. The very idea thrilled and horrified him.

"I can't," he whispered.

"Why not?" she asked, their lips a breath apart.

His hands trembled at his sides. "It isn't right."

Her dark eyes met his, determined and serious. "I am your wife," she charged. "It is my job to love you, to help you. And if you need me—if I can help you learn to control this magic, then by Allore's might, I want to." Her fingers tightened around his neck. "I want *you.*"

Deckard swallowed, his thoughts growing traitorous. She was right. If anything was to teach him control, it should be her, even if it meant losing himself to his carnal urges in the process. After all, she was his wife. Who better to lose himself to?

Without fully committing to the decision internally, Deckard found himself kissing her. The past days without her had finally taken their toll, and he couldn't withhold his desires any longer. Infinity wove past her lips and into him. His mind became a void of all but the woman in his arms. She consumed him, and the boundless energy twisted through his veins. A dull hum waved through his body, blocking all sounds outside the two of them. The calm of everything and nothing took over. His body warmed; his vision turned black.

Soon, they were twisted in the blankets of her childhood bed, bare skin allowing the magic to flow readily between them. Only the gold and onyx Relic remained, resting against her tanned flesh. His veins pounded with power, flooding him with the ecstasy of its vastness. It threatened to come undone under his skin, demanding its release.

Yet, as Deckard lost himself to his wife, his magic never surfaced. It remained within, whispering to him and tingling under his skin. But inexplicably, the urge remained placid and docile, seeming to be satisfied as he gave himself to Evylin.

And for the first time, Deckard realized the full influence of their Bond. *Evylin* granted him control over Space. It wasn't him who needed to take charge; it was her. When he let go, he allowed her to be his strength, and the rest was easy.

Finally, collapsing in each other's embrace, their physical and emotional love satiated, Deckard relaxed into his wife. "You were right," he whispered against her neck.

She chuckled softly, her chest expanding against him. "Of course I was," she murmured and wrapped her arms tighter around him. "I'm always right when it comes to matters of marital bliss."

Deckard smiled in amusement. The Relic pressed against him in their embrace, and for the first time, he didn't feel a tug on his magic. He kissed her jaw and said, "I will never doubt you again."

He wasn't foolish enough to believe that all was resolved. He knew the magic would still call to him again; he would still struggle with allowing it to consume him. But he had hope now. If he began to falter, he wouldn't try to control it on his own—he would reach out and let Evylin help him.

And as she'd promised, he knew she wouldn't let him fail.

23RD OF RADIA, 1574

"One day ahead of Blount," Thom said as they entered Olbury at last.

Deckard took a steadying breath, scanning the cobbled streets, optimistically confident that the Night Mage wasn't lurking nearby, waiting to ambush them. "We'd better make the most of it," he replied.

The port town bustled with merchants, fishermen, and residents. Lawmen patrolled, monitoring the comings and goings with casual interest. Estshire was a reasonably safe province. The greatest criminals were thieves and con men, like Rafferty, or gamblers and pit fighters, like Ethenn. However, as Olbury was the largest town in all the Shires, nearing the status of a city, it was known for a few more nefarious crimes, making the clear presence of the law necessary.

Nearly five months prior, Deckard had been to Olbury on his recruiting mission. The town had intrigued him even then, though he hadn't had much chance to explore. Large merchant ships were moored alongside smaller fishing trawlers and dories at the docks. While farmland surrounded the outskirts of the city, the majority of its revenue came from fishing and trade.

The Allundan language was met with a blend of Schonese and various other foreign languages and accents Deckard didn't recognize. Merchant stalls in the trade district were filled with men and women with unique features and manners of dress. The sharp, pungent scents of Jal'Khoyan spices, a nation in lower Giyda, contrasted sharply with the sweet aroma of caramelized nuts from the Denebergen stands, the northernmost empire in Matteire.

Evylin gaped around at the chaos and novelty. "Where are all these people from?" she asked.

"The varying nations of Terraeus," Isla said. "Olbury is the singular post of foreign trade in Allund."

"Though we intend to change that," Vayden added. "We'd like to see far more commerce and resources coming to our land."

Dismounting, they led their horses toward an inn, boarding them in the stables. However, they didn't bother to rent rooms. Their plans were already set.

With their shortened timeline, they would enter the Terrae Keep that evening. Though Ilain was the stronger Mage and could employ her Terrae magic if called to, Isla had a stronger connection to the resource. Therefore, she would lead their charge and defeat the Guardian. After recovering the Relic, they would then camp around the Keep, watching for Blount's arrival. They would be exhausted, but it was their best chance. If they could ambush Blount on his way down into the Keep, he and his men would bottleneck in the stairwell, unable to defend themselves well. With their four Relics in hand and a Bonded couple, they should manage his defeat handily.

As prepared as they could be and all feeling the urgency of their mission, the troop followed Isla and Ilain, who were guided by their Elemental magic toward the Terrae Keep. Outside of the port city, they wound through the rocky cliffs that lined the shore. The sea breeze coated them with salty air. Pebbles crunched under their boots on the cavernous beachside. The wild, green-blue ocean rolled around them as they traversed the craggy shore.

Nearly two hours later, they found the split in the cliffside. They squeezed through and into the antechamber below, Deckard's magic humming contentedly within him.

After the dedication he and Evylin had shown to their marital "practice" the previous two nights, he'd begun to find his center. Though he had yet to utilize their Bond in battle as a means of control in a heightened situation, he was going into this Keep with more hope than ever before.

They stepped into the antechamber of the Terrae Keep, emerald light pooling into the hall as they drew their weapons. A faint sense of nostalgia reached Deckard, a feeling that Evylin shared. He scanned the arched windows and domed ceilings. This was the last time they'd enter a Keep. And while he wouldn't miss the looming possibility of death, he would always remember the wonder and beauty of the magical worlds within.

Flora decorated the ironwork windows around them. They passed farther into the hall. Isla and Ilain stood at the front, ready to open the metal door. Ethenn held the Wind bow ready while Brea transformed the Night Relic into a staff of iridescent amethyst. A pulse of power came from Deckard's side as Evylin held the Space sword in her hand. The onyx blade seemed to absorb the emerald light around it while reflecting a rainbow of colors around its hilt.

Ilain paused at the door, looking over her shoulder at them. Isla and Vayden stood with her, with Thom and Rafferty next in line. Deckard and Evylin waited next while Brea and Ethenn took up the rear.

"This is it," Ilain said, her eyes locked behind Deckard's shoulder. He felt Ethenn shift behind him. She swallowed tightly. "I want to thank you all," she addressed the Ephrians, an unexpected glimmer of moisture in her eyes. "Without you, Auden and I would have failed long ago. You made this possible, and my brother's legacy will live on through our success."

A somber silence passed through the hall.

Finally, Thom raised his chin. "Into the fray," he said proudly.

With a nod, Deckard added, "Into the fight."

Ilain gave the brothers a soft smile. Then she turned to Isla. "Into the fray," she repeated.

Isla stepped forward, turned, and set her hand on the iron door. A booming *thunk* echoed into the hall. The door slid open with rolling clicks.

A momentary surge of panic raced through Deckard's limbs. He feared that he'd be consumed by the power of Space when he stepped over the threshold. But Evylin's fingers brushed his arm.

"Together," she said.

He looked down at her, taking comfort in her strength. "Together," he murmured, and hand in hand, they stepped into the Terrae Keep as one.

CHAPTER FIFTY-ONE

Vibrant greens and terrae-rich browns filled the Keep. A peaceful blue sky stretched miles above them, only a thin line between the thick trees that crowded it out of view. Abundant life burst forth all around them. The luscious trees towered higher than any building in Loclight. Their massive brown trunks and roots butted against one another while thick branches stretched wildly in all directions.

"The path is only wide enough for two of us at a time," Isla said as they clustered on the stairs. "We should do our best not to step outside of it."

The team shared nervous glances.

"You think something bad will happen if we do?" Rafferty asked.

Isla gave the trees a wary inspection. "I don't want to find out if I'm wrong."

"All right," Deckard said, taking a cautious step forward. "Two at a time. Isla, take Brea and lead us. Thom, I want you to watch their backs. Ethenn and Ilain, you'll go next with Raff and Vayden right behind you. Evylin and I will defend the rear."

The troop moved steadily to follow his orders, though he noted Ethenn and Ilain gave one another tight looks as they stepped into place. Still, they moved together down the path as instructed.

The nine of them moved quickly. Within moments, the hum of the Shades heralded their prompt arrival. It sounded like the rustling of a hundred thousand leaves. A great whisper of the terrae, coming to life in their ears.

Dirt and clay swirled into being as the Shades rose from the grass and dirt. And they never stopped growing. Large and bulky, these Shades dwarfed the others they'd encountered. Deckard worried that any hits they landed would deal twice the damage. He tightened his grip on his sword, feeling the tug of Space on his heart. Its whisper was softer than usual, a gentle urging rather than that furious demand from his dream. But he wasn't yet ready to draw on his magic. He couldn't risk losing control again.

Ethenn's silver arrows were the first to zip through the air, each hitting its mark. But it quickly became apparent that it would take multiple arrows to bring down only one Shade. Several of the creatures barreled onto the path as his targets exploded into mounds of dirt where they'd stood.

Deckard grimaced, knowing that the force of those giant clumps could cause severe damage if a person got trapped beneath their shower.

Wind magic ripped through several Shades as Isla and Brea fought their way forward. Evylin cut one down while Deckard staved off another. The Shade's death nearly knocked him off his feet when it burst into dirt.

Evylin tugged him out of the way. "Let me handle close combat, will you?" she said with casual humor. "I need you to thin out the pack."

Deckard spared her a glance as they rushed ahead toward the towering obelisk awaiting them. "I should wait for the Chamber," he said.

A column of fire burned up a Shade that got too close, its mound spilling onto their path. They veered around it as they ran, forced into single file until they passed.

"We can't let them get onto the path," Deckard called. "They'll block us."

"Are we sure we can't go into the grass?" Rafferty asked.

"Do you want to risk it?" Evylin replied.

With no more argument, Rafferty dropped his head and ran.

Their past experiences had taught them not to waste the precious moments between waves on anything less than an all-out sprint. They made it almost halfway down the trail by the time the second wave arrived. Since the creatures were larger, they moved more slowly but hit harder. A fact Deckard learned more intimately than he liked when an approaching Shade drove its fist into his chest before he could duck out of the way.

The impact stole his breath, and he was sure he heard a rib crack as he stumbled backward. Evylin reached out but was too slow to catch him before his foot landed in the grass. In an instant, the foot disappeared, the grass wrapping around his leg like an intertwining nightmare of ropes, pulling him down into the terrae.

Locked in combat, Evylin slashed violently with the Space sword, the power of her swing finishing off the Shade nearest her. It burst, clumps of dirt raining down upon them as the mound piled up at the edge of the path. The Shade that had attacked Deckard turned and reared back with both arms, swinging down to smash her.

Without thinking, Deckard raised his hand as his leg sank halfway into the dirt, the magic waiting at the surface of his consciousness, ready for his touch. Instinctively, onyx shards shot out from his hand to tear the creature apart, shooting through it like a thousand blades. The creature crumbled. Grabbing under his shoulders, Evylin wrenched him back on the path. They barely caught their footing before returning to the fight.

"The terrae will pull you down," Deckard yelled to the others. "*Stay* on the path."

With a mighty effort, he pushed down his magic and tightened his grip on his sword. He had to protect his energy. If he lost himself to the magic this early, he wouldn't have enough strength for the final battle to get them out.

The troop tore through the second wave, and giant piles of dirt crested the sides of the path, making their run precarious. As the third wave hummed into existence, they neared the chamber's entrance. With renewed strength, the Shades attacked mercilessly the closer they approached.

Surrounded, their team worked to break through the Shade's onslaught. At the front, Brea and Thom moved before and behind Isla to keep her path clear. The Mage sent out torrents of Wind and manipulated the dirt mounds of the fallen Shades to create columns of Terrae. She caused the grass to spring up their legs and rise, twisting up the creatures' torsos. It slowed them down enough for Ethenn's arrows to finish them with ease.

Though they thinned the oncoming horde, fighting with a sword grew more difficult by the second as the Shades pressed in. Deckard was about to sheath it when he was knocked flat on his back.

A Shade charged past him, clutching the back of Rafferty's coat. The weasel let out a startled yelp as the Shade yanked him off the path and rushed into the trees. Deckard scrambled to his feet. With a grimace, he gave chase.

Every step across the grass forced him to work twice as hard as normal. He tore his feet away from the terrae's grip each time. Then he leaped over the mounting dirt piles and plunged into the trees.

Deckard followed the faint shadow of the Shade, guided by Rafferty's call for help. The creature's hulking form scraped against the trunks and low-hanging limbs while Deckard struggled to vault over the unnatural, gargantuan roots. His ribcage pinched, but he ignored the pain with each breath. Already, the Shade was fading into the depths of the forest, and he feared losing sight of it with his slow movement.

Magic pulsed against his chest. His jaw clamped tightly, determined not to lose another comrade. He allowed the whisper to rise, its eagerness pressing with force against his tenuous hold. Deckard gritted his teeth against the compulsion to give himself over to the full weight of power and thrust a hand forward.

A shard tore after the Shade, a spiral of the Heavens glittering through the forest.

The obsidian spike hit its mark, piercing through the back of the creature's head. It erupted into dirt.

Rafferty's grunt reached his ears, but he couldn't see where the man had fallen.

Deckard rushed forward, scrambling through the roots. They seemed to shift under his feet even as he moved, causing him to wobble unsteadily. "Where are you?" he called, forward his only option.

A muffled cry reached him another thirty feet ahead. He hurried on, spotting the large mound of dirt. He climbed over the roots as he fought the terrae around him.

"I'm almost there," he called again.

Another now-fainter grumble replied, but it sounded like Rafferty was getting farther away.

Deckard broke over the tangled roots to stand before the mound of dirt. He had to keep moving his feet so the grass and roots didn't begin to pull him down. But he couldn't find Rafferty.

"Raff!"

A muted grunt came from his left, almost too faint to hear.

Deckard looked over to catch a single flash of white-blond hair before the shifting roots swallowed Rafferty whole.

Bounding over, Deckard searched the limbs for any way through. There was none.

With a deep breath, he summoned his magic, feeling the heat spread along his skin. "Don't move," he warned. Then Space tumbled out of him in arcs of black that sliced through the roots as though they were butter. They splintered apart, and the tree recoiled, revealing the soldier underneath.

Deckard reached down and pulled him free.

The man shuddered, coughing out dirt as Deckard dragged him to his feet.

"Come on," he ordered without giving him time to recover. "We can't stay in one place, or we'll both get trapped."

Rafferty wheezed but limped along as Deckard hopped from root to root. "Which way?" he asked weakly.

Deckard scanned the trees. They all looked the same. Every direction held an identical image all around them. They had no way to find their way back.

He continued forward, unable to stand still. "Give me a minute," he said.

"Are you an expert tracker all of a sudden?"

"No," he said, his thumb brushing his moonstone ring. He thought of Evylin, feeling for her presence inside his own soul. "But I am a Bonded Mage."

Deckard had become accustomed to feeling Evylin's presence within him. Initially, it had seemed strange to be constantly aware of her whereabouts. His attachment to her psyche and emotions was unusual. However, he had come to value it profoundly, especially in moments like these.

Deep within his core, Deckard found her, feeling the irresistible tug of her strength and grit, her excitement and adrenaline. Her feelings rose up within him as if they were his own, and he made a sharp right turn.

"This way," he said, tugging Rafferty along.

Racing back through the trees, Deckard and Rafferty followed the pull of Evylin's consciousness. Before long, they made it back to the chaos. Evylin, Ethenn, and Brea still fought fiercely, bringing down the last of the Shades. Ilain stood at the head of the troop, hands raised as she used Terrae magic to lift a giant mound of dirt from the path. Clumps of it flew through the air, clearing the pile. Thom and Vayden knelt at the base of the mound, working to pull Isla free.

"What happened?" Deckard asked, hurrying to their side.

"We tried to hold them back," Brea explained. "But there were too many. Isla got caught by their death knell."

As Ilain parted the dirt in two, the men helped Isla stand. She let out a small cry, grimacing as she tried to put weight on her foot. Vayden wrapped his arm around her waist, supporting her weight.

"I'm all right," Isla insisted, though she didn't try to pull away. "It's just a sprain."

Ilain stepped over, slightly out of breath. "We're fifty yards from the Chamber entrance," she said. "We need to get there now before the next wave comes. Once inside, I'll check to ensure it isn't broken."

"Let's go, then," Thom said, gesturing toward the cleared path. Together, he and Brea took the lead.

Vayden lifted Isla in his arms despite her protests and raced for the door. The soft beginnings of the rustling hum reached them just as they tumbled into the stairwell. He set his wife down on the stone steps, and Ilain crouched before her.

Evylin turned to Deckard and Rafferty, worry in her eyes. "Are either of you injured?" she asked, scanning both of them with a frantic inspection.

Deckard brushed her arm comfortingly. "We're fine."

"Speak for yourself," Rafferty grumbled. "I was nearly eaten by a tree."

Thom and Brea chuckled while Ilain stood. "It isn't broken," she said. "I could heal it, but—"

"No, save your strength," Isla said. "I've already used too much magic on my own to take down the Guardian. I'll lose consciousness if I do. Someone will have to carry me either way, but I *can* fight on the way out if I retain enough energy now."

"It'd be an honor to be your carriage, my dear," Vayden teased, helping her rise.

Ilain chewed on her lip. "I can heal it now," she insisted. "The two of us can take the Guardian down together, sharing energy."

"It will weaken you too much, Ilain." Isla held her gaze. "Terrae is not only your lowest Elemental resource, which you've already had to tap into to save me, but you aren't even supposed to manage Day. We can't risk you healing each of our minor wounds."

"That's why she's got Ethenn, though, right?" Rafferty said.

Ilain flinched, and Ethenn shifted awkwardly at Brea's side.

Deckard frowned, noting their discomfort for a second time since they'd entered the Keep. "What's wrong?" he asked.

"Nothing," Ilain said.

Ethenn dropped his eyes to the stone steps. "Would it help?" he asked Ilain.

She hesitated, facing away from him. "It would."

Without a word, he stepped forward and held out his hand.

Crouching back down, Ilain set one hand on Isla's ankle and the other in Ethenn's palm. After a quick burst of orange light, she released them both.

Immediately, Ethenn moved away. He looked up at Deckard. "We've decided to end our betrothal, sir," he said. "That's all."

The entire stairwell fell silent as the troop gaped at them.

Evylin's lips parted in shock. "Why?" she asked.

Ilain bore up, her expression turning faintly amused. "You can stop gaping at us now," she said. "We determined that our paths don't align, that's all. Now, shall we retrieve this Relic and get out of here?"

Though a long pause lingered, Deckard motioned toward the descending stairs. Slowly, the troop began their journey down. "Isla, do you still feel you can't take down the Guardian?" he asked.

"It wouldn't be wise," Isla admitted as she limped down the steps. Ilain's magic had given her the ability to walk again, but the ankle was clearly still sore. "Even with Ilain's help. If we want me conscious on the way out, that is."

Deckard pursed his lips, breathing through the aching pain in his side. "I don't think I could manage it," he said. "I've no concept of what Terrae magic feels like."

Ilain glanced over her shoulder at him. "I can manage it," she said, then cleared her throat. "But I will need support. From *any* Warrior."

There was a beat before Ethenn said, "I'll do it."

"You don't have to—"

"I'll do it, Ilain," he interrupted in a brusque manner.

She clamped her mouth shut and turned away.

Deckard and Evylin shared a look. Whatever the pair wanted to claim, the end of their betrothal clearly hadn't been as amicable as they made it sound. There was a clear layer of underlying anger and hurt between them. But it wasn't his place to question them on it.

Or was it?

Ethenn had requested that Deckard be his advocate in their betrothal. He'd wanted Deckard's advice. And since that first day, Deckard had failed to check in on the couple. He'd been so focused on each day of travel, on staying ahead of Blount, and on learning to control the magic within that he'd barely given it a thought. Perhaps he should have been more attentive to the young man's request.

Regardless, now was not the time to resolve this problem. They'd have all the time in the world once they recovered the Relic and stopped Blount.

The Terrae Chamber spread out before them as a forest brimming with life. The entire room glimmered with verdant growth. Emerald tiles peeked through swirls of grass. Vines twisted up the columns. And a glowing dais awaited them at the far end.

Taking their first steps into the Chamber, the Wind Relic pulsed in Ethenn's hand. It morphed into a sword, glowing with an inner silver light. He hesitated, then held out his hand to Ilain. "Stay close," he said.

Reluctantly, Ilain's fingers slipped through his, but she said nothing.

"Be fast," Thom advised, keeping his sword raised. "And don't die."

Weapons at the ready, they moved into the giant hall. The grass under their feet remained docile but gripped the soles of their boots, making each step sluggish. A gentle rumble vibrated along the ground, harkening the Guardian's arrival.

Deckard scanned the space, alert and ready for whatever creature might come at them. *The Living Land*, he remembered, *from the children's book.* Was it possible that such a creature existed?

The rumble grew louder, and the ground began to shake. They widened their stances to steady themselves as the quaking intensified. Once, Thom had to reach out, catching Brea's shoulder to keep his footing.

Suddenly, even the tiled floors began to shift. They watched as it gave way, morphing with the grass to form a massive beast. Brutish in build and bearing two bulging limbs with its trunk affixed to the terrae, the Guardian rolled back its thick shoulders to stand at its full height. Its head scraped the ceiling hundreds of feet above them. Fierce green eyes landed on them with far more intelligence than the terrae should own.

The Living Land, indeed.

Then the Guardian raised its two massive fists.

"Move!" Deckard ordered, and the team immediately sprang into action.

The fists lashed out in a sweep from right to left, forcing them all back and away. Ethenn pulled Ilain to the left around the pillars while the rest of the troop leaped out of the Guardian's range. Deckard dove, rolling to his feet beside Evylin. Together, they engaged the beast.

From the back of the troop, Vayden fired arrows while Isla propelled huge gusts of Wind in cutting swipes. With Brea in the lead, Rafferty and Thom dashed forward, slipping under the lumbering creature's guard to hack at its monstrous trunk, but only funneling more grass and stone into its form.

Evylin charged ahead, the Space sword drawn and glittering, and Deckard summoned his magic. He didn't care if it consumed him now. Faced with this ginormous Guardian, he knew it would take all the power they had to keep them alive.

The Living Land struck out, causing Evylin to drop into a slide as she approached. With ease, she hopped to her feet again. The Space sword spun in a luminescent arc as she twirled her wrist, slicing into the creature's base. It bellowed a low growl. Dirt poured from the cut.

Deckard planted his feet and raised his hands. The onyx shards trailed up his arms and across his torso. His vision turned dark. The glittering magic soared past Evylin, Thom, Rafferty, and Brea to plunge into the Guardian's form. They twisted their way through the marble and terrae torso and out its back, then rotated to repeat the process.

Together, Evylin and Brea cut giant slashes into The Living Land's trunk while Thom and Rafferty needled it with their mundane weapons. Vayden's arrows sank into the creature's form only to be sucked away. Isla's magic sloughed off chunks of dirt and stone. Great rivulets of soil poured from the punctures left by their assaults.

Maddened, The Living Land bellowed a thunderous cry. It swiped at them with greater fury and swelled in size. The ground shifted again, knocking Rafferty from his feet. Thom stumbled back, but Brea caught him, tugging him to the side. Evylin fought on, seemingly oblivious to the difficult terrain.

A great fist came at Deckard then. He spared it a momentary glance, his magic whispering steadily in his mind. He flicked one wrist toward The Living Land's oncoming blow. A crystalline band shimmered to life, pinning the fist to the ground.

The Guardian howled, and its anger shook the air around them. But the trap lasted only a second. The fist sank into the terrae to reform and free itself of the Space magic.

Evylin darted forward before The Living Land could rise from its stooped position. She leaped onto the arm and charged up its length. She'd barely scrambled to the shoulder before it resumed its full, towering height.

Deckard's stomach clenched, but he refused to worry about her. She was a Warrior. Battle was what she was made for.

While Evylin slashed at the Guardian's shoulder, neck, jaw, and ear, Deckard riddled it with holes. Colossal mountains of dirt began to crumble onto the tiled floors. Thom, Rafferty, and Brea scrambled away, unable to draw near without putting themselves in danger of being buried.

Enraged, The Living Land bellowed, swatting out furiously. Its arms sailed through the air. Brea shoved Thom down, avoiding a blow, but the fist landed in the center of Rafferty's chest. He flew back, slamming into a column. Then the Guardian convulsed in on itself, dissipating in a sudden shower of grass and terrae. And from the great height, Evylin began to fall.

Deckard thrust his hands out, his heart in his throat. A circular disk of obsidian crystal formed beneath her. Her body landed on it with a *thunk.*

"That hurt!" she called good-naturedly.

Deckard breathed easily, guiding the disk to drift to the ground. Evylin swung her legs over the edge and leaped the short distance down. He let the magic go.

Ethenn and Ilain approached from the far side of the room. The Terrae Relic glowed brightly in her hands.

Near his side, Brea eyed Deckard with interest. "You have fast reflexes," she noted.

"It's not the first time I've had to save her life that way," he said. A tingle rushed along his skin as the magic drifted around his hands. Though Space still murmured in his head, it hadn't overtaken him. Somehow, he was steady, working *with* the magic rather than against it. And when he released it, it didn't fight him.

Evylin's laughter soothed over him as she stepped up to their side. "Says the man who's nearly died every time we've entered a Keep," she bantered.

"I did just fine in the Wind and Time Keeps, thank you very much."

"Hey," Thom interrupted, kneeling at Rafferty's side. The weasel sat propped against the column he'd collided with. "We could use some help over here."

The group hurried over. Rafferty held his side, and his face bore a few scrapes, but he otherwise didn't look the worse for wear. "What's wrong?" Deckard asked.

"Not sure," Rafferty said, then gasped and grimaced. "It hurts to breathe, though."

Deckard let out a weak laugh. "I can relate," he said. "Do you think you can run?"

"Maybe," Rafferty said dubiously.

Ilain crouched next to him and set a hand on his chest. Rafferty let out a small grunt of pain as she prodded him. "You've got a fierce touch, lady flame," he grumbled through clenched teeth. "No wonder little Lox decided it wouldn't work out."

Ilain gave him a bland look but ignored the comment. "He's punctured a lung," she said. "He can run with us, but he can't fight."

"Can you heal it?" Deckard asked.

"The more healing I do, the more energy I lose," she said, and for the first time, Deckard noticed how tired she looked. "And the more difficult our exit will be."

Deckard pressed his lips together, drawing in a long breath. His side spasmed, but he tried to ignore it.

Evylin shifted at his side, looking up at him with sudden agitation. "You're not serious," she said accusingly.

Ignoring the pain, he furrowed his brow. "What?"

"I can feel what you feel, you idiot," she said, worried. "Why didn't you say you were injured?"

Everyone turned to him in shock.

"It's nothing," Deckard assured them. "Just a bruise, I'd imagine."

Thom shook his head and gestured to Ilain. "Check him," he said.

Deckard sighed as Ilain crossed to him. "Where?" she ordered. He gestured to his ribcage. She pressed on the wound lightly, then huffed. "Oh, yes," she said in a mocking tone. "You're completely fine. Just a cracked rib. No problem there."

"Jonn!" Evylin gasped. "When did this happen?"

"When the Shade knocked me off the path," he said, trying to placate her. "I'm fine, though."

"But it hurts?" Ilain asked.

"Yes, but it's manageable."

"A cracked rib is manageable?" Brea asked with skepticism.

Ilain dismissed her with a wave of her hand. "He's a Mage in a Keep. The magic that flows around us takes the edge off. And I'll grant that it's a very small crack, but it's got to make breathing hellish."

"I can run and fight," Deckard said. "That's all that matters."

Thom scoffed, and Evylin rolled her eyes.

Gathered together now, Ilain turned to Ethenn, holding out the emerald amulet in her hands. "I'd like the Wind Relic," she said.

Ethenn's brow furrowed curiously, but he made the exchange.

Thom voiced their collective question aloud. "Wouldn't it be better for you to carry Terrae since you're not as strong with it?"

"That's the exact reason I *shouldn't* keep it," Ilain said, hanging the Wind Relic around her neck. She flicked her fiery hair out from under its chain. "Wind is my second, which means it will drain far less energy from me when I use it. Terrae would wear me down far too fast. Now, help Rafferty up."

Thom did as requested, and Ilain looked up at Deckard. "Lead us out of here, Colonel," she said.

Deckard surveyed the troop in one quick sweep. "With Rafferty's injury, he'll need to be defended. Thom," his brother met his gaze, "can you handle that?"

"Don't worry," Thom said, then ruffled Rafferty's white-blond hair affectionately. "I'll get our little weasel outta here alive."

Rafferty slapped at his hands, then gasped in pain and grabbed his side again.

"Ethenn, Ilain—" Deckard gave them a searching look. "I'd still like you to work together."

Ilain raised her chin. "It isn't me who has the problem, Jonn."

Ethenn ground his teeth but said, "Whatever you command, sir."

"Good. Put aside your differences and take the back." Deckard turned to Brea. "Stick with Vayden and Isla. Focus on protecting them and supporting Thom if he needs it." He met Evylin's gaze. "We'll take the front."

Marching for the staircase, Evylin and Deckard took the lead. "You're sure about this?" she asked, worry glinting in the amber of her eyes.

"I promise," he brushed his hand against hers, "I'm just fine."

"Don't black out on me this time," she ordered. "I can't take that again."

"I won't leave you alone ever again."

They ascended the staircase, winding back to the top of the Keep. When they neared the door, Deckard reached for his magic once more, letting it coil up his arms. The heat of magic singed his veins, and the world grew shadowed.

Evylin reached for the door, meeting his gaze. Rather than the questioning he expected to see there, her countenance reflected nothing but unerring confidence in him and his magic. As his Warrior, she was ready to take on the Keep at his side, and it sent a surge of reassurance through him while his power whispered earnestly in his head.

At his resolute nod, Evylin opened the door. Deckard raised his hands, and a shower of onyx shards pierced the waiting wave of Shades. She slipped out and began to tear through them, her sword flashing in the light. Mountains of dirt exploded all around, crashing into each other as the creatures died. As if in slow motion, Deckard watched the powerful spray of dirt, realizing its descent would block their path. On instinct, he gestured in an upward arc. Glittering, twin walls of Space magic burst up, protecting their pathway.

Deckard hurried behind Evylin, the rest of the troop following. United in their attacks, Bonded Warrior and Mage led the charge with nearly unstoppable power. Space magic flew through the Keep, cutting down Shade after Shade. Evylin defended Deckard from any creature that neared their path. In response, his magic protected their perimeter with increasing spikes of power. Pure, raw force tore out of his body. It was incredible and intoxicating. Perhaps the only thing more truly stunning was the woman fighting at his side. His instincts drew him to tap into her magic as she waged battle beside him.

Evylin spun the Space sword with such grace and agility that she might have been dancing. A spin and a strike. A dip back before her arm flowed in a crushing upward blow. A glide forward as she lunged to pierce the attacker ahead of her.

And through it all, she radiated undiluted joy.

Deckard was in awe. This was Evylin in her purest form, the Warrior and the woman who'd captivated his mind and fascinated his heart. She was incredible and impossible. And she was his.

As a fresh wave of the Shades poured toward them, the Space sword pulsed with a shimmer. Deckard watched as darkness erupted from the blade, crystalline shards descending to wrap over her arm and across her body, sliding down to her feet. She was covered in a silhouette of his magic. It lashed out with each of her strikes, defending her as she fought.

With his chest filled with overpowering adoration, Deckard's magic intensified. Cold seeped into his mind, soothing the heat of his power. He knew this chill. It was the same sensation he'd experienced during their Bonding ceremony. It was her power, freshly alight in him.

The room came into focus, even as the shadows at the edges of his vision remained. Every one of Deckard's senses heightened. His perspective became nearly omnipresent, and he could see them all fighting together. He and Evylin led the charge, taking down Shade after Shade with almost no effort. They'd torn through the fourth wave already, though the fifth joined within moments.

At the back, Ilain and Ethenn worked together with similar harmony. They were disjointed at times, but all in all, they moved with near-impossible precision and grace. Another Warrior and Mage in perfect balance.

In the middle, Brea and Isla flowed together, though not with the same steadiness. Vayden and Thom kept Rafferty safe, handling themselves well. They'd made steady progress, already almost three-fourths of the way through the Keep.

It wasn't until the sixth wave that the creatures seemed to refine their attack, and the onslaught caught up to them. Hesitant to turn away from Evylin, Deckard sent a stream of shadows behind them. Several Shades came crashing down at the back of the fight. He threw up the walls of Space to protect the troop from the blowback of their deaths.

But a Shade broke past Vayden's defenses while Isla was distracted on the other side. Ethenn dove forward, taking the hit meant for Vayden. He rolled across the path with the Terrae bow tight in his grasp. But the Shades rushed him.

Ethenn was trampled in the stampede, groans audible under their assault.

Ilain expelled a giant cloud of fire that rumbled over the Shades. They burst into ash, falling weightlessly over Ethenn. He gasped for air at the release, his face twisted in pain.

Brea hurried forward with Vayden to haul Ethenn to his feet.

Seeing their trouble, Deckard called to Evylin, holding out his hand. Their eyes met with trust. Though she couldn't know his plan, he knew she could sense his urgency. She flipped the Space sword, slashed through a Shade, and dashed to his side.

The second their palms met, they disappeared in a cloud of black, reappearing at the back of the troop.

At their materialization, an explosion of shards cut through the Shades surrounding them, blowing the creatures back. Though they'd thinned out the front, Deckard wouldn't leave Thom undefended up there for long. He intended to just see the Calders, Ethenn, and Brea secure on their feet.

While Deckard and Evylin cleared out a mass of Shades, the wave grew less dangerous. Ilain sent more fire bolts sailing through the air. Isla's Wind magic sliced through the Shades in huge swaths. The path was clear, but Ethenn required both Vayden and Brea's support, his head lolling with a worrying droop.

As Evylin cut down another Shade, Deckard called to her. Hands clasped, they teleported back to the other side to stop the Shades again, who were bearing down on Thom and Rafferty. They reappeared in a burst of magic, immediately slicing through the creatures.

Rafferty cursed at their sudden appearance next to him. "Warn someone before you do that!" he called.

Deckard and Evylin were too busy taking down the remaining Shades and clearing their path to the exit to respond.

Rushing up the staircase, Deckard slammed his hand against the door. It rumbled open as he resumed the fight. The troop scrambled up the steps after him, hurrying into the antechamber. The last to leave, Deckard and Evylin defended their escape, a crystalline shadow of magic surrounding them both.

Once Ilain made it through the door, Deckard and Evylin slipped out last. The door shut, and they were free of the last and final Keep.

Their breath collectively heaving, Deckard and Evylin stood, frozen as one, as they stared in awe at one another. They'd done it: Fire, Day, Water, Night, Wind, Time, Terrae, and Space. All the Relics had now returned to Terraeus.

Part III: The Prince's Gambit

*I am days away from obtaining my prize, and then you will have my sole focus.
Do not grow weary in your journey. I have included another gift to finance
your endeavors. We will have our victory yet, Captain: your son's health and
my eternal destiny, as is our gods-given right.*

Excerpt from a letter from King Rouland Blount II to Captain Aune Comara

*Accounts of Rouland Blount II, Crown Prince of Wauld, often note his cunning
and ruthless nature. However, his godfather, Lord Sirraus Obel, Duke of
Pyralund County, contradicts these traits, arguing that they are not inherent
but a result of his father's brutality. Lord Obel's recounting of Rouland II as
a child reveals a young boy with a tender heart, one he hoped would alter the
course of their kingdom. He had hopes to nurture his godson, especially upon
the discovery of Rouland II's status as a Night Mage like the duke. However,
after Rouland II's arrival for training in Verlund Reach, it appeared the
damage had already been done.*

*Lord Obel recited a long-remembered quote from his godson that impacted
his choice to abandon the Blount monarchy. 'It is my right,' a young Rouland
II told his godfather, 'to wield this power not only as the crown prince, but as
a chosen of the gods. And I will prove to my father once and for all that his
son is not weak.'*

**Excerpt from A Complete History of West Auld, written by Lord Edmaund Fishere,
Earl of Mouroc, published posthumously in 1575**

Ephria City

CHAPTER FIFTY-TWO

At the sight of Deckard and Evylin glittering with the silhouette of Space morphing and moving around them, Thom frowned. He'd never witnessed anything so terrifyingly incredible as Warrior and Mage fighting side by side. Seeing the magic swirl around their forms was like catching them in an intimate embrace, much like when they'd Bonded. They were unity embodied.

And it made him more aware than ever that he didn't belong in their world.

Turning away as Deckard wrapped his arms around Evylin, Thom forced down the jealousy coiling in his gut. He didn't begrudge their happiness. But he did envy it.

Thom leaned against the windowsill between one of the arches in the antechamber. He worked to slow his heart rate as he scanned their troop. Rafferty stood to his left, his hand still pressed to his ribcage. Isla helped Vayden and Brea lower Ethenn to the floor. The hunter grimaced, his whole face aflame with a blush. Thom was beginning to wonder if the response was a nervous tic after all or something else entirely.

"I'll be fine," Ethenn said through gritted teeth. He handed the Terrae Relic to Brea with his right hand, the other clutched to his chest, its shape smashed and bent oddly. Vayden guided him to lean against the wall as Ilain knelt beside them, muttering under her breath.

When she began to check him over, Ethenn shied away from her touch. "I'm *fine*," he repeated. "Warriors heal themselves, right?"

Ilain's glare could have burned a whole village to the ground. "Give me your bloody hand," she demanded.

Ethenn's jaw tightened. His eyes darted to the side where Deckard and Evylin approached, their magic fully extinguished. Then he did as Ilain instructed.

With a gentle touch, she took hold of him. Her hands trembled, but she tested the swollen wrist. "I can see that you're scraped up," she said with a rote tone, like she'd shut off her emotions to perform the task. "But do you have any other injuries?"

Reluctantly, Ethenn pointed to his abdomen and left leg.

After checking the areas, Ilain scowled. "You bloody idiot," she muttered, but Thom could see the tears that pooled at the corner of her eyes. She settled her hands over Ethenn's wrist, preparing to heal it. "Yes, Warriors heal themselves over time. But with the bruising along your ribs, the contusions across your body, a torn sartorius muscle in your thigh, and the numerous fractures in your wrist and hand . . ." She seared him with a glare. "It would take about a year to heal all this purely on your own magic."

A sour grin pulled at Ethenn's lips. "Guess Thom has his chance to get me back for setting his leg."

Thom smirked, and Rafferty sniggered, though there was an unusual wheeze to the sound.

Ilain was far less amused.

A flare of bright orange light burst between their hands, and he convulsed. Clearly fighting to hold in a scream, he lost the battle. He cursed and glared at her even as she moved on to his leg. He shifted uncomfortably when she touched him, and Thom didn't have to wonder why. The muscle he'd torn was rather high on the inside of his thigh. Another flash of light, another snarl of pain from Ethenn, and Ilain pulled away.

"There," she said sharply. "I healed the fractures and the muscle. I don't have the energy to fix the rest in addition to Jonn and Rafferty's wounds. And as you said, your magic will heal you just fine. Give it about two weeks, but don't come crying to me when you can't sleep from the pain."

Ethenn massaged his now healed hand, still pressed against his chest. "You were right, Raff," he said, lips tight. "She's not much of a caring nurse, is she?"

Ilain's lips lifted in a sly grin, and Thom pitied the young man's folly. Her chin rose, the emerald light around them contrasting fiercely with her red hair. "I care for those who care for me," she said stolidly.

And with that, Ilain walked away. She stepped over to Rafferty first, healing his punctured lung with a flare of light.

"Is this it then?" Brea asked, breaking the awkward silence. "We've retrieved the Relic, and now we wait for Blount?"

Deckard nodded. "It's likely night at this late hour," he said as Ilain came to heal his cracked rib. "If our calculations were correct, we should only have to wait twelve to twenty hours before he arrives."

Her work complete, Ilain sat next to Thom. Her shoulders drooped, and her face was shadowed with exhaustion. "We need all the recovery we can get in that time," she said. From the rasp in her voice, it was clear that weariness was settling over her. "With our injuries, the depletion of our magic, and the energy we exerted, we have to rest if we want a chance to stand against him."

"We'll stick to the plan," Deckard said. "We can't risk going back to the town and missing Blount's arrival."

Thom wiped the last beads of sweat from his brow. "Then we know our roles," he said. "You and Ethenn up top. Ilain, Brea, and I will be on the beach."

They'd made their plan the previous night. With no time to spare, they had to be ready for Blount whenever he made his appearance. That meant setting up an ambush.

Deckard and Ethenn would be their lookouts on the clifftop. Once they spotted Blount, Deckard would teleport them down into the Terrae Keep's antechamber and alert Evylin, Rafferty, Isla, and Vayden.

And in the meantime, Thom, Brea, and Ilain would be a contingency on the beach. They would flank Blount's men, but if they were given the signal (they had come up with three separate signals to ensure their success), the trio would run as far as they could, taking the Wind and Space Relics with them.

No one liked the plan, but it was their only shot. If Blount defeated their ambush, they couldn't let him capture all the Relics. They couldn't take the Terrae Relic out of the Keep's antechamber yet; if Blount had any Terrae Mages with him, they'd feel its entrance into the world again. So while Deckard and Evylin would fight with the Night and Terrae Relics, they hoped their Bond was enough to stop Blount. If it wasn't, they would all be secure in the knowledge that Thom would get Ilain and Brea to safety. They would regroup with the Alliance, form a new plan, and take Blount down another day.

The plan was the only hope they had.

One by one, they gathered, said their goodbyes, and parted. Thom hugged Evylin tightly, worried it'd be the last time he'd see her.

"Be safe, all right?" he whispered during their lingering embrace. She'd come to mean so much to him over the last four months. She was a sister, a friend, a comrade, and a confidante. He trusted her more than anyone, aside from possibly Deckard, and his heart ached at the thought of never seeing her again.

Evylin gave him a final squeeze, just as Meria would have. "You as well."

Deckard's hug was scarcely less affectionate. The brothers clung to one another, the hurt of past decades all but gone. If nothing else, this mission had repaired their troubled relationship. It had changed Thom wholly. He no longer sought what he couldn't have. He only cared to be by his brother's side.

"I'll see you later," Deckard said when they broke apart.

Thom nodded, refusing to give in to his fear. "Don't miss me too much."

With a pat on Rafferty's back and a ruffle of Ethenn's hair, Thom shook Vayden's hand, nodded to Isla, and joined Brea at the stairs. Ilain took longer to say goodbye to Vayden and Isla, their words whispers in the antechamber. Ethenn stood as far from the woman as possible, his chin tucked into his chest.

Thom ran a hand along his jaw, studying them.

Brea nudged his elbow. "You're frighteningly obvious when you're scheming," she said.

"I'm not scheming," he replied. "I'm considering."

"Very different," she noted.

"Exactly."

At last, Ilain joined them. They ascended the staircase, ready to seek a hiding place among the rocky shoreline. The sky was speckled with stars as they stepped outside, but both moons were mere slivers, keeping the night darker than usual. Thom shivered from the damp breeze sweeping across the sea.

Waves crashed against the shore, spraying them with salty droplets. They found a hideout nearly a mile down the coast. Brea's magic would be their means of ensuring they saw Blount's arrival or heard the signal. A large outcropping of oblong rocks stood on their sides, creating a ring-like alcove that would hide them in its shelter and shadow. Though partially open to the sky, it rested on an angle where the tide couldn't reach them even at its highest point. They agreed that, during the night, only one of them should sit up at a time. The likelihood of Blount's arrival before morning was fortunately slim, and they needed rest.

"Why don't you two sleep first?" Thom suggested as they settled into the alcove. "We need you both at the height of your powers if we are to have any chance."

Though Ilain readily found a corner to curl herself away from the chilly sea breeze, Brea stayed by Thom's side. "You're cute when you're concerned about people," she teased as they sat.

"Cute?" Thom scowled in the darkness. "I don't like that."

Fondly, she smiled. "Wake me if you see something," she instructed, then lay down beside him. "Goodnight, *mi'caro*."

"Sleep tight, *demoloba*."

She lifted her head, eyes narrowed.

"If you have a nickname for me, I get to have one for you," he explained with a bright tone.

In the faint wash of moonlight, he watched Brea's brow lift. "So you chose to call me 'demonwolf'?"

"It's fearsome," he said. "And they scare the shit out of me, just like you."

With a light chuckle, Brea lay back down and fell asleep.

For hours, Thom watched the darkness. He glanced toward the cliffside, towering above them. Deckard and Ethenn were somewhere up there, keeping watch. He sent a silent prayer that they would be safe, as the most exposed members of their party.

With the long-awaited confrontation with Blount approaching, Thom let his thoughts roam to all the mistakes he'd made in his life. He considered Hewitt's charges. *"How do you best want to serve this world . . . Your purpose is whatever you make it; just make sure it's a worthy one."* And he thought of what Evylin had told him in Whickam Village. *"You're a much different man than when we met."*

Thom felt different. Everything about how he perceived himself had changed. Contrary to his overinflated sense of self, he was lowly, meek, and unworthy. He was a mortal among gods. And he felt like a fool, thinking he ever could have measured up to them.

He was tired of wanting more, of wishing he could be enough for them. He wanted a small life of little consequence where he didn't feel so inferior all the time.

"But you wouldn't be happy."

Thom propped his arms on his knees. The ocean receded and rose, again and again, fizzing around the pebbled shore.

"I'm under no illusions about your worth."

Ilain had told him that.

"You're far better and far more worthy than you think."

Those were Brea's words.

Why were so many women trying to get him to see his value? What had he done to deserve their admiration? None of them sought his affection, not even Brea. They were simply affirming his worth because they cared for him.

Was he worthy? He didn't feel it. But maybe you never did.

Maybe worth wasn't something you ascribed to yourself. Maybe it could only come from the people who loved you. And just maybe, it wasn't as great a burden as he thought.

"How do you best want to serve this world?"

Glancing over his shoulder at the two sleeping women, Thom was beginning to have an idea.

24TH OF RADIA, 1574

Thom woke to the bright light of a new day. After his extended shift, he'd woken Brea to trade places when he could no longer remain awake. He'd fallen into a dreamless sleep within moments, his exhausted body all too ready for rest.

Now, the sun was beating down, causing him to squint in its light. He sat up, the pebbled beach shifting under his weight. He brushed the sand from his hair and face as he looked over to find Ilain, not Brea, by his side.

"What time is it?" he asked.

Ilain glanced at the sky. "Close to ten in the morning, I'd assume."

"Huh." Thom scanned their alcove, then the shoreline. "Where's Brea?"

"She went to scout," Ilain replied. "I think she got bored sitting around."

Thom smirked. "Can't blame her." He unbuttoned his coat in the rising heat of the day. "No Blount yet, I take it?"

Ilain sat a couple of paces away from him, braiding small sections of her curly red mane. Even after a night of rest, she still looked haggard, though her eyes weren't as shadowed as last night. "No," she said in a flat, hollow tone.

"We got anything to eat?"

"In the pack."

Thom retrieved the pack they'd dropped in the corner of the ring-like rock alcove. Ilain had used it as a pillow the previous night. While they couldn't bring much with them, they made sure each group had supplies for after their excursion into the Keep. The pack held the most meager necessities, such as water, several small rations, and a few medical supplies. The Relics were safely tucked around Thom's neck, prepared to hand to Ilain and Brea should circumstances call for it.

With three strips of beef jerky in hand, a specialty from the stall of a Jal'Khoyan merchant, Thom returned to his seat. He sat next to Ilain, scanning the ocean and beach carefully. Gulls swooped overhead, and he thought he saw a whale crest the water in the far distance, but otherwise, the world was still.

"So," Thom broke the silence, "no more Ethenn, eh?"

Ilain turned to him, and he smirked as their gazes met.

With a perturbed roll of her eyes, she turned away again. "No more Ethenn," she confirmed.

"Wanna tell me about it?"

"Not particularly."

Thom tapped his knee against hers. "He's an idiot."

"Yes, I know," she replied.

A long pause hung between them.

"Why exactly—?"

Ilain interrupted him before he got the full question out. "Because he doesn't believe I love him back," she said.

Thom furrowed his brow. "Did you tell him you love him?"

"I did."

"Ah." Thom understood. This was what Ilain worried about from the start. Because of their previous deal—flirting to discourage Ethenn's advances—and Thom's bitter reaction to Ethenn's ratting him out to Deckard, the young Warrior still thought Ilain's interest only stemmed from the discovery of his power.

"I'm sorry, Ilain," Thom said genuinely. "This is my fault. If I hadn't—"

"No," Ilain interrupted again. "I mean, yes, it is partially your fault, but . . ." She paused, staring out at the sea. "I was a fool. Everything I thought I felt was selfish. I liked Ethenn from the start, yes, but I didn't love him—*truly* love him—until two weeks ago."

Thom turned to her, listening as she confessed her heart.

"He needs me," she whispered. "But I was too blind—too determined to have my own way, and now, he doesn't trust a word I say."

"But you do love him?" Thom asked.

She nodded slowly. "I would cross all five seas if he asked me to."

Remembering that Ethenn had named sea travel as her greatest fear, Thom couldn't help smiling. "That's pretty sacrificial of you," he noted.

"Love is sacrifice," Ilain said flatly. "And I have yet to sacrifice anything for him."

Thom blinked. "What are you willing to sacrifice?"

"Everything."

Picking at his fingernails, Thom turned away. No matter her role in the mistake, he was equally—if not more—to blame. It was his outburst, his lie, that had convinced Ethenn against Ilain's growing feelings. While she hadn't been in love with the young man at the time, she *was* interested. And he'd ruined her chances.

Thom cleared his throat. "So," he winced, "this is my mistake to fix."

Ilain turned to him, expression curious.

"I don't think Ethenn is going to believe you," he explained. "No matter what you say, he's going to assume that you're just trying to get him to be your Warrior. Which is probably because I told him you never had an interest and never would. He's got some self-esteem issues, it seems."

"He had a hard childhood," Ilain offered.

"So did we all," Thom muttered. With a dismissive shake of his head, he presented his plan. "It's going to take some time to repair this damage. Ethenn isn't going to believe me after one conversation. Even if I tell him the truth, he's going to doubt me. So keep loving him, all right? Sacrifice for him or whatever. I'll work on getting him to look past his insecurity and see that you did, in fact, fall in love with *him* and not his magic. Will that absolve me?"

Ilain scanned him. "It will."

"Fantastic." Thom turned back to the shore. "Now, we've just got to kill this bloody prince, and we can save your love life after."

It wasn't exactly a "purpose"—fixing Ilain and Ethenn's relationship—but it was a start.

After the last few days and weeks, Thom had come to a newfound understanding of himself. He liked caring for people. He liked helping his friends and seeing them happy. It made him feel useful. Instead of constantly seeking the love and devotion of others, he was ready to devote himself to loving them.

And one day, once they'd stopped Blount and raised Allund, perhaps he could find a true purpose, one that satisfied him more than anything else ever had.

"I apologized to Brea," Ilain said, breaking through his thoughts.

Thom swallowed the jerky in his mouth. "Yeah?"

"Yes." Ilain kept her gaze upon the sea. "I know her choosing you in the Keep wasn't malicious. It was hard . . . Brea has been friends with Isla and Vayden for years. They see her as family in many ways. And it seemed to me that she should accept us in the same manner. Yet, she and I never got along, and she constantly rejected Auden's attempts to get to know her."

Thom wanted to say that it was hard to accept someone's advances when you knew they were only interested in using you but kept the thought to himself.

"Her choosing you . . ." Ilain shook her head. "It felt like a final rejection of Auden, condemning him to a needless death."

A salty breeze ruffled their hair, causing Thom to bat some of her red curls away as they flew across his face. "Well," he said with gentleness as he pushed the hair behind her shoulder. "We've all made stupid mistakes, Ilain. This one is probably the most understandable of them all."

Ilain looked over at him, her green eyes glowing almost golden in the bright morning light. "Do you know something, Thom?" she said softly.

He raised his brow in expectation.

Her lips lifted in a smile. "I'm going to miss you."

"Am I going somewhere?"

She shook her head. "I am. When this is all over, I'll Bond with one of the other Warriors and return to the West. And while I'll miss Evie and Jonn and Rafferty and . . . and Ethenn . . . I think I'll miss you most."

Thom didn't know whether to feel honored or baffled. "Me?" he said.

She smiled brightly. "Don't let it go to your head. I just find you entertainingly ridiculous—wise one moment and idiotic the next."

"Ah." Thom grinned, settling back to rest against his palms. "Yes, well, I won't miss you."

"No?"

"Hm-mm. You're far too annoying, always making smart comments and encouraging me. I rather liked the cynicism and angst I harbored before meeting you."

"You could always return to it," she suggested.

"Without you around to torment me, I think I might actually manage it."

She returned his teasing smile. "Try not to forget everything I've taught you," she said pleasantly. "You've become a reasonable man, and I'd hate to see my hard work undone."

Thom chuckled, looking out over the crashing waves of the Allundan coastline. "I'll do my best," he promised.

CHAPTER FIFTY-THREE

While most of their team waited far below, Ethenn and Deckard kept watch on the cliffside. Neither thought a fire or a tent was wise; instead, they took turns resting under the stars in the high grasses while the other kept watch. The night was cold, restless, and never-ending.

The bruising on Ethenn's ribs caused him to grimace with almost every breath. The pain was a constant reminder of Ilain. He didn't begrudge her inability to heal all his wounds. If anything, he was more annoyed that she'd healed him at all.

She was being oddly gracious about his choice to break their betrothal. He'd taken away her lifelong dream. She deserved to be angry.

"I care for those who care for me."

Yes, she deserved to be angry.

But then, so did he.

Ilain had used him and his affection from the start. And when he'd tried to do the right thing, she'd tried to manipulate him once again.

So many of her words had filled Ethenn with false hope. She wanted him. They were meant for one another. She loved him.

They were lies. Manipulations to get what she wanted.

In the new morning, Ethenn sat on the edge of the cliff, his feet dangling over the side. Thousands of feet below, the rocky shore of the beach was covered by the high tide. Deckard sat several paces back, reading one of his books on Space magic. While the Mage sat in the shade of a tree, Ethenn let the sun beat down on him. He wasn't concerned about being spotted. Since he'd tapped into his Warrior magic the night before, thereby sharpening his senses, he'd see anyone coming before they got close.

After several hours of silence, Deckard came to join him on his watch, though he remained farther back from the edge. "Anything?" he asked.

Ethenn shook his head, gaze catching on the outcropping where Ilain and Thom sat up the slope of the shoreline. He'd seen Brea climb the rock face near them an hour ago. She slipped in and out of his sight every so often, but the last he'd seen, she was headed their way.

"May I ask a question?" Deckard said.

Ethenn glanced over his shoulder at the colonel. "About Ilain?" he assumed.

Deckard nodded.

Turning back to the ocean, Ethenn sighed. "Sure."

"Who broke off the betrothal?"

"Me."

"Why?"

Ethenn tightened his jaw. He didn't mind Deckard asking. If he were to speak with anyone, he thought the colonel would have the best answers for him. Ethenn looked up to Deckard. The man was everything honorable, just, and good, while he was everything broken, faulty, and weak.

"You'll burn in hell, you wretch."

Ethenn imagined his uncle was right about that. He'd gambled and fought. He'd leched—though not egregiously. He'd drunk to excess. He'd murdered. Allore wouldn't want a soul as black as his.

"A few reasons," Ethenn answered at last. "They all come down to the same thing, though. I'm not the right man for the job."

Deckard was silent, taking that in. Then he countered, "Did you ask her opinion on that matter?"

Ethenn couldn't help his bitter scoff. "I did not."

"Don't you think she deserves the chance to decide for herself?"

"I think she deserves a man whom she *loves*." Ethenn grimaced. "Or, more appropriately, a man who helps her realize there's more to life than getting her way. She's a politician. I'm a hunter. I can't be the man who stands by her side at the head of a kingdom or whatever Allund will be. But there has to be someone out there who can do that *and* make her better. I just realized that man isn't me."

Deckard hummed in thought.

"You warned us of this," Ethenn said. "You told me that a one-sided affection placed additional strain on a marriage. You said I lacked the intensity and shrewdness that she required." He breathed out a self-derisive chuckle. "You were right."

He heard Deckard shift behind him. "May I offer you new advice?" he asked.

Ethenn shrugged but welcomed whatever the colonel could offer him.

"Why do you love her?"

Hesitating, Ethenn looked over his shoulder. "That's a question, not advice."

Deckard grinned. "The question informs the advice."

Accepting it, Ethenn took a deep breath. His heart bled, thinking of her fondly, but he answered it anyway. "She's a liar," he said. "Everything she presents about herself isn't real. She's gentle, reserved, and tender. She's fragile. And I think . . . I love the *real* Ilain Calder. Not the brash, flippant Mage she presents to the world—though, I love that version, too, for other reasons."

Ethenn shook his head, staring up at the golden sun. "She deserves someone who makes her feel safe," he said. "Someone who can help her become that soft, compassionate version of herself. I thought maybe I could do it, but. . . ."

After realizing that Ethenn didn't intend to finish that statement, Deckard spoke. "What makes you think you can't?"

Ethenn smiled sadly. "Because I'm not safe."

He turned, swinging his legs back up so he could face Deckard. "I killed a man when I was sixteen," he confessed. "It was in the fighting pits, so nothing was done about it. It's an unspoken rule that stepping into the ring is forfeiting your life, as the clubs are illegal in the first place. You can't get the law involved without ratting on yourself. During that fight, the man kept taking cheap shots, and I'd already been angry because my uncle—" He cut himself off, not caring to admit his uncle's abuse to Deckard.

Clearing his throat, he began again. "I went into the fight angry, and I just kept getting angrier. Oftentimes, fighting makes it worse. The more I hit, the more I want to hit. Now that I know what I am, I guess it's the magic egging me on, but—" He licked his lips, but they still felt parched. "I punched the man so hard, he collapsed. I heard someone say something about a brain hemorrhage, though I don't know what that means. He was dead by the time he hit the floor. It's how I got the nickname 'Slayer.'"

Deckard listened with a strange expression. It was something between shock, disappointment, and pity.

Ethenn hated it.

Tightening his jaw, he got to the point. "I'm dangerous," he concluded. "After that incident, I was able to keep it together for a while. Occasionally, I'd slip up and cause serious injury, but I never killed anyone else. Then I nearly killed my brother-in-law. I nearly killed Thom too. All because I got so angry that I lost control."

He met Deckard's wary gaze. "So you see, don't you?" he asked. "You see why I can't be the right man for her. I'm not *safe*. How could I ever make her feel cared for enough to let go and be herself? How could I presume to be worthy to lead this nation beside her?"

A long silence passed as Deckard considered Ethenn's words. The wind rustled the tree a few feet away while the ocean rumbled far below. The colonel broke the pause. "Does she make you better?"

Ethenn blinked. "You mean, does she take the anger away?"

Deckard nodded.

He grimaced. "Sometimes."

"Perhaps that's enough," Deckard said thoughtfully. He met Ethenn's gaze with a dry grin. "I presume you know that my wife is friends with Ilain."

Ethenn scoffed wryly. "I've become aware of the fact."

"They talk."

"Mm."

Deckard's smile softened. "And my wife talks to me."

Ethenn narrowed his gaze, waiting.

"I would advise you to reconsider the end of your betrothal."

Drawing back, Ethenn sucked in a tense breath, but Deckard held up a hand, forestalling his reply. "She makes you better," he said, raising his brow. "And you make *her* better. Whether or not you see that, it's true. You've been together for a month. It took twice that for Evylin and me to grow comfortable in our marriage. It took three times that for us to figure out our relationship."

"This isn't about comfort," Ethenn said. "It's about what's best for her."

"Is it?" Deckard pierced him with a keen gaze. "Or are you protecting yourself?"

Ethenn frowned.

"I'm married to Evylin, remember?" The colonel grinned knowingly. "Warriors don't seem to trust easily."

"It isn't about trust either."

"It's about fearing that you aren't enough for her," Deckard surmised. "That, despite everything you feel, she'll never return your devotion. You'll only ever be a tool for her to use. A weapon. You fear that she'll make you a killer of her own design and for her own selfish purposes, is that it?"

Ethenn faltered for words. How had the colonel seen so clearly what Ethenn had yet to realize for himself? Yes, he feared that all Ilain wanted from him was his magic.

In her hands, under her influence, she could make him into the most frightful killer the world had ever seen. And all he wanted was to sink into obscurity, hiding away from the power that made him a vile heathen.

"These burns are nothing to the fiery fate that awaits you."

Vernon Loxley was a devout Allorian, proud of his piety. He and his family lived beyond reproach. They were the picture of perfect morality. That's what they claimed.

Ethenn was their one cause for shame.

"Your father would roll in his grave if he knew what you'd become."

On the clifftop, Ethenn's hands shook, and the heat crept up his spine. He hated his uncle. The man was cruel. He punished through false claims of superiority. He abused those he deemed lesser.

Ethenn never blamed the other religious men and women in the town. He saw how they lived their lives. Most were genuine, like Deckard. It was only the self-righteous who became hypocrites like his uncle.

But Vernon's affected piety didn't change the truth: Ethenn was a sinner, a killer, and a disappointment. His parents would be devastated if they saw what he'd become.

Ilain was meant to be his redemption. If he could love her well, perhaps he could absolve his sins. Now, he knew how wrong he was.

The sound of approaching footsteps broke him out of his reverie.

"I am a weapon," Ethenn concluded, turning back to Deckard. "No matter what, that's all I'll ever be good for." Though Deckard's expression said he disagreed, Ethenn rose quickly. "Brea's here," he announced.

Appearing over the rise a short distance away, Brea wore her dark braids loose, their length falling across her back. She'd left most of her weapons behind, it seemed; only her sword hung at her hip. Though she presumably wore many hidden daggers.

The men met her under the tree. "Is something wrong?" Deckard asked, leaning toward her with worry.

"Why would something be wrong?" Brea asked.

"You're supposed to be with Thom and Ilain."

She grinned. "I don't like sitting in one place for long periods of time," she said. "I thought I'd check in with you two. Have you seen anything?"

The men shook their heads. "Nothing," Ethenn said. "It's been absolutely quiet."

Brea pursed her lips and hummed, disappointed. "I suppose it's to be expected. There's a chance Blount won't show up today at all."

"What do we do in that event?" Ethenn asked.

"We'll decide that if the time comes," Deckard said.

"And what if he never arrives at all?" Brea rested casually against the tree. "How long will we wait for him to make an appearance that might not come?"

They frowned down at her. "He was headed for the Terrae Relic," Deckard said.

"To our best knowledge," she agreed. "But what if we were wrong? It would behoove us to consider every eventuality."

With a sigh, Deckard nodded. "I suppose you're right. Very well." He scanned the beaches. "If we've seen no sign of Blount by tomorrow evening, I suppose there's no point in staying. We can't wait here endlessly."

"You're willing to lose two days to Blount's whims?" Brea asked.

"What else can we do?"

Ethenn realized the suggestion behind Brea's words. "We could regroup with the Alliance," he said. "They have spies in Blount's circles. They could have heard something but were unable to get us a message in time. And even if they haven't, there's a chance they might know something to help us defeat Blount rather than continue wasting time here."

Deckard considered their proposal. "We did the calculations," he said. "Blount should arrive today. But you have a point; we may be wasting time. If he doesn't arrive by morning . . . I think we should reconvene and reconsider."

Brea straightened, a gratified look on her face. "Excellent," she said and turned to Ethenn. "Would you like to spar for a bit? I'm about to lose my mind."

Ethenn and Deckard shared a grin.

The hunter stepped forward, nodding at her. "That sounds like exactly the distraction I need."

CHAPTER FIFTY-FOUR

25TH OF RADIA, 1574

Waiting in the Terrae Keep's antechamber proved equal parts eerie and dull. Evylin hated being confined to the small, narrow hallway. The companionship wasn't bad, though.

Rafferty kept their spirits lively, while Vayden's and Isla's levelheaded conversation was a calming addition. Evylin enjoyed listening to the stories of their youth. Vayden had gotten into many dangerous and exciting predicaments during the time he paraded as Blount. And Isla was an undercover spy in her own right, working for the nobility as an aterian.

"We aterians are essentially glorified bodyguards," Isla said. "Once we've obtained the rank, we are available for hire from each Order. The wealthy are the only ones who can afford us, of course. As we are tied to our Order, *they* get most of our hire price. However, we are paid an annual sum."

While Evylin found the hierarchy of Mages and the Calders' stories interesting, she couldn't escape the tension of the horrible sensation that she was trapped. She could sense Deckard on the cliffside directly above her. Though the distance made it harder to decipher emotions, she could feel that he was mostly at rest. And she was sure he could feel that she was agitated.

When he appeared suddenly in the antechamber that morning, the four of them bolted up, expecting Blount's arrival. Deckard held his hands up soothingly. Evylin caught a swell of relief and worry from him as his eyes fell on her, then noted his wry smile.

"Blount hasn't arrived," he said.

Isla's brow furrowed. "He's now a day late."

Deckard nodded somberly. "It's worrisome," he admitted. "I've spoken with Brea, and we believe the best plan is to cut our losses here and leave."

Everyone exchanged skeptical looks.

"What losses?" Rafferty said. "We've got the Relic. Now, we're four and four with dear ol' prince-Mage. Though I can't say I'm thrilled about sitting for hours in this green hall for untold hours, what other options do we have? We can't traipse about the country until we run across Blount's path."

"No," Deckard agreed. "But we can meet with the Alliance."

Vayden and Isla raised their heads, expressions full of anticipation.

"Minister Molloy does live in Virwoud," Vayden commented. "We could go visit him, receive an update on Blount's movements, and make a new plan from there."

"It beats sitting around for an unknown number of days," Evylin said. "We can't let ourselves atrophy. While we waste away on meager rations and little activity, Blount remains at his prime."

"Our thoughts exactly," Deckard said. "Brea didn't mention the name of that minister, but whoever we visit, we should also meet with the Alliance to determine our next step. Whatever happens in the future, Blount didn't do as we expected. We obtained both Relics, but . . ."

Evylin recognized the prickle of Deckard's anxiety. "You're worried he's done something," she said.

Deckard met her gaze. "He isn't here," he said. "There could have been a delay in his travels. Or it could be something far worse."

With the ominous thought, their path was agreed upon: They would leave the Keep immediately and find the Alliance.

Blount's actions continued to be suspect. He'd been one step ahead of them from the start. Wherever he was, whatever he was doing, it didn't bode well for them now.

After gathering, they retrieved their horses from Olbury and left the town. Evylin was rather disappointed that she hadn't had the opportunity to explore the settlement more. It was exactly the sort of place Ryen had longed to visit, so full of life and people and brimming with a sense of adventure. But she promised herself that, one day, she and Deckard would return. Perhaps they'd charter a ship and take a journey across the sea, just as Ryen had always longed to.

Though the journey to Whickam Village was better taken as a two-day ride, they pressed hard into the night for the sake of speed. They arrived in the village well past respectful hours, the ivory and shadow moons still faint in the sky. A sheepdog barked at their unexpected arrival as they rode through the pastureland. While Thom, Ethenn, and Rafferty settled the horses, the rest of them hurried to the Glaas residence.

Reluctantly, Deckard rang the bell. Calyn appeared only moments later, peeping out tentatively, then throwing the door wide open when she recognized them. "You're back!" she exclaimed with excitement. "We weren't expecting you for another day or two. Where's Thom?"

Brea snorted while Evylin pressed her lips together. "Caring for the horses," she told her sister. "Might we come in?"

Calyn backed away, holding the door open for them.

"We're sorry for the late hour," Deckard said. "But our mission for the king requires haste."

"Not to worry," Calyn said, straightening the lace collar of her floral dress. "Mother has gone up to bed, but I believe Father is in his office. I can pull together a bite to eat if you're hungry?"

Evylin's nearly empty stomach grumbled at the thought. "That would be divine, Caly."

They gathered in the kitchen, where Evylin and Calyn scrounged together a simple meal of cured meats, a variety of cheeses, and some bread. It wouldn't be quite as filling as a meal, but it would do in the present circumstances.

While they clustered around the kitchen bench, eating and resting after their hard ride, Deckard offered his plan for the next day. They'd leave early for Virwoud, as Vayden and Isla suggested. Riding as fast as they could without causing harm to their mounts, it would take them roughly four days to reach the port city. Once there, they would seek out Minister Molloy—whom they referred to as Mr. Molloy in Calyn's presence—and hope that he could provide an update from the Alliance—whom they referred to as the king.

The bell rang again, and Calyn disappeared momentarily to open the door for Thom, Ethenn, and Rafferty. The men rushed for the remains of the food, stuffing their faces with nearly as much enthusiasm as Evylin.

"Oh, Corporal Loxley," Calyn broke in abruptly.

They all turned to her. Ethenn's thick eyebrows pulled together in confusion, a hunk of bread in one hand and a mouth full of cheese.

"I made a discovery," Calyn announced. "I knew I recognized your name. Though Evie went to town more often, Doli and I would regularly visit Cousin Nelle when we could. Especially when we were younger. But I was sure I knew the name Loxley, so I went digging through my old things, and wouldn't you know—I found it!"

Swallowing, Ethenn stared at her with evident confusion. "Found what?"

"Loxley!" she said proudly. "I'm friends with your sister, Terrina."

Ethenn flushed, a strange tension to the clench in his jaw.

"Isn't that wonderful?" Calyn continued, unaware of Ethenn's discomfort. "I'd forgotten her maiden name because, well, I called her Rina, and she called me Caly. But when she got married last year, I was invited to the wedding. Her husband is so handsome. I about died when I saw him. But it's so delightful, isn't it?"

Evylin watched with amusement as Ethenn took in her sister's overly enthusiastic explanation. His neck grew redder with the blush, and his jaw tensed. "Her marriage?" he asked.

"Well, yes, that too," Calyn said. "But I mean her pregnancy. You're going to be an uncle."

Everyone turned to Ethenn with congratulations, but Evylin caught the hardness in his glare as well as the shock in Ilain's.

Ethenn took a deep, steadying breath before muttering, "So it seems."

"What's more," Calyn continued, ignorant of the tension growing in the room, "I was reading through Rina's letters, and I discovered that your mother, Leannah, was the daughter of Harol Pinnette."

Evylin's brow rose, recognizing the name. "Pinnette?"

"Yes!" Calyn beamed. "Harol was our grandfather's nephew. Which means Corporal Loxley's mother and our mother are second cousins." She turned to Ethenn with joy. "*We're* cousins . . . Or third cousins. I think."

Evylin and Ethenn turned to stare at one another, mouths agape. They were related. Not closely, but still. They were family, and they'd never known it.

Evylin smiled. "I always knew I liked you," she teased.

Ethenn blinked, his expression unreadable. "We're family?"

"Seems that way."

Brea began to chuckle. "If Ethenn is Evylin's cousin," she said, turning to Thom, "that makes him *your* cousin too."

"By marriage," Thom said, a curious lift to his brow. His grin shifted slyly. "Why, Lainy," he exclaimed then. "That makes you my cousin too!"

Though Ethenn looked ready to protest, Ilain reached across the kitchen bench and slapped the back of Thom's head.

"Ow," Thom protested, rubbing the spot.

"So then," Isla said, "we're one big happy family. Look what love can do for a band like ours."

"Excepting the lovely lieutenant and myself, of course," Rafferty piped up.

"Nonsense," Brea said. "You're the brother they never wanted."

Lighthearted laughter swept through the room, lifting their road-weary hearts. It'd been too long since they'd laughed together like this. Too much darkness had crept into their lives. The loss of Hewitt and Auden. The weight of saving their nations. The responsibility of recovering the Relics. The fear of fighting Blount.

This laughter, this joy, this reminder of family was what they needed to keep them going.

Evylin took in the room's occupants with fresh joy. They were *family*. In their own strange way, admittedly, but in the end, they were all bound together. Granted, Ethenn and Ilain's betrothal seemed broken, but that didn't make their bonds as a group any less real.

For the first time in a long time, Evylin felt a rich sensation of peace. With these people by her side, she knew she could face any future.

"I see you're all back," Lawton said, appearing in the doorway. His serious gaze swept across the room, and they collectively sobered.

Deckard dipped his head in a slight bow. "Just for one night, sir. We apologize for the inconvenient hour."

"You're very welcome here," he said. "Though I would ask that you contain your gaiety. This is an old house, and the noise carries."

Evylin and Calyn shared a knowing look at the recurrent lecture.

Lawton raised a hand, an unopened letter in his grasp. "This came while you were gone."

Deckard took the letter with thanks. Lawton departed then, disappearing down the hall.

"You know, Eve," Rafferty said. "You're really nothing like your father."

"They're more alike than you'd think," Deckard said absentmindedly as he opened the missive.

Evylin pursed her lips in disapproval but was too distracted by the unsteady emotions drifting off Deckard to correct him. "What is it?" she asked.

A jolt of panic cut through the air just before Deckard met her gaze.

Evylin's heart dropped, knowing something dreadful had happened. "Jonn?"

"It's from Carlile," Deckard said weakly. He scanned the letter again, then announced, "Blount tricked us."

The troop jolted up from their relaxed postures, alert and tense. At the side of the room, Calyn watched uncertainly, entirely forgotten by the others.

Deckard held Evylin's gaze as he explained. "He never went to Carrickbrack. It was a diversion. The reports the Alliance received were false. Blount completely played us. He let us go after the Relics while he returned to Mouroc."

Evylin frowned, uncertain what gambit the prince had played.

Deckard's lips twisted ruefully. "He killed his father. He took the Waulden throne, assumed control of their army, and . . ." He paused and glanced at the letter as though wishing its words had changed. Then he said, "Rouland Blount II, King of Wauld, has marched on Ephria with the entire force of the Waulden Army and every aterian in the country. They aren't entirely certain of his expected arrival, but even with a force that large, I'd only expect it to take two weeks at most."

Evylin's lips parted in shock. Blount hadn't bothered retrieving the Relics because he knew they'd do it for him. Instead, he took the power he had, murdered his father, and subverted them in the most unexpected way.

"Ephria can't stand against a force like that," Evylin said.

Deckard sighed sadly. "That's not the worst part," he said. "After Isla's betrayal, he suspected there were spies among his people. Somehow, he found out about the Alliance, and he hunted them down in Wauld. Carlile says he doesn't know who lived and who died, but this letter . . . It was sent a week ago. Everything could have changed by now."

While the troop remained silent, taking in the news, Deckard continued, "The Alliance abandoned Mouroc. Carlile was waiting for confirmation to discover which of the ministers and members survived."

"My grandfather . . ." Brea whispered, and Thom set a hand on her shoulder comfortingly.

Deckard gave her an apologetic look. "Last they knew, Blount was marching toward Ephria City to overthrow King Ephren."

Calyn gasped, stepping up to Evylin's side, reminding her of her sister's presence. Calyn's hand slipped into hers, and Evylin squeezed to reassure her sister.

"Blount has issued a charge to the Alliance," Deckard concluded. "He has hostages. He demands that we give him the Relics, or he'll kill every last one of them."

"He'll kill them anyway," Isla said.

Deckard dipped his chin, a subtle admission that he suspected as much.

The chaos of expectant silence pressed into the room. Troop member after troop member exchanged looks, each of them on the verge of speech. Yet, they all held their tongues, turning to Deckard for answers.

"What do we do?" Evylin asked.

After a long, strained pause, Deckard drew back his shoulders and said, "We're going to Loclight. And we're stopping Blount for good."

CHAPTER FIFTY-FIVE

35TH OF RADIA, 1574

They rode hard for nine days straight, ignoring all settlements and comforts in preference for speed, stopping only for short bouts of rest and food. The week's delay it took for Carlile's letter to reach them, plus their week and a day's journey, meant anything could have happened since their last receipt of information. Blount and his army could be anywhere on their journey to Ephria's capital. They could arrive to find Loclight razed to the ground for all Deckard knew.

At the start, Vayden suggested continuing with their original plan. "We could still visit Minister Molloy," he said, his Waulden accent thickening in his worry. "He might have an update for us."

"And what if he doesn't?" Deckard said. "We would waste days journeying there. The Alliance needs us in Loclight. Whether we save King Ephren's life or not, we know Blount's destination. We can end this by stopping him now."

Deckard knew the pace at which an army could move. They weren't fast, but if his calculations were correct, he imagined Blount could cross the border and arrive in Ephria City by the end of two weeks. It was more than enough time to beat their small band there.

The troop rode harder than they ever had before. Their horses showed the strain each night, and Deckard worried they'd kill them if they kept up with their blistering pace. But they had little choice. If they arrived too late, the hundred thousand souls living in the city could be lost to Blount's mania. And though he felt little allegiance to King Ephren anymore, he couldn't let himself give up his past monarch's life either.

With the little spare time they had in the evenings, the Warriors trained with intensity. As if the pressure was refining them, Evylin and Ethenn showed marked improvement, tapping into their magic more quickly and fighting with more control than ever. Ilain and Isla spent extra hours working with Deckard as well, ensuring his connection to Space was as strong as possible.

Huddled over the light of the fire, Deckard and Evylin studied *Attachments of the Soul* from cover to cover. It was laborious but insightful, and he discovered that they'd only scratched the surface of their Bond's capabilities. While they discovered it would take decades to master their new connection, certain benefits, such as sharing fragments of one another's powers, could be tapped into presently.

Beyond that, the book helped him overcome his struggle with the Space Relic. Deckard realized Ilain was right; he simply needed to let go of his urge for control, trusting the magic and the Bond to help him channel it correctly. While he continued to struggle with allowing the magic to consume him, the compulsion wasn't nearly as strong.

None of their preparation eased their fears as they inched closer to Loclight each day.

On the morning of the thirty-fifth of Radia, they crested the hill that rose before the valley of Ephria City. The spring sun hung in the west, glittering across the Ónette Sea upon their evening arrival. The troop pulled their horses to a stop, devastation running through their ranks.

They'd arrived too late.

Purple banners with a golden crown imposed over a double moon had replaced the old crook and sword of Ephren's reign. Hundreds of tents littered the farmland before the outskirts of the city. Siege weapons and soldiers covered the terrae. Warships cluttered the ocean. Smoke and the dust of rubble still clouded the city air. They couldn't even see the palace through the dark haze.

Evylin's hand found Deckard's. Blount had taken their home.

In awe, they all stared, incapable of action.

"How did he lay siege to an entire city in . . ." Rafferty cast a dazed glance at the group. "Well, how long do you think it took him?"

"Blount has Mages in his army and Relics in his possession," Ilain said coldly. "Ephren has nothing. There was no defense against magic."

Deckard could hardly comprehend the scene before him. His home, his city—

they'd been brought low by the power of a tyrannical Mage. Lives had been lost, friends and comrades destroyed by one man's lust for power. And Blount's tyranny was only beginning. It would continue to spread across the land . . . unless someone stopped him.

"We're here now," Deckard said, breaking the silence. "The city has us."

With one final scan of the distressing scene, Deckard turned his horse. They couldn't just sweep through an entire war camp, hoping their power was enough. They'd fought innumerable Shades in the Keeps, but this was different. There were nine of them against thousands, non-magical and Mage, all at once. They'd have to sneak into the city, find Blount, and kill him to regain control.

The others followed Deckard back into the trees. "How do we stop him?" Thom asked.

"He'll be in the palace," Deckard said, "setting up his reign."

"All right," Thom dismounted beside him, "but you can't just walk in."

Deckard stepped up to the tree line, observing the city. The stone walls showed minimal damage despite the weapons of war. He wondered if Blount's Mages had negated the need for such tactics, the weapons' presence perhaps a mere show of force. Though the road to the city gate was open, no one was entering or exiting.

"It seems Blount has shut down travel," he noted.

"I bet he'd let us in," Rafferty snarked.

"I imagine he would," Vayden said. "But I don't think surrendering is our best option."

Brea pointed to the gate. "Is that the only entrance?"

"No," Deckard said. "There are two more gates to the east and west leading to the farms and ranches."

"Amid those houses?"

"Yes." Deckard gestured to the two districts in turn. "Those are the lands allocated to the farmers and ranchers. They're far less populated than the inner city."

Brea nodded. "There's nowhere to hide at either gate, is there?"

"No."

"Sneaking in isn't going to be easy," she said. "But it could be done . . . by the right people."

Deckard turned to her, expectant.

Brea held his gaze, stoicism on her face. "Rafferty, Ethenn, and I could slip through," she said. "I wouldn't trust anyone else to have the stealth for the mission."

"What good would that do us?" Rafferty asked. "I *am* incredibly fearsome, but I'm not sure the three of us alone are going to do much good against an army of Mages and Blount's four Relics."

"We could find another passage," Brea said. "Or we could seek out the Alliance."

"I have a question," Ethenn interrupted suddenly.

They turned to him.

"What's our aim here?" he asked. "Say we get inside and kill Blount. What's next? The entire Waulden Army waits outside the gates, plus however many Mages he has at his side. Do you expect them to listen to us, to serve us?"

Ilain gave him a snide grin. "Dear, do try to remember," her eyes sparkled proudly, "I am a goddess in their eyes. With the Relics in hand—and your generous assistance—I could wipe out each and every person who stands in our way."

Ethenn met her gaze dubiously. "Really?"

"No matter what you think," she said sharply, "I'm not a liar."

Ignoring the pointed comment, he turned back to Deckard. "What is our plan after we defeat Blount? Unleashing Ilain's wrath?"

"Hell hath no fury," Rafferty mocked, "like Ilain Calder."

Though Brea and Thom smirked, Deckard drew a hand along his jaw. Ethenn's point was valid. Even if they took the palace and defeated Blount, they'd be left with an entire army to face and would already be exhausted from the battle against the now-King of Wauld.

Seeing his hesitation, Ilain stepped forward. "Trust me," she said passionately. "Between my power and your Bond with Evylin, we *can* do this. We will have all eight Relics. No one can stand in our way."

Deckard met Evylin's gaze then, questioning her with a look. Could they do this? Were they strong enough?

"We have little choice," Evylin replied to his unspoken plea. "Either we fight Blount here—*now*—or we let him take the kingdom and wait for a better opportunity that may never come. He has four Relics. He can hole up in the city for as long as he likes, and we can do nothing to stop that."

"He knows we're coming for him," Isla agreed. "After years of working with Blount, I can tell you, he's not going to give us an easy path. We either take him today, or we hand him the reign of both countries for untold years."

"We don't know all our options," Deckard argued. "What if we rush into this battle and lose when we could have waited a day or two and come out the victors?"

"Blount is weakest now," Brea said. "He can't have finalized his takeover yet. While his men work to subdue the city, his force is divided. Once he establishes himself—likely within days due to the Mages working alongside him—it will be nearly impossible to unseat him."

"Acting now gives us the best odds," Thom said with a slow nod. "The city is in turmoil, forced to submit to a false leader. They'll not only be gratified to see Blount defeated, but once they learn it was the Alliance who did it, they'll welcome the new rule of Allund."

Deckard lifted his chin. It was true. If the people learned the Alliance was their savior, they'd flock to them. It was the best opportunity to win the people's goodwill at the outset of the new nation's establishment.

And he hesitated to afford them such a chance.

"I don't trust the Alliance," Deckard admitted, finally putting words to the fears he'd harbored silently for so long.

Ilain, Isla, Vayden, and Brea looked at him uneasily. Their frustration, confusion, and hurt were plain. With that declaration, it was as though he'd rejected each of them individually. By stating his distrust of the organization, he was veritably announcing his distrust of them.

Deckard shook his head. "You're so sure they're good and noble? All of you?"

"Do you think we'd be part of something that wasn't?" Ilain asked.

"I think," he said with gentleness, "perhaps they've duped you. Just as they did us."

Brea pulled herself to her full height—though nearly an entire foot shorter than Deckard—beside him. Her dark eyes met his steadily. "Your cynicism is puzzling," she said. "You live your life determined to be good and noble. You act as the ideal Allorian gentleman. Yet, you question the validity of an organization that believes the same values as you. Why? When you've lived with the Calders for three months—when you've traveled with Vayden, Isla, and me for three weeks—how can you question our sincerity? How can you not trust us?"

Deckard took a deep breath and shrugged. "Everyone has something they want," he said. "You each have specific goals, and the Alliance will help you achieve them."

"You think we're selfish? We have risked our lives for you." Her gaze darkened, and she dropped her voice so that only he and Evylin beside him could hear. "I risked *my* life for your brother's. How can you doubt *me* when you've seen through what few secrets I hold?"

Deckard blinked, hearing the unsaid. He'd recognized her affection for Thom from the start. It wasn't hard, but Brea was cunning enough to cover her fondness as friendship. But she'd never fooled Deckard.

Wetting his lips, Deckard forced himself to acknowledge the truth. The fact was, he did trust Brea. He trusted Ilain, Vayden, and Isla too. Their intentions were honorable. And if they genuinely believed in the Alliance's aims. . . .

"They use duplicitous means to accomplish their purposes," Deckard said, still contending for his point.

Brea smirked. "Not so differently from you. I believe Thom told you that I listen to conversations as a matter of course," she said. "I listened to your discussion with your father-in-law as well."

Deckard's brow rose in shock.

"And you lied through your bloody teeth the entire time."

Feeling wholly exposed by her accusation, Deckard drew back. Thom snorted, and Evylin set a hand over her mouth, a wave of humor washing out of her despite the tension in the group.

Deckard gave them both a perturbed look. But he couldn't deny that Brea was right. He had lied to Lawton Glaas the entire conversation. He'd assured him that Evylin wasn't a soldier; the king had simply granted her an honorary title. He'd created false personae for Brea and the Calders. He even told the magistrate that Hewitt's death was at the hands of a bear in his letters. At every turn, Deckard lied to make the truth palatable. And he'd done that his entire life.

The Alliance's duplicity seemed tame by comparison.

Scratching the back of his neck, Deckard didn't care to admit his crimes in front of his men. "I will concede that the Alliance may not deserve my full criticism," he said. "However, it does not solve the problem we face. Whether or not they're worth serving is a matter for another day. For now, we must find a way into the palace."

"Would you like us to dig a hole, Highlord?" Rafferty asked snidely.

Deckard sent him a sharp look, but Evylin set a hand on his arm. "I have a suggestion," she said. They turned to her, waiting. "In our party, we have a spy, a hunter, and a thief—"

"I'm an entrepreneur," Rafferty corrected.

"It's their job to be sneaky," she concluded.

"Technically," Thom said and pointed to Ethenn, "it's his job to sit in a tree waiting for a deer to pop its antlers into view."

"Which requires copious amounts of stealth," Evylin noted. She swept her arm in the direction of Vayden, Ethenn, and Rafferty. "Let *them* figure out our way in."

The three men exchanged looks, though they didn't appear opposed to the idea.

Deckard grinned at Evylin. "Seems you're onto something there," he said and turned to the men. "All right. If you were going to plan this mission, how would you do it?"

A long silence passed as the trio considered the task.

Ethenn spoke first. "We can assume Blount will be in the throne room," he said thoughtfully. "Where else would you set up your new reign?"

"I do my best plotting in the loo," Rafferty said. "And I bet the royal facilities are quite posh."

Vayden chuckled but shook his head. "Blount is a narcissist. I should know; I had to impersonate him."

"And you did such a splendid job, love," Isla teased.

"Thank you, darling." Vayden brushed a hand under his chin, eyes shifting toward the palace. "Ethenn is right. If Blount is in the palace, he'll want to be on the throne, making judgments. Which gives us a goal."

"We've been to the throne room before," Ethenn said. "I think I could lead us there."

Vayden turned to Ilain. "You lived in the palace for weeks. And you said that Carlile taught you about its secret passages and entrances, yes?"

"Four entrances, ten passages," she confirmed.

"Excellent. Then it merely comes down to finding our way onto the palace grounds, which we already know how to do thanks to our trip to the Space Keep."

"Which we can only do once we've passed through those pretty stone walls over there," Brea quipped.

Rafferty scanned the massive city walls. "Unfortunately, they're too high to scale," he said thoughtfully.

"Even if we could, Blount will have them guarded," Ethenn said.

"What about drainage gates?" Rafferty asked. "That worked when we saved our dashing Prince Ephren."

Vayden shook his head. "Blount was trained in warfare. There are many tales of sieges being won by slipping in through the sewers and drainage systems. He'll have them watched at the very least."

"Pity."

Deckard watched the men think with interest. Evylin leaned against the tree behind them, her arm brushing his, the touch a comfort, however light.

"We could wait for night," Rafferty said. "It'd be easier to move undetected then."

"It's a capital city with technology's latest advances," Vayden said. "They have lamps lighting the streets."

"Ah, yeah," Rafferty said. "I always forget about those. We didn't have them in Estshire." He tapped his nose in thought. "I suppose we don't want to cause a distraction."

Vayden shook his head. "That'll just draw attention to our presence."

"Blounty-boy does know we'll be coming for him at some point."

"But he doesn't know we're here as of yet," Vayden countered. "We don't want to alert him or his men." He grimaced then. "There is one thing we could try . . ."

"What's that, Vayd?" Rafferty asked.

"I look like Blount." Vayden shrugged. "It was my job to impersonate him before. I could do it again."

"Ooh," Rafferty nodded, "I do like disguises. We'll be your retinue. That could work."

"It couldn't," Ethenn interrupted.

"Why not?" Rafferty asked with annoyance.

Ethenn raised his brow. "Do *you* have nine disguises fit for a king and his royal guard hidden in your saddlebags?"

Rafferty pulled a face. "I suppose the kid's got a point."

Vayden sighed. "I'm out of ideas, then."

"I've got one," Ethenn said casually. "But first," he looked at Deckard, "how far can you jump?"

Deckard's brows pinched together in confusion. "As far as the average man, I'd guess."

Ilain snorted. "I believe he means magically." She flashed her fingers in a motion that mimicked a poof of air.

"Ah." Deckard tipped his head, recalling the details of his studies. His thorough practice over the last several weeks had afforded him a better understanding of the shocking ability. While he still wasn't entirely used to the sudden jolt that took him from one location to the next, he was growing more and more comfortable with the stomach-turning process. "I believe it's as far as I can sustain with my energy."

"It's unlimited?" Ethenn asked.

"Theoretically." This plan was already beginning to worry Deckard. "But I'm still developing my strength."

Ethenn glanced toward the city. "Are you strong enough to teleport into the palace itself?"

Deckard gaped at the young man, baffled by his suggestion.

A long silence stretched as they all considered this wild plan. Then Thom burst out with a nervous laugh.

"That's insane," he said. "Deckard can't jump nine people across *miles* of land."

"That's not what I'm suggesting," Ethenn said. "He only has to jump five of us, including himself."

Evylin huffed out a laugh at Deckard's side. He was no less bemused. "That will still take too much energy," he argued. "I'm not all-powerful, contrary to what you might think."

"You have the Space Relic," Ethenn countered. "You're Bonded. Beyond that, you can share energy with anyone you jump."

"It will weaken us," Ilain warned. "All of us."

"You're a bloody goddess," Ethenn returned. "You'll be fine."

A small, amused grin at his sharp rebuttal came to Ilain's lips, but she remained silent.

Ethenn held Deckard's gaze with fierce determination. "Forget jumping to the palace, in that case," he said. "If you want to defeat Blount, then we have to outsmart him. He knows we're coming. So let's let him think he's won."

Deckard frowned. "How?"

"Give him what he wants."

Tension filled the air as they all listened, skeptical of the plan he was presenting.

"We split up," Ethenn continued. "He *wants* us to come to him because he wants the Relics and Evylin. He will allow her to walk to the front gate and have his men bring her straight to him."

Deckard's chest constricted, but he let the young Warrior finish his plan. "Send Thom, Ilain, and Raff with Evie as a negotiation party. Blount will bring them right into the throne room to boast about his victory." Ethenn raised his brow. "Meanwhile, the rest of us will go with you, Colonel. You'll jump us past the walls and shroud us through the city, and we'll make our way onto the palace grounds through the same secret passage we took to reach the Space Keep. We'll work our way through the palace via one of Ilain's secret entrances and through the passageways."

Evylin met Deckard's gaze.

"The Bond will lead you to her," Ethenn continued. "And together, we will all defeat Blount, take back the Relics, and raise Allund."

"There are too many things that could go wrong," Deckard said. "Blount has his Mages in the city. My control over Night magic isn't that strong. Any Night Mage will recognize my shroud the moment they see it. It's costly to my magic, and I will weaken faster the more I use it."

Ethenn brushed the worry off. "You'll only need to use it if we run into trouble. We'll also have Vayden with us. Worst case, he'll pretend to be Blount long enough to cause them to hesitate while the rest of us take them out."

"Two Mages and two Warriors," Brea jested. "That's a rather appropriate guard for His Royal Highness."

"I've overthrown two countries now, *naladar*," Vayden said, his voice shifting into an imitation of Blount. "You may call me 'Your Majesty.'"

Ignoring their banter, Ethenn faced Deckard. "While Blount and his men are focused on the negotiation party, we'll sneak into the palace, sight unseen."

"We flank him," Thom surmised. "In a roundabout sort of way."

Deckard didn't like it. They'd be risking their lives. He'd be separated from Evylin, handing her over to the very man who was obsessed with Bonding with her. Yet, what choice did they have? The alternative was to go in together, putting everything on the line and hoping Blount didn't end them in one strike. Or they could divide, distract, and pray they lived to see another day.

Either way, Deckard thought, *there will be casualties.*

One option just provided the opportunity to lessen their losses.

"Might I mention," Thom said warily, "that the negotiation party will be putting themselves at Blount's mercy? Why wouldn't he just kill Ilain, Raff, and me and keep Evie for himself?"

"He won't want me dead right away," Ilain said. "He'll make my execution public. Pyra's Heiress at the mercy of his power paints a potent picture."

"That doesn't improve our odds, dear lady," Rafferty quipped.

Ilain smirked. "If it comes to it, I'll save you."

"Blount won't want to kill you right away," Vayden confirmed. "He'll want to prove his power by lording it over you. He's been slowly succumbing to the Deep over the past twenty years, driving him to irrational and cruel actions. Killing you too quickly will take away the joy of his victory. He'll be far more likely to torture you to death over time."

"Mm. We have such stunning choices before us," Thom grumbled.

Sighing, Deckard pinched the bridge of his nose. "Is this really our best option?" he asked. "Divide our party and *hope* that Blount's narcissism is enough to overcome his good sense?"

Evylin rested her hand on his arm, her touch comforting. "We've been preparing for this moment from the start," she said. "You, Ethenn, and Brea are completely unknown to him. If you come in with the Relics, there's no chance he'll defeat us. But if we're all together, if we fight as one, he'll know your powers. And we'll have lost our greatest asset, the element of surprise."

Ilain stepped forward then, the early evening sun beaming through the trees in shafts of light, making her hair look as if it were on fire. "This is our chance," she said. "I can protect them, Jonn. Together, Evylin and I are strong enough to free all four of us if things fall apart. And with the rest of you together, you can be our support."

Deckard's heart was in turmoil. He didn't want this—any of it. If he had his way, he'd take Evylin, return to Olbury, and sail across the sea to Audis on the southern shores of Matteire, where they could walk along the white sandy beaches, and he'd teach her to swim in the crystal blue waters.

The sunlight caught in her gaze, shifting the brown to amber. "We can do this,

Jonn," she promised. "Blount has used us from the start. He's manipulated us, tricked us, trapped us. I'd like to use him and his arrogance against him for once."

Her fingers tightened on his arm, but her gaze softened. Despite her confident demeanor, he felt the anxiety rippling around her. Nonetheless, it blended with determination. "Together," she whispered, "you and I are stronger than he could ever be. We can do this."

Deckard shook his head, not sharing her surety. "I'm not strong enough without you."

A gentle smile brought the dimples to her cheeks. "You're never without me anymore," she said, lifting his hand to kiss his moonstone ring. And he knew it was true. They were Bonded. She had become part of his very soul. Even if they were miles apart,

he could feel her. And he knew if all else failed—if he felt a surge of fear and panic too strong from her through their Bond—he could teleport straight to her. It might drain much of the energy he owned, but he could come to her rescue, even at the expense of the others.

Deckard's conscience twisted his gut. Could he abandon their friends to save his wife? Was that even laudable?

He prayed he wouldn't have to make that choice.

In his lingering indecision, Evylin reached up. She slipped the Space Relic out from beneath her coat, bringing the chain over her head. Then she placed the pendant in his palm. A thrill of magic shot up his arm, but unlike many times before, it stayed contained, like a greeting rather than a compulsion.

"You are strong enough," Evylin promised. She closed his fingers around the Relic. "You always said one man can make the difference." Deckard's heart stuttered as she looked up at him with pride shining in her gaze. "You *are* that one man," she said.

He wanted to deny it, to reject the weight of such responsibility. How could he be that man? How could he—a mere farm boy from Nettershire, a nobody, a failure of a soldier—be anything of significance?

But as he looked into Evylin's eyes, he realized: He was significant to her. And perhaps that was all that mattered.

With a deep breath to gather his courage, Deckard gave a single nod. Then he turned to the troop.

"Today," he said, "we do what thousands before us couldn't. Together, as a team, we will enter the city, stop Blount, and bring peace to Allund. Today, we will end the Centurial War."

CHAPTER FIFTY-SIX

After another hour of planning, the sun had dipped low in the sky, casting a rusty haze over the woods. The Relics were passed out—Night to Brea, Wind to Isla, Terrae to Ethenn, and Space to Deckard. Ilain sat with Vayden, giving him the exact directions through the palace grounds and the halls containing the known secret entrances and passages.

Ethenn and Brea covered themselves in extra weapons, preparing for every eventuality. Even Vayden added extra daggers to his person, carrying Brea's old bow and quiver as well. And while Deckard tightened the buckle on his sword belt, he removed his moonstone ring.

"You're not wearing your ring?" Evylin asked in surprise.

A strange emotion flowed from Deckard, and she sensed it was something between determination and resignation. "We already discussed this plan," he said. "If we want to trick Blount, he can't know I'm a Mage. I'll avoid using my magic for as long as possible, and when the time comes," he tucked the ring into her hand, wrapping her fingers around the stone and metal, "I'll simply summon it back."

Evylin smirked. "You're quite welcome for that discovery."

He gave her a wry smile and turned to the team. "While I'd like to say I have no doubts about this plan's success, I'm afraid I'm not that confident in myself. However," his chin rose as he surveyed each of them, "I am confident in each of you."

A swell of pride filled Deckard's manner. "Together, we've survived seven Keeps.

We've fought Guardians and Shades, Mages and mercenaries. We've evaded Blount six times now. Whatever comes of this day, we will survive this too."

"Don't get sappy on us, Colonel," Rafferty said despite an unusually weak grin on his lips.

Deckard gave him a nod. "Let's end this war, shall we?"

With resounding fervor, the troop agreed before moving to exchange their farewells. Vayden pulled Ilain into a long, protective hug. They whispered to one another, tears coming to their eyes, likely sharing the memory of Auden. Isla was at their side, gently rubbing circles on Ilain's back.

Thom, Rafferty, and Ethenn stood in a circle, giving each other masculine pats on the shoulders until Thom rolled his eyes and swept both men into one massive hug. "I love you idiots," he said.

Ethenn flushed lightly, muttering, "You too," while Rafferty rolled his eyes and shoved out of Thom's grasp.

"I preferred you when you were emotionally stunted," he said.

Evylin shook hands with Vayden and hugged Isla. Brea gave Evylin some final advice, then offered a kind farewell before turning to Thom.

"Be safe, *mi'caro*," she said.

"You too, *demoloba*," Thom replied.

One of her eyebrows lifted. "If we make it out of this alive, you're going to come up with a better nickname for me."

He smirked. "I'll see what I can come up with."

For a moment, Brea looked about to hug him. Then she slapped his cheek instead. "*Te'idita pé ai'amós*," she said rapidly.

Thom's brow furrowed. "I didn't catch all of that."

"You weren't supposed to." Brea winked and walked away.

Evylin eyed Thom, but Ethenn stepped before her nervously, and she turned to the young man.

"I, uh—" He cleared his throat and started again. "I hope this isn't the end," he said. "You've become rather important to me and . . ."

In his bashful silence, Evylin reached forward and pulled him into a hug. He tensed, all his muscles taut under her embrace. "We're family, remember?" she said, and he noticeably relaxed. "That makes you quite important to me too."

Slowly, cautiously, Ethenn returned the hug. "Be careful, please," he whispered.

"Only if you are," she teased.

They parted, sharing small smiles.

Evylin turned to share her last farewell, expecting to find Deckard at her side.

Instead, he stood off at the far end of the clearing with Rafferty. They talked quietly, but there was something strangely serious in their mannerisms. Then Rafferty sniggered, and Deckard rolled his eyes. They shook hands, and Deckard stepped away.

Evylin would have watched his approach, but Ilain came to stand before Ethenn, where he lingered near Evylin's side. The Fire Mage stopped an arm's length away, but Ethenn still took an uncomfortable step back.

Ilain held Ethenn's stare undaunted. "If there's a chance I'm going to die today, I'd like you to know something."

Ethenn clenched his jaw but listened in silence.

"You are enough," she said. "No matter what anyone else tells you, no matter what you've done or who you were before, you *are* enough. For me and everyone else."

Ethenn's brow furrowed, and his expression remained tight. "That's kind of you to say," he muttered.

"I'm not trying to be kind," Ilain said in that haughty manner of hers. Then her lips lifted in her signature wry grin. Her eyes twinkled with a knowing glint. "Do try to make it back to me, love. I'd be awfully disappointed if you didn't."

Despite Ethenn's baffled expression, Ilain turned on her heel, offered Deckard a quick farewell, and headed to her horse.

While the rest of the troop chuckled awkwardly at the exchange, Deckard's hand on Evylin's arm drew her attention to him. She looked up at him as regret and longing crashed into her like the waves against the shore. Instantly, she leaned against his chest as he enfolded her in his arms. His wool coat was rough against her cheek. He smelled of dirt and sweat, but it was oddly comforting. They'd been on the road for so long that the unwashed scent reassured her, knowing he was there.

Deckard pressed his lips to her temple, drawing her closer. She could feel the Space Relic beneath his coat, pressing against her collarbone. "Don't die," he whispered. "Please, don't die."

Dismay leached from his soul into hers. His fingers rubbed circles against her back, creating little spikes of magic to radiate across her skin. And yet, she knew, as desperately as they clung to one another, they were made for this. Bonded and powerful, they could change the world. While Deckard had worked so hard to give her the life she desired, for once, she would grant him the deepest secret of his heart. She would help him become more than simply an imitation of Euon Sergus.

Evylin would help Deckard be the man who made the difference for their people.

With no use for words, Evylin drew back just enough to lift her lips to his. Whatever promises she made, whatever platitudes she spoke, they would fade into nothingness. Only action lived forever.

So she kissed him for far longer and with far greater passion than was appropriate for the moment. Surrounded by trees, their friends, and the destiny ahead of them, Evylin reassured him of her love and her dedication through her caress. It was a promise that, today, they would fight and win. They would survive and change the nation together.

Deckard ended the kiss before she was ready, resting his forehead against hers. He cupped the back of her neck, his fingers tangled in her hair. "I love you," he whispered.

Evylin opened her eyes to meet his green-blue gaze. "I love you."

Deckard's thumb grazed her jaw. He pulled away. It felt like her body split in two when she separated from him. But she forced herself to join Thom, Ilain, and Rafferty at the horses.

Together, they watched the other five members of their troop mount up. The negotiation party would wait in the trees, giving Deckard and the others time to get into the city.

Evylin's eyes followed Deckard's every movement until he was out of sight, affixing his moonstone ring to the silver chain of her rosette necklace. And even then, she tracked their progress, feeling their soul-tie grow like a spool unraveling in her chest. The thread of his presence extended, but it didn't waver. She tracked him the entire way and felt when he took a short pause a mile east of their location. Then there was a jog toward the city walls. And then a flash of power came, surging deep within her core.

"It's time," Evylin said, knowing he'd just teleported them into the city.

Evylin, Thom, Ilain, and Rafferty mounted their own horses and left the woods, taking the wide road to Ephria City. While Rafferty chatted as usual, she was too busy tracking Deckard's progress. It would be slow. With or without a shroud, they'd have to move carefully through the city.

The golden sun dipped below the horizon. Evylin tensed as they approached the war camp's border. Several soldiers in dented and dirty armor affixed to their wool coats and bearing pikes stepped forward. One raised his hand, halting them.

"In the name of King Blount, I demand to know who approaches," the soldier said in a Waulden accent.

"Don't you recognize us?" Ilain crooned pleasantly.

The soldiers exchanged confused looks. "No," the leader said.

"You should," she quipped. "His Majesty has a writ out on us. Granted, it's only Evylin's and my likenesses so kindly displayed."

The Waulden men bore up in sudden understanding. "You mean—"

Ilain interrupted with a flourish of her hand. "I," she set her hand on her chest, "am Highlady Ilain Calder, ViceMage of the Order of the Flame and Pyra's Heiress."

"Do you think you're still the viceMage?" Thom asked lightly. "I would've thought they'd fired you by now."

Ilain ignored him. "This," her hand swept to Evylin, "is Private Evylin Deckard. And behind us are our friends, Captain Deckard and Corporal Rafferty."

"Pleasure," Rafferty said with a mock salute.

"We'd like to speak with His Majesty about terms of surrender on behalf of the Alliance," Ilain concluded.

The soldiers snapped into action, and Evylin smirked at their sudden baffled anxiousness. The head soldier began giving orders, sending for their general. He ordered the quartet off their horses and instructed the other soldiers to bind them.

Thom frowned. "We're here peacefully," he said. "There's no need for restraints."

"I'll be the judge of who needs restraining and who doesn't," the soldier snapped. "And I say *you* need particular restraining."

Rafferty sniggered. "He's not wrong, Thommy."

Subjecting themselves to the shackles, Evylin forced herself to remain calm. She felt along the tether between her and Deckard, finding that though his emotions were heightened with anxiety, it was a more subtle, slow feeling rather than the chaotic type that came with a fight. The others were safe, for now. That was what mattered.

A horse thundered to the camp's entrance. Its rider was a soldier with a purple cape tied to his epaulets and a black plume affixed to his hat. He dismounted immediately, and the men guarding the camp stepped out of his way. "What's this?" he demanded.

"The Calder woman and the Warrior, General Maurcus," the leader said. "They say they've come to surrender."

"I said we've come to *discuss* surrender," Ilain corrected.

The general scanned them with recognition. "Well," Maurcus said brightly, "I'm sure His Majesty will be pleased to receive you." To his men, he added, "Search them. Take their weapons and the Relics. And for Galatae's Heavens, remove those bloody shackles. They're the king's honored guests."

"You think we brought the Relics?" Rafferty snarked as the soldiers rushed to their orders. "We're a negotiation committee. We're not stupid."

"That's debatable," Thom said, readily offering his weapons to the soldiers once his hands were freed.

Though the men moved toward Ilain, she gave them a fierce glare. "If you so much as *try* to touch me, I will burn you to ash."

The men hesitated, looking to General Maurcus. He waved a dismissive hand. "Mages don't carry weapons," he said. His brow rose. "But I would request you open your collar, Highlady, to prove you don't carry the Relics."

"What if she's got one up her skirt?" Rafferty asked slyly.

Evylin sent him an annoyed look, but Maurcus wasn't bothered. "We will meet with Highlady Wendle at the palace to ensure there are no surprises," he explained.

Slowly, Evylin unsheathed her sword, handing it over along with each of her daggers. The belt felt abnormally light around her waist. Her jaw tightened as she handed over the moonstone dagger, its golden handle and silver blade glinting in the light, willing it to remain with the men until she called for it again. She slipped off the band of throwing knives she wore across her chest. Then she unbuttoned her coat and tugged open her collar so they could see she wasn't wearing a Relic. She turned out her pockets next.

Maurcus motioned to her boot. "I know you've got one more," he said.

Evylin smirked, reaching for the final dagger. "Blount remembers, does he?" She gave an amused hum. "I suppose he's not as dull as I thought."

With a faintly amused grin in return, the general accepted the dagger. "You may want to watch that tongue in His Majesty's presence," he said.

"Oh," Evylin shrugged casually, "but didn't you know? I'm his heart's greatest desire. I like to think he recognizes my matchless wit."

"It probably has more to do with your pleasingly firm—"

Thom elbowed Rafferty's stomach to keep him from finishing the comment.

With a steady eye, Maurcus watched them. He smiled again, but it was a tense expression now. "If you please, remount your horses, and I will escort you to His Majesty."

"What if I don't please?" Rafferty asked, though he did as requested anyway.

Maurcus led them on a parade through the war camp, a band of ten soldiers joining them. All around them, Waulden men—and a few women who seemed there as companions or nurses rather than soldiers—watched them pass. Either they recognized them, or word had already circulated through the camp.

When they reached the main gate of Ephria City, Evylin's stomach clenched, and her heart seized. The heads of King Ephren and his family were set on pikes affixed to the stonework, in full view for all to see. The prince and his sweet wife, Henriette. A child who bore the Ephren visage. Seretta and her father, the duke. Many others Evylin didn't recognize.

Another spike of dread seared through her, but it was fainter, and she knew it was Deckard. He'd sensed her distress.

Forcing herself to calm down, she sent a soothing wave toward him to tell him she was safe. At her side, Ilain gagged and averted her gaze. Evylin herself was torn between looking away and scanning the heads of the royals for Carlile. Was the old adviser safe?

Or had he been discovered as an Alliance member, and Blount was torturing him even now?

Since she didn't find the adviser among the dead, Evylin looked away and hardened her jaw. They passed through the gates. Two Mages with dark cloaks joined them, the double-moon crest marking them as Night Mages. They flanked Ilain, a special guard, likely intended to keep her from using magic.

Evylin scanned the city as they rode, trying to take in the details. Surprisingly, it showed few signs of siege. The bodies of Ephrian soldiers littered the streets. A few fires put off great clouds of smoke, while a handful of buildings showed wear from the initial attack of catapults. Large boulders remained lodged in buildings or scattered along damaged streets. However, it appeared that the siege hadn't lasted long, as most of the city's buildings were intact.

Yet, an eerie silence left the air pregnant with tension. The only people in sight were the occasional band of Waulden soldiers, a Mage often with them, patrolling the streets. The shops and stalls were closed. The windows of most houses were shuttered, their curtains drawn. She thought she saw a child peering out of an upper window, but it might've been a cat.

The banners of Ephria were already either torn down or replaced with those of Wauld. The homeless cowered in the alleys, ignored by their army escort. A lamplighter walked the streets with his small ladder and satchel. He stopped at each wrought-iron lamp, opening the lantern to give light to the fading day. He paused in his work, quickly ducking his head at the group's approach as if he could dip out of sight.

Absentmindedly, Evylin reached for her rings. She didn't like seeing the way Blount had overtaken her home. Given what little time she'd spent in the city, somehow her heart had attached to it, as though it belonged to her and Deckard. Knowing Blount had walked their streets, laying claim to their home, riled her innermost being.

As they passed through the Quarter District and into the Military District, the streets widened. And there, the bodies of the fallen soldiers thickened. Green and gray uniforms filled the streets. They passed the barracks, the gates hanging open as hundreds of bodies poured out, layered on top of one another in rows where they'd fallen. Evylin shared a look with Thom, and his face blanched. Blount's men had slaughtered the whole of the Ephrian Army stationed within Loclight. Her heart clenched, thinking of her brother-in-law, Druan. Had he escaped Blount's attack, or was he among the dead too?

In the center of the street leading to the barracks stood a large wooden gallows, several bodies hanging from its ropes. Their officer insignias shone in the last flare of sunset. The triple braid of General Rand caught her gaze the most.

Evylin turned away. She couldn't feel smug at his demise. She wouldn't wish the end he'd suffered for anyone except Blount and his men.

Looking ahead, Evylin saw the palace's white stone rooftops come into view. She kept her eyes on it the rest of the way, only allowing a spare glance at their home as they passed. Blount's magic hadn't caused cataclysmic destruction to the city, but he'd still brought death to her home.

Evylin sought Deckard's presence once again. He was nearer now, somewhere north of her. A quarter of a mile away. Likely near the entrance to the palace grounds.

Finally, they reached the palace. Its cheery grounds remained immaculate, though Waulden soldiers filled the grass and gardens. The evening light was nearly gone, casting a light grayish-purple hue over the world. They came to a stop at the end of the gravel drive. Soldiers came forward to surround Evylin, Thom, Ilain, and Rafferty. The general led them into the palace, where a female Mage dressed in scarlet was waiting.

"Hello, Ivetta," Ilain said merrily. "It's been too long."

The woman gave her an annoyed glare. "A thousand years would be too soon, Highlady Calder," she said coldly.

Ilain leaned over to Thom. "Ivetta was always jealous of my power," she said.

"Are you sure it wasn't just your personality?" Thom asked.

Ilain tutted at him just before Ivetta, a Fire Mage, took her into a side room. A few minutes later, they reemerged. "No weapons, no Relics," the woman told General Maurcus.

However, Ilain bore a burning red mark on her left cheek. It bubbled at the edges, revealing that Ivetta had used her magic. Evylin and Rafferty bristled while Thom made a movement as if to step toward the Mage. Soldiers impeded him, but the general glared at the woman.

"His Majesty said unharmed," Maurcus snarled.

"He said it about the Warrior." Ivetta sent Evylin a scowl before bearing herself up. "He said nothing about Pyra's Heiress."

"No matter," Ilain said calmly. She closed her eyes and took a deep breath, and the burn mark began to slowly fade with a glimmer of golden orange. Once it was fully gone, her pale cheek soft and pink again, Ilain smiled at Ivetta. "I'm immune to such barbarity."

General Maurcus motioned, and they followed him through the marble halls. Despite Blount's banners throughout the city, his men couldn't remove all the marks of Ephren in the palace. The ceilings still depicted the Estshire hills. Paintings of Ephren's descendants had been torn and destroyed but still hung on the walls. The emerald color of Ephria still filled the home, seen within its furnishings and decor.

When they reached the hall to the throne room, Evylin's heart sped up. She searched for Deckard. He was very near now. A story below her, several hundred feet away. Anxious but steady.

Soldiers filled the hall, observing as they proceeded. Two attendants pulled open the grand double doors. The green marble of the room shone beneath the glorious chandelier. The stained glass window appeared dim, shrouded in the shadows of the night outside. Above them, the Shepherd King loomed on the ceiling, crook and sword in hand, witnessing his kingdom being reclaimed by the Mage currently seated on his marble throne.

Blount sat forward on the dais, chin in his hand as he listened to a soldier whisper his report. His golden hair was impeccably trimmed and slicked back, devoid of a crown. His sharp blue gaze flickered across the room, and Evylin could tell the moment he spotted her. A shift came to his expression as though narrowing in. He held up a hand, halting the soldier's words.

The man stepped back, and Blount rose. He whispered a single sentence. The soldier bowed and left. Then Blount turned to the approaching group. He wore a black coat with deep amethyst braids and golden buttons, giving him a kingly and militaristic appearance all at once. He looked so much like Vayden that it gave Evylin an unexpected pause. Yet, there was a hardness in his bearing that she'd never witnessed in his half-brother.

Around his neck hung the four Relics. The flickering ruby of Fire, the pulsing yellow topaz of Day, the rippling sapphire of Water, and the rhythmic diamond of Time. Their golden chains clinked softly as he stepped off the dais.

Their party came to a stop, General Maurcus at their head. Evylin did a quick count of the room: twenty soldiers and somewhere around fifteen Mages. Not impossible but certainly not ideal.

"Your Majesty," Maurcus said, bowing low. "Highlady Calder, Private Deckard, Captain Deckard, and Corporal Rafferty have come to negotiate terms of surrender."

Blount didn't so much as glance at Maurcus. He walked across the emerald marble, his soldiers parting for him. A slow, casual smile came to his lips as he approached. His sharp gaze scanned Evylin from head to toe as he walked, taking in her muddy boots, road-worn clothes, and long-unwashed braid. Then they met her eyes.

Evylin's cheek twitched, remembering the kick he'd landed there months ago.

"Welcome, my Warrior," he said with cruel fondness, still a few strides away. "I'm so glad you could join me at last."

CHAPTER FIFTY-SEVEN

"He doesn't look that scary," Rafferty muttered to Thom behind Evylin.

Blount's long stride drew him one step closer to their party as he scanned each member for the first time. "You have a very interesting taste in companions, Evylin," he said. "Last time you were with Highlord Calder. This time, his sister accompanies you. Where is our other good friend?"

While Ilain shifted beside Evylin, her dress rustling, she gave no other indication that Auden's mention bothered her.

When Blount stepped closer to Evylin, Thom moved up to stand at her side like a guard. "He's a bit busy at the moment," he said calmly.

Blount paused, regarding Thom slowly. Evylin could practically see his thoughts working to place this man. Surely, he remembered Thom. He'd been one of his captives.

As the memory dawned on him, a sly grin came to Blount's face. "You're the wrong Deckard," he said.

Thom shrugged casually. "I've been told that my whole life."

Blount hummed at the quip and turned to Evylin. "Where is your husband?"

With an internal search, she made a quick check on Deckard's location—he was moving toward them from the back of the palace—and she raised her brow. "With Auden," she lied. "They're watching the Relics while we give our terms to you."

The sound of Blount's genuine laughter filled the air. "Your terms," he repeated. "That's about as amusing as the idea that your husband would allow you to surrender yourself without guaranteeing your safety. You see, I spoke with Oriane before her death—"

When Evylin's brow furrowed, Ilain clarified, "Renaul."

"Ah, yes." Blount gave Ilain a snide look. "I suppose you wouldn't have known her first name."

"Your mistress," Evylin said. "The one you killed."

Blount shrugged callously. "She was a disappointment in more ways than one. But it's no matter. Less competition for you, dear."

"I'd rather gouge out my eyes," Evylin said.

"They'd heal, you know." Blount scanned her. "Once we're Bonded, the recovery would be even faster. I wonder if they'd be the same color, though."

"Blood doesn't change, no matter what alterations you make," Ilain noted.

"Mm." Blount looked as bored as he sounded. "As I was saying," he stared down at Evylin, his height several inches taller than even Deckard, "if your husband isn't here, it leads me to believe you have a plan that makes him think he can get you back."

"We have an offer for you," Evylin admitted.

He regarded her with interest. "Unless it's the Relics, I don't want it."

"Not even if it's me?"

That caused Blount's eyes to darken greedily. Thom and Rafferty shifted, but Ilain remained still and silent.

"You?" Blount said, disbelief tingeing his tone. "And you think I'll believe that your husband will allow this arrangement?"

"Under the correct terms, he will," Evylin said. "I will Bond with you, as you wish, according to Renaul, and you will return Ephria to the Alliance's authority. You may have Wauld and me, but not Ephria or the Relics."

He looked disappointed, as though she thought him foolish, but she quickly added, "Aside from the Night Relic, of course. Bonded to me, you can carry it without any ill effects. And the Alliance won't stop you."

His expression shifted then. Standing this close, she could see the subtle differences between Rouland Blount II and Vayden Calder. Blount's eyes were a true sky blue; Vayden's held a darker tinge. A small scar marred Vayden's hairline; Blount bore no blemishes. Blount's face showed no signs of age; Vayden's wrinkles showed his maturity.

"Is this your version of a peace treaty?" Blount asked.

"It is."

"And your husband won't mind giving you to me?"

At the mention of Deckard, Evylin checked on his progress. He was nearer, approaching at a faster rate than before. She couldn't read his emotions through her anxious heartbeat and the wariness she felt in Blount's presence, but she recognized the slight uptick in his own worry.

Evylin forced herself to calm her heart rate for his sake. She didn't want to cause concern for him when the trap was almost ready. Blount was in their hands. She just needed to stall a little longer.

"I will be your Warrior," Evylin lied. "Nothing else."

Blount gave a soft chuckle. "I'm told that can't last."

"Neither can my husband's life. As a Warrior, I will outlive him by more than a century. Once he dies—of *natural* age—I will be yours, wholly."

Blount reached out, cupping Evylin's chin. He dipped his head. "What if I don't care to wait that long?" he asked.

Evylin forced herself not to squirm under the violent pressure of his grasp. "I hear patience is a virtue."

"I've never been virtuous," Blount said flatly. He released her then. "No. I reject your terms."

Evylin blinked, her heart stalling with disappointment at his unwillingness to play along with her scheme.

"I won't entertain this childish game anymore. You're amusing, Evylin. I like that. But don't ever make the mistake of treating me as though I'm a fool ever again." His eyes gleamed with cruelty. "I won't refrain from retribution if you do."

Having experienced Blount's retribution in the Water Keep, Evylin didn't doubt his sincerity.

"I have decades of experience in warfare," Blount said. "I have studied a millennium's worth of history and politics. Should I acquiesce to this ridiculous farce of an offer, I would, at best, be faced with another war with your *Alliance* a century from now."

"Why would you care?" Rafferty asked. "You'll be dead, right?"

"I'll be Bonded," Blount said. His eyes darted arrogantly toward Ilain. "And I'll have another means of survival, thanks to our brethren of old."

Evylin furrowed her brow, but a sharp laugh burst out of Ilain. "You aren't serious," she said in blatant amusement. "You believe you can find the sandgem?"

"The what?" Rafferty said, eyes bright at the word "gem."

"It's an ancient magical artifact," Ilain explained, "*rumored* to give eternal life to its bearer. But it was lost to time, along with nearly all other magical antiquities."

"Money and power can buy you many things, Highlady Calder," Blount said.

"I wish you the best of luck," Ilain said sarcastically.

Blount ignored her. "Now, understanding my eternal destiny, you can see," he said to Evylin, "I couldn't accept your bargain even if it was genuine because I'm not interested in ruling Wauld alone. I want all of the Isle of Allund under my command."

"You don't believe our offer is genuine?" Evylin asked. She would have been bothered by his perception if Deckard hadn't been on the other side of the door.

"No," Blount said. "I'll still Bond with you, of course, and perhaps I'll let your husband remain with us. I do relish the idea of him watching while I bend you to my will."

Evylin's heart thumped at the confidence in his gaze. "I'm afraid that doesn't suit me," she said bitingly.

"I'm afraid I don't care, darling."

With that, Blount raised his hand. Evylin flinched, sure he was going to hit her. Instead, he snapped.

The throne room doors swung open. Dread spiraled through her as she got a clear read on Deckard's emotions for the first time since they'd entered the palace: bone-deep dread.

Then she saw him.

A troop of soldiers escorted Deckard, Ethenn, Vayden, Isla, and Brea into the room. Shackles bound them all. It took four soldiers to carry all of Ethenn and Brea's weapons. Their uniforms were mussed, and several of them bore bloody scrapes. They'd been captured.

Worse, at the head of the party, Lord Sirraus Obel, Duke of Flamesend Crest, Night Mage, and supposed Alliance member, led the way.

Deckard's eyes met Evylin's as they were brought into the room. He held his mouth in a rigid line. Worry leaped out of him in waves. Whether it was due to their capture or specifically Obel's betrayal, Evylin didn't know.

Thom swore under his breath. "You traitor," he said as Obel drew near.

"That's right, Captain," Blount said. "My godfather has been quite helpful to me in bringing an end to your so-called Alliance. And now, he's caught your friends sneaking around the palace." He *tsked*. "Such improper behavior as guests of your new monarch."

Blount's hand landed on Evylin's shoulder, gripping it tightly. "As it is," he said. "We're all here now, so the festivities can begin."

"Festivities?" Evylin asked, scanning their troop. Ethenn bore a cut on his cheek, and a smear of blood marred his coat. Some of Brea's hair had pulled loose from the low bun she wore. Vayden bore a split lip. Isla looked rather unscathed, aside from a swelling bump on her forehead.

But Deckard had a vicious slash going from his temple down across his cheek, the wound narrowly missing his eye. It wept a slow crimson streak despite its shallow depth.

Blount ignored Evylin's question as Obel stepped forward. "We found these on them, Your Majesty," he said, the glowing Relics hanging from his hand.

A pleased smile came to Blount's lips. He released Evylin to take up the Relics. Night beamed amethyst, Wind swirled gray tourmaline, and Terrae radiated emerald.

Evylin furrowed her brow before she caught herself.

Gratefully, Blount was distracted, slipping the three Relics next to the other four around his neck. "Where's the Space Relic?" he asked Deckard.

"We've yet to retrieve it," Deckard lied apologetically.

Blount's skeptical gaze said he didn't believe the claim, but Rafferty piped up. "It took us bloody forever to get to Estshire," the weasel said with a shrug. "We were on our way here to fetch it when we heard about your grand coronation. Congratulations, by the way. I think you'll look ruddy fantastic in Ephren's crown."

The quickness of Rafferty's lie shouldn't have surprised Evylin. That was his job, smuggling things in and out of places. He knew how to think on the fly. But the memory of Deckard speaking with the weasel so intently before they'd parted made her suddenly suspicious.

Blount turned to Obel for confirmation. The duke raised his dark brow in an unconcerned manner. "We searched them thoroughly," he promised. "None of them have it."

Blount hummed, disappointed. "Very well," he said. "We'll find the Keep after the ceremony."

Evylin hesitated at the term, uncertain of what ceremony to which he referred, but Blount kept speaking. "Well now," he surveyed the troop, "it isn't every day you get such a grand reception from your enemies. Shall we officially meet one another? I love making new friends."

He stepped up to Deckard first. "You're the illustrious Colonel Deckard, I take it. You have a beautiful wife."

"I'm aware," Deckard said calmly.

"It's a pity that you're so mundane," Blount said with a flippant scan of Deckard. "You don't deserve her."

"No man could."

A wry grin lifted Evylin's lips. He *would* find a way to compliment her in a situation such as this.

Blount chuckled, the sound light. He returned to Evylin's side, eyes on Deckard even as he slid his hand over Evylin's shoulder and up her neck. To her disappointment, a rush of magic raced along her skin. "On the contrary," he said. "She'll find I'm quite her equal."

Deckard's eyes met hers knowingly. She could sense his annoyance as well as his security. But he was unexpectedly calm, given their situation. The dread of his entrance had shifted, lightening to mild uncertainty.

His eyes, shifting more green than blue, returned to Blount's face. "I'd advise you to get your hands off my wife," he said, his tone ice-cold.

"You're not in a position to threaten anyone, Colonel." Blount's smile remained. "She'll be your widow soon enough. Let's not rush it, shall we?"

Blount's hand slid down her back before he shoved her toward Obel. "Keep a close eye on her," he charged.

Obel's hands clamped around Evylin's arm, holding her at his side.

Blount stepped up to Vayden then. He scanned his near twin. Side by side, it was easier to see their differences. They weren't so impossibly identical as on their own.

"And who is this?" Blount asked.

"Vayden Calder," Obel said. "The spy I told you about."

Blount smirked at the name. "Oh, yes. My half-brother, and—" He looked at Ilain, awareness dawning on his face. "Yours. Where's your other brother?"

Ilain's jaw twitched, and Vayden swallowed, crestfallen.

"Ah," Blount said. "How did he go?"

"The Terrae Keep," Ilain replied weakly.

"Unfortunate," Blount remarked. "I had hoped to have my revenge against him. Oh, well." He patted Vayden's chest. "I suppose killing you in front of *her* will be justice enough." A nod of his head indicated Ilain.

Then he turned to Isla. "Darling Freye."

"Buttercup," Isla replied, mocking his snide mannerism.

Rafferty snorted as Blount pursed his lips. "When did you hear that?" he demanded.

"Oriane was not quiet during copulation," Isla said.

That earned a full-on chortle from Rafferty.

"Always clever," Blount said, eyes burning with malevolence. He took her face in his hands, drawing her closer even as he towered over her. Vayden tensed, but Isla didn't so much as flinch. "I liked you once."

"I remember," Isla said.

"Do you also remember what you said to me?"

"'I prefer non-magical men,'" she said. "It wasn't a lie."

"You said you like to subjugate them."

"*That* was a lie."

"Along with so many other things, I'm sure." Blount drew her face toward his, forcing her a step closer. "I don't mind that you rejected me, Islaren. It's your betrayal

I can't stand. Despite your rebuff, I trusted you. I kept you in my confidence, called you a friend."

"You don't have friends," Isla said. "You have playthings. Vassals. Slaves. You use them up and throw them away when they displease you, just like Oriane."

His gaze hardened, though his thumbs brushed gently across her cheeks. "If you wished to be free of my service, darling Freye, all you had to do was say the word."

"No," Vayden murmured just before Blount tightened his grip on Isla.

Isla's eyes flashed toward her husband as Blount brought his mouth to hers. But it wasn't a kiss of passion or affection. It was a magical inhale that swept Isla's body of air. Her figure jerked, going rigid. Vayden and Ilain cried out in alarm, yanking on their guards' holds. But the men held them back, keeping them from rushing Blount.

Almost as soon as it began, Blount pulled away. Evylin swore she could see a shimmer of wind drift between their lips as the Wind Relic glowed brightly on his chest. Then he let her drop.

Isla hit the floor with a sickening *thump*.

Evylin gaped at her still body, uncomprehending of what had just occurred.

"Isla!" Vayden wept, ripping himself violently from the arms of his captors. He fell to the marble in his attempt to get to her side. Blount held up a hand to halt his men when they moved to hold him back.

With no sign of emotion, Blount watched as Vayden scrambled to his wife's side. He pulled her onto his lap, his shackled hands fumbling to clutch her to his chest.

Looking down at the couple, Rafferty paled. "Is she . . . ?"

"Dead?" Blount asked, watching his half-brother's grief with something like morbid fascination. "Yes."

Evylin's heart broke, seeing Vayden sob over his wife's limp form. She thought of their daughter, Reyana, who would never see her mother again. Tears came to her eyes as she looked at Ilain, who wept silently as well. She'd lost her brother, and now she'd lost a sister as well.

It wasn't right. The Calder family had lost too much. They'd sacrificed far too much. And in the blink of an eye, Isla was taken from them too.

Bored by the dramatics, Blount moved on to Brea. The woman stared down at her dead friend, lips parted and body trembling. But she met Blount's gaze with fierce, dry eyes.

"And who are you?" he asked.

Though Obel started to introduce her, Brea spoke over him. "My name is Breata Lohen. You just killed my best and oldest friend. So I think it is only fair that I kill you."

Blount grinned with amusement. "Traitors don't deserve life."

"Tyrants don't deserve life either."

With a grunt, Blount reached out to grab her face. Brea whacked his hand away with her fists, the shackles jingling with the movement. "You touch me," she hissed, "and I'll drive my sharpest dagger up your *cúos*."

Blount's eyes glinted, suddenly fascinated. "Ah, you're a Warrior," he said with awe.

Brea didn't reply.

"Good." Blount moved to Ethenn then. "You're Ephrian, obviously," he said, dismissing him. But then he paused, studying him. His feet shifted as he glanced back at Evylin and Brea in turn.

He faced Ethenn again. "Surely not. Another Warrior?"

"I don't see how that's any of your business," Ethenn said blandly.

Blount chuckled, gleeful. "Well, this is splendid fun," he said. "I'll enjoy dissecting you at a later time. I've always been interested in discovering what fuels a Warrior's magic. You aren't connected to the resources, and yet you're so powerful."

"What makes you think he's a Warrior?" Rafferty asked. "After all, the kid's just got a funny look to him. There's not really anything magical about that."

Ethenn glared at his friend, but Obel said, "Rouland has studied magic thoroughly over his lifetime. While Warriors are vastly rare these days, he's managed to discover their tells. Their aura is chief among them. You become accustomed to it long enough, and you can sense it readily."

Blount had moved from Ethenn's side, crossing to Ilain, who was still crying, watching her brother cling to her dead sister-in-law. "Highlady Calder," Blount called.

When Ilain didn't respond, he slapped her across the face.

Ethenn clenched his fists, but the five guards holding him kept him from moving.

Ilain met Blount's gaze then, a hand pressed to her red cheek. "Yes, Your Majesty?" she said with marked contempt.

"I have need of your services," Blount said. He beckoned to her. "Come with me."

Led by her guards, Ilain walked behind Blount. He strode across the marble to Evylin. He gripped her wrist, yanking her from Obel.

Prepared, Evylin leaned into the force of Blount's pull, crashing into him and driving him back. It caused him to stumble, so Evylin slipped her foot out to trip him. Then she swept her clasped hands up into his jaw, making contact with a sharp smack. He grunted and released her, stumbling backward from the force of her blow.

Freed, Evylin darted toward Deckard. If she could get to him, she could break him free of his captors, get one of their weapons, and together, they could rescue their friends.

An amethyst shadow slammed into Evylin's back, sending her careening to the floor. She hit the tiles hard but used the momentum to roll to Deckard's side. She scrambled to rise, only for a foot to land on her chest.

"I wouldn't," Blount said, standing over her. His boot pressed violently against her sternum, making it hard to breathe.

Evylin's eyes darted to Deckard's, so close by. A wave of sorrow passed through the air between them. "We'll be all right," he whispered tenderly.

He was such a splendid liar. But this time, Evylin struggled to believe him.

The guards had pressed all their friends to their knees, knives at their throats. Vayden still wept, Isla's body beside him. Thom knelt at Deckard's side, fear in his gray-blue gaze. Rafferty and Ethenn were next, Brea at the far side. All of them stared helplessly as Blount pulled Evylin to her feet.

"Now . . ." Blount gestured to the guard holding Deckard. The soldier took his knife and drove it into Deckard's shoulder.

Deckard grimaced, a deep grunt eliciting from him.

Evylin felt the blade as though it had stabbed her own shoulder, a fire racing through her arm. Was that part of the Bond? She'd not experienced Deckard's physical pain before.

Still, her husband held her gaze steadily until Blount forced her eyes to him.

"Should I have any more trouble from you," the Night Mage growled, "I will let my men carve him apart one limb at a time. Understood?"

Evylin dipped her chin, anger racing through her. "Yes," she said flatly.

"Good." He tugged her along behind him. "Sirraus, are we ready?"

"As much as we can be," Obel said. "We need the final details from Highlady Calder."

"Then get it," Blount said testily. He pulled Evylin up the dais steps toward the throne.

Obel dragged Ilain with him. "We have a Mage of each resource and two moonstones—one white, one black," he told her. "But what else are we lacking?"

Ilain's brow furrowed, staring up at Obel. "What are you talking about?"

"The Bonding ceremony," Obel said, impatient. "We have the Mages and moonstones. What else do we require for you to Bond His Majesty, King Rouland Blount II, to Private Evylin Deckard?"

Ilain gaped at the duke while Evylin's breath caught. Blount intended to Bond with her at that very moment. He couldn't because she was already Bonded, but he would figure that out soon enough.

Then a more startling revelation came to her: Obel was at her and Deckard's Bonding ceremony. He knew what they needed just as well as Ilain.

The duke was playing Blount.

Suddenly, Evylin felt a wave of focus sweep through the room and the moonstone ring that pressed against her collarbone on the silver chain vanished. Her body thrummed with power, responding to Deckard's rising magic. She glanced over her shoulder to find him watching her, but his expression was impassive.

He already had a plan.

"I won't do it," Ilain spat, jerking in Obel's grasp.

"If you don't," Blount said, "I will kill your only remaining brother."

Ilain glanced at Vayden. She hesitated, but Evylin knew she must understand the truth as well. She knew Obel was on their side. The tide had turned in their favor. They just had to play along until the opportune moment.

"Now," Blount said sharply, "tell us what we're missing."

Ilain paused, her acting surprisingly strong. "I—" She glanced at Evylin. "I'm sorry."

Evylin chewed on her bottom lip, not trusting herself to play her own role well.

Ilain turned to Obel. "Two Warriors," she said. "One male, one female."

Blount laughed. "How perfect." He beckoned to the men holding Ethenn and Brea. "Bring them forward."

"We—we're not dressed right," Ilain argued. "This is to be a sacred event. There are protocols and rituals. And there are far too many people here. The ceremony is meant to be intimate and holy. You must treat it as such if you want me to proceed."

Blount gave her a bored stare. "I'm not sending away my men to give you better odds at fighting me. Perform the ceremony, or I will start killing your friends one at a time."

Subdued, Ilain pressed her lips together and gave a tense nod. She guided them each into the proper positioning, with Blount and Evylin facing one another, the eight Mages—including Obel—behind them. Ethenn and Brea stood on either side of Ilain, along with all their guards.

"You can't wear the Relics," Ilain said then.

Blount scoffed. "Do not play games with me, Highlady."

"I'm not," she said fiercely. "Their magic will impede the union. If you want a secure Bond, you'll remove them. Otherwise, it will fail to take hold."

Blount looked at Obel for confirmation. "I have not studied the institution enough to know whether or not it is true, Your Majesty," the duke said.

With a sharp nod, Blount gestured to the guards holding Thom. One of them took out a dagger and drove it into his gut.

Evylin sucked in a shallow breath as Deckard called in panic to his brother. Thom slumped forward, blood rapidly staining his coat. Brea looked ready to fight the entire room to get to him. Ethenn and Rafferty gaped with panic on their faces.

"I wasn't lying, you bloody bastard!" Ilain yelled through fresh tears.

He glared at her, unmoved.

"Fine," she ground out. "Be united by a faulty Bond. See if I care. Join right hands."

With force, Blount took Evylin's right hand. She kept reminding herself that Deckard had a plan. This wasn't the end. They wouldn't lose.

But Isla was dead, and Thom was bleeding out—*again*. They were scattered through the room. And at last count, there were thirty-nine soldiers and seventeen Mages present in the throne room, thirty-nine non-magical and seventeen magical beings barring them from victory.

"Fire, Day, Water, Night, Wind, Time, Terrae, and Space," Ilain began, her voice taut. "This is the foundation of Terraeus, the resources of life."

Evylin stared up at Blount, the words creating a strange déjà vu in her magically heightened senses. A gentle wave of adoration swept over her from the far side of the room.

"From the dawn of creation," Ilain continued, "Allore formed Warriors and Mages from his very soul, setting them as gatekeepers and anchors of his power, charging them to be caregivers and servants to all."

Inexplicably, Evylin found herself smiling, remembering her ceremony with Deckard. She remembered his tender gaze and gentle touch. The tingle of magic spread across her skin.

Blount's brow furrowed at her wistful gaze.

Ilain's voice grew stronger as she spoke. "To Bond is to release who you are alone and fasten who you are together."

Clarity came to Evylin's mind. Time slowed, and she saw the room with an omniscient gaze, perceiving each heartbeat. It wasn't just her Warrior senses that had heightened this time, though. She could sense the heat building under her skin and the world tinged black with the silhouette of Space.

Evylin remembered Ilain's words from their ceremony. *"Not double-sided but never-ending—singular and whole."*

Singular and whole.

Warrior and Mage.

Evylin and Deckard.

A sudden weight settled into Evylin's left hand—light and metallic and small enough to conceal easily. She tightened her grip, feeling the cool touch of the golden scrollwork.

Her smile grew into a smirk.

"What are you smiling about?" Blount said, interrupting Ilain's speech.

Evylin shrugged playfully. "Oh, I'm just a happy person, generally. It used to annoy my uncle, whom you killed, by the way. I've been meaning to repay you for that."

Blount's grip tightened on hers. "You can hold a grudge as long as you like," he said, with a bitter snarl. "But you're mine now. And one day, you'll love me more than any other."

"Actually," Evylin quipped, "I won't."

His gaze hardened.

"You see—" The world slowed. With her left hand, Evylin raised the returned Bonding dagger to thrust the silver blade into Blount's chest. The moonstone in the pommel shimmered under the light of the chandeliers. "I'm already Bonded."

The room exploded with magic.

Blount stumbled back, the blade protruding from his pectoral. With a thought, Evylin summoned it back, and it landed in her right hand.

Angered, Blount sent out a fierce amethyst shadow. It crashed into Evylin, knocking her back.

Around them, Ilain and Obel engaged the other Mages while Brea and Ethenn struggled to fight in their chains. Elemental and Existential magic erupted in dazzling flares. With her omnipresent vision, Evylin saw the black crystals of Space tearing through the guards holding Deckard, Thom, Rafferty, and Vayden. Together, they rose and joined the fray, though Thom struggled with the gaping wound in his gut. Pausing for but a moment, Deckard set a hand on his brother's stomach, a bronze light pulsing to heal him.

With the battle raging, Evylin focused on Blount. He sneered at her, something like respect entering his gaze. "You're more cunning than I expected," he said. "Who'd you find to Bond with?"

"In truth, he found me." Evylin ducked under another shadow that narrowly missed her. She spun, flicking her wrist as she faced the Night Mage again. The dagger embedded itself in his thigh, and he cried out. The blade returned to her summons. "I did welcome his advances, though. He's awfully charming, you see."

Blount charged Evylin, slashing with his hands, sending out shadows, waves, and torrents of all other magic. Evylin dodged them, some with more success than others. She sensed that her friends had procured weapons for themselves. Deckard took down several soldiers, and, finally, his and the others' chains dissolved through his powers.

More Mages and soldiers pressed in around them. An eruption of Terrae magic blasted Rafferty across the marble floor to the foot of the dais. Ethenn defended Thom's weak side, doing twice the work. Brea fought beside Vayden, both of them wielding the broadswords of fallen Waulden soldiers.

Heat and burning flesh seared the air. Ilain appeared beside Evylin, her hands raised. A flame roared toward Blount, but he lifted a hand, the Fire Relic flickering on his chest. He took hold of the fire and controlled it, rolling it inward on itself before turning it back to hurl at Ilain. The fireball hit her square in the chest, tossing the woman across the dais.

Obel stepped up, throwing a deep purple shadow surging toward Blount. Again, Blount controlled the attack with the added power of the Relics. "Traitor!" he accused, hurling the magic back at his godfather. "You were supposed to be with *me*."

Obel barely deflected the shadow's blow and was forced a step back. "I *was* with you," he shouted back. "Until I saw the man you'd become."

"A god?"

"A tyrant like your father."

Blount attacked with renewed fury. Deep amethyst shadows swirled around him, growing and undulating. They surrounded the dais, choking the rest of the room from sight. Evylin tried to dart closer to attack, but Blount's control of the magic was too strong. Any step she took, the shadows erupted, slamming into her and sending her reeling backward.

Obel tried to fight at her side, but he was now the focus of Blount's attacks. Shadow after shadow pummeled the duke. He threw his hands up to block the attacks. But one slipped past his defenses, striking him like a whip. He shuddered against the pain.

"Eve." Rafferty popped up beside Evylin, a singular knife in his hand. The blade was bloody, and his face was splattered with gore. Yet, he wore a bright smile.

Evylin and he ducked behind the throne as Blount's shadows lashed out at them. "I'm a little busy, Raff," she said. "Did you need something?"

"It's more that *you* need something," Rafferty said with a wily grin.

Blount's Mages appeared through the shadows. Evylin and Rafferty jumped up, dodging the sudden fresh onslaught of magic. She grimaced as a bolt of Day slammed into her shoulder. She twisted, flicking her dagger toward the Mage. It landed in the precise center of his throat. Blood spurted from the wound as Evylin called the blade back.

"Here," Rafferty said, pulling a hand from his pocket. He tossed a small, glittering object toward Evylin.

The gold pendant hit Evylin's hand. Instantly, it transformed. The onyx blade of the Space sword rippled with power, filling Evylin with a renewed sense of energy. A surge of magic swept through her, and Deckard's magic swelled in response across the throne room. She didn't have long to appreciate it as the Mages continued their attacks.

With Rafferty at her side, Evylin dashed forward through the violet and amethyst shadows around them. They slashed and sliced. At close range, the Mages weren't nearly as dangerous. They struggled to create bursts of magic large enough to inflict true damage. Evylin and Rafferty dispatched them easily, their months of teamwork turning them into a frightful force.

"How did you get this?" Evylin asked, spinning away from a crackling flame.

"Your noble husband isn't quite as boring as he seems." Rafferty dropped to a crouch, hamstringing one of the Mages before he was even aware of his presence. "He teleported the bloody thing right into my pocket when we entered the throne room. A contingency plan, he called it."

Evylin slashed with the glittering sword. "Remind me to kiss him later."

"It's me who deserves your thanks."

"Then remind me to kiss you later too."

"I'll hold you to that."

As the last Mage crumpled, Evylin turned to find Ilain fighting at Obel's side. But Blount was still too strong, the Relics granting him vast wells of power. The pendants glowed around his neck. Flashes of red, yellow, blue, purple, gray, white, and green filled the shadows around him like colorful lightning strikes. His attacks were so fierce that all Ilain and Obel could do was defend themselves.

Evylin raced forward, but she wasn't fast enough.

In one coiling purple shadow, Blount's magic slammed into Obel and Ilain with more power than Evylin had ever seen. Its force was like the bomb at Renaul's estate, rocking the very ground under her feet. The Alliance Mages tumbled away through the air. Obel crashed into the throne, landing against the base. He didn't move, either unconscious or . . .

Ilain flew clear off the dais, crashing hard against the tile floor. Evylin heard a sickening *crack* as her head slammed on the marble. Vayden and Ethenn called out, even as they continued to fight. With the Waulden soldiers and Mages surrounding the troop, only Evylin and Rafferty were near enough to check on the woman.

Evylin left the task to him.

Charging up the steps, Evylin brandished the Space sword. Blount sent a gust of wind laced with the shadow of Night. Pointlessly, Evylin slashed the sword out. But to her surprise, the blade caught the magic, absorbing it.

Blount took a step back in surprise. "You little liar," he seethed. "You do have it."

Feeling the heat of Deckard's magic creeping up her arms, Evylin's vision darkened once more. "I lied about a lot of things." A tingle worked across her skin as Space magic coiled around her. "A vice I picked up from my husband."

Blount gaped at her, truly shocked. "He's a bloody Space Mage?"

"It surprised me too."

The Night Mage's blue eyes flared violently. "And you're Bonded?"

"We are."

A cruel smile came to his lips. "That means I only have to kill one of you."

"You can try," Evylin challenged, then rushed him.

Blount sent out torrents of magic, each one with increasing power. If he wasn't careful, he would burn up all his energy and pass out. Though Ilain had noted Blount's impressive skill in the past. Evylin wondered if they had the power to overcome him at all.

The crystalline shards around Evylin deflected Blount's strikes, but she felt each blow zapping more energy from her limbs. She couldn't sustain her defense forever. An aggressive approach might be the only way to defeat the Mage.

Striking out, Evylin took the offensive. She stepped boldly toward him, and Blount had to step away from the range of her sword, throwing more shadows and flares, flames, and waves. She pressed in close to crowd his defenses. He raised a hand as she slashed, the blade slicing open the palm of his hand. But he flexed his fingers past the pain, and the diamond pendant flared with a white glow against his chest.

Within an instant, Evylin was frozen. Her muscles were incapacitated, locked in Time. No matter how hard she tried, her body was wholly halted.

His bleeding hand shook, betraying his early signs of fatigue, and Blount glared at her. He reached out, curling his fingers around the hilt of the Space sword, wetting her fingers with his blood. "I'll take that," he said, ice-blue eyes piercing her with their rage.

A sudden hand appeared on Blount's shoulder. Then Rafferty's head popped into view. "Afraid not, chap," he said, driving a sword from behind through the Night Mage's stomach.

Blount howled in pain, jerking away. The Space Relic clattered to the floor, and Evylin dropped to the ground as he released the Time magic.

Blount whirled, the sword still in his back. He set a stunning blast of Day out around him, dazing both Evylin and Rafferty. Then he snatched Rafferty's collar as the man tried to scramble away.

The Night Mage's hand closed around Rafferty's neck, knuckles white as a shadow of the darkest amethyst seeped between his fingers. "That's twice you've stolen from me, thief."

Fumbling for the Space Relic, Evylin struggled to her feet. But Blount threw his free hand behind him, hitting her with a shocking cloud of Night. The wave caused her body to convulse, her fingers loosening around the Relic.

"I'm—" Rafferty gasped as the shadow crept along his skin. His veins protruded, turning a sickening dark purple beneath his pale skin. His fingers trembled as he tugged at Blount's grip. Then he wheezed, "An entrepreneur."

Blount grunted as Rafferty used his final strength to kick out, hitting the tip of the sword sticking out of the Night Mage's gut. He drove it down, cutting a violent gash through Blount's torso.

But Blount didn't let go.

Instead, his fist tightened, and Rafferty went rigid, the amethyst veins cutting ridges all along his pale skin. Then his body fell limp, his last breath stolen.

Horror and fury lit within Evylin, though her muscles still spasmed from the Night magic. Blount tossed Rafferty's dead body aside. He reached behind himself to pull the sword from his stomach. With a trembling hand, he cauterized the wound with a swift flare of Day magic.

Somehow, Evylin found her way to her feet, the Space sword back in her hand. Her head was light, and she stumbled over the first steps. Haphazardly, she darted up the staircase. Blount raised his hands, a roiling amethyst cloud forming between them.

An iridescent black silhouette flashed, and Evylin skidded to a stop. Deckard stood on the dais, his body acting as a shield. Space coiled around his entire form, his energy restoring her. "I'd ask you not to threaten my wife," he said placidly. "I'm rather protective of her."

Blount spared a solitary glance at the rapidly declining number of his men. He took a step back, moving down the top of the stairs. "I'm afraid this isn't the end I had in mind for today."

"It's the end you're going to get," Deckard replied. A hundred black shards rose with his hands. "Together?"

Evylin raised the Space sword. "Together."

As Evylin sprinted forward, Deckard's magic soared along with her. In the time it took to blink, Blount faded into nothingness under a shroud. However, though he was hidden from the physical eye, Evylin and Deckard could both sense him, her Warrior magic surging through them both.

With heightened senses, they could see the slight shimmer of Blount's form as he ran for the side door. His footsteps pounded, and the acrid scent of his fear could not hide from their ascendant magic.

The chase was hardly a chase at all. Blount didn't even get to turn around as the Space sword and crystalline shards found their target, slicing through him. His body sagged, and his concentration fumbled. The Shroud dissipated.

Blount crashed to the marble floor, gasping for air. Evylin and Deckard stood over him. The Night Mage stared at Evylin, a trickle of blood escaping the edge of his mouth. "I . . ." He coughed, a clot seeping onto his lips. "I . . . deserved it. And you."

Evylin furrowed her brow. Even in death, he was unrepentant. "Why you more than anyone else?" she asked.

"I had . . . power," he wheezed. "I deserved . . . it all."

Evylin frowned. Was that all that qualified him?

Shaking her head, Evylin sighed. "It never would have been enough."

Blount coughed again, his body trembling. The Relics around his neck dimmed. "Never . . . enough," he whispered brokenly, sky-blue eyes staring up at the painted ceiling. His eyes found the Shepherd King, sword raised on the fields of Estshire above them.

Evylin watched as the light of the Relics fully faded. Deckard's hand rested on her shoulder. Though she expected relief at Blount's end, she only felt pity. He'd wanted nothing but the same as her—"more."

More power, more respect, more love.

Blood pooled around Rouland Blount II, ViceMage of the Order of the Night and momentary King of Wauld and Ephria. The seven Relics lay without life on his chest. His beautiful coat was riddled with holes. He'd killed, he'd ruled, he'd grasped the greatest power in the world. But it never would have been enough.

"What would be reason enough to live?"

She knew the answer now.

Life was enough. Anything more was a gift.

Leaning into Deckard's touch, the sudden silence of the room felt oppressive to Evylin. The fight had stopped, the death of Blount proclaiming their victory but at great cost.

"It's over," Evylin whispered. "It's finally over."

Part IV: The Republic of Allund

That I would never carry this burden has never been my wish. It is a great honor to be granted such responsibility as the trust of my fellow man.
Quote attributed to Euon Sergus, circa 617

Do not mourn those who can never be forgotten, for they will live eternally.
Nikleby Draaw, from The Prince of the Living Wood

One day, Kit, we'll change the world, you and me.
Ryen Glaas, age eleven, to his cousin, Evylin

HARMOUTH
BROUNES
DUNBRIA
OLLOONEY
RHUNAUR
CARRICKBRACK
AULTON
WESTFOR
TINIEN
LINCASTE
EPHRIAN
FELBORNE
WESSHIRE
AUCHROIM
FELSTON
EDGE
AUBINGHAM
CAULTO
ORDER
OF THE
WIND
SUTTERLUND
REACH
FAURAMERS

CHAPTER FIFTY-EIGHT

The moment Blount fell, the fighting ceased. Evylin and Deckard took the Relics from Blount's corpse, and what Mages and soldiers remained stood down and dropped their weapons.

Ethenn had never been more grateful for a fight to end. His muscles were strained, his mind distracted. Magic had funneled through him, fiercer than ever before. He'd watched helplessly as Ilain's body was thrown to the marble. He could smell the blood seeping from the wound on her forehead. His heart contracted, but he didn't allow himself to let his guard down.

Deckard and Evylin approached, Brea and Ethenn stepping up to their side to be their backup. Obel was unconscious, Thom was pale from blood loss, and Vayden was weak with fatigue—both emotional and physical. It was clear by the dubious looks in the eyes of the enemy Mages that they doubted the strength of the troop's victory.

Ignoring their opponents, Deckard stepped to Thom's side. He set a hand on his stomach, a flash of bronze and a pulse of the Day Relic fully healing the wound that he'd merely cauterized before. Thom sucked in a relieved breath and hefted his sword.

"All good?" Deckard asked.

Thom nodded, the color returning to his face. "Prime as ever."

At the display of power, the Mages squirmed. Whether or not they wanted to admit it, Deckard and Evylin's Bond made them better suited to carry the Relics than Blount. And their strength wouldn't falter for quite some time, should they be contested. With how few enemies remained in the throne room, the odds weighed heavily in the Bonded couple's favor.

With a wary eye on the Wauldeners, Deckard beckoned Ethenn and Brea. "Here," he said, handing them each a Relic: Fire for Ethenn and Wind for Brea.

"We have work to do," Deckard charged as the Relics transformed into weapons.

As one, the remaining members of the troop stepped forward. They addressed the small crowd of soldiers and Mages. General Maurcus and Highlord Baurun were their respective leaders. A quick discussion of surrender took place, but Ethenn was too distracted to pay attention to the details. He knew there was an argument; General Maurcus challenged Deckard and Evylin's ability to withstand the resistance of the entire Waulden Army. Highlord Baurun, with his sharp blue eyes regularly darting to the Relics, quelled that argument.

Ethenn kept a firm grip on the Fire sword in his hand. His Warrior senses still alert, his thoughts kept diverting to the faint yet steady breaths of Ilain. She was alive: injured and unconscious, yet alive.

Tension remained palpable in the room. While they maintained control in the throne room, everyone outside those walls was unaware of the power shift. Deckard instructed Maurcus to send out an order for his men to stand down. It was a tenuous situation. One wrong move could undo everything they'd achieved.

However, Maurcus and Baurun finally agreed to work with Deckard, seeming to understand that if they got on his good side, they might find a place for themselves in this new world that was rapidly forming around them all.

That was the thing, Ethenn supposed. The thrones of Wauld and Ephria were empty. There were no more kings, no more governments. Someone had to take leadership, or there would be anarchy. Maurcus and Baurun were leaders in their own right. They understood this. And they attached themselves to the victors readily.

Over time, peace settled in, allowing the troop to relax enough to check on each other. Brea went to Obel, finding his pulse steady. As Deckard's party had snuck through the palace halls, they'd run across a patrol of soldiers. Obel had appeared as well. Despite the initial shock of his appearance, he immediately began to aid the troop, taking down Blount's men in a surprise attack. He explained that he'd done all he could to prevent Blount's annihilation of the Alliance. He'd been the one to send warnings to the Ephrian ministers and even managed to help many members escape Wauld.

Obel had falsely assisted Blount's investigation, pretending to have no prior knowledge of the Alliance, which meant he'd had to facilitate the deaths of those members he couldn't get out. Through his research, he'd "learned" information about Vayden and other members of the organization. But he never gave Blount details that would lead directly to them.

Though Deckard and Ethenn were skeptical of his sincerity as they questioned him in the hall, Vayden, Isla, and Brea trusted the duke. And when Obel kept Deckard, Brea, and Ethenn's magic a secret when a new band of soldiers discovered them in the halls, Obel pretending to be their prisoner, Ethenn realized they'd made the right call.

With the Day Relic, Deckard restored Obel to consciousness. They needed his knowledge of the Alliance to bring the nations under full control, and his assistance would also lend credence to their cause amongst the greater ranks of the Waulden Mages.

Yet, their victory hardly felt like a success, with Rafferty and Isla lost.

They'd laid their friends out at the foot of the dais. Vayden, Evylin, and Brea cried openly. Thom had tears in his eyes. Deckard and Ethenn controlled their emotions better than the rest.

But Ethenn's heart broke, seeing his friend lying on the emerald marble, lifeless, his skin nearly as pale as his white-blond hair.

Evylin pressed a kiss to Rafferty's cheek and whispered, "You were better than you liked to pretend. Not a thief or a smuggler. You were a hero."

Ethenn nearly cried then.

However, they didn't have time to languish in their grief.

With Obel's help, they took control of the palace. The few remaining Mages sat placidly in the corner, awaiting instruction. Obel called for the palace's head of staff, informing him of the situation. His nobility granted him an understanding of how to set up new leadership. Maurcus and Baurun deferred to his commands. They knew him and trusted him. They were pleased to work with him, knowing that he had great influence in the current Waulden government and that it would spare their lives.

While servants came to care for Isla and Rafferty's bodies, others offered to prepare a recovery room for Ilain. Vayden went with her when the time came.

Deckard requested that Thom and Ethenn follow Obel's coordinates to the Alliance's safehouses, seeking out any surviving members. They needed to restore order to the kingdom, and their small troop wouldn't be enough.

Stepping out into the late night, tension pulsed within Ethenn's skull. He was grateful for the task, removing him from the politics of the throne room. With a letter in General Maurcus's hand and the Fire Relic, they had little to fear from the Waulden soldiers patrolling the city.

The late-night sky was a rich purple, stars glittering in the depths of the Heavens. The ivory moon glowed with half of its face, while the shadow moon showed a mere sliver.

"Well," Thom sighed as they walked out of the palace gate, "that was . . ."

Ethenn didn't reply. There was no conclusion to that sentence. It *was*. It was everything—every emotion in Terraeus. And Ethenn hated it.

Thom halted, and Ethenn turned to look over his shoulder. A pained expression twisted Thom's face. "What have we done?" he asked.

Ethenn blinked. "We ended the Centurial War."

Thom cursed, pressing his hands to his face. "Rafferty's dead."

A tremor worked through Ethenn's hands. He tightened his jaw, nodding.

"We lost our best friend."

Ethenn refused to allow the grief to penetrate his demeanor.

"Did you hear me?" Thom demanded.

"Of course I heard you," Ethenn returned dully. "But right now, we have a job to do."

Thom scowled. "Why aren't you more upset by this?"

"You think I'm happy right now?" Ethenn snapped, heat blistering along his neck. "I'm furious! But what am I supposed to do? Fall down and weep? We have a job to do," he repeated. "Raff is gone, yet thousands of others are relying on us to save them. This world still needs fixing. I'll grieve later."

Thom studied him, a strange look on his face. His eyes flickered to the Fire Relic around Ethenn's chest. Already, it tugged on his heart, warping his thoughts. Passion swirled in his chest. He wanted to unleash his anger and hurt. He wanted to tear down everything in sight. But he forced himself to focus on the knowledge that Ilain—the fearsome Fire Mage who experienced these impulsive feelings constantly—would deny herself and save the world before falling apart with grief.

Thom seemed to understand that too.

"Come on," he said, clapping Ethenn on the shoulder. "Let's get this done then."

39TH OF RADIA, 1574

Four days passed in constant chaos, one demand flowing after the next.

Upon finding the hidden Alliance members—Carlile among them—Ethenn and Thom brought them to the palace, where they took over the government. It felt like a runaway horse, wholly out of Ethenn's control. The city was firmly under Alliance authority, its leaders giving the troop new orders every moment.

Gratefully, some of those commands were to rest. They requested that Deckard, Evylin, Brea, and Ethenn keep the Relics until better guards could be procured.

The days passed in a blur of politics and mundanity. Setting up a country was far more laborious than Ethenn expected. It was slow and arduous. There were so many things to consider: the current state of security, daily routines, the new military regime, law and order, and so much more. Ethenn had a perpetual headache through it all.

While most of the Ephrian members of the Alliance had escaped Blount's attack, they still mourned the loss of hundreds of Waulden members, as well as a few of their own. Yet, they worked hard and carried on through their grief. Sacrifice was expected in the Alliance, after all. But they also took the time to hold a funeral, remembering the lives of their lost members—specifically Isla—and Rafferty.

Vayden was understandably distraught, but even he was steadily working through the outward expression of his pain, remaining always at Ilain's side.

Ethenn hadn't spent much time around Ilain. That was one gratifying part of the work the Alliance asked of him. While he was busy working with the military or training with Brea, who insisted on maintaining the same schedule of training as before in case of another attack, he was often kept separate from the Fire Mage. And when they were in the same room, there really was no cause to speak.

It wasn't until the second day that Ethenn had even learned of Ilain's recovery. She simply showed up in the council room—a grand but narrow space filled with a long table, green velvet chairs, and ornate murals on the walls—in a velvet red gown with a mourning flower pinned to the breast. The Alliance's Administration did most of its work in the council room, often holding meetings to determine its next move. Ethenn had stood at Brea's side, as he most often did due to his assignments, trying not to stare at Ilain from across the room.

Everyone greeted Ilain enthusiastically, gladdened to see her well. And she did look better. Only the faintest scratch marred her forehead, though sorrow lingered in her eyes.

They hadn't spoken a word to one another in that meeting or any other.

Several Waulden members arrived in the city over those days. Some had made it across the border before Blount's slaughter of the city. Others came out of hiding to assist in the government's development.

The remaining Waulden ministers were among these newcomers, their numbers narrowed by three who had fallen to Blount's rage. Archminister Fishere was, most notably, one who had fallen. Ethenn didn't recognize the names of the other two.

While Winton Dudleye was promoted to interim archminister, the announcement of two of the three new interim ministers caused Ethenn's stomach to swirl.

Daulton and Rowana Calder, parents of Vayden, Auden, and Ilain, now sat with the Administration, overseeing the work. In their sixties, the couple made a handsome pair. Daulton looked so much like Auden that it caused Ethenn to take a second look despite his lighter red hair turning a coppery white with age. Rowana herself had golden-white hair and the same cunning eyes as the Calder siblings. Both were tall and willowy, their pale faces lined with wrinkles. And they were inordinately kind.

Their presence was frightening.

Ethenn hadn't yet had a proper introduction to the parents, which was admittedly intentional. He didn't know if they were aware of his previous relationship with Ilain, but he didn't relish looking Daulton Calder in the eyes, knowing he'd shared a bed with the man's daughter, then jilted her.

Thankfully, Ethenn's work kept him out of any of the Calders' presence for quite some time. He and Brea spent their days with other Warriors and restructuring the military. It was rigorous work. He often felt like he was simply Brea's right hand, running to and from different locations, delivering her messages, or gathering supplies. He didn't mind being her lackey. It was an easy, out-of-the-way job.

Evylin wasn't so lucky. As a Bonded Warrior, she was required to sit in the meetings at Deckard's side, politicking and strategizing. On the few occasions they'd had the chance to share a meal and catch up, she'd lamented how boring it all was. "I wish I could train with you and the others," she said.

Ethenn didn't blame her. All eleven Alliance Warriors had escaped Blount's attack. Half had come to Ephria, while the others remained in Wauld to secure the government there. Emmaas joined them in Ephria, helping to train the new soldiers.

The Warriors worked as a seamless team. General Waaver commanded the troops, managing them and creating new orders within the rule of Allund. New officers were named, and letters were sent to the various outposts in Ephria, alerting them of the regime change. The Ephrian Army was no more; they were part of Allund now.

On the fourth morning, Ethenn prepared to join the others in the barracks. The Alliance required him to reside in the palace due to his charge over the Fire Relic. He'd offered it back now that Ilain was awake, but they suggested he continue to carry it. He didn't like it. It made him feel brash and reckless. He was far more reactive with it around his neck. It was troublesome.

But he slipped it over his head again, tucking it beneath his shirt.

As Ethenn buckled his sword belt, there was a knock at his door. Thom stood on the other side. "What are you doing here?" Ethenn asked at the sight of his friend.

For the time being, Thom worked primarily as a liaison between the Ephrian Army and the Allundan military. Though he wasn't a high-ranking officer, his reputation was known due to his assignment to the Order of the King. And he'd been in the service long enough to know who would react favorably to the Alliance's regime and who wouldn't. That meant he and Ethenn often crossed paths but rarely spent time together.

Ethenn didn't like that either.

"We've been summoned," Thom said cheerily. He leaned against the doorframe. "Sounds as though the Administration has got their ducks in a row enough to debrief us now."

Ethenn furrowed his brow. "All of us?"

Thom shrugged. "Sounds that way."

"Ah." Ethenn shoved Thom into the hall. "Lead the way, then."

"We're meeting in the council chamber," Thom said as they walked. "Apparently, the ministers think it's less stuffy than the throne room, but I disagree. I don't like standing at the end of a table while they all prattle on."

"You don't like many things," Ethenn noted.

Thom grinned. "That's true."

They walked in silence for a moment.

"Have you talked with Ilain recently?" Thom asked.

"No," Ethen said flatly.

Thom eyed him. "Why not?"

"There isn't really anything to say."

"That's certainly not true. There are many things to say. 'Hello. How are you? I've missed you. Please, for the love of Allore, take me back.'" Thom smirked. "Would you like more examples?"

Ethenn ignored him.

"You're being an idiot," Thom said.

"I'm being practical," Ethenn argued. "She deserves a life better than marriage to a man she doesn't love."

Thom rolled his eyes. "You're so bloody blind," he muttered. "All right, look, I promised to fix this, so I'm gonna fix it." He grabbed Ethenn's sleeve, pulling him to a stop. "What I said after the Time Keep—it was a lie. I thought you'd figured that out, but it seems you haven't. Ilain didn't ask me to flirt with her because she didn't have an interest in you—it was because she *did*."

Ethenn frowned at the confusing words. "What?"

Thom nodded vehemently. "Ilain liked you, evidently from the start. But she couldn't be with someone who wasn't a Warrior, so she tried to discourage you so neither of you would get your hearts broken. Convoluted, I know, but true."

Staring up at his friend, Ethenn considered his words. There was no reason for Thom to keep lying. What he said was what he understood to be the truth. Ilain genuinely had feelings for Ethenn from the beginning—or at least, an attraction to him.

The sudden revelation sent a spiral of heat up his spine.

Ilain liked him—she'd had an interest in him. Yet, she'd denied them both because she was too dedicated to the Alliance. The truth hardly made it better.

With a low scoff, Ethenn decided it wasn't enough. "It's too late," he said. "If she had said something sooner, maybe things would be different, but . . ."

"But what?" Thom said irritably. "She likes you; you like her. Go find that woman, haul her into a room, and make her your wife for real."

Ethenn gave him a flat glare. "We're not betrothed anymore," he said. "And beyond that, I don't want to be with her."

"Why the bloody hell not?"

"Because whatever she felt, I'm not the right man," Ethenn said. "If she's going to spend her life ruling this country, she needs someone who can rule at her side. I'd muck it up."

Thom raised his brow. "As the reigning champion of muck-ups, I can guarantee that you won't. It's not in your blood."

"Hedonistic rat."

Ethenn shut out the voice of his uncle and turned down the hall, ignoring Thom's encouragement.

When they arrived at the council chamber, an attendant opened the door and nodded respectfully. The vaulted ceilings and large windows created a sense of spaciousness, and morning light flooded in, keeping the space bright.

The ministers were already seated at the table. Eight men and eight women of all ages, complexions, and stations. They greeted the two men with welcoming smiles. Though Ethenn had spent the last four days around them, he still couldn't remember all their names.

Deckard and Evylin were also there, along with Brea. They all shared greetings, and Thom stepped up to Brea's side. "Morning, *bon'florá*," he quipped.

She raised her brow disapprovingly. "Did you just call me 'pretty flower'?"

He shrugged. "I'm workshopping. The Schonese don't have a word for 'dryad.'"

"That's because we don't believe in fairy stories," she said. "Try again."

"As you say, *pel'dagas*."

Brea rolled her eyes.

Standing on Thom's other side, Ethenn glanced around the room. The ministers were talking casually among themselves, plates of pastries and cups of tea before some of them. A servant offered the soldiers cups as well. Brea and Ethenn alone accepted— he needed the wakeful power of the olifera leaf in the traditional Ephrian blend. Evylin declined but requested some of the pastries, to which Thom and Brea seconded the request.

Shortly after, the door opened again. Vayden stepped in first. He wore a brown coat with a calluna flower pinned over his left breast—the symbol of mourning in the moors of Wauld. He was clean-shaven and pulled together, but the dark circles remained beneath his eyes.

His daughter, Reyana, had come to Ephria along with her grandparents. From Ethenn's understanding, father and daughter spent most of their time together. However, the girl was not with him that morning.

Instead, Ilain walked in after her brother. The bright light streaming through the windows lit up her fiery hair. As striking as ever, she wore a pale blue dress embroidered all along the bodice with golden beads. The sleeves draped down to flow with the soft skirt. She, too, wore a calluna affixed to her gown. Yet, she carried her chin high, showing no other signs of her state of mourning.

Ethenn looked away before she could catch him staring.

"Good morning," the woman at the head of the table said. Archminister Essen of Ephria was a pretty older woman with dark skin and light chestnut eyes. Her silver-shot black hair coiled tightly like a halo around her head. "Thank you all for joining us. Though we wish it were under more joyful circumstances, I'm afraid we have matters of state to attend to."

Ethenn straightened. Matters of state. What a bizarre thing for him—the Slayer of Trollenston—to be involved in.

"Presently," Archminister Essen continued, "the countries once known as Wauld and Ephria are in shambles. This is to be expected in an overthrow of monarchies. However, we had hoped to be better prepared for the timing of such events. As King Blount II chose to murder his father along with the Ephrian royal bloodline, the kingdoms have since been thrown into upheaval."

The archminister informed them about all matters across the continent. Ephria posed a simpler challenge since they were already within the palace after the fall of the Ephren reign. Restoring the Allundan rule was straightforward with the previous leadership removed. However, they expected to spend several months uniting the nobles, mending relationships with them, and ensuring the military received appropriate orders.

Given their intention to divide the rulership into four provinces on the country's eastern side, it should not pose significant challenges to restoring peace. However, such a governmental modification would only be implemented upon achieving more effective control over Wauld, which presented its own challenges.

The neighboring country was in turmoil. Following the assassination of the first King Blount, the attempted seizure of Ephria, and King Blount II's subsequent death, true authority was absent in the nation. Blount's son, Rouland III, was not yet two years old and was the designated heir. Since Blount's death had occurred just four days ago and the news was just reaching the palace, the royal family remained largely unaware of how to handle the overthrow in their own country. A few Alliance members still held positions within the government, managing to keep the nation stable while preventing any but the Alliance from regaining power. Yet, this arrangement was highly volatile.

"Therefore," the Waulden archminister, Dudleye, said, "we need to provide new authority as we establish the Allundan government within the western half of our continent."

Archminister Essen smiled brightly. "Highlady Calder and Corporal Loxley, we would like you to be our official delegates for this task." Ethenn's stomach dropped as the woman continued, "Which means we shall perform your wedding and Bonding ceremonies immediately."

Realizing for the first time that no one had informed the Alliance of their broken betrothal, Ethenn stared open-mouthed, unsure how to break the news. His face heated. Surely, Ilain should do it. She had worked with them for far longer. She was likely friends with many of the ministers. In fact, her parents were sitting just to Ethenn's left.

But what if she didn't? This was the perfect opportunity for her to force him to follow through or else make a fool of himself in front of the governors of their new country.

"Forgive me, Archminister," Ilain said, her melodic accent filling the room. "I'm afraid that won't be possible."

An awkward silence passed as the sixteen ministers looked from Ilain to Ethenn to each other and back. Daulton and Rowana Calder looked greatly confused, scanning Ethenn with pointed uncertainty.

He shifted uncomfortably as Archminister Dudleye said, "I'm afraid I don't understand. Edmaund, Allore rest his soul, informed us of your betrothal. He marked your marriage to be officiated upon the reestablishment of Allund or in a year's time, whichever came first. Allund is being established, and we'd like to complete the wedding."

Ethenn could practically feel the other troop members holding their breaths.

"Yes, that was the arrangement," Ilain said calmly. She held her shoulders back and her head high and didn't so much as glance at Ethenn once. "However, we came to a mutual decision to end our betrothal."

Ethenn tried not to react to that statement, but the Fire Relic around his neck flared. *Mutual?* It hadn't been mutual. She'd fought him every step of the way. So why wasn't she fighting now?

Baffled and somewhat irritated, Ethenn heard himself huff.

The entire room turned to him.

Body flushing molten hot, Ethenn dipped his head.

"Was there something you wished to add, Corporal Loxley?" one of the ministers asked.

When he looked up, Ethenn realized it was Rowana Calder, her knowing gaze darting between him and her daughter.

Forcing himself not to squirm, Ethenn shook his head. "No, ma'am," he said deferentially.

Thom jabbed him in the ribs, and Ethenn glared up at him but held his tongue.

While the ministers still appeared bemused, Archminister Dudleye turned back to Ilain. "Very well. As you know, Highlady Calder, the position of Chancellor of Doorstunds Reach is dependent upon your Bonding. We would still like *you* to take that role." He raised his bushy white brows. "There are eleven other Warriors within our organization. You may choose to marry any of them, and they would readily accept."

A hush fell over the room, and Ethenn's stomach twisted. *Don't do it,* he thought. If she married any of them, it would be as bad as marrying him. She didn't love them. She didn't want them. And he couldn't fathom her living life in such a resigned state.

Ethenn's hands began to tremble, so he clasped them behind his back. His eyes darted toward Ilain, finding a sad smile on her face. "I'm afraid, Archminister, that I can't do that."

Her words failed to penetrate Ethenn's brain. She was . . . refusing?

"I appreciate your nomination and support, but I don't want it," Ilain concluded. "Not at the price it will cost me."

Ethenn gaped at her. She was *refusing* the position. Why?

Thom slugged Ethenn's arm then, and he grunted. The entire room turned to face him again.

Ethenn cleared his throat but kept his head down.

Taking pity on him, Archminister Essen spoke. "We are admittedly disappointed, Highlady," she said, and Thom poked Ethenn's side. "But we accept your choice. We shall send word to those in the west to instate Highlord Grey Trumane and Captain Alma Maarsh as the new Highlord Chancellor and Highlady Commander of Verlund Province."

Another prodding from Thom.

Ethenn sent him a glare but otherwise ignored him.

"They will then be sent to Mouroc to facilitate the expansion of Allund. Should you be so willing, we'd like you to travel to join them. As to our eastern governing—"

"Are you bloody insane?" Thom burst out at last.

The ministers froze, staring at them.

"Not you," Thom said, waving a hand at the men and women at the table. He whirled on Ethenn. "What is wrong with you?"

Under normal circumstances, Ethenn might have been wise enough not to rise to the bait. But he was wearing the Fire Relic, so to hell with decorum. "I'm not the one with the problem," Ethenn shouted back. "You jab me again, and you'll have a broken finger."

"Oh, stop being a sodding twit." Thom shoved him then—not hard but strong enough to cause Ethenn to shuffle. "You heard what she just said, and you're *still* going to coddle your ego?"

"Thom," Deckard called under his breath.

Thom brushed his brother off. "He needs to grow up," he said.

A caustic laugh slipped out of Ethenn. "Congratulations, Thom. You've discovered a new level of hypocrisy," he retorted.

"Oh-ho! I'm in awe of your cutting wit," Thom said dryly. "Do you mind taking two seconds to think through what she just said?"

Ethenn glared at his friend. "I don't need two seconds. I heard her clearly. She's refusing the position because she—" He paused, realizing specifically what she'd said. He leaned around Thom, taking in Ilain, who stood there, lips parted and eyes darting between the men with uncertainty.

"Hang on," Ethenn said, taking a step forward. He pointed at Ilain. "What price?"

Ilain blinked, her jade green gaze vibrant in the light. An uncharacteristic nervous laugh slipped out of her. "We can discuss this later," she said.

"No, we can discuss it now. What price?" Ethenn pressed with undue confidence.

"Ethenn—"

"Ilain, answer the bloody question."

She blinked. "I think you need to give someone else the Fire Relic."

"And I think you need to stop deflecting," he returned. "What did you mean?"

Ilain opened her mouth, but no words came out. She fidgeted uncomfortably, her fluttery sleeves rippling around her with each movement. "I would rather not discuss this in front of . . ." Her hand gestured wildly at the ministers.

"You're the one who brought it up in front of . . ." He waved his hand in a mocking of her gesture.

Ilain curled her upper lip at him. "And you ignored it until Thom pestered you."

"I'm a little slow sometimes," Ethenn said truthfully. He tipped his chin toward her. "Tell me what you meant. What price aren't you willing to pay?"

Ilain took a step back as though she were afraid of him. Her beaded dress glittered, its pale blue like the faded sky on a clear winter day. "I . . ." Ilain's voice was almost soundless as she fought for words. "It's you."

Ethenn's brow drew together, the Fire Relic stirring the emotions inside of him. It was him. He was the price she wouldn't pay. But . . . "What does that mean?"

A gentle smile came to Ilain's lips. "I think you know."

"Pretend I don't."

She chuckled lightly. "I can't become the Highlady Chancellor," she said. "Not if it means marrying someone else."

Ethenn blinked as her words sank in. "Hm."

Her brow quirked. "Hm?"

"Mm-hm." Ethenn drew in a long breath. "So you won't marry someone else because you meant it. I didn't believe you, but you—you did; you meant it that night?"

A faint blush swept across her pale skin. "I did."

"You love me?"

"I do."

"That's . . ." He heaved a sigh. "That's bloody fantastic." Immediately, Ethenn turned to the ministers. "Is our betrothal still valid?"

An air of collective confusion swept over the room. The ministers cast fleeting glances at each other while their friends tried to stifle their laughter. Archminister Essen and Archminister Dudleye shared a knowing look.

"As we were only now informed that you wished to end it, the contract still remains, which means that, yes, you are legally betrothed," Dudleye said.

"Ilain is my wife?" Ethenn asked, pointing toward her.

"Yes."

"Great." Ethenn shuffled on his feet, fighting the urge to let out a whoop of joy. "In that case, Ilain and I would like to be married and Bonded without delay, as previously discussed. You lot figure out the paperwork and details to perform both of those ceremonies tonight, and you can send us wherever the hell you like after that. In the meantime, my wife and I have some things to, uh . . . take care of."

Without bothering to wait for their reply, Ethenn strode across the room, grabbed Ilain's hand, and pulled her out the door before anyone else could get out a word. He marched her through the halls, trying to remember which path would get them back to his room the fastest.

"You really need to give that Relic to someone else," Ilain said, breaking through his concentration. "You're starting to become dangerously impetuous."

"Admittedly, four days with it has weakened my threshold for caution," he quipped.

"But as we're going to Bond in somewhere around twelve hours, I'm not sure it matters much."

Ilain tugged on his arm, forcing him to a stop beside her. "Ethenn," she wore a look of awe, "are you sure?"

"You love me?" he asked.

Her expression softened tenderly. "Yes."

"For how long?"

"Truly?" She shrugged, causing her sleeves to flutter like flowers in the breeze. Her fingers brushed his forearms. "When you told me about these."

Realizing she meant his scars, he furrowed his brow. "Why—?"

"I loved you before then, I'm sure, but it was at that moment I realized that I would give up anything—" She gripped his hands, pulling them to her chest. "*Anything* to see you happy."

And she had, Ethenn understood. She'd willingly rejected the Alliance and the future she'd prepared for the last thirty years . . . for him.

Ethenn kissed her then. Deep and full. The Fire Relic burned against his chest with excitement, but his magic sent a cooling spiral through his veins. Ilain returned the kiss, still clutching his hands as though desperately afraid to let him go.

Drawing back, Ethenn tugged her closer. "I'm sorry," he said immediately. "I was a fool. The things I said—"

"You didn't know." Ilain's gaze was soft. "And you were right. The whole time I've known you, I've been trying to protect myself by manipulating you and lying to you. That's why I pushed you to seal our betrothal before we were ready." Her voice dipped lower. "*I* was the fool, Ethenn. From the moment we met, I knew you were different. And I feared that my heart would attach itself to you, so I pushed you away. Then you turned out to be a Warrior, and I knew you wouldn't believe me . . . So I tried to convince you of my affection without ever being vulnerable enough to tell you the truth."

Seeing the glimmer of tears in her eyes, Ethenn's chest tightened. They stood along a walkway under the light of a large window, in full view of the palace. He supposed he ought not to be concerned since he'd just kissed her, but he thought this conversation should be held somewhere less public.

Swiftly, Ethenn drew Ilain through the hallways, down the final few curves toward his bedroom. There, he shut them in, drawing her toward the small settee that sat against the wall. He guided her to sit, though the flickering urges of the Fire Relic kept him standing.

"Ilain," he began, flexing his hands at his sides, "whatever the path before us, I want you to know now: I'm not a good man. I've made numerous mistakes, I'm prone to violence, and I refuse to trust people because I've been hurt too many times. But I don't want to be that man anymore."

And so, Ethenn told Ilain about his past. He told her about his parents, Fredrik and Leannah, and his sister, Terrina. He didn't leave out any details of their family life or their upbringing. He didn't hesitate to tell her about Vernon and his abuse, the years spent in the fighting pits, or the accidental murder of his fellow fighter. He explained Terrina's marriage, his presumed killing of her husband, and his subsequent volunteering to become a soldier to escape the wrath of the law.

He trusted her with everything because he didn't want to be a weapon any longer, and he thought perhaps Deckard was right: Ilain could make him better. The true Ilain Calder, the gentle, reserved, and tender woman she was within, was perfectly suited to quell the fire within him purely with her love.

And with everything in him, he hoped that his loyalty, determination, and ferocity might make her feel safe and cared for enough to become that woman in full.

CHAPTER FIFTY-NINE

38TH OF HYDRAE, 1574

One month had passed since the establishment of Allund.

After Ethenn and Ilain's offhanded acceptance of the position in Mouroc to help facilitate the government's control on the western half of the continent and their abrupt departure from the council chamber, the Administration had requested Deckard and Evylin do the same there in Loclight.

"It will be temporary," Archminister Essen assured. "We have much to do to gain the faith of the people. We feel that with your assistance, we can accomplish it well."

They were granted time to confer, but they didn't need it. After the first four days, Deckard and Evylin had seen this request coming and chose to accept it. As Thom had said, someone had to ensure the country gained good, honorable leaders. Deckard could help with that process as they worked alongside the Alliance. And he could determine for himself just how truly noble they were.

And there was the promise of the short-term nature of the assignment. "A month or two at the most," Essen said.

Ethenn and Ilain's wedding and Bonding ceremony marked a turning point for the troop. For the first time in months, they were to part. The newlywedded Loxley couple, along with Vayden and Reyana, would return to Wauld—now West Allund—while the Deckards and Brea remained in Ephria—now East Allund. Due to their Bonds, the couples were given charge over the Relics of their halves of the continent, four and four. It was the natural choice, though they required Thom and Vayden to carry the extra three

Relics as a guard against the influence of the Warriors' and Mages' dispositions. That meant that the Bonded couples also became a sort of bodyguard to the non-magical men.

"See," Ilain teased Thom when the announcement was made. "You are special, after all."

With the choice of delegates made, the Alliance requested that Brea stay with Evylin to continue her training and help reform the Eastern Army. She accepted without hesitation.

Deckard and Evylin spent much of the following days with the ministers, Carlile, and Obel, determining East Allund's next steps. There was plenty to figure out within the palace's halls and in the capital city, so they started a running list of tasks to complete during their first days as delegates.

Two days after Ethenn and Ilain's Bonding, which allowed them time to celebrate their marriage, the troop came together for a final dinner before the West Allund party headed to Mouroc the following morning. It was already evident that the marriage had positively influenced the couple. Ethenn's demeanor shifted significantly. In the short span of time, he'd become more confident and expressive, speaking up more often— though his contributions were still less than most people in the room, it was a notable improvement for him. Ilain also seemed more self-assured. While she continued to joke and maintain her playful nature, a composed and thoughtful sense of self began to moderate her previously flippant and unpredictable behaviors.

The two of them worked well together, their internal flames easing each other, providing a safety of heart where each could truly be themselves. This convinced Deckard that he was correct in Olbury—Ethenn and Ilain did need each other, and their lives would be better with one another in them.

In the morning, Ethenn and Ilain departed alongside the western ministers, Vayden, and Obel, taking the Fire, Night, Wind, and Time Relics with them. It felt strange to watch them leave, and Deckard sensed immediate sorrow radiating from Evylin. Just the night before, she had confided in him that she didn't want them to go. They had become family to her, especially after discovering that Ethenn was her true cousin. She couldn't bear to part with them, fearing they might not meet again for a long time.

Deckard felt similarly. After leaving his family nearly thirteen years ago to travel with the Ephrian Army, he was accustomed to saying goodbye. This felt different, like a piece of who they were was going away with the Loxleys.

Deckard perceived another unspoken inner turmoil within Evylin. Since Blount's death and the true beginning of their Alliance work, she exhibited signs of a deepening depression. Initially, he attributed it to the aftermath of months of battles and loss. However, he saw how she watched Thom, Ethenn, and Brea interacting with each other and the soldiers over the weeks. She wasn't disappointed or dejected; she felt confined.

At that moment, Deckard asked to meet with Archminister Essen and pushed for a return to their home. Having spent considerable time in the palace, he recognized that escaping the Alliance's unrelenting scrutiny would allow Evylin to feel liberated once more.

Essen disapproved of removing the Day, Water, Terrae, and Space Relics from the palace but consented upon Deckard's prolonged insistence. As the palace was set to become the Order of the Heavens, he proposed repurposing it now. She agreed and began clearing unnecessary people from the halls with Carlile's help to develop Allund and the Order. This led to Thom returning home as well and Brea relocating to the barracks.

During the subsequent month, Allund gradually evolved into a stable yet deliberate government. Understandably, individuals in both the East and West expressed their dissent. The nobility in the West voiced their grievances due to the loss of their privileges. Conversely, the Alliance garnered widespread support among the general populace, who embraced the alteration in government. Consequently, the Western faction redirected its efforts toward identifying collaborators and potential replacements while striving to avert further conflict.

The situation in the East presented a stark contrast. A greater number of nobles were informed about the Alliance than the general populace, attributable to Carlile's initiatives among the upper echelons of society. This approach effectively facilitated the establishment of new governmental policies and procedures; however, it inadvertently resulted in a pervasive sense of discontent among the commonwealth. This unrest was particularly exacerbated by the increasing prevalence of negative suggestions regarding the influence of Mages and the practice of magic governing their territory.

Recognizing the growing struggle, the Alliance decided to address the issue through the cultivation of personal relationships. They dispatched Deckard and Evylin as ambassadors, accompanied by Thom and a few others. First, they traveled to Norhels and met with various magistrates en route.

During their first day within the port city, Deckard led Evylin through the streets with purpose. "Where are we going?" she asked curiously.

"I have something to pick up," he said.

He brought her to a small stable, where a young man was in the process of reshoeing a horse. He looked up on their arrival, asking them to wait a moment before finishing his task and stepping forward.

"What can I do for you?" the man asked, wiping his hands on his apron.

"Good afternoon," Deckard said, holding out a folded receipt. "I'm Colonel Deckard, and I boarded my horse here a while back on the provision that she might be rented out for labor. I'd like to reclaim her."

At his side, Evylin smirked but remained silent as the young man reviewed the receipt. "I'm just the hand," he said once he'd inspected the note, "but I'll get my boss to confirm, and we'll get your horse back to you in a jiffy."

Once all was in order, the farrier brought the sleek black mare to his side. Despite the months apart, she readily recognized him, whinnying gently as he stroked her neck. "It's good to see you again, girl," he whispered fondly.

As they left the farrier, Evylin crossed her arms, eyeing her husband with amusement. "Are you finally going to tell me her real name?" she teased.

Deckard grinned. "I told you before: The hostler named her Calyn."

Evylin rolled her eyes. "The moment we get back to Loclight . . ."

"I'll lead you to him myself," he promised.

While establishing the Order of the Day in Norhels, they assured the public that Mages weren't evil, power-hungry villains, and Warriors were more than mere legends. After several days of working with the Alliance in the city, they returned to Olbury to complete the same task. At each of their stops, they encountered a predictable mixture of goodwill and skepticism. Some individuals were more quickly persuaded, while others remained entirely resistant. Nevertheless, they collectively regarded the experience as a success.

Evylin quite enjoyed the return to travel. Though she regularly lamented the loss of Ethenn and Ilain, Deckard could sense her renewed joy as they journeyed through the country again, particularly when they passed through Whickam Village on their way to Virwoud.

The Glaas family was shocked to learn of Evylin and Deckard's magical abilities. Lawton seemed skeptical at first but readily accepted the new course of things.

"Are you to be our new king and queen, then?" the magistrate asked with ready pride in his gaze as though it was *his* will that brought Deckard and Evylin together in the first place.

"No," Deckard said immediately. "We are soldiers, facilitating the government's establishment only."

"Besides," Evylin added in a lighthearted tone, "there won't be any kings or queens in Allund."

"What else could there be?" Calyn asked, her dark eyes curious as she listened.

"Allund is an oligarchal democracy," Deckard explained. "We will be called a republic. During our conversations, the ministers informed us that there are to be eight provinces governed by chancellors and commanders—one Mage and one Warrior per province. It will work almost like a fief where the governors will supervise the land and its people, but they will work for the people rather than for the government."

Calyn blinked, then turned to Thom beside her. "Do you understand that?" she asked.

Thom shook his head, an amused grin on his lips. "Not really," he admitted.

They stayed an extra three days in Whickam Village. It was a welcome reprieve, though Deckard had to admit he grew bored with the humdrum life rather more quickly than he expected. Evylin couldn't sit still either, adding to his anticipation of their departure. They were intending to travel to Virwoud next on the same mission, facilitating the reconstruction of the Order of the Sea. However, they received a summons from the Alliance, calling them back to Loclight early.

While the magistrates of East Allund would still need time to accept the new reign, the country as a whole was flourishing under the assistance of the noblemen and women who were already on the Alliance's side, and the work in Norhels was moving more swiftly than they anticipated.

On their last day in Whickam Village, Deckard—urged by Evylin—persuaded Lawton to let Calyn accompany them on their return journey. After much cajoling, Deckard managed to convince the magistrate that his daughter would have better odds of finding a husband in the city than in their tiny village. And it helped that Thom was paying the young Glaas daughter kind attention. Guiltily, Deckard even allowed himself to hint that Thom might be more amenable to marriage if he had time to fall in love with the girl.

Lawton assented.

When Deckard asked Evylin why she wanted her sister to join them so much, she said, "Because Calyn is growing up. You can see it in the way she acts and in the way she listens to our conversations. She *wants* to understand."

"And you don't think that's just because she wants Thom's attention?" he pressed.

Evylin gave him a knowing smile. "She wrote to me, Jonn. After our last visit, she sent me a letter in Loclight telling me how, for the last several months, she's discovered that there's more to life than this village. When I left with you, she began a journey of self-reflection. She isn't the same as me; she doesn't long for adventure. But she does want more."

"More of what?"

"Life."

And though Deckard was apprehensive, he understood Calyn's desire. Even more, he was glad to make Evylin happy. After everyone she'd lost, either to death or the demands of the Alliance, the companionship of her sister cheered her up. She fostered Calyn's growth and exploration of the world while taking comfort in her more simplistic view of life.

Over the next week, they returned to Loclight. No longer the capital of Ephria, the Allundan banners of white and black embroidered with eight stars—four gold and four silver—hung on the wall. Soldiers casually patrolled the streets in light gray coats. Merchants sold books about Mages, and a few had managed to find tales about Warriors. The citizens had recovered from the siege, calling out praise as they rode through the streets. Everything Ephrian was done away, and only Allund remained.

"This is incredible," Calyn muttered, staring in awe as they passed over the cobblestones. "I've never seen such large buildings. Or so many people."

Evylin smiled. "Just wait until you see the palace."

Calyn's jaw dropped at the mere thought.

"Don't gape," Thom teased. "No husband will claim you if you look like a fish."

Her mouth shut with a click of her teeth, and she blushed.

"Ignore him," Deckard advised kindly. "He's prone to exaggeration."

"Though gaping isn't very ladylike," Evylin said.

As Deckard rode to the barracks to return their horses, he sensed Allund's increasing influence. After Blount's annihilation of the army within the city, it required a great effort to regain a military presence. To the great sorrow of Evylin's family, Lieutenant Druan Silvaa, the husband of their eldest daughter, was caught in Blount's attack. He died defending the city, leaving Euna a widow and her five daughters without a father. Deckard was saddened by the news as well, remembering the kind man and wishing he might have come to know his brother-in-law better.

However, with the war concluded, most Ephrian soldiers were granted the choice to return home or sign new contracts and join the Allundan Army. Consequently, fewer soldiers occupied the barracks, and Sergeant Maac Byan, the husband of Evylin's sister, Albina, was able to return to his wife and daughters. Despite the losses, the army was under the steady hand of the Warriors from the Alliance. While several Warriors embarked on missions across the East, three stayed in the city to manage the soldiers.

Those three were easily noticeable when they entered the barracks' courtyard. Soldiers in the Allundan Army donned gray coats, while Warriors sported black. This color distinction quickly highlighted those with magical abilities and, therefore, greater authority.

As General Waaver conversed with another non-magical officer on the walkway above, Colonel Reid and Brea, recently promoted to captain, sparred below. Reid had quickly established himself as a true friend in the brief time they knew him. He was accommodating and respectful, yet an underlying hint of danger led one to wonder if he was always up to something. Despite both appearing to be in their late twenties, they learned that Reid was actually fourteen years older than Brea. His well-groomed black hair, stout build, and piercing gray eyes struck Deckard as a mixture of Thom and Hewitt upon their first meeting. However, Reid was the traditionally short Easterner. Surprisingly, he exhibited a unique personality that combined Deckard's composed friendliness with Rafferty's playful spirit and sense of adventure. An unexpected blend if ever there was one.

As their horses' hooves clacked through the courtyard, Brea glanced in their direction, giving Reid the chance to disarm her. However, she didn't give up; instead, she opted to drop low and sweep his legs while he anticipated her surrender. Thom applauded as Calyn watched with wide-eyed wonder.

The two Warriors hurried over to greet them as they dismounted. "That," Thom said, slapping Reid on the shoulder, "was a sloppy finish, my friend. Aren't colonels supposed to be better than that?"

"She cheated," Reid replied, giving Brea a mock frown. "Disarmed is disqualified."

"And losers rely on qualifications to justify their loss," Brea said, then shoved him aside to hug Evylin. "Thank Allore, you are back. No place has the right to be so boring."

"Boring? This place is magnificent!" Calyn exclaimed, stepping up to Evylin's side.

"Oh," Brea gasped at the young woman's sudden appearance. She glanced at Thom before turning back to Calyn. "I didn't realize you were coming to Loclight, Calyn."

"It's a pleasure to see you again, Brea," Calyn said with a tiny curtsy. "Evie and Deckard were kind enough to let me stay with them for a while."

"How nice," Brea muttered, though it didn't sound sincere.

"It's good to be back," Deckard said, shaking hands with both Warriors. "Have we missed much the past four weeks?"

"Not too much, Colonel," Reid replied, standing tall with his shoulders back. Despite not being an official member of the Allundan Army yet—his new contract still pending—Deckard was permitted to retain his rank. "There have been a few young recruits causing trouble lately and some attempts to incite a rebellion among the rabble, but overall, the city is functioning well."

"Count on Reid to focus on the negative," Brea teased before adding, "We've had half of the Ephrian troops sign their Allundan contracts throughout the East, and about two-thirds of those remaining have returned home. We're still waiting for word from the rest. However, things are going well, and we've received a positive response from the current officers regarding the change in command."

Brea turned to Thom. "Which reminds me," she smirked, "I'm afraid your rank has been revoked, as you haven't signed your Allundan contract yet."

"Forgive me," Thom mocked. "But I haven't been offered an Allundan contract."

"I believe it's sitting on General Waaver's desk if you'd like to sign it."

"I'd be honored," he replied. "Did I get a promotion, too, Captain?"

Brea's eyes twinkled merrily. "Of a sort."

Thom narrowed his gaze suspiciously. "What sort?"

Reid clapped him on the arm. "Ah, don't worry, friend. Your contract is ready for signing, and you're back to military life as a major."

It took a moment for the words to register before Thom stammered, "A major? I don't want to be a training officer!"

Reid and Brea exchanged proud grins. "I told you he'd fall for it," she said.

The colonel sighed good-naturedly, then fished out a silver coin and placed it in Brea's waiting palm. "Don't spend it all in one place," he quipped.

"It was a joke?" Thom asked.

Evylin chuckled and slipped her arm through Calyn's. "Come on," she said, gesturing to the others. "We ought to get home."

"Don't we need to get our things?" Calyn asked.

"Nah," Thom grumbled. "These idiots will send our things once they've unloaded."

"But not yours," Brea said slyly. "As you're no longer a soldier, I'm afraid you'll have to pick it up yourself."

Thom reached across the small space between them, tugging Brea into a hug. It was typical for them to engage in playful or platonic touches, like nudges or gentle pats. They often rested their arms on each other's chairs or leaned in to share whispers. However, wrapping his arms around her and pulling her tightly against his chest was a level of affection Deckard was unaccustomed to witnessing.

Deckard also sensed Brea's surprise at their unexpected closeness. Cautiously, she wrapped her arms around Thom's waist, her forehead pressing against his chin awkwardly. In the past month, Deckard hadn't noticed any romantic growth between his brother and the Warrior, and, having spent most of that time apart, he chose not to question Thom about it. His brother tended to overthink his emotions, and Deckard understood how much his friendship with Brea mattered to him. Deckard wanted to avoid presuming any infatuation or romance where it was unwarranted.

However, as Thom and Brea's embrace lasted just a bit longer than what would typically be deemed socially acceptable, Deckard worried he might need to have a conversation with his brother after all.

As though recognizing the uncomfortable situation he'd put them in, Thom backed up and cleared his throat. He gave Brea's shoulder a smack with a terse, "It's good to see you again, *dulá*." Then he pushed past her to walk toward the gate.

Brea turned to Deckard and Evylin in confusion.

"Don't ask me," Deckard said dryly. He grinned at both Brea and Reid. "We'll see you both tomorrow, I'm sure."

"Oh, Colonel," Reid said before they could turn away.

"Please, call me 'Deckard.'"

"I don't think I should."

"You should," Evylin said. "What did you need?"

"Lord Carlile requested I inform you," Reid explained. "The Administration wishes to meet with you first thing tomorrow."

Deckard shared a look with Evylin. "Yes, their letter said they'd want a debriefing of the trip."

Reid shook his head. "Things have changed. It's to be an official meeting on behalf of Allund. They want Captains Deckard and Lohen there too."

Tension coiled in Deckard's chest. Though the country was thriving even without an official ruling system, it couldn't continue indefinitely. Decisions were already delayed, and without a clear chain of command, progress was stalling. The Alliance was prepared to advance to the next phase of their plans. They would attempt to impose the roles of commander and chancellor on Evylin and him, leaving them with no alternatives. The archminister would frame it in such a way that refusing the position would be akin to rejecting the best interests of their countrymen.

However, after witnessing Evylin's decline within the palace and the pressure they faced, Deckard vowed to himself that they wouldn't accept. He would refuse the position, even if it compromised his principles.

Deckard thanked Reid for the update and made an effort to ensure his farewell didn't come off as curt or hostile. He trailed Thom through the gate, guiding Evylin and Calyn back home. Upon their return, Thom got busy preparing a meal while Deckard heated water for everyone to clean up. Their belongings, including Thom's, arrived quickly, giving them a clear task for the evening: namely, unpacking. Deckard appreciated having something to do with his hands while he mulled over the upcoming meeting.

Evylin noticed his irritation, as she always did lately, but she kindly chose not to press him when he offered excuses to avoid the conversation. Instead, she wrapped up her unpacking, gave him a sweet kiss on the cheek, and headed off to help Calyn settle in.

With her away, Deckard's thoughts spiraled irrationally. He worried that his conscience wouldn't allow him to refuse the Alliance. If they played on his sense of duty, could he deny them? And what if Evylin changed her mind? If she reconsidered and determined that she wanted to rule, he couldn't refuse her.

Deckard's frustrations grew during the hour he spent carefully unpacking, rearranging, and bathing. He was meticulous while shaving, even defining the hairline at the back of his neck. To Evylin's dismay, he'd resumed shaving after the reinstatement of Allund. If he were to work as an official of a nation, he believed he should appear as professional and respectable as possible.

His eyes were drawn to the Space Relic resting on the bed as he dressed after his bath. Ever since their appointment as ambassadors of Allund, the Alliance had requested that Deckard wear the Relic visibly. They claimed it would establish him as a Mage in the eyes of the people and help dispel any fear surrounding their kind. This assignment made him uneasy. Occasionally, he still felt a nagging desire to use his power, and while he had come to master its pull, that did not make him any more comfortable with the weight of responsibility it represented to him.

More than anything, Deckard longed to be a soldier again. He wanted the Allundan Army to offer him a contract so he could resume his role as an officer. Being a Mage was exhausting. Politicking was taxing. He yearned to return to insignificance, to fade into obscurity now that their mission was complete.

Deckard slipped the Space Relic over his head, tucking the cold metal pendant beneath his tunic. He didn't care if the Alliance wanted him to appear as an elite Mage. He was home. He would allow himself one night off.

Adopting a better mood, Deckard went down to dinner. Together, Thom and Evylin had finished their preparations for the meal. They all sat around the table, said their prayer over the food, and began to answer Calyn's many questions about the city, the Alliance, their previous travels, and life outside of Whickam Village.

Deckard found himself pleasantly bemused during dinner. With Evylin by his side and Thom and Calyn across from them, it was like they were a real family. He finally had the dream he'd always wanted: a wife he loved, a good relationship with his brother, and the hope of a happy future.

Deckard smiled at the thought. He realized that no matter what came or the pressures the Alliance placed on them, he could be happy because he had his family.

As the meal continued, Deckard watched Thom and Calyn carefully. His brother hadn't indicated again his desire to be with the young woman, though he treated her with far more kindness and consideration than in the past. He didn't think Thom had feelings for Calyn, at least not romantic ones, but perhaps he could learn to.

That thought gave Deckard pause. *Should* Thom learn to love Calyn that way? They would make a handsome couple, that was clear. Thom was dashing with his dark hair and sharp gaze. Calyn was lovely with her demure smile and richly tanned complexion. Now that Thom had overcome his insecurities, he acted with chivalry and grace. As Calyn matured, she bore a new refinement and sensibility. They chatted pleasantly, treating one another with deference and affection. But was their camaraderie a result of attraction? Or was it more platonic in its care?

After witnessing Thom's strange behavior with Brea, Deckard wasn't sure what to think. But he decided he'd better find out the truth.

Rising from the table after dinner, Deckard caught Thom's gaze. "I'm thinking of going out for a drink," he said. "Would you care to join me?"

Thom and Evylin stared at Deckard in shock.

"You want to go to the tavern?" Thom asked.

Deckard nodded. "After all this travel, I'd like to relax."

Thom turned to Evylin, who shrugged.

"All right," Thom said uncertainly. "I could go for a pint."

"Can I come?" Calyn asked, eager. "I've never been to a tavern."

"No," Thom said without hesitation. "It's no place for a lady."

"I've gone many times," Evylin countered.

"You're not a lady," Thom teased.

Deckard could see that Calyn was about to press, so he said, "Forgive us for abandoning you, Calyn. I'd like some time with my brother, as I'm sure you'd appreciate time alone with Evylin."

Calyn's expression shifted with understanding. "Oh, yes." She nodded vehemently. "I understand perfectly. The relationship of a sibling is profoundly important. You're good to desire quality time with your brother."

Evylin pressed her lips together as though holding in a laugh, and Thom rolled his eyes, evidently seeing through Deckard's request.

"Shall we get to it?" Thom said, standing.

Evylin rose to gather the dishes and kissed Deckard's cheek. "Don't stay out too late," she whispered.

Deckard forced his expression to remain stolid. Surreptitiously, he brushed her thigh, hidden by the folds of her skirt. "I won't," he promised, then followed Thom to the door.

CHAPTER SIXTY

Thom

"So," Thom began, sitting in the booth at the back of the tavern, "what did you want to talk about?"

Across from him, Deckard unbuttoned his coat. They both wore street clothes for the first time in months. Since their appointment with the Third Volunteer Company, they'd either been traveling as officers, on their mission, or on Alliance business. It felt good to be out of the rigid military coats and regalia. They'd both forgone cravats, too, making them appear like any other common man. Though Thom could still see the gold chain of the Space Relic peeking through his brother's collar. Thom had left the other Relics with Evylin, thinking them safer in the house than in a tavern.

Deckard thanked the barmaid as she delivered a pint of ale and a glass of wine. "I'd like to know about your intentions," he said without preamble.

Thom pulled a face, lifting his ale. "My intentions," he repeated dramatically. "Don't you sound like a protective father?"

Though Deckard tried to ease his expression, it didn't work. "I'm simply checking in on you," he said. "We haven't spoken in a while, and I'd like to know if you're feeling the same as before."

"Mm." Thom drank the red ale slowly, considering his reply. He looked over the tavern, surveying the soldiers and other patrons. Living in the Military District, taverns were prevalent. Deckard had never frequented them, but Thom had. He had story after story to tell from the raucous evenings spent in their warm walls.

But recently, Thom had no desire to spend time in taverns. They reminded him too much of Rafferty and the friendship he'd lost.

With a sigh, Thom set his pint down. "You mean, do I still wish for mundanity?"

"More or less."

He shrugged. "Yes."

Deckard narrowed his gaze thoughtfully. "What does that look like to you?"

"I'm not sure," he admitted. "Probably soldiering. I'd like to sign my contract if they'd ever bloody offer it to me."

Deckard hummed in agreement as he sipped his wine.

"But," Thom continued, "I'd also like to stay with you and Evie. So whatever that looks like, I'll do it. Aside from that . . . I'd like a family. A wife. Some children. Maybe a dog."

"What kind of dog?"

"One of those Shireland Collies. The black and white ones, with the spots on their noses."

"Ah. They're quite trainable, I've heard."

"Good with kids too." Thom leaned forward. "But you're not interested in dogs, are you?"

Deckard grinned. "Not particularly."

"You want to know if I intend to woo Calyn," Thom surmised.

"I believe you've already wooed her," Deckard said lightly. "I'd like to know if you intend to wed her."

Thom tapped his fingers along the handle of his tankard. He'd asked himself that question many times over the last several weeks. Ever since they'd returned to Whickam Village on their mission to retrieve the Relics and he'd seen her again, he wondered what he felt toward the young woman. She was pretty; that was certain. And she'd changed. She'd matured. He'd come to understand that even better over the last week.

No longer was Calyn Glaas an impetuously-in-love, foolhardy girl. She was still romantic, innocent, and even ignorant, but she also bore a distinct desire to grow. It was charming. And she would make an excellent wife.

But for some reason, Thom couldn't convince himself to want her.

"No," he said. "I don't want to marry her."

Deckard's posture eased as though he'd been holding his breath and could finally let it out. "Good."

Thom scoffed into his ale. "You didn't approve?"

"I told you before," his brother raised his brow, "she's not serious enough for you.

Despite all your sarcasm and flippancy, you feel far deeper than most people. And you need a wife who can understand that."

Thom didn't bother replying.

Deckard shifted, obviously uncomfortable with his next words. He took another sip of wine, then asked, "And what about Brea?"

Thom frowned, meeting his brother's gaze with confusion. "What about her?"

"What are your intentions toward her?"

Struggling to comprehend the catalyst of this question, Thom gaped at Deckard. "I'm rather confused," he said. "Brea and I are friends."

"Perhaps," Deckard said disbelievingly. "But she has admitted feelings for you, hasn't she?"

Thom smashed his lips together. He regretted telling Deckard about that. Though Brea hadn't requested that Thom keep her past with Adie secret, it felt almost like a betrayal to reveal it. And now, Deckard was using it against them.

"Yes, all right?" Thom shook his head. "She had feelings for me. *Before.* But she's also made it perfectly clear that she didn't want those feelings. She made her promise to the Alliance; she intends to Bond with whomever they wish, and what's more, she told me she's talking to a few of them. Through letters mostly, but Highlords Wilkinsone and Grames are both here in Ephria, so she's seen them on occasion. She said Grames has a good sense of humor and darker hair than most Wauldeners, which is a plus for her. Granted, he's apparently about six-foot-five, so they'd have quite the journey to share a kiss."

Thom tried to chuckle at the joke, but the thought of Brea kissing anyone made his stomach pinch.

Deckard noticed. "You like her," he said.

Thom shook his head again. "Not like that."

"No?"

He squirmed under his brother's inspection. "No," he said, then illogically added, "Even if I did, she's moved on."

Deckard's brow quirked. "You know that for a fact?"

He hesitated. "Yes."

"How?"

Thom had no reply.

Deckard wore a knowing grin. "Let's say you're wrong. She does still have feelings for you, and she would abandon her promise to the Alliance to be with you." He set his forearms on the table, clasping his hands. "Would you accept her offer?"

Thom stared at him, mouth clamped tightly shut. He fidgeted with his tankard, tapping an uneven rhythm on the rim. "I don't like this game," he muttered.

Deckard drew in a long, understanding breath. "Right," he murmured, drawing a hand over his mouth.

"Stop," Thom said flatly.

Deckard met his gaze, silent.

With a small, dejected shake of his head, Thom said, "Just . . . stop trying to figure this out, all right? I know nothing can come of it. That's why I'm refusing to accept it. I don't have feelings for her. I can't."

"But you do," Deckard confessed for him.

Thom swallowed, the truth locked deep inside of him. Yes, he had feelings for Brea. If she abandoned her promise to the Alliance in order to be with him, he'd take her in an instant. No one had ever made him feel so seen, so cared for. Not even Deckard.

Breata Lohen was strange. She was blunt, rude, and downright terrifying. But she was also the gentlest soul he'd ever met.

"We can't be together," Thom said quietly. "She's the last single female Warrior in the Alliance. The last in Allund, from what we know. They'd never approve of our marriage, and she wouldn't break her promise to them. I wouldn't ask her to."

Running a hand through his hair, Thom scoffed at his ridiculous desires. "She deserves better than me anyway."

Deckard appraised Thom slowly. It was clear he was trying to deduce the truth behind Thom's words. In Thom's entire life, he'd never had a serious relationship with a woman. He'd chased different girls. He'd even carried on a secret affair with a widow during his time as a sergeant in Worthing, a tiny village in the foothills of Felbourne province. It was a sin he wasn't particularly proud of but had long repented of in the kirk.

But for all his life, Thom had looked for a woman's affection. He thought it would make him whole, that it would fill the void of his insecurities.

He'd come to learn romantic love wasn't enough. He had to be enough for himself first before he could give himself wholly to another.

But he still *wanted* someone to love him. He *wanted* to be enough for her too.

"You're far better and far more worthy than you think."

"Thom," Deckard began cautiously. His brows pinched together, showing his concern. "Do you love Brea?"

Thom took a moment to consider the question. "Are you asking if I love her or if I'm in love with her?"

Deckard tipped his head to the side. "Is the answer different?"

A second passed before Thom nodded.

"Then I'm asking both."

Thom thumbed his nose, took a swig of ale for courage, and said, "Yes, I love her. I want her to be happy with or without me. Whether I'm in love with her is . . . uncertain."

Deckard seemed as puzzled by the answer as Thom felt. "If she weren't a Warrior, would you pursue her?"

Thom chuckled self-derisively. "Ah, but she is a Warrior."

"Pretend she wasn't."

"I can't," Thom said. "That's part of what makes her *her*. It's part of what makes me—" He cut himself off, not ready to be so open yet.

Deckard sighed. "Do you intentionally get yourself into difficult situations, or are such situations inexplicably attracted to you?"

A sour laugh escaped him. "Unfortunately, I think it's a bit of both."

"I see." Deckard sipped his wine, a thoughtful expression across his face, then pronounced, "You're in love with her."

Thom shrugged. "Maybe."

Shaking his head, Deckard grinned kindly. "No, Thom," he insisted. "You *are* in love with Brea. You're willing to sacrifice your happiness to let her have her own. Even if that means you can't be with her."

The truth of the sentiment hit Thom then: He was bloody in love with Breata Lohen. If given the chance, he'd marry her. If she asked, he'd pull down both moons for her.

Thom dropped his face into his hands. "This is shit," he said, the words muffled by his palms.

Deckard chuckled. "This is love," he said. "It hurts, but it's worth it."

"Is it?" Thom demanded, hands dropping to the table. "If you're you, then fine, sure, it's worth it. Everything you and Evie went through hurt, but you ended up together. Love was worth the pain because, in the end, you're together. But what about me? Is it worth loving someone you'll never be with? Someone who will never even know how much they mean to you?"

Deckard frowned. "You don't intend to tell her?"

Thom glared at him. "You can't be serious."

"Why?"

"That would go against the very thing you just said proves my love for her."

Deckard looked entirely baffled. "How so?"

"If love is self-sacrificing, then how can I possibly be selfish enough to even offer the lesser option to her?" Thom said. "How could I ever ask her to let go of everything she's worked toward for the past thirty years—shit, that's longer than I've been alive. How could I ask her to give that up for *me*?"

"I thought you said she doesn't have feelings for you anymore," Deckard quipped. He raised a placating hand at Thom's annoyed glare. "Love is self-sacrificing, yes. But you're forgetting that it takes two people to be in love. She gets to sacrifice as well. And, at the end of the day, you'll find that neither of you felt like you were sacrificing much at all because you're together, and isn't that the thing you want most in the world anyway?"

Thom slumped in his seat. He eyed his brother irritably. "I hate you, you know? You and your bloody good advice."

Picking up his wine, Deckard raised it in a mock toast. "I'll stop giving it if you'd like."

Thom scoffed but sobered quickly. "I don't want to lose her friendship, Jonn. If it comes down to being her friend or losing her because I decided to take a risk, I'd choose the friendship."

"You could be happy that way?"

"Happy?" He grimaced. "Most of the time. At least I'd have her in my life."

Deckard ran a hand along his smooth jaw. "Before we go any further, I'd like to go on record and tell you that I am not particularly in favor of your marrying a woman old enough to be our mother. That bothers me, and I don't really care to see you live with the problems that may arise with her extended life."

At Thom's frown, Deckard smiled. "However," he said knowingly, "in the interest of your happiness, I'm going to remind you of something. Nearly two months ago, Brea told you frankly that she had feelings for you. And, from my recollection, your friendship didn't falter or fade by even a fraction. And if you could be so understanding and loyal . . ." He shrugged. "Can't you be man enough to give her the chance to do the same?"

Thom hesitated, a fight of fear and hope mixing in his stomach. "I don't know," he admitted.

"Either way," Deckard said, "I think she'd appreciate your honesty."

Thom pinched the bridge of his nose. "I wish you weren't so damn right all the time," he lamented.

"I'll take that as a compliment."

"I didn't mean it as one," Thom jested. He lifted his ale. "Well, here's to my singleness. I think that after I've made a fool of myself in front of the woman whom I like best in the world, I'll give up trying for a while. Maybe Rafferty had the right idea about monogamy. It's not worth the heartache."

Deckard shook his head. "You're far too dramatic."

"It's what makes me charming," Thom snarked and drained the rest of his ale.

CHAPTER SIXTY-ONE

39TH OF HYDRAE, 1574

For the first time in weeks, Deckard enjoyed a moment of peace as he woke to the gentle light of dawn. Usually, the prospect of meeting with the Alliance and hosting Calyn would have him jumping into action. But today, he chose to embrace the stillness, happily setting aside any expectations of the upcoming meeting and the obligations that came with entertaining guests.

Deckard leaned against his pillow, pulling Evylin closer to him, and surveyed the room. A small piece of blue fabric peeked out from the edge of the wardrobe on Evylin's side. He decided to be charmed by her carefree nature as he shifted his gaze to the long windows on their right. The thin curtains provided a soft, dreamy view of the early morning skyline. He could see the wispy, white clouds drifting alongside the dark gray rooftops. In the distance, the cheerful sound of birds chirping filled the air, and he watched one land on the windowsill for a brief moment before it fluttered off to its next adventure.

Deckard traced a circle on the delicate fabric of Evylin's nightdress. The muted clatter of carts passing on the streets below reached him as the sun climbed higher, and its orange-yellow light filtered through the linen curtains. Deckard furrowed his brow at the brightening rays. Though he consistently woke with the sun, he hadn't realized how inconvenient the thin curtains would be for Evylin.

Despite being a heavy sleeper, the brightness of the morning often aggravated her already grumpy mood. Even while she remained asleep in his arms, he could feel her nose pressing against his shoulder to escape the light.

Deckard decided that new curtains were necessary—dark, thick ones that wouldn't let a single ray of sunlight through. Indeed, the entire residence required redecoration. The place appeared stark, devoid of the necessary furnishings to run a household, including a proper tea set and a suitable parlor for hosting guests. The property currently lacked all the elements that would make it a home.

Though Evylin hadn't complained, Deckard couldn't shake off the sense of barrenness. He wanted to create a space where she felt completely at home, like it belonged to them forever.

However, Deckard couldn't be certain that this would remain their home forever. Given his promise to let Evylin choose their future, she could either decide to stay or leave. There was a possibility that she'd want to depart Loclight to distance themselves from the Alliance and the Relics.

Deckard stared blankly at the window as he let his musings take over, pondering what adventure would most fulfill Evylin. Over the last month, it became clear that she would not thrive in one location for long. Her spirit had visibly waned even during their brief time in Loclight, repairing the government. Having nearly explored everything the Allundan continent offered, Evylin might prefer to venture into entirely new lands. Exploring Giyda or Matteire could offer the life she truly desired.

Absorbed in his thoughts, Deckard failed to notice Evylin gradually waking up until she stretched, momentarily freeing herself from his embrace before sinking back down to snuggle in closer. "Good morning," she whispered into his neck.

Deckard rested his cheek on the crown of her head. "Good morning, my love."

In her languid state, Evylin lounged against him while Deckard massaged her back. These soothing, intimate moments were the ones Deckard treasured most. Being close to her, feeling her heartbeat, and basking in the tenderness they shared fulfilled all his lifelong hopes.

Evylin pressed a series of kisses along his neck, then propped herself halfway onto his chest to gaze down at him. She reached up to caress his jaw, cheek, and temple with her fingers. "I suppose we should get up," she said. "We have a meeting to attend."

Deckard tightened his arm around her waist, purposefully blocking thoughts of the Alliance meeting. For once, he was unconcerned about their possible tardiness or even the risk of missing it entirely. What mattered to him was simply being with her, savoring the happiness she brought him before confronting a world that expected more than he was prepared to offer.

Deckard smiled up at her, rubbing his hand over her shoulder and arm. "We should go somewhere," he said.

A gentle laugh escaped Evylin, highlighting the dimples on her cheeks. "We just returned," she reminded him. His lack of a reaction caused her smile to broaden. "Where should we go?"

"Anywhere you like," he promised.

"Anywhere?"

"Anywhere in this world."

Evylin laughed again, her lungs contracting against his chest with the activity. "What if I want to go somewhere out of this world?"

"Then I'll find a way."

She scrunched her nose in playful delight. "That's awfully generous."

As Deckard entwined his fingers in her hair, he let his smile fade, allowing her to grasp the sincerity in his tone. "I mean it, Evie," he murmured. "Wherever you wish to go, we'll go together."

Her head tipped to the side, likely feeling the urgency of his emotion. "You mean . . . now?"

He nodded.

Evylin's smile turned to a smirk. "We can't leave, Jonn."

"Why not?"

"There are several reasons. First, the Alliance is counting on us to help finalize Allund. Second, we have the Relics, and we can't exactly take them with us. Nor can we leave them behind unattended. Third—"

"None of that matters," Deckard said, interrupting her. He didn't care about her reasons; he had his own. "I made a promise to you. I told you that I would take you anywhere you wanted to go. I intend to follow through."

Evylin's concern faded, and her dimples reappeared. "I've seen nearly the whole of Allund. Because of our marriage. Because of you." She shrugged. "Consider your promise fulfilled."

Disappointment shadowed his chest. Throughout their marriage thus far, Deckard knew of one thing that made Evylin happy. Now, she was taking it away, leaving him with nothing to offer her.

"And I know you, Jonn," she continued, caressing his face. "Well enough to realize you won't walk away when you're needed. When you have the power to change the world."

Deckard tried to breathe through his frustration. "I only care about changing your world," he whispered tenderly.

"You already have," she said, brushing her fingers along the bridge of his nose. "And you're a Mage. You're meant to live for more than just me."

"And what if I don't want to be a Mage?"

"I'd be rather sad if you weren't."

He met her gaze, a glowing amber in the morning light. "You would?"

Evylin nodded, her wavy hair dancing around her face with the motion. "Why?"

"If you weren't a Mage," she whispered, "then I wouldn't be your Warrior."

Deckard cupped her face in his hands as a profound wave of devotion flowed from Evylin's skin into his. "You will always be mine," he vowed. "Just as I will always be yours. Whether as Warrior, Mage, or whatever else this world grants to us."

The morning's lateness and the impending meeting couldn't stop Deckard from delighting in the moment with Evylin. He was determined to indulge in her kisses and love for as long as she allowed, even for all eternity if possible. They ignored their obligations in the pursuit of their passion, losing themselves in their love.

It made them dreadfully late for breakfast.

On any other day, Deckard would have been bothered by Thom's annoyed yet amused smirk at their delayed arrival. Normally, he would have felt embarrassed when Calyn innocently inquired if it was typical for city folks to sleep in. Under different circumstances, he would have hurried to the meeting for which they were already late. However, Deckard let Evylin enjoy a complete breakfast while he leisurely sipped a second cup of black tea.

"Brea will be there already," Thom grumbled, his knee bouncing under the table.

"You can leave without us if you'd like," Deckard suggested.

"To stand around and wait for you to arrive while they ask me why you're late? No thanks."

Calyn ripped her toasted rye bread apart to pair with her sausage. "Evie's always late to everything. I'm surprised they're not accustomed to it."

Thom shot her a sidelong glance. "Deckard is never late to anything."

"Which should earn me some understanding," Deckard said as he reluctantly finished the small bowl of porridge that Evylin placed before him.

"Don't worry," Evylin reassured Thom. "I'm almost finished, and then we can go."

"I still have half a cup," Deckard countered.

"Then you'd better drink it fast," she said with a smirk before turning to her sister. "Are you ready, Caly?"

Thom's brow furrowed. "Will they approve of her joining the meeting?"

Evylin shrugged. "If they don't want her listening, they can have someone show her around the palace."

Shortly thereafter, they departed. As Thom said, Brea was there when they arrived. The ministers received their lateness and Calyn's presence with welcome understanding.

They requested that Highlady Grenwood, a Day Mage, show Calyn around the palace while they spoke. Calyn's momentary disappointment faded as the charming blonde Mage engaged her in conversation, complimenting her pretty floral dress and offering to show her the art gallery the Ephren kings had filled throughout their reigns.

Once the doors closed behind the two women, Archminister Essen turned to the four gathered. "Thank you, Colonel, Captain, and Private Deckard, for your efforts over these past weeks. You have exceeded our expectations in everything we set out for you to achieve. Thanks to your success, we can now proceed to the next stage of implementing the Allundan rule."

Essen rested her wrinkled brown hands on the table. "We, the Ministers of East Allund, are needed in Aulton at the Aulden Palace."

Deckard and Thom shared a puzzled glance. Nearly two centuries ago, Aulton served as the capital of Auld. The Aulden Palace was where the eight Mages governed Auld collectively. Nevertheless, the inaugural King Ephren made it his mission to obliterate both the city and the palace as his first decree as the official King of Ephria. Stories of the devastation and brutality involved in the city's downfall had become legendary within the Ephrian Army.

"Have you managed to rebuild Aulton?" Deckard asked in awe.

Archminister Essen shook her head. "Not wholly, but it's on its way."

"It was said to be brought to rubble," Thom noted.

Essen grinned. "Terrae Mages are especially skilled in such recovery efforts. While the city lay in ruins, the palace remained mostly intact. It would have taken years for Ephren to demolish such a structure, and he didn't have that kind of time."

"So you're leaving," Deckard said, bringing it back to the point. "I take it you want us to watch over the city for you while you're gone?"

"No, no." Essen waved a hand to dismiss the idea. "You'll be coming with us."

Deckard, Evylin, and Thom drew back their shoulders in collective surprise, standing a bit taller.

Brea remained relaxed as if this was the news she'd expected. "It's time, then?" she asked.

"Yes, it is," Essen confirmed. "As you four accompany us to Aulton, so will Corporal and Highlady Loxley and Mr. Calder accompany the Ministers of West Allund. Here in the East, Highlady Grenwood and Colonel Geis are to be presently married and Bonded. Therefore, they will join us too. We have many trusted Mages and Warriors who will help our clerks keep both the West and East stable during your absences."

Deckard felt a spike of excitement from Evylin. Not only were they to continue traveling, but they'd also see their friends again.

Essen took a breath before continuing, "While both the Western and Eastern ministers will stay in the city for some time, this will be a short trip to Aulton for the rest of you. It is our intention to finalize the governmental rule of Allund while there. Should all go well, you shall return home within the matter of a week."

It was as Deckard feared, then. They were going to press them into service. He wet his lips, uncertain how to proceed. "If I may ask, Archminister Essen," he began, attempting not to sound too frustrated, "why are we necessary to this finalization of the nation?"

"We value your opinion, Colonel," Essen said kindly, then added, "And it's a bit of a reward. We intend to celebrate, you see. It is the dawning of our nation. Many feasts and dances will be held, and as your team was instrumental in our victory, we'd like you to be our guests of honor."

Nudging his moonstone ring, Deckard drew in a steadying breath. It was a celebration. Yet, he couldn't help worrying that the excursion would end up being a coronation that they didn't want.

Evylin entwined their fingers. He felt a conflict within her. The undercurrent of excitement remained, but there was also hesitation. "When are we to leave?" she asked.

"Tomorrow morning," Essen said.

"So soon?"

"I'm afraid so," the archminister said, giving the three Deckards an apologetic smile. "I know you've been traveling for four weeks, but we have another long journey ahead of us, and the country cannot wait much longer."

Deckard understood that. The country needed firm authority. It needed law and order. Security and stability.

But Deckard didn't want to be part of that authority, not when it tied Evylin and him to the nation's responsibility.

They should have run away together. He should have taken her to Audis and those white sand beaches while he had the chance. Now, they were destined for the captivity of rulership or the derision of their nation. And he worried they couldn't endure either fate.

CHAPTER SIXTY-TWO

6TH OF PYRA, 1574

The archminister hadn't lied when she said Aulton was still under construction. In fact, Evylin thought she greatly understated the amount of work that still needed to be done.

Nestled on a vast plateau in the mountains, Aulton resembled a blend of ruin and renewal. The contrast was clear in the lush, overgrown greenery and the ancient, weathered stone of the city. It was as if the growth and decay were at odds, with dilapidated buildings and crumbling walls juxtaposed with bustling activity and the magical rebuilding carried out by the new residents.

Several miles away, Evylin could see the Aulden Palace rising in the center of the city. It was a vague shadow in the distance, a beacon of regrowth. She didn't know much about the Aulden Mages or their city, but Deckard had told her what he'd learned through his personal studies and the tales he'd heard during life in the army.

Aulton was a remnant of the past, showcased by its unique architecture and layout. In contrast to the tall, angular buildings of greater Allund, which were characterized by their symmetry, wrought iron accents, and traditional designs, Aulton embodied the ancient Isle culture, preserved since the era when the Aterian Relics were sealed away.

As they drew closer, Evylin finally grasped what Deckard had described. The ancient city, over a thousand years old, was arranged in a circle of dense foliage, a patchwork of buildings, and winding streets. Some of the broken russet-brown and gray stone walls still stood, displaying the grand turrets and spiked battlements that encircled the massive city. The city gate featured a rusted portcullis, its arch half-demolished. One of the gate doors lay flat on the ground, the terrae long ago beginning its reclamation.

Even in the bright sunlight, Evylin felt she was entering a haunted city from one of her novels. She could easily picture the lingering ghosts of the past in Aulton. The abandoned homes and shops built of weathered stone created a sinister atmosphere. Twisting vines marred the façades, and wild branches shattered the windows. The cobblestone streets were in ruins, prompting them to steer their horses and carriages cautiously.

However, they passed through this forest of destruction to find the grand revitalization of which Archminister Essen had spoken.

Slowly, the buildings began to transform, their ancient architecture restored to its former glory. Soaring towers, pointed arches, grand tracery, and intricate carvings adorned every structure. Homes, businesses, kirks—Deckard called them chapels, stating that kirks were meant for the Shires. Everything appeared decorative and overwrought to Evylin's eyes. And it was gloriously beautiful.

As they entered this renewed section of the city, the streets became smoother. The plant life was tamed, vibrantly flowering in early summer. Blossoms of yellow, pink, and white brightened the once-dreary homes. The very air and aura of Aulton lightened.

Everywhere she looked, men and women worked upon the buildings, using tools and magic to advance the city. A few soldiers roamed, while many workers carried weapons, though she noted they were often just daggers. Despite this, a sense of peace and focus prevailed as they worked, indicating that the threat of attack didn't worry them.

As they arrived at the heart of central Aulton, Evylin discovered a glimpse of its former beauty. Purposely arranged manicured trees and flower beds infused the dry, stone city with vitality. An intricate fountain trickled water to the side of the road, with benches positioned around it, inviting passersby to enjoy the tranquility it offered.

The restoration all seemed to bloom outward from the city center, where the majestic Aulden Palace towered above them. Fashioned more as a citadel than a palace, its stunning tan stone walls soared high with arches and columns that reminded Evylin of the Keeps. Its cylindrical shape mirrored the city around it, the palace reaching an impossible thirty stories. Above that, eight statues rose majestically into the clouds, adding to its already grand stature. Its width was beyond Evylin's estimation, and she wondered how long it would take to get from one side to the other.

All in all, Evylin determined that this city was the most stunning and thoughtfully designed place she had ever encountered. Loclight and Mouroc couldn't compare to its splendor.

The streets led up to Aulden Palace, where stone walkways transitioned into lush gardens. At the forefront of their group, the two soldiers who had joined them at the gate came to a stop as they approached the massive staircase that ascended to a pair of oak and iron doors. Servants rushed forward to assist the ministers as they exited their carriages. A third carriage had been offered to Deckard and the team, but they opted to ride their own horses instead. Even Calyn decided to ride alongside them, asserting that she wasn't a child and didn't require coddling.

"In that case," Evylin had told her sister, "you'd better wear trousers. If you're going to be an adventurer, you should look the part."

At the foot of the steps, two strangers greeted them with broad smiles. One was a tall, pallid man wearing a long navy coat, and the other was a blonde woman in a gray overcoat adorned with a colorful glass brooch at her collar.

"Welcome, everyone," the man said as they bowed together. His deep voice carried a Western accent, and as he stood, Evylin noticed his eyes gleaming with a green flash. "I'm Highlord Wilkinsone, and this is Clerk Fairburne. We are delighted to have you here in Aulton. Ministers, if you will follow me, I shall escort you to your rooms. Colonel and Private Deckard, Captain Lohen, Captain Deckard, Miss Glaas—" he gestured to the woman beside him, "Clerk Fairburne will guide you to your chambers."

"Please, call me Gisele," the woman said, her own lilting accent apparent as she spoke.

As the servants and soldiers tended to the horses, carriages, and luggage, the parties followed the highlord and Gisele through the grand entrance into an awe-inspiring foyer. Light poured in from every direction through cross-hatched iron and glass windows. The ceilings soared twenty feet at their lowest point, arching above with intricately painted domes. The foyer seemed endless, curling around to the left and right and dotted with columns supporting the weight of the structure.

The vast room bustled with people dressed similarly to the pair who had received them. Some wore long robes of varying colors—predominantly green, blue, red, gray, and yellow—while a few donned white robes adorned with colorful patches, marking them as Mages. However, the majority sported coats and dresses, adorned with brooches or pins like those worn by Gisele, indicating they were likely non-magical members of the Alliance.

If not for the unique uniforms, Evylin might have overlooked the lone man across the room. He was dressed similarly to their own group, wearing dark brown trousers, riding boots, and a light linen jacket that hung open over a tan shirt. The man was conversing with a shorter individual clad in a gray uniform.

"Vayden!" Thom called.

The man lifted his blond head, a welcoming smile spreading across his face the instant he saw their team. "About time you all showed up," he said, hurrying over to meet them. The man with whom Vayden spoke followed him at a respectful distance while Gisele stepped aside, a patient expression on her face as she waited for them.

Thom and Vayden grasped hands and patted each other on the back. He shared a more affectionate embrace with Brea before offering Calyn a courteous bow and shaking Deckard's and Evylin's hands. "It's great to see you all again," he said, his voice radiating a warmth that was missing when he departed Loclight a month ago. Though his blue eyes still held a sheen of sadness, it was evident that the month since Isla's loss had fostered the beginning stages of healing despite the calluna flower on his jacket.

Deckard patted his shoulder and grinned back. "Great to see you as well. Did your daughter come with you?"

Vayden nodded. "Yes, she's in the apartments with Ilain and Ethenn. As I'm not my sister, I don't require five hours of scrubbing to look my best, so I decided to figure out this maze of a building with Cris here."

When Vayden gestured to the young man, Evylin noticed that after they greeted their friend, Brea had moved past them to speak with him. Playfully, she tapped the youth on the chin and laughed as he shook his head at her, the pair talking quietly while the others were greeting each other.

Brea brought him over. "Everyone," she said, placing her hand on his arm. "This is my nephew, Cristopher Lohen."

"You can call me Cris," the young Lohen said with a subtle Schonese accent. The family resemblance was clear through his round face, full brows, and well-defined cheekbones. However, he bore bronze-brown skin rather than Brea's richer, creamy brown complexion.

"Nephew?" Calyn gasped. "But you look . . ."

"The same age?" Brea asked, smirking. "Yes, that tends to happen when your aunt is a Warrior."

Cris's sly grin was a replica of his aunt's. "It's an unfortunate truth in our family," he said, then gave Calyn a more genuine smile, his long lashes framing his rich gaze handsomely. "You get used to it."

A pink flush came to the young woman's temples, her brown eyes wide as a slow, shy smile came to her lips.

Evylin rolled her eyes at her sister before turning to face Vayden. "When did you get here?" she asked.

"This morning," he said. "We could have pushed hard the night before and made it but figured there was no real rush. It was a short trip over from Blaucklake, so we managed it in a couple of hours."

"I take it you haven't found any good taverns yet, then?" Thom asked, nudging his friend's arm.

Vayden laughed but pointed to Cris. "Not yet, but we've got a local here who I'm sure would be more than pleased to show us the sights."

"Perhaps another time," Gisele said, then motioned to the hall awaiting them. "For now, we still have a ways to go."

Vayden and Cris promised to see them at dinner, calling goodbyes as they followed Gisele.

The clerk escorted them deeper into the palace. They traversed an arched hallway that seemed to extend forever, ascended four flights of stairs, and continued around the palace. As they climbed, the exquisite design remained consistent. Warm light streamed through the windows in radiant beams, gently illuminating the cream-colored stone interior. Allundan banners appeared throughout without seeming gaudy or out of place.

Gisele reduced her pace as the hall concluded with double doors guarded by two Allundan soldiers. Observing the group, the guards swung open the doors, allowing the clerk to guide them into the spacious chamber beyond. Mirroring the city's grandeur, the room featured towering columns, painted ceilings, and multiple windows along the far right wall. Three couches flanked a sizable fireplace, and a large golden chandelier hung overhead, its candles flickering softly. To the immediate left, there were two doors leading off the room, while a narrower hallway extended from across the way.

Above the fireplace hung a large painting depicting an obsidian sky adorned with silver and golden starlight, cerulean and crimson nebulae, and amber shadows. The room featured a thick rug, plush pillows, onyx curtains, black marble vases, and various décor, which echoed the theme of Space.

Evylin felt Deckard tense beside her.

"Welcome to your chambers," Gisele said, folding her hands in front of her as she paused just inside the door. "This apartment is designed to accommodate esteemed guests from the Loclight province of East Allund. To your left is a study and a storage room, while the bedrooms and bathing chambers are down the hall. Your belongings will arrive shortly, but if you find anything missing or need assistance, please let one of the servants or your guards know, and we will ensure you are taken care of."

As she spoke, a middle-aged woman emerged from the hall. Her dark brown hair was styled in a bun, and her round face radiated friendliness. She wore an outfit like that of the clerk, but she also sported an ivory apron embroidered with a patch of the same colorful pattern instead of a brooch.

"Hello," the woman said warmly, her accent unmistakably Ephrian. "I'm Lora Wilumson, the head of staff for the Loclight apartments. If you need anything at all, please feel free to ask me."

Evylin smiled, though her excitement waned as Deckard's whirlwind of emotions tugged at her heart. Aulton was magnificent and awe-inspiring, the palace stunningly surreal, their apartment extravagantly lavish, and the people inside delightful. Yet, she couldn't enjoy it, knowing of his growing discomfort.

"It's a pleasure to meet you, ma'am," Deckard said politely.

"Dinner will start at seven," Gisele informed them. "As Mr. Calder mentioned, the palace is a bit of a maze when you aren't used to it, so I'll be back to escort you to the dining hall. Until then, take your time, get comfortable, and I'll see you in a few hours."

With that, the clerk walked out the doors, and the guards shut them behind her.

"Now then," the head of staff said, stepping closer. "There are eight rooms in the apartment, all ready for occupancy. Those men should have your things up in no time, so we'll need to know where you want us to put them. I've also got the two baths drawn up and ready with hot water. Those Fire and Terrae Mages managed some kind of heating system, so it won't take long to get the rest of you cleaned up as well. Who would like to go first?"

The five of them exchanged amused and amazed glances.

Evylin stepped forward. "*Mrs*. Wilumson?"

"Yes, dear?"

"Perhaps you could give us a quick tour of the apartment first, and then we'll make our decisions about rooms and who will freshen up first."

The woman complied and led them through the hall, cheerfully showcasing each bedroom, even though they were identical, as well as the two bathing chambers. Every room mirrored the parlor's design with onyx, ivory, and crystal elements. A servant's entrance was located at the back of the hall for more convenient cleanup and service.

Thom chose the first room closest to the parlor. Brea opted for the room two doors away, and Calyn chose the one right next to hers. Deckard let Evylin decide, so she settled on the room at the far end of the hall, which provided ample separation from the group.

In the following hours, additional staff members arrived to ensure that their visit was graciously accommodated with refreshments and snacks. After all five guests had refreshed themselves, they replenished the bathroom linens, rekindled the fires in the bedrooms and the parlor, and departed with a reassurance that they would remain merely a call away.

Evylin closed the bedroom door after the last servant left and turned to find Deckard standing before the fire, rubbing his clean-shaven jaw. His hair was damp from his bath, and he wore a tunic loose over his trousers, but she could sense the weight in his heart. All throughout their journey to Aulton, which had taken a little under a week, she'd sensed this discontentment radiating from him. She knew it had something to do with his doubts about the Alliance, but she hadn't pressed him, understanding his need to process in solitude before explaining his heart.

Evylin stepped around the settee to stand behind him and wrap her arms around his waist. Given their height difference, she had to rise onto her toes to rest her chin on his shoulder. "You're pouting, my love," she whispered teasingly.

A slight sense of gratitude pulsed out of him as he settled his hands over hers. "I'm sorry," he said.

She ran her thumbs along the bottom of his ribcage. "You don't need to be. You're uncertain, and that's understandable."

"They're just so . . . good. And gracious. Everyone here is happy. Too happy, almost. It can't be real."

Evylin peered up at him. "You're upset because they're too nice?"

"It's foolish, I know."

After a moment of studying him, his brows notably pinched together, she smirked. "You think they'll ask us to take over Loclight as chancellor and commander?"

"Yes."

"I suppose that's a fair assumption, but I fail to see the problem. We've already agreed to say no."

Deckard shifted, wrapping his arm around her shoulders to pull her into his side and look down at her. "We did," he said. "Is that still what you want?"

Evylin held his gaze steadily. She hadn't abandoned the quest she'd taken up in Whickam Village. She'd made a second vow at Ryen's graveside: to prove Deckard's worth to him—to show him he was loved. Their mission and work with the Alliance had taken precedence, but she never forgot. And she was slowly working to earn his unwavering trust as he had with her.

Because that was something Evylin had learned about her husband. No matter how caring and noble he was, he didn't fully trust her. He loved her, but he feared offering her the darkest parts of his soul.

Reaching up to kiss his cheek, Evylin said, "I want what you want."

Deckard smirked in disbelief.

She tugged on the hem of his tunic. "Jonn," she said gently, "you said it yourself: The Alliance is good. They won't press us into service."

He stared at the fire abjectly, his thumb tracing circles on her bicep.

Evylin narrowed her gaze, trying to understand the disappointment within him. Why should their goodness worry him? If he truly wanted to be free of the responsibility that came with the position—which she wasn't convinced of—then shouldn't he take their honorable nature as a boon?

The absurdity of the truth hit Evylin, and she chuckled. "Oh, Jonn."

"What?" he asked, clearly surprised by her affectionate mirth.

She gave him a wry grin. "You don't want them to be good because, if they are, you'll feel bad saying no."

Deckard pressed his lips together, a self-derisive humor easing the discomfort within him. "I don't like you," he bantered.

"Mm, but you love me."

"That I do."

Deckard leaned down and kissed her, but she pulled away before he could make it any more passionate. "Now," she said brightly, "stop worrying. We're in an impossible palace surrounded by our friends and what's sure to be a feast like no other. Whatever the Alliance asks of us, we'll tackle those challenges later. For now, can you enjoy being here? With me? With our friends?"

Though there was a tinge of hesitation from him, Deckard smiled. "I'll do my best."

Another hour later, they were dressed in their finest. The Alliance provided clothing for them, having taken their measurements and any particular requests they had while still in Loclight to prepare for the grand celebration of the rebirth of their nation. Evylin hadn't cared what she wore so long as it was exceptionally elegant. However, Deckard had given the tailors his own requests for her gown: a dark green velvet dress heavily embroidered with silver everbloom ivy all along the bodice, skirt, and sleeves. The square neckline provided ample display for her rosette necklace from Hewitt while preserving a modest cut per Eastern sensibilities.

She felt regal in the gown but also cared for, knowing that Deckard had ensured Ryen and Hewitt's inclusion in this grand moment.

Deckard was given a white military-style coat with a high collar and black detailing to signify his status as a Space Mage. Though she had no doubt he cared little for the distinction, she thought it made him look sufficiently like an officer. And even better, the black silk cravat made the color of his eyes pop more green than blue, which she found especially alluring.

They discovered Thom seated near the fire in a light silver-blue coat and black trousers. He stood upon their entrance, smiling. "Well, don't you look positively imposing?" he teased.

Evylin brushed his sleeve playfully. "You look rather handsome yourself."

"Really?" Thom's chest puffed out as he brushed back some of the dark hair that drooped onto his forehead.

"That color brings out your eyes," she confirmed.

"Why, thank you." Thom edged closer to whisper so only she could hear. "It's the sixth today, remember?"

Evylin sucked in a sharp breath at the reminder. "That it is," she said.

They exchanged a sharp nod while Deckard watched curiously.

Calyn's giggle in the hall announced the arrival of the rest of their party. Together, Calyn and Brea stepped into the parlor. They were both so very different in general, and their appearance only emphasized the fact. Calyn's soft brown hair was tucked and braided into a ladylike bun, little wisps dancing around her face. She wore a lavender-blue dress with fluttering sleeves, a demurely wrapped V to the neckline, and glittering beads all along the waistband and skirt. Her light tan skin glowed in the evening light, and Evylin was struck by the maturity of her little sister's appearance. Calyn was truly a woman, in mind and form.

At the young woman's side, for perhaps the first time ever, Brea's dark black hair was out of its braids. It hung in a thick curtain of curls around her shoulders, the top pinned back elegantly. If that wasn't odd enough, she wore a flowing, colorful gown of pastel blue with floral appliqués—one perched on the shoulder as the others trailed down like a spray of heather across the Western moors.

"Oh!" Thom said abruptly, interrupting Brea and Calyn's conversation.

The women stopped, looking at him in surprise.

Thom shuffled awkwardly. "Ah." He winced, cleared his throat, and started over. "You ladies look lovely."

While Brea wore a knowing grin, Calyn beamed bashfully. "And you look dashing, Thom," she said. She plucked at her chiffon skirt. "How marvelous that we all selected blue."

"Indeed," Brea said dryly.

"Though I think your coat and your dress match better," Calyn noted to Thom and Brea. "Mine's a bit too purple to truly match."

"I think your dress is perfect," Brea said. She patted Calyn's arm. "Thom, why don't you escort Calyn? She is your sister-in-law, after all."

"Oh, well—"

Deckard cut Thom off, surprising Evylin by saying, "Actually, I'll be escorting both Evylin and Calyn."

"You will?" Evylin asked, bemused.

"Mm," he said. "It's only proper, as I'm the closest thing she has to a father here in Aulton."

At that moment, Gisele, the clerk, knocked and entered to guide them to the banquet hall. Though Evylin shared a dubious look with her sister, they did as Deckard requested, each hooking their hand into the crooks of his arms, leaving Thom to offer his arm to Brea.

Gisele guided them through the dim glow of the sunset-tinged halls and down two flights of stairs. Oil lanterns hung on the columned walls, and their footsteps echoed on the stones. Gisele offered tips on how to navigate the palace and pointed out the locations of the most significant rooms. After about ten minutes, they arrived at the dining hall, and Evylin felt overwhelmed by the flood of directions that she knew she would probably forget.

As men and women poured into the hall, they brought with them the lively buzz of conversation and excitement. The expansive space was filled with numerous tables where both magical and non-magical folks gathered together, sharing laughter and stories. Everyone was dressed in their finery, proudly wearing signs that identified them as Warriors, Mages, clerks, and various other roles she didn't recognize. While scanning the room, she spotted a few familiar faces, but the one she recognized most was Highlord Aterian Jarrad Hoult, the Terrae Mage who had helped them escape from Renaul. At his side was a beautiful young woman with golden brown hair, and in his arms, he held a little boy.

At the far end of the room, a platform was occupied by a series of tables arranged in a U-shape. Some ministers were already seated, while others were just coming in. Right in front of the platform stood a long table with all its seats vacant, although six individuals nearby were busy handling what appeared to be small pieces of paper.

A spike of anticipation lit in Evylin, and Deckard's burgeoning joy met her grip on his arm. They watched as Vayden leaned against the back of a chair, chatting with two men, and Ilain playfully swatted at a piece of paper in Ethenn's hand, which the young man skillfully kept out of her reach. She tugged at the sleeve of his black coat, both smiling brightly, while Reyana, Vayden's daughter, stood to the side, watching their fight with a hand covering her laughter.

Unconsciously, Evylin's footsteps sped up, desperate to see her friends. Her family.

Deckard gently unhooked her hand from his arm. "Pardon me, Clerk Gisele," he called, and the woman turned back. He set his hand on the small of Evylin's back, ushering her forward. "We can find our way from here."

With apparent understanding, Gisele smiled and stepped out of their way.

Evylin didn't bother waiting. She lifted her skirt and hurried down the aisle of tables. Several people took notice, but she didn't care.

One of the men Vayden conversed with—Brea's nephew, Cris—spotted them approaching and alerted his companions. Vayden turned, grinning, and then reached over to pat his sister's shoulder. Ilain's fiery hair flickered as she spun around to see where her brother was pointing. The moment she recognized them, Ilain darted past the men.

With the flurry of movement and the vibrant yellow of her gown, Ilain looked just like the fire she wielded. The women crashed into one another in a furious embrace filled with laughter, smiles, and teary eyes. Elation erupted through Evylin. She'd missed Ilain far more than she'd ever imagined possible. The woman's bright spark and unerring confidence, her fierce loyalty and ready affection were a noticeable absence from her life. Evylin never wanted to let her go.

"Oh, Evie, I've missed you," Ilain said before she pulled back. "Alma is a good Warrior, and she's a nice person, but she's not like you."

"I'm glad to hear it," Evylin replied. "I'd hate to think you'd found someone to replace me."

"Never," Ilain promised, clasping Evylin's hands in hers.

Ethenn appeared behind his wife, a respectful grin tugging at his lips as he approached. He nodded to Deckard behind the women and then turned to Evylin. "Hello," he said, as if not wanting to interrupt.

Ignoring his more reserved nature, Evylin pushed past Ilain to sweep the young man into her arms next. He hugged her back readily—an improvement from his typical demeanor—and it felt just like hugging Ryen. They were different men in so many ways, but Ethenn had become so much of what Ryen had been to Evylin. A friend, a confidant, a brother.

"I don't like being apart from you two," Evylin pronounced when she and Ethenn parted.

"We don't like it either," Ethenn agreed.

Deckard greeted the couple then as Thom, Brea, and Calyn arrived at their side.

"Then move back East, would you?" Thom said. "It's boring without you and your obnoxious wife. Oh, hello, Ilain, I didn't see you there. That's such a drab dress you're wearing; you practically blend into the room around you."

"Ha," Ilain mocked. "I didn't miss you at all."

"I'd be worried if you did."

Despite their snipes, the pair shared a warm hug.

The troop gradually returned to the table, immersed in greetings and chatter.

Everyone was excited to reunite, eagerly asking each other questions and expressing how much they regretted their separation. Reyana was more reserved than before her mother's passing but greeted them all with kindness. Calyn initiated a discussion with Cris, who readily indulged her curiosity on various topics. Vayden then introduced them to the other man at his side, Captain Alan Aalgar.

"You probably know my father," Alan said. "Major Aalgar, the Warrior."

They were all quite familiar with Aalgar, a fair yet firm trainer who worked his soldiers in a manner similar to Hewitt, though with more professionalism. Thom and Alan hit it off as they discussed the army from a non-magical perspective.

As the final ministers took their seats and the banquet seemed ready to start, Captain Aalgar excused himself, and the troop rushed to find their places around the table. Small, folded cards indicated each seat's assigned occupant, and Evylin recognized them as the slips of paper Ilain and Ethenn had been arguing over as they approached. Though Ethenn held a chair out for Ilain, she settled into the seat up the table, next to Deckard at the head, wearing a superior smirk.

A flicker of cunning passed through Ethenn's dark brown eyes, and his lips twitched with humor. He pulled the chair completely out from beneath the table, grabbed the back of Ilain's seat, and, with one deft show of strength, scooted it over next to Vayden before taking hold of the empty chair and sitting down beside Deckard.

Ilain shot a scowl at her husband. "Sorry," he said, his tone hardly conveying remorse.

Just as Evylin hoped, the dinner turned out to be an extraordinary feast. Servants continuously presented tray after tray of delicious roasted, cured, and smoked meats, followed by bowls overflowing with potatoes, fresh vegetables, savory soups, and a delightful array of dried and fresh fruits. Pastries and warm loaves of bread seemed to magically appear just when they were needed. Their cups were kept brimming with the finest Schonese wine, and the conversation sparkled with life.

Evylin was happier than she'd been in some time, surrounded by her friends and food. After so long traveling and working for the Alliance, it was refreshing not to think about Allund's welfare or the looming responsibilities of the future. For tonight, she could live in the moment with the man she loved, her sister, her brother, their closest friends, and the memories they shared.

Even Deckard relaxed, enjoying the company. She could feel the worry sloughing off him with each passing moment. His shoulders eased, his laughter came readily, and he smiled constantly. Everything was as it ought to be.

And for the first time, Evylin truly understood Deckard's reluctance to accept the rulership of Loclight Province. If they became rulers, they would have to part from

Ethenn and Ilain for good. Perhaps they'd meet every year or so for political gatherings like this one, but they would practically be on opposite ends of the country. Their lives would be distant and separate.

She didn't want that.

As the servants started to clear the tables, Archministers Dudleye and Essen stood to speak to the audience. They offered special acknowledgments to the troop who had rescued their country, gesturing toward Evylin and the other honored guests. The entire room erupted in applause, giving them a standing ovation that made her blush from the attention.

Archminister Dudleye raised his hand to restore order in the room. "Since we've all had our fill, please adjourn to the ballroom, where there will be music, dancing, and drinks enough to sate even a kraken's thirst."

Laughter rang out as the people rose. Reyana hopped up, kissed her father's cheek, and hurried off to join her friends.

However, Dudleye continued to speak, his eyes on their table. "Colonel Deckard," he said, "if you and your team would remain behind, we'd like a word."

CHAPTER SIXTY-THREE

Deckard, halfway out of his chair, suddenly froze, a twist of anxiety in his stomach. The weight of the meal and wine felt even more burdensome as he looked at Evylin. Her expression went slack upon meeting his gaze. It seemed the Alliance was prepared to reveal their heavy-handed request after all.

Deckard stood up completely, unable to find an excuse to refuse the meeting. "Of course," he said, raising his voice over the loud footsteps of the hundreds leaving the dining hall. "Would you prefer that we stay at our table?"

"Oh, no." Archminister Essen waved her hand. "We'll go somewhere more comfortable, shall we?"

Deckard turned to the table where the others stood. Calyn watched him and Evylin with her lips pressed together in anxious expectation. "Excuse me, but my sister-in-law," he motioned toward her, "can she join us?"

"I'm sorry, but no," Essen responded. "This meeting is reserved for those who were on the team to retrieve the Ateri Relics. Shall we arrange for Clerk Fairburne to take her back to your apartment?"

Deckard glanced at Calyn, who looked disappointed. She clearly wanted to attend the dance, but without a chaperon or at least one acquaintance, it would be improper.

"I can take care of her, sir," Cris Lohen addressed Deckard, drawing the rest of the table's attention.

"I bet you can," Thom muttered slyly.

Brea jabbed her elbow into his stomach, causing him to gasp. She held Deckard's gaze steadily. "My nephew is as honorable as they come," she promised. "He will be sure Calyn is safe and cared for."

After checking with Evylin, Deckard nodded. "Thank you, Mr. Lohen," he said. "We would appreciate that."

When Cris offered his arm to Calyn, a soft pink flush worked across her cheeks. She accepted his escort, and they walked toward the door together.

The ministers proceeded to guide the troop through a side entrance from the dining hall. They navigated through more winding corridors, eventually arriving at a cozy meeting room. The walls bore murals of the western moors and eastern Shires, and several large tables formed an unconnected square. The ministers sat around three of the tables while the troop took the chairs at the fourth.

A fireplace blazed at the rear of the room while several servants busily arranged fresh glasses of wine at each table setting. The ministers swiftly settled into the divide between East and West: Archminister Essen on the right, Archminister Dudleye on the left. The Calder parents sat on the Western side as well, retaining their interim roles.

As though they'd rehearsed, the troop sat down, leaving the center seat for Deckard. He wet his lips, steeling himself, and took the seat.

Essen and Dudleye exchanged a nod before the woman spoke. "Thank you all for coming to this late meeting," she said, her dark eyes sparkling in the room's warm glow. "Although we've just arrived, we want to provide you a day of rest and celebration tomorrow, so we thought it wise to handle these matters right away."

Those around Deckard shared glances, although none of them spoke as they awaited the Eastern archminister's next words.

"First," she beamed at them, "let us express our genuine gratitude: We owe you a debt of thanks. For everything you've done and all you've sacrificed, we are forever grateful to you."

The chorus of acknowledgment and gratitude expressed by the other ministers resonated throughout the room for a brief moment. It was, much like all else in Aulton, as authentic as Deckard could conceive. Their remarks were strikingly sincere.

However, it didn't ease the tightness coiling in his stomach.

Archminister Essen clasped her hands in a prayer-like gesture. "With the Alliance in control and Allund gaining momentum, we can advance now. While several matters still need to be addressed to ensure the nation's smooth operation and integrity, that process will require time.

"Given the current relationship between the Alliance and the people, we feel we can confidently set our sovereigns in place. You have all protected the Relics well, but we wish them to be granted to the Bonded Warriors and Mages who will be their bearers for the next century or more. Over time, we believe the Relics will add to the stability and vitality of our nation. But they are also great threats to our safety, as the ancient Mages understood."

Dudleye nodded, taking over the lead as he said, "A millennium ago, the ancient Mages locked the Ateri Relics away due to the wars and greed caused by their power. This kept the vilest of Mages from obtaining their deep power, but it also caused our world to deteriorate. The creatures of legend faded, the weather shifted, and magic waned. With their return, we will experience a righting of Terraeus to the world Allore intended it to be. However, this comes with the weight of protecting these Relics well.

"Once the world discovers the truth and power of these Relics, they will come for them," Dudleye concluded. "Our chancellors and commanders of each province will be responsible for keeping them safe."

Deckard wanted to squirm but forced himself to remain still. However, he did allow himself to ask, "Do you mind explaining what the rule of Allund looks like in your eyes?"

At his question, the ministers turned surprised looks their way. "You don't know?" Archminister Essen asked.

"We were never told," Evylin replied.

During their travels, Auden and Ilain disclosed fragments of the Alliance's plans for the nation; however, the complete narrative remained unknown to them. Their knowledge was limited to the involvement of Mages and Warriors in government and the ministers' efforts to maintain the organization in the interim. The information provided still lacked clarity and official confirmation. As they faced a nation that they had contributed to establishing, Deckard felt that they were entitled to this degree of transparency now.

The ministers looked to Ilain, who pursed her lips. "Our minds weren't exactly on the minutiae of governmental policy," she offered.

Dudleye raised his hand to gain everyone's attention. "Allow me to clarify. The Allundan government has two elements: a democratic republic and an oligarchy. The republic includes the Administration." He gestured to the fifteen individuals beside him. "Every four years, a vote will be taken to choose the ministers for each province. Some ministers might change while others stay, based on the election results. Each of Allund's provinces—four in the East and four in the West—must have one male and one female representative. These representatives shall serve the people and their concerns.

"Each settlement will have magistrates to ensure a direct line of communication. To prevent corruption and biased voting, an annual census will be conducted. This will align with the yearly search for magic in each settlement, offering an accurate representation of the population. When voting begins, citizens from each settlement will be verified against the census records. A minister must be at least thirty-five years old and demonstrate good standing in their community to qualify for the position. To promote fair name recognition, candidates will submit a summary of their achievements for posting by the magistrates, ensuring everyone has an equal opportunity. Other forms of campaigning will not be allowed.

"The Administration's aim is to ensure that the oligarchy remains aware of the people's needs and wishes. The ministers will function both as advisors and checks on power. We want our leaders to consider the public in all their actions, whether magical or otherwise. This is not a rule of oppression but a rule of service."

Dudleye inhaled deeply before he spoke again. "The oligarchy," he declared, "will govern with the goal of maintaining unity throughout the nation while ensuring the safety of its citizens. It will consist of the heads of the eight provinces—or what are currently called the eight Orders. Each province will be overseen by a Bonded couple who will train the next generation of Mages and Warriors to safeguard and serve the populace, just as they were initially intended to do.

"The Administration will personally select these magical rulers for their initial term. In subsequent iterations, the Head of the Order will choose the heirs. Since these rulers may live hundreds of years before their heirs take over, this role will necessitate ongoing selections. We have several magical methods to guarantee a continuous line of heirs for this position."

The archminister clasped his hands on the table. "Does that satisfactorily answer your question?"

The tension in Deckard's stomach was nearly so strong that he struggled to breathe. The explanation answered his question, but not with any degree of satisfaction. At least, not personal satisfaction.

If he set aside his ties to the government and evaluated the plan carefully, he could recognize its many merits. Naturally, there were some gaps and questions that came to mind, but he didn't believe this brief response represented the entirety of what the Administration could provide. They had been developing this plan for generations. The Alliance was established soon after the Centurial War commenced but originated far before the divide of Ephria and Wauld, carrying back to the time when the Aulden Mages ruled with tyranny. They would undoubtedly have responses to any inquiries he might raise.

Unable to formulate any response through his dry throat, Deckard nodded.

"Excellent," Archminister Essen said. "That leads us nicely to the point of this meeting. As we prepare for the final phases of establishing Allund's government, we hold some aspirations for your futures within it."

Deckard struggled to stay seated as Essen spoke. He wanted to pace and work through the internal conflict within him. But he held himself still, feeling Evylin's anxiety at his side, melding with his.

"Corporal and Highlady Loxley," Essen said with a knowing grin. "It may not surprise you, but we would like to officially ask you to accept the role of Highlady Chancellor and Highlord Commander of the Order of the Flame. You would govern the Doorstunds Province in the southwest of Allund, which includes the counties of Doorstunds Reach, Highloft Moors, Idlevere, Faurfield, and Vlaugmira. We believe that both of you would serve not only as powerful but also as capable and kind-hearted leaders. We have faith in your ability to guide the Order of the Flame with your understanding and wisdom."

Ethenn placed his hand over Ilain's on the wooden table. Her gold and silver moonstone ring reflected the firelight.

"Mr. Calder," Essen continued, prompting Vayden to straighten next to his sister, "we ask you to lead the guard in Doorstunds Province as the general overseeing the chancellor's and commander's security. We believe no one is more qualified to protect your sister and her husband than you. With your extensive background and training, along with your deep love for family, we are confident you will fulfill this role with honor and diligence."

Vayden's bright blue eyes kept flickering between his parents, Ilain and Ethenn, and the ministers, but he didn't speak.

"Captain Lohen—" Brea lifted her gaze at the mention of her name. "We would like you to Bond and rule with one of our candidates for chancellor. Highlords Wilkinsone, Humes, and Grames have all expressed their interest in being your partner. We would support your marriage to any of them, or another Mage, should you so desire. You have proven yourself a strong, brave, and insightful Warrior. If you think our desire for your union and Bonding stems from your gender alone, let us clarify that this is not our main motivation. We recognize you as a natural leader and a true servant of the people."

Thom adjusted in his seat next to Brea, pulling his arm away from resting casually on the back of her chair. Yet, the Warrior herself showed no reaction to their appeal.

"Colonel and Private Deckard," Essen continued.

Deckard's stomach tightened, and Evylin grasped his hand under the table.

"We request that you accept the position of Highlord Chancellor and Highlady Commander of the Order of the Heavens. You would oversee Loclight Province in the north of Allund, which includes the counties of Loclight, Hartfolley, Tindon, Dunbriar, Maasters, and Harmouth. After these past five months, we have no doubt that both of you exemplify noble leadership and inspire loyalty among your peers. You represent everything we in the Alliance believe defines good sovereigns: honor, selflessness, trustworthiness, and devotion."

The compliments had no impact on Deckard. He wasn't interested in hearing how well he would perform in the role. What he truly wanted was assurance that the position was wholly unavailable to him, that he wouldn't have to refuse to serve his fellow countrymen.

Heat burned beneath Deckard's skin as his emotions surged. A wave of fear coursed through him, stemming not only from within but also from Evylin. He could feel her distress at the announcement, evident in her trembling hands.

"Lastly, Captain Deckard," Essen said, and Thom turned from his inspection of Deckard and Evylin to face the ministers. "We ask you to lead the guard in Loclight as its general. We believe you are exceptionally suited for this role. Your commitment to your brother and sister-in-law, your support for your friends, and the competencies that aided you on your mission strongly endorse you over anyone else for the position. Additionally, you have prior experience as an officer. We have complete trust in you for this responsibility."

A storm of emotion rolled through Thom's gray-blue eyes as he ran a hand over his jaw. But he nodded to acknowledge the request.

Deckard felt his panic intensify. Everything was moving too quickly and becoming overly complex all at once. If he and Evylin declined the position, they would also deny Thom his potential appointment. Deckard couldn't gauge from his brother's response whether or not he desired to be a general, but he suspected that Thom's personal discomfort stemmed more from the Alliance's plans for Brea's future than his own.

Although he anticipated that Archminister Essen would ask for their response and acceptance, Deckard flinched when she spoke again.

"All these hopes," she said, her mature voice filled with tenderness, "are nothing more than that. They are *requests* alone."

A chill rolled down Deckard's back, and Evylin's fingers tightened on his encouragingly.

"Your team has provided invaluable service to our country," Essen said with a smile. "We don't require you to accept these roles; you have already done so much for our nation. Now, it's our opportunity to do something for you. The Alliance presents these roles as options. We envision you in these positions, but the choice to accept or decline is yours."

Deckard didn't know whether to be grateful or disappointed. Evylin had been right earlier; it was harder for him to decline in the face of their goodwill. From the start, the members of the Alliance had given their lives to the cause selflessly. Who was he to do any different?

Essen continued speaking. "We present these positions to you tonight to give you time to think about them," she explained. "Tomorrow, after you've rested and reflected, we will meet again. At that time, we would like you to either accept the offers or, if you wish, propose your own requests to us. You can ask for any job and any compensation, and if it's in our power to grant it to you, we will."

Deckard met Evylin's hopeful gaze. Their offer seemed both impossible and incredible. The Alliance was presenting an opportunity for them to have everything they desired. Any future they wished for was laid out before them.

A short gasp of disbelief escaped Deckard.

"We can have anything we want?" Thom asked in amazement.

"Unless there are any questionable or disreputable petitions you may possess," Dudleye stated, followed by a chuckle shared with the majority of the ministers. "We shall make every effort to approve and fulfill all of them."

"Anything?" Ethenn asked. "If we didn't want what you just offered and instead said . . . I don't know—that we wanted to move to Schon, would you let us?"

Another chuckle. "We would."

"We could go home?" Deckard asked, finally finding his voice. "We could return to our lives before and walk away from all of this; you wouldn't stop us?"

"You could, and we wouldn't."

Deckard leaned back in his seat.

Everything was in front of them. Every option they could ever come up with was within their grasp.

He could return to his former life. He could abandon his role as a Mage. He could become a soldier and build the family he'd always envisioned with Evylin by his side. This time, she could also be a soldier. They could reside in their home in Loclight, spending more than just a few nights there. They could explore together. Serve alongside each other.

Or they could explore the world like she'd always intended with Ryen. They could sail the five seas, see all that Terraeus had to offer, and become legends worth five hundred tales.

And at last, Deckard would fulfill his promise to Hewitt. He would give Evylin the life she'd dreamed of.

The life she'd always deserved.

CHAPTER SIXTY-FOUR

The door shut behind their troop with a soft *thump*. Thom didn't know how to feel. Their offer was incredible and exciting, and their requests were heartening and gratifying.

Yet, standing in the stone corridor with his brother, Evylin, their friends, and the woman he was coming to realize he loved, Thom found himself immeasurably disappointed. The night had come, shrouding them all in darkness, lit only by the gentle golden-amber glow of oil lamps mounted on the columned walls. It was as though the world was reflecting the inner turmoil inside Thom. Hope and dejection.

The Alliance presented him with a thrilling dream job and the opportunity to have anything he desired (within reason). Yet, they wanted Brea to marry a Mage; they'd even given her a choice of whom. And she'd already told him she would accept.

"It is my burden to carry on with my promise to the Alliance."

"You shouldn't have to do that, Brea."

"It's all I have left."

But it wasn't all she had.

She could have *him*.

Following behind the others as they meandered absently down the hall, Thom nearly scoffed at the thought. And yet, what could he offer Breata Lohen, the most impressive, strong, and intelligent woman he knew? She was magical. He was not. She would live another century. He would likely die within half that time. She was destined for greatness and a soul-deep connection. He could offer her nothing but mundanity and meager affection.

"So," Ethenn said, breaking the silence and Thom's disdainful thoughts, "that is . . ." He didn't finish the sentence, scratching the back of his head.

Ilain immediately brushed down the hair he'd mussed. "It is exciting," she said decisively, though she didn't sound convinced herself. "We can all take the next day to consider our futures. In the meantime," she grabbed her husband's hand, "I'd like to dance."

Though Ethenn gave her a disgruntled look at the thought, Thom grasped onto the idea. "Almighty, yes," he said. "We should certainly join the party. I could use a drink right about now."

Though Vayden and Brea offered amused chuckles, Thom noticed that neither Deckard nor Evylin showed any sign they'd heard the discussion around them. In the shadowy hall, they stood side by side, holding hands and gazes, locked in some silent conversation.

"You two all right?" Thom asked, taking a step closer.

As though startled out of their private reverie, Deckard and Evylin whipped toward him with wide eyes. Evylin took a deep breath before saying, "Yes. We're fine."

The smile she offered wasn't quite believable, but before Thom could press the issue, she added, "You all go on. Jonn and I . . . We need to discuss some things."

At her side, Deckard cupped her arm gently. He gave Thom a grateful nod, trusting him to take care of the others.

Thom returned the gesture. "I'll have a glass in your honor," he teased. He tilted his chin toward the stairs. "We'll make your excuses and see you in the morning."

Though the others shifted with disappointment behind him, the appreciative and relieved smiles of Deckard and Evylin were all Thom cared to see.

While the couple made for the staircase, Thom turned to Brea. He proffered his arm. "Shall we drown ourselves in Schonese wine, *mi'ambrosá*?" he said.

Pulling her dark, watchful stare from Deckard and Evylin's retreating forms, Brea took his arm. "Those names are getting better," she quipped dryly.

"I consulted my Schonese dictionary for that one."

"No wonder it sounded forced."

Vayden shook his head, coming alongside them as Ethenn and Ilain led their way to the ballroom. "May I give you some advice, Thom?" Vayden said.

"By all means," Thom replied.

"Schon is a playful yet direct country. Poetry is seen as frivolous. Delicate nicknames like 'my stunning one' are regarded as flippant." A flicker of wistful sorrow passed over his expression as he likely thought of Isla, before his face resumed its wry tilt. "If you want to woo a Schonese woman, don't use flowery speech. Be candid. She'll like it better."

Though Brea showed no signs of discomfort, Thom struggled not to tense at Vayden's pointed comment. Thom hadn't thought his true feelings for Brea were that obvious. He liked her, he desired her, but he never intended to "woo" her. Even after his revelation of loving her, he knew he'd have to let her go. Why give himself false hope?

Plastering a smirk on his lips, Thom kept his head high. "Then it's decided," he said and clutched Brea's hand in the crook of his elbow dramatically. "I shall henceforth call you *mi'stelá briantes*."

Brea immediately scrunched her nose. "Brilliant star?" she said incredulously. "I'm nothing like a star."

"That's the point," Thom said.

As they reached the ballroom, Ethenn paused to guide Ilain in first, tossing Thom a knowing look over his shoulder.

Thom held the young man's gaze. It didn't matter what anyone else thought. He wasn't going to take Brea from a life filled with joy, luxury, and power so she could dally with him in the dullness of normality.

Their arrival sparked enthusiastic cheers. Many rushed forward to greet them, eager to share drinks or a dance. Amid shaking hands and receiving manifold introductions, Thom quickly lost sight of Brea as he lingered near Vayden's side. The older man recognized all the Alliance members who came over, skillfully carrying the conversations for Thom, who smiled and nodded, contributing only the necessary comments.

Shortly, Cris Lohen approached with Calyn at his side. Her cheeks were flushed from the heat of the room and wine, but she looked clearheaded and uncorrupted enough. Perhaps Brea's nephew really was honorable.

Calyn stepped away from Cris with a thankful, momentary farewell and grasped Thom's arm. "Where are Evie and Deckard?" she asked brightly.

"My brother has polluted your sister, I'm afraid," Thom remarked. "He's taken her off to bed."

Calyn wrinkled her nose. "But it's only nine o'clock," she said innocently.

Thom decided not to make his euphemistic jest clearer. "Jonn is a tremendous bore."

"No matter." Calyn brushed her hand through the air, her newfound composure diminished in the festivities. She tugged on his arm. "You must dance with me. This is the grandest party I've ever attended. And the musicians! They're divine."

Thom smiled at her, grateful for the escape from the politicking and small talk. "Yes, yes," he patted her hand, "I'm yours to do with as you please."

Letting Calyn carry him into the heart of the room, Thom tried to remember his minimal dance lessons with his mother. He'd never been a skilled dancer, though he enjoyed the levity of a reel or an up-tempo waltz. He tended to stand at the back of the party, drinking and making snide comments. But tonight, he preferred the distraction of Calyn's effusive, sweet chatter over the scornful ruminations of his thoughts.

"Cris asked me to dance with him," Calyn said as Thom attempted to lead her with grace across the polished wooden floors. At his raised brow, she concluded, "I told him no."

He frowned. "Why?"

"I didn't think I should say yes."

"Again . . . Why?"

Calyn chewed on her lip—a bad habit on the dance floor when a clumsy trip could cause painful consequences. "Well, we've just been acquainted."

"You've never danced with an acquaintance before?"

"I have."

"Then why not him?"

She gave Thom a bashful look. "I find myself . . ."

At her hesitation, Thom smirked. "You're attracted to him?"

Her expression grew worried. "Are you angry?"

Thom huffed. "Why would I be angry?"

"Because you—" Calyn paused, and her eyes narrowed. "You're courting me. Men are usually jealous when their intended is attracted to another man."

"My intend—" Thom nearly tripped, baffled. "Calyn," he said sharply, "we are not courting."

She looked genuinely surprised. "We're not?"

"No."

"You're sure?"

Thom worked to withhold his incredulous laughter. "Quite sure."

"Oh." Calyn stared over his shoulder as they danced, deep in thought. Then she said, "Father said you had intentions toward me. That's why he allowed me to come with you all—so I could win your heart and marry you."

Pressing his lips together, Thom cursed Deckard's likely hand in that farce. "Mm, yes, well . . . No, my only intentions toward you are to help you find a good husband who is *not* me."

With a steady nod, Calyn continued to look thoughtful. "Do you mind if I say I'm glad?"

Thom grinned dryly. "You don't want to marry me?"

She gave him a playful look that reminded him quite a lot of Evylin. "To be honest,

I did want to once. But over time, I realized that I don't find you all that attractive beyond your looks."

"I'm hurt."

She heard his sarcasm, used to the Shires' banter. "That's one of the reasons," she admitted, pinching his shoulder. "You're too mocking. It makes me feel naive and slow-witted."

Thom's expression softened. "I'm sorry," he said. "I don't mean to make you feel that way. But I'm glad you don't have any more designs on me than I do on you. And if you'd like to dance with Cris, I won't stop you."

He considered it further, then added, "Though if he's anything like his aunt, I warn you, his remarks might be even more cutting than mine."

"Oh, no!" Calyn insisted. "Cris is the model of a gentleman. Though he's clever, he was very attentive too."

Thom smirked. "That could have something to do with his attraction to you."

Calyn blushed. "Do you think so?"

"He's watching us presently," Thom noted. "As he's done constantly for the last half hour. I'm quite certain."

Calyn giggled lightly, her bright smile filling Thom's heart. He liked this young, impetuous girl. She reminded him of the best parts of Meria and Evylin. She was a wonderful sister to add to his life.

"Come on," he said, twirling her toward the edge of the dance floor. "It's time for you to dance with your Schonese *caréso*."

"What does that mean?"

"It's their word for 'sweetheart.'"

Calyn gasped with excitement. "You speak their language?"

"Bits," Thom admitted. "I'm not fluent by any means, but I'm learning."

"For Brea?" she asked.

Thom frowned at her. They were near enough to Cris now that he didn't care to discuss the topic, so he simply said, "No, for myself." Then he turned to Cris with a smile. "I heard that my sister rejected your dance on a misunderstanding," he began.

Cris gave a kind, if abashed, smile. "It was of no consequence," he said.

"It was," Calyn said. "I was misinformed and thought it inappropriate. However," she smiled up at Thom, "my *brother* has cleared it up for me."

Watching them uncertainly, Cris chuckled. He brushed a hand through his thick curls. The hair brushed the collar of his moss-green coat. "If you're sure," he said, then faced Calyn wholly, "I would be honored to share a dance with you, Miss Glaas."

Calyn beamed at him, and Thom all but shoved her into the young man's arms. "Dance the night away," he said.

Thom watched while the pair returned to the twirling couples on the floor. There was an awkwardness in their shy glances and longing looks. The attraction was clear, but there was a regard in Cris's eyes that Thom recognized. It was the same look he'd seen Deckard and Evylin share in Whickam Village all those months ago. He liked her because he saw something in her. A part of her soul spoke to his. Neither of them was magical, yet they shared a sudden, certain bond.

It wasn't love at first sight. It was hope. It was a sense that there was someone who could make your life a little more whole than it'd been before.

Thom smiled sadly. He'd never experienced that feeling. No one had looked at him with that same knowing. And he envied it.

Suddenly, a woman slid her arm through Thom's. He looked down to find fire-bright red hair flashing in the light of the party.

"Ah," he greeted snidely, "if it isn't my least favorite person."

"You love me, and you know it," Ilain replied. She followed his gaze to the dancing couple. "Lost another one, eh?"

"I'm destined for celibacy."

"As someone who waited forty-three years to find her husband, let me tell you—" She gave him a twinkle-eyed smile. "It's bloody worth it."

Though Thom wasn't as undefiled as she presumed, he chuckled. "I'm afraid Bonding isn't in my future."

"Perhaps not." Ilain pulled him to walk alongside her. "We have another meeting to attend."

Thom furrowed his brow. "With whom?"

"Each other."

"You and I?" He scoffed. "Shall we solve Terraeus' problems together? Or do you need marital advice?"

"I'd go to literally everyone but you for that."

"I'm the one who got Ethenn to kiss you if you'll remember."

"After doing expressly what I asked you not to do."

"It worked, didn't it?"

They made their way to the back corner of the ballroom, where the lights were softer and the music quieter. Though partygoers still mingled, the atmosphere was much more tranquil. Small tables aimed at fostering relaxed, intimate conversations were thoughtfully arranged in the corner. Seated at one of these tables were Ethenn, Vayden, and Brea, the trio evidently waiting for them.

Thom smiled. "*This* is the 'each other' you meant," he realized.

"Yes," Ilain said, breaking off from him. "Now, sit down. We have much to discuss."

Taking the free seat beside Brea and finding a ready decanter of wine and a spare glass awaiting him, Thom settled in. He smirked at Ethenn. "Your wife made overtures to me," he sniped.

Ethenn didn't flinch. "I'm not worried."

"Because I'm too honorable."

A sly grin came to his lips. "Because if you'll remember, I feel what she feels," he said. "And she feels decidedly motherly toward you."

"Enough of that," Ilain said, calling their impromptu meeting to order. "We all have some decisions to make, and I want to ensure we make the right ones. Now, obviously, Deckard and Evie will become chancellor and commander of Loclight—"

"They won't," Thom said.

Ilain shot him a perturbed glare. "Don't be ridiculous. They were made for the job."

Pouring the wine, Thom shrugged. "Doesn't mean they'll take it."

"They should," Brea said, bemusement in her tone. "As Ilain said, it suits them perfectly. He is a servant, and she is a soldier. What better leaders could we have?"

"A goddess and a hunter?" Vayden quipped.

Ethenn lifted his brow self-mockingly. "It does sound foolish when you put it that way," he admitted. "While Ilain has been trained for this her whole life, who am I to run a country?"

"We'd be running a province, dear," Ilain said. "That's only one-eighth of the country."

He gave her a flat look and said, "I love you."

She linked their hands on the tabletop.

"You make an adorably bizarre couple," Thom noted. He leaned back in his chair. "Listen, I don't know what to tell you. Yes, Jonn and Evie should take the position. No, they won't take it because she loves him, and he's scared of responsibility."

Brea narrowed her eyes. "I don't think you know your brother very well."

"I know him better than anyone but Evylin. And unless she finds some way to convince him otherwise, he'll refuse the position."

The others exchanged wary looks.

Vayden turned to Ilain and Ethenn. "I assume you'll accept it, though?" he said.

With their chairs nearly pressed side to side and her full yellow skirt draped around them, it was hard to tell where Ethenn began and Ilain ended. "It's what we always intended," he admitted.

Ilain nodded, unusually silent.

Thom narrowed his eyes. "You're undecided?"

"No," she said too quickly. Ethenn squeezed her hand on the table, and she sighed. "Maybe. It's just hard—being apart from you all. After all this time, after becoming family . . . We don't want to be distant from you, but. . . ."

"But this is who you were made to be," Brea concluded.

Ilain ducked her head, and Ethenn drew her closer supportively.

Vayden sat with his hands resting in his lap. He stared across the room, likely watching his daughter with her friends. The calluna flower remained on his lapel in memory of Isla. Though the father and daughter were still in mourning, it was clear they were trying to move forward with the new nation. "Whatever you choose," he said decisively, "I'll do the same."

Ilain's gaze softened as she faced her brother. "You don't have to do that, Vayd. You and Rey have a home in Faurna. I don't want you giving that up just to be with me."

"It isn't just to be with you," he insisted. "Reyana and I need a fresh start. I want to be with my daughter. Isla and I lost years with her because of our work. Now, our home is filled with memories of that loss. Whether you take the chancellorship or move to be near Deckard and Evylin . . . I think it would do us good to come with you. We could use the presence of family to make us whole again."

With somber, comforting smiles, Ilain and Ethenn accepted the answer.

"What about you, then, Thom?" Vayden asked. "Will you take the job with or without Deckard and Evylin's acceptance?"

Thom let out a huff. "No. Like you, I'll go where my family goes. If, by some miracle, they choose the position of chancellor and commander, I'll consider the post. But I won't be counting on it."

Sharing nods, they all sipped their wine, the corner falling silent for a few moments.

"And you, Brea?" Ilain asked gently. "You've got three suitors, it seems. Would you accept Wilkinsone, Humes, or Grames?"

Brea hesitated, taking a longer drink, and Thom angled farther to the side in his chair.

"I'm undecided," Brea said at last. "I only just met Humes tonight. He's . . . nice, I suppose, but he's a Wind Mage, and I'm not particularly interested in living in West Allund."

"You said you liked Grames," Thom offered, hating himself for it. He took another sip to cover his grimace.

Brea smirked as though remembering something. "He has a fine wit," she said. "I could probably be happy with him."

Ethenn, Ilain, and Vayden eyed her curiously.

"You don't have to take the position," Ethenn said. "They found another female Warrior two weeks back, near the border. She's an army widow with three children, and after talking with her, she's agreed to remarry and Bond with Highlord Everlye, the Time Mage."

"But I would be their fourth," Brea said. "Balance is imperative to magic—to Allore. And, therefore, to the Alliance as well. Presently, they have two female Warriors settled for commandership. If Evylin and I both take the other roles, it would put us in balance with four male and four female commanders."

"And if Evie doesn't take it?" Thom asked.

"Then I'm sure they could scour the eastern half of the continent and find one more female Warrior to make up the difference."

"Why not make it two?" Ethenn said. "If you don't love these men—if you don't want to be with them, why make yourself?"

A glimmer of tears appeared on Brea's lower lashes. "It's what we do in the Alliance," she said softly, repeating Isla's words from so long ago. "We sacrifice everything for the sake of a better future."

Vayden reached over then, taking Brea's hand.

Thom continued to sip his wine. The warmth of its aged grapes burned on his tongue. He wanted to curse the sacrificial nature of the Alliance, but they weren't forcing this future on Brea. They'd offered it as a mere option. She could have anything she wanted, yet *she* was the one willing to marry for utility and not love.

"I had love with Adie. I don't care to replace it."

If Thom had been alone, he might have smiled bitterly. Brea had already told him more than a month ago: No matter her attraction to him, she didn't want him. She'd experienced love, and she wanted to preserve its memory.

"Well," Ilain said, her tone hinting at sourness, "it sounds as though we're all undecided."

Vayden finished his wine and stood. "I'm not," he said. "Where you go, Lainy, I'll go. For now, I'm going to dance with my daughter."

They said goodnight, and Vayden disappeared into the crowd.

Ethenn shifted in his chair next. "I think we need to have a long talk," he told Ilain.

She nodded solemnly. "Probably without the influence of wine. Otherwise, I may forgo all conversation and get right to the lovemaking."

While her husband wore a bashfully amused smirk, Thom snarled. "Ilain, some of us don't care to hear about your exploits," he noted.

"Then don't listen," Ilain returned, tugging a quite willing Ethenn behind her as she departed.

Shaking his head, Thom scoffed. "Those two scare me," he remarked drolly.

Brea propped her feet onto Vayden's vacated chair. "I think they're rather cute," she said. "In Schon, we're very open with our intimacy. *Nos efétes, nos amés.*"

Thom furrowed his brow, attempting to translate. "No regard, no love?"

"*Efétes* is better translated as affection, but yes, the meaning is much the same."

"A Schonese proverb?"

She smirked, lifting her wine glass. "Advice," she said. "From *mi'abeya.*"

"Your grandmother was a romantic?"

"Most Schonese are."

Thom raised his brow. "You're not," he said.

She reached over and slapped his cheek, though not hard enough to hurt. "I am the most romantic soul you'll ever meet," she said with a sharp yet playful tone. "I've just acted as a soldier around you, and there is no time for romance on the battlefield."

"Well, I'll have to disagree with you there," Thom quipped. He offered her a wry smile. "You saved my life, and I find that quite romantic."

She gave him a derisive frown.

"Besides," Thom continued, gesturing to her form, lounging in the chair. "This is a decidedly unsoldier-esque look. I'd venture to call it downright feminine."

"I am a woman."

"I noticed."

A pleased smile spread across her full lips, illuminating her dark eyes. She truly was beautiful. The soft blue of her dress enhanced her tawny skin, giving it a deeper golden hue—a blend of her dark-skinned Ephrian and bronze-complexed Schonese heritage. Its flowing fabric swooped low, revealing more of her sculpted décolletage than the Shires would deem appropriate. Her tight curls danced whimsically around her cheeks and shoulders. If he had been more of a scoundrel, he would have devoted the whole evening to trying to seduce her.

As it was, he held his attraction in with a tight rein.

"So," Brea said, changing the subject, "what will you ask for? If Evylin and Deckard refuse the position, would you really want to go with them *wherever*?"

Without hesitation, Thom nodded. "I'll stay with them no matter what."

"What if they want to live in Estshire with her family?"

Thom chuckled at the notion. "They won't go for that. Neither of them desires to live in a small village. At worst, they'll opt to leave Loclight for a different city."

She poured them both another glass of wine, and Thom envied her inability to feel the effects of alcohol. It was already lightening his thoughts enough to allow him to give her leering looks as before. His eyes darted down to her neckline at the thought.

"You're a good brother, you know?" she said, startling his attention back up. "You always have been."

Thom scoffed nervously as she handed him the wine glass. "Not always."

"Ever since I've known you."

"You've known me at my least difficult state," he said, passing her an amused glance. "And even then, I was still quite difficult."

"You've never been difficult to me."

"That's because I like you."

The second the words passed his lips, Thom's stomach dropped.

Brea paused, her glass halfway to her lips. Seated side by side, he was glad she wasn't looking directly at him as he hid his mortification behind a sip.

With a friendly pat on his hand, Brea broke the awkward silence. "I'm glad, *mi'caro*," she said.

Thom bristled. Ever since their conversation, he'd increasingly disliked the nickname. Once, she'd said it with teasing affection. Now, she used it almost derisively, like she was mocking the feelings she once held for him.

"And are we to expect an announcement soon?" Brea asked.

Thom frowned. "In regard to what?"

She gave him a knowing look. "Your engagement."

His frown grew. "Engagement—?" He realized then. "You mean to Calyn?"

"She told me you are courting," she explained. "I'm proud of you. She's a very sweet girl, and I think you will be happy together."

Caught between amusement and annoyance, Thom shook his head. "I know I'm prone to making mistakes, Brea, but that's not one of them."

She stared at him in confusion, so he clarified. "I'm not courting Calyn. There was a misunderstanding, but she and I are not together. In fact, I think your nephew is winning her heart right now." He frowned then, looking out across the ballroom. "I hope he's not taking too much advantage of my absence."

Brea sat forward, giving him a dangerous view of her cleavage. Instantly, he averted his gaze as she asked, "You aren't pursuing her hand?"

"Allore's might, no!"

"Why not?" Brea asked, sounding truly disappointed. "She's young, beautiful, open, and caring. What's more, I think she'd do well for you."

Thom gaped at her, baffled. Why was Brea supportive of him marrying another woman? Did she not feel the same ache of indignation at the thought of him with anyone but her?

"I could never be with Calyn," he said.

Brea's brows drew together. "Oh, Thom." She sounded almost pitying. "You could if you tried. Her heart is open to you, and she would love you as you've always deserved. You don't have to be alone."

The truth her words held meant nothing to Thom. It didn't matter that Calyn was charming and lovable; Thom knew he could never be happy with her. He could love her as a sister but never as a wife. He could never truly be *in love* with her.

Rapping his knuckles against the table, Thom fought down his agitation. "Brea, I know I've made jokes in the past, but let me make this clear: I have no romantic interest in Calyn. I never have, and I never will. I think it would be a terrible thing for me to pretend I did just because I don't want to be alone."

Though Thom's tone was determined, Brea scanned him doubtfully.

An incredulous laugh slipped out of him. "Why don't you believe me?" he demanded.

"It isn't that I don't believe you, *mi'caro*. It's that I don't understand why you wouldn't pursue a relationship with her. You find her attractive, don't you?"

"Yes, but—"

"And you think she's a charming girl, yes?"

"Yes, but Brea—"

"You *could* love her," she insisted. "If you tried, you could let go of your self-doubt and find that you're worth being loved too."

The words sprang to Thom's lips in that instant. As he maintained her gaze—so gentle and full of warmth—he felt suspended in time and place, every emotion he had ever felt for her rising to the forefront. From the moment he met Breata Lohen, she had only astonished him. She was remarkable. Moreover, she believed he was worthy of love.

Thom thought about letting the words slip out. He truly did. But he surrendered himself to the role she'd relegated him to long ago. "Because I'm handsome, strong, and a total shit?"

"Your finest qualities, indeed," Brea said, raising her glass in a mock cheers.

Encouraged by her lighthearted reply, Thom advanced the joke. "Or is it because I'm not magical? And we unfortunate souls have to discover *something* worth living for."

"Luck of the draw, *mi'caro*," she said with a sly grin. "I did not ask for my magic any more than you asked not to have it."

"You know," he said, setting his glass on the table, "for a time, I thought I wanted it. That it would improve my life and make me more important. But I don't believe I'd enjoy it much."

"Too much responsibility?"

Thom's response lacked the same lightness. "Too much life," he confessed. "I've made countless mistakes and outlived too many friends. I wouldn't want another century or more in this world."

Brea remained silent, opting instead to sip her wine.

At her side, Thom admired her profile. Her pert nose added a charming accent to her features. Her small silver earrings sparkled in the light of the many candles. Her chin, cheekbones, and forehead showcased striking, powerful lines. She exuded a fierce and imposing presence—stunning and awe-inspiring, standing apart from every other woman in the world, but not just for her beauty.

Breata Lohen was truly unique in every aspect. She exuded unwavering confidence. Strong and self-assured, she moved with both power and elegance. Despite her small, slender frame, she commanded respect and was never seen as delicate. It was futile to try to intimidate, deceive, or discourage her. She wielded truth and wit as potent tools. He believed nothing could deter her once she committed to a goal.

Thom smiled at the wonderful woman next to him and spoke before he could second-guess himself. "There would be one benefit to being magical."

Brea grinned, ready for another joke. "What's that?"

Thom downed the rest of his wine, let the glass *plunk* against the table, and reached across to draw one of her tight curls free of the others. As if turned to stone, Brea's dark eyes widened as he ran his fingers over the silky strand.

Thom let his smile drop away to ensure she knew this was no joke at all as he said, "I could have you."

Brea inhaled deeply as if to speak, but Thom leaned down and kissed her cheek, silencing her. Her skin was warm against his lips, but he didn't linger. He tucked her curl behind her ear, gently stroked the line of her sharp cheekbone, and withdrew in one smooth motion.

"Goodnight, *mi'cara*," he said and left her sitting there alone at the table as he exited the ballroom, laughter and music echoing through the halls around him.

CHAPTER SIXTY-FIVE

Leaving their friends behind to enjoy the party, Evylin and Deckard walked back through the dark halls of the Aulden Palace. She'd heard someone say during the dinner that they intended to rename it, though they were waiting until the coronation to let the chancellors and commanders determine its final name. A menial-sounding task, but somehow, it carried a weight to it.

The halls were shrouded in a foreboding gloom. Shadows clung to the arched windows and columned walls, broken only by the faint glow of lanterns. Their footsteps reverberated on the stone staircases, with only the rare sound of a casual patrol to break the silence. It was a tranquil night, one that should have brimmed with revelry and joy.

Yet, here they walked, somber and uncertain.

Evylin felt Deckard's growing agitation throughout the meeting. He was glad to know they served a worthy organization but embittered at having them place responsibility upon him. She wished he could understand. . . .

When they arrived at the Loclight apartment, two new guards opened the doors for them. The parlor was alight with a low-burning fire. She ignored the comfortable space, heading instead for the privacy of their room. Whenever Thom, Calyn, and Brea returned, she didn't want to be in the middle of their debate.

Deckard kept up with her until they stepped into the room. He shut the door, letting her drift deeper into the suite. The attendants had clearly come in to turn down the bed and prepare the room for rest. Low lamplight cast a warm glow over the space. The hearth crackled behind its metal fire screen. The blankets were turned down, and the windows were open to let in the cool night air.

Evylin paced to stand behind one of the settees. The suite was grand, with abundant space. She supposed it was intended for the chancellor and commander of Loclight to have an escape while in Aulton.

Absentmindedly, she kicked off her slippers, letting her toes curl against the plush rug.

Deckard approached, his manner hesitant. "Why are you nervous?" he asked gently.

Realizing that she'd started tugging on her rings, Evylin blew out a half-amused chuckle. "I don't want to let you down," she confessed, her voice quiet.

He drew back, eyes narrowed in confusion. "How could you possibly—?"

"This is it, right?" Evylin interrupted. She shrugged, tossing her hands and letting them fall into the folds of her skirt. "You made me a promise: Whatever I asked, you'd do. You offered me the future—whatever future I want. And now, it's up to me to choose."

A heartbeat passed as Deckard drew in a long breath. "You know," he said softly, "whatever our future together, I will be happy knowing that you're happy. There is no wrong choice."

Evylin's lips turned up in a wry, uneasy grin. "Of course, there's a wrong choice, Jonn. There's *always* a wrong choice."

"Not in this case."

"No?"

"No," he insisted.

Evylin's chest constricted with frustration.

Deckard's brow pinched together. "Why does that answer bother you?" he asked.

"Oh, Jonn." She dropped her face into her hands. "Because I love you," she said. "And I want you to be happy too. Thus, there *must* be a wrong choice because if I choose something that you don't want—"

"Evylin." He took hold of her shoulders, smiling kindly at her. "My happiness is not tied to my getting my way."

Feeling the need to push his goodness, to reveal to him his disregard for the obvious, she said, "Then if I told you that my choice was to accept the Alliance's offer—to become Chancellor and Commander of the Order of the Heavens—you would be fully happy?"

Worry flashed through his eyes, and his demeanor grew unsettled before he could mask his emotions. "Yes," he lied.

Evylin couldn't help the laugh that escaped her.

"I *would*," he pressed. "Because if that is the future you want, I'd accept it."

Evylin moved out of his touch to stand before the fireplace. She questioned the fairness of his request, placing the burden of their life solely on her. Nonetheless, she couldn't ignore the essence of his plea. He wasn't asking her to decide because he was unwilling; rather, he wanted to secure her happiness above all else.

But there was one immense fault in his request.

"I don't know what I want," Evylin said, turning back to him. "I left Whickam Village because I made a promise to Ryen. I fulfilled that promise. But all that time, it wasn't what *I* wanted. My actions were for *him*. Now . . ."

Hewitt's words came back to her. *"What would be reason enough to live?"*

Evylin smiled humorlessly. "I don't know what life I desire."

Silence met her confession. She wasn't sure if he delayed his response because he was waiting for her to elaborate or if he was unsure of what to say. But then he stepped forward.

Deckard brushed her hair over her shoulder, his fingers grazing her jaw and neck, trailing down to her shoulder and upper arm. He caressed her gently, warming the skin under her gown. "If you don't know," he said with the greatest tenderness, "then I'll do whatever I can to help you discover the answer."

As Evylin gazed into his eyes, which glimmered a soft green-gold in the firelight, she recalled all the reasons for her love. There was no denying his physical attractiveness. His eyes, always reminiscent of shifting oceans, the strong contours of his brow, cheekbones, and jaw, the genuine expressiveness of his features, the toned musculature of his physique, and his overall calm demeanor all contributed to his appeal. Yet, her feelings went deeper than mere attraction.

Evylin loved Deckard for his goodness—in every way. He was heartfelt. He exemplified trustworthiness and loyalty, showed tenderness and calmness, and embodied superior morals and a friendly demeanor. Even though he was somewhat reserved with others, he shared everything with her. And he was willing to sacrifice any part of himself for her, always eager to give.

Setting her hand over his, Evylin whispered, "Please."

Gently, Deckard kissed her temple, his hand sliding down her arm to entwine their fingers as he guided her across the room. They settled at the edge of the bed, the mattress yielding to their weight, their hands resting on the plush comforter between them.

"How do we . . . ?" Evylin asked, words failing as she held his gaze.

Deckard tipped his head to the side. "I suppose the first step is figuring out what it is you want out of life."

"How do we do that?"

He hesitated far longer than she expected. "Do you have any ideas currently? Any thoughts on what you *might* want? Any dreams of how the future might look?"

After a few seconds' consideration, Evylin shook her head. "Not really."

"Nothing at all?"

"I mean, if I *really* think about it, I guess I imagine myself traveling and fighting, but . . ." She let out a deep breath. "I don't know how much of that is actually what I want and how much of it is residual from the past twenty-seven years of my life. We've been traveling and fighting for six months now. How do I know whether I actually want more or if I'm just . . . used to it?"

A small smile tugged at the side of Deckard's mouth. "Do you like traveling?"

"Yes."

"Do you like fighting?"

"Yes."

"Then why wouldn't you want them to be in your future?"

It was a valid point, but traveling and fighting had many drawbacks, which had caused Evylin to question her dreams ever since they left Whickam Village. However, she thought the biggest reason *not* to include them in her future was potentially sitting right in front of her.

"Do you like traveling?" she asked.

Deckard pressed his lips together, revealing his displeasure with the question. He believed their conversation should focus on her rather than himself. However, he replied, "Sometimes."

"Do you like fighting?"

"Not particularly."

"Not even as a Mage?"

"Evie—"

"I'm curious." She tightened her grip on his fingers. "And you said you'd help me."

"How does this help?"

"Because I have no ideas, Jonn," she lamented. "All I can think of is more of the same: asking the Alliance if they'd like us to run errands like this for them forever. But I don't know if that's truly what I want or if it's just my lack of imagination."

Deckard sighed, his eyes dropping to his lap. An air of frustration and conflict surrounded him. "Do you want help with ideas?"

Evylin angled toward him. "Do you have some?"

He nodded hesitantly. "A few."

"Then, by all means, tell me."

Deckard ran his hand along his jaw, staring across at the fire now. "There are several paths we could take. And all these ideas could be altered to fit whatever you'd like best."

He cleared his throat. "Initially, we could follow your suggestion and ask to serve as their . . . errand runners, I suppose. This role might be open to interpretation, leading us to tackle a variety of tasks, which could bring a decent level of excitement and adventure. On the flip side, it might also become quite routine and tedious. There's a possibility we'd end up acting more like diplomatic representatives for the nobles rather than engaging in anything truly thrilling."

Evylin had not thought of this possibility, and she now questioned how she had missed it. The likelihood seemed to favor the last option. Going from one noble to another to make sure they were fulfilling their duties and had all they required would be much more about politics than adventure.

"If you didn't want to take that risk," Deckard continued, "or simply wanted more than that position could offer . . . We could leave Allund."

Evylin grinned dryly. "And go to that white beach in Audis?"

He responded to her humor with a serious stare. "If you're interested," he remarked. "Or we could set sail across the sea to Schon and embark on a brand-new adventure— something entirely unknown. We could earn a living using our skills and never experience a dull moment again."

As Evylin furrowed her brow, she came to the conclusion that the idea wasn't as thrilling as it initially appeared. After all the traveling and exciting adventures that they had experienced over the last six months, she found the notion of a boring routine quite appealing. Not forever, perhaps just a month or so. But ideally, she wanted a few weeks to enjoy the peacefulness of monotony.

Deckard guided her hand onto his thigh and placed his other hand over it. "If you're concerned about being distant from everyone," he said, searching her eyes with genuine concern, "don't worry. I'm sure Thom would come along, and I believe we could persuade Brea to join us too. Vayden might even be open to the idea of a fresh start there. However, I doubt Ilain would want to leave, so we'll have to exclude her and Ethenn from our plans."

Evylin considered him, her lips parting slightly. "You've thought this through, haven't you?"

He shrugged. "I've considered many ideas."

"But this one more than the others?"

"More than some but not more than all."

Unsure whether she truly wanted to know the answer, Evylin fiddled with the blended moonstone in his ring. "And which idea have you considered the most?"

Deckard averted his gaze, tilting his head away from her. "It's inconsequential."

"Please tell me." She traced her fingers along the back of his hand and down to his wrist.

Without lifting his gaze, he responded with an almost regretful tone. "We could return to how things used to be. I could be an officer again, and we could settle in Loclight. We could forget that we were ever anything more."

Expressing those thoughts appeared to spark Deckard's bravery, and his gaze returned to her face. "We could relinquish our magic and lead ordinary lives. We could start a family, and you could manage the home and our daily matters. Or you could join me in the army. I could seek assignments that keep me in the city—ones that wouldn't separate me from you and our children for more than a week or two at a time if it's absolutely necessary.

"All of this," he freed one hand to gesture around the room, "would fade into mere memory. It was an adventure we shared, something unique to us that we could never forget. But we would finally be free of every obligation and the pressure to be anything other than ourselves—only bound to each other and our children."

Evylin heard the longing in every word he uttered. Yet, she also sensed the underlying fear.

Deckard's vision for their family—imagining them happily living in the city while he returned to being an officer—wasn't just a simple fantasy. Though she had asked him about his dreams before, he had never offered the truth of his hopes. Now, she could feel the unease that his real wishes brought to the surface. He might find it hard to acknowledge, but deep down, she understood that this wasn't his genuine desire. It was more of a compromise. This was the dream he convinced himself was enough to protect him from disappointment if he ever fell short of the aspirations that he truly cherished.

Hewitt's voice echoed in her mind. Every word he had ever spoken to her about Deckard, every piece of advice he had given her regarding her husband, came flooding back.

From the moment Deckard delivered his speech in Whickam Village, Hewitt declared that he understood what the captain desired. He believed Deckard's goal in joining the Ephrian Army was to emulate the legend he admired so much, aspiring to become a legend himself.

Hewitt expressed it clearly at his grave: This was why he chose Deckard for Evylin. He understood that Deckard's desires aligned perfectly with hers and that he could be more than just her husband—he could truly offer her everything she deserved.

Hewitt's final charge whispered to her: *"He's yours . . . Care for him the way he cares for you. He deserves that too."*

A soft smile came to Evylin's lips. She turned her face up to Deckard, in awe of his goodness and worth. "I love you," she whispered.

Deckard's expression pinched with confusion before easing tenderly. "I love you," he replied.

Evylin drew him close, their lips meeting with a light touch. It became so clear for her, everything she wanted for her life. Every question she had was whisked away in the memory of Hewitt's words. *"He's yours."*

Evylin rested her forehead against her husband's. "Can we stop?" she whispered, eyes closed as she reveled in the weight of his arm wrapped around her waist. "Just for the night, can we let this go and figure it out tomorrow?"

His nose brushed against hers as he nodded slowly. "If that's what you want," he replied, the words tickling her lips.

"That's what I want," she said, kissing him again.

Evylin surrendered to Deckard's touch, embracing the yearning growing inside her. His fingers entwined in her hair, intensifying the kiss. She sensed his initial worries melting away as his passion flared. It was slow, fulfilling, and powerful.

The world was flawed, and their lives might never match their hopes, but perhaps that was for the better. In her first twenty-six years, Deckard hadn't appeared in her dreams, yet now, she found it hard to imagine a day without him. She felt that anything she once wished for would be greatly lacking in his absence.

Still attired in their finery, it required some time and adjustment for them to proceed. But soon, Deckard's coat lay crumpled on the ground beside his boots, tossed there by Evylin. The remainder of his apparel followed shortly thereafter. Her lustrous dress lingered for a while longer due to the more intricate fastenings that they had to work through.

But soon enough, Deckard enfolded Evylin under the blankets. And as he kissed her, she knew her answer. She knew the future she wanted. For the first time ever, Evylin knew what was "more" and what was less in her life.

Now, she just needed to figure out how to tell him.

CHAPTER SIXTY-SIX

"I rather like being married," Ilain remarked. She played with the fire in the hearth absentmindedly, making it leap behind the metal screen. Without a magical quest, she had little regular use for her magic, and she found herself seeking out flames to manipulate with a twirl of her finger.

Lounging on one of the settees in their suite, Ethenn ran his thumb along her ribcage, sending a tiny spiral of magic across her skin. A contented emotion filled the air around them. Now Bonded, she'd readily grown used to feeling his emotions, a benefit of their union she greatly enjoyed.

"I expect you should," Ethenn said casually.

Ilain leaned closer against his chest, dropping her head back to look up at him. "Because you're such a splendid husband?"

"Well, I am," he replied with dry humor. "But I meant that marriage is *intended* to be enjoyable."

With a light chuckle, Ilain turned back to the fire. The fabric of her full skirt rustled as she stretched her legs to the length of the settee. "What are we going to do?"

"Be happy for the next two hundred years."

"I meant about—"

"I knew what you meant," he interrupted, then placed a kiss on the back of her head. He rested his mouth there, murmuring into her hair, "I don't know."

Ilain chewed on the inside of her cheek. "This was supposed to be the easy part," she lamented. "I always knew that once Allund was raised, I would become Highlady

Chancellor of Doorstunds Reach. That was my future from the beginning. Why is it so hard for me to accept that now?"

"It's probably my fault," Ethenn said apologetically.

Ilain tipped her head back to meet his gaze. "Why would it be your fault?"

"We're Bonded," he noted. "Your emotions are affected by mine. You can probably feel that I'm hesitant, and it's causing you to doubt yourself."

"Hm." Ilain picked at the beading on her skirt. "Why *are* you hesitant?"

He shrugged. "It's like you said earlier: They're our family. Evylin and I actually share blood, even if it is distant. You know how important that is to me."

Ilain did know. Before their marriage, Ethenn had explained everything about his past. He fought in the taverns and worked constantly for Terrina's sake. When Terrina was sold off to Bastien Muirren, it felt to him as though he'd lost his last family member—his only reason for living.

Discovering his relation to Evylin was like learning he had a second sister. For the first time in a long time, it gave Ethenn hope that he could still belong and had a purpose. There could be a reason for him to live and fight beyond the anger urging violence under his skin.

Ilain threaded her fingers through Ethenn's. "It's important to me too," she whispered.

"And if we take the position," Ethenn concluded, "we'll be weeks away from them. We won't see them for years at a time."

Ilain stared dejectedly at the flames dancing low in the fireplace. The Doorstunds Province apartments were decorated in the red tones of Fire. A crimson rug splayed over the stone floor. Lush scarlet drapes hung open around the windows, and a light breeze drifted in to cool the room. In the mountains, Aulton grew quite hot in the summer. Nearer the sun, it heated the great city like a stove.

"We could make that a condition of our acceptance," Ilain said hopefully. "If we take the position, they have to allow us time to visit at least once a season."

A sardonic knowing filled the air. "We'll be governing a province, Ilain. We can't just travel to visit family whenever we want."

She sighed. "Then we don't accept it."

Ethenn hesitated, his reluctance palpable. "What else would we do?"

"We're a Mage and a Warrior," she said. "Bonded, need I remind you. We would make splendid bodyguards."

He chuckled, his ribcage pressing against her back. "And who are we going to protect?"

"Jonn and Evylin, of course."

"Why would—?" He started over, understanding. "Thom doesn't think they'll take it."

"Of course they will," she insisted. "It may take time, but Evylin will help him see reason."

"You think she wants it?"

"No. It's Jonn who wants it. He's just too pious to admit it."

Ethenn paused. "That doesn't make sense."

"It makes perfect sense, dear. You're just not looking at it correctly."

He didn't argue, though she could feel that he wasn't convinced.

Ilain patted his arm placatingly. "Don't worry. They'll accept, and we can join them in Loclight as one big happy family. And worst case, if they don't accept, we'll simply request to go wherever they go."

Ethenn nodded. "I like that."

"Me too."

Resting her head against his shoulder, Ilain settled in. It wasn't the future she'd originally imagined for herself, but somehow, it felt right. She'd always held a secret desire to be free of her impending duty. It was weighty, considering herself as a ruler. In this version of their lives, Ilain would simply get to live as Ethenn's wife, enjoying the tranquil life for which she'd always wished.

The press of Ethenn's lips against her neck drew her to close her eyes. Yes, she quite liked marriage. And Ethenn truly was a splendid husband. With their ever-growing trust, his reservation had eased. He was still quiet and temperamental—she had to watch how often she teased him lest he become annoyed—but he'd grown vastly more tender and caring. He was steadier, as though her magic and his had combined to level out his inner fire.

It soothed the ember within Ilain too.

Ethenn's hand glided across Ilain's waist, his fingers tracing the crystal beads and embroidery on the dress. She'd chosen the gown to represent her brother. Golden yellow like Day. Auden might not have survived their mission, but he was in the Heavens now, watching over them proudly. The Alliance had accomplished its goal. Magic was restored to full power (a slow return, though Ilain could already feel a subtle burgeoning within her each time she touched her power), and Allund was a unified nation once again.

After all his hard work and sacrifice, Auden's life would not be in vain.

A sudden thought struck Ilain, stilling her under her husband's amorous touch.

Ethenn's lips paused, his affection halting on her bare shoulder. He lifted his head, looking at her. "What is it?" he asked.

Ilain blinked at the fire. How had she forgotten? She was a miserable excuse for a sister.

"Ilain?"

"I can't," she whispered.

"Can't what?"

"I can't do this."

Ethenn furrowed his brow. "I hate to inform you, love, but we've already done this about a hundred times."

Ilain turned to him with a scrunched-up nose. "We've only been married for a month," she said.

He shrugged lightly. "I rounded up."

She smirked. "That isn't what I was referring to, anyway."

"What were you referring to?"

Forcing herself to sit up, Ilain pulled out of his arms. She shifted on the crimson settee to face him fully. "I made a promise to Auden," she said.

Ethenn's chin lifted with ready understanding. He took her hands comfortingly.

"I told you about Maura," Ilain began. "She's locked in the Deep, dying slowly. If she isn't healed, she'll be lost forever. It was Auden's aim to save her."

"By Bonding," Ethenn noted.

Ilain nodded. "He thought that if he became the Day Chancellor, with the power of the Relic and his amplified magic, he could find a means of a cure. That's what Day does, after all. It heals."

Staring into Ethenn's dark eyes, Ilain knew he understood without her even having to say the rest. But she continued anyway. "I have to use the Alliance's favor to press for this cure. They'll try to help, yes, but . . . If I don't put my everything into it, it may never happen. Maura can't wait much longer. And I must save her. For Auden."

Ethenn nodded. "They'll agree, of course," he said. "But you're not a Day Mage, and only so much can be done."

"But if you and I go to the Order of the Day," she said, "if we add our powers and skills into searching for this cure alongside the Day Chancellor and Commander, we can ensure that it comes."

Slowly, Ethenn lifted his chin. "That will only take a few years, Allore willing. What will we do then?"

"Rejoin our friends?" Ilain suggested.

Ethenn smiled. "I'd be happy with that."

Still, Ilain was unsettled.

Ethenn tugged on her hand gently. "Tell me."

"It's nothing. I just—" Ilain stared at their hands. She wore only two rings now: the white and black moonstone, shining in its elegant gold and silver fitting, and her wedding gift from Ethenn—an intricate golden band designed to look like two gilda lilies holding a ruby between them. She'd already begun to slowly infuse power into both rings, storing it up for a time she might need it most.

"For the past thirty years of my life," she whispered, almost to the rings themselves, "*this* is who I was meant to become. I was supposed to be Highlady Chancellor. Now . . ."

She met Ethenn's patient gaze again. "What will I be when this is over?"

Tenderly, Ethenn lifted her chin, his thumb grazing her jawline. "Who you've always been," he said. "Highlady Ilain *Loxley*, the most powerful Fire Mage in two centuries, a bloody goddess, and . . ." He leaned closer as he whispered, "My wife."

A bashful smirk came to Ilain's lips. "I still think we should have taken my last name."

"I'm not that progressive," he said, closing the gap.

Just before their lips met, she murmured, "Bloody prude."

CHAPTER SIXTY-SEVEN

7TH OF PYRA, 1574

For the first time in their marriage, Evylin awoke before Deckard. She stared at him in the wan morning light, smiling softly to herself. In the heat of summer, they slept with the windows open and the curtains drawn back. A single sheet remained over their entangled limbs, aiding their cool temperature.

Impatient, Evylin wondered how Deckard could stand waking before her. He didn't often linger in bed with her, but he must have gone mad with the boredom on the occasions that he did.

Still, she lay in his arms, studying his features. He looked older than when they'd first married. Not in any great way; he bore no more wrinkles or physical signs of aging than before. Rather, it was a weightiness to his features. A refinement that gave him a sense of responsibility.

It worried her. She was about to ask him to accept even more of that weight. Would he resent her for it?

Absentmindedly, Evylin began to trace the lines of freckles across his skin. They were soft, almost indistinct in places, dotting his pale flesh intermittently. There was one on his chest that she'd always thought looked like a star. It made her smile, thinking he'd been marked by the Heavens from the start.

"Are you trying to tickle me?" Deckard muttered sleepily.

Evylin startled at his abrupt greeting. "No," she said with amusement. His eyes were still closed, but the corner of his mouth was lifting in a grin. "I'm just bored, waiting for you to wake up."

"I get the best sleep of my life," he yawned, "and you decide to wake me because of your impatience?"

"Something like that." Evylin leaned down, pressing a kiss to his cheek. She rolled farther on top of him, and he finally met her gaze. "Good morning."

"Good morning," he said warmly.

His arms tightened around her waist, and Evylin leaned her forehead on his. "Happy birthday."

A slow, playful smile appeared on Deckard's face, crinkling the corners of his eyes. "You remembered."

"Just barely," she admitted. "I had to write it down and have Thom remind me too."

Deckard cupped her face in his hands, kissed her softly, and then leaned back, his entire being flooded with joy. "As I told you before," he said tenderly. "I don't care if you remember these kinds of things."

"You also told me not to get you a gift. And I didn't listen to that either."

He frowned lightly then, and she sensed that his reprimand wasn't sincere. He appreciated her thoughtfulness.

"Don't get too excited," she warned. "It isn't quite so tangible as your gift to me."

Deckard's eyes narrowed in interest. "Oh?"

She nodded. "But I think we should sit up. You may not be able to unwrap it, but our current position could be somewhat distracting."

A sly glint appeared in Deckard's eyes as his hands slid lower down her back. "I wouldn't mind being distracted."

Evylin laughed and pulled away. "Quit that," she commanded, quickly escaping his grasp to roll off the bed. "Or I'll just have to keep your gift."

"I thought that *was* my gift."

Evylin rushed to their trunks with a huff and grabbed a tunic for each of them. Although she enjoyed his teasing and their flirtations, this situation required more sobriety than their previous state of undress. She tossed him the shirt and slipped on her own before climbing back onto the bed and crossing her legs.

Deckard didn't argue; he simply followed her lead. Leaning against the pillows and headboard, his demeanor revealed his easy mood. The yellow morning light revealed more copper in his hair than usual, and his eyes sparkled with a bright blue. He fiddled with his moonstone ring, which she had observed becoming more of an unconscious habit rather than a sign of anxiety. His warm smile and cheerful demeanor were contagious.

Evylin grasped his hands. "Honestly," she admitted, "I forgot to get you a gift."

A soft, airy chuckle escaped Deckard.

"Now, I'm actually grateful I did. Because I believe this is the best option I could have discovered."

He brought her hands to his lips, kissing the backs of them. "Whatever it is," he vowed, "it will be the best gift I've ever received."

"Well, let's not put too much pressure on it," she muttered.

Deckard lowered their hands to the bed between them, and she inhaled deeply. She met his eyes and said, "This is my gift to you: I am at your side, no matter what."

A bemused pinch pulled Deckard's brows together.

"Throughout my life, I've sought one thing: to see Ryen's and my dream come to life. I achieved that. Yet, over all that time, I've come to understand that it wasn't enough. I crave adventure, yes, but that isn't all I want. I also desire a home, security, and happiness. I long for both adventure and normalcy, yet I know now that neither choice will ever be enough."

Evylin scooted closer. "Do you remember," she said, "when we released Hewitt, and I asked him about—about his 'more'?"

"I remember." Deckard's smile had vanished, leaving confusion heavy around him. "I can't say I fully understood it, but I grasped the sentiment."

"Well," she said, lightly tracing her fingers along the back of his hand, "I always wanted to escape Whickam Village, convinced there had to be 'more' to life. I believed there was something grand out there that would make life truly worthwhile. Since childhood, I've thought that something was adventure, as Ryen and I imagined.

"But the moment I left, I recognized that the world mirrored my home. Each settlement felt identical; some were just bigger or smaller, but they all shared a commonality. I considered then that perhaps the world wasn't as exciting as I expected. Yet, I held out hope that genuine adventures were waiting for me."

She smiled. "Then we saved the prince, met Mages, fought a dragon, and . . . We had every adventure Ryen and I had planned—aside from becoming pirates, of course." They shared a laugh before she self-derisively concluded, "And it was horrible."

Deckard's smile disappeared as she tightened her grip on his hands. "Death terrifies me, Jonn," she confessed. "The thought of losing you, Thom, Ilain, Ethenn, Brea, Vayden, or anyone else is paralyzing. I hadn't recognized before how significant the fear of death can be in adventure."

Sympathy enveloped them as Deckard leaned closer. She sensed his desire to offer comfort, although he struggled to find the right words. That was fine with her; she already had plenty to express herself.

"Regardless of my fears," Evylin held their hands tightly together, "I've realized one truth: I'm a Warrior. Though travel can be uneventful and adventure carries its price, my love for it endures. Deep down, a part of me will always yearn for more of it."

Evylin paused, her face flushing and her throat going dry with the emotions swelling inside her. She focused on their hands for a moment, struggling to retrieve her courage and find her voice.

Meeting her husband's affectionate gaze filled her with the strength she needed.

"With that in mind," Evylin emphasized her words with strength and clarity, "I now understand that my past dreams aren't sufficient. They don't truly enhance this world. If you told me right now that you wanted us to remain here in Aulton, working as clerks in this palace and never traveling again, I wouldn't feel sad. If you expressed a desire to return to Nettershire and take over your father's farm, I would be happy to accompany you. If you decided to move to gloomy West Allund and live in dismal Dunneshead, I would follow you there."

Although Deckard appeared apprehensive, they both laughed at the last one.

"I would do any of those things for you," Evylin promised. "Because I finally know the answer."

A heartbeat passed, and Deckard tilted his head to the side. "What answer?"

Evylin smiled at him, feeling perhaps lighter and happier than ever. "It's you," she said. "You're my 'more.'"

If Evylin ever doubted Deckard's affection for her, the wonder and warmth in his gaze, along with the love and joy he felt at that moment, dispelled any uncertainty permanently.

Evylin found herself smiling brightly. "This world is so much richer with you by my side and far less vibrant when you're not there." She continued with determination, "So I won't decide our future. I won't choose who we become or what path we take because I trust that you'll stand by me no matter what, regardless of your true feelings.

"I won't allow you to endure a future less than you are," she asserted. "I want your happiness to match mine. You deserve to be happy, Jonn, and to become the man you aspire to be."

A brief flicker of fear glimmered in Deckard's eyes. He cleared his throat. "I don't know who that man is," he said.

"Don't you?" Evylin asked soothingly.

The breath he exhaled sounded labored. "Who do you want me to be?"

"I want you to be *you*."

Deckard scoffed and shook his head. There was a certain level of exasperation around him, but she could tell it wasn't aimed at her. Instead, it was directed at himself.

"Who do *you* want to be?" she asked.

Pulling one hand free, Deckard ran it along his jaw. "I don't know."

"You don't know, or you don't want to say?"

That brought an edge of irritation toward her. Yet, it vanished instantly as he sighed, "I don't want to admit it."

"I know."

"It's . . . it's not easy, you know," he whispered. "Wanting to be like that."

"Like Euon Sergus?"

He hesitated, then nodded.

"Like a legend?"

He winced. "That makes me sound like an egotistical maniac."

Evylin brushed a hand over his cheek. "No," she said, holding his gaze lovingly. "It makes you sound like Ryen and me."

A small, embarrassed smile appeared on his lips. "You understand, don't you, that everything you just shared, I feel the same way about you? I would gladly give up everything I am to make your life what you desire. I would leave everything behind for you."

"Yes, I understand," she said. "But do you realize I'm giving you a chance to do just that? To choose between becoming the legend you've always dreamed of being or becoming the man you believe you *can* be."

Deckard's entire body froze. Even his breathing stopped as fear seeped from him into her hands. "I don't want it, Evie."

She softened her expression, understanding he needed reassurance in this decision. "Is it that you don't want it, or that you doubt you can achieve it?"

"I don't want it."

"Why not?" she pressed. "After all this time—after thirty-three years of life—when it's finally in front of you, why don't you want it anymore?"

Deckard frowned. "Because it's too difficult, Evylin. Being that man, being that perfect, is too difficult. Throughout my entire life, I have repeatedly denied myself because I believed there was a greater standard to meet." He shook his head, struggling to articulate his feelings. "I have put in immense effort to be selfless, honorable, and decent for those around me. I have done everything possible to mirror Sergus, yet I have failed time and again. I failed my brother. I failed Hewitt and Auden. I've failed you more times than I'd like to count. How could I possibly think I could assist my country in this way? I do not consider myself the right man for this responsibility. I am not Sergus, and I never will be."

Evylin knelt before Deckard on the soft bed, cupping his face in her hands. "Who do you want to be?" she asked. "If you can't be him, then who will you become? A farmer? A soldier? A mercenary?"

"I want to go home," he murmured, embracing her tightly. "I want to take you back to Loclight and stay there forever."

Evylin bit her bottom lip to suppress a smile at the sweet sentiment. "And what happens when you get bored?"

"I'd never get bored. I'd have you."

"After just one week, I'd drive you insane." She shook her head. "That's not you, Jonn."

"Who am I, then?" Deckard pleaded, sincerity and hope evident in his voice, emotions she hadn't anticipated.

Evylin smiled, gently brushing her fingertips through the waves of his hair. "You are a servant, a leader, a Mage, and my husband." She pressed a firm, reassuring kiss to his lips. "And I won't allow you to be anything less than that."

Deckard lowered his eyes and turned his head away. A hush fell over them as a whirlwind of emotions swirled around him—conflict, confusion, anxiety, and a glimmer of hope. In that brief moment, it was clear he was wrestling with worries that were far too complex for an instant reply.

As she observed him grappling with his inner struggles, Evylin moved closer. Leaning in, she whispered softly into his ear, "I don't want you to be Sergus." She kept her voice warm and reassuring, and she felt his grip tighten around her as she continued, "I want you to be you."

Deckard buried his head in her neck, remaining silent.

"You're far better than Sergus anyway."

Evylin tenderly rubbed her hand over Deckard's back, letting him battle the storm of emotions within him. Minutes passed by like whispers. Time seemed to stand still as he navigated his internal conflict. But Evylin didn't mind; she found joy in holding him close, savoring the moment as he moved toward the same feeling of freedom that she now cherished.

At first, the thought of self-sacrifice was quite daunting for her. The idea of possibly giving up everything made her question whether she was truly making the right choice. However, Evylin remembered that Deckard had faced the same dilemma for her. He was ready to make such a brave sacrifice, fully aware that she would never settle for a quiet life as a housewife, tending to the home as she waited for his return. That just wasn't who she was. He had given her the freedom to decide, knowing full well that her heart was set on a life of adventure.

Evylin was determined to show Deckard the same understanding and support.

All those months ago in Whickam Village, Hewitt saw that Deckard was Evylin's perfect match. *"If you sacrifice the man you truly desire to become, you can't be the man she needs."*

A man who would never settle for the mundane or the simple. A man who would opt for the difficult path because it was the right one. A man who would confront his fears of failure to serve his ruler and countrymen.

Even if, in this case, it made him that ruler.

Deckard placed his hands on Evylin's arms and withdrew slightly. His green-blue eyes locked onto hers. He attempted to speak but initially found no words. After a deep inhale, he tried once more.

"From childhood," he stated, his voice firm and heartfelt, "I aspired to be like Sergus. I yearned to be remembered for my excellence. I put in great effort to achieve that, Evie. I truly did."

"And you are."

"I'm not, " Deckard maintained, shaking his head. "I'm a selfish failure, and I've disappointed countless people."

Evylin offered him a reassuring smile. "You're not the type to quit, Jonn. I understand you, and I know your desire to become a legend goes beyond mere excitement. It may have begun that way, but that's not the essence of who you are. Everything you are, you give to others. That isn't selfish. Everything you undertake, you put in your best. That isn't failure. To everyone you meet, you offer all that you are. You've never let anyone down."

"I'm not good enough."

"Yes, you are."

"I will fail."

"Maybe," she conceded. "But you'll never stop trying to make it right. You'll take care of this nation better than anyone else could."

Deckard lowered his head. "You think we should accept the position, then."

Evylin took a deep breath, choosing her words wisely. "I believe," she began, "you need to be certain you won't regret turning it down."

He pressed his lips into a thin line, remaining silent. The air was thick with disappointment as his hands went still on her.

Concerned she had put undue pressure on him, Evylin lifted his chin. "Jonn," she said with kindness, "it doesn't matter to me. No matter what you decide, I want you to be happy, and I want you to know we made the right decision. Whatever that may be— whether leading the Loclight Order, serving in the Allundan Army, traveling to the beaches of Audis, or tilling the fields in the Shire—I will stand with you."

Deckard scanned her face. "No matter what?"

"No matter what."

A deep, prolonged sigh escaped his lips, so thick and heavy that she wondered how long he might have been carrying it with him.

Deckard pressed his forehead to hers. "This . . ." he whispered, shaking his head. A bittersweet wave of relief and pain enveloped him. Yet, his voice emerged clear and firm. "This is who we were destined to be. This was the future Hewitt envisioned for us. This has always been our life: service and adventure.

"It's who we are," he said, straightening to smile with the light of hope in his eyes. "A Warrior and a Mage. It would be a mistake to try to be anything else."

Evylin controlled her emotions, gripping them tightly as she sought clarity. "Are you certain? You're not just saying this because you believe it's what I want to hear?"

"No," Deckard promised. "I *do* believe it's what you want to hear, but I'm not saying it for that reason. It's what I want as well."

"Oh, thank Allore," Evylin said, unable to contain her relief any longer.

Deckard chuckled as she threw her arms around him. "I thought you didn't care."

"Of course I care," she exclaimed, pulling back to study his handsome face. "I don't want to be a farmer's wife. I married a captain with the intention of traveling the country, not living in a cottage and wasting my life cooking your dinners."

"You've never made me dinner."

"Pardon me, but I made your dinner the first night we met. Or at least, I made the vegetables."

Deckard smirked playfully. "Did you? They were particularly fine vegetables."

"Don't mock me," she said, draping her arms around his shoulders. "I helped prepare all the meals you enjoyed at my family's house, and I'm an excellent cook."

"I'll take your word for it."

Evylin allowed her laughter to fade. "Are you sure?" she asked again.

Deckard smiled, and a wave of true contentment washed over her, confirming its authenticity. "I'm absolutely certain."

"So we'll accept it?"

"Yes," he said, kissing her. "We'll accept it."

CHAPTER SIXTY-EIGHT

Thom tossed and turned throughout the night. Over and over, he ruffled his hair, his head in his hands as he stared wide-eyed at the ceiling. Although he knew he must have fallen asleep at some point, he had no memory of doing so. Instead, he drifted through a series of wakeful moments until he finally sat up on the edge of his bed, the rising sun casting an orange glow across the room.

What a bloody idiot you are, Thom thought.

He pushed off the bed, unable to bear his reproachful, embarrassed thoughts any longer. He'd been such a fool. What man in his right mind made such an egregious overture to a woman who had only moments before pointedly told him that she thought he should marry another? Whatever feelings Brea had held in the past for him, it was clear that she had no intention of forsaking her vow to the Alliance for any reason, let alone for *him*.

Grumbling at his insanity, Thom dressed in a hurry. He hoped the others weren't up yet. He could grab a quick breakfast and sneak out of the apartment, avoiding Brea until after their appointment with the Administration later that afternoon. Then he'd work up the courage to apologize to her and congratulate her on whichever Mage she chose to marry.

The good news was that, shortly, they'd likely live on opposite sides of the continent. Whichever of the Mages she Bonded with, they would take her away. Wilkinsone's affinity was to Water, Humes's was to Wind, and Grames's was to Terrae. Even if, by some miracle, Deckard and Evylin took the position in Loclight, he'd be weeks away from any of the other Orders, meaning he wouldn't have to worry about awkwardly running into Brea any time soon. And after a few years, they could laugh it off like the joke it was.

Tugging his cravat looser than was strictly standard, Thom stepped out of his suite. He entered the parlor to find Mrs. Wilumson setting the small dining table with a smorgasbord of breakfast. It smelled of hearty sausage, herbaceous potatoes, buttery bread, and fragrant tea. The room was filled with light, as the windows were open to the early morning breeze. Songbirds crooned from their perches.

And Thom regretted even waking as he took his first step into the parlor.

Seated at the table, Brea thanked Mrs. Wilumson for the cup of tea she'd just handed to her. She'd braided her tight black curls back this morning in thick plaits before pinning them into a bun at the base of her neck. Dressed in a subdued tunic, vest, and skirt, she appeared more Warrior-like as usual. The sunlight caught on her brown skin, making her look like a radiant angel.

As Mrs. Wilumson moved to depart, Thom silently mouthed a particularly vile curse. Though Brea was seated facing the wall, there was no doubt in his mind that she already knew he was there. The woman heard everything—thus the silent curse rather than a muttered one.

Forcing himself to man up, Thom steeled his bravery. If he could face down dragons, *vængebjörn*, bloodwolves, and all other manners of mythological creatures, he could handle an awkward conversation with the woman he loved.

Thom drew back his shoulders and approached the table. "Morning," he said casually. He took the seat across from Brea—though not directly—and reached for the teapot.

"Good morning," Brea replied with a polite smile.

Throat as dry as the wind outside the stone palace, he inquired, "Did you sleep well?"

Brea blinked, pausing for only a moment as she filled her plate. "I did," she said. "These beds are rather luxurious."

"Like everything here," Thom noted.

"Yes."

Hearing the curious tilt to her tone, Thom sipped his tea, then settled the cup back on the cotton tablecloth. "So," he began, "I think I should probably address the, uh . . . rather unintentional statement I made last night."

Brea's sharp brow arched, but he kept talking before she could reply. "We were drinking, and though I was not drunk, wine is known to make me act in less than the wisest manner at times." The words came out stilted and forced. He cleared his throat. "What I mean to say is—"

"Good morning!" Calyn called in a cheerful singsong as she flounced into the room in a bright pink dress.

Thom did curse audibly then.

Calyn narrowed her eyes reprovingly. "That's not polite, Thom," she said.

"You scared me," he grumbled as she took the seat next to Brea.

Tucking a few of her brown waves behind her ear, Calyn wrinkled her nose. "I merely said good morning."

Brea patted her hand. "He's a miserable grouch when he wakes," she said by way of explanation. "I had the unfortunate pleasure of experiencing that daily while we traveled."

"Can something be an unfortunate pleasure?" Calyn asked, gathering her own breakfast.

Brea smirked, lifting her teacup to her lips. "I can't think of any better way to describe him."

Unsure if that was Brea's way of offering her unspoken forgiveness, Thom grinned warily. "Ha-ha," he mocked.

Her smile grew, but she turned back to her breakfast.

"Are you feeling all right?" Calyn asked him suddenly.

Thom frowned. "Of course I am. Why wouldn't I be?"

"Well, you left the party early. Cris had to walk me back."

"I'm sure you were devastated."

She ignored his quip. "And now, you look sort of . . . pallid. There are an awful lot of shadows on your face, particularly under your eyes."

"I didn't sleep well," Thom said tersely.

"Did you drink too much?" Calyn asked.

"No."

Brea looked up, meeting Thom's gaze with a sly glimmer in her dark eyes. "Perhaps we ought to call the doctor," she said. "Sometimes, the weak-bodied develop what's called 'air sickness' this high in the mountains. It would be a pity if you were bedridden the rest of our time in the city, *mi'caro*."

Brea spoke with a daring spark that allowed Thom to breathe again. It was as if by her teasing she was offering to overlook the awkward truth if he chose to do so. She seemed determined not to let their friendship waver, just as he hadn't let hers falter either.

Grateful for her kindness, Thom returned her smile, albeit a bit more nervously than usual. "I'm quite hale, *demoloba*," he replied.

"Are you sure?" Calyn asked, leaning forward with worry. "I've never seen you so haggard."

Thom gave her a flat look, but Brea brushed Calyn's concern away. "Don't worry, Caly. I'll keep an eye on him. Now, tell me, did you enjoy your evening with Cris?"

"Oh, yes!" Calyn said, a light blush coloring her cheeks. "He's quite charming and an excellent dancer. I was worried that it wouldn't be appropriate to share so many sets with him, but as I didn't know anyone else, I didn't feel right accepting many other partners anyway."

"All Schonese men are trained dancers," Brea said matter-of-factly. "We highly prize dancing in our culture."

"I've never seen you dance," Thom said, surprised.

Brea turned a cunning grin his way. "You've never asked me to."

He blanched and chose to let the taunt go. Turning away, he looked at Calyn. "Cris was a gentleman, right? He didn't try anything untoward?"

Calyn's jaw dropped along with her eyes. "Of course not," she said sharply, though she shifted with discomfort in her seat.

Thom studied her knowingly. "He kissed you," he surmised.

Her dark gaze flew back to his face, her cheeks turning the color of the Fire Relic. Thom nodded. "I knew it."

"It was on the cheek, if you must know," Calyn insisted. "Nothing inappropriate."

"But still, rather forward."

Brea made a face. "Kissing on the cheek is a greeting and a farewell in Schon," she said.

"Well, we aren't in Schon, are we?" Thom returned. He thought about commenting that Brea had never kissed his cheek in any manner but decided it was best to refrain.

"Decidedly not," Brea said before turning to Calyn. "While I'm sure Cris meant it more affectionately with you, I am also sure it wasn't intended to be forward."

Calyn looked between them, chewing on her bottom lip in a manner that resembled Evylin. "Do you think he's . . . He wouldn't be interested in forming an attachment," she said. "Surely, not so soon."

Brea shrugged. "I'm not sure. I've yet to speak with him on the subject."

Calyn nodded with enthusiastic understanding as Deckard and Evylin entered the parlor. Thankfully, their arrival put an end to Thom and Brea's more personal conversations. They weren't scheduled to meet with the Administration until later in the afternoon, leaving the morning free for relaxation and exploration.

After breakfast, Thom murmured a subtle "Happy birthday" to Deckard while the women prepared to leave. Then they met up with Ethenn, Ilain, Vayden, and Reyana. Brea excused herself to spend the morning with her family, easing Thom's discomfort even more. Though part of him never wanted to be apart from her, another part of him was glad for the separation. It allowed him to think of other matters.

Such as what he was going to do with the rest of his life.

One of the Alliance clerks gave their party a tour of the Aulden Palace grounds. The sprawling palace featured a training ground suitable for the grandest military in the world, along with numerous dance halls, apartments, and governmental offices. The clerk informed them that the official administrative work of Allund would take place within the palace walls. It would function as their central command, while the chancellors, commanders, and ministers would enact the laws across the land.

Thom wondered where he fit into this new world of theirs. He would follow Deckard and Evylin so long as they'd let him, but he had no idea what that future would look like. He didn't think he'd make a good general, so it was just as well that they wouldn't accept the position in Loclight. Perhaps they could all become soldiers together.

Though he considered speaking with them about their requests to the Alliance, he decided against it. With their friends around, he knew Deckard wouldn't want to discuss it, nor did he care to reveal his own thoughts on the subject.

The day flew by faster than Thom preferred, and before long, Calyn and Reyana went off together while the clerk escorted the rest of them to the throne room of Aulden Palace, where Brea was already waiting.

Situated on the palace's lowest floor and at its very center, the throne room awaited them. Its breathtaking design reminded Thom of the Keeps. Eight tall, arching entrances lined the circular space. Constructed from the same creamy stone as the rest of the palace, the grand room featured no columns for support, as it seemed to have no ceiling. Rising high above, a glass and iron roof allowed sunlight to pour in. Thin rectangular windows positioned along the room's walls provided light to the other spaces in the palace.

Eight thrones were positioned on tall platforms, with stone staircases winding around their bases for easy access to the seats. Yet, both the thrones and the expansive platforms they occupied remained unoccupied.

The ministers were arranged in a semicircle on the far side of the room. "Good afternoon," greeted Archminister Essen, her aged face lighting up with a smile. "I hope you all had a restful night and morning?"

A chorus of their approval resonated throughout the vast room. Thom struggled to concentrate amidst its overwhelming grandeur.

"We don't wish to take up your whole afternoon, so we'll get to the point, shall we? Do you feel you've each had ample time to consider your reward?"

A pause lingered as the troop exchanged glances. Ilain edged closer to Ethenn's side while Vayden stood behind them. Brea turned to Thom, who pressed his lips together and shrugged before glancing at Evylin and Deckard.

After assessing the entire team one by one, Deckard stepped forward. "I think most, if not all of us, feel that we've had sufficient time to consider, ma'am," he stated as if he were speaking to a commanding officer rather than an elderly woman.

Archminister Essen's smile broadened, and her pleasure was reflected through the expressions of her fellow ministers. "Wonderful," she said, bringing her hands together in delight. "Don't hesitate to ask for anything you need or desire."

Deckard turned back to the group, his gaze darting nervously to Evylin as if he were afraid to speak first.

Ilain stepped forward, her eyes sparkling with something like hesitation. "I suppose we might as well be the ones to get us started," she said, flashing her husband a warm smile.

Ethenn's neck flushed slightly, yet he nodded. "Ilain and I have spoken, and we feel we must ask . . ." He paused, glancing at his wife. At her nod, he smiled, encouraged. "We would ask that you allow us to spend however long it takes with the Order of the Day, seeking a cure for the Deep. It was the greatest wish of Highlord Magister Auden Calder that this task be accomplished, and together, Ilain and I would like to see that task fulfilled."

Taken aback, the ministers exchanged confused looks. Thom himself was surprised at first, but knowing they were seeking a cure for Maura, he understood completely.

Archminister Dudleye spoke first. "Is this a refusal of the positions of chancellor and commander?"

"As we are incapable of being in two places at once," Ilain said with a lighthearted apology, "yes, it is."

"We could grant that the resources and effort be placed into this discovery for you, Highlady," Dudleye said. "You needn't go to Norhels yourself."

"I must, though," Ilain said. "I promised my brother I would see this done. If I don't attend to it myself, I cannot feel that I've honored his memory with my best effort."

A muttering of questions spread among the ministers. They mentioned the idea of interim rulers in Ilain and Ethenn's places, but the fact was, there was no guarantee of how long it would take for this cure to be found. It could be months, years, or decades. Possibly even a century. Ilain hoped it would be within a handful of years, for Maura's sake, but she could not say with any certainty.

After a long, regretful conversation, the ministers granted the request. "You will," Dudleye finally said, "henceforth be known as Highlord and Highlady Loxley until such a time as you have discovered this cure and chosen your next path. And we will pursue another couple to lead our people in Doorstunds Province."

Ilain and Ethenn shared a contented smile, and Thom knew they'd made the right choice. Together, the pair would make excellent leaders, but this choice wasn't about their personal desires or skills. In the Alliance, they made sacrifices, and this was their sacrifice.

"It seems," Vayden said, setting a hand on Ilain's shoulder, "that I've found my request as well. I don't know what good I can do toward this cure, but my daughter and I would request to go with Ilain and Ethenn. Whatever their path, it is mine also."

The siblings exchanged a warm smile as the ministers granted their approval.

Deckard offered his best wishes to Ilain, Ethenn, and Vayden before facing the ministers again. Evylin intertwined her fingers with his as they exchanged a long, curious glance, one that suggested both excitement and trepidation, as if they were on the brink of something significant.

A momentary flash of worry made Thom question if they would request some future that he would be incapable of joining.

"Evylin and I," Deckard said, "have decided to accept the appointment as Chancellor and Commander of Loclight Province."

Thom's breath whooshed out of his lungs, and Ilain nudged Ethenn.

"This is the life we desire," Deckard said confidently. "A life devoted to serving our people. We will do everything in our power to govern the province and the Order of the Heavens with honor and justice."

"However," Evylin said with a playful lilt in her voice, "we ask for the ability to travel regularly. We miss our friends and family, and many of them won't be in Loclight with us."

The ministers nodded readily, and Archminister Essen brushed her hand through the air. "We can make arrangements for that," she assured them. "Is that all?"

"For now," Evylin said.

"Very well." She turned to Thom. "Should we presume that you'll accept your post as well, *General* Deckard?"

Thom paused for an extended moment to consider this new path. He had envisioned a situation in which Deckard and Evylin accepted the appointment but never thought it would actually happen. Now, he found himself uncertain about his next steps. He questioned whether he could be an effective head of the guard or if he'd fail as he'd failed so many things in life.

"I, uh—" Thom cleared his throat and took a single step forward. "I'm sorry, I know I want to stay with Jonn and Evie, but . . . I don't think I'd like the position."

Deckard watched him with his ever-steady brotherly affection while Evylin smirked. "You don't want to protect us?" she teased.

"I tried that once," Thom bantered. "It didn't work out well."

A moment of silence passed before Essen asked, "Do you need more time?"

Thom nodded. "If you don't mind."

"Well then, Captain, we'll grant you an extension," she said. "We do not wish to rush any of you."

Thom gave her a small bow. "Thank you, ma'am. I greatly appreciate it."

The archminister dipped her head in return, then straightened. "And Captain Lohen, what is your request?"

Thom took a deep breath, resisting the urge to turn back to Brea too quickly. She rested one arm on the other, her fingers touching her mouth in contemplation. Her deadpan gaze startled him, a look far too serious for his taste.

"Captain?" the archminister repeated.

Brea lowered her arms and walked past Thom toward the ministers. With her chin held high, she spoke. "Ministers, I appreciate this opportunity and the trust you extend toward me with your offer to become a commander in our nation. You hold me in high regard, and I acknowledge that honor. However, I must decline your request."

Thom's stomach quaked. Had she just . . . ?

"I have no desire to be a commander," Brea continued. "Mistakenly, I made a promise to the Alliance long ago when I was a youth, and I lost someone very dear to me because of it. I was prepared to keep that promise as a sacrifice. But I cannot do it."

There was a moment of silence before one of the female ministers from the east gave Brea an encouraging smile. "While we are surprised, we fully respect your decision," she said.

Brea bowed her head in gratitude. "I do wish to serve the Alliance," she said vehemently. "Which is why I would ask that you allow me to become the head of chancellor and commander Deckards' guard."

While everyone else started in shock, Thom chuckled.

Brea turned to look at him as if seeking his permission.

"Take it," he said, smiling. "You'll be far better at it than I would."

She paused briefly to smile back at him.

"If that's the job you want, Captain," Archminister Essen said with a warm, matronly smile, "then we would be happy to offer it to you." And why wouldn't they? Brea would undoubtedly be the finest general the world had ever known.

"Thank you," Brea replied, yet she remained in place. She clenched and unclenched her fists at her side. "I have one more request."

"You do?" Essen asked.

"Yes, ma'am." Brea lifted her chin another inch. "In the past two months, I've made some wonderful new friends, but I also lost my oldest and closest one." Brea and Vayden exchanged a somber glance. "If Isla's death taught me anything, it's not to let my fears keep me from what I most desire."

She shifted her dark stare then, meeting Thom's gaze as she concluded, "Or from the man I love."

The words struck everyone in the room, a current of shock running through the space. Like he'd just suffered a punch to the stomach, Thom took a step back, a faint gasp escaping him. The ministers pulled back, wearing surprised and confused looks. The troop members shifted their focus between Thom and Brea.

"I would ask," Brea continued, still holding his gaze, "that you approve my marriage to Thom Deckard."

Thom's mouth dropped open.

Brea's brows raised in question. "If he'll have me."

The whole room held its breath, eagerly anticipating Thom's reply. But what could he say? He loved her deeply and wanted her by his side. Still, a little voice nagged at him, whispering that their relationship might not be meant to be. It told him she was too perfect, and he was a mere mortal. She was incredible, while he was so far below her.

Desperate for help, Thom turned to Deckard. He received exactly what he expected: his brother's kind and supportive smile paired with a firm nod of approval.

Thom couldn't suppress the small scoff that escaped him. Trying to gather his thoughts, he ran a hand through his hair and then passed it over his face. "Are you sure?" he asked Brea. "I'm not good enough for you."

"Probably not," she said, her cunning smirk in place. "But I love you, regardless."

"You shouldn't," he advised.

"Too late, *mi'eló*."

Mi'eló. My only.

Hearing those words fall from her lips didn't strike Thom the way he thought it would. He didn't experience an electrifying rush or an incredible warmth igniting his soul. He didn't feel instantly complete or whole. His past was riddled with mistakes, and he had years of redemption ahead of him. Yet, a wonderful sense of joy washed over his heart, knowing that, for once, *he* was the one someone chose.

As Thom took three tentative steps closer, he examined her face, studying its angles, curves, and contours. In her dark eyes, he saw hope and sincerity despite the worry and intensity etched into her lowered brows. Nerves and humor flickered at the corners of her lips. He had admired her beauty countless times, but at this moment, she appeared more captivating than ever.

Thom gently traced his finger along her jawline, lifting her chin. "It's too late," he repeated, "for both of us."

"Is that a yes?" she asked. "You'll have me?"

"Only if you'll have me," he promised.

"I wouldn't want anyone else."

The overwhelming urge to kiss her pressed upon him. He'd thought about it multiple times in the past. Even during moments when he considered them just friends, he'd occasionally wondered what the press of her lips on his would feel like. However, he never allowed these thoughts to develop until his discussion with Deckard a week prior. Now, it was difficult to think of anything *but* kissing her.

Despite having gained confidence that he could—and perhaps should—kiss her, he hesitated. It shouldn't be here. Not in front of the ministers and their friends. Certainly not for the first time.

Forcing himself to look up, Thom stared at the ministers. "Will you approve our marriage?" he demanded.

The ministers were silent, exchanging uncertain looks. "We . . ." Archminister Essen looked to Archiminister Dudleye. "We need to discuss it?"

The man shrugged. "Technically, we should."

"You promised to approve any requests we made," Brea said sharply. Her hand grasped Thom's, and he stared down at them in astonishment.

Am I really engaged? The thought was fleeting and abstract, and his attention quickly returned to the men and women who would decide his fate.

"Within reason," one of the western ministers said.

Deckard stepped forward. "And how is this unreasonable? You said that you fully respect her choice to marry for love. This is your chance to demonstrate that."

Essen raised a placating hand. "It is our policy to take each marriage of magical persons very seriously," she said. "As they are reflections of Allore's power himself, we believe they have a responsibility—"

"Oh, shove your responsibility," Deckard said in a very uncharacteristic fashion.

Thom's eyes went wide as Evylin's hand flew to her mouth with barely contained laughter.

Deckard stood at the forefront of the group, contending for his brother. "Will you break your promise just because it conflicts with your plans? Are you going to compel her to marry someone to shape the world to your liking? Is that truly the kind of nation we envision Allund to be?"

Several ministers wore disgruntled looks, but Archminister Dudleye waved his hand through the air. "We never said we wouldn't approve it, Chancellor Deckard," he said soothingly. "No, this isn't what we hoped for, but you are right. We aren't a tyranny, and we won't start Allund by breaking a promise to the very people who risked everything to help us raise it."

Nods of support came from nearly every minister.

"We had an agreement, and we will honor it," Dudleye promised. "Together, Archminister Essen and I and the whole of the Administration approve this marriage."

Cheers rang out from their friends on either side, yet Thom and Brea simply exchanged smiles. He grasped her other hand, drawing her an inch closer.

Not here, he reminded himself. *Not yet. But soon.*

"Archminister," Thom called, still looking down at Brea.

"Yes, Captain Deckard?" Dudleye replied.

"I know what reward I want."

"What's that?"

"A house," he said with a bright smile. "Right next door to Deckard and Evie's. And I want to work for my wife."

Brea smirked. "I won't go easy on you just because we're married."

"I wouldn't expect you to."

"That's all?" Dudleye asked, sounding genuinely surprised.

"That's all I need."

"Very well," the western archminister replied. "Having heard all your requests, we will initiate the necessary processes to fulfill them. Once again, our gratitude to your troop is beyond words. We will forever be in your debt. If there are no further matters, you may be excused."

While Deckard and Ilain expressed their gratitude to the ministers, Thom and Brea quickly made their exit. They hurried through the archway into the bustling, column-lined halls. He felt lost with so many people moving around, but she guided him confidently to the right without hesitation.

"Brea," Thom whispered as she tugged him through the busy halls.

She smiled as she glanced over her shoulder. "What?"

As Thom glanced to the left and right, he noticed an empty room ahead and quickly took the lead. They entered, and he closed the door and fixed his gaze on her. "Brea."

"What?" she asked again.

"I love you."

She smiled, brighter and more beautiful than ever before.

Taking her face in his hands, Thom marveled at how his racing heart had not yet burst from his chest. Her skin was so soft beneath his fingers, her face tilted toward him, open and full of hope.

"I was so afraid," he whispered, his voice barely rising above the flood of emotions inside him. "I thought I'd ruined everything last night—that I'd pushed you away."

"You didn't," she reassured him, placing her hands on his wrists.

"I can see that now."

"I wouldn't have said anything," she said. "I wouldn't have asked to marry you if you hadn't . . ."

His eyes darted between hers. "You wouldn't have?"

"Of course not. I never thought . . . I didn't believe you desired anything beyond friendship. I was content with that."

"So was I," he confessed, savoring the way his thumb glided along her cheekbone. "But that changed."

Gently, she ran her hands down his arms and stepped closer. "Thom," she whispered now, "there are many challenges ahead for us. I spoke with my grandfather about his marriage; my grandmother was non-magical, too, and their life together, while beautiful, was fraught with difficulty and pain. He had to watch her age while he stayed the same. She endured ridicule for being with a man presumably so much her junior. While he remained in his prime, she became frail and weak. We won't have an easy life, you and I."

Hearing the warning she was giving him—*he* would endure ridicule from those who didn't understand as he grew old and gray while she remained youthful, and *he* would age into feebleness while she maintained her vitality and vigor—Thom couldn't find it in him to care.

"Easy is boring," he said.

Brea raised an eyebrow, a mischievous smile forming on her full lips, drawing his attention to her mouth as she continued, "You've always been difficult, haven't you?"

"Absolutely," he affirmed, dipping down toward her. Their lips nearly met just as she tugged back lightly.

"Well then," she said playfully, her breath mingling with his, "perhaps I should make this a little more challenging for you."

"I'd rather you didn't."

"I thought easy was boring?"

"Brea." He wound one arm around her waist. "*Mi'cara*," he whispered in her ear. "There's nothing about you that could ever be boring."

"And nothing about you could ever be easy, *mi'eló*."

Thom smiled and leaned in, laughing softly as he brought his face closer to hers again. "I love you," he repeated. "Though I've foolishly said those words to others in the past, I now know—with complete certainty—that you are the only one I've ever truly meant it about. The only one who's made me fully understand what love is."

"Thom," she whispered, setting a hand along his jaw.

"What?"

Brea didn't speak but drew Thom closer, rising on her toes to press her lips to his in a long and far-overdue kiss.

CHAPTER SIXTY-NINE

24TH OF PYRA, 1574

The Alliance spent the next two weeks preparing for the coronation of the Allundan oligarchy. While Deckard and Evylin were brought up to speed on the finer points of Allund's structure and administration through various meetings, the ministers worked to find suitable replacements for Ethenn and Ilain.

As the Loxleys had effectively abdicated, they moved into the Loclight suites, along with Vayden and Reyana, granting their troop time to be together again. Though Deckard and Evylin were often busy during the days, they spent the evenings with their friends, and he could feel how grateful she was for that. They would still have to part from the Loxleys and Calders before long, but they wouldn't be as far as West Allund. And when they discovered the cure, they hoped to join the rest in Loclight.

During their meetings, Deckard and Evylin also met with the other chancellors and commanders. During their mission to retrieve the Relics, they'd met the Night Mage, Grey Trumane, in Mouroc, but this was their first chance to meet Alma, his Warrior bride. They were a unique pair; Grey displayed a bright, dry sense of humor, while Alma reminded Deckard of a female version of Hewitt, her manner gruff and no-nonsense. Evylin liked her tremendously.

When Deckard met the other Bonded couples, he assessed their character with thoughtful care. These were the individuals set to take on leadership roles in their country. He was desperate to ensure they were capable and pleasant. He was relieved to find that, overall, they fit the bill.

Once all preparations had been finalized for the coronation, the date was set, and the ministers granted the troop a three-day leave to recuperate and unwind. These were to be their final days in each other's company for a considerable duration. After the coronation, their lives would set out on different paths. With the future they'd worked for closer than ever, a sense of unease settled in Deckard's stomach; he still didn't feel ready for the responsibility he was about to assume. However, he knew that with Evylin and Thom beside him, he couldn't fail. They wouldn't let him.

On the night before the coronation, the troop gathered in the parlor. Sitting in the Loclight apartments wasn't quite like the old times around the campfire. So much had changed, yet the same laughter and companionship prevailed. They missed Hewitt, Auden, Rafferty, and Isla but were joined by Calyn and Cris—who were officially courting, as he had received a letter of permission from Magistrate Glaas only the previous day—and Reyana, who often spent her time with her father or Brea.

Only a day after meeting with the ministers, Thom and Brea had married. They didn't want to wait, opting for a small ceremony with only the troop as witnesses. Although Deckard still wasn't thrilled about the discrepancies in their age and magic, he was genuinely happy for his brother. Thom had grown significantly as a man over the past year. Deckard attributed this growth largely to Brea's influence. She had a way of bringing out the best in Thom and pushing him in ways no one else seemed able to accomplish.

In Deckard's eyes, Brea was surprisingly companionable. As she was to be their head of the guard, she had already begun working closely with Deckard and Evylin to plan how they would run Loclight. The more time Deckard spent with Brea, the better they got along. He found her levelheadedness and candid manner refreshing and often sought her advice on difficult decisions.

With their time together in Aulton, Deckard was able to see that the rest of their friends had grown as well.

Over the last nearly two months of marriage, Ethenn and Ilain had become a synchronous team. They worked well alongside each other, tempering their more intense traits while encouraging their more subdued ones. The young hunter had become confident and caring, and the highlady was attentive and knowledgeable. Although Deckard felt they would have made admirable rulers, he was proud of them for choosing to seek a cure for the Deep. He considered it a noble pursuit befitting them both.

Even Vayden wore a steadier smile than he had in quite some time. Isla's death still seemed to haunt him, but over the last two weeks, he had spoken with Deckard and Thom about his plans for the future. Although he didn't regret the effort he and Isla had put into the Alliance, knowing it had secured the fate of the country they dreamed of for their daughter, he mourned the years lost with his wife. While he would work to help Ethenn and Ilain find the cure, he was determined to dedicate the rest of his life to cherishing his time with Reyana. The teenage girl was healing from her own grief, but she was coping better than Deckard had expected. Vayden attributed this to the influence of his parents.

"Admittedly," he said, "my mother was more present in Rey's life than Isla. Reyana loved her mother, but . . . She didn't know her well. That was a choice Isla made, and it is a choice we'll have to live with."

It was a brutal yet honest truth. Deckard prayed he would never have to make such a choice regarding his children.

Deckard and Evylin, too, had undergone significant changes since their journey began. Almost a year ago, when Deckard arrived in the quaint Whickam Village, he had no idea he was on the verge of a life-altering introduction. Upon entering that dining room, he'd encountered the most notable woman in existence—the extraordinary, resilient, and adventurous individual who, by some stroke of Allore's will, became his wife.

What began as a mutually beneficial arrangement evolved into what Deckard could only describe as a magical union. Or perhaps, better stated, the divine influence of Allore's power flowing through their veins.

Regardless of its origins, the undeniable connection between Deckard and Evylin was something that neither could articulate. And he didn't often desire to attempt to do so.

He was simply content to love the woman who had changed his life forever.

Too soon, their leave expired, and the day of coronation arrived.

Following a late night spent in the company of their friends, Deckard and Evylin enjoyed a prolonged morning in bed. Mrs. Wilumson finally roused them by persistently knocking on their door until they awoke. Almost immediately, she directed Deckard out of the room to allow the servants to prepare them for the coronation.

"We are married, Mrs. Wilumson," Evylin said, laughing as the older woman nearly pushed Deckard out the door. "There's no reason Jonn and I can't dress in the same room."

"This is a special occasion, dear," Mrs. Wilumson argued. "You'll both thank me later."

With that, the door closed in Deckard's face. A servant instructed him to follow to the next room. Over an hour later, Deckard appeared in an all-black uniform adorned with fine fabrics and intricate golden embroidery that made him feel both regal and confined, like a bird in a gilded cage. He was requested to bear the Relic and to leave it hanging to glitter over his coat. The servant clarified that each Mage and Warrior involved in the ceremony had received specific outfits tailored to their resource and province.

Deckard contemplated that Loclight, as the site of the Order of the Heavens, would present a somewhat somber image, considering the dark attire they were obliged to don. At least, that was his thought until Evylin graced him with her presence in the foyer. He had regarded her as spectacular on numerous occasions in the past; however, she now represented a truly royal transformation. The lustrous silk of her obsidian gown billowed around her like a crystalline shadow, with only the bodice tailored to her figure, covered in shining silver beads like stars, while the skirt and cape-like sleeves flowed elegantly around her.

The servants had styled her hair in an elegant bun, keeping the off-the-shoulder neckline exposed. She'd donned her usual rosette necklace, and the moonstone dagger was secured at her waist. Her silver and onyx earrings glimmered in the light, and her dimples revealed her amusement as he gazed upon her.

"That's quite the expression you're wearing," she teased, standing before him.

Deckard took her hands but spoke to Mrs. Wilumson instead. "My apologies, ma'am," he said. "You were right. This is a wonderful surprise."

"You look quite dashing yourself," Evylin said, straightening his already perfectly straight cravat. "Such kingly attire! A crown will suit you quite nicely."

That caused Deckard to frown. "We don't have to wear crowns, do we?"

Brea entered, wearing a black gown, which had a distinctly militaristic flair. "Of course not," she replied, flashing him a knowing smile. "Crowns are unnecessary and ostentatious."

"Thank Allore."

Brea continued as if he hadn't replied. "You *will* wear an insignia befitting your station, however."

Deckard, both intrigued and concerned, arched his brow at her. "I take it I'll get jewelry, and Evylin will receive a weapon."

The women laughed, but Brea neither confirmed nor denied the assumption. Thom, Calyn, Ethenn, Ilain, Vayden, and Reyana all arrived in the parlor shortly, each dressed in black. Deckard scanned their friends. He thought to ask why they'd wear the color of Space as well, but he realized the significance readily: This was their means of showing their support and allegiance to Deckard and Evylin.

For a spare moment, Deckard thought he might cry. Then a gentle sweep of encouragement from Evylin met him in the air, and he bolstered his emotions.

"Thank you all," Deckard said, meeting each of their gazes. "This is . . ."

Smiles met his pause as his friends—his *family*—awaited his final words. Evylin slipped her hand under his arm, looking up at him with radiant joy.

Deckard lifted his chin. "I don't deserve this life," he said. "A year ago, I accepted a mission that I hoped would propel me one step forward in my career. Instead, it brought me all of you. I wish I could say I was selfless enough not to desire this moment. That would be a lie.

"Since I was a boy, I hoped to matter in this world. On the cusp of becoming an oligarch," he scoffed at the sentiment, "I find myself doubting my ability to lead justly. Yet, I know now that the future isn't solely up to me."

Deckard set his hand on Evylin's, meeting her rich brown gaze. "My success isn't mine alone. I only fail if I forget to rely on those standing beside me. My desire was to be like Euon Sergus—a legend the world could never forget. But I forgot the key to Sergus's success. Which is rather embarrassing because I spent nearly three months making the same speech at every settlement in the Shires."

Chuckles met his self-mocking statement.

Running his thumb along his wife's fingers, which were curled around his bicep, Deckard turned to scan his troop. "With his dying breath, Sergus didn't take credit for his actions. He simply said he'd done his duty, and the men who aided him were the only thing that made his actions possible."

Deckard smiled. "*You* made this possible," he concluded. "Without you, Evylin and I would not be here. You all made the difference in my life. And I will endeavor to deserve your support from this day forward."

A crowd of proud, kind gazes met Deckard's speech. Ilain and Calyn wiped at the wet corners of their eyes. Surprisingly, Thom, too, seemed to be fighting tears. He sniffled, and Brea patted his arm teasingly. Ethenn held his head high, a soldier honoring his commanding officer. Vayden and Reyana smiled, the father's arm around his daughter's shoulders. And Evylin . . .

At his side, Evylin looked up at him with undying love. She squeezed his arm. "You made the difference for us," she said softly. "Without you . . . *we* would fall."

Recognizing the line from his speeches in the Shires so long ago, Deckard chuckled lightly so that he wouldn't cry.

Mercifully, the clerk, Gisele, chose that moment to arrive. There would be no grand procession to the throne room. Just their small party, walking through the arched halls of the Allminous Palace, as the oligarchy had agreed to call it. *Allminous*. The ancient Allundan Gaelic for "Allore's land."

They entered the throne room alongside the other chancellors and commanders, along with their retinues. As each party stepped into the grand hall, they found hundreds already assembled. The crowd filled the center of the room, gazing in awe at the entering oligarchs. The troop joined the crowd as witnesses to the coronation, while Brea stayed with Deckard and Evylin, serving as their guard.

Gisele guided the trio a few more feet to the right and pointed to the staircase leading up to one of the daises. "Here is the throne of the Loclight Province," she said with a smile. "Archminister Essen and Minister Maarsh are already here."

While Deckard had originally been surprised that they would host the archminister within Loclight, they'd been informed that both archministers would return to the original capital cities. Though the true capital of Allund would be Aulton, the most populated cities were still Loclight and Mouroc. With each new archminister elected, they would also move to the respective cities as representatives of the people.

At the base of the dais, Deckard hesitated. The staircase, wide enough for two, felt like a threshold. If he ascended those stone steps, he would accept their nation's fate. It didn't seem right. He was a lowly captain from Nettershire, a farmer's son with a slow, painstaking military career ahead of him. How had he gained the favor of a nation to become its ruler, albeit one of sixteen?

But Deckard wasn't the same man he'd been when he embarked on his journey. He wasn't just a farmer's son. He was a Mage. And he wasn't alone. He had his wife beside him and his family behind him. He hadn't reached for this position of authority; the duty had been offered to him.

And he would serve his people with his entire heart and body until the end of his days.

Together, Deckard and Evylin ascended the dais.

Archminister Essen and Minister Maarsh welcomed them at the summit with warm smiles. They exuded a regal presence in elegant black and gray robes adorned with colorful brooches akin to those worn by the clerks.

"Please," Archminister Essen said, stepping out of the way, "take your seats."

Deckard and Evylin gazed beyond the ministers toward the vacant thrones on the dais. Crafted from the same ivory stone as the palace and adorned with ebony velvet cushions, the weight of what was about to unfold struck Deckard like a cascading torrent.

Evylin gripped his arm tighter, and a surge of compassion washed over him. She knew his fears, his hopes, his dreams—every self-ambitious desire that drove him and caused him to doubt himself. Her touch was her offer of strength, her reminder of how she would not let him fail during this momentous occasion. Deckard glanced down to see the creamy light streaming through the room, turning her eyes the most vibrant amber.

"Jonn," she whispered affectionately. No further words were needed.

Deckard inhaled deeply and guided her to the thrones. Brea and the ministers trailed behind, moving to stand beneath a black banner adorned with eight gold and silver stars at the back of the dais. The emblem of Space.

Once all the thrones were occupied and the room was full to nearly bursting with witnesses, Archministers Essen and Dudleye—positioned on the directly opposite daises—advanced to request silence.

"Ladies and gentlemen," Archminister Essen announced, her voice resonating throughout the hall, "we extend our sincerest gratitude for your presence here today as we commemorate the inception of our great nation. Following years marked by struggle, conflict, and diligent labor, we have triumphantly witnessed the fall of the oppressive monarchies of Blount and Ephren, heralding the dawn of a new era characterized by liberty rather than tyranny and suppression. Today, we formally invest our newly appointed leaders with the authority to govern and safeguard our collective interests."

Dudleye continued in her stead, stating, "With careful consideration and profound trust in the magical members of our society, the Administration of Allund has selected our new sovereigns. Bonded Mages and Warriors, who have demonstrated their fidelity and honor, shall be inducted as the servants of Allore, as preordained at birth."

Applause and cheers resounded throughout the hall as the archministers withdrew. For a brief moment, Deckard was surprised at the unanimous public approval of the royalty. However, he realized it was not the royals they approved of. None of the magical individuals poised to be enthroned would wield absolute authority. They were highlords and highladies, akin to the nobility, entrusted with a parcel of land to steward and ensure the well-being of the populace. The success of their governance would be contingent upon the efficacy with which they attended to the needs of the people.

They were not to be supreme rulers. They were safeguards and champions, and they answered directly to their people.

Deckard reached over and took Evylin's hand, seated on his left. She turned to him, her smile a wellspring of hope and joy. No matter what lay ahead, they were about to embark on an extraordinary adventure, one that would require their lifelong commitment. It was a journey they would gladly endure together.

"Esteemed citizens of Allund," Archminister Essen declared to the tumultuous assembly, "let the coronation of our sovereigns commence."

Two ministers advanced to the left of their dais as a clerk, bearing a marble box, ascended the stairs to the thrones of Doorstunds Province. The chancellor and commander rose from the opulent red velvet cushions. The crimson banner positioned behind them bore intricately embroidered gold and silver flames. Both individuals wore expressions of joy; the man was adorned in a crimson and black uniform and the woman in an elegant ruby gown.

The troop had met the replacements taking the role intended for Ethenn and Ilain earlier in the week. Highlord Commander Vecent and Highlady Chancellor Pol Haadge were a striking duo of opposites. Pol bore golden curls, pale skin, and a flame-bright personality (though much more sweet-tempered than Ilain). Vecent's cedar-brown skin and stocky build revealed his Setshire heritage, while his reserved demeanor exuded temperate wisdom. Though the pair had not been in love upon their marriage, they seemed to genuinely admire one another.

Deckard smiled as the clerk approached the ministers, Daulton and Rowana Calder, and subsequently opened the box. The Calders extended their hands to retrieve the insignias contained within. Meanwhile, Pol and Vecent stood, and the general of their guard watched attentively from behind the throne.

"I, Interim Minister Daulton Calder, hereby charge you, Highlady Chancellor Pol Haadge, to lead the Doorstunds Province of Allund with your wisdom and insight."

Pol dipped her head in a humble bow as the minister draped a thin gold and gem-encrusted chain with a small ruby pendant over her neck.

"I, Interim Minister Rowana Calder, hereby charge you, Highlord Commander Vecent Haadge, to protect the Doorstunds Province of Allund with your equity and strength."

Vecent also bowed as Rowana pinned a platinum and ruby badge to the lapel of his coat next to where the flickering Fire Relic hung.

The ministers stepped back. "Do you both swear to uphold these charges?" Daulton asked.

"We do," the Bonded couple said together.

"Then," Rowana continued, "by the authority vested in the Administration of Allund, we hereby appoint you as overseers of the Order of the Flame and sovereigns of Doorstunds Province."

Another round of applause rang throughout the hall. Deckard watched Ethenn and Ilain carefully, noting their shared look of acceptance. They'd given up this path for an unknown future. Yet, Deckard didn't spot a trace of doubt in their expressions.

The coronation proceeded in a clockwise manner around the assembly. Beneath the yellow, sun-embroidered banner of Day, Highlady Chancellor Nessa and Highlord Commander Sidney Geis were appointed as overseers of the Order of the Day and sovereigns of Helsford Province, located in the northeastern region of Allund. Having collaborated with Deckard and Evylin in Loclight for an extended period, Nessa and Sidney had proven to be both amicable and wise, leading Deckard to confidently conclude that they would serve as effective leaders for the populace in that region, as well as valuable allies to Ilain and Ethenn's cause.

The banner, adorned with sapphire and decorated with motifs of the sea, swayed gracefully in the gentle breeze that flowed through the hall as Highlady Chancellor Pennie and Highlord Commander Aarl Swartz were appointed as overseers of the Order of the Sea and sovereigns of Portlund Province, which included what was previously recognized as the southwestern region of Ephria.

Highlord Chancellor Grey and Highlady Commander Alma Trumane were placed in charge of the Order of the Night and the Verlund Province. For the Order of the Wind, Highlady Chancellor Oriel and Highlord Commander Sean Olsen were assigned to Sutterlund Province. In Vaura Province, Highlord Chancellor Nicholson and the newly discovered Highlady Commander Ailsa Everlye were to oversee the Order of the Age. Finally, Highlady Chancellor Wintie and Highlord Commander Samel Feelds were tasked with the Order of the Terrae and the governance of Shirelund Province, which contained the Deckards' childhood homes.

At last, their coronation came.

Gisele ascended the steps as the ministers advanced to greet her. Deckard rose alongside Evylin. He clasped her hand tightly, staving off the anxiety that shot tremors through his body. He caught a bead of anxious anticipation woven in the excitement radiating off her, but she held her head high, undaunted in the face of the vast charge that lay ahead of them.

The archminister approached, gleaming insignia in her hand. "I, Archminister Linne Essen, hereby charge you, Highlord Chancellor Jonn Deckard, to lead the Loclight Province of Allund with your wisdom and insight."

Deckard remained as still as possible while she affixed a gold badge to his coat. Up close, he could see the design more clearly as it rested by the Relic around his neck. It was an eight-sided star, inlaid with onyx and moonstone—a beautifully crafted, intricate piece.

"I, Minister Ross Maarsh, charge you, Highlady Commander Evylin Deckard, to protect the Loclight Province of Allund with your equity and strength."

Evylin lowered her head for the man to fasten the platinum and onyx chain around her neck. It sparkled brilliantly in the late morning light as she turned to look up at Deckard, her expression a mix of disbelief and laughter. Even as she stifled her amusement, her dimples filled her face with joy.

Deckard shared her astonishment. Far beyond his wildest imagination, this was not the person he envisioned becoming. Yet, as he stood beside Evylin on the dais, he realized he wouldn't want to be anyone else.

"Do you both swear to uphold these charges?" Minister Maarsh asked.

"We do," Deckard and Evylin replied in unity.

"Then by the authority vested in the Administration of Allund," Archminister Essen announced, "we appoint you as overseers of the Order of the Heavens and sovereigns of Loclight Province."

As the last of Allund's sovereigns was appointed, the hall erupted in a cacophony of applause and cheers. The old ways were gone, and magic was renewed.

The Republic of Allund had arrived.

CHAPTER SEVENTY

13TH OF TERRAEN, 1578

The ministers honored their word. Amidst their service to the country over the next four years, Evylin and Deckard had regular opportunities to visit family and friends. While they often remained in Loclight due to their responsibilities—Evylin training with the Warriors and Deckard collaborating with the Mages while managing the province— every day brought something new. Though the work was not always thrilling, Evylin appreciated the variety it offered.

Additionally, the Alliance conceded to their wish to continue residing in their home located in the Military District. This arrangement allowed Evylin to conveniently reach the barracks while Deckard had a quick journey to the Order's headquarters, located in the old Ephrian palace. Each morning, they would separate to pursue their respective duties, with Brea accompanying Evylin and Thom going with Deckard.

While Norhels was a week's journey away, they saw Ethenn and Ilain as regularly as they could—though it wound up being once a season at the most. However, they were making grand progress on the cure, with Maura's body now transferred to the Order of the Day, where they cared for her, ensuring she didn't succumb to death in the pursuit of her healing.

The Loxleys and Calders were quite happy. After their short stint as interim ministers, the Calder parents sold their home in Faurna to move to East Allund with their family. Though Vayden remained single, he enjoyed his quiet life near the sea. He and his father bought land to raise horses together. Reyana had blossomed into a stunning young woman, studying dutifully at her aunt's side. Though she wasn't magical, she wished to assist the research for the cure in whatever way she could.

During a trip to Loclight the previous month, Ilain announced her pregnancy. Thom teased Ethenn mercilessly about becoming a father, but the once-young hunter had matured into an immovable highlord. He didn't flinch at the suggestion of his impending duties as a father but proudly stated that he looked forward to every challenge it presented. As this would be their first child, Ilain firmly believed it would be a boy whom they would name Auden. Ethenn offered no objections.

The Deckard family was quite pleased with their lives as well. The Order of the Heavens, while the smallest of the Orders with only fifteen Space Mages and a few dozen Warriors, was nonetheless known for its remarkable qualities.

Deckard proved to be an exceptional leader who dedicated himself to mastering Space magic and encouraged the Mages of the Order to do the same. He was well-liked, as was to be expected, because he treated everyone with respect and shared his knowledge freely. Their enclave was marked by calmness, control, and commitment to the craft. The Mages embodied the deep peace and steadiness of Space itself.

Deckard had found a protégé within the Order, a young man named Oren Brennen. The year prior, Evylin and Deckard had been called to West Allund to recover the sixteen-year-old, who had accidentally sliced through an entire city block while running for his life from zealous Waulden-regime sympathizers, known as The Sterling. These zealots clung to the Faith of Eight, seeking Blount's children—legitimate or not—as the legal heirs to his throne.

Oren was one of these illegitimate heirs.

While attempting to escape The Sterling, Oren's magic revealed itself with unrestrained violence, and the teenage boy was terrified. From the moment they found him in Verlund Province, Deckard took him under his wing and ensured he learned everything he knew. Oren proved to be a promising Mage.

Best of all, Deckard was now utilizing his office at home. With limited literature available on the study of Space, he took the initiative to document his findings, aiming to eventually author books on the topic for others to explore. He urged the other Mages to follow his lead.

As for Evylin's contributions to Allund, the Warriors of the Order were renowned for their immense strength, intelligence, and readiness to act. Their techniques rivaled those of any other Order, although Evylin hesitated to claim all the credit. She based their training on everything Hewitt had taught her and led with the support of Brea and Emmaas's knowledge behind her. She took pleasure in the work and appreciated the excellent company.

Eventually, Colonel Valen Reid joined the Order of the Day, carrying with him many skills he had acquired from the Order of the Heavens, which Evylin was pleased to learn were equally beneficial in Norhels. In the third year of Allund, the Administration requested Evylin's insights for the Orders still refining their training programs. Although drafting the letters was a tedious task, Deckard assisted her, making the work far more bearable.

Brea led the Order Guard with a strong and steady demeanor, and her soldiers admired her with deep loyalty. She dedicated herself to ensuring that Evylin, Deckard, and the entire province were safe, while Thom, as Lieutenant General, managed the Allundan Army within the city. Together, they formed an effective team. Thom became the supportive brother, devoted friend, loving husband, and brave soldier Evylin always knew he could be, his daily happiness surpassing her greatest hopes for him.

In their first year of marriage, Thom and Brea welcomed their first daughter, Isla. She was a delightful baby, and Thom became the most devoted father one could imagine. Evylin was surprised that Brea wanted children so soon, but when she inquired, Brea replied, "I have one life, Evylin. One life to fill with as much goodness and love with Thom as possible. The best way to enhance that life is to include more of him in it. What better way than through our children?"

Two years later, they had their second daughter, Rosa.

Between the two girls, Evylin and Deckard welcomed their own firstborn. While he had wished for a daughter, she desired a son. Her wishes prevailed. He accepted his defeat the moment he cradled his son. Ryen Deckard inherited his father's green-blue eyes, but he bore his mother's dark hair.

The family often engaged in a lively debate about whether Ryen, Isla, or Rosa would possess magic. Thom insisted they all would, while Brea pointed out that it was unlikely any of them would inherit it. Meanwhile, Deckard and Evylin tried to remain indifferent. They had one life, after all. They would fill it with as much joy and love as they could, no matter the trials they'd face.

Entrusting the province to Emmaas, the ministers, the clerks, and their Order, the Deckard family returned to Nettershire late in the year to visit Stocburrough. Every year, Deckard prioritized a trip around their anniversary, and Evylin persuaded him to visit his family this time.

"It's not very romantic," he contended, "celebrating your fifth anniversary in a small village surrounded by family."

Evylin embraced him. "No, but we'll have a built-in babysitter. If that doesn't spark romance, I'm not sure what will."

"Being intimate in your childhood bed isn't exactly romantic either, Evie."

"Then I suppose we'll just have to find somewhere else," she teased.

Regardless of his objections, they traveled to Nettershire with Thom and Brea. Their family was ecstatic upon their arrival. Serah and Meria continuously played the role of hosts, while Mathes and Vaan queried them about Loclight, the Order, and their work. Little Isla toddled off to play with Liliette and young Jonn, while the three youngest children—Ryen, Rosa, and Ivana, Meria's third child—played together inside the house.

They planned to stay for a week, and Evylin observed how Deckard immediately relaxed upon entering the village. With each visit to his family, she noticed how he shed some of the burdens he carried in his daily life. Occasionally, she felt remorse for encouraging him to leave the simpler life he once desired, but then she recalled his true nature and his passion for his work. He was content, and so was she. She had no doubt that they'd made the best decision.

On the third morning of their stay, Evylin woke to find Deckard beside her. This unusual occurrence was even rarer during their visits with his family. However, she had expected it this morning.

"Happy anniversary," she whispered, snuggling closer to his side.

Deckard ran his hand along her arm and kissed her forehead. "Happy anniversary, my love."

"I have a surprise for you."

"Do you?"

She nodded. "But first, we have to get up."

"Do we have somewhere to be?"

"Actually, we do."

"Oh? And what engagement have I forgotten in this meager village?" he teased.

Evylin smirked at him. "It's more a promise than an engagement."

"Do explain."

"Almost five years ago, you vowed to teach me how to swim, and now you are finally going to fulfill that promise."

Deckard fought to control a hearty laugh so as not to wake the sleeping Ryen on a spare mattress at the foot of their bed. "Evie, it's mid-autumn. The lakes will be frigid."

"Are you going to break your promise?" she challenged.

"Do you want to freeze?"

She rolled her eyes at him. "It won't be that cold."

It *was* that cold.

Despite the chill, Deckard taught her to swim, and after half an hour, they became somewhat acclimated to the water's temperature.

"Was it worth it?" Deckard asked as they treaded water under the cavern of the concealed pool.

With her arms wrapped around his neck, Evylin smiled, even as a shiver ran down her spine. "Yes," she said. "It was all worth it."

"All?" he inquired, his eyes shifting to green in the dim light of the rocky outcrop he'd brought her to. "I meant the lesson in the ice we're swimming in. What are you talking about?"

"The same," she said with a shrug. "And everything else too."

Deckard smiled and drew her closer, wrapping her legs around his waist. "Everything else, you say? Referring to the past five years?"

"Referring to us. Deciding to marry a man I had known for just three days. Deciding to love you."

"Ah, yes." He tilted his head down. "That 'everything else.'"

They floated in the water for a while, relishing their closeness, until Deckard eventually decided he'd had enough, claiming the water was too cold for sensible people to swim in. Evylin asserted she wasn't sensible, yet she followed him out regardless. After drying off and changing into fresh clothes, they strolled to the hillside where their horses awaited. A few miles from the village, they chose to bask in the sun, at its peak in the sky. Though the autumn chill permeated the terrae beneath them, the heat of the day and their additional layers helped them to regain their warmth.

Evylin unraveled her damp braid and toweled off the ends while Deckard looked up at her.

"You know," he whispered, "you were right."

"I know," she said with a smirk. "What was I right about this time?"

"Everything."

She laughed and tossed the towel aside. Leaning into him, she kissed his lips quickly as his arm encircled her waist. "Referring to the past five years?" she teased.

"Referring to us."

She nodded. "Referring to us," she repeated tenderly.

Deckard's smile softened as she ran her fingers through his hair. It was dark with water, though the sun was quickly drying it back to its reddish tint. "Thank you for being brave enough to marry me," he whispered.

"Thank you for being brash enough to marry me."

"Are you happy, Evylin?"

Tilting her head, Evylin struggled to find the right words to convey her happiness. She had Deckard, their Ryen, her friends, her family, and a life full of adventure. Nothing in her imagination compared to the world she lived in now.

"Beyond my wildest dreams," she affirmed. "Are you happy, Jonn?"

Deckard entwined his fingers in her hair and drew her nearer. "More than I ever hoped," he whispered just before kissing her—softly, deeply, and enduringly.

Amid the gentle chirping of birds, the scent of grass beneath them, and the sun's warm embrace, Evylin could sense the depth of his love through kisses like these. They didn't need a Bond to tell her how truly happy he felt. Not when he kissed her like this. Not when he held her so tightly.

Evylin paused, grinning too broadly to keep kissing. "Are you ready for your surprise?" she whispered.

Deckard grinned up at her, tracing her jawline with his thumb. "You're pregnant."

Evylin gaped at him, her mouth falling open. "How did you know?"

His hand grazed her stomach. "I feel what you're feeling, remember?" he teased. "You've been extra tired, irritable, and wistful."

"Irritable?" Evylin poked a finger into his rib, causing him to lurch beneath her with laughter. "I'm a delight when I'm with child."

"I wouldn't begin to deny that."

She poked him firmly again.

"What was that for?" he demanded.

"For spoiling my surprise," she said, giving him another poke.

Deckard grabbed her waist tightly, allowing him to gain the advantage of rolling her over onto the drying grass. He interrupted her next attack with another kiss, even as their laughter shook them. Gradually, his kisses served their purpose well, settling them into the serenity of affection.

"I take it you're hoping for a girl again?" she remarked as they lay contentedly in each other's embrace.

Without a word, Deckard nodded.

"Why?"

He traced the contours of her face with his finger as if committing every detail to memory. "Because she would be just like you."

"You don't know that."

"She'd be your daughter, wouldn't she?"

She smirked. "I do believe so."

He arched his right eyebrow. "Then she'd be perfect."

Somehow, the compliment made Evylin blush, even after all their years together. "What if it's another boy?" she asked, her voice softer than normal.

"Then I'll love him as much as I love Ryen, and he'll be just as wonderful."

"Ryen is pretty wonderful, isn't he?" she asked proudly. Though only a year old, their little boy was already sweet and tenderhearted. She hoped he was having fun with his cousins in their absence. He'd cried at their departure, and it took every bit of her will to walk out the door.

Deckard smiled. "That he is."

"Your mother mentioned that he resembles you at his age—he loves stories and is always thoughtful toward others." Evylin had the sudden urge to embrace her son, wishing they would have brought him with them.

"Really?" Deckard said, curling a few damp waves around his finger. "He reminds me more of you. Headstrong and far too clever for this world. If he possesses magic, I'm confident he'll become a Warrior."

Looking up into Deckard's gentle gaze, she found herself hoping that their son wouldn't be magical. In fact, she hoped none of their children would be. The weight of being a Mage or a Warrior was just as significant as the rewards it offered. While she dreamed of them living as long as she and Deckard, she also yearned for them to enjoy lives with less responsibility.

Evylin ran her hand along Deckard's arm as she rested in his embrace. "Jonn," she whispered.

"Yes, Evie?"

"I learned something recently."

"What's that?"

"My 'more' has changed."

The pinch in Deckard's brow appeared, and she smiled. "Don't worry," she said, reaching up to smooth the crease away. "You're still part of it."

"I'm relieved," he said with a chuckle. "I'd hate to think you were weary of me."

"Never," she vowed, holding him close.

"Then tell me," he prompted. "How has your 'more' changed?"

Taking a moment to reflect on her feelings, Evylin paused. "I suppose it hasn't changed so much as it has grown," she corrected herself. "Now, I see that what matters most to me in this world—what is worth living for—it's still you, but it's also Ryen. And now, it includes our other child as well. No matter what challenges life throws at us, life is enough because I have each of you."

The purest smile tugged at Deckard's lips, lighting up his green-blue eyes, which sparkled with joy. "Evylin," he uttered her name as if it were the most beautiful word in existence.

"Yes, Jonn?"

"I love you."

"I love you."

Together on the dry grass plain of Nettershire, Evylin rested her head against Deckard's shoulder. She closed her eyes, feeling his contentment pulse through her along with the shared sentiment from the Space Relic he wore around his neck. The Relic had begun to convey its emotions to them both in subtle waves of energy, no matter which of them was wearing it. It was something all the Bonded couples experienced, as they'd learned from their discussions with their fellow chancellors and commanders.

Evylin smiled, the gentle cool of her magic fluttering across her skin as Deckard traced circles over her arm. After five years, her love for him had only grown, and she couldn't fathom how it would expand in the wake of the centuries ahead of them. As always, her heart panged at the thought that their Ryen and this new life burgeoning inside her might not be part of their prolonged existence. Her world felt so full with the "more" of her children. She couldn't bear a day without them.

Yet, after everything they'd endured, the truth Hewitt taught her remained ever certain: It was up to her to choose what "more" looked like for her life. Death and heartbreak were inevitable, but along the way, new family and hope could be found. She'd lost her cousin, her uncle, and many dear friends throughout their journey. And she'd found a husband, a brother, a vast family, two children, and so many more companions who made her life even more complete.

In her heart, Evylin could almost feel Hewitt's presence as he surely smiled down at her from the Heavens.

Life was enough because of the people at Evylin's side, those who remained and those who'd departed. And she would never forget their love, so long as she lived.

Also Available from V.K. Dixon

WARRIORS & MAGES
Fire & Night
Sword & Shadow
Relics & Thrones

ARCHIVES OF THE WARDEN
Lake of Glass
Vault of Stone
The Raven's Cry
Veil of Mist
The Wolf's Howl
Of Spirit & Ether (Coming Spring 2026)
Book Seven (Coming Fall 2026)

Acknowledgments

In November of 2019, Evylin and Deckard's story came to me. It was the first time in a long time that I had a clear inspiration for a story. I was desperate to recapture the spark of creativity that had once permeated my life as a teen and college student, so with the encouragement of my husband, I set out on a journey: I challenged myself to write the complete trilogy now known as *Warriors & Mages* to prove that I could be an author.

Now, here we are in November of 2025 and I'm writing the acknowledgements for the third book.

In the past six years, this story has changed my life in so many ways. Not only because it gave me the courage to pursue my dreams of being an author, but because it taught me so many lessons. Evylin's internal journey of discovering her "more" relates very closely to my own struggles of feeling that life never measures up to expectations. While she and I are very different in many ways, I will forever be grateful to her for giving me the chance to grow and understand that "more" isn't always as tangible or epic as we might dream. Sometimes—most times—"more" simply means being surrounded by those we love.

So, thank you to all those I love! You make my world full.

Josh, your support, love, and encouragement for this story gave me hope. You are the reason I had the strength to pursue this dream. But beyond that, your goodness, consideration, and strength gave me the inspiration to write a hero with that same measure of selfless devotion. I am daily in awe of your constant faithfulness and love.

To Sam and our second little one: I hope one day you read this story and learn the same truth I did through its pages. Life is enough because of the people at your side.

To my editor, Brittany: Your guidance and teaching over these years has given me so much confidence and hope. I will forever be grateful to you for your friendship as well as our work together.

To my readers: Six years ago, you were a dream to me—a lofty goal I didn't know if I'd ever achieve. Your support has fulfilled that dream, and I could never say thank you enough!

Thank you to every Kickstarter backer, to my paid Substack subscribers, to my ARC readers, my street team, and everyone along the way who has supported this story in any way. Writing can feel like such a lonely, hopeless pursuit at times, and you have stunned this author with your kindness, friendship, and care. I will be forever grateful to each of you!

And thank you to God—for this story, for the people you've sent me, and for the chance to write for you. Let every word and every breath be a symbol of you and your kingdom, for now and forever.

About the Author

V.K. Dixon writes fantasy and romance novels filled with found family, lasting love, and unique magic. She believes that the extraordinary gives us a deeper desire for the things beyond us—the things of God.

www.ingramcontent.com/pod-product-compliance
Lightning Source LLC
Chambersburg PA
CBHW030904300726
48970CB00001B/8